a Song for Arbonne

Also by Guy Gavriel Kay

THE FIONAVAR TAPESTRY, a trilogy
The Summer Tree
The Wandering Fire
The Darkest Road

Tigana

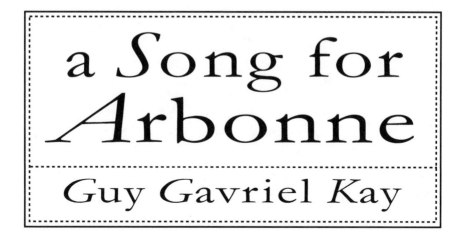

a Song for Arbonne

Guy Gavriel Kay

CROWN PUBLISHERS, INC.   NEW YORK

Published by Crown Publishers, Inc.,
201 East 50th Street, New York, New York 10022
Member of the Crown Publishing Group

Originally pu blished in Canada by Penguin Books Canada Ltd. in 1992
CROWN is a trademark of Crown Publishers, Inc.
Manufactured in the United States of America
Library of Congress Cataloging-in-Publication Data

Kay, Guy Gavriel.
A song for Arbonne / Guy Gavriel Kay. – 1st U.S. ed.
p.   cm.
I. Title.
PR9199.3.K39S6   1993
813'.54—dc20   92-29134
CIP

ISBN 0-517-59312-2

10 9 8 7 6 5 4 3 2 1
First American Edition

*This book is dedicated, with love,
to the memory of my father,
Dr. Samuel K. Kay,
whose skill and compassion as a surgeon
were enhanced all his life by a love for language and literature —
a love he conveyed to his sons, among so many other gifts.*

ACKNOWLEDGEMENTS

A lthough this is a work of fiction, I am once again indebted to the skill and industry of a great many scholars writing about the period that has provided me with my sources. Many of them, not surprisingly, are French: Georges Duby, Emmanuel Le Roy Ladurie, Phillippe Aries. I have also been instructed by the works of, among others, Urban Tigner Holmes, Frances and Joseph Gies and Friedrich Heer. My access to the troubadours, both their works and their history, has primarily been by way of Frederick Golden, Paul Blackburn, Alan Press and Meg Bogin.

A *Song For Arbonne* was substantially written during two long periods in the countryside near Aix-en-Provence. It is a pleasure to acknowledge the gracious welcome and assistance extended by certain people there who have since become friends: Jean-Pierre and Kamma Sorensen and their son Nicolas, and Roland and Jean Ricard.

I continue to be fortunate in having access to the critical and professional abilities of a number of people. Among them are my agents, Linda McKnight in Toronto and Anthea Morton-Saner in London. It is also past time to record the stimulation and support I have long received from the friendship and example of the immensely gifted George Jonas. Finally, and as always, there is Laura.

A Note on Pronunciation

It will likely be evident to the reader that the French language has provided the basis for most of the proper names herein. There is one caveat to this. Historically, the language of what is now the south of France (Provence or Languedoc or Aquitaine), unlike modern French, normally involved the pronunciation of a final 's'. I have followed this, and, accordingly, names such as Aelis or Cauvas ought to have their final consonant sounded.

From the vidan of the troubadour, Anselme of Cauvas . . .

Anselme, who has ever been acknowledged as the first and perhaps the greatest of all the troubadours of Arbonne, was of modest birth, the youngest son of a clerk in the castle of a baron near Cauvas. He was of middling height, dark haired, with a quiet manner in speech that was nonetheless wondrously pleasing to all who heard him. While yet tender in years, he showed great skill and interest in music and was invited to join the celebrated choir of the Cauvas sanctuary of the god. It was not long, however, before he felt the beginnings of a desire to make music very different from that acceptable in the service of the god, or indeed of the goddess Rian in her temples. And so Anselme left the comforts of the chapel and choir to make his way alone among the villages and castles of Arbonne, offering his new songs shaped of tunes and words such as he had heard sung by the common folk in their own speech . . .

He was later brought into the household of Duke Raimbaut de Vaux and honoured there, and in time his prowess came to the attention of Count Folquet himself, and Anselme was invited to pass a winter in Barbentain. From that time was Anselme's fortune assured, and the fate of the troubadours of Arbonne likewise made sure, for Anselme swiftly rose high in the friendship and trust of Count Folquet and in the esteem and very great affection of the noble Countess Dia. They honoured him for his music and his wit, and also for his discretion and cleverness, which led the count to employ him in many hazardous tasks of diplomacy beyond the borders of Arbonne . . .

In time, Count Folquet himself, under the tutelage of Anselme of Cauvas, began to make his own songs, and from that day it may be said that the art and reputation of the troubadours has never been diminished or endangered in Arbonne, and has indeed grown and flourished in all the known countries of the world . . .

·PROLOGUE·

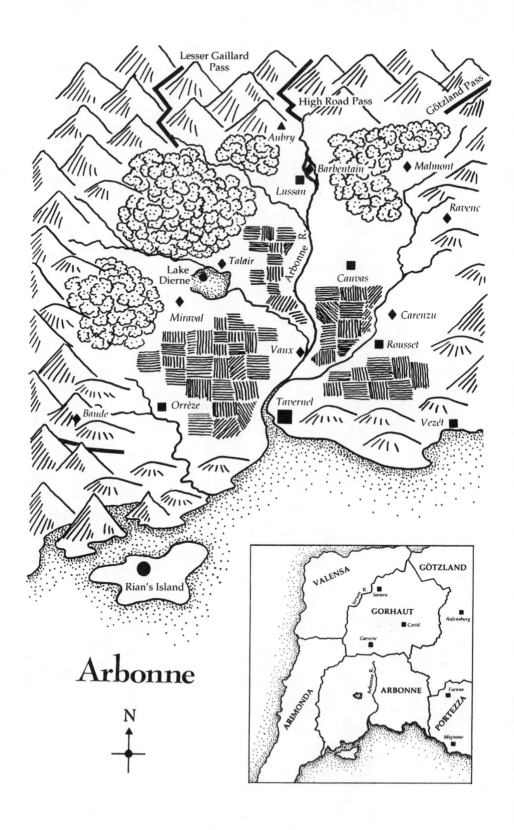

Lesser Gaillard
Pass

High Road Pass

Götzland Pass

Aubry

Barbentain

Malmont

Lussan

Ravenc

Arbonne R.

Talair

Cauvas

Lake
Dierne

Carenzu

Miraval

Rousset

Vaux

Orrèze

Tavernel

Baude

Vezét

Rian's Island

Arbonne

N

VALENSA

GÖTZLAND

Iersen R.

Savaric

GORHAUT

Aulensburg

Cortil

Garsenc

ARIMONDA

Arbonne R.

ARBONNE

Lucuna

PORTEZZA

Mignano

On a morning in the springtime of the year, when the snows of the mountains were melting and the rivers swift in their running, Aelis de Miraval watched her husband ride out at dawn to hunt in the forest west of their castle, and shortly after that she took horse herself, travelling north and east along the shores of the lake towards the begetting of her son.

She did not ride alone or secretly; that would have been folly beyond words. Though she was young and had always been headstrong, Aelis had never been a fool and would not be one now, even in love.

She had her young cousin with her, and an escort of six armed corans, the trained and anointed warriors of the household, and she was riding by pre-arrangement — as she had told her husband several days before — to spend a day and a night with the duchess of Talair in her moated castle on the northern shore of Lake Dierne. All was in order, carefully so.

The fact that there were other people in Castle Talair besides the duchess and her ladies was an obvious truth, not worthy of comment or observation. A great many people made up the household of a powerful duke such as Bernart de Talair, and if one of them might be the younger son and a poet, what of that? Women in a castle, even here in Arbonne, were guarded like spices or gold, locked up at night against whoever might be wandering in the silence of the dark hours.

But night, and its wanderers, was a long way off. It was a beautiful morning through which they now rode, the first delicate note of the song that would be springtime in Arbonne. To their left, the terraced vineyards stretched into the distance of the Miraval lands, pale green now, but with the promise of the dark, ripe summer grapes to come. East of the curving path, the waters of Lake Dierne were a dazzle of blue in the light of the early sun. Aelis could see the isle clearly, and the smoke rising from the three sacred fires in Rian's temple there. Despite her two years on the other, larger island of the goddess far to the south in the sea, Aelis had lived her life too near to the gather and play of earthly power to be truly devout, but that morning she offered an inward prayer to Rian, and then another — amused at herself — to Corannos, that the god of the Ancients, too, might look down with favour upon her from his throne behind the sun.

The air was so clear, swept by the freshness of the breeze, that she could already see Talair itself on the far shore of the lake. The castle ramparts rose up, formidable and stern, as befitted the home of a family so proud. She glanced back behind her then and saw, across the vineyards that lay between, the equally arrogant walls of Miraval, a little higher even, seat of a lineage as august as any in Arbonne. But when Aelis looked across the water to Talair she smiled, and when she looked back at the castle where she dwelled with her husband she could not suppress a shiver and a fleeting chill.

'I thought you might be cold. I brought your cloak, Aelis. It is early yet in the day, and early in the year.'

Her cousin Ariane, Aelis thought, was far too quick and observant for a thirteen-year-old. It was almost time for her to wed. Let some other girl of their family discover the dubious joys of politically guided marriages, Aelis thought spitefully. But then she was quick to withdraw that wish: she would not have another lord such as Urté de Miraval visited upon any of her kin, least of all a child as glad-hearted as Ariane.

She had been much the same herself, Aelis reflected, not so long ago.

She glanced over at her cousin, at the quick, expressive, dark eyes and the long black hair tumbling free. Her own hair was carefully pinned and covered now, of course; she was a married woman, not a maiden, and unloosed hair, as everyone knew, as all the troubadours wrote and the joglars sang, was sheerest incitement to desire. Married women of rank were not to incite such desire, Aelis thought drily. She smiled at Ariane though; it was hard not to smile at Ariane. 'No cloak this morning, bright heart, it would feel like a denial of the spring.'

Ariane laughed. 'When even the birds above the lake are singing of my love,' she quoted. 'Though none can hear them but the waves.'

Aelis couldn't help smiling again. Ariane had the lyric wrong, but it wouldn't do to correct her, it might give too much away. All of her ladies-in-waiting were singing that song. The lines were recent and anonymous. They had heard a joglar sing the tune in the hall at Miraval only a few months before during the winter rains, and there had been at least a fortnight's worth of avid conjecture among the women afterwards as to which of the better-known troubadours had shaped this newest, impassioned invocation of the spring and his desire.

Aelis knew. She knew exactly who had written that song, and she also knew rather more than that — that it had been composed for her, and not for any of the other high-born ladies whose names were being bandied about in febrile speculation. It was hers, that song. A response to a promise she had chosen to make during the midwinter feasting at Barbentain.

A rash promise? A deserved one? Aelis thought she knew what her father would have said, but she wondered about her mother. Signe, countess of Arbonne, had, after all, founded the Courts of Love here in the south, and Aelis had grown into womanhood hearing her mother's clear voice lifted in wit or mockery in the great hall at Barbentain, and the responding, deep-throated laughter of a circle of besotted men.

It was still happening now, today, probably this very morning amid the splendours of Barbentain on its own island in the river near the mountain passes. The young lords of Arbonne and even the older ones and the troubadours and the joglars with their lutes and harps and the emissaries from over all the mountains and across the seas would be dancing attendance upon the dazzling countess of Arbonne, her mother.

With Guibor, the count, watching it all, smiling to himself in the way he had, and then assessing and deciding affairs of state afterwards, at night, with the glittering wife he loved and who loved him, and whom he trusted with his life, his honour, his realm, with all his hope of happiness on this side of death.

'Your mother's laughter,' he'd said to Aelis once, 'is the strongest army I will ever have in Arbonne.'

He'd said that to his daughter. She'd been sixteen then, newly returned home from two years on Rian's Island in the sea, newly discovering, almost day by day, that there seemed to be avenues to beauty and grace for herself, after an awkward childhood.

Less than a year after that conversation her father had married her to Urté de Miraval, perhaps the strongest of the lords of Arbonne, and so exiled her from all the newly charming, flattering courtiers and poets, from the wit and music and laughter of Barbentain to the hunting dogs and the sweaty night thrustings of the duke he'd decided needed to be bound more closely to his allegiance to the ruling counts of Arbonne.

A fate no different from that of any daughter of any noble house. It had been her mother's fate, her aunt's in Malmont to the east across the river; it would be black-haired Ariane's too, one day — and night — not far off.

Some women were lucky in their men, and some found an early widowhood — which might actually mean power here in Arbonne, though not, by any means, everywhere in the world. There were other paths as well: those of the goddess or the god. Her sister Beatritz, the eldest child, had been given to Rian; she was a priestess in a sanctuary in the eastern mountains near Götzland. She would be High Priestess there one day — her parentage assured at least so much — and wield her own measure of power in the intricate councils of Rian's clergy. In many ways, Aelis thought, it was an enviable future, however remote it might be from the laughter and the music of the courts.

On the other hand, how close was she herself to such music and such laughter in Miraval, with the candles and torches doused just after dusk and Duke Urté coming to her in the night through the unlatched door that linked their rooms — smelling of dogs and moulting falcons and sour wine, in search of temporary release and an heir, nothing more?

Different women dealt with their destinies in very different ways, thought dark-haired, dark-eyed Aelis, the lady of Miraval, as she rode under green-gold leaves beside the rippling waters of Lake Dierne with vineyards on her left and forests beyond.

She knew exactly who and what she was, what her lineage meant to the ferociously ambitious man she'd been given to like a prize in the tournament at the Lussan Fair: Urté, who seemed so much more a lord of Gorhaut in the cold, grim north than of sun-blessed Arbonne, however full and ripe the grapes and olives might grow on his rich lands. Aelis knew precisely what she was for him; it didn't need a scholar from the university in Tavernel to do that sum.

There was a sudden sound, an involuntary gasp of wonder beside her. Aelis stirred from reverie and glanced quickly over and then beyond Ariane to see what had startled the girl. What she saw stirred her own pulse. Just ahead of them, off the road beside the lake, the Arch of the Ancients stood at the end of a double row of elm trees, its stones honey-coloured in the morning sunlight. Ariane hadn't taken this ride before, Aelis realized; she would never have seen the arch.

There were ruins of the Ancients all over the fertile land named for the Arbonne River that watered it: columns by the roadside, temples on cliffs by the sea or in the mountain passes, foundations of houses in the cities, bridge stones tumbled into the mountain streams and some still standing, some still in use. Many of the roads they rode or walked today had been built by the Ancients long ago. The great high road beside the Arbonne itself, from the sea at Tavernel north to Barbentain and Lussan and beyond them into and through the mountains to Gorhaut, was one of the old straight roads. All along its length were marker stones, some standing, many toppled into the roadside grass, with words upon them in a language no one living knew, not even the scholars of the university.

The Ancients were everywhere in Arbonne, the simple sight of one of their ruins or artifacts, however unexpected, would not have drawn a cry from Ariane.

But the arch by Lake Dierne was something else again.

Rising ten times the height of a man, and almost as broad, it stood alone in the countryside at the end of its avenue of elms, seeming to master and subdue the gentle, vine-clad landscape between the forests and the lake. Which, Aelis had long suspected, was precisely the purpose for which it had been raised. The friezes sculpted on both the near face

and the far were of war and conquest: armoured men in char-
iots carrying round shields and heavy swords, battling others
armed with only clubs and spears. And the warriors with the
clubs were dying on the friezes, their pain made vivid in the
sculptor's art. On the sides of the arch were images of men and
women clad in animal skins, manacled, their heads bowed and
averted in defeat, slaves. Whoever they were, wherever they
now had gone, the Ancients who had set their marks upon
this land had not come in peace.

'Would you like to see it more nearly?' she asked Ariane
mildly. The girl nodded, never taking her eyes from the arch.
Aelis lifted her voice, calling ahead to Riquier, the leader of
the corans detailed to ride with her. He dropped hastily back
to her side.

'My lady?'

She smiled up at him. Balding and humourless, Riquier
was much the best of the household corans, and she was, in
any case, prepared to smile at almost anyone this morning.
There was a song winding through her heart, a song written
this winter, after the festive season, in response to a promise
a lady had made. Every joglar in Arbonne had been singing
that song. No one knew the troubadour who had written it,
no one knew the lady.

'If you think it safe,' she said, 'I should like to stop for a
few moments that my cousin might see the arch more closely.
Do you think we could do that?'

Riquier looked cautiously around at the serene, sunlit
countryside. His expression was earnest; it was always earnest
when he spoke with her. She had never once been able to make
him laugh. Not any of them, actually; the corans of Miraval
were men cut from her husband's cloth, not surprisingly.

'I think that would be all right,' he said.

'Thank you,' Aelis murmured. 'I am happy to be in your
hands, En Riquier, in this as in all things.' A younger, better-
educated man would have returned her smile, and a witty one
would have known how to reply to the shameless flattery of
the honorific she had granted him. Riquier merely flushed,
nodded once and dropped back to give his orders to the rear
guard. Aelis often wondered what he thought of her; at other
times she wasn't really sure she wanted to know.

'The only things that belong in that one's hands are a sword or a flask of unmixed wine,' Ariane said tartly and not quite softly enough at Aelis's side. 'And if he deserves a lord's title, so does the man who saddled my horse.' Her expression was scornful.

Aelis had to suppress a smile. For the second time that morning she had cause to wonder about her young cousin. The girl was disconcertingly quick. Despite the fact that Ariane's words reflected her own thoughts exactly, Aelis tendered her a reproving glance. She had duties here — the duties of a duchess towards the girl-woman who had been sent to her as a lady-in-waiting for fostering and to learn the manners proper to a court. Which was not, Aelis thought, going to happen in Miraval. She had considered writing her aunt at Malmont and saying as much, but had so far refrained, for selfish reasons as much as any others: Ariane's brightness, since she had arrived last fall, had been a source of genuine pleasure, one of the very few Aelis had. Not counting certain songs. *Even the birds above the lake are singing of my love...*

'Not all men are made for gallantry or the forms of courtliness,' she said to her cousin, keeping her voice low. 'Riquier is loyal and competent, and the remark about the wine is uncalled for — you've seen him in the hall yourself.'

'Indeed I have,' Ariane said ambiguously. Aelis raised her eyebrows, but had neither time or inclination to pursue the matter.

Riquier cantered his horse past them again and swung off the path, angling through the roadside grass and then between the flanking trees towards the arch. The two women followed, with corans on either side and behind.

They never reached it.

There was a crackling sound, a surge and rustle of leaves. Six men plummeted from branches overhead and all six of Urté's corans were pulled from their horses to tumble on the ground. Other men sprang instantly from hiding in the tall grass and raced over to help in the attack. Ariane screamed. Aelis reared her horse and a masked assailant rushing towards her scrambled hastily back. She saw two other men emerge from the trees to stand in front of them all, not joining in the fight. They too were masked; they were all masked. Riquier was down, she saw, two men standing over him. She wheeled her horse, creating room for herself, and grappled at her saddle for the small crossbow she always carried.

She was her father's daughter, and had been taught by him, and in his prime Guibor de Barbentain was said to have been the best archer in his own country. Aelis steadied her horse with her knees, aimed quickly but with care and fired. One of the two men in the road before her cried out and staggered back, clutching at the arrow in his shoulder.

Aelis wheeled swiftly. There were four men around her now trying to seize the horse's reins. She reared her stallion again and it kicked out, scattering them. She fumbled in the quiver for a second arrow.

'*Hold!*' the other man between the trees cried then. 'Hold, Lady Aelis. If you harm another of my men we will begin killing your corans. Besides, there is the girl. Put down your bow.'

Her mouth dry and her heart pounding, Aelis looked over and saw that Ariane's frightened, snorting horse was firmly in the grasp of two of their attackers. All six of Urté's corans were down and disarmed, but none seemed to have been critically injured yet.

'It is you we want,' the leader in front of them said, as if answering her thought. 'If you come gently the others will not be further hurt. You have my word.'

'*Gently?*' Aelis snapped, with all the hauteur she could manage. 'Is this a setting for gentleness? And how highly should I value the word of a man who has done this?'

They were halfway to the arch, among the elms. To her right, across the lake, Talair was clearly visible. Behind her, if she turned, she could probably still see Miraval. They had been attacked within sight of both castles.

'You don't really have a great deal of choice, do you?' the man before her said, taking a few steps forward. He was of middling height, clad in brown, with a midwinter carnival mask, unsettlingly incongruous in such a place as this, covering most of his face.

'Do you know what my husband will do to you?' Aelis said grimly. 'And my father in Barbentain? Have you any idea?'

'I do, actually,' the masked man said. Beside him, the one she had wounded was still clutching his shoulder; there was blood on his hand. 'And it has rather a lot to do with money, my lady. Rather a lot of money, actually.'

'You are a very great fool!' Aelis snapped. They had surrounded her horse now, but no one, as yet, had reached for the reins. There seemed to be about fifteen of them — an extraordinary number for an outlaw band, so near the two castles. 'Do you expect to live to spend anything they give you? Don't you know how you will be pursued?'

'These are indeed worrisome matters,' the man in front of her said, not sounding greatly worried. 'I don't expect you to have given them much thought. I have.' His voice sharpened. 'I do expect you to co-operate, though, or people will start being hurt, and I'm afraid that might include the girl. I don't have unlimited time, Lady Aelis, or patience. Drop the bow!'

There was a crack of command in the last sentence that actually made Aelis jump. She looked over at Ariane; the girl was big-eyed, trembling with fear. Riquier lay face down on the grass. He seemed to be unconscious, but there was no blade wound she could see.

'The others will not be hurt?' she said.

'I said that. I don't like repeating myself.' The voice was muffled by the festive mask, but the arrogance came through clearly.

Aelis dropped her bow. Without another word the leader turned and nodded his head. From behind the arch, having been hidden by its massive shape, another man stepped out leading two horses. The leader swung himself up on a big grey, and beside him the wounded man awkwardly mounted a black mare. No one else moved. The others were clearly going to stay and deal with the corans.

'What will you do with the girl?' Aelis called out.

The outlaw turned back. 'I am done with questions,' he said bluntly. 'Will you come, or will you need to be trussed and carried like an heifer?'

With deliberate slowness, Aelis moved her horse forward. When she was beside Ariane she stopped and said, very clearly, 'Be gallant, bright one, they will not, they *dare* not do you any harm. With Rian's grace I shall see you very soon.'

She moved on, still slowly, sitting her horse with head high and shoulders straight as befitted her father's daughter.

The leader paid her no attention, he had already wheeled his mount and had begun to ride, not even glancing back. The wounded man fell in behind Aelis. The three of them went forward in a soft jingling of harness, passing under the Arch of the Ancients, through the cold shadow of it, and then out into sunlight again on the other side.

They rode through the young grasses, travelling almost due north. Behind them the shoreline of Lake Dierne fell away, curving to the east. On their left Urté's vineyards stretched into the distance. Ahead of them was the forest. Aelis kept her silence and neither of the masked men spoke. As they approached the outlying pines and balsams of the wood Aelis saw a charcoal-burner's cottage lying just off the lightly worn path. The door was open. There was no one in sight, nor were there any sounds in the morning light save their horses and the calling of birds.

The leader stopped. He had not even looked at her since they had begun to ride, nor did he now. 'Valery,' he said, scanning the edges of the forest to either side, 'keep watch for the next while, but find Garnoth first — he won't be far away — and have him clean and bind your shoulder. There's water in the stream.'

'There is usually water in a stream,' the wounded man said in a deep voice, his tone unexpectedly tart. The leader laughed; the sound carried in the stillness.

'You have no one to blame for that wound but yourself,' he said, 'don't take your grievances out on me.' He swung down from his horse, and then he looked at Aelis for the first time. He motioned for her to dismount. Slowly she did. With an elaborately graceful gesture — almost a parody given where they were — he indicated the entrance to the cottage.

Aelis looked around. They were quite alone, a long way from where anyone might chance to pass. The man Valery, masked in fur like a grey wolf, was already turning away to find Garnoth, whoever that was — probably the charcoal-burner. Her arrow was still in his shoulder.

She walked forward and entered the hut. The outlaw leader followed and closed the door behind him. It shut with a loud click of the latch. There were windows on either side, open so that the breeze could enter. Aelis walked to the centre of the small, sparsely furnished room, noting that it had been recently swept clean. She turned around.

Bertran de Talair, the younger son, the troubadour, removed the falcon mask he wore.

'By all the holy names of Rian,' he said, 'I have never known a woman like you in my life. Aelis, you were magnificent.'

With some difficulty she kept her expression stern, despite what seeing his face again, the flash of his quick, remembered smile, was suddenly doing to her. She forced herself to gaze coolly into the unnerving clarity of his blue eyes. She was not a kitchen girl, not a tavern wench in Tavernel, to swoon into his arms.

'Your man is badly wounded,' she said sharply. 'I might have killed him. I sent specific word with Brette that I was going to shoot an arrow when you stopped us. That you should tell your men to wear chain mail under their clothing.'

'And I told them,' said Bertran de Talair with an easy shrug. He moved towards the table, discarding his mask, and Aelis saw belatedly that there was wine waiting for them. It was becoming more difficult by the moment, but she continued to fight the impulse to smile back at him, or even to laugh aloud.

'I did tell them, truly,' Bertran repeated, attending to the wine bottle. 'Valery chose not to. He doesn't like armour. Says it impedes his movement. He'll never make a proper coran, my cousin Valery.' He shook his head in mock sorrow and then glanced over his shoulder at her again. 'Green becomes you, as the leaves the trees. I cannot believe you are here with me.'

She seemed to be smiling, after all. She struggled to keep control of the subject though; there was a real issue here. She could easily have killed the man, Valery. 'But you chose not to tell him *why* he ought to protect himself, correct? You didn't tell him I planned to shoot. Even though you knew he would be the one standing beside you.'

Smoothly he opened the bottle. He grinned at her. 'Correct and correct. Why are all the de Barbentain so unfairly clever? It makes it terribly difficult for the rest of us, you know.

I thought it might be a lesson for him — Valery should know by now that he ought to listen when I make a suggestion, and not ask for reasons.'

'I might have killed him,' Aelis said again.

Bertran was pouring the wine into two goblets. Silver and machial, she saw, not remotely belonging in a cabin such as this. She wondered what the charcoal-burner was being paid. The goblets were each worth more than the man would earn in his whole life.

Bertran came towards her, offering wine. 'I trusted your aim,' he said simply. The simple brown jacket and leggings became him, accenting his burnished outdoor colour and the bronze of his hair. The eyes were genuinely extraordinary; most of the lineage of Talair had those eyes. In the women, that shade of blue had broken hearts in Arbonne and beyond for generations. In the men too, Aelis supposed.

She made no motion towards the extended goblet. Not yet. She was the daughter of Guibor de Barbentain, count of Arbonne, ruler of this land.

'You trusted your cousin's life to my aim?' she asked. 'Your own? An irrational trust, surely? I might have wounded you as easily as he.'

His expression changed. 'You did wound me, Aelis. At the midwinter feast. I fear it is a wound that will be with me all my life.' There was a gravity to his tone, sharply at odds with what had gone before. 'Are you truly displeased with me? Do you not know the power you have in this room?' The blue eyes were guileless, clear as a child's, resting on her own. The words and the voice were balm and music to her parched soul.

She took the wine. Their fingers touched as she did. He made no other movement towards her though. She sipped and he did the same, not speaking. It was Talair wine, of course, from his family's vineyards on the eastern shores of the lake.

She smiled finally, releasing him from interrogation for the moment. She sank down onto the one bench the cottage offered. He took a small wooden stool, leaning forward towards her, his long, musician's fingers holding the goblet in two hands. There was a bed by the far wall; she had been acutely aware of that from the moment she'd walked in, and equally aware that the charcoal-burner was unlikely to have had a proper bed for himself in this cottage.

Urté de Miraval would be a long way west by now in his favourite woods, lathering his horses and dogs in pursuit of a boar or a stag. The sunlight fell slantwise through the eastern window, laying a benison of light across the bed. She saw Bertran's glance follow hers in that direction. She saw him look away.

And realized in that instant, with a surge of unexpected discovery, that he was not nearly so assured as he seemed. That it might actually be true what he'd just said, what was so often spun in the troubadours' songs: that hers, as the high-born woman, the long-desired, was the true mastery in this room. *Even the birds above the lake...*

'What will they do with Ariane and the corans?' she asked, aware that unmixed wine and excitement were doing dangerous things to her. His hair was tousled from the confining mask and his smooth-shaven face looked clever and young and a little bit reckless. Whatever the rules of the courtly game, this would not be a man easily or always controlled. She had known that from the first.

As if to bear witness to that, he arched his brows, composed and poised again. 'They will be continuing on their way to Talair soon enough. My men will have removed their masks by now and declared themselves. We brought wine and food for a meal on the grass. Ramir was there, did you recognize him? He has his harp, and I wrote a ballad last week about a play-acting escapade by the arch. My parents will disapprove, and your husband I rather imagine, but no one has been hurt, except Valery by you, and no one will really be able to imagine or suggest I would do you any harm or dishonour. We will give Arbonne a story to be shocked about for a month or so, no more than that. This was fairly carefully thought out,' he said. She could hear the note of pride.

'Evidently,' she murmured. *A month or so, no more than that? Not so swiftly, my lord.* She was trying to guess how her mother would have handled this. 'How did you arrange for Brette in Miraval to help you?' she temporized.

He smiled. 'Brette de Vaux and I were fostered together.

We have had various . . . adventures with each other. I thought he could be trusted to help me with . . . '

'With another adventure, my lord?' She had her opening now. She stood. It seemed she didn't need to think of her mother after all. She knew exactly what to do. What she had dreamt of doing through the long nights of the winter just past. 'With the easy matter of another tavern song?'

He rose as well, awkwardly, spilling some of his wine. He laid the goblet down on the table, and she could see that his hand was trembling.

'Aelis,' he said, his voice low and fierce, 'what I wrote last winter was true. You need never undervalue yourself. Not with me, not with anyone alive. This is no adventure. I am afraid . . . ' he hesitated and then went on, 'I am greatly afraid that this is the consummation of my heart's desire.'

'What is?' she said then, forcing herself to remain calm despite what his words were doing to her. 'Having a cup of wine with me? How delicate. How modest a desire for your heart.'

He blinked in astonishment, but then the quality of his gaze changed, kindled, and his expression made her knees suddenly weak. She tried not to let that show either. He had been quick to follow her meaning though, too quick. She suddenly felt less sure of herself. She wished she had somewhere to set down her own wine. Instead, she drained it and let the empty goblet drop among the strewn rushes on the floor. She was unused to unmixed wine, to standing in a place so entirely alone with a man such as this.

Drawing a breath against the racing of her heart, Aelis said, 'We are not children, nor lesser people of this land, and I can drink a cup of wine with a great many different men.' She forced herself to hold his eyes with her own dark gaze. She swallowed, and said clearly, 'We are going to make a child today, you and I.'

And watched Bertran de Talair as all colour fled from his face. *He is afraid now*, she thought. Of her, of what she was, of the swiftness and the unknown depths of this.

'Aelis,' he began, visibly struggling for self-possession, 'any child you bear, as duchess of Miraval, *and* as your father's daughter — '

He stopped there. He stopped because she had reached up even as he began to speak and was now, with careful, deliberate motions, unbinding her hair.

Bertran fell silent, desire and wonder and the sharp awareness of implications all written in his face. It was that last she had to smooth away. He was too clever a man, for all his youth; he might hold back even now, weighing consequences. She pulled the last long ivory pin free and shook her head to let the cascade of her hair tumble down her back. *The sheerest encitement to desire.* So all the poets sang.

The poet before her, of a lineage nearly as proud as her own, said, with a certain desperation now, 'A child. Are you certain? How do you know that today, now, that we . . .'

Aelis de Miraval, daughter of the count of Arbonne, smiled then, the ancient smile of the goddess, of women centred in their own mysteries. She said, 'En Bertran, I spent two years on Rian's Island in the sea. We may have only a little magic there, but if it lies not in such matters as this, where should it possibly lie?'

And then knowing — without even having to think of what her mother would have done — knowing as surely as she knew the many-faceted shape of her own need, that it was time for words to cease, Aelis brought her fingers up to the silken ties at the throat of her green gown and tugged at them so that the silk fell away to her hips. She lowered her arms and stood before him, waiting, trying to control her breathing, though that was suddenly difficult.

There was hunger, a kind of awe and a fully kindled desire in his eyes. They devoured what she offered to his sight. He still did not move, though. Even now, with wine and desire racing through her blood, she understood: just as she was no tavern girl, he in turn was no drunken coran in a furtive corner of some baron's midnight hall. He too was proud, and intimately versed in power, and it seemed he still had too keen a sense of how far the reverberations of this moment might go.

'Why do you hate him so much?' Bertran de Talair asked softly, his eyes never leaving her pale, smooth skin, the curve of her breasts. 'Why do you hate your husband so?'

She knew the answer to that. Knew it like a charm or spell of Rian's priestesses chanted over and over in the starry, sea-swept darkness of the island nights.

'Because he doesn't love me,' Aelis said.

And held her hands out then, a curiously fragile gesture, as she stood, half-naked before him, her father's daughter, her husband's avenue to power, heiress to Arbonne, but trying to shape her own response today, now, in this room, to the coldness of destiny.

He took a step, the one step necessary, and gathered her in his arms, and lifted her, and then he carried her to the bed that was not the charcoal-burner's, and laid her down where the slanting beam of sunlight fell, warm and bright and transitory.

PART I

Spring

CHAPTER·1

There was very little wind, which was a blessing. Pale moonlight fell upon the gently swelling sea around the skiff. They had chosen a moonlit night. Despite the risks, they would need to see where they were going when they came to land. Eight oars, rising and falling in as much silence as the rowers could command, propelled them out across the line of the advancing waves towards the faint lights of the island, which was nearer now and so more dangerous.

Blaise had wanted six men only, knowing from experience that missions such as this were best done relying on stealth and speed rather than numbers. But the superstitious Arbonnais who were Mallin de Baude's household corans had insisted on eight going out so that there would be, if all went well, nine coming back when they were done. Nine, it appeared, was sacred to Rian here in Arbonne, and it was to Rian's Island they were rowing now. They'd even had a lapsed priest of the goddess go through a ritual of consecration for them. Blaise, his men watching closely, had reluctantly knelt and permitted the drunken old man to lay gnarled hands on his head, muttering unintelligible words that were somehow supposed to favour their voyage.

It was ridiculous, Blaise thought, pulling hard at his oar, remembering how he'd been forced to give in on those issues. In fact this whole night journey smacked of the absurd. The problem was, it was as easy to be killed on a foolish quest in the company of fools as on an adventure of merit beside men one respected and trusted.

Still, he had been hired by En Mallin de Baude to train the man's household corans, and it had suited his own purposes

19

for his first months in Arbonne to serve a lesser baron while he quietly sized up the shape of things here in this goddess-worshipping land and perfected his grasp of the language. Nor could it be denied — as Mallin had been quick to point out — that tonight's endeavour would help to hone the corans of Baude into a better fighting force. If they survived.

Mallin was not without ambition, nor was he entirely without merits. It was his wife, Blaise thought, who had turned out to be the problem. Soresina, and the utterly irrational customs of courtly love here in Arbonne. Blaise had no particular affection, for good and sufficient reasons, for the current way of things in his own home of Gorhaut, but nothing in the north struck him as quite so impractical as the woman-driven culture here of the troubadours and their joglars, wailing songs of love for one lord's wife or another. It wasn't even the maidens they sang of, in Corannos's name. It seemed a woman had to be wed to become the proper object of a poet's passion in Arbonne. Maffour, the most talkative of the household corans, had started to explain it once; Blaise hadn't cared enough to listen. The world was full of things one needed to know to survive; he didn't have the time to fill his brain with the useless chaff of a patently silly culture.

The island lights were nearer now across the water. From the front of the skiff Blaise heard one of the corans — Luth, of course — offer a fervent, nervous prayer under his breath. Behind his beard Blaise scowled in contempt. He would have gladly left Luth back on the mainland. The man would be next to useless here, good for nothing but guarding the skiff when they brought it ashore, if he could manage to do even that much without wetting himself in fear at owl noises or a falling star or a sudden wind in the leaves at night. It had been Luth who had begun the talk earlier, back on shore, about sea monsters guarding the approaches to Rian's Island — great, hump-backed, scaly creatures with teeth the size of a man.

The real dangers, as Blaise saw it, were rather more prosaic, though none the less acute for that: arrows and blades, wielded by the watchful priests and priestesses of Rian against falsely consecrated men come in secret in the night to the goddess's holy island with a purpose of their own.

Said purpose being in fact extremely specific: to persuade one Evrard, a troubadour, to return to Castle Baude from his self-imposed exile on Rian's Island in the depths of righteous indignation.

It was all genuinely ridiculous, Blaise thought again, pulling at the oar, feeling the salt spray in his hair and beard. He was glad that Rudel wasn't here. He could guess what his Portezzan friend would have had to say about this whole escapade. In his mind he could almost hear Rudel's laughter and his acerbic, devastating assessment of the current circumstances.

The story itself was straightforward enough — an entirely natural consequence, Blaise had been quick to declare in the hall at Baude, of the stupidity of the courtly rituals here in the south. He was already not much liked for saying such things, he knew. That didn't bother him; he hadn't been much liked in Gorhaut, either, the last while before he'd left home.

Still, what was an honest man to make of what had happened in Castle Baude last month? Evrard of Lussan, who was said to be a modestly competent troubadour — Blaise was certainly not in a position to judge one man's scribblings against another's — had elected to take up residence at Baude in the high country of the south-western hills for a season. This had redounded, in the way of things down here, to the greater renown of En Mallin de Baude: lesser barons in remote castles seldom had troubadours, modestly competent or otherwise, living with them for any length of time. That much, at least, made sense to Blaise.

But, of course, once settled in the castle, Evrard naturally had to fall in love with Soresina and begin writing his dawn-songs and liensennes, and his cryptic trobars for her. That, also in the way of such things here, was precisely why he had come, with the less romantic incentive, Blaise had caustically observed, of a handsome monthly payment out of Mallin's wool revenues from last autumn's fair in Lussan. The troubadour used a made-up name for his Lady — another rule of the tradition — but everyone in the vicinity of the castle, and surprisingly soon everyone in Arbonne who mattered at all, seemed to know that Evrard of Lussan, the troubadour, was heart-smitten by the beauty and grace of young Soresina de Baude in her castle tucked in a fold of the high country leading to the mountain passes and Arimonda.

Mallin was enormously pleased; that too was part of the game. A lovestruck troubadour exalting the baron's wife enhanced Mallin's own ardently pursued images of power and largess.

Soresina, of course, was thrilled beyond words. She was vain, pretty and easily silly enough, in Blaise's jaundiced opinion, to have precipitated exactly the sort of crisis with which they now found themselves dealing. If it hadn't been the one incident, it would have been another, he was sure of it. There were women like Soresina at home, too, but they were rather better kept in hand in Gorhaut. For one thing, their husbands didn't invite strangers into their castles for the express purpose of wooing them. However Maffour might try to explain the strict rules of this courtly game of love, Blaise knew an attempt at seduction when he saw one.

Soresina, manifestly uninterested in the newly resident poet in any genuinely romantic way — which no doubt reassured her husband more than somewhat — nonetheless contrived to lead Evrard on in every manner possible, given the constraints imposed by the extremely crowded spaces of a small baronial castle.

Mallin's yellow-haired wife had a ripe body, an infectious laugh and a lineage substantially more distinguished than her husband's: something that always added fuel to the fires of troubadour passion Blaise had been told by the discursive Maffour. He'd had to laugh; it was all so artificial, the whole process. He could guess, too easily, what acid-tongued Rudel would have said about this.

In the meantime, the celebrated southern spring came to Arbonne, with many-coloured wildflowers appearing almost overnight in the meadows and the high slopes about Castle Baude. The snows were reported to be receding from the mountain pass to Arimonda. As the poet's verses grew in heat and passion with the quickening season, so did the throbbing voices of the joglars who had begun arriving in Baude as well, knowing a good thing when they saw one. More than one of the corans and castle servants had private cause to thank the troubadour and the singers and the erotic atmosphere they'd induced for amorous interludes in kitchen and meadow and hall.

Unfortunately for him, Evrard's own cause was not aided by the all-too-evident reality that he was short, yellow-toothed and prematurely losing what thin hair he'd once had. Still, according to the great tradition, troubadours were supposed to be loved by the high ladies of culture and grace for their art and their fierce dedication, not for their height or hair.

Trouble was, Soresina de Baude didn't seem to care much for the great tradition, or that part of it, at any rate. She liked her men to look like the warlike corans of the great days past. Indeed, she'd made a point of telling Blaise as much shortly after he'd arrived, looking artlessly up at his tall, muscled form and then glancing down and away in transparently feigned shyness. Blaise, somewhat used to this sort of thing, had been neither surprised nor tempted. He was being paid by Mallin and had shaped his own code in such matters.

What Evrard of Lussan shaped, later that spring, was something else. In brief, the little troubadour, having downed a considerable quantity of unmixed Miraval red wine with the corans one night, finally elected to translate his fiercely impassioned verses into modestly passionate action.

Inflamed by a joglar's fervid rendition of one of his own ballads earlier that evening, the troubadour had left his sleeping place late at night and stumbled along dark and silent corridors and stairways to Soresina's door, which happened, unfortunately for all concerned, to be unlocked: Mallin, young, healthy, tall enough, and rather urgently seeking heirs, had but lately left his wife for his own chamber nearby.

The intoxicated, verse-enraptured poet had entered the pitch-black chamber, felt his way over to the canopied bed and planted a lover's kiss upon the lips of the satiated, sleeping woman he was busily making famous throughout Arbonne that spring.

There were a good many schools of thought evolving, in the aftermath of the event, as to what Soresina should have done. Ariane de Carenzu, queen of the Court of Love since the countess, her aunt, had passed the title to her, had proclaimed a session to rule on the matter later in the year. In the meantime, every man and woman Blaise encountered in the castle or outside it seemed to have an opinion on what he himself regarded as an entirely predictable, utterly trivial event.

What Soresina had done — quite naturally, or very unfortunately, depending on one's perspective — was scream. Roused from post-coital dreaming, then realizing who was in her chamber, she cursed her stunned, besotted admirer, in a voice heard by half the castle, as a rude, ill-bred peasant who deserved a public whipping.

What Evrard of Lussan, wounded to the core of his all-too-sensitive soul, had done in turn was leave Baude Castle before sunrise, proceed directly to the nearest sanctuary of the goddess, receive benediction and consecration and, making his way to the coast, cross by boat to Rian's Island in a retreat from the harsh, ungrateful society of women and castles that could so abuse the unstinting generosity of his art.

Safely on the island, away from the terrible storm and strife of the world beyond, he had begun soothing and diverting himself by composing hymns to the goddess, along with some undeniably witty satires on Soresina de Baude. Not by name, of course — rules were rules — but since the name he used now was the same one he'd coined to exalt the long-limbed elegance of her form and the dark fire of her eyes, no one in Arbonne was left even slightly in ignorance on this particular point. The students in Tavernel, Blaise had been given to understand by a seriously distressed Mallin, had taken up the songs and were amplifying them, adding verses of their own.

After a number of weeks of this, En Mallin de Baude — his wife an increasing object of amusement, his castle on the verge of becoming a byword for rustic bad manners, his conciliatory letters to Evrard on the island pointedly unanswered — elected to do something drastic.

For his own part, Blaise would probably have arranged to kill the poet. Mallin de Baude was a lord, if a minor one; Evrard of Lussan was no more than a travelling parasite in Blaise's view. A feud, even a dispute between two such men, would have been unthinkable in Gorhaut. But this, of course, was woman-ruled Arbonne, where the troubadours had a power in society they could never have dreamt of anywhere else.

In the event, what Mallin did was order Blaise and his corans to cross to the goddess's Island secretly by night and bring Evrard back. The baron, of course, couldn't lead the expedition himself, though Blaise had enough respect for the man to believe he would have preferred to. Mallin would need some distance from the escapade, though, in the event that they failed. He had to be able to say his corans had conceived the scheme without his knowledge or consent, and then hasten to a temple of Rian and make appropriate gestures of contrition. It was all made particularly neat, Blaise had thought, by the fact that the leader of the corans of Baude that season just happened to be a hired mercenary from Gorhaut who didn't, of course, worship Rian at all and might be expected to perpetrate such a sacrilege. Blaise didn't mention this thought to anyone. It didn't even really bother him; this was simply the way of things at a certain level of the world's affairs, and he had more than a little familiarity with it.

Soresina, languishing and aghast at what an instinctive scream and outburst had wrought, had been energetically primed by a succession of visiting neighbouring ladies, rather more experienced in the ways of poets, as to how to deal with Evrard on his return.

If Blaise and the corans got to the island. If they found him. If he chose to return. If the sea monsters of Luth's dark dreams chose not to rise up above their skiff, towering and dreadful in the pale moonlight, and drag them all down to death in the watery blackness.

'Towards those pines,' Hirnan, who was navigating, muttered from the front of the skiff. He glanced back over his broad shoulder at the looming shadow of the island. 'And for the love of Corannos, keep silent now!'

'Luth,' Blaise added softly, 'if I hear a sound from you, any kind of sound from now until we're back on the mainland, I will slit your throat and slide you overboard.'

Luth gulped, quite noisily. Blaise elected not to kill him for that. How such a man had ever been consecrated a warrior in the Order of Corannos he could not understand. The man could handle a bow well enough, and a sword and a horse, but surely, even here in Arbonne, they had to know that there was more to being a coran of the god than those skills. Were there no standards any more? No pride left in a corrupt and degenerate world?

He looked back over his shoulder again. They had rowed very close now. The pines were around towards the western side of the island, away from the sandy northern beaches and the glowing lights beyond that marked the three temples and the residences. Hirnan, who had been here before — he hadn't said why and Blaise hadn't pushed him — had said there was no chance of landing undetected on any of those northern beaches. The servants of Rian guarded their island; in the past they had had cause to fear more than a single skiff of corans searching for a poet.

They were going to have to try to get ashore in a harder place, where the forest pines gave way, not to sand, but to rocky cliffs and boulders in the sea. They had rope with them, and each of the corans, even Luth, knew how to handle himself on a rock face. Castle Baude was perched high in the wild country of the south-west. Men who served there would not be unfamiliar with cliffs or crags.

The sea was another matter. Hirnan and Blaise himself were the only ones entirely at ease on the water, and on Hirnan's shoulders now rested the burden of getting them close enough, amid sharp and shadowed rocks, to make it possible to come ashore. Privately, Blaise had told him that if the best they could find was a sheer cliff face, they didn't really have a chance. Not at night and with the need for absolute silence and with a poet to bring back down. In addition to which —

'Couch oars!' he hissed. In the same instant Maffour, beside him, snarled the same words. Eight rowers swiftly lifted their oars from the water and sat rigidly still, the skiff gliding silently towards the island. The sound came again, nearer now. Motionless, bent low for concealment, Blaise strained his eyes into the night, searching by moonlight for the boat he'd heard.

Then it was there, a single dark sail against the starry sky, skimming through the waves around the island. In the skiff eight men held their breath. They were inside the circling path of the sailboat, though, very near — dangerously near, in fact — to the rocky coast. Someone looking towards them in this faint light would almost certainly see nothing against the dark bulk of the island; and the guards, Blaise knew, would probably be looking outward in any case. He relaxed his fingers on his oar as the small boat continued past them, cutting across the wind, a beautiful thing in the moonlight.

'The goddess be praised!' Luth murmured with reflexive piety from up front beside Hirnan.

Cursing himself for not having sat the man next to him, Blaise flung a furious look over his shoulder in time to see Hirnan's hand shoot out and grip his benchmate fiercely on the arm in a belated effort to silence him.

'Ouch!' Luth said. Not quietly. At sea. In a very calm night.

Blaise closed his eyes. There was a moment of straining silence, then:

'Who is there! In Rian's name, declare yourselves!' A grim male voice rang out from the sailboat.

His brain racing furiously, Blaise looked over and saw the other boat already beginning to swing about. They had two choices now. They could retreat, rowing frantically, and hope to lose the guards in the darkness of the sea. No one knew who they were; they might not be seen or identified. But the mainland was a long way off, and eight men rowing had little chance of outracing sails if they were pursued. And this one sailboat could have others with it very soon, Blaise knew.

He hated retreating anyhow.

'Only fisherfolk, your grace,' he called out in a wavering, high-pitched voice. 'Only my brothers and myself trawling for lampfish. We're terrible sorry to have wandered out so far.'

He lowered his voice to a snarled whisper. 'Get three of the ropes over the side, quickly! Hold them as if you were fishing. Hirnan, you and I are going into the water.' Even as he spoke he was removing his boots and sword. Hirnan, without a question asked, began doing the same.

'It is interdicted to come so near the goddess's Island without leave. You are subject to Rian's curse for what you have done.' The deep voice across the water was hostile and assured. The boat was still turning; it would begin bearing down upon them in a moment.

'We are not to kill,' Maffour whispered anxiously from beside Blaise.

'I know that,' Blaise hissed back. 'Do what I told you. Offer them a tithe. Hirnan, let's go.'

With the last words he swung his feet across the low railing and slipped silently over the side of the skiff. On the other side, balancing his motion exactly, Hirnan did the same. The water was shockingly cold. It was night, and early yet in the spring.

'Truly, your graces, as my brother says, we had no intention to transgress.' Maffour's apologetic voice carried across the darkness. 'We will gladly offer a tithe of our catch for the holy servants of blessed Rian.'

There was a silence from the other boat, very much as if someone were weighing a sudden temptation. That, Blaise had not expected. To his right he spotted Hirnan's dark head bobbing towards him. He motioned, and the two of them began swimming quietly towards the other boat.

'Are you fools?' The second voice from the sailboat was a woman's, and cold as the ocean waters. 'Do you think you can make redress for trespass in the waters of the goddess by offering a load of fish?'

Blaise grimaced. The priestesses of the goddess were always harsher than the priests; even a short time in Arbonne had taught him that much. He heard the sound of flint being struck, and a moment later, cursing silently, saw a lamp lit in the sailboat. A glow of orange light fell upon the water but offered only slight illumination. Praying that the six corans in the skiff would have the sense to keep their heads down and faces hidden, he gestured for Hirnan to move closer. Then, treading silently in the sea, he put his mouth to the other man's ear and told him what they had to try to do.

Holding the lamp high while Maritte guided their craft, Roche the priest peered ahead into the night. Even with the flame, even by the light of the waxing pale moon, it was difficult to see clearly. Certainly the skiff they were approaching was one such as the fisherfolk of the shore used, and he could make out the lines of the trawling nets over the side, but there was still something odd about this encounter. For one thing, there seemed to be too many men in the skiff. He counted at least five. Where were they going to put their catch with so

many men on board? Roche had grown up by the sea; he knew
more than a little about trawling for lampfish. He also loved
— more than a little — the taste of the succulent, hard-to-
find delicacy, which is why he'd been shamefully tempted by
the offered tithe. Maritte, mountain-born, had no such weaknesses to tempt her. Sometimes he wondered if Maritte had
any weaknesses at all. He would not be particularly unhappy
when their shared tour of duties ended next week, though he
couldn't claim to regret the three obligatory nights in bed
together. He wondered if she had conceived by him, what a
child born of the two of them would be like.

It really did seem to be a fishing boat. Manned by too
many men most likely because they were afraid, venturing so
near the island. It happened more often than it should, Roche
knew. The deep waters around Rian's Island were a known
ground for lampfish. A pity, he sometimes thought — aware
that this was perilously near to heresy — that all fish and
fauna on or about the island were sacred to the goddess in her
incarnation as Huntress, and so not to be pursued in any way
by mortal man or woman.

One really couldn't entirely blame the fisherfolk of Arbonne for occasionally yielding to the lure of that rare and delicate taste and once in a while venturing perhaps a little nearer
the island than they ought. He wondered if he dared turn to
Maritte and offer that thought, in the spirit of compassionate
Rian. He forebore to do so. He could guess what she would say,
mountain-born, hard as mountain rock. Though not so much
so in the dark, mind you, surprisingly softened by passion and
its aftermath. The three nights had been worth it, he decided,
whatever she'd have said now to his suggestion.

What Maritte did in fact say in that moment, her voice
suddenly harsh, was: 'Roche, these are not fisherfolk. Those
are only ropes, not nets! We must —'

That was all, lamentably, that Roche heard. Even as he
leaned quickly forward to peer more closely at the skiff,
Roche of the Island felt himself pulled bodily out of their
small boat, the lantern flying from his hand to douse itself
hissing in the sea.

He tried to cry out, but he hit the water with a smack
that knocked the wind from his lungs. Then, as he desperately

sucked for air, he went under an advancing wave, swallowed a mouthful of salt sea water and began retching and coughing. There was a hand holding him from behind in a grip like a blacksmith's. Roche coughed and gasped and coughed, and finally cleared his lungs of water.

He drew one normal breath and then, as if that had been a patiently awaited signal, received a blow from the haft of a knife on the side of his head that rendered him oblivious to the icy chill of the water or the beauty of moonlight on the sea. He did have an instant to realize, just before all went black, that he hadn't heard a sound from Maritte.

Blaise was briefly afraid, as he manoeuvred the unconscious priest back into the sailboat with Hirnan's help, that the other man, anxious not to err, might have killed the woman with his blow. After he had clambered with some difficulty into the boat he reassured himself. She would have a lump like a corfe egg on her temple for a few days, but Hirnan had done well. He spared a moment to grip the other man briefly on the shoulder in approbation; such things mattered to the men one led. He had some experience of that, too — on both sides of the equation.

The sailboat was neat and trim and well equipped, which meant plenty of rope. There were also blankets against the night chill and an amount of food that might have been surprising had the priest not been so plump. He stripped the unconscious man of his sodden shirt, then swaddled him in one of the blankets. They bound and gagged both the man and the woman, though not so tightly as to cripple them, and then steered the boat towards their own skiff.

'Maffour,' he said, keeping his voice low, 'take charge there. Follow us in. We're going up to find a landing place. Luth, if you prefer, you can kill yourself now before I get to you. It might be more pleasant.' With some satisfaction he heard Luth moan in distress. The man believed him. Beside Blaise in the sailboat Hirnan grunted with a sour, chilled amusement. With a degree of surprise Blaise recognized within himself the once-familiar sensation of sharing competence and respect with another man on a task of some danger.

Danger, yes, rather more evidently now, given what they

had just done to two of Rian's anointed. But tonight's was still a quest of sheerest stupidity — as to that Blaise's opinion was not about to change simply because they had dealt neatly with their first obstacle. Shivering and wet, rubbing his arms in an effort to generate necessary warmth, he realized, though, almost against his will, that he had enjoyed the moments just past.

And, as so often seemed to happen, the surmounting of a crisis seemed to incline chance or fate or Corannos the god — one or all of them — to show favour in the next stage of a difficult enterprise. Hirnan grunted again a few minutes later, this time with a note of satisfaction, and a second afterwards Blaise saw why. Gliding westward, as close to shore as he dared, Hirnan had brought them abreast of a small inlet among the rocks. Blaise saw trees above, their tops silvered by the high moon, and a gently sloping plateau beneath them giving way to a short cliff down to the sea. An almost perfect place for a landing, given that the beaches were barred to them. The inlet would offer shelter and concealment for the two boats and the climb to the plateau was unlikely to be difficult for men used to the steepness of the goat runs above the olive trees near Baude.

Hirnan guided the two craft carefully into the cove. In the boat he quickly lowered sail and set about dropping anchor. In the skiff, Maffour, without a word spoken, looped one of the ropes about his shoulders and, leaping to the nearest of the rocks, adroitly scrambled up the short face of the cliff to the plateau. He tied the rope to one of the pines above and dropped it over for the rest of them. *Two good men here*, Blaise thought, realizing that he really hadn't given much thought at all, in the time he'd been here, to taking the measure of the corans of Mallin de Baude. He acknowledged inwardly that Mallin had been right in at least one thing: the truest test of a man's mettle was a task where the danger was real.

Hirnan finished with the anchor and turned to Blaise with an arched eyebrow of inquiry. Blaise glanced down at the two tied-up clerics in the boat. Both were unconscious and would likely be so for awhile. 'We'll leave them here,' he said. 'They'll be all right.'

The men in the skiff were already proceeding up

Maffour's rope towards the plateau. They watched the last one climb, then Hirnan stepped carefully from the boat to one slippery boulder and then another before reaching the rope and smoothly pulling himself up the rock face. Behind him, Blaise did the same. The salt of the wet rope stung his palms.

On the plateau he set his feet squarely on solid ground for the first time since leaving the mainland. The sensation was odd, as if there were a tremor in the earth beneath him. They were standing on Rian's Island, and illicitly consecrated, Blaise thought unexpectedly. None of the others seemed to have reacted, though, and a moment later he grinned with wry amusement at himself: he was from Gorhaut, in the god's name — they didn't even worship Rian in the north. This was hardly a useful time to be yielding to the superstitions that had afflicted Luth all night.

Young Giresse, without a word, handed him his boots and sword, and Thiers did the same for Hirnan. Blaise leaned against a tree to pull on the boots and buckled his sword belt again, thinking quickly. When he looked up he saw seven tense men looking at him, waiting for orders. Deliberately he smiled.

'Luth, I have decided to let you live to trouble the world a little longer yet,' he said softly. 'You'll guard the two boats here with Vanne. If those two down below show signs of rousing I want them rendered unconscious again. But conceal your faces if you have to go down to do it. If we are very lucky none of us will have been recognized when this is over. Do you understand?'

They seemed to. Luth looked almost comically relieved at the assignment. Vanne's expression by moonlight showed a struggle to conceal disappointment — a good sign actually, if he was sorry to be missing the next stage of their journey. But Blaise was not about to leave Luth alone now with any task, however simple. He turned away from them.

'Hirnan, I take it you can find the guest quarters once we reach the temple complex?' The red-headed coran nodded briefly. 'You lead then,' Blaise said. 'I'm behind you, Maffour's rear guard. We go in single file. No words unless vital. Touch each other for warnings rather than speak. Understood?'

'One question: how do we find Evrard when we get there?' Maffour asked quietly. 'There must be a great many dwellings in the complex.'

'There are,' Hirnan murmured.

Blaise had been privately worrying about the same thing. He shrugged though; his men weren't to know what was concerning him. 'I'm assuming he'll have one of the larger ones. We'll head for those.' He grinned suddenly. 'Then Maffour can walk in and wake him with a kiss.' There was a ripple of laughter. Behind him, Luth giggled loudly but controlled himself before Blaise could turn.

Blaise let the tension-easing amusement subside. He looked at Hirnan. Without another word spoken the coran turned and stepped into the the forest of the holy Island of the goddess. Blaise followed and heard the others fall into line behind. He didn't look back.

It was very dark in the woods. There were sounds all around them: wind in the leaves, the chitter of small animals, the quick, unsettling flap of wings alighting from a branch above. The pines and the oak trees blocked the moon except in the occasional place where a slant of pale silver fell across their path, strangely beautiful, intensifying the blackness as soon as they had moved on. Blaise checked his blade in its scabbard. It would be close and awkward ground here if anything large chose to attack. He wondered if any of the big hunting cats made their home on Rian's Island; he had a feeling they did, which was not reassuring.

Hirnan, threading his way around roots and under branches, finally struck a rough east-west track in the wood and Blaise drew a calmer breath again. He was surprisingly conscious of where they were. Not that he had any real superstition in him, but there was something about this forest that, even more than the thought of tawncat or boar, would make him very happy when they left. In fact, that same truth applied to all of this island, he realized: the sooner they left the more pleased he would be. Just then a bird of some sort — owl or corfe almost certainly — landed with a slight, rushing sound of wings in air in the tree directly above him. Luth, Blaise thought, would have soiled his clothing. Refusing to look up, he moved on, following Hirnan's shadowy form eastward towards the temples of the goddess worshipped here in the south as a huntress and a mother, as a lover and a bride, and as a dark and final gatherer and layer-out, by moonlight, of the dead. *If we're luckier than we deserve,* Blaise of Gorhaut thought grimly, more unsettled than he really wanted to acknowledge, even to himself, *maybe he'll be outside singing at the moon.*

Which, as it happened, was exactly what Evrard of Lussan was doing. Troubadours seldom in fact sang their own songs; musical performance was seen as a lesser art than composing. It was the joglars who did the actual singing, to the music of varied instruments. But here on Rian's Island there were no joglars now, and Evrard had always found it a help when writing to hear his own words and evolving tune, even in his own thin voice. And he liked to compose at night.

They heard him as they approached the sanctuary grounds, emerging from the blackness of the forest into moonlight and a sight of distant lanterns. Drawing a breath, Blaise registered the fact that there were no walls around the guest quarters south of the temple complex, though a high wooden palisade surrounded the inner buildings where the priests and priestesses would be sleeping. There didn't appear to be any guards manning the ramparts behind those walls, or none that could be seen. Silver light fell on the temples, lending a soft white shimmer to the three domes.

They didn't have to go that way. On the extreme southern edge of the goddess's compound, not far from where they stood, there was a garden. Palm trees swayed in the gentle breeze, and the scent of roses and anemones and early lavender drifted towards them. So did a voice.

> *Grant, bright goddess, that the words of my heart*
> *Find favour and haven in the shrine of your love.*
> *Yours are the seafoam and the groves in the wood*
> *And yours ever the moonlight in the skies above...*

There was a brief, meditative pause. Then:

> *And yours the moonlight that falls from above...*

Another ruminating silence, then again Evrard's voice:

Yours is the moonlight and the stars overhead
And the moonlit seafoam and each forest grove.

Blaise saw Hirnan glancing at him, an ironic look on his expressive face. Blaise shrugged. 'Mallin wants him back,' he murmured. 'Don't look at me.' Hirnan grinned.

Blaise stepped past the other man and, keeping to the shadowy cover at the edge of the wood, began working his way around towards the garden, where the thin voice was still essaying variants of the same sentiment. Blaise wondered if the clergy and the other guests of Rian minded having their sleep disturbed by this late-night warbling. He wondered if it happened every night. He had a suspicion, knowing Evrard of Lussan, that it might.

They reached the southern end of the wood. Only grass, silvered by moonlight, open to view from the walls, lay between them and the hedges and palms of the garden now. Blaise dropped down, remembering with an eerie, unexpected vividness as he did the last time he'd performed this kind of manoeuvre, in Portezza with Rudel, when they had killed Engarro di Faenna.

And now here he was, fetching a sulky, petulant poet for a minor baron of Arbonne so the baron's wife could kiss the man on his balding brow — and the god knew where else — and say how extremely sorry she was for chancing to scream when he assaulted her in bed.

A long way from Portezza. From Gorhaut. From the sort of doings in which a man should properly find himself engaged. The fact that Blaise loathed almost everything about Gorhaut, which was his home, and trusted at most half a dozen of the Portezzan nobility he'd met was, frankly, not relevant to this particular truth.

'Thiers and Giresse — wait here,' he whispered over his shoulder to the youngest two. 'We won't need six men for this. Whistle like a corfe if there's trouble coming. We'll hear you. Maffour, you've been told what speech to give. Better you than me, frankly. When we get to the garden and I give you the sign go in and try, for what it's worth. We won't be far.'

He didn't wait for acknowledgements. At this point, any halfway decent men would know as well as he did what had to be done, and if there were any legitimate point to this mission in Blaise's eyes, it was that he might begin to get a sense of what these seven Arbonnais corans he was training were like.

Without looking back he began moving on elbows and knees across the damp cool grass towards the hedgebreak that marked the entrance to the garden. Evrard was still carrying on inside; something about stars now, and white-capped waves.

In his irritation with the man, with himself, with the very nature of this errand, he almost crawled, quite unprofessionally, squarely into the backside of the priestess who was standing, half-hidden, beside the closest palm to the entranceway. Blaise didn't know if she was there as a guard for the poet or as a devotee of his art. There really wasn't time to explore such nuances. A sound from the woman could kill them all.

Fortunately, she was raptly intent on the figure of the chanting poet not far away. Blaise could see Evrard sitting on a stone bench at the near end of a pool in the garden, facing away from them, communing with himself, or the still waters, or whatever poets did their communing with.

Disdaining finesse, Blaise surged to his feet, grabbed the woman from behind and covered her mouth with one hand. She sucked air to scream and he tightened his grip about her mouth and throat. They were not to kill. He disliked unnecessary death in any event. In the silence he had been trained to by the assassins of Portezza, Blaise held the struggling woman, depriving her of air until he felt her slump heavily back against him. Carefully — for this was an old trick — he relaxed his grip. There was no deception here though; the priestess lay slack in his arms. She was a large woman with an unexpectedly young face. Looking at her, Blaise doubted this one would have been a guard. He wondered how she'd got out from the compound; it was the sort of thing that might someday be useful to know. Not that he planned on coming back here in a hurry, if ever.

Laying the priestess carefully down beneath the palm tree, he motioned Maffour with a jerk of his head to go into the garden. Hirnan and Thulier came silently up and began binding the woman in the shadows.

Yours the glory, bright Rian, while we mortal men
Walk humbly in the umbra of your great light,
Seeking sweet solace in the —

'Who is there?' Evrard of Lussan called without turning, more peeved than alarmed. 'You all *know* I must not be disturbed when I work.'

'We do know that, your grace,' Maffour said smoothly, coming up beside the man.

Edging closer, hidden by the bushes, Blaise winced at the unctuous flattery of the title. Evrard had no more claim to it than Maffour did, but Mallin had been explicit in his instructions to the most articulate of his corans.

'Who are you?' Evrard asked sharply, turning quickly to look at Maffour in the moonlight. Blaise moved nearer, low to the ground, trying to slip around to the other side of the bench. He had his own views on what was about to happen.

'Maffour of Baude, your grace, with a message from En Mallin himself.'

'I thought I recognized you,' Evrard said haughtily. 'How *dare* you come in this fashion, disturbing my thoughts and my art?' Nothing about impiety or trespass or the affront to the goddess he was currently lauding, Blaise thought sardonically, pausing next to a small statue.

'I have nothing to say to your baron or his ill-mannered wife, and am in no mood to listen to whatever tritely phrased message they have cobbled together for me.' Evrard's tone was lordly.

'I have come a long way in some peril,' Maffour said placatingly, 'and Mallin de Baude's message is deeply sincere and not long. Will you not honour me by hearing it, your grace?'

'Honour?' Evrard of Lussan said, his voice rising querulously. 'What claim has anyone in that castle to honour of any kind? I bestowed upon them a grace they never deserved. I *gave* to Mallin whatever dignity he claimed — through my presence there, through my art.' His words grew dangerously loud. 'Whatever he was becoming in the gaze of Arbonne, of the world, he owed to me. And in return, in return for that — '

'In return for that, for no reason I can understand, he seeks your company again,' Blaise said, stepping quickly forward, having heard quite a bit more than enough.

As Evrard glanced back at him wide-eyed, attempting to rise, Blaise used the haft of his dagger for the second time that night, bringing it down with carefully judged force on the balding pate of the troubadour. Maffour moved quickly to catch the man as he fell.

'I cannot begin to tell you,' Blaise said fervently as Hirnan and Thulier joined them, 'how much I enjoyed doing that.'

Hirnan grunted. 'We can guess. What took you so long?'

Blaise grinned at the three of them. 'What? And interfere with Maffour's great moment? I really wanted to hear that speech.'

'I'll recite it for you on the way back then,' Maffour said sourly. 'With all the "your grace's" too.'

'Spare us,' said Hirnan briefly. He bent and effortlessly shouldered the body of the small troubadour.

Still grinning, Blaise led the way this time, without a word, down towards the south end of the garden, away from the sanctuary lights and the walls and the temple domes, and then, circling carefully, back towards the shelter of the wood. If these were the corans of a lesser baron, he was thinking to himself, and they turned out to be this coolly competent — with one vivid exception — he was going to have to do some serious reassessing, when they got back to land, of the men of this country of Arbonne, even with its troubadours and joglars and a woman ruling them.

The one vivid exception was having, without the least shadow of any possible doubt, the worst night of his life.

In the first place, there were the noises. Even at the edge of the woods, the sounds of the night forest kept making their way to Luth's pricked ears, triggering waves of panic that succeeded each other in a seemingly endless progression.

Secondly there was Vanne. Or, not exactly Vanne, but his *absence*, for the other coran assigned to guard duty kept wilfully abandoning Luth, his designated partner, and making his own way down the rope to check on the two clerics in the sailboat, then going off into the forest itself to listen for the return of their fellows, or for other less happy possibilities. Either of these forays would leave Luth alone for long

moments at a time to cope with sounds and ambiguous shift-
ings in the shadows of the plateau or at the edges of the trees,
with no one to turn to for reassurance.

The truth was, Luth said to himself — and he would have
sworn to it as an oath in any temple of the goddess — that he
really wasn't a coward, though he knew every man here would
think him one from tonight onward. He *wasn't* though: put
him on a crag above Castle Baude in a thunderstorm, with
thieves on the slopes making off with the baron's sheep, and
Luth would be fierce in pursuit of them, sure-footed and deft
among the rocks, and not at all bad with his bow or blade when
he caught up with the bandits. He'd *done* that, he'd done it last
summer, with Giresse and Hirnan. He'd killed a man that night
with a bowshot in darkness, and it was he who had led the other
two back down the treacherous slopes to safety with the flock.

Not that they were likely to remember that, or bother to
remind the others of it, after tonight. If any of them lived
through tonight. If they ever left this island. If they —

What was that?

Luth wheeled, his heart lurching like a small boat hit by
a crossing wave, in time to see Vanne making his way back
onto the plateau from yet another survey of the woods. The
other coran gave him a curious glance in the shadows but
said nothing. They were not to speak, Luth knew. He found
their own enforced silence almost as stressful as the noises of
the night forest.

Because they weren't just noises, and this wasn't just
night-time. These were the sounds of Rian's Island, which was
holy, and the eight of them were here without proper consecration, without any claim of right — only a drunken ex-
priest's mangling of the words of ritual — and they had laid
violent hands on two of the goddess's truly anointed before
they'd even landed.

Luth's problem, very simply, was that he was a believer
in the powers of the goddess, profoundly so. If that could
really be called a problem. He'd had a religious, superstitious
grandmother who'd worshipped both Rian and Corannos
along with a variety of hearth spirits and seasonal ones, and
who'd known just enough about magic and folk spells to
leave the grandson she'd reared helplessly prey to the terrors

of precisely the sort of place where they were now. Had he not been so anxious not to lose face among the other corans and his baron and the big, capable, grimly sardonic northern mercenary Mallin had brought to lead and train them, Luth would certainly have found a way to back out of the mission when he was named for it.

He should have, he thought dismally. Whatever status that withdrawal would have cost him was as nothing compared to how he'd be diminished and mocked because of what had happened tonight. Who would ever have thought that simple piety, a prayer of thanks to holy Rian herself, could get a person into so much trouble? How should a high country man know how bizarrely far sound — a murmured prayer! — could carry at sea? And Hirnan had *hurt* him with that pincer-like grip of his. The oldest coran was a big man, almost as big as the bearded northerner, and his fingers had been like claws of iron. Hirnan should have known better, Luth thought, trying to summon some sense of outrage at how unfair all of this was turning out to be.

He jumped sideways again, stumbled, and almost fell. He was grappling for his sword when he realized that it was Vanne who had come up to him. He tried, with minimal success, to turn the motion into one of alertly prudent caution. Vanne, his face blandly expressionless, gestured and Luth bent his head towards him.

'I'm going down to check on them again,' the other coran said, as Luth had despairingly known he would. 'Remember, a corfe whistle if you need me. I'll do the same.' Mutely, trying to keep his own expression from shaping a forlorn plea, Luth nodded.

Moving easily, Vanne negotiated the plateau, grasped the rope and slipped over the side. Luth watched the line jerk for a few moments and then go slack as Vanne reached the rocks at the bottom. He walked over to the tree that Maffour had tied the rope to and knelt to run a practised eye over the knot. It was fine, Luth judged, it would continue to hold.

He straightened and stepped back. And bumped into something.

His heart lurching, he spun around. As he did, as he saw what had come, all the flowing blood in his veins seemed to dry up and change to arid powder. He pursed his lips and tried to whistle. Like a corfe.

No sound came out. His lips were dry, as bone, as dust, as death. He opened his mouth to scream but closed it silently and quite suddenly as a curved, jewelled, inordinately long dagger was lifted and held to his throat.

The figures on the plateau were robed in silk and satin, dyed crimson and silver, as for a ceremony. They were mostly women, at least eight of them, but there were two men besides. It was a woman, though, who held the crescent-shaped blade to his throat. He could tell from the swell of her body beneath her robe, even though she was masked. They were all masked. And the masks, every one of them, were of predatory animals and birds. Wolf and hunting cat, owl and hawk, and a silver-feathered corfe with golden eyes that glittered in the moonlight.

'Come,' said the priestess with the blade to Luth of Castle Baude, her voice cold and remote, the voice of a goddess at night. A goddess of the Hunt, in her violated sanctuary. She wore a wolf mask, Luth saw, and then he also realized that the ends of the gloves on her hands were shaped like the claws of a wolf. 'Did you truly think you would not be found and known?' she said.

No, Luth wanted frantically to say. *No, I never thought we could do this. I was sure we would be caught.*

He said nothing. The capacity for speech seemed to have left him, silence lying like a weight of stones on his chest. In terror, his brain going numb, Luth felt the blade caress his throat almost lovingly. The priestess gestured with a clawed hand; in response, Luth's feet, as if of their own will, led him stumbling into the night forest of Rian. There were scented priestesses of the goddess all about him as he went, women masked like so many creatures of prey, clad in soft robes of silver and red amid the darkness of the trees, with the pale moon lost to sight, like hope.

Coming back through the forest, Blaise felt the same rippling sensation as before through the soles of his boots, as if the earth here on the island had an actual pulse, a beating heart. They went faster now, having done what they had come to do, aware that the priestess by the garden might be missed and found at any time. Blaise had dropped back to let Hirnan, carrying the unconscious poet, guide them once more, with a sense of direction seemingly unerring in the darkness of the woods.

They left the forest path and began to twist their way north again through the densely surrounding trees, small branches and leaves crackling underfoot as they went. No moonlight fell here, but they had their night vision now, and they had been this way before. Blaise recognized an ancient, contorted oak, an anomalous sight in a strand of pine and cedar.

Shortly afterwards they came out of the woods onto the plateau. The moon was high overhead, and Maffour's rope was still tied around the tree, their pathway down to the sea and escape.

But neither Vanne nor Luth was anywhere to be seen.

His pulse prickling with a first premonitory sense of disaster, Blaise strode quickly to the edge of the plateau and looked down.

The sailboat was gone, and the two bound clerics with it. Their own skiff was still there, though, and Vanne's body was lying in it.

Beside Blaise, Maffour swore violently and made his way swiftly down the rope. He sprang over the boulders and into the skiff, bending quickly over the man lying there.

He looked up. 'He's all right. Breathing. Unconscious. I can't see any sign of a blow.' There was wonder and the first edge of real apprehension in his voice.

Blaise straightened, looking around the plateau for a sign of Luth. The other corans stood in a tight cluster together, facing outwards. They had drawn their swords. There was no sound to be heard; even the forest seemed to have gone silent, Blaise realized, with a tingling sensation along his skin.

He made his decision.

'Hirnan, get him into the skiff. All of you go down there. I don't know what's happened but this is no place to linger. I'm going to take a fast look around, but if I can't see anything we'll have to go.' He glanced quickly up at the moon, trying to judge the hour of night. 'Get the skiff free and give me a few moments to look. If you hear me do a corfe cry start rowing hard and don't wait. Otherwise, use your judgment.'

Hirnan looked briefly as if he would protest but said nothing. With Evrard of Lussan slung over his shoulder like a sack of grain, he made his way to the rope and down. The other corans began following. Blaise didn't wait to see them all descend. With the awareness of danger like a tangible presence within him, he drew his sword and stepped alone into the woods on the opposite side of the plateau from where they'd entered and returned.

Almost immediately he picked up a scent. Not of hunting cat or bear, nor of fox or badger or boar. What he smelled was the drifting fragrance of perfume. It was strongest to the west, away from where they had gone.

Blaise knelt to study the forest floor in the near-blackness. He wished Rudel were with him now, for a great many reasons, but in part because his friend was the best night tracker Blaise had ever known.

One didn't have to be expert, though, to realize that a company of people had passed here only a short time before, and that most if not all of them had been women. Blaise swore under his breath and stood up, peering into the darkness, uncertain of what to do. He hated like death to leave a man behind, but it was clear that a large number of priests and priestesses were somewhere ahead of him in the woods. *A few moments*, he had told Hirnan. Could he jeopardize the others in an attempt to find Luth?

Blaise drew a deep breath, aware once again now of that pulsing in the forest floor. He knew he was afraid; only a complete fool would not be afraid now. Even so, there was a core truth at the root of all of this for Blaise of Gorhaut, a very simple one: one did not leave a companion behind without an attempt at finding him. Blaise stepped forward into the darkness, following the elusive scent of perfume in the night.

'*Commendable*,' a voice said, immediately in front of him. Blaise gasped and levelled his blade, peering into blackness. 'Commendable, but extremely unwise,' the voice went on with calm authority. 'Go back. You will not find your fellow. Only death awaits you past this point tonight.'

There was a rustling of leaves and Blaise made out the tall, shadowy form of a woman in the space in front of him. There were trees on either side of her, as if framing a place to stand. It was very dark, much too black for him to see her face, but the note of assured command in her voice told its own grim story about what had happened to Luth. She hadn't touched Blaise, though; no others had leaped forth to attack. And Vanne had been unharmed in the skiff.

'I would be shamed in my own eyes if I left and did not try to bring him out,' Blaise said, still trying to make out the features of the woman in front of him.

He heard her laughter. 'Shamed,' she echoed, mockingly. 'Do not be too much the fool, Northerner. Do you truly think you could have done any of this had we not permitted it? Will you deny feeling the awareness of this wood? Do you actually believe you moved unknown, unseen?'

Blaise swallowed with difficulty. His levelled sword suddenly seemed a hapless, even a ridiculous thing. Slowly he lowered it.

'Why?' he asked. 'Why, then?'

Her laughter came again, deep and low. 'Would you know my reasons, Northerner? You would understand the goddess on her own Island?'

My reasons.

'You are the High Priestess, then,' he said, shifting his feet, feeling the earth's deep pulsing still. She said nothing. He swallowed again. 'I would only know where my man has gone. Why you have taken him.'

'One for one,' she said quietly. 'You were not consecrated to this place, any of you. You came here to take a man who was. We have allowed this for reasons of our own, but Rian exacts a price. Always. Learn that, Northerner. Know it as truth for so long as you are in Arbonne.'

Rian exacts a price. Luth. Poor, frightened, bumbling Luth. Blaise stared into the darkness, wishing he could see this woman, struggling to find words of some kind that might save the man they'd lost.

And then, as if his very thoughts were open to her, as if she and the forest knew them intimately, the woman lifted one hand, and an instant later a torch blazed in her grasp, illuminating their small space within the woods. He had not seen or heard her striking flint.

He did hear her laugh again, and then, looking at the tall, proud form, at the fine-boned, aristocratic features before him, Blaise realized, with a shiver he could not control, that her eyes were gone. She was blind. There was a white owl, a freak of nature, resting on her shoulder, gazing at Blaise with unblinking eyes.

Not really certain why he was doing so, but suddenly aware that he had now entered a realm for which he was terribly ill equipped, Blaise sheathed his sword. Her laughter subsided; she smiled.

'Well done,' Rian's High Priestess said softly. 'I am pleased to see you are not a fool.'

'To see?' Blaise said, and instantly regretted it.

She was undisturbed. The huge white owl did not move. 'My eyes were a price for access to a great deal more. I can see you very well without them, Blaise of Gorhaut. It was you who needed light, not I. I know the scar that curves along your ribs and the colour of your hair, both now and on the winter night you were born and your mother died. I know how your heart is beating, and why you came to Arbonne, and where you were before. I know your lineage and your history, much of your pain, all your wars, your loves, the last time you made love.'

It was a bluff, Blaise thought fiercely. *All* the clergy did this sort of thing, even Corannos's priests at home. All of them sought control with such arcane incantations.

'That last, then,' he dared say, even here, his voice rough. 'Tell me that last.'

She did not hesitate. 'Three months ago. Your brother's wife, in the ancient home of your family. Late at night, your own bed. You left before dawn on the journey that has brought you to Rian.'

Blaise heard himself make a queer grunting sound as if he'd been punched. He could not help himself. He felt suddenly dizzy, blood rushing from his head as if in flight from the inexorable precision of what he had just heard.

'Shall I go on?' she asked, smiling thinly, the illuminating torch held up for him to see her. There was a new note in her voice, a kind of pitiless pleasure in her power. 'You do not love her. You only hate your brother and your father. Your mother for dying. Yourself a little, perhaps. Would you hear more? Shall I tell your future for you now, like an old crone at the Autumn Fair?'

She was not old. She was tall and handsome, if no longer young, with grey in her dark hair. She knew things no one on earth should ever have known.

'No!' Blaise managed to say, forcing the word out. 'Do not!'

He feared her laughter, her mocking voice, but she was silent and so was the forest around them. Even the torch was burning without sound, Blaise realized belatedly. The owl lifted its wings suddenly as if to fly, but only settled itself again on her shoulder.

'Go then,' Rian's High Priestess said, not without gentleness. 'We have allowed you the man for whom you came. Take him and go.'

He should turn now, Blaise knew. He should do exactly as she said. There were things at work here far beyond his understanding. But he had led seven men to this place.

'Luth,' he said sturdily. 'What will be done to him?'

There was a strange, whistling sound; he realized it had come from the bird. The priestess said, 'His heart will be cut out while he lives. It will be eaten.' Her voice was flat, without intonation. 'His body will be boiled in a vat of very great age and his skin peeled from his bones. His flesh will be cut into pieces and used for divination.'

Blaise felt his gorge rising, his skin crawled with horror and loathing. He took an involuntary step backwards. And heard her laughter. There was genuine amusement, something young, almost girlish in the sound.

'Really,' the priestess said, 'I hadn't thought I was so convincing as all that.' She shook her head. 'How savage do you think we are? You have taken a living man, we take a living man from you. He will be consecrated as a servant of Rian and set to serve the goddess on her Island in redress for his transgression and yours. This one is more a cleric than a coran in any case, I think you know as much. It is as I told you, Northerner: you have been permitted to do this. It would have been different, I assure you, had we chosen to make it so.'

Relief washing over him like a stream of water, Blaise fought a sudden, uncharacteristic impulse to kneel before this woman, this incarnated voice of a goddess his countrymen did not worship.

'Thank you,' he said, his voice rough and awkward in his own ears.

'You are welcome,' she said, almost casually. There was a pause, as if she were weighing something. The owl was motionless on her shoulder, unblinking, gazing at him. 'Blaise, do not overvalue this power of ours. What has happened tonight.'

He blinked in astonishment. 'What do you mean?'

'You are standing at the very heart of our strength here on this island. We grow weaker and weaker the further we are from here, or from the other isle in the lake inland. Rian has no limits, but her mortal servants do. I do. And the goddess cannot be compelled, ever.'

She had built up a veil of power and magic and mystery, and now she was lifting it for him to see behind. And she had called him by his name.

'Why?' he asked, wonderingly. 'Why do you tell me this?'

She smiled, almost ruefully. 'Something in my own family, I suspect. My father was a man prone to take chances with trust. I seem to have inherited that from him. We might need each other, in a time not far from tonight.'

Struggling to absorb all of this, Blaise asked the only question he could think to ask. 'Who was he? Your father?'

She shook her head, amused again. 'Northerner, you seek to lead men in Arbonne. You will have to grow less bitter and more curious, I think, though it might be a long road for you. You should have known who was High Priestess on Rian's Island before you came. I am Beatritz de Barbentain, my father was Guibor, count of Arbonne, my mother is Signe, who rules us now. I am the last of their children yet alive.'

Blaise was actually beginning to feel as if he might fall down, so buffeted did he feel by all of this. *The skiff*, he thought. *The mainland*. He urgently needed to be away from here.

'Go,' she said, as if reading his thoughts again. She raised her hand very slightly and the torch instantly went out. In the suddenly enveloping darkness, Blaise heard her say in her earlier voice — the sound of a priestess, speaking with power:

'One last thing, Blaise of Gorhaut. A lesson for you to learn if you can: anger and hatred have limits that are reached too soon. Rian exacts a price for everything, but love is hers as well, in one of her oldest incarnations.'

Blaise turned then, stumbling over a root in the close night shadows. He left the wood, feeling moonlight as a blessing. He crossed the plateau and remembered, somehow, to untie Maffour's rope and loop it about himself. Finding handholds in the rock face, he descended the cliff to the sea. The skiff was still there, waiting some distance away from shore. They saw him by the light of the high, pale moon. He was going to swim out, almost prepared to welcome the cold shock of the water again, but then he saw them rowing back for him and he waited. They came in to the edge of the rocks and Blaise stepped into the boat helped by Maffour and Giresse. He saw that Evrard of Lussan was still unconscious, slumped at the back of the skiff. Vanne was sitting up, though, at the front. He looked a little dazed. Blaise was not surprised.

'They have kept Luth,' he said briefly as they looked at him. 'One man for one man. But they will do him no harm. I will tell you more on land, but in Corannos's name, let's go. I need a drink very badly, and we've a long way to row.'

He stepped over to his own bench and unwrapped the rope from his body. Maffour came and sat beside him again. They took their oars, and with no other words spoken, backed quietly out of the inlet Hirnan had found and turned the skiff towards land, towards Arbonne, rowing steadily in the calm, still night.

To the east, not long afterwards, well before they reached the shore, the waning crescent of the blue moon rose out of the sea to balance the silver one setting westward now, changing the light in the sky and on the water and on the rocks and trees of the island they were leaving behind.

CHAPTER·2

Some mornings, as today, she woke feeling amazingly young, happy to be alive to see the spring return. It wasn't altogether a good thing, this brief illusion of youth and vitality, for its passage — and it always passed — made her too achingly aware that she was lying alone in the wide bed. She and Guibor had shared a room and a bed after the older fashion until the very end, a little over a year ago. Arbonne had observed the yearfast for its count and the ceremonies of remembrance scarcely a month past.

A year wasn't very long at all, really. Not nearly enough time to remember without pain private laughter or public grace, the sound of a voice, resonance of a tread, the keen engagement of a questioning mind or the well-known signs of kindled passion that could spark and court her own.

A passion that had lasted to the end, she thought, lying in bed alone, letting the morning come to her slowly. Even with all their children long since grown or dead, with an entirely new generation of courtiers arising in Barbentain, and younger dukes and barons taking power in strongholds once ruled by the friends — and enemies — of their own youth and prime. With new leaders of the city-states of Portezza, a young, reckless-sounding king in Gorhaut, and an unpredictable one as well, though not young, in Valensa far in the north. All was changing in the world, she thought: the players on the board, the shape of the board itself. Even the rules of the game she and Guibor had played together against them all for so long.

There had been mornings in the year gone by when she had awakened feeling ancient and bone cold, wondering if she had not outlived her time, if she should have died with the husband she'd loved, before the world began to change around her.

Which was weak and unworthy. She knew that, even on the mornings when those chill thoughts came, and she knew it more clearly now, with the birds outside her window singing to welcome the spring back to Arbonne. Change and transience were built into the way Corannos and Rian had made the world. She had accepted and gloried in that truth all her life; it would be shallow and demeaning to lament it now.

She rose from her bed and stood on the golden carpet. Immediately one of the two girls who slept by the door of her chamber sprang forward — they had been waiting for her — carrying her morning robe. She smiled at the young one, slipped into the robe and walked to the window, drawing back the curtains herself on the view to the east and the rising sun.

Barbentain Castle lay on an island in the river and so below her, down past the tumbling rocks and forbidding cliffs that guarded the castle, she could see the flash and sparkle of the river rushing away south in its high spring torrent, through vineyard and forest and grainland, by town and hamlet and lonely shepherd's hut, past castle and temple and tributary stream to Tavernel and the sea.

The Arbonne River in the land named for it — the warm, beloved, always coveted south, sung by its troubadours and joglars, celebrated through the known world for its fruitfulness and its culture, and for the beauty and grace of its women.

Not the least of which women, not by any means the least, had been she herself in the lost days of youth and fire. The nights of music, with a many-faceted power in her every glance and lifted eyebrow, when candlelight cast a warming glow on silver and gold and a glittering company, when the songs were always of love, and almost always about love of her.

Signe de Barbentain, countess of Arbonne, stood at her bedchamber window on a morning in spring, looking out over the sunlit river of the land she ruled, and the two other women in the room with her, preparing to attend to her needs, were far too young, both of them, to have even a hope of understanding the smile that crossed her face.

In fact, for no reason she really knew herself, Signe was thinking of her daughter. Not of Beatritz, wielding power within her own domain on Rian's Island in the sea; not of Beatritz, her last child living, but of Aelis, her young one, so long dead.

> Even the birds above the lake
> Are singing of my love,
> And even the flowers along the shore
> Are growing for her sake.

Twenty-two, no, twenty-three years now since young Bertran de Talair — and he had been *very* young then — had written those lines for Aelis. They were still being sung, remarkably, in spite of all the verses the troubadours had spun since those days, all the new rhyme schemes and metres and the increasingly complex harmonies and fashions of today. More than two decades after, Bertran's song for long-dead Aelis was still heard in Arbonne. Usually in springtime, Signe thought, and wondered if that had been the early-morning half-awake chain of associations that had led her to remember. The mind did strange things sometimes, and memory wounded at least as often as it healed or assuaged.

Which led her, predictably, to thoughts of Bertran himself, and what memory and loss and the unexpected shapes they had taken had done to him in twenty-odd years. What sort of man, she wondered, would he have become had the events of that long-ago year fallen out differently? Though it was hard, almost impossible really, to imagine how they could have turned out well. Guibor had said once, apropos of nothing at all, that the worst tragedy for Arbonne, if not for the people actually involved, had been the death of Girart de Talair: had Bertran's brother lived to hold the dukedom and father heirs, the younger son, the troubadour, would never have come to power in Talair, and the enmity of two proud castles by the lake might never have become the huge reality it was in Arbonne.

Might-have-beens, Signe thought. It was seductively easy to wonder — of a winter's night before a fire, or amid the drone of bees and the scent of summer herbs in the castle garden — about the dead, imagining them still living, the differences they might have made. She did it all the time: with her lost sons, with Aelis, with Guibor himself since his passing. Not a good channel of the mind, that one, though inevitable, she supposed. *Memory*, Anselme of Cauvas had written once, *the harvest and the torment of my days.*

It had been some time since she'd seen Bertran, she thought, pulling her reflections forward to the present, and rather longer since Urté de Miraval had come to Barbentain. Both of them had sent messages and surrogates — Urté his seneschal, Bertran his cousin Valery — to the yearfast of Guibor's passing. There had been a killing among their corans, it seemed — not an unusual event between Miraval and Talair — and both dukes had felt unable or unwilling to leave their castles then, even to mourn their dead count.

Signe wondered, not for the first time in the month gone by, if she should have commanded them to be present. They would have come, she knew; Bertran laughing and ironic, Urté grimly obedient, standing as far apart from each other in all the ceremonies as dignity and shared high rank allowed.

She hadn't felt, somehow, like issuing that order, though Roban had urged her to. The chancellor had seen it as an opportunity to publicly assert her control over the fractious dukes and barons of Arbonne, bringing to heel the two most prominent of all. An important thing to do, Roban had said, this early in her own reign, and especially with what was happening in the north, with the peace treaty signed between Gorhaut and Valensa.

He was almost certainly right; Signe had known he was, particularly about the need to send a clear signal north to the king of Gorhaut and his counsellors. But somehow she had hated the thought of using Guibor's yearfast — not the *first* one, surely — in such a bluntly political way. Could she not be allowed, for the one time, to remember her husband in the company only of those who had freely come to Barbentain and Lussan to do the same? Ariane and Thierry de Carenzu; Gaufroy de Ravenc and his young bride; Arnaut and Richilde de Malmont, her sister and brother-in-law, almost the last, with Urté, of their own generation still ruling in the great castles. These had all come, and so, too, had virtually every one of the lesser dukes and barons and a deeply affecting number of the other folk of Arbonne: landless corans, artisans of the towns, brethren of the god and priests and priestesses of Rian, farmers from the grainlands, fisherfolk from the sea, shepherds from the hills by Götzland or Arimonda, or from the slopes of the northern mountains that blocked the winds from Gorhaut, carters and smiths and wheelwrights, millers and merchants from a dozen different towns, even a number of young men from the university — though Tavernel's unruly students were legendary for their aversion to authority of any kind.

And all of the troubadours had come to Barbentain.

That had been the thing that moved her most of all. If one excepted Bertran de Talair himself, every one of the troubadours of Arbonne and all the joglars had come to share in the remembering of their lord, to offer their new laments and make sweet, sad music to mark the yearfast of his dying. There had been poetry and music for three days, and much of it had been rarely crafted and from the heart.

In such a mood, with so many come willingly in a spirit of shared sorrow and memory, Signe had felt profoundly unwilling to compel the presence of anyone, even two of the most powerful — and therefore most dangerous — men in her land. How could she be blamed for wanting the spirit of the yearfast and its rituals to be unmarred by the long wrangle between Miraval and Talair?

The problem, and the reason she was still dwelling upon this, was that she knew what Guibor IV, count of Arbonne, would have done in her place. In terms admitting of no possible ambiguity her husband would have demanded their presence before him during any remotely similar event, whether of mourning or celebration, in Barbentain itself or in the temples of god or goddess in Lussan town beside the river.

On the other hand, she thought, and the smile on her still-lovely face deepened almost imperceptibly, had she herself been the one being mourned instead of Guibor, Bertran de Talair would have been with the others in Barbentain for her yearfast, come feud or river flood or fire or blight to the grapes. He would have been there. She knew. He was a troubadour as much as he was anything else, and it had been Signe de Barbentain who had begun the Court of Love and shaped with her own personality the graceful, elegant world that had let the poets and the singers flourish.

Aelis her daughter might have inspired Bertran's passion and his youthful springtime song, still sung after more than twenty years; Ariane her niece might be queen of the Court of Love now; but Signe had had a hundred verses and more written for her in fire and exaltation by a score of troubadours who mattered and at least twice as many who didn't, and every song written for every noblewoman in Arbonne was, at least in part, a song for her.

But this was unworthy, she thought wryly, shaking her head. A sign of old age, of pettiness, competing in this way — even in her own mind — with Ariane and the other ladies of Arbonne, even with her poor, long-dead daughter. Was she feeling unloved, she wondered, and knew there was truth in that. Guibor was dead. She ruled a court of the world now, not a simulated, stylized court named for love and devoted to its nuances. There were differences, great differences that had altered, and not subtly, the way the world dealt with her and she with it.

She should have ordered the two dukes to come last month; Roban, as usual, had been right. And it might even have been good for her, in the usual, strange, slightly hurtful way, to see Bertran again. It was never a wise idea in any case to let him go too long without a reminder that she was watching him and expecting things of him. No one alive could truthfully claim to have a large influence on the duke of Talair and what he chose to do, but Signe thought she had some. Not a great deal, but some, for many reasons. Most of which led back those twenty-three years or so.

He was said to be in Baude Castle now, of all places, high in the south-western hills. The situation had stabilized — for the moment — between Talair and Miraval, and Signe could guess how the story of Evrard of Lussan and Soresina de Baude would have been irresistible for Bertran in his endless, disruptive careen.

It *was* a delicious piece of gossip. Beatritz had already sent private word of what Mallin de Baude had done, abducting the aggrieved poet from Rian's Island. She should have been outraged at the tidings, Signe knew — and Beatritz should *certainly* have been — but there was something so amusing in the sequence of events, and the poet had clearly been wearing out his welcome on the island by the time the corans had come and taken him away.

Not that any of that tale would reach the ears of most of the people in Arbonne. Mallin would hardly want word of his impiety to spread — which is undoubtedly why he'd not led the mission himself — and Evrard of Lussan would scarcely be thrilled with a public image of himself knocked unconscious and carried back like so much milled grain in a sack to the castle from which he'd fled in such high dudgeon.

On the other hand, the story of Soresina's very public contrition and her open-armed, kneeling welcome of the poet was certainly going the rounds of the castles and towns. That part of the tale Evrard would encourage for all he was worth. Signe wondered if he'd bedded the woman after all. It was possible, but it didn't much matter. On the whole, and however improbably, it looked as if everyone might end up happy in this affair.

Although that optimistic thought certainly didn't factor in the moods and caprices of En Bertran de Talair, who was, for reasons of his own, currently bestowing the honour of his presence on the doubtlessly overwhelmed young couple in Castle Baude. Mallin de Baude was reported to be a man of some ambition; he wanted to rise in the world, to move among the circles and the councils of the great, not remain mewed up in his eyrie among the sheep and goats and terraced olive trees of his family estates. Well, the great of the world, or one of them at any rate, had come to him now. Mallin was probably about to discover some of the implications of his dreaming.

Signe shook her head. There was folly at work here, she had no doubt. Bertran often essayed his wilder escapades in the spring; she had come to that realization long ago. On the other hand, she supposed it was better that he pursue whatever it was that had drawn him to those high pastures near the Arimondan passes than the killing matters of earlier in the year.

In any case, she had no real leisure to spend dwelling on such affairs. Ariane ruled the Court of Love now. Signe had Gorhaut to deal with, a dangerous peace signed in the north and rather a great deal more. And she had to do it alone now, with only the memory — *the harvest and the torment of my days* — of Guibor's voice to guide her along the increasingly narrow paths of statesmanship.

There was a new fashion among the younger troubadours and nobles — she even thought Ariane might approve of it: they were writing and saying now that it was ill-bred, in bad taste if not actually impossible, for a wife to love her husband. That true love had to flow freely from choices made willingly, and marriage could never be a matter of such free choice for men or women in the society they knew.

The world was changing. Guibor would have laughed at that new conceit with her, and said exactly what he thought of it, and then he might have taken her in his arms and she could have laced her hands in his hair and they would have proven the young ones wrong in this, as in so many other things, within the private, enchanted, now-broken circle of their love.

She turned from the window, from the view of the river below, from memories of the past, and nodded to the two young girls. It was time to dress and go down. Roban would be waiting, with all the needs of the present, imperious in their clamour to be addressed, drowning — as in a flooding of the river — the lost, murmuring voices of yesterday.

†

There was, of course, no light where he had chosen to keep watch, though there were brackets for torches on the walls of the stairwell. It would have been a waste of illumination; no one had any business coming up these stairs after nightfall.

Blaise settled himself on one of the benches in the window recess nearest the second-floor landing. He could see the stairs and hear any movement on them but would be hidden from anyone coming up. Some men would have preferred to be visible, even torchlit, here on guard, to have their presence known and so function as a deterrent to anyone even contemplating an ascent. Blaise didn't think that way: it was better, to his mind, to have such designs exposed. If anyone was planning to make their way towards Soresina de Baude's chambers he wanted them to try, so he could see them and know who they were.

Though, in fact, he knew exactly who such a person would be tonight if there was to be an attempt, and so did Mallin de Baude — which is why Blaise was on guard here, and Hirnan, equally trusted, equally discreet, was outside the walls beneath the baroness's window.

Bertran de Talair had a twenty-year reputation for being exceptionally determined and resourceful in pursuit of his seductions. Also successful. Blaise had no real doubt that if the troubadour duke of Talair did manage to make his way to Soresina's bed his reception would be considerably different from what Evrard of Lussan's had been earlier in the year.

He made a sour face, thinking about that, and leaned back, putting his booted feet up on the opposite bench. He knew it was unwise on guard duty at night to make himself too comfortable, but he was used to this and didn't think he would fall asleep. He had kept night watch over a number of different things in his time, including, as it happened, the women's quarters in more than one castle. Guarding the womenfolk, virtually imprisoning them at night, was a part of the ordinary round of life in Gorhaut. No hint there, not even a trace, of this subversive Arbonnais custom of encouraging poets to woo and exalt the women of the land. The lords of Gorhaut knew how to protect what was theirs.

Blaise had even felt a carefully concealed satisfaction when Mallin de Baude, after a week of watching their very distinguished and equally notorious guest charm his wife, had asked his hired northern mercenary to quietly arrange protection for Soresina's rooms during En Bertran's last night in Castle Baude. A balding, rumpled poet like Evrard was one thing, evidently, but the most celebrated nobleman in Arbonne was another. Soresina's manner the past few days had offered proof enough of that.

Blaise had accepted the assignment and arranged to post Hirnan outside without so much as a word of comment or a flicker of expression on his face. The truth was, he liked Mallin de Baude and would have thought less of him had the baron been oblivious or indifferent to the nuances that had been shaped since de Talair's arrival in their midst, not long after Evrard had departed again.

Remarkably enough, amusingly even, everyone in Castle

Baude seemed to have been happy in the aftermath of the raid on Rian's Island. In part because virtually no one knew there had been a raid. As far as the folk of the castle and the countryside around were concerned, all they knew — all they needed to know, Mallin had stressed repeatedly to Blaise and the corans — was that Evrard of Lussan had reconsidered his position and had returned to the castle, escorted, by pre-arrangement, by a group of Mallin's best men and the northern mercenary who was leading and training them that season.

Hirnan and Maffour, who apparently knew Luth's grand-mother, had been given the task of conveying to her what had happened to the hapless coran. They returned with Maffour grinning wryly and Hirnan shaking his big head in bemusement: far from being distressed at her loss, the woman had been thrilled by their tidings. Her grandson serving the goddess on Rian's Island had been a prophetic dream of hers years ago, the two corans reported. Blaise had lifted his eyebrows in disbelief; he was clearly not going to be able to understand the Arbonnais for a long time yet, if ever. Still, the woman's attitude was useful; an outcry of loss from her would have proven embarrassing.

In the meantime, Soresina's public reception of the prodigal poet had been almost touching in its emotion. 'There's an actress in that one,' Maffour had whispered drily to Blaise as they stood to one side of the castle forecourt and and watched the young baroness kneel and then rise to salute the troubadour with a kiss on each cheek and a third one on the lips.

'There is in all of them,' Blaise had replied out of the side of his mouth. Nonetheless, he too had been feeling rather pleased that morning, a sensation that continued when it became clear that although Evrard was not going to linger in Baude Castle — no one really wanted him to — he seemed to have accepted his abduction with a good humour that matched Mallin's own.

The poet offered one quickly-fashioned verse with an elaborately strung-together set of images about emerging from a dark cave, drawn upwards by a glow of light that turned out to be the radiance of Soresina de Baude. He used another name for her, of course, but the same one as it had been all along. Everyone knew who the woman was. Everyone was happy.

The troubadour left Baude at the end of a week with a jingling purse, an assuaged self-esteem and a more than slightly enhanced reputation. No one in Arbonne would know exactly what had transpired in this remote castle in the highlands, but it was evident that Evrard of Lussan had somehow been wooed back by the baron and his wife, and had been handsomely rewarded for his indulgence of their earlier errors. Among other things, the power of the troubadours, both in their person and through their satires and encomiums, had been subtly augmented by the enigmatic sequence of events. That part Blaise didn't much like, but there wasn't anything he could do about it, and this wasn't his home in any case. It shouldn't matter, he told himself, what follies Arbonne strayed into, or continued with.

The corans of Baude had been making wagers amongst each other all week — wagers never likely to be settled one way or another — as to just how far Soresina's contrition had gone, or rather, how far it had allowed the poet to go. Blaise, scrutinizing the woman and the man narrowly on the morning of Evrard's departure, had been quite certain that nothing untoward had happened, but this was not the sort of thing he wagered upon or talked about, and he kept his peace. He did accept an additional purse from Mallin over and above his wages that month; the baron was so caught up in his new style of noble largess that Blaise actually spent part of a morning doing calculations and then musing on how long Mallin was going to be able to sustain this sort of thing. Rank and position in the hierarchy of nobility didn't come cheaply, in Arbonne or anywhere else. Blaise had wondered if the baron really understood all the implications that were likely to arise from his pursuit of status in the world.

And then, about ten days after Evrard's departure, one of the more immediate implications had arrived, preceded by an envoy with a message that had thrown Baude Castle into a chaos of preparation.

At the top of the dark stairway Blaise shifted his seat on the stone bench. It would be nice, he thought briefly, to have a beaker of wine up here; not that he'd ever really have allowed himself such an indulgence. He knew at least two men who had died, drunken and asleep, when they should have been on watch. He had, as it happened, killed one of the two himself.

It was silent in the castle; he felt very much alone, and a long way from home. An unusual feeling, that one: home hadn't meant much to him for a long time. People still did, though, sometimes, and there was no one here who was really a friend yet, or likely to become one in the time he was allowing himself at Castle Baude. He wondered where Rudel was tonight, what country, what part of the world. Thinking of his friend led him back to the cities of Portezza, and so, inevitably perhaps in the silence of night outside a woman's rooms, to memories of Lucianna. Blaise shook his head. *Women*, he thought. *Was there ever one born to be trusted since the world was made?*

And that thought, not a new one for him this year, would take his memories straight home if he let them, to his brother and his brother's wife, and the last time — as the High Priestess of Rian had somehow known — he had lain with a woman in love. Or, not love. The priestess had known that too, uncannily. He had felt shockingly open and exposed before her blindness in the forest that night, and not overly proud, after, of what she had seen in him. He wondered if her vision was deep enough, in whatever way she saw such things, to reach back to roots and sources and an understanding of why men — and women — did the things they did.

Blaise wondered if he himself really understood the events of that short, hopeless attempt to return home four months ago. It had been pure impulse that had led him back, or so he'd thought at the time, bidding farewell to Rudel at the Götzland Pass to go back to Gorhaut and his family home for the first time in almost a year. What was a country, what was a home? He looked out through the narrow archers' window. The blue moon was high, almost full. Escoran they named it in Gorhaut — 'daughter of the god' — but they called the blue moon Riannon here, for their goddess. There was a power to naming so, a choosing of alignments. But the moon was the same, wasn't it, whatever mortal man chose to call it, lending her strange, elusive light to the landscape east of the castle?

Pale Vidonne — which bore the same name everywhere — wouldn't rise for some time yet. If someone were actually making a foray from outside, climbing up to the window, it would be fairly soon, in the denser shadows while the blue moon rode alone. It was a mild night, which pleased Blaise for Hirnan's sake outside. It was unlikely in the extreme that any sane man would actually attempt to scale the outer wall of the castle in pursuit of a seduction, but as long as they were assigned to guard duty they might as well do it properly. Blaise had had that attitude to things as a boy, and nothing in his adult years had made him find cause to change.

He couldn't see Hirnan down below, of course, but the moonlight showed the hills in the distance, and the fields where the lavender would soon flower, and the winding road that climbed from them up to the castle. Lavender would make him think of Lucianna again if he wasn't careful. Resolutely, Blaise turned his mind to the task at hand, to where he now was, to this matter of Bertran de Talair, with all its implications.

On a bright, windy morning seven days ago, with spring fully arrived and the first wildflowers gleaming in the sun like a many-coloured carpet laid down for royalty, three horses had been seen making their way up the slow, circuitous path to the castle gates. A trumpet blew erratically from the ramparts, the portcullis was raised with a dangerous celerity, almost maiming one of the men handling the winches, and Blaise had assembled with the corans and most of the household in the forecourt. Mallin and Soresina, splendidly jewelled and attired (a great deal more expense there; Blaise happened to know exactly what fur-trimmed Portezzan samite with gold thread in the weft would have cost), rode out to honour the arriving trio.

Blaise saw a brown horse, a grey, a rather magnificent black. An elderly joglar with the by now familiar harp and lute was riding the brown; a broad-shouldered coran of middle years sat the grey with the ease of many seasons in the saddle. Between the two of them, bareheaded in the sunshine and the wind, clad in nondescript brown fustian without adornment of any kind, rode Duke Bertran de Talair, come to pay — inexplicably — a visit to the appropriately over-whelmed young baron and baroness of Castle Baude.

As the small party rode into the castle forecourt, Blaise, staring with frank curiosity, saw that de Talair was a man of slightly more than middle height with a lean, ironical face, clean-shaven in the Arbonnais fashion. He was almost forty-five years old, Blaise knew from the corans' reports, but he didn't look it. His eyes were indeed as blue as the gossip had them; even at a distance the colour was disconcerting. There was a scar on his right cheek, and he wore his hair cropped unfashionably short, revealing that the top part of his right ear was missing.

Most of the world, it seemed, knew the story of how he had come by those injuries, and what he had done in turn to the hired assassin from Portezza who had inflicted them. As it happened, Blaise knew the son of that man. They had served a season in Götzland together two years back.

As events unfolded over the next hours and days, it swiftly became apparent to Blaise that the duke's reasons for being there were at least threefold. One, obviously, was Mallin, and a wide-ranging, many-faceted attempt to enlist the emerging, ambitious young baron to Bertran's allegiance in the long power struggle with Urté de Miraval for pre-emi-nence in the western part of Arbonne, if not the country as a whole. That much, in fact, Hirnan and Maffour had guessed well before the duke had arrived.

The second lure for Bertran, almost as evidently, had been Soresina. En Bertran de Talair, never wed, though linked to an extraodinary number of women in several countries over the years, seemed to have an almost compulsive need to per-sonally acquaint himself with the charms of any celebrated beauty. Evrard of Lussan's verses, if they had done nothing else, had clearly piqued the curiosity of the duke.

Even Blaise, who didn't like her, had to admit that Soresina had been looking quite magnificent of late, as if Evrard's proclamation of her charms had somehow caused her fair-haired beauty to ripen, her dark, flashing eyes to become even more alluring, that she might come to equal in reality the elaborate fancies of his verse. Whatever the cause, there was something almost breathtaking about the young baroness

of Castle Baude that week, and even men who had lived in
her presence for some time would find themselves turning dis-
tractedly towards the sound of her lifted voice and laughter in
a distant room, forgetting the path of their own thoughts.

Blaise would have spent more time wondering how
Bertran de Talair sought to reconcile an attempt to cultivate
the friendship of Mallin de Baude with an equally fervent if
slightly more discreet pursuit of the baron's enticing young
wife had it not emerged very quickly that the third reason for
the duke's presence among them was Blaise himself.

On the very first evening, after the most elaborate and
expensive repast Baude Castle had ever seen — there were
even spoons for the soup, instead of the usual chunks of bread
— Bertran de Talair lounged at his ease beside his hostess and
host and listened as Ramir, his joglar for more than two
decades, sang the duke's own compositions for the best part of
an hour. Even Blaise, jaundiced as ever on this subject, was
forced to concede privately that — whether it was the elderly
joglar's art or Bertran's — what they were listening to that
night was of an entirely different order from the music of
Evrard of Lussan that had been his own first introduction to
the troubadours of Arbonne.

Even so, he found this writing of verses a silly, almost a
ludicrous pastime for a nobleman. For Evrard and those like
him, perhaps it could be understood if one were in a tolerant
mood: poetry and music seemed to offer a unique channel
here in Arbonne for men, or even women, who might never
otherwise have any avenue to fame or modest wealth or the
society of the great. But Bertran de Talair was something else
entirely: what possible *use* were these verses and the time
wasted in shaping them for a lord known to be one of the foremost fighting men in six countries?

The question was still vexing Blaise, despite the fact that
he'd allowed himself an extra cup of wine, when he saw de
Talair lean across, setting down his own wine goblet, and
whisper something in Soresina's ear that made her flush to the
cleavage of her pale green gown. Bertran rose then, and Ramir
the joglar, who had evidently been waiting for such a movement, stood up neatly from the stool he'd been sitting upon
while he played and held forth his harp as de Talair stepped

down from the dais. The duke had been drinking steadily all night; it didn't seem to show in any way.

'He's going to play for us himself,' Maffour whispered excitedly in Blaise's ear. 'This is rare! A very high honour!' There was a buzz of anticipation in the hall as others evidently came to the same awareness. Blaise grimaced and glanced over at Maffour disdainfully: what business had a fighting coran to be growing so agitated over something this trivial? But he noted, glancing at Hirnan on Maffour's far side, that even the older coran, normally so stolid and phlegmatic, was watching the duke with undeniable anticipation. With a sigh, and a renewed sense of how hopelessly strange this country was, Blaise turned back to the high table. Bertran de Talair had settled himself on the low stool before it. *Another love lyric*, Blaise thought, having had a season of Evrard, and having noted the glances that had already begun to pass between hostess and noble guest during the meal. As it happened, he was wrong.

What Bertran de Talair gave them instead, in a highland hall at the very beginning of that summer, amid candles and jewels and silk and gold, with early lavender for fragrance in bowls along the tables, was war.

War and death in the ice of winter, axes and swords and maces clanging on iron, horses screaming, and the cries of men, eddies of snow beginning to fall, breath-smoke in the bitterly cold northern air, a wan red sun setting and the chill pale light of Vidonne rising in the east over a field of death.

And Blaise knew that field.

He had fought there, and very nearly died. Far to the south, here in woman-ruled, woman-shaped Arbonne, Bertran de Talair was singing to them of the Battle of Iersen Bridge, when the army of King Duergar of Gorhaut had beaten back the invaders from Valensa in the last battle of that year's fighting.

The last battle of a long war, actually, for Duergar's son, Ademar, and King Daufridi of Valensa had signed their treaty of peace at the end of the winter that followed, and so ended a war that had lasted as long as Blaise had lived. Leaning forward now, his hand tightening around his goblet, Blaise of Gorhaut listened to the resonant chords Bertran drew from his harp in waves like the waves of battle, and to the clear, deep, chanting voice as it came, inexorably indicting, to the end of the song:

Shame then in springtime for proud Gorhaut,
Betrayed by a young king and his counsellor.
Sorrow for those whose sons were dead,
Bitter the warriors who had battled and won —
Only to see spoils claimed by their courage
Disposed and discarded like so much watered wine.

Shame in the treaty and no pride in the peace
Ademar allowed to vanquished Valensa.
Where were the true heirs of those who had died
For the glory of Gorhaut on that frozen field?
How could they sheathe their shining blades
With triumph gained and then given away?

What manner of man, with his father new-fallen,
Would destroy with a pen-stroke a long dream of glory?
And what king lost to honour like craven Daufridi
Would retreat from that ice-field not to return?
Where went the manhood of Gorhaut and Valensa
When war was abandoned and pale peace bought

By weak kings and sons long lost to their lineage?

A last chord, stern and echoing, and Bertran de Talair was done. There was absolute silence in the hall, an entirely different order of response from the grateful laughter and applause that had greeted the joglar's earlier offerings of love and springtime.

In that stillness Blaise of Gorhaut grew painfully aware of the pounding of his heart, still beating to the rhythm of the duke's harsh chords. Men he had known all his life had died on that field by Iersen Bridge. Blaise had been not twenty helpless strides away, with frozen bodies piled between, when Duergar his king had pitched from his horse, an arrow in his eye, crying the god's name in agony, his voice towering over the battlefield like the giant he had been.

Five months later Duergar's son, Ademar, now king in Gorhaut, and Galbert, his Chief Counsellor, High Elder of Corannos, had negotiated the treaty that, in exchange for hostages and gold and King Daufridi's daughter to wed when she came of age, gave Valensa all of the northlands of Gorhaut down to the line of the Iersen River. The very fields and villages Daufridi and his warriors had been unable to take with their swords in three decades of war they had won a season later with the smooth words and sly diplomacy of their hired Arimondan negotiators.

Not long after that, Blaise of Gorhaut had left home on the circuitous journey through several countries that had brought him to this hall in Arbonne, a year from the season of that treaty.

His reverie ended with the abrupt, unsettling realization that Bertran de Talair, who had done no more than nod when Blaise was first presented to him in the morning, was staring across the room at him now from the low stool where he sat, one leg gracefully extended. Blaise straightened his shoulders and returned the gaze steadily, grateful for whatever masking his beard afforded. He wouldn't have wanted his thoughts read just then.

En Bertran drew his fingers quietly across the harp. The notes hung, delicate as glass, as the table flowers, in the stillness of the hall. As quietly, though very clearly, the duke of Talair said, 'What do you think, Northerner? How long will it hold, this peace of yours?'

Some things grew clear to Blaise with those words, but even as they did, other mysteries took shape. He drew a careful breath, aware that everyone in the great hall was looking at him. Bertran's gaze in the torchlight was uncannily blue; his wide mouth was quirked in an ironic smile.

'It is no peace of mine,' Blaise said, keeping his tone as casual as he could.

'I thought not,' said Bertran quickly, a note of satisfaction in the light voice, as if he'd heard more than Blaise had meant to say. 'I didn't *think* you were down here for love of our music, or even our ladies, fair as they are.'

As he spoke, the blue eyes and the smile — not ironic at all suddenly — had been briefly redirected towards the high table and the lone woman sitting there. His long fingers were moving once more across the strings of the harp. A moment later, the duke of Talair lifted his voice again, this time in exactly the kind of song Blaise had expected before. But something — and not merely the mood of a night — had been changed for Blaise by then, and he didn't know how to respond this time to an Arbonnais lord singing words of his own devising about the glory to be searched for in a woman's dark eyes.

The next day the corans of Baude put on a display in the fields below the castle village, charging with lances against a bobbing wooden contraption got up — as it was everywhere — to look like a racoux from the ghost tales of childhood, complete with whitened face and jet-black hair. Mallin had declared a holiday so the villagers and workers in the fields could join the castle household in cheering on the warriors. Blaise, cautiously pleased with the men he'd been training, was careful to seem competent himself but not flamboyantly so. In three of the four runs he made, he sent the racoux rocking properly backwards on its stand with a spear thrust dead on the target of its small shield. The fourth time he contrived to miss, but only by a little, so the cleverly constructed adversary didn't spin round — as it was balanced to do — and fetch him a blow with its wooden sword on the back of the head as he thundered past. It was one thing not to look ostentatious in a setting such as this, it was another to be knocked from one's horse onto the dusty ground. In Gorhaut, Blaise remembered, some of the racoux wielded actual swords, of iron not wood. Some of Blaise's fellow trainees in those days had been badly cut, which of course increased the concentration young men placed on their mastering of the skills of war. There were simply too many distractions here in Arbonne, too many other, softer things a man was expected to think about or know.

　　When it came time for the archery tests, though, and Bertran's cousin Valery joined them at the butts, Blaise was grimly forced to concede that he hadn't met an archer in the north, or even his friend Rudel in Portezza, who could shoot with this man, whatever distractions to training and the arts of war Arbonne might offer. Blaise was able to vie with Valery of

Talair at forty paces, and Hirnan was equal with both of them.
The two of them were level with their guest at sixty paces as
well, to Mallin's evident pleasure, but when the marks were
moved back — amid the loud shouts of the festive crowd — to
eighty paces, Valery, not a young man by any means, seemed
unaffected by the new distance, still finding the crimson with
each soberly judged and smoothly loosed arrow. Blaise felt
pleased to keep all his own flights anywhere on the distant targets, and Hirnan, scowling ferociously, couldn't even manage
that. Blaise had a suspicion that Bertran's cousin would have
fared as well at a hundred paces if he had chosen to, but Valery
was too polite to suggest such a distance and the exhibition
ended there, with applause for all three of them.

They hunted the next day. Soresina, clad in green and
brown like a forest creature of legend, flew a new falcon for
the first time and, to her prettily expressed delight, the bird
brought down a plump hare in the high fields north of the castle. Later, beaters in the fields stirred up a loud-winged plen-
itude of corfe and quail for their party. Blaise, familiar with
the unwritten rules of hunting in this sort of company, was
careful not to shoot at anything until he was certain neither
Mallin nor the duke had a line on the same prey. He waited
until the two nobles had each killed several birds and then
allowed himself two at the very end with a pair of swift arrows
fired into the line of the sun.

On the third night there was a storm. The sort of cata-
clysm the mountain highlands often knew in summer. Lightning streaked the sky like the white spears of Corannos, and
after the spears came the god's thunder voice and the driving
rain. The wind was wild, howling like a haunted spirit about
the stone walls of the castle, lashing the panes of the windows
as if to force its way in. They had firelight and torches, though,
in the great hall of Baude, and the walls and windows were
stronger than wind or rain. Ramir the joglar sang for them
again, pitching his voice over the noises outside, shaping a
mood of warmth and close-gathered intimacy. Even Blaise had
to concede that there were occasional times, such as this, when
music and the attention to physical comforts here in the south
were indeed of value. He thought about the people in the hamlets around the castle though, in their small, ramshackle

wooden homes, and then about the shepherds up on the mountains with their flocks, lashed by the driving rain. Early to bed in the wild night he pulled the quilted coverlet up to his chin and gave thanks to Corannos for the small blessings of life.

The morning after the storm dawned cool and still windy, as if the onset of summer had been driven back by the violence of the night. Bertran and Valery insisted on joining with the men of Castle Baude in riding up into the hills in the thankless, wet, necessary task of helping the shepherds locate and retrieve any of the baron's sheep scattered by the storm. The sheep and their wool were the economic foundation of whatever aspirations Mallin de Baude had, and his corans were never allowed to nurture the illusion that they were above performing any labours associated with that.

It was two hours' steep ride up to the high pastures, and the better part of a day's hard, sometimes dangerous work at the task. Late in the afternoon, Blaise, swearing for what seemed to him entirely sufficient reasons, clambered awkwardly up out of a slippery defile with a wet, shivering lamb in his arms to see Bertran de Talair lounging on the grass in front of him, leaning comfortably back against the trunk of an olive tree. There was no one else in sight.

'You'd best put that little one down before she pisses all over you,' the duke said cheerfully. 'I've a flask of Arimondan brandy if it suits you.'

'She already has,' Blaise said sourly, setting the bleating lamb free on the level ground. 'And thank you, but no, I work better with a clear head.'

'Work's done. According to your red-headed coran — Hirnan, is it? — there's three or four sheep who somehow got up to the top of this range and then down towards the valley south of us, but the shepherds can manage them alone.' He held out the flask.

With a sigh, Blaise sank down on his haunches beside the tree and accepted the drink. It was more than merely Arimondan brandy, one sip was enough to tell him as much. He licked his lips and then arched his eyebrows questioningly. 'You carry seguignac in a flask to chase sheep on a hill?'

Bertran de Talair's clever, oddly youthful face relaxed in a smile. 'I see that you know good brandy,' he murmured with deceptive tranquillity. 'The next questions are how, and why? You are trying extremely hard to seem like just another young mercenary, a competent sword and bow for hire like half the men of Götzland. I watched you during the hunt, though. You didn't bring down anything till the very end, despite half a dozen clear opportunities for a man who can hit a target every time at eighty paces. You were too conscious of not showing up either Mallin de Baude or myself. Do you know what that says to me, Northerner?'

'I can't imagine,' Blaise said.

'Yes, you can. It says that you've experience of a court. Are you going to tell me who you are, Northerner?'

Schooling his face carefully, Blaise handed back the handsome flask and settled himself more comfortably on the grass, stalling for time. Beside them the lamb was cropping contentedly, seeming to have forgotten its bleating terror of moments before. Despite insistent alarm bells of caution in his head, Blaise was intrigued and even a little amused by the directness of the duke's approach.

'I don't think so,' he said frankly, 'but I've been to more than one court in the past, in Götzland and Portezza both. I *am* curious as to why it matters to you who I am.'

'Easy enough,' said de Talair. 'I want to hire you, and I prefer to know the backgrounds of the men who work for me.'

This was too fast in too many ways for Blaise to run with. 'I've been hired already,' he said. 'Remember? Mallin de Baude, youngish fellow, a baron in Arbonne. Pretty wife.'

Bertran laughed aloud. The lamb lifted its head and looked at them a moment, then resumed her own affairs. 'Really,' said the duke, 'you belie your country's reputation with jests like that: everyone knows the Gorhautians have no sense of humour.'

Blaise allowed himself a thin smile. 'We say the same thing back home about the Götzlanders. And Valensans smell of fish and beer, Portezzans always lie, and the men of Ari-monda mostly sleep with each other.'

'And what do you say back home,' Bertran de Talair asked quietly, 'about Arbonne?'

Blaise shook his head. 'I haven't spent much time back home in a long while,' he said, dodging the question.

'About four months,' de Talair said. 'That much I checked. Not so long. What do they say?' His hands were loosely clasped about the flask. Late-afternoon sunlight glinted in his short brown hair. He wasn't smiling any longer.

Neither was Blaise. He met the clear blue gaze as directly as he could. After a long moment he said, in the silence of that high meadow, 'They say that a woman rules you. That women have always ruled you. And that Tavernel at the mouth of the Arbonne River has the finest natural harbour for shipping and trade in the world.'

'And Ademar of Gorhaut, alas, has no sheltered harbour on the sea at all, hemmed in by Valensa on the north and womanish Arbonne to the south. What a sad king. Why are you here, Blaise of Gorhaut?'

'Seeking my fortune. There's less of a mystery than you might want to make out.'

'Not much of a fortune to be found chasing sheep for a minor baron in these hills.'

Blaise smiled. 'It was a start,' he said. 'The first contract I was offered. A chance to learn your language better, to see what else might emerge. There are reasons why it was a good idea for me to leave the Portezzan cities for a time.'

'Your own reasons? Or those of Ademar of Gorhaut? Would there by any chance be a spy behind that beard, my green-eyed young man from the north?'

It had always been possible that this might be said. Blaise was surprised at how calm he felt, now that the accusation was out in the open. He gestured, and de Talair handed him the brandy flask again. Blaise took another short pull and wiped his mouth with the back of his hand; the seguignac was really extraordinarily good.

'Indeed. Very important information to be gathered up here,' he said, finding himself for some inexplicable reason in a good humour. 'I'm sure Ademar will pay handsomely for a precise numbering of the sheep in these hills.'

Bertran de Talair smiled again and shifted position, resting on one elbow now, his booted feet stretched out in front of him. 'This could be just a start, as you say. An entry to our councils.'

'And so I cleverly lured you into offering me a position

by failing to shoot well on a hunt? You do me too much credit, my lord.'

'Perhaps,' said de Talair. 'What does Mallin pay you?'

Blaise named the figure. The duke shrugged indifferently. 'I'll double that. When can you start?'

'I'm paid through to a fortnight from now.'

'Good. I'll expect you at Talair three days after that.'

Blaise held up a hand. 'One thing clear from the start. The same thing I told En Mallin de Baude. I'm a mercenary, not a liegeman. No oaths.'

Bertran's lazy, mocking smile returned. 'But of course. I wouldn't dream of asking you to swear to anything. I wonder, though, what will you do if Ademar comes south? Kill me in my sleep? Could you be an assassin as well as a spy?'

Which, as it happened, was nearer to the bone than was at all comfortable. Blaise thought suddenly of the High Priestess of Rian on her island in the sea. He looked down at his hands, remembering Rudel, a moonless night in Portezzan Faenna, the garden of a palace in that dangerous city, fireflies, the scent of oranges, a dagger in his hand.

He shook his head slowly, bringing his mind back to Arbonne, to this high plateau and the disturbingly perceptive man looking steadily at him now with those vivid blue eyes.

'I'm no more a sworn man of Ademar's than I will be of yours,' Blaise said carefully to Bertran de Talair. He hesitated. 'Do you really think he might come south?'

'*Might*? In Rian's holy name, why else did he make that peace with Valensa I'm trying so hard to undermine with my songs? You said it yourself: woman-ruled Arbonne. Our count dead, an ageing woman in Barbentain, no obvious heir in sight, wine fields and grainlands and a glorious port. Men who do nothing but write songs all day and yearn like callow boys for a woman's cool hand on their brow at night . . . of *course* Ademar's going to come down on us.'

Blaise felt his mood changing, the pleasant fatigue of a day's hard labour chased away by the words as clouds were blown by the mountain winds. 'Why are you hiring me, then?' he asked. 'Why take that chance?'

'I like taking chances,' Bertran de Talair said, almost regretfully. 'It is a vice, I'm afraid.' The High Priestess, Blaise remembered, had said something much the same.

Bertran shifted position again, sitting up now, and took a last pull of the seguignac before capping the flask. 'Maybe you'll end up liking us more than you think. Maybe we'll find you a wife down here. Maybe we'll even teach you to sing. Truth is, I had a man killed this spring, and good men are hard to come by, as I suspect you know. Leading a successful raid on Rian's Island so soon after you got here was no mean achievement.'

'How do you know about that?'

Bertran grinned again, but without mockery this time; Blaise had the odd sensation of being able to guess what that smile might do to a woman the duke wanted to charm. 'Anyone can kill a corfe on a hunt,' de Talair went on, as if Blaise hadn't spoken at all. 'I need someone who knows when *not* to kill one. Even if he won't tell me how he learned that or who he is.' He hesitated for the first time, looking away from Blaise, west towards the mountains and Arimonda beyond. 'Besides which, for some reason you've made me think of my son the last few days. Don't ask me why. He died as an infant.'

Abruptly he stood. Blaise did the same, seriously confused now. 'I didn't think you had ever married,' he said.

'I didn't,' Bertran said carelessly. 'Why, do you think it is time?' The sardonic, distancing smile was back. 'A wife to warm my old bones at night, children to gladden the heart in my declining years? What an intriguing thought. Shall we discuss it on the way down?'

He had begun walking towards his horse as he spoke, and so Blaise, perforce, did the same. It had grown colder now on this windy height, the sun hidden behind a grey mass of swiftly driven clouds. As an afterthought Blaise looked back and saw that the lamb was following. They mounted up and began to ride. From the crest of the ridge they could see Mallin and the rest of their party gathered east of them and below. Bertran waved briefly and they started down. Far in the distance, beyond meadow and wood and the other men, the castle could be seen, with the lavender fields in shadow beyond.

On the way down, in the interval before they reached the others, the matter Bertran de Talair chose to raise had nothing at all to do with marital bliss, belated or otherwise, or with the soothing accoutrements of a quiescent old age.

And now, remarkably or predictably, depending on how one chose to consider things, there came the unabashed glow of a candle from the curve of the stairway below the window niche where Blaise was keeping watch. Not even an attempt at stealth, he thought grimly. He heard the quiet sound of footsteps steadily ascending. As promised, though Blaise hadn't really believed it on the hillside.

'I imagine you'll be posted on watch outside the baroness's rooms on my last night. I wouldn't go up until then in any case . . . too many complications otherwise, and it isn't really decent. No,' Bertran de Talair had said on that ride down the chilly slope, 'I'll wait till the end, which is always best. I can count on your discretion, I take it?'

For a long moment Blaise had had to struggle to control his anger. When he'd replied, it was in the best equivalent he could manage to the duke's casual tones. 'I would suggest you not rely on any such thing. I have accepted an offer of service from you, but that begins a fortnight from now. For the moment Mallin de Baude pays me and you would be advised to remember that.'

'Such loyalty!' de Talair had murmured, gazing straight ahead.

Blaise shook his head. 'Professionalism,' he'd replied, keeping his temper. 'I am worth nothing in the market for fighting men if I have a reputation for duplicity.'

'That is an irrelevance. Nothing that affects a reputation will emerge from a dark stairway with only the two of us to know.' De Talair's tone was quietly serious. 'Tell me, Northerner, would you impose your own values in matters of love and night on all the men and women that you meet?'

'Hardly. But I'm afraid I will impose them on myself.'

The duke had glanced across at him then and smiled. 'Then we shall probably have an interesting encounter a few nights from now.' He'd waved again at Mallin de Baude down below and spurred his horse forward to join the baron and his men for the rest of the ride back down to the castle.

And now here he was, without even a token attempt at deception or concealment. Blaise stood up and stepped from the window nook onto the stairway. He checked the hang of his sword and dagger both and then waited, his feet balanced and spread wide. From around the curve of the stairs the glow of flame gradually became brighter and then Blaise saw the candle. Following it, as if into the ambit of light, came Bertran de Talair, in burgundy and black with a white shirt open at the throat.

'I have come,' said the duke softly, smiling behind the flame, 'for that interesting encounter.'

'Not with me,' said Blaise grimly.

'Well, no, not really with you. I don't think either of us suffers unduly from the Arimondan vice. I thought it might be diverting to see if I could fare better in the room at the top of these stairs than poor Evrard did some while ago.'

Blaise shook his head. 'I meant what I told you on the hills. I will not judge you, or the baroness either. I am a sword for hire, here or elsewhere in the world. At the moment En Mallin de Baude is paying me to guard this stairway. Will it please you to turn and go down, my lord, before matters become unpleasant here?'

'Go down?' Bertran said, gesturing with the candle, 'and waste an hour's fussing with my appearance and several days of anticipating what might happen tonight? I'm too old to be excited by temptation and then meekly turn away. You're too young to understand that, I suppose. But I daresay you do have your own lessons to learn, or perhaps to remember. Hear me, Northerner: a man can be forestalled in matters such as this, even I can be, whatever you might have heard to the contrary, but a woman of spirit will do what she wants to do, even in Gorhaut, and most especially in Arbonne.' He lifted the candle higher as he spoke, sending an orange glow spinning out to illuminate both of them.

Blaise registered the fact of that quite effective light an instant before he heard a rustle of clothing close behind him. He was turning belatedly, and opening his mouth to cry out, when the blow cracked him on the side of the temple, hard enough to make him stagger back against the window seat, momentarily dazed. And a moment, of course, was more than enough for Bertran de Talair to spring up the three steps between them, a dagger reversed in one hand, the candle uplifted in the other.

'It is difficult,' said the duke close to Blaise's ear, 'extremely difficult, to protect those who prefer not to be protected. A lesson, Northerner.'

He was wearing a perfume of some kind, and his breath was scented with mint. Through unfocused eyes and a wave of dizziness, Blaise caught a glimpse beyond him of a woman on the stairs. Her long yellow hair was unbound, tumbling down her back. Her night robe was of silk, and by the light of the candle and of the moon in the archers' window Blaise saw that it was white as a bride's, an icon of innocence. That was all he managed to register; he had no chance for more, to move or cry out again, before Bertran de Talair's dagger haft rapped, in a neat, hard, precisely judged blow, against the back of his skull and Blaise lost all consciousness of moonlight or icons or pain.

When he awoke, he was lying on the stone floor of the window niche, slumped back against one of the benches. With a groan he turned to look out. Pale Vidonne, waning from full, was high in the window now, lending her silver light to the night sky. The clouds had passed, he could see faint stars around the moon.

He brought up a hand and gingerly touched his head. He would have a corfe egg of his own on the back of his skull for some days to come, and a nasty bruise above the hairline over his right ear as well. He moaned again, and in the same instant realized that he was not alone.

'The seguignac is on the seat just above you,' said Bertran de Talair quietly. 'Be careful, I've left the flask open.'

The duke was sitting on the other side of the stairwell, leaning back against the inner wall at the same level as Blaise. The moonlight pouring in through the window fell upon his dishevelled garments and the tousled disarray of his hair. The blue eyes were as clear as ever, but Bertran looked older now. There were lines Blaise couldn't remember seeing before at the corners of his eyes, and dark circles beneath them.

He couldn't think of anything to say or do so he reached

upwards — carefully, as advised — and found the flask. The seguignac slipped down his throat like distilled, reviving fire; Blaise imagined he could feel it reaching out to his extremities, restoring life to arms and legs, fingers and toes. His head ached ferociously, though. Stretching cautiously — it hurt to move — he reached across the stairway and handed the flask to the duke. Bertran took it without speaking and drank.

It was silent then on the stairs. Blaise, fighting off the miasma of two blows to the head, tried to make himself think clearly. He could, of course, shout now and raise an alarm. Mallin himself, from his own room down the hall from Soresina's, would likely be the first man to reach them here.

With what consequences?

Blaise sighed and accepted the return passing of the seguignac from the duke. The flask gleamed palely in the moonlight; there were intricate designs upon it, most likely the work of Götzland master smiths. It had probably cost more than Blaise's monthly wages here in Baude.

There really was no point in crying out now, and he knew it. Soresina de Baude had chosen to do — as Bertran had said — exactly as she wished. It was over now, and unless he, Blaise, stirred up an alarm and roused the castle it would probably be over with little consequence for anyone.

It was just the *dishonesty* of it all that bothered him, the image — yet another — of a woman's duplicity and a man's idle, avid pursuit of pleasure at another's expense. He had somehow hoped for more of Duke Bertran de Talair than this picture of a jaded seducer putting all his energy into achieving a single night with a yellow-haired woman married to someone else.

But he wouldn't raise the alarm. Bertran and Soresina had counted on that, he knew. It angered him, the easy assumption that his behaviour could be anticipated, but he wasn't enough provoked to change his mind simply to spite them. People died when spite like that was indulged.

His head was hurting at back and side both, two sets of hammers vying with each other to see which could cause him more distress. The seguignac helped though; seguignac, he decided sagely, wiping at his mouth, might actually help with a great many matters of grief or loss.

He turned to the duke to say as much, but stopped, word-less, at what he saw in the other's unguarded face. The scarred, ironic, worldly face of the troubadour lord of Talair.

'Twenty-three years,' Bertran de Talair said a moment later, half to himself, his eyes on the moon in the window. 'So much longer than I thought I would live, actually. And the god knows, and sweet Rian knows I've tried, but in twenty-three years I've never yet found a woman to equal her, or take away the memory, even for a night.'

Feeling hopelessly out of his element in the face of this, Blaise felt an unexpected moment of pity for Soresina de Baude, with her unbound hair and her white silk night robe in the room above them. Unable to summon any words at all, suspecting that none that he could ever think of would be remotely adequate to what he had just heard, he simply reached back across the stairway and offered the seguignac.

After a moment En Bertran's ringed hand reached out for it in the moonlight. De Talair drank deeply, then he drew the stopper from some recess of his clothing and capped the flask. He rose slowly, almost steady on his feet and, not bothering with another candle, started down the winding stairway with-out another word or a glance back. He was already lost to sight in the darkness before the first curve took him away. Blaise heard his quiet footsteps going down, and then those, too, were gone and there was only silence and the moon slowly passing from the narrow window, leaving behind the stars.

CHAPTER·3

Ademar, king of Gorhaut, slowly turns away from the diverting if extremely messy struggle taking place in front of the throne between the carefully maimed hound and the three cats that have been set upon it. Not even acknowledging the half-clothed woman kneeling on the stone floor in front of him with his sex in her mouth, he looks narrowly over at the man who has just spoken, interrupting this double amusement.

'We are not certain we heard you correctly,' the king says in his unexpectedly high voice. The tone however is one his court has come to know well in little over a year. Not a few of the fifty or so men assembled in the audience chamber in the king's palace at Cortil offer silent thanks to Corannos that they are not the recipients of that gaze or that tone. The handful of women present might have different thoughts, but the women do not matter in Gorhaut.

With an elaborate casualness that fools no one, Duke Ranald de Garsenc reaches for his ale and drinks deeply before answering. To his credit, the more attentive eyes among the court note, de Garsenc's hand is steady as he sets the heavy flagon down again. Looking across the wooden trestle table at the king, he lifts his voice. 'I understand you were talking about Arbonne this morning. I simply said, why don't you marry the bitch? She's a widow, she's heirless, what could be simpler?'

The king's extremely large, ringless hands descend absently to first loop themselves in the long black hair and then to briefly encircle the ceaselessly working throat of the girl on her knees in front of him. He never actually looks

down at her though. Beyond her, the old hound has now
fallen; it is lying on one side panting raggedly, blood streaming from a great many wounds. The cats, starved for five days,
are avidly beginning to feed. Ademar smiles thinly for a
moment, watching, and then makes a sudden moue of distaste
as the dog's entrails begin to spill onto the floor. He gestures,
and the handlers spring forward to seize the four animals and
bear them from the room. The cats, ravenous and deranged,
make high-pitched shrieking sounds that can be heard even
after the doors at the far end have closed behind them. The
smell of blood and wet fur lingers, mixed with stinging smoke
from the fires and spilled beer on the tables where the high
lords of Gorhaut are permitted by ancient custom to sit and
drink in the presence of their liege.

Their liege closes his eyes at just that moment. His large,
well-knit body stiffens and an expression of pleased surprise
crosses his fair-skinned, full-bearded features. There is an
awkward silence in the room as courtiers see reason to scruti-
nize their fingernails or the dark beams of the ceiling. With a
sigh, Ademar slumps back on the throne. When he opens his
eyes again it is to look, as he always does when this particular
amusement reaches its climax, at the women of his court,
gathered near the windows to the left of the throne. The more
discreet among them are looking assiduously down and away.
One or two are visibly discomfited. One or two others are
equally flushed, but for what seem to be different reasons, and
these are the ones whose eyes gaze boldly back at Ademar's.
Screening the king's lower body with her own, the kneeling
woman attends to the points and drawstrings of his garments
and carefully smooths his breeches and hose before tilting her
head up for permission to withdraw.

Slouching back in his throne, Ademar of Gorhaut looks
down at her for the first time. With an indolent finger he
traces the contours of her lips. He smiles, the same thin smile
as before. 'Attend to the duke of Garsenc,' he says. 'My
father's former champion seems a man sorely in need of the
ministrations of a proper woman.' The girl, expressionless,
rises and paces gracefully across the floor towards the man who
had interrupted the king's pleasure a moment before. There is
a ripple of coarse laughter in the room; Ademar grins,

acknowledging it. Beside the window one woman turns away suddenly to look out over the misty grey of the landscape. Ademar of Gorhaut notices that. He notices a great deal, his court has come to realize in the short period of his reign.

'My lady Rosala,' the king says, 'turn not away from us. We covet the sunshine of your countenance on a day so dreary as this. And it may be your husband will be well pleased to have you learn a new skill as you watch.'

The woman called Rosala, tall, yellow-haired and visibly with child, delays a long moment before obeying the command and turning back to the room. She nods her head formally in response to the king's words but does not speak. The other girl has by now slipped under the long table and can be seen settling herself in front of Duke Ranald de Garsenc. The duke's colour is suddenly high. He avoids looking towards the side of the room where his wife stands among the women. A few of the lesser courtiers, bright-eyed with amusement and malice, have strolled over to stand by his shoulder, glancing downwards with an intense simulation of interest at what is now taking place beneath the table. Ranald stares straight ahead, looking at no one. This amusement of the king's has taken place before, but never with a lord of so high a rank. It is a measure of Ademar's power, or the fear he elicits, that he can do this to a man who was once King's Champion in Gorhaut, however many years ago that was.

'Marry the bitch,' the king repeats slowly, as if tasting the syllables on his tongue. 'Marry the countess of Arbonne. How old is Signe de Barbentain now, sixty-five, seventy? An astonishing suggestion ... how is she with her mouth, does anyone know?'

Several of the men and one of the women by the window titter with laughter again. None of the foreign envoys is in the room at the moment; given the current subject matter, an extremely good thing. Rosala de Garsenc is pale, but her square, handsome features betray no expression at all.

On the other side of the room her husband abruptly reaches for his flagon again. This time he spills some ale as he brings it to his lips. He wipes his moustache with a sleeve and says, 'Does it matter? Would anyone imagine I speak of more than a marriage of acquisition?' He pauses and glances, almost involuntarily, downward for an instant, and then resumes. 'You marry the crone, pack her off to a castle in the north and inherit Arbonne when she dies of fever or ague or whatever else the god sees fit to send her. Then you follow through with your marriage to Daufridi of Valensa's daughter. She may even be old enough to bed by then.'

Ademar has turned in his seat to look fully at him, his pale eyes unreadable above the yellow beard. He says nothing, chewing meditatively on one end of his long moustache. There is a stir at the far end of the room, made louder by the silence around the throne. The great doors swing open and the guards let someone through. A very large man in a dark blue robe enters, striding purposefully forward. Seeing him, Ademar's face lights up. He grins like a mischievous child and glances quickly back at Ranald de Garsenc, who has also taken note of the man entering, though with a very different expression on his face.

'My dear High Elder,' the king says, his tone brightly malicious now, 'you are narrowly in time to observe how we value our cousin, your son, and his wise counsels. Our well-beloved Mistress Belote is even now assuaging him with his lady wife's full approval. Will you come make this a family affair?'

Galbert de Garsenc, High Elder of Corannos in Gorhaut, Chief Counsellor to the King, disdains to even glance at his son, nor does he appear to acknowledge the amusement in the room that takes its cue from the king's brittle tone. He stops not far from the throne, a bulky, formidable presence, and inclines his large, smooth face towards Ademar, saying merely, 'What counsels, my liege?' His voice is deep and resonant; though he speaks quietly it fills the large chamber.

'What counsels, indeed! Duke Ranald has just advised us to marry the countess of Arbonne, send her off north and inherit her sun-drenched country when she succumbs in her decrepitude to some lamentable pestilence. Would this be a thought you and your son have devised together?'

Galbert, the only clean-shaven man in the room, turns to look at his son for the first time as the king finishes speaking. Ranald de Garsenc, though very pale, meets his father's gaze without flinching. With a contemptuous twist of his mouth, Galbert turns back to the king.

'It would not,' he says heavily. 'Of course it is not, my liege. I do not devise with such as he. My son is fit for nothing but spilling ale on himself and occupying tavern sluts.'

The king of Gorhaut laughs, a curiously joyous, high-pitched sound in the dark-beamed, shadowed room. 'Tavern sluts? In the name of our blessed god! What a way to speak of the noble lady his wife, my lord Galbert! The woman bearing your grandchild! Surely you do not think —'

The king stops, hilarity vivid in his face, as a flagon of ale hurtles across the room to strike the High Elder of Corannos full on his broad chest. Galbert stumbles heavily backwards and almost falls. At the long table Ranald rises, hastily pushing his semi-erect member back into his clothing. Two guards step belatedly forward but pause at a gesture from the king. Breathing heavily, Ranald de Garsenc points a shaking finger at his father.

'Next time I might kill you,' he says. His voice trembles. 'Next time it may be a knife. Take note for your life. If you speak so of me again, anywhere where I might hear of it, it may mean your death and I will submit myself to whatever judgment of that deed Corannos makes when I leave the world.'

There is a shocked silence. Even in a court not unused to this sort of thing, especially from the de Garsenc clan, the words are sobering. Galbert's rich blue robe is stained with dark ale. He fixes his son with a glance of icy contempt, easily a match for Ranald's impassioned rage, before turning back to the king. 'Will you allow such an assault upon your High Elder, my liege? An attack upon my person is an insult to the god above us all. Will you sit by and let this impiety go unpunished?' The deep voice is still controlled, resonantly pitched, soberly aggrieved.

Ademar does not immediately reply. He leans back once more against the heavy wooden seat-back of the throne, stroking his beard with one hand. Father and son remain on their feet, rigid and intense. The hatred between them lies heavy and palpable in the room, seeming denser than the smoke of the fires.

'Why,' says King Ademar of Gorhaut, at length, his voice sounding even higher and more querulous after the

High Elder's deep tones, 'is it such a foolish idea for me to wed Signe de Barbentain?'

Abruptly Duke Ranald sits again, a tiny smile of vindication playing about his lips. Impatiently he moves a knee to forestall an obedient attempt by the woman beneath the table to resume her attentions. On the far side of the room he notices that his wife has turned away again and is staring out the window with her back to the king and the court. It has begun to rain. He looks at Rosala's profile for a moment, and a curious expression crosses his own features. After a moment he lifts his flask and drinks again.

The only thing I really don't know, Rosala de Garsenc is thinking just then, looking out at the cold, steady, slanting rain and the mist-wrapped eastern moors, *is which of them I despise most.*

It is not a new thought. She has spent a remarkable amount of time trying to decide whether she more hates the erratic, usually inebriated man she'd been forced to wed by the late King Duergar, or the dangerously cunning, Corannos-obsessed High Elder of the god, her husband's father. If she chooses, as today, to take the thoughts one small, very natural step further, it is easy to include Duergar's son, now King Ademar of Gorhaut, in that blighted company. In part because she is uneasily, constantly aware that when the child she now carries is born she is going to have to contend with the king in a very particular way. She doesn't know why he has singled her out, why her manner seems to have captivated him — goaded him, more likely, she sometimes thinks — but there is no denying the import of Ademar's flat, pale gaze and the way it lingers on her, especially in that dangerous time of night here in Cortil after too much ale has been drunk around the banquet tables but before the women are permitted to leave.

One of the reasons, perhaps unfairly, that she despises her husband is for the way in which he will notice the king staring at her and indifferently turn away to his dice cup or his flagon. The duke of Garsenc ought surely, Rosala had thought, in the early months of her marriage, to have more pride in him than that. It appeared, though, that the only people who could arouse Ranald to anything resembling passion or spirit were his father and brother, and that, of course, was its own old, bleak story. It sometimes seems to Rosala that she has been part of their tale forever; it is hard to remember clearly back to a time when the lords of Garsenc have not trammelled her tightly about with their festering family griefs. It had been different at home in Savaric, but Savaric was a long time ago.

The wind is rising now, coming about to the east, sending droplets and then a gusty sheet of rain through the window to strike her face and the bodice of her gown. She doesn't mind the cold, she even welcomes it, but there is a child to think of now. Reluctantly she turns away, back to the smoky, stale, crowded room, to hear her husband's father begin to speak to the issue of forced marriages and conquest in the warm bright south.

'My liege, you know the reasons as well as I, so, indeed does every man in this room, save one perhaps.' The glance flicked sideways at Ranald is so brief as to carry its own measure of bone-deep contempt. 'Even the women know my son's folly when they hear it. Even the women.' Beside Rosala, Adelh de Sauvan, who is venal and corrupt and newly widowed, smiles. Rosala sees that and looks away.

'To wed the countess of Arbonne,' Galbert goes on, his rich voice filling the room, 'we would need her consent. This, she will not give. Ever. If she did, for whatever reason, maddened by woman's desire perhaps, she would be deposed and slain by the assembled dukes of Arbonne before any wedding could take place. Think you that the lords of Carenzu or Malmont or Miraval would sit by and watch us so easily stake a claim to their land? Even a woman should be able to see the folly in such a fatuous thought. What, my liege, do you think the troubadour lord of Arbonne would do at such a time . . . think you that Bertran de Talair would stand by and let such a marriage take place?'

'That name is forbidden here!' Ademar of Gorhaut says quickly, leaning abruptly forward. Two spots of unnatural colour show in his cheeks above the beard.

'And so it should be,' Galbert says smoothly, as if he'd expected exactly that response. 'I have as much reason as you my liege to hate that schemer and his godless, discordant ways.'

Rosala smiles inwardly at that, keeping her features carefully schooled. It was little over a month ago that de Talair's latest song had reached the court of Gorhaut. She remembers the night; wind and rain then, too, a trembling, whey-faced bard obeying Ademar's command, singing the duke of Talair's verses in a voice like rasping iron:

> Shame then in springtime for proud Gorhaut,
> Betrayed by a young king and his counsellor.

And more, much more, and worse, in the creaking, barely audible mumblings of the terrified singer while a wind blew on the moors outside:

> Where went the manhood of Gorhaut and Valensa
> When war was abandoned and pale peace bought
>
> By weak kings and sons long lost to their lineage?

Rosala can almost find a kind of warmth in her heart at the memory of the torchlit faces around her that night. The expressions of the king, of Galbert, the furtive glances that flitted about the hall from one newly landless lord or coran to another as the driving music brought the force of the words home, even in the timid voice of the singer. The bard, a young trovaritz from Götzland, had almost certainly owed his continued life to the presence in the great hall of Cortil that evening of the envoy from his own country and the undeniable importance of keeping peace with King Jörg of Götzland at this juncture of the world's affairs. Rosala had no doubt what Ademar would have liked to do when the music ended.

Now he leans urgently forward again, almost rising from the throne, the two bright spots vivid in his cheeks and says, 'No man has as much reason as we do, Galbert. Do not exalt yourself.'

The High Elder gently shakes his head. Again the rich voice encompasses the room, so warm, so caring, it can so easily deceive one into thinking the man is profoundly other than he is. Rosala knows about that; she knows almost everything about that by now.

'It is not in my own name that I take umbrage, my liege,' says Galbert. 'I am as nothing, nothing at all in myself. But I stand before you and before the eyes of all those in the six countries as the voice of the god in Gorhaut. And Gorhaut is the Heartland, the place where Corannos of the Ancients was born in the days before man walked and woman fell into her ruin. An insult to me is a blow delivered to the most high god and must not be tolerated. Nor will it be, for all the world knows your mettle and your mind in this, my liege.'

It is fascinating, Rosala thinks, how smoothly, how effortlessly, Galbert has shifted the matter at hand. Ademar is nodding his head slowly; so are a number of the men in the hall. Her husband is drinking, but that is to be expected. Briefly, Rosala feels sorry for him.

'We would have thought,' the king says slowly, 'that Daufridi of Valensa would share our attitude to this provocation. Perhaps when we next receive his envoy we ought to discuss the matter of Bertran de Talair.'

Daufridi has all our land north of Iersen now, Rosala finds herself thinking bitterly, and knows that others will be framing the same thought. *He can afford to tolerate insults from Arbonne.* Her family's ancient estates along the Iersen River are right on the newly defined northern border of Gorhaut now; Savaric had not been so exposed ever before. And there are men in this room whose lands and castles have been given away; they are part of Valensa now, ceded by treaty, surrendered in the peace after being saved in the war. King Ademar is surrounded by hungry, ambitious, angry men, who will need to be assuaged, and soon, however much they might fear him for the moment.

It is all so terribly clear, Rosala thinks, her face a mask, blank and unrevealing.

'By all means,' Galbert the High Elder is saying, 'raise the matter with the Valensan envoy. I think we can deal with a shabby rhymester by ourselves, but it would indeed be well to have certain other matters understood and arranged before another year has come and gone.'

Rosala sees her husband lift his head at that, looking not at his father but at the king.

'What matters?' Duke Ranald says, loudly, in the silence. 'What needs to be understood?' It is only with an effort sometimes that Rosala is able to remember that her husband was once the most celebrated fighting man in Gorhaut, champion to Ademar's father. A long time ago, that was, and the years have not sat kindly on the shoulders of Ranald de Garsenc.

Ademar says nothing, chewing on his moustache. It is Ranald's father who replies, the faintest hint of triumph in the magnificent voice. 'Do you not know?' he asks, eyebrows elaborately arched. 'Surely one so free with idle counsels can riddle this puzzle through.'

Ranald scowls blackly but refuses to put the question again. Rosala knows he doesn't understand; again she feels an unexpected impulse of sympathy for him during this latest skirmish in his lifelong battle with what his father is. She doubts Ranald is the only man here bemused by the cryptic byplay between the High Elder and the king. It happens, though, that her own father, in his day, had been a master of diplomacy, high in the counsels of King Duergar, and Rosala and one brother were the only two of his children to survive into adulthood. She had learned a great deal, more than women tended to in Gorhaut. Which, she knows, is a large part of her own private grief right now, trapped among the de Garsenc and their hates.

But she *does* understand things, she *can* see them, almost too clearly. If he is sober enough, Ranald will probably want her thoughts tonight when they are alone. She knows the heavy, hectoring tone he will use, the scorn with which he will quickly dismiss her replies if she chooses to offer any, and she also knows how he will go away from her after and muse upon what she tells him. It is a power of sorts, she is aware of that; one that many women have used to put their own stamp, as a seal upon a letter, upon the events of their day.

But such women have two things Rosala lacks. A desire, a passion even, to move and manipulate amid the fever and flare of court events, and a stronger, worthier vessel in which to pour their wisdom and their spirit than Ranald de Garsenc is ever going to be.

She doesn't know what she will tell her husband if he asks for her thoughts that evening. She suspects he will. And she is almost certain she does know what his father's designs are and, even more, that the king is going to move with them. Ademar is being guided, as a capricious stallion by a master horsebreaker, towards a destination Galbert has likely wanted to reach for more years than anyone knows. King Duergar of Gorhaut had not been a man susceptible to the persuasion of anyone in his court, including his clergy — perhaps especially his clergy — and so the High Elder's access to real power dates back only to the precise moment when a Valensan arrow, arching through a wintry twilight, found Duergar's eye in that grim, cold battle by Iersen Bridge a year and a half ago.

And now Duergar is dead and burned on his pyre, and his handsome son rules in Cortil, and there is a peace signed in the north disinheriting a quarter of the people of Gorhaut, whether of high estate or low. Which means — surely *anyone* could see it if they only stopped to look — one thing that will have to follow. Instinctively, a motion of withdrawal as much a reflex as a forest creature's retreat from a tongue of flame, Rosala turns back to the window. It is springtime in Gorhaut, but the grey rains show no signs of ending and the damp chill can ache in one's very bones.

It will be warmer, she knows, warmer and softer and with a far more benevolent light in the sky, in Arbonne. In woman-ruled Arbonne, with its Court of Love, its wide, rich, sun-blessed lands, its sheltered, welcoming harbours on the southern sea and its heresy of Rian the goddess ruling along-side the god, not crouched in maidenly subservience beneath his iron hand.

'We will have much to speak of yet,' Galbert de Garsenc is saying, 'before summer draws fully upon us, and to you my liege will rightly fall all decisions that must be made and the great burden of them.' He raises his voice; Rosala does not turn back from the window. She knows what he is about to say, where he is taking the king, taking all of them.

'But as High Elder of Corannos in this most ancient, holy land where the god was born, I will say this to you, my liege, and to all those gathered here. Thanks to your great wisdom, Gorhaut is at peace in the north for the first time in the life-time of most of those here. We need not draw axe and sword to guard our borders and our fields from Valensa. The pride and the might of this country under King Ademar is as great as it has ever been in our long history, and ours is still and ever the holy stewardship through the six countries of the power of the god. In these halls walk the descendants of the first corans — the earliest brothers of the god — who ever bestrode the hills and valleys of the known world. And it may be — if you, my liege, should decide to make it so — that to us will fall a scourging task worthy of our great fathers. Worthy of the greatest bards ever to lift voice in celebration of the mighty of their day.'

Oh, clever, Rosala thinks. *Oh, very neatly done, my lord.* Her eyes are fixed on what lies beyond the window, on the mist rolling in over the moors. She wants to be out there alone on a horse, even in rain, even with the child quickening in her womb, far from this smoky hall, these voices and rancours and sour desires, far from the honey-smooth manipulations of the High Elder behind her.

'Beyond the mountains south of us they mock Corannos,' Galbert says, passion now infusing his voice. 'They live under the god's own bright sun, which is his most gracious gift to man, and they mock his sovereignty. They demean him with temples to a woman, a foul goddess of midnight and magics and the blood-stained rites of women. They cripple and wound our beloved Corannos with this heresy. They unman him, or they think they do.' His voice sinks again, towards intimacy, the nuanced notes of a different kind of power. The whole room is with him now as in the toils of a spell, Rosala can sense it; even the women beside her are leaning forward slightly, lips parted, waiting.

'They think they do,' Galbert de Garsenc repeats softly. 'In time, in our time if we are worthy, they shall learn their folly, their endless, eternal folly, and holy Corannos shall not be mocked in the lands of the Arbonne River ever again.'

He does not end on a rousing note; it is not yet time. This is a first proclamation only, a beginning, a muted instrument sounded amid smoking fires and a late, cold spring, with slanting rain outside and mist on the moors.

'We will withdraw,' the king of Gorhaut says at length in his high voice, breaking the stillness. 'We will take private counsel with our Elder of the god.' He rises from the throne, a tall, handsome, physically commanding man, and his court sinks low in genuflection like stalks of corn before the wind.

It is so clear, Rosala is thinking as she rises to her feet again, *so clear what is to come.*

'Do tell me, my dear,' Adelh de Sauvan murmurs, materializing at her elbow, 'have you any late tidings of your much-travelled brother-in-law?'

Rosala stiffens. A mistake, and she knows it immediately. She forces herself to smile blandly, but Adelh is a master at catching one unawares.

'Nothing recent, I fear,' she answers calmly. 'He was still in Portezza, the last we heard, but that was some months ago. He doesn't communicate very much. If he does, I shall be most certain to convey your anxious interest.'

A weak shaft, that one, and Adelh only smiles, her dark eyes lustrous. 'Please do,' she replies. 'I would think *any* woman would be interested in that one. Such an accomplished man, Blaise, an equal, a rival even to his great father I sometimes think.' She pauses, precisely long enough. 'Though hardly to your dear husband, of course.' She says it with the sweetest expression imaginable on her face.

Two other women come up just then, blessedly freeing Rosala from the need to frame a reply. She waits long enough for courtesy to be served and then moves away from the window. She is cold suddenly, and wants very much to leave. She cannot do so without Ranald, though, and she sees, with a brief inward yielding to despair, that he has refilled his flagon, and his dice and purse are on the table in front of him now.

She moves towards the nearest of the fires and stands with her back to the blaze. In her mind she goes back over that short, unsettling exchange with Adelh. She cannot stop herself from wondering what, if anything, the woman could possibly know. It is only malice, she finally decides, only the unthinking, effortless malice that defined Adelh de Sauvan even before her husband died with King Duergar by Iersen Bridge. An instinct for blood, something predatory.

Rosala has a sudden recollection, involuntary and frightening, of the starving cats and the torn, dying hound. She shivers. Unconsciously her hands come up to rest upon her

belly, as if to cradle and shelter from the waiting world the life
taking shape within her.

†

The light was the extraordinary thing, the way in which the
sun in a deep blue sky seemed to particularize everything, to
render each tree, bird on the wing, darting fox, blade of grass,
something vividly bright and immediate. Everything seemed
to somehow be *more* of whatever it was here, sharper, more
brilliantly defined. The late-afternoon breeze from the west
took the edge off the heat of the day; even the sound of it in
the leaves was refreshing. Though that, on reflection, was
ridiculous: the sound of the wind in the trees was exactly the
same in Gorhaut or Götzland as it was here in Arbonne; there
just seemed to be something about this country that steered
the mind towards such imaginings.

A troubadour, Blaise thought, riding through afternoon
sunshine, would probably be singing by now, or composing, or
shaping some quite unintelligible thought based on the symbolic language of flowers. There were certainly enough
flowers. A troubadour would know the names of all of them,
of course. Blaise didn't, partly because there were varieties of
extravagantly coloured wildflowers here in Arbonne that he'd
never seen before, even among the celebrated, rolling countryside between the cities of Portezza.

The land here was beautiful, he conceded, without
grudging the thought this time. He wasn't in a grudging mood
this afternoon; the light was too benevolent, the country
through which he rode too genuinely resplendent at the
beginning of summer. There were vineyards to the west and
the dense trees of a forest beyond them. The only sounds were
the wind and the chatter of birds and the steady jingle of harness on his horse and the pack pony behind. In the distance
ahead Blaise could see at intervals the blue sparkle of water
on a lake. If the directions he'd been given at last night's inn
were correct, the lake would be Dierne and Castle Talair
would be visible soon, nestled against the northern shore. He
should be able to make it by day's end at a comfortable pace.

It was hard not to be in a good humour today, whatever
one's thoughts might be about country and family and the

slowly darkening tenor of events in the world. For one thing, Blaise's leave-taking at Baude four days ago had been a genuinely cordial parting. He'd worried for a time about how Mallin would receive his defection to the ranks of the corans of Bertran de Talair, but the young lord of Castle Baude seemed to have almost expected Blaise's announcement when it came, two days after En Bertran rode off, and even — or so it seemed to Blaise — to almost welcome it.

There might, in fact, have been pragmatic reasons for that. Mallin was a comfortable but not a wealthy man, and the expenses of aspiring towards a place of honour on the higher ramparts of the world might have begun to give him pause. After a fortnight's extravagant entertainment of the troubadour lord of Talair, it was possible that Mallin de Baude was not averse to some measures of economizing, and seasoned mercenary captains such as Blaise of Gorhaut were not inexpensive.

On the morning of Blaise's departure, Mallin had wished him the blessing of the god and of Rian the goddess as well; this was Arbonne, after all. Blaise accepted the one with gratitude and the other with good grace. He'd surprised himself with the degree of regret he felt bidding farewell to the baron and to the corans he'd trained: Hirnan, Maffour and the others. He hadn't expected to miss these men; it seemed as if he was going to, for a little while at least.

Soresina, in the last days before he went, was a different, more unsettling sort of surprise. The simple truth was, however much Blaise might want to deny it, that the lady of Castle Baude, always an attractive woman and aware of it, seemed to have grown in both dignity and grace in a very short period. Specifically, the short period since Bertran de Talair's visit to the highlands. Was it possible that a single furtive night with the duke could have effected such a change? Blaise hated the very notion, but could not deny the poised courtesy of Soresina's subsequent treatment of him, or the elegance of her appearance at her husband's side in the days that passed between Bertran's departure and Blaise's own. There was not even the shadow of a hint in her expression or manner of what had taken place on the stairway below her chambers so little time ago. She did seem pensive at times, almost grave, as if inwardly coming to terms with some shift in her relations with the world.

Soresina was with Mallin when the baron and his corans rode part of the way with Blaise on the morning he took leave of the western highlands. She'd offered him her cheek to kiss, not merely her hand. After the briefest hesitation Blaise had leaned sideways in his saddle and complied.

Soresina had glanced up at him as he straightened. He remembered a glance she'd offered him shortly after he'd arrived, when she'd told him how she liked men after the older fashion, warlike and hard. There was an echo of that now, she was still the same woman after all, but there was also something else that was new.

'I hope some woman elsewhere in your travels through Arbonne persuades you to remove that beard,' she said. 'It scratches, Blaise. Grow it back, if you must, when you return to Gorhaut.'

She was smiling at him as she spoke, entirely at ease, and Mallin de Baude, visibly proud of her, laughed and gripped Blaise's arm a last time in farewell.

There had been a number of farewells in his life during the past few years, Blaise thought now, three days after that morning departure, riding amid the scent and colours of wildflowers, past the green and purple beginnings of grapes on the vines, with blue water in the distance beckoning him with flashes of mirrored sunlight. Too many goodbyes, perhaps, but they were a part of the life he'd chosen for himself, or had had chosen for him by his birth and his family's rank, and the laws, written or unwritten, that guided the country of Gorhaut through the shoals of a rocky world.

There had been regret, anger at twists of fate, real pain in Portezza the last time he was there, but it seemed that in the end he truly was most content as he was now, on his own, answerable to no man — and certainly no woman — save for service honourably owed by contract freely entered into. There was little that was greatly unusual about any of the patterns of his life. It was a well-enough trodden path in the lives of younger sons of noble families in the world as they knew it. The eldest son married, fathered other children, inherited all: the lands — fiercely guarded, scrupulously undivided — the family goods, and whatever titles had been earned and not lost as one monarch succeeded another in Gorhaut. The daughters of such houses were expensively dowried pawns, though often vital ones, married off to consolidate alliances, expand holdings, lay claim or seige to even higher rank for the family.

Which left little enough for the other sons. Younger sons were a problem, and had been so for a long time, ever since the dwindling sizes of partitioned estates had changed the system of inheritance. All but barred from a useful marriage by virtue of their lack of land or chattels, forced to leave the family dwellings by friction or pride or sheerest self-protection, many entered the clergy of Corannos or attached themselves to the household corans of another high lord. Some followed a third, less predictable course, going out into the world beyond the country of their birth, alone on the always dangerous roads or more often in smaller or larger groupings to seek their fortune. In a season of war they would be found at the battlefields; in the rarer times of tranquillity they would be stirring up strife themselves with a restless champing at the bit of peace, or maiming and hammering each other in the tournament mêlées that moved with the trade fairs from town to town through the known lands of the world.

Nor was this pattern only true in Gorhaut. Bertran de Talair, until his older brother died childless and he became the duke, had been among this roving number in his own day, one of the most celebrated, bringing a sword and a harp, both, and later a joglar expensively outfitted in his livery, to battlefield and tournament in Götzland and Portezza and watery Valensa in the north.

Blaise of Gorhaut, years later, and for a variety of reasons, had become another such man, ever since he'd been anointed as a coran by King Duergar himself.

He'd left home with his horse and armour and weapons and his skills with them, skills that had travelled well and not without profit — most of it banked in Portezza now with Rudel's family. It was a life that had left him, riding alone under the sun of summer in Arbonne, untied and untrammelled by the bonds that seemed to ensnare so many of the men he knew.

He would have scorned the question and the questioner both, but if asked that day, Blaise would have said that he was not an unhappy man, for all the bitterness that lay behind him at home and among the dangerous cities of Portezza. He would have said he knew the future he wanted for himself, and that for the foreseeable future it was not unlike the present through which he rode, in whatever country it might chance to fall. He wasn't particular about that, he would have said. If you kept moving there was less chance of putting down roots, forming bonds, caring for people . . . learning what happened when those men or women you cared for proved other than you had thought them. Though he would never have said that last aloud, however assiduously a questioner pursued.

Cresting the last of a series of ridges, Blaise saw the blue waters of Lake Dierne clearly for the first time. He could make out a small island in the lake with three plumes of white smoke rising from fires burning there. He paused a moment, taking in the vista that spread before him, and then rode on.

No one had cautioned him otherwise, or offered any warning at all, nor had he asked any questions, and so when he went forward from that ridge Blaise took what was clearly the more direct, less hilly road, riding straight north towards the lake and the beginnings of what was to be his destiny.

The well-worn path went along the western shore of Lake Dierne, with faded milestones of the Ancients along the way, some standing, some toppled into the grass, all testifying mutely to how long ago this road had been laid down. The island wasn't very far away — a good swimmer could cover the distance — and from the path Blaise could now see that the three white plumes of smoke were carefully spaced along the midline of the isle. Even he was sufficiently aware after a season in Arbonne to realize that these would be holy fires of Rian. Who else but the clergy of the goddess would burn midday fires in the heat of early summer?

He narrowed his gaze across the dazzling blue water. He could make out a handful of small boats at anchor or pulled up on the sands of the island's nearer shore. One boat with a single white sail was tacking back and forth across the lake into the breeze. Watching, Blaise's thoughts went back to the

High Priestess with her owl in the blackness of night on Rian's other island, in the sea. After a moment he looked away in the bright sunshine and rode on.

He passed the small hut that held and kept dry wood and kindling for the signal fires that would summon the priestesses when those on the shore had need, whether for childbirth or healing or surrendering the dead. He resisted the impulse to make a warding sign.

A little further along the path he saw the arch.

He stopped his horse again. The pack pony trudging behind with his goods and his armour bumped up against them and then placidly lowered its head to crop at the grass by the road. Blaise was staring at that arrogant, monumental assertion of stone. The soldier in him understood it at once, and admiration vied with an inward disquiet.

There were figures carved along the top of the arch, and there would be friezes along the sides as well. He didn't need to go nearer to study them; he knew what the sculptor's art had rendered there. He had seen such arches before, in northern Portezza, in Götzland, two in Gorhaut itself near the mountain passes, which seemed to be as far north as the Ancients had established themselves.

The massive arch offered its own clear testimony as to what those who built it had been. Where the milestones by the long, straight roads told of continuity and the orderly, regulated flow of society in a world now lost, the triumphal arches such as this one spoke to nothing but domination, the brutal grinding down of whoever had been here when the Ancients came to conquer.

Blaise had been to war many times, both for his country and for his own purse as a mercenary, and had known both triumph and defeat on widely scattered battlefields. Once, by the frost-rimed Iersen Bridge, he had fought among ice and blowing snow past the bitter death of his king through to a twilit winter victory that had then been alchemized into defeat in the elegantly phrased courtiers' treaty of the spring that followed. That one had changed him, he thought. That one had changed his life forever.

The arch standing here at the end of a procession of planted trees told a hard truth that Blaise knew in his soldier's bones to be as valid now as it had been centuries ago: when you have beaten someone, when you have conquered and occupied them, you must never let them forget the power that you have and the consequences of resistance.

What happened when the arches remained but those who had so arrogantly raised them were dust and long departed was a question for milk-fed philosophers and troubadours, Blaise thought, not for a fighting man.

He turned his head away, unsettled and unexpectedly angered. And it was only when he did so, wresting his attention from the massive arch, that he became aware, belatedly, that he was no longer alone on this shore of Lake Dierne under a westering sun.

There were six of them, in dark green hose and tunics. The livery meant they were unlikely to be outlaws, which was good. Rather less encouraging was the fact that three of them had bows out and arrows to string already, levelled at him before any words of greeting or challenge had been spoken. What was even more ominous was that the obvious leader, sitting his horse a few feet ahead and to one side of the others, was a rangy, dark-skinned, moustachioed Arimondan. Experience in several countries, and one sword fight he preferred not to remember except for the lesson it had taught him, had led Blaise to be exceptionally wary of the swarthy warriors of that hot, dry land beyond the western mountains. Especially when they appeared at the head of men who were aiming arrows at his chest.

Blaise held out his empty hands and lifted his voice into the wind. 'I give you greetings, corans. I am a traveller on a high road of Arbonne. I mean no offence to anyone and trust I have given none.' He was silent, watching, and left his hands out to be seen. He had defeated four men once at a tourney in Aulensburg, but there were six here, with arrows.

The Arimondan twitched his reins and his horse, a genuinely magnificent black, moved forward a few restive paces. 'Fighting corans carrying armour sometimes give offense merely by their existence,' the man said. 'Who is it that you serve?' He spoke Arbonnais flawlessly, with scarcely a trace of an accent. He was clearly no stranger to this land. He was also observant. Blaise's armour was well wrapped under cloth on the pack pony; the Arimondan would have deduced what it was by shape.

But Blaise, too, was used to watching men closely, especially in a situation such as this, and out of the corner of his eye he saw one of the archers lean forward with the question, as if hanging upon the answer.

Blaise temporized. He had no real idea what was happening here. Outlaws on the roads were one thing, but these men were clearly trained and just as clearly asserting control over this part of the road. He wished he'd studied a map more closely before leaving Baude. It would have helped to know whose lands these were. He ought to have asked more questions at last night's inn.

He said, 'I am traveling in peace on an open road. I mean no trespass. If such is your complaint, I will gladly pay a fair toll.'

'I asked a question,' the Arimondan said flatly. 'Answer it.'

Hearing that tone, Blaise felt his mouth go dry, even as a familiar anger began rising in him. He had his sword, and his bow was ready to hand in the saddle quiver, but if the three men behind the Arimondan knew how to shoot there was little hope in trying to fight. He considered cutting the rope that tied the pony to his grey and making a run for it, but he hated leaving his armour behind almost as much as he hated fleeing from an Arimondan.

'I am not in the custom of detailing my affairs to strangers with bows drawn,' he said.

The Arimondan smiled slowly, as if the words were an unexpected gift. He gestured with his left hand, a negligent, graceful movement. All three archers loosed arrows. An instant later, with a queer, grunting sound, Blaise's pack pony collapsed behind him. Two arrows were in its neck and one was just below, near the heart. The pony was dead. The archers had already notched three more arrows.

Feeling the colour leave his face, Blaise heard the Arimondan laugh. 'Tell me,' the man said lazily, 'will you preserve what you call your customs when you are naked and bound face down in the dust to serve my pleasure like a boy bought for an hour?' The two other men, the ones without bows, had moved without visible instruction in opposite directions, cutting off both paths of flight for Blaise. One of them, Blaise saw, was smiling broadly.

'I asked a question,' the Arimondan went on softly. The wind had dropped; his voice carried in the stillness. 'The horse dies next if I am not answered. In whose service do you ride, Northerner?'

It was his beard, of course; it labelled him like a brand marked a thief or blue robes a priest of Corannos. Blaise drew a slow breath and, fighting hard to hold down his anger, sought shelter in the shade of the great — as Rudel had more than once put it.

'En Bertran de Talair has hired me for a season,' he said.

They shot the horse.

But Blaise had had his clue from the one archer's straining manner the first time the question had been asked, and he had kicked his legs free of the stirrups even as he spoke. He landed on the far side of the screaming stallion and pulled his bow free and the dying horse downwards towards him in the same motion so that it offered protection when he dropped behind it. Firing from an almost prone position he killed the northernmost coran and, turning, shot the one guarding the southern path in the neck before the three archers could loose another volley. Then he dropped flat.

Two arrows hit his horse again and the third whizzed above his head. Blaise rose to one knee and fired twice, at speed. One archer died, screaming like the horse, and the second dropped in silence with an arrow in his throat. The third man hesitated, his mouth falling open with dismay. Blaise notched his fifth arrow and shot him calmly in the chest. He saw bright blood stain the dark green tunic before the man fell.

It was suddenly extremely quiet.

The Arimondan had not moved. His magnificent black thoroughbred was still as a statue, though with nostrils flared wide.

'Now you *have* given offense,' the dark-skinned man said, his voice still silky and soft. 'I see that you can shoot from hiding. Come now and we will see if you are a man among men with a sword as well. I will dismount.'

Blaise stood up. 'If I thought you a man I would do so,'

he said. His voice sounded oddly hollow to his own ears. The too-familiar pounding was in his head and his rage was still with him. 'I want your horse. I will think of you with pleasure when I ride it.' And with the words he loosed his sixth arrow and took the Arimondan through the heart.

The man rocked violently backwards with the impact, clinging to his last seconds of life under the brilliant sun. Blaise saw him draw a dagger then, one of the wickedly curved, bejewelled blades of his own country, and plunge it, even as he began to topple from his saddle, deep into the throat of his black stallion.

The man hit the ground as his horse surged high into the air on its hind legs, screaming in rage and fear. It came down and rose again immediately, trumpeting, lashing out with its hooves. Blaise notched a last arrow and let it fly, with passionate regret, to put the glorious creature out of pain. The stallion dropped and then rolled on one side. Its legs kicked out one more time and then were motionless.

Blaise stepped forward, moving around his own dead horse. The stillness in the clearing was eerie, broken only by the nervous whickering of the archers' mounts and the sound of the breeze picking up again. He realized that no birds were singing now.

A short while ago he had imagined that the wind of Arbonne in the leaves and vines whispered of refreshment and ease, of easy grace here in the warm south. Now there were six dead men in the grass by the side of the road. Not far away, looming in silence at the end of its avenue of elms, the massive arch looked down upon them all, keeping its secrets, bearing its own grim friezes of battle and death carved long ago.

Blaise's anger began to drain away, leaving behind the disorientation and nausea that seemed always to follow combat. Battle seldom fazed him now after so many years of it, but the aftermath left him vulnerable for a long time, trying to come to terms with what he was capable of doing when the fury of war swept over him. He looked across the grass at the Arimondan and shook his head. He had wanted, for a moment, to walk over and cut the dead man into pieces, to make things easier for the carrion dogs when they came. He swallowed and turned away.

As he did he saw a small boat with a white sail pulling
up to the stony shore of the lake on the far side of the road.
There was a grating sound as the craft grounded itself, and
Blaise saw two men help a woman to alight. His heart
thumped once, hard. The woman was tall, robed in crimson
fringed with silver, and she had an owl on her shoulder.

Then he looked more closely, and with a second glance,
undistorted by memory or fear, he saw that this was not the
High Priestess from Rian's Island in the sea. This one was
much younger and brown-haired and, manifestly, she had eyes
with which to see. Nor was her bird white, as the one on the
other island had been. She was a priestess, though, and the
two men with her and the one other woman were also clergy
of Rian. The boat was the one he'd seen tacking into the wind
before. Beyond them, on the isle, the three plumes of smoke
still rose into the summer sky.

'You are fortunate,' the woman said, walking steadily
across sand and gravel to stand before him on the grass beside
the road. Her voice was mild but her eyes, appraising him,
were steady and unreadable. Her hair was heavy and hung
down her back, not covered or pinned. Blaise endured her
scrutiny impassively, remembering the blindness of the High
Priestess who had seen right through him nonetheless.
He looked at the bird this one carried on her shoulder and
felt an echo of the anxiety he'd felt in the forest on the
island. It was almost unfair; the aftermath of combat left him
susceptible to this.

'I daresay I am,' he said, as calmly as he could. 'I could
not have expected to prevail against six. It seems the god has
favoured me.' That last was a challenge of sorts.

She didn't rise to the bait. 'And Rian as well. We can
bear witness for you that they attacked first.'

'Bear witness?'

She smiled then, and that smile, too, took him back to
the High Priestess in her night forest. 'It would have served
you better, Blaise of Gorhaut, to have been more curious
about affairs in this part of the world.'

He didn't like her tone, and he didn't know what she was
talking about. His uneasiness increased; the women in this
country were unimaginably difficult to deal with.

'How do you know my name?'

Again the secretive, superior smile, but this time he had expected it. 'Did you imagine that once having been allowed to leave Rian's Island alive you were free of the goddess? We have marked you, Northerner. Thank us for it.'

'Why? For following me?'

'Not following. We have been waiting for you. We knew you were coming. And as to the why . . . hear now what you should have learned already for yourself. A fortnight past, the countess in Barbentain had an edict proclaimed that any further killings among the corans of Talair or Miraval would result in property of the offending party being ceded to the crown. The troubadours and the clergy are carrying the tidings, and all the lords of Arbonne have been cited by name and formally bound to impose the edict by force if need be. You might have cost En Bertran a part of his land today had we not been here to give a report in your defence.'

Blaise scowled, in part with relief, in part because this was indeed something he should have made a point of knowing before. 'You will forgive me if I do not express dismay,' he said. 'I must admit I would not have valued his vineyards over my life, however much he proposes to pay me in wages.'

The priestess laughed aloud. She was younger than a first impression had suggested. 'Our forgiveness hardly need concern you . . . in this, at least. But Bertran de Talair is another matter. He might have fairly expected an experienced coran to avoid giving provocation before even arriving at his castle. There *is* an eastern way around the lake if you hadn't noticed, one that does not pass by the vineyards of Miraval.'

The situation was, Blaise had to admit, becoming belatedly clear. And indeed, had he known these lands belonged to Urté de Miraval — or taken some pains to know — he would certainly have gone the other way. It was no secret, even to Blaise after a short time in Arbonne, that for reasons that apparently went years back into the past, the present lords of Miraval and Talair had no love for one another.

Blaise shrugged, to cover his discomfiture. 'I have been riding all day, this path seemed easier. And I thought the countess of Arbonne stood surety for the safety of the roads in her land.'

'Barbentain is a long way off, and local hatred will usually overmaster larger laws. A wise traveller will know where
he is, particularly if he rides alone.'

Which also was true, if arrogantly spoken by someone so
young. He tried not to dwell on the arrogance. Clergy of all
kinds seemed to have it as a collective quality. One of these
days, though, he was going to have to try to sort out why he
was so reluctant to pay more attention to the gossip, or even
the geography and divisions of land here in Arbonne.

Behind the priestess he saw three other small boats being
drawn up on the shore. Men and women in the robes of Rian
disembarked and made their away over the grass to where the
dead were lying. They began lifting the bodies and carrying
them back to the boats.

Blaise glanced over his shoulder to where the Arimondan lay beside his slain horse. He turned back to the priestess. 'Tell me, will Rian welcome such as he?'

She did not smile. 'She waits for him,' the priestess said
calmly, 'as she waits for all of us. Welcome and grace are other
matters entirely.' Her dark eyes held his own until Blaise
looked away, beyond her, past the isle in the lake, to where a
castle could be seen on the northern shore.

She turned and followed his gaze. 'We will take you if you
like,' she said, surprising him. 'Unless you want one of their
horses for yourself?'

Blaise shook his head. 'The only one worth having was
killed by its rider.' He felt a sour amusement suddenly. 'I will
be grateful for passage. Doesn't it seem apt . . . that I should
arrive at Talair Castle in a craft of the goddess?'

'More apt than you know,' she said, not responding to his
tone at all.

She gestured, and two of the priests moved to collect
Blaise's armour and goods from the dead pony. Blaise himself
took his saddle from his mount and, following the tall,
slender form of the priestess, walked over grass and stone to
her boat.

They put his gear on board as well, and then the craft was
pushed free of the shore and with the west wind in the one
sail and the sun low now behind them it went skimming across
the waters of Lake Dierne.

As they approached the castle, Blaise registered with a practised, approving eye how well defended it was, poised on a crag above the lake with the water coming around on three sides and a deep moat carved to the north. A cluster of men had come down to the pier to wait for them. There was another boat already there, with two priests and a priestess in it; tidings would have preceded them then. As they drew near Blaise recognized Valery, Bertran's cousin, and then, surprisingly, Bertran himself stepped forward to neatly catch the rope thrown by the priest at the prow.

The duke of Talair crouched to tie their craft to an iron ring set in the wooden dock, then he straightened, looking expressionlessly at Blaise. There was no hint in his gaze of the eerie, late-night intimacy of their last conversation. *Twenty-three years*, Blaise remembered, suddenly. The last thing he'd heard this man say, in the dark of a stairway, speaking of a woman long ago: *So much longer than I thought I would live.*

'Welcome to Talair,' Bertran said. The scar on his cheek was prominent in the clear light. He was dressed much as he had been when he came to Baude, in a coran's clothing made for the outdoors. His hair was uncovered, disordered by the wind. He smiled thinly, a crook of his mouth. 'How does it feel to have made an enemy before you even report?'

'I have my share of enemies,' Blaise said mildly. He felt calmer now; the ride across the lake and the memory of that dark stairwell in Baude had taken away the last of his battle mood. 'One more or one less should not matter greatly. The god will take me when he is ready.' He raised his voice slightly on that last, for someone else's benefit. 'Do you really think the duke of Miraval will bother hating me for guarding my life when attacked?'

'Urté? He could,' Bertran said judiciously. 'Though it wasn't him I was thinking of, actually.' He looked for a moment as if he would explain, but then he turned instead and began walking towards the castle. 'Come,' he said over his shoulder, 'there is meat and drink inside and after we will help you choose a horse from the stable.'

Broad-shouldered, greying Valery stepped forward and extended an arm. Blaise hesitated a moment, then grasped it, pulling himself forward onto the dock. His gear had already been lifted up by three other men. Blaise turned back to the boat. Already the line had been untied and the small craft was beginning to glide back out over the water. The young priestess had her back to him, but then, as if aware that he was looking, she turned.

She said nothing, nor did Blaise as the distance between boat and shore slowly increased. Her hair gleamed in the still warm light of the setting sun. The owl on her shoulder gazed away to the west. *More apt than you know*, she had said on that western shore, responding with weighty sobriety to an attempted irony. He didn't understand what she'd meant, he didn't understand it at all, and within him a spark of rekindled anger blazed. He'd meant to say goodbye and to thank her, but instead he watched for another moment and then turned away impassively.

Valery was waiting for him. Bertran's cousin had a wry expression on his face.

'Six men?' he said. 'Fair to say you aren't arriving quietly.'

'Five, and a catamite from Arimonda,' Blaise said tersely. His anger was mostly gone though; he felt tired more than anything else. 'I was riding quietly enough, and on the road. They shot my horse.'

'The Arimondan,' Valery murmured, looking out to sea after the withdrawing boat. 'Remind me to tell you about him later.'

'Why bother?' Blaise said. 'He's dead.'

Valery glanced curiously at him a moment, then shrugged. He turned and began walking. Blaise fell into step beside him. The two men went along the length of the pier and then up the narrow, increasingly steep path towards the castle of Talair. They came to the heavy doors, which were open, and they passed within to the sound of music playing.

PART II

Midsummer

CHAPTER·4

W alking briskly through the crowded streets, calling cheerful replies to people she knew and to some she didn't, Lisseut was reminded over and again why the Midsummer Carnival in Tavernel was her favourite time of the year. Colours and crowds and light, the knowledge of a season's touring ended with time before another began, the hinge and axis of the year. Midsummer was a time between times, a space in the round of the year where all seemed in suspension, when anything might happen or be allowed. After nightfall, she thought, that would certainly be true in a variety of ways.

A masked figure clad in green and bright yellow sprang in front of her, arms outspread; in a mock growl that clashed with his birdlike costume he demanded an embrace as passers-by laughed. Sidestepping neatly, Lisseut pirouetted out of his grasp. 'Bad luck to kiss a singer before sundown!' she called over her shoulder. She'd made that one up two years back; it seemed to work. And by sundown she was usually with friends and so shielded from anyone coming to assert a deferred claim.

Not that the claims would ever be a serious problem. Not here, and not for her — too many people knew who she was by now, and even among the wildest of the students, the joglars and troubadours had an exalted status in Tavernel, even more so during Carnival. It was a debauched season, but one with its hierarchies and rules nonetheless.

As she crossed Temple Square, where the silver domes of Rian's principal shrine faced the square, golden towers of Corannos's, the south breeze brought her an almost forgotten tang of salt from the port. Lisseut smiled, glad to be back by the sea after a long winter and spring touring inland and in the mountains. Reaching the far side of the square, she was suddenly overwhelmed by the smells of cooking food and remembered that she hadn't eaten since midday on the road. Easy enough to forget to eat in haste to be in town, knowing how many friends she'd not seen for a year would be arriving that day and the next. But the smells reminded her that she was ravenous. She nipped into a cookshop and emerged a moment later chewing on a leg of fried chicken, careful to keep the dripping grease from staining her new tunic.

The tunic was a present to herself after a very successful spring in the eastern hills, her best tour yet by far. First at the goddess's own temple for a fortnight, and then at lofty Ravenc Castle, where Gaufroy de Ravenc had been more than generous to her and to Alain of Rousset, the troubadour with whom she'd teamed up that season. She'd even had untroubled nights there in a room all to herself with a wonderfully soft bed, since En Gaufroy evidently preferred Alain's charms to her own. Which was fine with Lisseut; Alain's clever verses, her own singing and whatever took place in the lord's chambers at night had led Gaufroy into a humour of exceptional largess when it came time for the two of them to leave.

When she'd briefly parted with Alain at Rousset town a few days after — he was planning to spend some time with his family before coming down to Tavernel, and she was committed to a performance at Corannos's shrine near Gavela — he was highly complimentary about her work and invited her to join him on the same circuit in a year's time. He was an easy man to work for and Lisseut found his songs well-crafted if less than inspired; she had had no hesitation about agreeing. A few of the other troubadours might offer richer, more challenging material for a joglar — Jourdain, Aurelian, certainly Remy of Orreze — but there was much to be said for Alain's relaxed congeniality, and something also to be said for the bonus his night-time skills offered with the priests and lords at certain temples and castles. Lisseut considered herself honoured to have been asked; it was her first repeat contract after three years on the roads, and the joglars of Arbonne fought and schemed for such offers from the better-known troubadours. She and Alain were to seal the agreement at the Guildhall before Carnival ended. A great many contracts would be negotiated and sealed this week; it was one of the reasons virtually all the musicians made a point of being there.

There were other reasons, of course; Carnival was sacred to Rian, as all Midsummer's rites were, and the goddess was patroness and guardian of all music in Arbonne, and so of all the itinerant performers who crossed back and forth along the dusty roads singing songs and shaping them in the name of love. One came to Tavernel at Midsummer at least as much in homage to Rian as for anything else.

That said, it had to be conceded that Carnival was also the wildest, least inhibited, most enjoyable time of the year for anyone not in mourning, or incapacitated, or dead.

Lisseut finished her chicken leg, paused to wipe her hands with elaborate fastidiousness on the apron of a portly, grinning fruit seller, and bought an orange from him. She rubbed it quickly on his crotch for luck, drawing ribald laughter from the crowd and a groan of mock desire from the man. Laughing herself, feeling glad to be alive and young and a singer in Arbonne in summer-time, Lisseut continued down towards the harbour and then right at the first crossing lane and saw the familiar, much-loved sign of The Liensenne swinging above the street.

As always, it felt like coming home. Home was really Vezét, of course, on the coast further east with the famous olive groves climbing up behind it, but this, the original 'Tavern in Tavernel' for which Anselme of Cauvas had written his song years and years ago, was a kind of second home for all the musicians of Arbonne. Marotte, the proprietor, had served as a surrogate father and confidant for half the younger joglars and poets in his day, including Lisseut herself when she had first said goodbye to her parents and her home and followed her troubadour uncle onto the road, trusting in her voice and music to feed her and her mother-wits to keep her alive. Less than four years ago, that was. It seemed a much longer time. Grinning, she jauntily tipped her feathered hat to the lute-playing figure on the signboard — it was said to be a rendition of Folquet de Barbentain, the original troubadour-count himself — nodded back at a broad wink from one man amongst a crowd of half a dozen playing pitch-coin outside the door and stepped inside.

She knew her mistake the instant she did so.

Knew it even before Remy's exultant, skirling howl of triumph assaulted her ears over the din, even before Aurelian, standing next to Remy, intoned 'Nine!' in a voice deep as doom, even before she saw the flushed hilarious crowd of musicians holding a dripping, moustachioed, furiously expostulating Arimondan upside-down over the accursed basin of water, preparing to dunk him again. Even before the covey of coin-pitchers outside pushed quickly in right behind her, cackling in glee.

She *knew* this tradition, in Rian's holy name! What had she been *thinking* of? She'd even nodded like a fatuous bumpkin at the people gathered outside waiting for the ritual ninth to enter, thus making it safe for them to follow. Friendly, simple-minded Lisseut, nodding happily on her way to a ducking only the ignorant were supposed to receive.

And now Remy, looking quite unfairly magnificent, bright hair in ringlets on his forehead, damp with perspiration, blue eyes positively glittering with hilarity, was swiftly approaching, followed by Aurelian and Jourdain and Dumars and even — oh the perfidy of it all! — the laughing figure of Alain, her erstwhile partner, along with fully half a dozen others, including Elisse of Cauvas, who was enjoying this unexpected development quite as much as she might be expected to. Lisseut registered Elisse's mocking smile and furiously cursed her own stupidity again. She looked around frantically for an ally, spotted Marotte behind the bar and pitched a plea for help at the top of her highly regarded voice.

Grinning from ear to ear, her surrogate father shook his head. No help there. Not at Midsummer in Tavernel. Quickly, Lisseut turned back to Remy, smiling in her most endearingly winsome fashion.

'Hello, my dear,' she began sweetly. 'And how have you been this —

She got no further than that. Moving as gracefully as ever, Remy of Orreze, her former lover — every woman's former lover, someone had once said, though not bitterly — slipped neatly under her instinctive, warding gesture, put a shoulder to her midriff and had her hoisted in the air before Lisseut could even try to phrase some remotely plausible reason why she should be exonerated from the water-ducking. A dozen pairs of hands, both before and behind, hastened to assist him in bearing her aloft like some sacrifice of the Ancients towards the ducking basin by the bar.

Every year! Lisseut was thinking, grasped too tightly to even struggle. *We do this every cursed year! Where was my brain just now?*

In the chaos around her she noticed that Aurelian had already turned back to the door to resume his counting. Remy had her around the waist from below and was tickling now, which was inexcusable, given what he ought to have remembered about her. Cursing, giggling helplessly, Lisseut felt her flailing elbow crack into something and was unconscionably pleased a second later to note that it was Elisse who staggered back, swearing like a soldier herself and holding a hand to the side of her head. Holy Rian must have guided her elbow; there was no one else in the room she would actually have wanted to hit! Well, with the exception of Remy, perhaps. She frequently wanted to hit Remy of Orreze. Many of them did, when they weren't listening intently to some favoured joglar singing his newest song.

Lisseut saw the basin loom beneath her. She felt herself being swung completely upside-down. Her feathered hat, which was also new, and expensive, flew from her head undoubtedly to be crushed underfoot amid the densely packed, raucously shouting crowd. Through the arc of a swiftly inverting world she glimpsed her dripping-wet Arimondan predecessor being unceremoniously bundled aside. Dragging a quick breath of tavern air into her lungs, still cursing herself for a dewy-eyed fool, Lisseut closed her eyes tightly as they swung her down into the water.

It wasn't water.

'Marotte!' she cried, spluttering and gasping when they finally lifted her out. 'Marotte, do you know what he's done! This isn't —'

'*Down!*' Remy commanded, cackling uproariously. Lisseut frantically sucked air again just before she was once more submerged.

They held her under for a long time. When she finally surfaced, it took all her strength to twist her neck towards the bar and croak, 'It's *wine*, Marotte! Cauvas sparkling! He's using —'

'*Down!*' Remy shrieked again, but not before Lisseut heard a howl of outrage from Marotte.

'What? Cauvas? Remy, I'll flay you alive! Are you dunking people in my best —?'

Pushed back under, her ears stopped, Lisseut heard no more, but a small, inner glint of satisfaction made the last ducking easier to endure. She even took a quick swig of the wine before they pulled her out for the third and final time. Cauvas sparkling gold was not something young joglars tasted very often, even conceding that being dunked head first into a basin of it after an oiled and perfumed Arimondan was not the connoisseur's preferred mode of consumption.

They swung her out and righted her in time for Lisseut to see a red-faced Marotte confronting Remy across the bar top.

'Carnival tithe, Marotte!' the fair-haired darling of the troubadours was saying, eyes alight with mischief. 'You'll make more than enough off all of us this week to cover the cost.'

'You madman, this is a sacrilege!' Marotte expostulated, looking as truly outraged as only a lover of fine wines could. 'Do you know what Cauvas wine *costs*? And how many bottles you've wasted in there? How in the name of Rian did you get into my cellars?'

'Really, Marotte,' Remy retorted with lofty, exaggerated disdain, 'did you really expect a padlock to keep me out?' A number of people laughed.

'*Seven!*' Aurelian said crisply, his low voice cutting through the hilarity in the room. Everyone — including Lisseut, vigorously drying her face and hair with the towel one of the servers had kindly offered — turned expectantly towards the door. A young, red-headed student came in, blinked a little at the scrutiny he was subjected to and made his way uncertainly towards the bar. He ordered a flagon of ale. No one paid him any attention. They were watching the entrance.

They didn't have long to wait. The eighth person in was a broad-shouldered, competent-looking coran of middle years. As it happened, a number of those in the tavern knew him very well, including Lisseut. But before she had a chance to properly register and react to the enormity of what was about to happen the next man, the ninth, had already passed through the door.

'Oh, dearest god!' Marotte the innkeeper murmured, in an entirely uncharacteristic appeal to Corannos. In the abrupt silence his voice sounded very loud.

The ninth was Duke Bertran de Talair.

'Nine,' said Aurelian, an unnecessary confirmation. His voice was hushed, almost reverential. He turned to Remy. 'But I really don't think . . .' he began.

Remy of Orreze was already moving forward, his handsome face shining, a wild, hilarious look in the blue eyes beneath the damp ringlets of his hair.

'*Hoist him!*' he cried. 'We all know the rules — the ninth is ducked in Rian's name! Seize the duke of Talair!'

Valery, the coran, Bertran's cousin and old friend, actually stepped aside, grinning broadly as he sized up the situation. The duke himself, beginning to laugh, held up both hands to forestall the swiftly approaching Remy. Jourdain, very drunk already, was right behind Remy, with Alain and Elisse and a handful of others following a little more cautiously. Lisseut, mouth open in disbelief, realized in that moment that Remy was actually going to do it: he was about to lay hands on one of the most powerful men in Arbonne in order to dunk him in a tub of water. Correction, she thought, a tub of vintage, insanely expensive sparkling Cauvas wine. Remy — mad, cursed, blessed, impossible Remy — was going to do it.

He would have, if another man, clad in the blue-on-blue colours of Talair but with a full, reddish-brown beard and features that stamped him unmistakably as from Gorhaut, had not stepped forward from the doorway behind Bertran just then and levelled a drawn blade at Remy's breast.

Remy's reckless, giddy motion was carrying him forward over the slippery floor too swiftly to stop. From her place by the basin, Lisseut, hands flying to her mouth, saw the whole thing clearly. Bertran quickly spoke a name, but even before he did the man with the sword had shifted it aside. Not all the way, though, just enough for the tip to glance off Remy's left arm and away.

It drew blood. The man had meant to draw blood, Lisseut was almost certain of it. She saw her former lover come to an awkward, stumbling halt and clutch at his arm below the shoulder. His hand came away streaked with crimson. She couldn't see his expression, but it was easy enough to guess. There was a collective growl of anger from the musicians and students gathered in The Liensenne. The rule against drawn blades in taverns was as old as the university; indeed, it was one of the things that had permitted the university to survive. And Remy of Orreze, for all his impossible ways, was one of *them*. One of their leaders, in fact, and the big man who had just bloodied him with a blade was from Gorhaut.

In that tense moment, with the scene in the tavern on the brink of turning ugly, Bertran de Talair laughed aloud.

'Really, Remy,' he said, 'I don't think that would have been a good idea, much as Valery might have enjoyed suspending his own good judgment long enough to see me ducked.' He flicked a sidelong glance at his cousin who, surprisingly, flushed. The bearded man with the drawn sword had not yet sheathed it. Now he did, at a nod from de Talair.

'I think Aurelian might have been trying to tell you as much,' En Bertran went on. Lanky, dark-haired Aurelian had indeed remained by the bar, not far from Lisseut. He said nothing, watching the scene with sober, careful attention.

'You know the rules of Carnival,' Remy said stoutly, his head high. 'And your hired northern lout has just broken the city laws of Tavernel. Shall I report him to the seneschal?'

'Probably,' Bertran said carelessly. 'Report me as well. I should have told Blaise about the sword laws before we came. Report us both, Remy.'

Remy gave a hollow laugh. 'Much good that would do, me sending the duke of Talair to justice.' He paused, breathing hard. 'Bertran, you're going to have to decide one day: are you one of us, or are you a duke of Arbonne. By all rights you should be upside-down now over that basin, and you know it.'

Genuinely amused, ignoring the presumption of Remy's using his name without a title, de Talair laughed again. 'You should never have left your studies, my dear. A little more Rhetoric would have done you a world of good. That is as false a dichotomy as ever I've heard.'

Remy shook his head. 'This is the real world, no scholar's cloudland of dreams. In the real world choices have to be made.'

Lisseut saw the duke's amused expression change then, and even at a distance she was chilled by what succeeded it. It was as if de Talair's tolerance had just been taken past some breaking point.

'And are you now going to tell me,' he said coldly to Remy of Orreze, 'how things operate in the real world? Are you, Remy? With two Arimondans here that I can see and a table from Portezza, none of whom I know, and a Götzlander at the bar, and the goddess knows how many others upstairs in Marotte's bedrooms . . . you are going to tell me that in the real world, as you choose to conceive of it, a duke of Arbonne should have let himself be dunked in a barrel of water just now? I can tolerate insolence sometimes, but I'm afraid I can't indulge it. Think, lad. Sober up a little and use your brain.'

'It isn't water,' someone said. Uneasy laughter slid through the grim stillness that had followed the duke's words. Lisseut could see a crimson flush on the back of Remy's neck. She looked over at Aurelian; he was gazing back at her. They exchanged a glance of shared apprehension and concern.

'He filled the basin with Cauvas gold, my lord,' Marotte added, bustling busily out from behind the bar now, striving to lighten the mood. 'If you want him bloodied again I'll be pleased to volunteer.'

'A whole basin of Cauvas?' En Bertran was smiling again, helping the innkeeper. 'If that is true I may have been too hasty. Perhaps I *should* let myself be ducked!' There was a gust of relieved laughter; Lisseut found herself breathing more easily. 'Come on, Remy,' the Duke added, 'let me buy us a bottle while Blaise takes care of that arm he cut.'

'Thank you, no,' said Remy with stiff pride. Lisseut knew all about that pride; she shook her head in exasperation. 'I'll look after it myself.' He paused. 'And as it happens, I prefer drinking with other musicians during Carnival, not dukes of Arbonne.'

His head high, he turned his back on Bertran and walked across the room and through the door beside the bar towards the chambers at the rear of the inn. He went past

Lisseut without even acknowledging her presence. A moment later, Aurelian offered Bertran an apologetic grimace, shrugged at Lisseut and followed Remy out, pausing to collect a pitcher of water and clean towels from Marotte.

It was all very interesting, Lisseut thought. Ten minutes before, Remy of Orreze had been utterly in command of this room, a man in his element, shaping the mood of a late afternoon at Carnival. Now he suddenly seemed to be no more than a young inebriate, his last words sounding childish more than anything else, for all the proud dignity of his exit. He would know it, too, she realized, which probably accounted for the aggrieved tone she'd heard creeping into his voice at the end.

She actually felt sorry for him, and not because of the wound, which didn't appear to be serious. She was fully aware of how much Remy would hate knowing she felt that way. Smiling inwardly, Lisseut happily resolved to make a point of telling him later — a first measure of retaliation for her ruined tunic and trampled hat. Remy's art might demand respect and admiration, and his manic humour and inventiveness had shaped memorable nights for all of them, but that didn't mean there was no room for the taking of small revenges.

Looking over towards the duke, Lisseut saw the bearded Gorhaut coran glancing about the crowded room of musicians with an undisguised look of disdain on his face. She was suddenly sorry he'd been the one to wound Remy. No one should be allowed to draw a blade against a troubadour in this tavern and then wear an expression like that afterwards; particularly not a stranger, and most particularly not one from Gorhaut. *Until the sun dies and the moons fall, Gorhaut and Arbonne shall not lie easily beside each other.* Her grandfather used to say that, and her father had continued to use the phrase, often after returning from the Autumn Fair in Lussan with whatever profit he'd made from his olives and olive oil, trading with the northerners.

Lisseut, her anger rising, stared at the big coran from the north, wishing someone in the room would say something to him. He looked insufferably smug, gazing down on them all from his great height. Only Aurelian was as tall a man, but Aurelian had gone with Remy, and the lean musician, for all his unassuming brilliance, would not have been the man to face down this one. With a quick shrug that was more characteristic than she knew, Lisseut stepped forward herself.

'You are arrogant,' she said to the northerner, 'and have no business looking so pleased with yourself. If your liege lord will not tell you as much, one of us will have to: the man you injured may have been frivolous just now in a Carnival mood, but he is twice the man you are, with or without an illegal blade, and he will be remembered in this world long after you are dust and forgotten.'

The mercenary — Blaise, the duke had called him — blinked in surprise. Up close he seemed younger than she'd first guessed, and there was actually a slightly different look in his eyes than Lisseut had thought she'd seen from by the bar. She wasn't certain what name to put to it, but it wasn't precisely haughtiness. Bertran de Talair was grinning, and so, unexpectedly, was Valery. Lisseut, registering their glances, was abruptly reminded that she was dripping wet from tangled hair to waist, and her new blouse was probably a dreadful sight and clinging to her much more closely that it should, in all decency. She felt herself flushing, and hoped it would be seen as anger.

'And there you have it, Blaise,' the duke was saying. 'Dust and forgotten. And more proof for you — if ever you needed it — of how terrible our women are, especially after they've been held upside-down. What would happen to this one back in Gorhaut? Do tell us.'

For a long time the bearded coran was silent, looking down at Lisseut. His eyes were a curious hazel colour, nearly green in the lamplight. Almost reluctantly, but quite clearly, he said, 'For speaking so to an anointed coran of the god in a public place she would be stripped to the waist and whipped on her belly and back by officers of the king. After, if she survived, the man so insulted would be entitled to do whatever he wanted with her. Her husband, if she had one, would be free to divorce her with no consequences at law or in the eyes of the clergy of Corannos.'

The silence that followed was frigid. There was something deathly in it, like ice in the far north, infinitely removed from the mood of Carnival. *Until the sun dies and the moons fall . . .*

Lisseut suddenly felt faint, her knees trembled, but she forced her eyes to hold those of the northerner. 'What, then, are you doing here?' she said hardily, using the voice control she'd so arduously mastered in her apprenticeship with her uncle. 'Why don't you go back where you can do that sort of thing to women who speak their mind or defend their friends? Where you could do whatever you wanted with me and no one would gainsay you?'

'Yes, Blaise,' Bertran de Talair added, still inexplicably cheerful. 'Why don't you go back?'

A moment later, the big man surprised Lisseut. His mouth quirked sideways in a wry smile. He shook his head. 'I was asked by the man who pays my wages what would be done to you in Gorhaut,' he answered mildly enough, looking straight at Lisseut, not at the duke. 'I think En Bertran was amusing himself: he has travelled enough to know exactly what the laws on such matters are in Gorhaut, and in Valensa and Götzland, for that matter — for they are much the same. Did I say, incidentally, that I agreed with those laws?'

'*Do* you agree with them?' Lisseut pursued, aware that this room, among all her friends, was probably the only place on earth where she would have been quite so aggressive.

The man called Blaise pursed his lips reflectively before answering; Lisseut was belatedly realizing that this was no thick-witted northern lout.

'The duke of Talair just now humiliated a troubadour you say will be famous long after I am forgotten. He as much as called him an uneducated, drunken schoolboy. At a guess, that will have hurt rather more than the scratch from my blade. Will you agree that there are times when authority must be asserted? Or, if not, are you brave enough to turn that fire of yours against the duke right now? I'm the easy target, an outsider in a room full of people you know. Would that be a part of why you are pushing me like this? Would it be a fair thing to be doing?'

He was unexpectedly clever, but he hadn't answered her question.

'You haven't answered her question,' said Bertran de Talair.

Blaise of Gorhaut smiled again, the same wry, sideways

expression as before; Lisseut had a sense that he'd almost been expecting that from the duke. She wondered how long they'd known each other. 'I'm here, aren't I?' he said quietly. 'If I agreed with those laws I'd be home right now, wouldn't I, very likely wed to a properly disciplined woman, and very likely plotting an invasion of Arbonne with the king and all the corans of Gorhaut.' He raised his voice at the end, quite deliberately. Lisseut, out of the corner of her eye, saw the Portezzans at their booth by the near wall exchange quick glances with each other.

'All right, Blaise,' Bertran said sharply, 'you have made your point. That is rather enough, I think.'

Blaise turned to him. Lisseut realized that his eyes had not left hers from the time she'd approached, though his last point, whatever it actually was, had clearly been meant for the duke. 'I think so too,' the big coran said softly. 'I think it is more than enough.'

'*Enough of what?*' came an assured voice from the doorway. 'Is something over too soon? Have I missed an entertainment?'

When Bertran de Talair grew pale, Blaise knew, the scar on his cheek became extremely prominent. He had seen it happen before, but not like this. The duke had gone rigid with anger or shock but he did not turn around. Valery did, very swiftly, moving so that his body was between Bertran's and the door.

'What are you doing here?' said de Talair, his back to the person addressed. His voice was cold as winter moonlight. Blaise registered that fact and moved, belatedly, to stand beside Valery. Even as he did, the crowd of men and women between them and the door was shifting awkwardly out of the way to reveal, as a parting curtain before a stage, the man standing in the entrance to the tavern.

He was huge, Blaise saw, robed in extravagantly expensive dark green satin trimmed with white fur, even in summer. Easily sixty years old, his grey hair cropped close like a soldier's, he stood lightly balanced, for all his size, and his posture was straight-backed and arrogant.

'What am I doing here?' he echoed mockingly. The voice was memorable, deep and resonant. 'Isn't this where the

singers are? Is this not Carnival? Cannot a man seek the solace
and pleasure of music at such a time?'

'You hate musicians,' Bertran de Talair said harshly, biting off his words. He still had not turned. 'You kill singers,
remember?'

'Only the impertinent ones,' the other man said indifferently. 'Only those who forget where they are and sing
what they should not. And that was a long time ago, after all.
Men can change, surely, as we move towards our waiting
graves. Age can mellow us.' There was nothing mellow about
that tone, though. What Blaise heard was mockery, savage,
acid-dipped.

And suddenly he knew who this had to be.

His eyes flicked to either side of the speaker, taking the
measure of the three green-garbed corans flanking him. All
wore swords, regardless of whatever laws Tavernel might have,
and all three looked as if they knew how to use them. He had
a flashing memory of a path by Lake Dierne, six dead men in
the spring grass. The crowd had fallen well back, leaving a
cleared space around the two parties by the door. Blaise was
aware that the slim, brown-haired woman, the one who had
accosted him, was still standing just behind him.

'I will not banter with you,' Bertran said quietly. His back
was still to the door, to the huge man standing there with malice in his flint-grey eyes. 'One more time, why are you here,
my lord of Miraval?'

Urté de Miraval, framed massively in the doorway of
The Liensenne, did not reply. Instead his heavy gaze, eyes
deep-hooded in his face, swung over to look at Blaise. Ignoring Bertran's question as if it had been asked by an impor-
tuning farm labourer, he fixed Blaise with an appraising
scrutiny. He smiled then, but there was no lessening of the
malice in his expression.

'Unless I am greatly wrong,' he said, 'and I do not think
I am, this will be the northerner who is so free with his bow
to shed the blood of other men.' The corans beside him shifted
slightly. The motion, Blaise noted, freed space for their swords
to be drawn.

'Your corans shot my pony and my horse,' Blaise said quietly. 'I had reason to believe they were minded to kill me.'

'They would have been,' Urté de Miraval agreed, almost pleasantly. 'Should I forgive you six deaths for that reason? I don't think I shall, and even if I were minded to, there is another aggrieved party in the case. A man who will be exceedingly happy to learn that you are here tonight. He might even join us later, which will be interesting. So many accidents happen amid the crowds of Carnival; it is one of the regrettable aspects of the celebration, wouldn't you agree?'

Blaise read the transparent threat; what he didn't know was its origin. From Valery's stiffened posture he sensed that the other man did.

'There is a law passed regarding killings between Miraval and Talair,' Bertran's cousin said sharply from Blaise's side. 'You know it well, my lord duke.'

'Indeed, I do. So, if it comes to that, did my six slain men. If only our beloved countess in Barbentain could pass laws that guarded against the mishaps of a riotous night in the city. Would that not be a pleasant thing, a *reassuring* thing?' His eyes swung back from Valery to Blaise and settled there, with the predatory quality of a hunting cat.

And with that, Bertran de Talair finally turned to confront the man in the doorway.

'You frighten no one,' he said flatly. 'There is nothing but sour rancour in you. Even the grapes on your land taste of it. A last time, my lord of Miraval, for I will not permit this exchange to continue: *why are you here?*'

Again there was to be no reply, or not from the man addressed. Instead, a woman, hooded and cloaked, stepped around him and into the room from where she'd been hidden behind his bulk.

'Oh dear, oh dear, oh dear!' she said. 'This isn't *at all* what I wanted to happen.' The words were contrite and distressed; the tone was as far from such feelings as it could possibly be. In that lazy drawl Blaise heard boredom and vexation, and more than a hint of power. *Not another one,* he thought. *Not another of these women.*

Astonishment and a different kind of anger flashed in the eyes of Bertran de Talair.

'Ariane, what, precisely, do you think you are doing? Is this a game? If so you have overreached yourself.'

Ariane. Ariane de Carenzu, who was queen of the Court
of Love. The woman so sharply addressed brought up one
elaborately ringed hand and cast back her hood, shaking free
her hair with an unconcerned motion.

She's married, though, Blaise thought stupidly. *Her hair is
supposed to be bound up, even in Arbonne.* It wasn't. Her hair
was thick and raven dark, and as he watched it fell in waves
down her back, liberated from the transitory confines of the
hood. There was a confused, excited murmur in the room.
Looking at the woman standing beside Urté de Miraval,
momentarily unable, in fact, to look away from her, Blaise
thought he understood why.

'Overreach?' she said now, very quietly. 'I don't think
I allow language like that even from a friend, Bertran. I
wasn't aware that I needed permission from you to visit
The Liensenne.'

'You need no such thing. But you also know that — '

'I know only that the duke of Miraval was kind enough
to invite me to join his company this evening to observe the
delights of Carnival, and I was happy to accept. I would also
have thought, evidently wrongly, that two high lords of
Arbonne might, for tonight at least, lay down a petty feud
they carry, at least enough to be civil in the company of
women and on the night dedicated to the goddess.'

'A petty feud?' Bertran echoed, incredulity in his voice.

Urté de Miraval laughed. 'This is becoming tedious in
the extreme,' he said. 'I came to hear what passes for music
this season in Tavernel, not to bandy words in a doorway with
a choleric degenerate. Whose songs are we hearing tonight?'

There was a stiff, short silence, then:

'Mine,' said Alain of Rousset clearly. 'We will hear my
songs, if you like. Lisseut, will you be good enough to sing
for us?'

It was, she thought much later, when she had space for
calmer reflection on the turbulent events of that night, not so
greatly surprising when looked at in a certain light. Remy and
Aurelian were both out of the room, and Bertran was certainly
not going to have his own verses sung at Urté de Miraval's
request; of the troubadours who remained, Alain had more
ambition than most and as much right to step forward as any,

and since she'd just finished a season of touring with him it was perfectly logical that he ask her to perform.

All such clear thinking came afterwards, though. At the moment, Lisseut was aware only that she had just been humiliatingly inverted in a tub of Cauvas gold wine, that there was a spreading puddle beneath her feet, that her clothing was ruined, her hair soaked, and in such a resplendent condition she was now being asked to sing — for the first time — in the presence of three of the most powerful personages in Arbonne, one of whom also happened to be the most celebrated troubadour of their day.

She made a small, gulping sound in her throat, hoping immediately after that no one had heard. The big coran from Gorhaut turned, though, and favoured her with an ironic scrutiny from behind his thick, reddish beard. She glared fiercely up at him, and that brief surge of anger, as much as anything else, calmed her momentary attack of fright. With what she hoped was a casual gesture she tossed the towel she was still holding to the bearded man and turned to Alain.

'I would be honoured,' she said, as calmly as she could. Alain's face, visibly contending with anxieties of his own, didn't much help her to relax. She understood, of course: the troubadour was boldly seizing an unexpected chance to make a bid for wider renown — and was handing her the opportunity to do the same. A moment such as this, singing in The Liensenne at Midsummer Carnival before the dukes of Talair and Miraval and the reigning queen of the Court of Love . . . Lisseut blinked and swallowed. If she thought too much about the potential implications of what seemed about to happen she would probably make herself sick.

Fortunately, the next face she focused on was Marotte's, and the delighted encouragement she read in the innkeeper's visage was exactly what she needed. Someone brought her a harp, someone else placed a low stool and a floor cushion in the usual place near the booths on the left-hand wall, and somehow Lisseut found herself sitting there, holding and tuning the harp, even as she adjusted the cushion for comfort.

She was still wet, if not actually dripping any more, and she'd had no time at all to prepare. Glancing up, she saw Duke Bertran walking over, a thin smile playing about his lips. It didn't reach his eyes, though. With Urté de Miraval in the room, Lisseut doubted if En Bertran could actually be amused by anything. The duke removed his lightweight summer cloak and draped it loosely over her shoulders.

'You'll catch a chill otherwise,' he said mildly. 'If you leave it draped so, it won't get in the way of your hands.' The first words he'd ever spoken to her. He turned and walked away, to sink gracefully into one of the three cushioned chairs Marotte had hastily provided near the performing area. Lisseut had a moment to absorb the fact that she was now wearing the midnight-blue cloak of the duke of Talair before Alain of Rousset, two spots of excitement showing on his cheeks, came over and said, softly, for her ears alone, 'The "Garden Song," I think. Sing it, don't shout it, Lisseut.'

The troubadours' ancient, standard injunction to their joglars rang almost unheard in Lisseut's ears. What registered was that in his choice of song Alain was offering her another gift. She smiled up at him, confidently she hoped. He hesitated a moment, as if about to say more, but then he too withdrew, leaving her alone in the space where music was made.

Lisseut thought of her father, as she always did when she needed to find serenity and sureness, then she looked out over the slowly quieting crowd and said, pitching her voice carefully, 'Here is a liensenne of the troubadour Alain of Rousset. I sing it tonight in honour of the goddess and of the Lady Ariane de Carenzu, who has graced us with her presence here.' Better that, she thought, than trying to sort out some kind of precedence. She was conscious though, very conscious, that she was wearing En Bertran's cloak. It was scented with an elusive fragrance. She didn't have time to decipher what it was. What she did realize, as she always did before she sang — a fleeting awareness but real as the stones of a wall — was that moments like this, with music about to follow, were why she lived, what made her feel most truly alive.

She began with the harp alone, as Gaetan, her father's brother, had taught her years ago, letting the audience settle, and then, when the stillness was deep enough, she sang.

When you came into my garden,
When you came to tell me of your love,

The one moon in the sky
Seemed brighter than the sun
And a white light was shining in my heart.

When you took me in your arms,
To whisper words of a long desire,
The scents of the garden
Were my garments in the dark
And day a distant rumour of despair

It was a well-made song, if not a brilliant one. Alain knew his craft and he was young enough to be maturing still. The special thing though — the gift this song offered Lisseut — was that it was written for a woman's voice. There weren't many, which was why the female joglars of Arbonne spent much of their time transposing tunes written for male voices and ignoring as best they could the obvious inappropriateness of most of the themes.

In this piece Alain had changed a great many elements of the traditional liensenne, shifting the narrative to the woman's point of view, while keeping enough of the familiar motifs to leave the audience in no doubt as to what they were hearing and appraising. Lisseut, keeping her instrumental ornamentation to a minimum, took them through it, serving the song as best she could, in simplicity. It was a long tune — most of the formal liensennes were, for audiences would balk and complain at the absence of elements they were expecting. The troubadour's challenge in this kind of song lay in using all of the familiar motifs while making them vivid and new, in whatever ways his art allowed. Lisseut sang the rising of the second moon, the customary menace of jealous, prying eyes, a formulaic, if rather clever stanza on the three flowers that traditionally sheltered lovers, another on the trusted friend watching out from beyond the wall with his mood-shattering warning of sunrise, and the lovers' parting words.

It was honest, professional work, and she knew she had the listeners with her. Even here, with an audience as profoundly versed as this one was, Lisseut knew, the way she sometimes did in the midst of performing, that she was doing justice to Alain's words and music. She was holding some-

thing in reserve, though, for the ending, for the place where
Alain of Rousset had surprised even himself by reaching for
something more than the usual closing platitudes of love triumphant and enduring and had found instead the rather more
painful integrity of art.

Lisseut allowed herself the briefest pause, no more, for
more would be to point the change, the new thing, too greatly
and mar the effect; then she pitched her voice upwards
towards sorrow and sang the last verse of the song.

> *When you come to say goodbye,*
> *When you come to say that you will wed,*
> *Do one thing for me*
> *In memory of love,*
> *Bring balm for the breaking of my heart.*

She looked at Bertran de Talair for a moment as she
began, then at the bearded coran behind him, but she ended
gazing out over the heads of her listeners at the doorway
beside the bar through which Remy and Aurelian had gone.
A reprise of the opening notes, as an echo of what had passed,
a chord for the watchman, a chord for the garden nights that
were gone, and she was done.

In Bertran's blue cloak the brown-haired girl looked delicate
and fragile, not exalted, Blaise thought. She was more clever-
looking than formally beautiful, but there was no missing —
even for him — the purity of her voice, and the unexpected
sadness at the very end of the song caught him for a moment.
He didn't know the new thing that note of sorrow represented, but he could hear the sound of it, and the meaning of
the words took his mind down unusual channels. Not for long
of course: he wasn't inclined to that sort of thing, by background or experience — but for just a moment Blaise of
Gorhaut, looking at the slender woman sitting on the low
stool with Bertran de Talair's cloak around her, held, in his
mind's eye, a clear image of a woman in a garden, weeping for
the loss of love.

'Oh, wonderful,' Ariane de Carenzu said in an oddly
wistful voice, far removed from her imperious tones of before.

The words carried clearly in the stillness that followed the last notes of the harp, and with them came the release of a tautness like the tension of a drawn bow in the room. Blaise drew a long breath and noted, with some surprise, that most of the people around him were doing the same.

There would have been other cries of approval doubtless, a swelling of applause to honour the singer and the troubadour who'd written the song, but just then the door to The Liensenne banged loudly open, letting in raucous noises from the darkening street outside. Blaise turned quickly to look and saw who was standing there, and the shape and nature of the evening changed entirely in that moment.

He was looking at the man he had killed on the black horse by Lake Dierne.

CHAPTER·5

*I*t wasn't, of course. It wasn't the same man; the dead remained dead, even here in Arbonne, even on Midsummer Eve. But the dark-skinned, arrogant look was the same, the heft and build, the muscled, dangerous quality of the Arimondan was exactly as Blaise remembered it from that afternoon by the lake with the Arch of the Ancients just beyond.

And the man was gazing at him with a look compounded equally of hatred and fierce joy.

Beside Blaise, Valery said quickly out of the side of his mouth, 'I did mean to tell you before. I should have. His brother, same birth. Be very careful.'

Blaise registered this without taking his eyes off the Arimondan by the door. The man was clad in the green livery of Miraval and he, too, wore a sword, the curved blade of his own country.

Urté de Miraval rose, without haste; so too, on the other side of Ariane de Carenzu, did Bertran. The lady remained sitting, though she had turned in her chair to glance over her shoulder at the door.

'Quzman,' said the duke of Miraval, 'I wondered where you were, and so long. See, as I promised you, there is a Gorhautian coran here you have expressed a desire to meet.'

'I do see that,' said the Arimondan. His voice was deep, almost musical. He smiled. 'I am most pleased. In my country we have a saying: murderers must be dealt with swiftly lest the green grass wither beneath their tread. Will you come outside with me, or do you only fight from a distance?'

'It was not murder,' said Valery sharply before Blaise

could reply. 'The priests and priestesses of Rian's Isle were wit-
nesses and have told their tale.'

The man called Quzman seemed not to have heard.
There was something uncanny about his smile, the way his
entire being seemed focused upon Blaise. Once, in a Götzland
castle, Blaise had seen a man look at another in that way, and
death had followed before the night was done. Now, in
response to the nakedness of this challenge, Blaise felt his own
anger rekindling, a memory of the encounter by the lake, the
luxuriously articulated, ugly words of the Arimondan on the
black horse.

'You do seem distressed,' he said to the man by the door,
keeping his own voice relaxed, almost lazy, in the way his
friend Rudel or even Bertran de Talair would say this thing.
'Tell me, did I kill your brother or your lover there? Or were
they one and the same?'

'Careful!' Valery whispered urgently again. But Blaise
had the pleasure of seeing the Arimondan's smile stiffen into
something harsh and artificial, a rictus, as of death.

'You have a foul murderer's tongue, Northerner.' It was
Urté de Miraval. 'I do not see why we should suffer it to wag
freely among us, and then carry back a spy's tales to Ademar
of Gorhaut.'

So that was brought into it too, now. Predictably.

'That last is the thought of a fool,' said Bertran calmly.
'And as for murder: this man was set upon by while riding in
peace on the countess's high road. His pony was slain and his
horse, and six cowards in your service sought to kill him. I
would not speak so glibly of murder, my lord of Miraval. I
might, instead, give a passing thought to the competence of
my corans were it my own six killers who were slain by one
man alone.'

'These are words,' said Quzman of Arimonda contemptuously. 'Words and posturings, the sad vices of Arbonne.
This man and I can end this alone outside, no one else need
be part of it. Unless he is truly afraid. As for the new law
you mention . . .'

He took two strides into the room, graceful as a hunting
cat, and knelt before Urté. 'My lord, matters touching upon
the honour of my family compel me to ask leave to withdraw

from your service for a time, that my actions need have no bearing on your own affairs. Will you grant me leave?'

'*He will not,*' said a clear, cold voice. The only voice in the room that could have tried to wield authority in that moment.

They all turned to her. Ariane de Carenzu had not troubled to rise or even fully turn to face the men. She was still looking over her shoulder, casually, her black hair tumbling down the back of her chair. There was nothing casual about her words though. 'In the name of the countess of Arbonne I forbid this duel. There is a land price placed on deaths between Talair and Miraval. It has been proclaimed and posted and cannot be evaded — understand me, my lords — by sham devices of this sort. I will not let the countess be mocked. Nor will I allow this night of the goddess to be marred in such a way. I hold you both strictly accountable, my lords, for the conduct of your men.'

'Surely so, but if he leaves my service —' Urté de Miraval began.

'He requires your consent and you will not give it.'

The woman's voice was precise and authoritative, the flat tone of someone absolutely versed in command. Even after months in Arbonne, Blaise found it disconcerting to see the two dukes so accepting of a woman's unveiled note of power.

He opened his mouth to speak, his own anger strong within him, and received a hard elbow in the ribs. '*Don't do it!*' Valery muttered, as if reading his mind.

He probably had, Blaise thought — the path of his thinking would have been clear enough. Blaise was, by his own insistence, not bound to Bertran de Talair by any oaths of fealty. He was a hired mercenary and could end his contract at any time, forfeiting only whatever pay was due to him and as yet untendered and freeing himself to fight the Arimondan, without seeking a by-your-leave from anyone, including this black-haired woman who styled herself a queen, if only of the troubadours' Court of Love.

He drew a slow breath, met Valery's gaze for a moment and held his peace. He looked around the room. No one else seemed to have dared to move. With mild surprise he saw that the girl with the harp, still wearing Bertran's blue cloak, was staring at him from across the room. He couldn't read her gaze from a distance, but he could guess. She had thrust herself forward to defend the honour of the troubadour he'd wounded. She would probably be quite content if he died by a curved, bejewelled Arimondan sword.

His gaze swept past her and upwards. On the upper storey of the inn, men and women had crowded to the railings, first for the music and now for what had followed. Most of their faces were hidden by the cross-beams; a procession of legs lined the hallway above his head, cut off at the trunk. It was odd, in a way, an audience of feet and calves and thighs in variously coloured hose.

'You came here bearing a message, I think,' Ariane de Carenzu continued, in the silence that had followed her last speech. She was looking at the Arimondan, Quzman. 'Is it about the boats on the river?'

The man glanced over at her. He had remained kneeling before Urté de Miraval. They were both large, exceptionally handsome men; it was a pose that might have been carved in relief on the stone wall of a chapel of Corannos in Gorhaut.

'Yes,' the dark-skinned man said finally. 'It was about the boats.'

'They are beginning now?'

'They are.' He offered no title or any courtesy at all to the woman.

'Then you will duel each other so for our amusement at Carnival,' said the lady of Carenzu with a swift, flashing smile that was radiant and yet infused with capricious malice.

'A game?' the Arimondan said, with derision. A ripple of anticipation and relief was sweeping across the room. Blaise saw Bertran turn quickly away to hide a smile.

'It is almost all a game,' Ariane said softly, in a rather different voice. 'We play it, all of us, through our nights and days, until the goddess takes us home. But hear me again,' she added calmly, 'if any man of either of your parties dies tonight I will hold it as murder and tell the countess as much.'

'I haven't been on the river in years,' said Bertran, an apparently inconsequential remark. He seemed to be struggling, with only partial success, to keep a thread of laughter out of his voice.

Urté de Miraval heard it. 'And I in decades,' he said, rising to the bait. 'But I will give you that, and twenty years' advantage of age and still best you, my lord of Talair, in any action that a man may honourably do among men.'

At that, Bertran did laugh aloud. With a whiplike malice of his own that Blaise did not fully understand, he said, 'Only among men? A prudent concession my lord, under the circumstances.'

Urté de Miraval's head snapped back, as if from an actual lashing. It was the first time he'd lost his composure, Blaise realized, and wondered why. Something he'd overheard weeks ago tugged vaguely at his memory: there was a woman somewhere at the root of what lay between these two.

'Bertran,' began Ariane de Carenzu sharply, 'I do not think that —'

'Ariane, have done! You have imposed your will here, and we are mindful of you. Do not overreach; it is a failing. I told you when you walked in and I have told you as much before.' Bertran's blue eyes as he wheeled to face her were hard and carried their own measure of authority now. 'We will play games tonight on the river for your amusement. No one will be killed, by your command. Be content with what you may control. The past is not in your province.'

'Indeed it is not,' said Urté de Miraval very softly, his self-control regained. Blaise had to lean forward to hear him. 'None of the dead are. Men or women. Even children. Even children, if it comes to that.'

Which, for some reason, drew a response from Bertran de Talair. He turned from the dark-haired woman to look full into the face of the other duke standing not far away. There was a suddenly dangerous stillness in the room again, a sense of genuine menace radiating outward from where the two men stood.

'It comes to that,' said Bertran finally, his own voice little more than a whisper now. 'Oh, believe me, my lord, it does.'

As the two of them locked gazes to the manifest exclusion of everyone else in the tavern, in the world, Blaise of Gorhaut realized, rather late, that the hatred here, the palpable weight of whatever lay in the past between them, was of a depth and texture infinitely greater than he had understood.

Beside him Valery muttered something under his breath that Blaise could not quite hear.

'Come,' Bertran added, breaking free of the frozen stare, his tone a sudden, exaggerated parody of ritual, 'let us go. Let us all go forth by the light of the mingled summer moons to make sport on the river for the queen of the Court of Love.'

He moved towards the door without looking back. Valery followed quickly. Blaise glanced around the tavern one more time. Ariane de Carenzu's expression was odd now, vulnerable for the first time. People were beginning to stir, shaking their heads, blinking vaguely, as if freed of an enchanter's cast spell. On the upper landing the legs were moving, black and white hose, white and blue, wheat-coloured and russet, crimson and gold, pale and forest green — the brilliant colours of festival time.

He watched for another moment, thinking about the words just spoken, nagged by the thread of a thought, and then moved with the crowd out the doorway and into the noisy street. On the way he passed very close to Quzman the Arimondan, closer than he needed to, in fact. He made a point of smiling as he did.

Valery was waiting just outside the door. A man and a woman masked as a crow and a fox bumped into Blaise as they stumbled past, laughing uproariously. The man carried an open flask of wine, the woman's tunic was mostly unbuttoned. In the light of the lanterns above the doorway of The Liensenne, her breasts showed clearly for a moment. There was laughter ahead of them and behind and a constant, cacophonous sound of noisemakers being whirled and banged and thumped.

'You don't have any of this in Gorhaut, I suppose,' said Valery companionably, as if nothing of note had happened in the tavern. Blaise realized that he liked Bertran's cousin for this relaxed, unruffled quality, as much as for anything else. Just ahead of them the duke was walking amid a cluster of musicians, including the woman who had sung for them; she was still wearing Bertran's blue cloak.

'Hardly,' he said shortly, by way of reply, but he tried to keep the criticism out of his voice. What should he say to Valery: that he found this whole night's goddess-inspired exercise in lechery demeaning and vulgar, unworthy of any man who aspired to serve his country and his god?

'I meant to tell you that there were two Arimondans,' Valery said after a pause. There was riotous sound all around them; a young boy raced past, violently whirling a noisemaker shaped like the head of a bull. Two laughing women leaned precariously far out of a window overhead, trading ribald jests with those passing in the crowded street.

'I'm sure,' Blaise said drily. 'Why didn't you?'

Valery glanced briefly at him. 'You didn't seem interested.' He said it mildly, but Blaise heard the nuance in the words. 'You haven't seemed much interested in anything. I wonder why you travel, sometimes. Most men leave home to learn about the wider world. You don't seem to want to know.'

A different sort of elbow in the ribs. Blaise thought of stating as much, but after a moment said only, 'Some men leave home to leave home.'

After a moment Valery nodded. He didn't pursue the matter. Turning right, he followed Bertran and the troubadours up a darker laneway leading away from the sea.

'How good are you with small boats on water?' he asked after a moment.

'Passable,' said Blaise cautiously. 'What, exactly, are we about to do?'

'A question!' said Valery of Talair, grinning suddenly. He looked younger, and very like his cousin when he smiled. 'You actually asked a question!'

Almost against his will Blaise laughed. He sobered quickly, concentrating, as Valery of Talair began to explain. Then, when Valery was finished and they had come to the river and Blaise saw what was there — the people, and the strung lights like glittering stars come down, the lanterns and faces in the windows of the merchant houses along the river, the ropes across the water mooring the rafts, the small boats waiting and others drifting downstream towards the invisible sea, some already capsized with men swimming beside them — he laughed aloud again, helplessly, at the childlike frivolity of it all.

'Oh, Corannos,' he said, to no one in particular, 'what a country this is.'

But they had caught up with the others by then, the troubadours and joglars amid the crowd on the riverbank, and Bertran de Talair turned back to look at him.

'We know that,' he said levelly over the noise. 'Do you?'

The river and the sea and the night were sacred to Rian, and Midsummer was holy to her, but Carnival was also a time when the order of the world was turned upside-down — sometimes literally, as in a vat of water, or Cauvas gold, Lisseut thought ruefully. The goddess was celebrated that night through Arbonne in laughter and amid noise and flowing wine and otherwise forbidden linkings in the darkness of cobbled laneways or grassy mews, or beds in houses where doors were left unlocked this one night of the year.

It was also celebrated in the city of Tavernel, and had been for years beyond number, with the challenge of the Boats and Rings on the river, here where the Arbonne came home to the sea after its long journey south from the mountains of Gorhaut.

Grateful for the hooded cloak Duke Bertran had forgotten or neglected to reclaim, Lisseut tried with only marginal success to pick up the thread of excitement and anticipation that had carried her into The Liensenne earlier in the day. It was still Carnival, she was still among friends and had even had — though there had been no time to properly absorb this — what appeared to be a spectacular success. But the presence of hatred, both ancient and new, was too strong now for her to regain the blithe mood of before. She looked over at the grim figure of Urté de Miraval and at the sleek Arimondan beside him, and she could not suppress a shiver, even within the cloak.

You kill singers, remember? So En Bertran had said to the duke of Miraval. Lisseut didn't know if that was true; if it was, then it had happened before her time and was not something anyone talked about. But Urté had not denied it. *Only those who sing what they should not,* he had replied, unperturbed.

Laughter, jarring incongruously with her thoughts, drew her attention to the river and, in spite of herself, she was forced to smile. Jourdain, who prided himself on his athleticism even more than Remy did, had pushed his way through the crowd to the water's edge and, prudently removing his expensive boots, was evidently about to be the first of their group to try the boats.

Lisseut cast a quick glance up at the sky, just as Jourdain did, and saw that the moons were both clear of clouds and would be for a few moments. That mattered, she knew. It was hard enough to grasp the rings in a whirling, bouncing toy of a boat without contending with the added problem of not being able to see them.

'Are you sure you wouldn't prefer to be ducked in the basin?' Alain of Rousset called out from the safety of the bank. 'It's an easier way to soak yourself!'

There was laughter. Jourdain said something impolite, but he was concentrating on stepping down and then settling himself in the tiny, bobbing craft that two men held close to the dock. He took the short, flat-bladed oar one of them offered him, glanced once more at the two moons — one waxing, one just past full — and nodded tersely.

They let the boat go. To screams of encouragement, Jourdain shot like a cork from a bottle out into the swiftly racing river.

'Ten copper pieces he doesn't make three rings,' Alain cried loudly.

'Done!' said Elisse, who was sleeping with Jourdain that season.

'And ten more from me,' Lisseut added quickly, more to wager against Elisse than for any other reason. 'Are you good for it?'

'More than good,' Elisse replied with a toss of her golden hair. 'I've been touring with *real* troubadours this spring.'

It was such a patently envious, silly gibe that Lisseut burst into laughter. Alain's aggrieved expression showed that he couldn't quite see it that way. Lisseut squeezed his arm and then continued to hold it as they watched Jourdain do battle with the river.

Sober or not, he steered smoothly enough across the current to the first raft and, without apparent effort, reached up and across to gracefully pluck the garland of olive leaves that had been looped on a pole hanging out over the water. The priestess on the first raft quickly raised her torch to signal success. A shout of approval went up along both sides of the river. People were massed all the way down the banks to the final strand of rope running across the stream, and there were almost as many leaning out of windows in the high houses.

Paddling vigorously, leaning his body far over to one side, Jourdain angled his boat back the other way, trying to move across the river before the current took him sweeping past the second raft. He made it, barely, had an instant to steady himself and then reached upwards — the second ring was higher of course — and plucked the garland. He almost slipped, toppling back into his boat and very nearly falling out. But another torch was lifted and another shout went up.

Jourdain's near-fall cost him precious time, though, and when he righted himself properly and seized the oar again Lisseut, even at a distance, saw him make a swift decision to eschew the third raft near the far bank and head straight downriver towards the fourth. It was the number of garlands that counted, not the sequence.

It was also a wrong decision. Running straight downstream, Jourdain's tiny boat, seeming little more than a chip of bark in the racing Arbonne, accelerated dramatically as he approached the fourth moored raft.

'Do you want to pay us now?' Alain said to Elisse.

Despite the wager, Lisseut winced in anticipation as Jourdain, flying down the river, bravely rose to his feet as the moored raft hurtled towards him. He reached upwards and over for the elusive garland.

He didn't even come close. With a whoop they could hear all the way upstream at the starting pier his feet went flying from under him, the boat shot out into the stream and Jourdain, seeming to defy the pull of earth, hung horizontally above the river, bathed in moonlight for a suspended moment, before plunging into the Arbonne with a splash that sent a fountain of water upwards to soak the priest on the raft and those who had gathered there to see the contest.

He almost doused the torch, but he was nowhere near the garland. Two men leaped quickly off the raft to assist him in the water — people had been known to drown in this game — and Lisseut breathed more easily when she saw them pulling Jourdain towards one of the anchored boats near shore. From a distance they saw him raise an almost jaunty hand to show that he was all right.

'What is the best so far,' Bertran de Talair asked in a quiet tone that brought Lisseut swiftly back to the reality of why they were here.

'One man has all four, my lord,' said the nearest of the boatmen crouched at the end of the pier. 'But he fell at the very beginning of the rope crossing, so no one has finished the course so far.'

'Good,' said the duke of Talair, stepping towards the end of the dock. 'With your agreement, my lord,' he said, turning towards Urté, 'I will give you a target to shoot for.'

Urté de Miraval made a negligent gesture that signalled assent. Not bothering to remove his boots, Bertran stood quietly as the boatmen manoeuvred the next small craft into position. Valery and the bearded coran from Gorhaut had moved down beside him, Lisseut saw. A murmur of sound, gathering and swelling as it went, began to race along the banks of the river carrying the news of what was about to happen.

Lisseut looked upwards, and in that same moment most of the others on the pier did the same. A bank of clouds, moving swiftly eastward with the breeze, had cut across the face of white Vidonne and would soon obscure the blue light of Riannon as well.

'Let me go first,' said Valery of Talair, stepping past the duke in the shadows. 'Wait for the moons. No one has challenged me so it doesn't matter if I miss.' He quickly unbuckled his sword and handed it to one of the boatmen. He looked over his shoulder and Lisseut was close enough to hear him say, 'Follow my line, Blaise. If you overshoot the third raft do everything you can to slow down before you reach the fourth — unless you're partial to the taste of river water.'

The Arimondan beside Urté laughed at that. It was not a pleasant sound, Lisseut thought, looking over quickly. The man frightened her. She turned away, back to the river, hoping the Arimondan hadn't noticed her staring at him.

Valery was in the boat with the flat paddle to hand. He grinned up at Bertran. 'If I get wet it's your fault.'

'Of course,' his cousin said. 'It always is.'

Then the boat was gone, out into the high, swift current of the river. A moment later, straining to see amid the shadows, Lisseut was made to understand something about the skills of men: Jourdain the troubadour was an athlete, and gifted, in the prime of his youth, but Valery of Talair was a professional coran, trained and hardened, and very experienced.

He snapped up the first wreath effortlessly, the boat turning back the other way almost before the priestess's torch had been raised and the responding shout had gone up along the bank. The second ring, which had initiated Jourdain's precipitate descent towards a watery immersion, was negotiated almost as easily and Valery, unlike the troubadour, kept both his balance and his control of the boat, paddling strenuously back across the river with a second triumphant torch lofted behind him and screams of wild approval on each bank.

'They think he's the duke,' little Alain said suddenly, and Lisseut realized that it was true. The word that En Bertran was to run the river had gone racing down the banks before the clouds had come and Valery had taken his place. These screams and cries were those the people of Tavernel reserved for their favourites — and the troubadour duke of Talair had been one of those for most of his life.

Meanwhile, Valery, approaching the third of the moored rafts, stood up smoothly in his bobbing craft — making a perilous feat seem easy — and stretched up and over to snatch the third of the olive laurels from its pole. He dropped back down into the boat and began paddling furiously across the water, leaning into the task as the people watching from riverbank and overhanging window and the crowded boats moored against the shore stamped and roared their most extreme approval.

The angle back to the fourth and final raft was the most acute by far and Valery was working for all he was worth to avoid being carried downstream past the ring; Jourdain had jumped for the laurel here and smacked into the water. Valery of Talair pulled hard to the upstream edge of the raft, let his small craft turn with the current and then stood, smoothly again, and without evident haste or urgency lifted his paddle upward and swept it along the pole suspended high above the raft and out over the river — and he caught the olive ring thereby dislodged as his craft went hurtling beneath.

That is what it looked like to Lisseut, a long way upstream with swift clouds obscuring the moons and men and women jostling and shouting around her as the priest of Rian's signifying torch was thrust triumphantly skywards far down along the Arbonne. For some reason she glanced over at the coran from Gorhaut: an unconscious grin, an almost boyish expression of pleasure, showed in his face, making him look different suddenly, less austere and formidable.

'My cousin, too, is worth six men — no, a dozen!' Bertran de Talair said happily, looking at no one in particular. There was a stirring among the green-garbed corans of Miraval. Lisseut, feeling particularly sharp just then, doubted that En Bertran had spoken carelessly — there were verbal daggers in almost everything he and the duke of Miraval said in each other's presence. Ariane, her hair swept up again and hidden beneath her hood, said something to Urté that Lisseut could not hear. Ariane stepped forward beside Bertran, the better to see Valery approach the end of the course.

The rope across the river was the last obstacle. An enormous round shield with a hole drilled in its centre hung exactly halfway across with the rope passing through it. Whichever side of the shield his boat passed under, the competitor's task was to leap up, seize the rope and then pull his way hand over hand under or over or around the shield — an exceptional achievement in itself — and then all the way to the opposite bank.

Every one of the men who had made it this far would be formidably agile and strong. Ropes across water would not customarily faze them. This one was different. This one was virtually impossible. It had, for a start, been coated with attentive, careful malice in layers of beeswax. Just before being strung across the water it had also been oiled extravagantly with the purest olive oil from the celebrated groves and presses in the hills above Vezét. Then it was strung across the Arbonne in such a fashion that it sagged just low enough in the middle to force the hapless adventurer who had adroitly made it this far to pull his way hand over slippery hand along a cruelly upward inclination towards the dismally remote platform on the bank where triumph and glory awaited.

Lisseut, in three years of watching this contest on the river at Midsummer Carnival, had never seen anyone come close; she'd never even seen anyone cross the shield. She *had* seen quite a few undeniably graceful men made to look comically helpless as they struggled to find a way across the shield in the middle, or found themselves hanging on grimly, as if pinned down by the bright watching moons, unable to move at all while their legs kicked helplessly above the racing river.

There was a point to all this, she knew; during Carnival there was a point to everything, even the most apparently trivial or licentious activities. All the inversions and reversals of this night of the goddess, suspended outside the rhythms and the round of the year, found their purest emblem in these torchlit and moonlit images of gifted men rendered helpless and inept, forced either to laugh at their own predicament while themselves suspended on a slick rope or, if too grimly serious to share the hilarity, bear the mockery of a shrieking crowd.

No one, though, was mocking Valery of Talair that night, and there was nothing even faintly hilarious about him as he guided his tiny boat straight towards the shield. Approaching the rope, he stood up again and, without hesitation, with a neat, precise, economic movement, hurled himself up towards it just to the left of the shield. Tucking his knees in tight to his chest like a tumbler performing at a banquet he let his momentum swing him around in an arc at the top of which he released his precarious grip on the slippery rope and rose gracefully into the air — to come angling back down, as if it were the easiest, most natural thing in the world on this night or any other night, on the other side of the shield barrier.

For all the relished anticipation of comic failure, the people of Tavernel and those assembled in the city for its Carnival knew excellence when they saw it. They exploded with exultant approval of such stylish mastery. The shouts and applause assaulted the ears. Lisseut, back on the launching pier, heard a bark of delighted, surprised laughter beside her and turned in time to see the Gorhautian coran's bearded face completely unguarded now with pleasure. He caught her quick glance this time though; their eyes met for an instant and then his flicked away, as if he were embarrassed to have been so observed. Lisseut thought of saying something but changed her mind. She turned back to watch Valery deal with the rope.

And so saw, by a trick, an angle, a flaring of torchlight far down the dark river, how the arrow — white-feathered, she would remember, white as innocence, as winter in midsummer, as death — fell from the summit of its long, high arc to take the coran in the shoulder, driving him, slack and helpless, from the rope into the river amid laughter turned to screaming in the night.

Blaise saw it too, out of the corner of his eye. He even marked, purely by reflex, with a professional's instinct, the two tall, dark-timbered merchant houses along the bank whence an arrow descending at that angle could have been let fly. And he, too, saw, by torchlight and the elusive gleam of the blue moon now riding free of the clouds, the white feathers Lisseut had seen. There was a difference, though. The difference was that he knew what those feathers meant, and the nagging thought from the tavern earlier in the evening grew fully formed and terrifying in his mind.

By then he was running. A mistake, because the Carnival crowd was densely packed along the water's edge, and the rope from which Valery had fallen was a long way down the river. Pushing and swearing, using elbows and fists, Blaise forced his way through the shouting, roiling mass of people. Halfway down he glanced over at the river and saw Bertran de Talair paddling furiously in one of the small boats — which, of course, is what he ought to have done himself. Blaise's curses turned inward and he redoubled his efforts. One man, drunken, masked, snarled an oath and pushed back hard as Blaise elbowed his way past. Without even looking, unbalanced by fear, Blaise sent the man reeling with a forearm to the side of his head. He couldn't even be sorry, though he did wonder — a reflex again — about the possibility of a knife in the back. Such things happened in frightened crowds.

By the time he reached the pier by the rope the boatmen had taken Valery of Talair from the river. He was lying on the dock. Bertran was there already, kneeling beside his cousin with a priestess and a man who looked to be a physician. The arrow was embedded in Valery's shoulder; not, in fact, a killing wound.

Except that the feathers and the upper shaft of the arrow were white and the lower shaft, Blaise now saw, coming up to the pier, was of night-black ash, and he had seen black-and-white leggings above him on the second-floor landing of The Liensenne when the singer had finished her music and they were all preparing to leave. A sickness passed through him like a churning wave.

Valery's eyes were open. Bertran had his cousin's head cradled in his lap now; he was murmuring steady, reassuring words. The physician, a thin, beak-nosed man with greying hair tied back with a ribbon, was conferring tersely with the priestess, eyeing the black-and-white shaft with resolution. He was flexing his fingers.

'Don't pull it,' Blaise said quietly, coming to stand above the four of them.

The doctor looked up quickly, anger in his eyes. 'I know what I'm doing,' he snapped. 'This is a flesh wound. The sooner we have the arrow out the sooner we can treat and bind it.'

Blaise felt tired suddenly. Valery had turned his head slightly and was looking up at him. His expression was calm, a little quizzical. Forcing himself to meet the coran's level gaze, Blaise said, still softly, 'If you pull the shaft you'll tear more flesh and the poison will spread the faster. You may also kill yourself. Smell the arrow if you like. There will be syvaren on the head, and very likely on the lower shaft.' He looked at the physician.

An animal-like fear showed in the man's face. He recoiled involuntarily. In the same moment, with a small, fierce sound of denial, Bertran glanced up at Blaise. His face had gone white and there was horror in his eyes. With sorrow and a slow, hard rage gathering together within him like clouds around the heart Blaise turned back to Valery. The wounded coran's expression had not changed at all; he had probably had an intuition, Blaise thought. Syvaren acted quickly.

'That was meant for me,' Bertran said. His voice was like a scrape in the throat.

'Of course it was,' Blaise said. Knowledge was in him, a cold certainty, the taste of it like ashes on his tongue.

'It was none of our doing, I will swear it by the goddess in her temple.' Urté de Miraval's deep voice rang out. Blaise hadn't heard him approaching.

Bertran did not even look up. 'Leave us,' he said. 'You will be dealt with later. You are a desecration wherever you walk.'

'I do not use poison,' de Miraval said.

'Arimondans do,' said Bertran.

'He was on the launching pier with us the whole time.'

Blaise, sick with knowing, opened his mouth to speak, but the priestess was before him.

'Leave off wrangling now,' she said. 'We must take him to a temple. Will someone find a way to carry him?'

Of course, Blaise thought. This was Arbonne. Valery of Talair, even though he was a coran, would not find his end in the sanctity of the god's house. He would pass to Corannos amid the dark rites of Rian. With a distaste that was akin to a fresh grief, Blaise turned away from the priestess; she had covered her head with a wide hood now. He saw that Valery's eyes were upon him again, and Blaise thought he understood the expression this time.

Ignoring the others, even Bertran, he knelt on the wet dock beside the dying man. 'Be sheltered ever in the god,' he said huskily, surprised by the difficulty he had in speaking. 'I think I know who did this. I will deal with him for you.'

Valery of Talair was pale as parchment beneath the moons and the torches. He nodded his head once, and then he closed his eyes.

Blaise rose. Without looking at anyone or staying for further words he strode from the dock. Someone made way for him; he realized only later that it had been Quzman, the Arimondan. Others also fell back before him but he was scarcely aware of any of them. There were those ashes in his throat and a queer blurring to his sight. Syvaren on the arrow. White feathers, white-and-black shaft. Blaise reached inward for the rage he needed, and it was there, but he could not ride it. There was too much grief, cold and clammy, coiled in tendrils as a mist in winter: half for Valery behind him and half for what he walked towards now, tall and grim as an image of the Ancients on a frieze, amid the flurrying torches and the smoke and noise and masks and, yes, in the distance, still the laughter of Carnival.

I will deal with him for you. Last words to a dying man, fellow coran of the god's long, hallowed brotherhood, a friend very nearly, here amid the goddess-shaped strangeness of Arbonne. And they were likely to have been a lie, those last words, the worst sort of lie.

CHAPTER·6

Lisseut, if asked in the midst of that swirling, suddenly horrific night, or even after, with time and a quiet place to think things through, would not have been able to say why she slipped free of Bertran de Talair's tell-tale blue cloak, ignored Alain's urgent cry behind her and followed the man named Blaise away from the torchlit pier and into the warren of dark, twisting lanes that led away from the river.

It might have been something about the way he had left the dock, the headlong ferocity, brushing past the Arimondan as if the man did not exist. Or something perhaps in the stricken expression she saw in his face as he went blindly past them all and plunged into the crowd. She had heard the word *poison* ripple back like a snake from where Valery lay. They were taking him to the largest temple of Rian. Men were hastily readying a sail canvas, slinging it between poles. They would move him on that. The crowd would make way in silence until they passed, bearing death, then it would be loud again, wilder than before, with flamboyant murder suddenly added to the intoxicating mixture of Carnival — something else by which to remember the night.

The troubadours and joglars would go to the temple, she knew, to wait and watch in a vigil outside the walls, many for Bertran's sake and some for Valery's. Lisseut had been part of death-watches before. She didn't want to join one tonight.

She followed the coran from Gorhaut.

She had to force her way against the press of the crowd. People were hurrying towards the river, drawn by rumours of some excitement or disaster, the coinage of festival time. Twisting past bodies, Lisseut smelled wine and cooked meats, roasted nuts, sweet perfumes, human sweat. She knew a brief, flurrying panic when she was trapped for a moment in a cluster of drunken merchant seamen from Götzland, but she twisted free of the nearest of them and hurried on, looking for the man she was following.

His height made it easier. Even in the thronged laneways she could make him out ahead of her, moving against the crowd, his hair a bright red when he passed under the torches set in the walls of the dilapidated old warehouses. This was not the choicest part of Tavernel. Blaise of Gorhaut plunged onwards, taking turnings seemingly at random, moving more quickly as the crowds thinned out away from the water. Lisseut found she was almost running in order to keep him in sight.

Incongruous in one dim, crooked laneway, she saw a woman, gowned magnificently in green silk, furred and bejewelled, with an elaborate fox mask, reach out for Blaise; he didn't even break stride to acknowledge her presence. Lisseut, hurrying along behind him, was made suddenly aware of her own damp, straggling hair and ruined shirt. Trivialities, she told herself sternly; a white-feathered arrow had been launched tonight with poison on its head, and it had been meant — it took no brilliance of insight to know — for the duke of Talair and not the cousin who had quietly taken his place in that small boat on the river.

Blaise of Gorhaut stopped abruptly at a crossing of lanes and looked around him for the first time. Lisseut quickly ducked into a recessed doorway. She almost fell over a man and a woman leaning back against the wall in the darkness beside the door, locked in an embrace. The lower part of the woman's gown was pushed up about her waist.

'Oh, good,' the woman drawled sensuously, glancing languorously at Lisseut, a ripple of amusement in her voice. Her mask had slipped back from her eyes and hair, dangling loosely down her back. The man laughed softly, mouth at her throat. Both of them reached out in the same instant, slender fingers and strong ones, to draw Lisseut into their embrace. 'Good,' the woman said again, a whisper, half-closing her eyes. There was a scent of wildflowers about her.

'Um, not really,' Lisseut said awkwardly, stirred against her will. She spun free of both of them.

'*Then farewell love, ah, farewell ever, love.*' The woman sang the old refrain with an unexpected plaintiveness marred by a giggle at the end as the man whispered something in her ear.

Back in the street, in the wavering, uneasy shadows between wall torches, Lisseut quickly donned the woman's mask. It was a cat; most of the women chose cat masks tonight. Ahead, she saw Blaise throw out a hand to stop a trio of apprentices. He asked a question. Laughing, they answered and pointed; one of them offered a flask. Lisseut saw Blaise hesitate and then accept. He squeezed a jet of dark wine down his throat. For some reason, watching, that made her uneasy.

He took the lane forking right, where they had pointed. She followed, passing the apprentices with quick sidelong steps, prepared to run; it was too dark here, not enough people. She reached the fork and looked along the lane to the right. It was even quieter there, running up and away from the river and the market square. The houses became steadily more impressive, more evidently prosperous, the roadway better lit than before with lanterns burning in ornate sconces on outside walls — one of the surest signs of wealth. Two girls, evidently servants, called cheerfully down to her from where they leaned out over a carved stone balustrade. Lisseut kept moving. Blaise, walking swiftly with his long strides, had already turned a corner up ahead. She began to run.

By the time she reached that next crossing of streets and turned right again as he had done, Lisseut realized where they were, even before she saw, in the square at the top of the street, the off-centred tower loom grimly above the largest red-stoned building.

This was the merchants' quarter, where the banking houses and mercantile operations of several countries had their headquarters in Tavernel, Arbonne's deep-harboured gateway to the world. That tower at the top of the road was a deliberate, intimidating echo of the great tower of Mignano, largest of the Portezzan city-states, and the massively formidable palaces on either side of the street leading to the square sheltered the Arbonne contingents of the lucid, careful merchants of those wealthy cities.

The noises of Carnival were distant now. Lisseut slipped
into an archway, peering out carefully as Blaise of Gorhaut
went past one massive doorway and then another. She saw
him stop finally, gazing up at the coat of arms above a pair of
iron doors. There were lights on in that house, on the upper
levels where the sleeping quarters would be. There was no one
else in the street.

Blaise stood motionless for what seemed to her a long
time, as if deliberating something difficult, then he looked
carefully around him and slipped down a narrow alley that ran
between that house and the one north of it. Lisseut gave him
a moment, then stepped out from her archway and followed.
At the entrance to the alley she had to hold her breath for a
moment, almost choking in the midden smell that came from
it. Kneeling for concealment, her eyes keen in the darkness,
she saw the coran from Gorhaut hoist himself smoothly to
scale the rough stone wall running behind the house where
he had stopped. There were more lights glowing softly from
beyond that wall. She saw him silhouetted for a second
against them before he let himself down on the other side.

It was time to go back to the river. She now knew where
he had gone. She could find out who owned this house in the
morning, report the incident to whoever seemed appropriate. Duke Bertran was the obvious person, or perhaps the
countess's seneschal in Tavernel. Perhaps even Ariane de
Carenzu, who had bound the men of Talair and Miraval to
keep the peace this night. Morning would tell her what to do;
she could consult with friends, with Remy, Aurelian. It was
time to go back.

Discarding her mask, gritting her teeth, Lisseut went
down the fetid alley, past the point where the Gorhautian had
scaled the wall and, further along, she found an overturned
wooden crate. There were always crates in alleyways. Rats
scattered in several directions as she stepped carefully up onto
it. From there it was just possible to lift herself to the top of
the wide wall. She lay flat on the stone, motionless for a long
time. Then, when she was sure she'd not been seen or heard,
she cautiously lifted her head and looked down.

It was an intricate, formal garden, carefully tended. A
plane tree grew just inside the wall and its branches offered

some concealment for her, which mattered, for Riannon, the blue moon of the goddess, rode free just then of what seemed the last of the cloud cover for a time. Above, through the screen of leaves, Lisseut could see the stars, brilliant in the summer sky. A bird was singing in the branches of the tree.

Below her, on a close-cropped grassy expanse, Blaise of Gorhaut stood quietly beside a small, round pool into which a sculpted fountain was splashing water. There were flowers planted around the border of the fountain and more of them laid out in patterns through the ordered space of the garden. Lisseut smelled oranges and lemons, and there was lavender near the southern wall. Behind her rats scrambled in the dank alley.

On a small patio near the house a stone table had been laid with meats and cheeses and wine. There were tall white candles burning.

A man slouched in a chair by that table, hands laced behind his head, long legs extended, his features obscured by shadow. Blaise was looking at him. He had not spoken or moved since she'd arrived at her place of concealment on the wall. His back was to her. He seemed carved of stone himself. Lisseut's heart was beating rapidly.

'I will confess that I wondered,' said the man by the table lazily, speaking Portezzan with elegant, aristocratic precision. 'I wondered if you were in a clever vein tonight and would come. But see, I did give you the benefit of the doubt — there is food and wine for two, Blaise. I'm glad you're here. It has been a long time. Do come and dine with me. It *is* a Carnival night in Arbonne, after all.'

He stood then, leaning across the table into the light as he reached for the wine. By the shining of the two moons and the candles and the glowing, graceful lanterns swinging from tripods among the trees, Lisseut saw that he was slender and bright-haired and young and smiling, that his loose silk tunic was night-black with wide, full sleeves, and his leggings were black and white, like Arsenault the Swordsman in the puppet shows she remembered from childhood — and like the arrows she saw lying in plain sight in their quiver by the table.

'You still use syvaren, I see,' said Blaise of Gorhaut

calmly. He didn't move any nearer to the table. He spoke Portezzan as well.

The fair-haired man made a face as he poured from a long-necked decanter. 'An ugly thing, isn't it?' he said with distaste. 'And amazingly expensive these days, you have no idea. But useful, useful at times. Be fair, Blaise, it was a *very* long shot in a breeze and uncertain light. I didn't plan anything in advance, obviously, it was sheerest good fortune I happened to be in the tavern when that river challenge was made. And then I had to count on Duke Bertran being skillful enough to make it as far as the rope. Which I did, and which he was, Corannos shelter his soul. Come now, you might have congratulated me by now on hitting him from so far. The right shoulder, I take it?' He turned, smiling, a glass of wine in each hand, one extended towards the other man.

Blaise hesitated, and Lisseut, all her senses alert, knew with certainty that he was wrestling with whether to tell the assassin of his error.

'It was a long shot,' was all he said. 'I don't like poison though, you know that. They don't use it in Arbonne. Had you not done so they might have thought the killing was by one of Urté de Miraval's men. It wasn't, I take it?'

The question was ignored. 'Had I not done so there wouldn't have been a killing. Only a duke with a wounded shoulder and a quadrupled guard, and I'd be out a rather spectacular fee.'

'How spectacular?'

'You don't want to know. You'll be jealous. Come, Blaise, take your wine, I feel silly standing with my hand out like an almsman. Are you angry with me?'

Slowly, Blaise of Gorhaut walked forward over the grass and took the offered goblet. The Portezzan laughed and returned to his seat. Blaise remained standing beside the table.

'In the tavern,' he said slowly, 'you would have seen that I was with the duke, one of his men.'

'Of course I did, and I must say it surprised me. I'd heard a rumour at the Aulensburg tourney — you were missed in Götzland, by the way, you were talked about — that you were in Arbonne this spring, but I doubted it, I really didn't know you liked singing so much.'

'I don't, believe me. But it isn't important. I'm employed by the duke of Talair, and you saw as much in the tavern. Didn't that mean anything to you?'

'A few things, yes, but you won't like them and you won't want to hear them from me. You *are* angry with me, obviously. Really, Blaise, what was I supposed to do, abandon a contract and payment because you happened to be on the scene trading insults with an Arimondan catamite? I gather you killed his brother.'

'How much money were you paid?' Blaise asked again, ignoring that last. 'Tell me.'

The fair, handsome head was in shadow again. There was a silence. 'Two hundred and fifty thousand,' the Portezzan said quietly.

Lisseut suppressed a gasp. She saw Blaise stiffen in disbelief.

'No one has that much money for an assassination,' he said harshly.

The other man laughed, cheerfully. 'Someone does, someone did. Deposited in advance with our Götzland branch, in trust for me on conditions. When word comes of the musical duke of Talair's so sad demise the conditions are removed. Götzland,' he said musingly, 'is a usefully discreet place sometimes, though I suppose it *does* help to have a family bank.'

The man still seemed amused, eerily so, as if there was some private jest he was savouring at Blaise's expense. Lisseut was still reeling inwardly, unable to even comprehend the size of the sum he had named.

'Payment in Portezzan coinage?'

Laughter again, on the edge of hilarity now, the sound startling in the quiet formality of the garden. A slow sip of wine. 'Ah, well now, you are fishing for information, my dear. You were never good at that, were you Blaise? You don't like poison, you don't like deceptions. You aren't at all happy with me. I've clearly gone to the bad since we parted. You haven't even asked for news of Lucianna.'

'Who paid you, Rudel?'

The question was blunt, hard as a hammer. Blaise's wine glass was set down on the table, untouched; Lisseut saw that it shook a little. The other man — who had a name now — would have seen that too.

'Don't be stupid and tiresome,' the Portezzan said. 'When have you ever revealed who hired you? When has anyone you respected done so? You of all men know I've never done this for the money in any case.' A sudden, sweeping gesture encompassed the house and the garden. 'I was born to this and all it represents in the six countries, and I'll die with it unless I'm more stupid than I plan to be, because *my* father happens to like me.' He paused. 'Drink your wine, Blaise, and sit down like a civilized person so we can talk about where we're going next.'

'We aren't very civilized in Gorhaut,' said Blaise. 'Remember?' There was a new note in his voice.

The man in the chair cleared his throat but did not speak. Blaise did not move from where he stood.

'I see it now, though,' he said softly. Lisseut could barely hear him. 'You've had too much wine too quickly, haven't you? You didn't mean to say all of that did you, Rudel?' He spoke Portezzan extremely well, much better than Lisseut did herself.

'How do you know? Perhaps I did,' the other man replied, an edge to his tone now. 'Lucianna always said that good wine at night made her — '

Blaise shook his head. 'No. No, we aren't talking about Lucianna, Rudel.' He drew a breath and, surprisingly, reclaimed his own goblet and drank. He set it down again, carefully. 'You told me too much. I understand now why you find all of this so diverting. You were paid in Gorhaut coinage. You were hired for that insane amount of money to assassinate the duke of Talair in the name of Ademar, king of Gorhaut. But on the orders and doubtless the instigation of Galbert, High Elder of Corannos in Gorhaut.'

In shadow the other man slowly nodded his head. 'Your father,' he said.

'My father.'

Lisseut watched as Blaise turned away from the table and the lights on the patio and walked back towards the fountain. He stood gazing down at the rippling waters of the artificial pool. It was difficult to see his face.

'I didn't know you were with Talair when I accepted the contract, Blaise. Obviously.' The Portezzan's voice was more urgent now, the amusement gone. 'They wanted him killed for some songs he wrote.'

'I know. I heard one of them.' Blaise didn't look up from the pool. 'There's a message in this. My father likes sending messages. No one is safe, he's saying. No one should think about crossing him.' He turned with a harsh gesture. 'You're *meant* to tell the fee, you know. If you don't, believe me they will. It'll get out. That's a message in itself. How far he'll go if he has to. The resources they can command. You've been used, Rudel.'

The other man shrugged, unruffled. 'We are always used. It is my profession, it's yours. People hire us to serve their needs. But if you're right, if they really intend to make sure everyone knows who paid for this and how much, then you had better think seriously about coming away with me.'

'Why?'

'Think about it. In your clever vein, Blaise. What happens to you here when your own secret's broached? When people learn who you are — and that your father killed the duke of Talair while you were supposed to be guarding him. I have some idea why you came away to Arbonne in the first place — and no, we don't have to talk about it — but you can't stay here now.'

Blaise crossed his arms over his chest. 'I could deal with that problem. I could turn you in. Tonight. I am employed by the duke of Talair, I'd be doing my duty.'

Lisseut couldn't see his face clearly, but from the voice that emerged from shadow she knew the man named Rudel was amused again.

'The late, lamented, poetical duke of Talair. He wrote one song too many, alas. Really, Blaise. Your father ordered the killing, your old comrade-in-arms performed it? Stop being stupid. You are going to be blamed for this. I'm sorry if what I've done makes things briefly awkward for you, but the only thing to do now is figure out where we'd like to go and leave. Have you heard, by the way? Lucianna is married again. Shall we visit the newlyweds?'

There was another silence. 'Where?' Blaise asked quietly.

Lisseut had a sense that the question came against his will.

'Andoria. To Borsiard, the count, a fortnight ago. My father was there. I wasn't invited, I'm afraid. Neither, evidently, were you, though I would have thought you'd have heard.'

'I hadn't.'

'Then we must visit them and complain. If he hasn't been cuckolded yet you can take care of that. I'll create a distraction of some kind.'

'How? By poisoning someone?'

The man named Rudel stood up slowly. In the light now, his features could be seen to have gone still; no trace of amusement remained. He set down his cup of wine. 'Blaise, when we parted a year since I was under the impression we were friends. I am not certain what has happened, but I don't have the same impression at the moment. If you are only angry for tonight, tell me, and explain why. If you are more than that, I would appreciate knowing as much, so I can act accordingly.'

Both men were breathing harder now. Blaise uncrossed his arms. 'You took a contract from my father,' he said. 'Knowing what you knew, you took a contract from him.'

'For two hundred and fifty thousand Gorhaut gold coins. Really, Blaise, I —'

'You have always said you don't do this for the money. You just said it again here. Your father *likes* you, remember? You're going to *inherit*, remember?'

'And are you jealous of that? As jealous as you are of any other man who is close to Lucianna?'

'Careful, Rudel. Oh, please be careful.'

'What will you do? Fight me? To see which one of us can kill the other? How stupid are you going to be about this, Blaise? I had no idea you were with the duke of Talair. By the time I knew I could not withdraw from a job I'd accepted. You are as much a professional as I am. You know this is true. I took your father's contract because it was by far the largest sum of money ever offered in our time for a killing. I admit it, I was flattered. I liked the challenge. I liked the idea of being known as the man who was worth that much as an assassin. Are you going to try to kill me for that? Or are you really wanting to kill me for introducing you to my cousin, who decided not to change her nature just because you appeared on the scene and wanted her to? I told you exactly what Lucianna and her family were before you ever saw her. Remember? Or do you prefer to just hide within your anger, hide away from everyone you know, down here in Arbonne, and forget such painful things? *Be honest with yourself, what is my sin, Blaise?*'

Lisseut, flat on the wall, screened by the leaves of the plane tree with a bird now silent in the branches above, heard what she should not have heard and felt her hands beginning to tremble. This was too raw, too profoundly private, and she was sorry now that she had come. She was spying on this garden exactly like one of the evil, envious audrades who spied on the lovers in all the dawnsongs, bent on ruin and malice. The steady, quiet splashing of the fountain was the only sound for a long time. There were usually fountains in the songs, too.

When Blaise next spoke it was, surprisingly, in Arbonnais. 'If I am honest with myself and with you, I will say that there are only two people on earth, one man and one woman, it seems I cannot deal with, and you are linked with both of them now, not just the one. It makes things . . . difficult.' He took a deep breath. 'I'm not going to leave Arbonne. Among other things, it would seem an admission of a guilt I do not bear. I will wait until morning before I report to the appropriate people who it was who shot that arrow. You should have no trouble being out to sea on one of your father's ships before that. I'll take my chances here.'

The other man took a step forward into the full light of the candles on the table and the torches. There was no levity or guile in his face now. 'We have been friends a long time and have been through a great deal together. If we are enemies now I will be sorry for it. You might even make me regret taking this contract.'

Blaise shrugged. 'It was a great deal of money. My father tends to get what he wants. Did you ever ask yourself why, of all possible assassins in the six countries, he hired the one who had been my closest friend?'

Rudel's face slowly changed as he thought about this. Lisseut saw it happen in the glow of the light. He shook his head. 'Truly? Would that have been it? I never even thought of that.' He laughed softly again, but without any amusement now.

'With my pride, I simply assumed he'd judged me the best of all of us.'

'He was buying a friend I had made for myself in the world away from home, away from him. Be flattered — he decided your price would be very high.'

'High enough, though I confess I'm less happy now than I was a moment ago. Tell me one thing, though. I think I do know why you left us all and came away by yourself, but why stay now? What has Arbonne done to buy you and hold you? What was Bertran de Talair that you will cast your lot in this way?'

Blaise shrugged again. 'It has done nothing, really. Certainly not to buy me. I don't even like it here, truthfully. Too much goddess for me, as you might have guessed.' He shifted a little, from one foot to the other. 'But I have a contract of my own, just as you did. I'll wrap that up as honestly as I can, and then see where I end up. I don't think I'm casting any lots, really.'

'Then think again, Blaise. Think harder. If your father was sending a message to the world by killing the duke of Talair what shall we take that message to be? What is Gorhaut telling us all? My father says there is a war coming, Blaise. If it comes, I think Arbonne is doomed.'

'It is possible,' said Blaise of Gorhaut, as Lisseut felt the colour leaving her face. 'As I say, I will see where I am in a little while.'

'There is nothing I can do for you?'

Lisseut heard a tired amusement in Blaise's voice. 'Don't let the wine make you sentimental, Rudel. I am going to report you as an assassin at sunrise. You had best begin making your own plans.'

The other did not move. 'There is one thing,' he said slowly, as if to himself. He hesitated. 'The factors in all of the Correze branch houses will be sent a letter from me ordering them to receive and conceal you should the need ever arise.'

'I will not go to them.'

It was Rudel's turn to sound amused. 'That much is out of my control. I can take no responsibility for your pride. But the letter will be written. I take it you are leaving your money with us?'

'But of course,' said Blaise. 'With whom else should I trust it?'

'Good,' said Rudel Correze. 'The one thing my father most hates is investors withdrawing their accounts. He would have been deeply unhappy with me.'

'I would regret being the cause of such unhappiness.'

Rudel smiled. 'If I had not seen you, Blaise, I should be an extravagantly pleased man tonight, flushed with my great success. I might even go out and join the Carnival. Instead I am rendered curiously sad and forced to take a night voyage, which never agrees with my digestion. What sort of a friend are you?'

'One who is not an enemy, at any rate. Be careful, Rudel.'

'And you. That Arimondan will kill you if he can.'

'I know. If he can.'

There was a silence. 'A message for Lucianna?'

'None at all. The god guard you, Rudel.'

Blaise took a step forward and the two men clasped hands. For a moment Lisseut thought they would embrace but they did not. She moved silently back along the wall, felt below in darkness with her feet for the wooden crate and slipped down into the odours of the alleyway. She heard the rats again as she moved quickly back towards the street. As she left the alley, she picked up her mask, discarded on the street, and put it on. She wanted some sort of barrier between herself and the world just then, and what she still wanted, even more than before, was a quiet time and a clear head that would let her think.

She didn't think she was going to get either tonight.

She went back down the empty street away from the square at the top, past the massive iron doors that were the entrance to what she now knew was the Arbonnais palace of the House of Correze. She knew the name, of course. Everyone knew the name. She had stumbled into something very large and she didn't know what to do.

A little further down she came to the arched doorway she'd watched from before, when Blaise went down the alley. She slipped back into it, looking out from behind the elongated eye-slits of her mask.

She didn't have long to wait. Blaise of Gorhaut came striding out of the alleyway a few moments later. He stopped in the street and looked up at the stern, square tower of Mignano. She knew why now, she knew more than she should, or even wanted to know: Mignano was controlled by the Delonghi family, it had been for a great many years, and the only daughter of Massena Delonghi was a woman named Lucianna, twice married, twice widowed prematurely.

Three times married, she corrected herself. To Count Borsiard d'Andoria now. She wondered, briefly, why a man of power and means would marry her, knowing her family's ambition, knowing her own reputation. She was said to be very beautiful. How much could beauty excuse or compel?

Blaise had turned away from the tower and was coming back down the street, walking quickly. The lantern light burnished his hair again, and the full beard.

She didn't know, until the moment she actually called his name, that she was going to do so. He stopped, a hand moving swiftly to his sword, then wavering before it dropped to his side. A woman's voice; he wouldn't fear a woman. Lisseut came out from her archway into the light. Her mask was on. She reached up and removed it; the makeshift coiling she'd done with her hair came undone as she did, and she felt the tangled tendrils coming down about her face. She could imagine what she looked like.

'Ah,' he said. 'The singer.' Some surprise in his voice, not a great deal. Not a great deal of interest, either. At least he recognized her. 'You are a long way from the Carnival here. Do you want an escort back to where there will be people?'

His tone was courteous and detached, a coran of the god doing his sworn duty by someone in need. It hadn't even *occurred* to him why she was here, she realized. She was merely an Arbonnais female, presumably in need of assistance.

Her mother had always said she did too many things on impulse and that it would cost her one day. It already had, more than once. It was probably about to do so again, she thought, even as she opened her mouth.

'I followed you,' she said. 'I was on the garden wall under the plane tree. I heard what you both said, you and Rudel Correze. I'm trying to decide what to do about it.'

She was briefly gratified at the level of astonishment that showed in his face, even behind the beard — as much a screen in its own way as all the masks were tonight. The feeling didn't last long. It was entirely possible, she realized, that he might kill her now. She didn't think so, but it was possible.

She braced herself for his fury. She thought, in the uncertain light, that she saw it come, a lifted head, a narrowed gaze upon her. He had stabbed Remy, she remembered. He had killed six men by Lake Dierne. His hands remained still, though. She saw him working out implications, surprise and anger giving way to a flatly professional appraisal. He was quick to control himself; had she not watched him earlier in the garden spilling wine in response to a woman's name spoken she would have thought him a cold, grim man.

'Why?' was all he said finally.

She'd been afraid of that question. She still didn't have an answer. She wished her hair was pinned properly, that her clothing was clean and dry. She felt like a street urchin. Her mother would be so ashamed.

'You seemed to be hurrying somewhere,' she said hesitantly. 'The way you left the pier. I think I was very . . . irritated with you in the tavern, I wanted to . . . know more.'

'And now you do.' He sounded more tired than angry, actually. 'So, what will you do?' he asked.

'I was hoping you would tell me,' Lisseut said, looking down at the cat mask in her hands. 'I heard you say that you were going to stay instead of leaving with him. I heard him say there might be a war, and I . . . I heard who paid for the killing.' She forced her head up to meet his gaze.

'My father,' he said bluntly. 'Yes, go on.'

She felt her brow knit with concentration. 'I'm not famous for my self-discipline, but I don't want to go charging into something that is out of my depth.'

'Oh, really,' he said with mild sarcasm. 'How restrained of you. More people should think that way. But the obvious question is: why trust me? Why are you telling me this on a dark street when no one in the world knows we're here together or knows what you just heard? Why are you asking Galbert de Garsenc's son what to do? You know who he is, you know who I am now. You know that Rudel Correze, my friend, is the man who killed Valery. You spied, you learned things that are important. Why are you standing with me now? Do you care so little for your life, or are you simply ignorant about what happens in the real world to people who do things like this?'

She swallowed. He was not an easy man, not at all. She pushed her hair back from her eyes again; it was snarled, miserably.

'Because I believe what you said to him. You didn't know I was there, you had no reason to lie. You had nothing to do with this killing. And you said you would not leave Arbonne and . . . and then you didn't tell him he killed the wrong man.' She felt her forehead smooth as she realized the truth of what she was saying. These *were* her reasons; she was discovering them as she spoke. She even smiled. 'I think you are an uncivilized northerner upon whom the better things in life are wasted, but I don't think you're evil and I do think you meant what you said.'

'Why,' said Blaise of Gorhaut in an odd, musing voice, 'am I so completely surrounded by sentimental people tonight?'

She laughed aloud. A moment later, as if surprised by himself, Blaise grinned crookedly. 'Come on,' he said. 'We shouldn't be seen in this neighbourhood. Connections will be made.' He began walking back down the wide street. His long strides made no concession to her size and she had to take quick, skipping steps to keep up. It was, in fact, irritating again, and after a short while she grabbed his sleeve and with a vigorous tug forced him to slow his pace.

'The god wouldn't want you to make me run,' she murmured. He opened his mouth and then closed it. She thought he had nearly laughed but wasn't sure, glancing up in the uncertain light and shadow.

It was then though, unfortunately, hand holding his sleeve, that she remembered that it was Carnival night, Midsummer Eve. It was said in Tavernel to be bad luck to lie alone tonight. She felt her mouth go dry. She swallowed and let go of his sleeve. He didn't even notice, striding along beside her at a more decent pace, broad-shouldered and competent, with the celebrated, notorious Lucianna Delonghi somewhere in his past. Unbidden, the image of the entwined couple in the dark laneway came vividly back to her. *Oh, good,* the woman had said, in a voice made husky by desire, and their hands had reached out to draw her into a shadowed sanctity.

Lisseut shook her head and swore to herself, breathing deeply of the night air. This was, of course, all Remy's fault. Before him such thoughts, such images, would have been alien to her. Well, mostly alien.

'Why are you letting him leave?' she asked, to change the pattern of her thoughts, to break the silence. There were more people around them now; mostly couples at this point in the evening she noted, and quickly suppressed that thought. 'Because he's your friend?'

Blaise glanced down at her. She wondered if her voice sounded strained. He hesitated. Lisseut had a quick, flaring sense that if she had been a man he wouldn't have. He did answer, though. 'Partly that, obviously. We have been through . . . a great many things together. But there's more to it. Rudel Correze is an important man. He's his father's son, and his father is a *very* important man. If he's captured here we would have to decide what to do with him, and that could prove awkward. If a war comes, the cities of Portezza will be important, for money, and possibly more than that.'

She took another chance. A large chance. '*We?*' she asked.

He was silent for a few strides. 'You are,' he said finally, 'a clever woman, and obviously a brave one.' She thought of sketching a mock bow in the roadway but refrained. 'I suggest you try hard not to become too sentimental about this. I'm a professional coran, at the moment under contract to Duke Bertran, who is not dead though a man I had come to like is. In my profession one gets used to the deaths of people one likes, or one finds another profession. I could as easily be in Aulensburg serving Jörg of Götzland by this autumn, and if he decides to join Gorhaut and if there is a war . . . I'll be back here and fighting for him against you. You must understand that. For now, I try to serve, as best I can, the needs of the man who pays me.'

'Payment is all? Wouldn't you fight for Gorhaut because it is your country? Only for that reason, money aside?' She found that she was breathing hard again.

He fell silent as they walked, looking over and down at her. Their eyes met for a moment, then he glanced away. 'No,' he said finally. 'Once I would have. Once I did. Not any more.' He drew a slow breath. 'Not since Iersen Bridge. I am a professional coran. Payment is all.'

'And you can change sides that easily? There are no attachments that matter? No people, no principles?'

'You started the evening attacking me,' he murmured. 'Is it becoming a habit?'

Lisseut felt herself blushing.

'If you are fair,' he went on, 'you will acknowledge that there are principles behind what I do. Attachments are dangerous in my profession. So is sentiment.'

'You've used that word at least four times tonight,' she said, more tartly than she'd intended. 'Is that your only word for human affection?'

He laughed again, surprising her. 'If I concede you the point will you leave it?' he asked.

He stopped in the street. They were back among the crowds now. Someone jostled her going past. Blaise laid a hand on her shoulder as she turned to look at him. 'I don't think I'm up to debating with you in the street tonight. I think I'd lose.' He gazed down at her soberly, a professional again, assessing a situation. 'You asked me earlier what you should do. I intend to speak to En Bertran in the morning. He should not be taxed with this tonight, I think that is obvious, quite aside from what I promised Rudel Correze. I will tell him everything that happened, including my decision to let Rudel have a chance to leave. I expect he'll agree with that, eventually, if not immediately. I'll also tell him who paid for that arrow. I promise you these things. If you don't trust me to do this, you can be there when we meet in the morning.'

It was more than she could have expected, rather a great deal more. She said, however, being what her mother had always said she was, 'You'll tell him everything? Including who you are?'

His expression did not change; he'd been expecting the question, she realized. He had already begun taking her measure; it was a curious thing to realize.

'If you insist that I do so, I will. I cannot stop you from telling, in any event. I don't go about killing women who learn too much. I can only ask you to let me be the judge as to when and whether to reveal that, as events unfold.' He hesitated again. 'I mean no harm to anyone you care about.'

She thought of Remy, with a sword wound in his shoulder. She said, hardily, trying to sound cool and experienced, 'Fine. I can give you that. But then I had better not be there when you speak to Bertran or he'll summon me after, alone, and ask me what else I heard — and I'm not very good at lying.' She was conscious of his hand still on her shoulder.

He smiled. 'Thank you. You are generous.'

Lisseut shrugged. 'Don't be sentimental,' she said.

He laughed aloud, throwing his head back. An artisan with a noisemaker ran past them just then, producing a terrifying blast of sound. Blaise winced.

'Where shall I leave you?' he asked. 'At the tavern?'

He had taken his hand from her shoulder. It was Midsummer Eve, in Tavernel. She said, 'You don't have to leave me . . . actually. It is Carnival and the night has some time yet to run. We could share a bottle of wine, if you like, and . . . and, well if you *are* staying in Arbonne for a while longer you should know some of our customs.' She looked away, despite herself, along the crowded street. 'It is said to be . . . unlucky to spend tonight alone in this city.'

Her mother had always said she would end up disgracing the family. She could blame her uncle for taking her out into the wide world as a singer. She could blame Remy of Orreze. She could blame the holy rites of Rian in Tavernel on Midsummer Eve.

She could wait, biting her lip, for the man with her to say, with devastating politeness, 'Thank you. To both things. But I am not of Arbonne, truly, and if it brings me ill luck or no, a coran I admired has died tonight and my own customs require that I keep vigil for him in a house of the god.'

'All night?' She looked back up at him. It took some courage.

He hesitated, reaching for words. Lisseut said then, knowing it was ill advised, 'I don't know what happened in Portezza, obviously, but I am not like that. I mean, I don't normally — '

He put a hand over her mouth. She felt his fingers against her lips. 'Don't say it,' he murmured. 'Leave me that much as my own.'

He was an uncivilized northerner, she thought. He had stabbed Remy in the arm. *Until the sun falls and the moons die,* her grandfather and her father used to say, *Gorhaut and Arbonne shall not lie easily beside each other.* His fingers withdrew, he withdrew back into himself, behind his own mask. It was only the dangerous associations of Midsummer Eve, she told herself, and the disturbing intimacy of what she'd heard in that garden. There were other men to be with, men she knew and trusted, men of talent and wit and courtesy. They would be back at The Liensenne, in the downstairs room or upstairs with Marotte's wine and cheeses and their own harps and lutes and songs, celebrating Rian through the remaining hours of the goddess's most holy night. It was not likely she would have to lie alone.

Unless, in the end, she wanted to. With an unexpected sadness within her, Lisseut looked away beyond the man she was standing with, struggling to regain the diamond-bright mood of exhilaration that seemed to have slipped away from her somewhere in this strange night among the crowds and the music and the noisemakers and the one arching arrow and the words she'd heard spoken beside the plashing of a fountain.

And so it was, looking away along the crowded street, that she saw before he did the six men in crimson livery who now came up and surrounded them carrying torches, bearing swords.

Their leader bowed gracefully to Blaise of Gorhaut. 'It would be a great courtesy,' he said, with perfect, grave formality, 'if you would come with us.'

Blaise looked quickly around; she could see him trying to take the measure of this new situation. He looked back at Lisseut, seeking a clue or explanation in her eyes; she had known he was going to do that. He didn't know the livery, of course. She did. She knew it well. And didn't much feel, just then, like helping him. How, she thought, surprised by her own swift anger, was a bedraggled joglar from Vezét's olive groves to compete with this sort of thing on a night of Rian?

'I don't think,' she said, 'that you are going to have your vigil with the god after all. I wish you joy of the night and the year.' And took a shallow, fleeting satisfaction in the incomprehension that showed in his eyes before they took him away.

One of the men in crimson escorted her back to The Liensenne. Of course. They were flawlessly versed in such niceties. They had to be, she thought sourly, they were meant to be an example to all the world.

CHAPTER·7

*E*ven when he saw the peacocks in the extravagantly lit inner courtyard of the house where they brought him, Blaise wasn't sure where he had come. He had no sense of immediate danger from the five men escorting him, but, equally, he was under no illusion that he could have refused their courteously phrased request.

He was surprisingly weary. He'd been more honest with the singer, the straggle-haired girl named Lisseut, than he would have expected to be, especially after what she'd done. But if he'd been entirely truthful he would have added, at the end, that his desire for a vigil in a house of the god was at least as much for the cool silence such a solitude would afford as it was to mourn and honour Valery of Talair's passing to Corannos that night.

He had rather a great deal to think about and try to deal with just now, and wine and whatever might follow on a decadent night in Tavernel with a singer — however spirited and clever she might be — was not going to ease his heart or his mind tonight. Things seemed to have suddenly become difficult again.

His father had paid a quarter of a million in gold to Rudel Correze to kill the duke of Talair.

A clear message meant for all the world, and another, hidden, for his younger son alone: *See what I have to work with, my errant child. See what I will deny you for refusing me. How I strip away even your friendships. Learn the cost of your folly. How could you ever have dreamt of gainsaying me?*

Was there any place on the surface of the earth where he might go and not be brought back, face to face as before the

169

polished, merciless, self-revealing surface of a mirror, with Galbert, the High Elder of Corannos in Gorhaut?

And there was more, even more than that tonight. Lucianna was married again. Another sort of mirror that, distorting and dark: guttering candles beside a ravaged bed, the god's moon passing from a window, an eastern songbird in an ornate cage singing to break the heart — images so raw the eyes of memory flinched away.

He had come in the stillness of winter through the passes to Arbonne as to a place of haven or refuge, where he had never been before, would probably not be known, might serve in quiet anonymity whatever petty lord in whatever remote mountain fastness might offer him an adequate recompense. Where he might not ever hear her name spoken, whether in admiration or desire or contempt, or be forced to deal with all the hurting, hoarded memories from Portezza: images framed in the intricate textures of carpeting and tapestries, cushions of woven silk, vases and drinking cups of marble and alabaster, and weaving through them all, like a drifting veil of smoke, the sensuous, elusive scents he had come to know perilously well in the women's wing of the Delonghi palace in many-towered Mignano a year ago.

What is my sin, Blaise? Rudel was like that. A knife in the voice and in the thought behind. Quicksilver bright, insubstantial as a moon on water sometimes, then sharp and merciless and deadly as . . . as an arrow dipped in syvaren. And the sharpness in his perceptions, as much as in anything else. A man from whom it was difficult to hide.

For the sin, the transgression, lay — and Rudel knew it, they both knew it — in his having given Blaise exactly what he wanted. In taking a Gorhaut coran still numb with shock and anger in the aftermath of the Treaty of Iersen Bridge and drawing him away, first to Aulensburg and the ale-sodden, hunt-obsessed court of Jörg of Götzland, and then down south by stages in fair, flowering springtime to something else, something entirely otherwise.

To the cities of Portezza and their intrigues, the delicate pleasures of subtle, wealthy men with sidelong smiles, and the infinitely versed women of those warring, brilliant city-states. And one windswept night, with distant thunder sounding on the hills north of Mignano, there had been Lucianna Delonghi's night-black hair at the head of a banquet table, the flash of her jewellery, the equally flashing wit with unsettling traps and double meanings everywhere, the mocking laugh, and then, astonishingly, what she was afterwards, elsewhere, under the painted canopy of a bed, clad only in the dazzle of that jewellery...what happened when mockery left the laughter but the laughter remained.

That was Rudel's sin. And so, being honest, Blaise was forced to say there was really no sin at all, only a doorway offered — and with a warning, as well — through which he himself had walked, scarred by wounds from a winter battle when his king had died, into the seeming warmth of a firelit, candlelit, scented sequence of rooms, from which he'd emerged a season later with wounds that went deeper by far.

The peacocks were arrogantly unafraid. One of them seemed inclined to challenge their right to cross the courtyard before it turned and strutted away, opening the glorious panoply of its tail. Under the moons and in the blaze of torches there was something extravagant and profligate about the fan of colours on display. In his memories of Lucianna, too, there was little daylight; it all seemed to have happened in darkness or by candlelight, extravagant, profligate, in one palace or another, and once, on a steaming, airless summer's night not to be forgotten, with Rudel in Faenna when they had killed her husband on a contract for her father.

As they approached the end of the courtyard a pair of doors were opened by a footman in the dark red livery. Behind him, in a wide hallway, bearing flame in a slender candlestick, a lady-in-waiting stood, in the same colours, with white at wrist and throat and binding her dark hair. The footman bowed, the woman sank low in a curtsey. The candle in her hand did not even waver. 'Will you honour me by following?' she asked.

Blaise was still under no illusions. Two of the guards had remained, he noted, waiting just inside the doorway. He was almost inclined to berate them all, to demand an end to this protracted charade of courtesy, but something in the perfection, the gravity of it, made him hold his peace. Whoever it was who had sent for him very clearly placed an exaggerated value on such things; it might be a useful piece of information.

And it was with that thought, following the woman's neat-footed progress down a corridor and up a wide, curving flight of stairs, with two guards in careful step behind him, that Blaise understood where he had to be, and something the singer had said, at the end, became belatedly clear to him.

They stopped before a closed door. The woman knocked twice and opened it; she stepped aside, gesturing with easy grace for Blaise to pass within. He did. They closed the door behind him, leaving him in that room without attendant or guard.

There was a fireplace, not lit. Candles in sconces on the walls and on tables placed around a richly furnished and carpeted room done in shades of dark blue and gold. Wine on one table, he saw, goblets beside a flask. Two, no, three doorways opening to inner rooms, a pair of very deep, high-backed chairs facing the fire. The windows on the outer wall were open to the breeze; Blaise could hear noises of revelry from below. There was a familiar, hard bitterness in him now, and a curiosity he could not deny, and a third thing, like the quickening hammer of a pulse, beneath both of these.

'Thank you for coming,' said Ariane de Carenzu, rising from a divan on the far side of the room. Her black hair was still down about her shoulders, as it should not have been. She was dressed as before, jewellery upon her like fire and ice.

'I would accept the thanks if I had had a choice in the matter,' Blaise said grimly. He remained just inside the doorway, assessing the room, trying not to stare too intently at the woman.

She laughed aloud. 'Had I been certain you would elect to come I would have been happy to grant you that choice.' Her smile made it clear she knew exactly what she was saying. She was very beautiful, the dark hair framing and setting off flawless white skin. Her dark eyes were wide-set and serene, the mouth was firm, and in her voice Blaise heard the note of control he had registered in the tavern when she had issued a command to the dukes of Talair and Miraval, and both had accepted without demur.

The women of Arbonne, he thought, trying to summon anger like a shield. He folded his arms across his chest. A little more than a year ago, on a spring night with the god's thunder outside on the northern hills, he had answered a different kind of summons to another black-haired woman's chambers. His life had been changed that night, and not, in the end, for the better.

There is wine by the fire, Lucianna Delonghi had said then, lying across her bed beneath the canopy of coupling figures. *Shall we begin with that thirst?*

There was no bed here, no lit fire, and the woman with him now poured the wine for both of them herself, and then neatly, without artifice, walked over to offer him a goblet. He took it without speaking. She did not linger beside him but turned and walked back to the divan. Almost without knowing he was doing so, Blaise followed. She sat and gestured with one hand and he took the chair she indicated. She was wearing perfume, a subtle scent, and not a great deal of it. There was a lute on a table at one end of the divan.

She said, without preamble, the dark brown eyes steady on his, 'There are a number of matters we might wish to consider, you and I, before this night is over, but do you want to begin by telling me what happened after you left the river?'

He was tired, and his mind and heart had been dealt double blows tonight, but he was not so far unmanned as that.

He even found himself smiling, though he could not have said why. Perhaps the pure challenge of it, the directness of what she seemed to be trying to do. 'I might,' he murmured. 'I might possibly want to tell you, but until I know who else is listening at the door behind you I would prefer to keep my own counsel, my lady. You will forgive me.'

He had expected many things, but not delight. Her laughter chimed with her two hands clapping happily together, the long fingers momentarily obscuring the rubies about her throat.

'Of course I will forgive you!' Ariane de Carenzu cried, 'You have just won me a wager of twenty-five silver barbens. You really shouldn't work in the service of men who undervalue you so much.'

'I object to that,' said Bertran de Talair, entering the room from the door behind her. 'I did not underestimate

Blaise. I might *possibly* have judged your charms to be rather more distracting than they seem to be of late.'

'I know your lute,' Blaise said briefly. 'I may not think much of your music, but I know the instrument.' He was making an effort to keep his composure. He wasn't really looking at Bertran, either, because another woman, very tall, had walked in behind the duke. This one had grey in her dark hair and she was blind and there was a white owl on her shoulder. The last time he'd seen her was on an island in the sea when she'd told him the secrets of his own heart in the night dark of a forest.

'You might at least have *tried*,' Bertran went on plaintively, addressing Ariane. 'I'm minded to renege on our wager. You were about as seductive as a wet goat in a cave.'

'Spare us a recitation of your preferences,' Ariane replied sweetly.

It was the High Priestess of Rian, her blank eye sockets turned unerringly to where Blaise had risen from his chair, who told him the thing he most needed to know, as de Talair threw back his head in laughter.

'The wounded coran will live. He should be completely recovered after the shoulder injury heals.'

'That cannot be,' Blaise said, his mind clamping shut in denial. 'There was syvaren on that arrow.'

'And he owes you his life for telling them as much by the river,' the priestess went on gravely. She was robed in a gown grey as the streaks in her hair. Her skin was darkened and roughened by sun and wind and the salt of the sea, a complete contrast to Ariane's alabaster smoothness. 'They brought him to me in the temple here, and because I knew what this was and because it happened tonight, I was able to deal with it.'

'You can't, though. You *can't* cure a man poisoned by syvaren. No surgeon in the world can do that.'

She permitted herself the small, superior smile he remembered. 'That last is true, at any rate. Nor could I have done so if too much time had passed and if I had not been in a consecrated place. It is also Midsummer Eve. You should have cause to remember, Northerner, that the goddess's servants can do things you might not expect when we are centred in her mysteries.'

'We burn women in Gorhaut when they traffic in the magics of darkness.' He wasn't sure why he'd said that, but he did indeed recall the apprehension he'd felt on the island, the pulsing of the forest floor beneath his feet, and something of that was coming back now. He was also remembering, as through a tunnel of smoke and years, the first witch-burning he'd ever seen. His father had pronounced the excoriation and had had both his young sons stand by him and watch.

The High Priestess of Rian was no longer smiling. 'Fear makes men label women's power an act of darkness. Only fear. Consider the price of that: no woman would have dared try to save Valery of Talair if that arrow had been loosed in Gorhaut.' She paused, as if waiting for a response, as a tutor with her charge. Blaise said nothing, keeping his face as impassive as he could. The owl flapped its wings suddenly but settled again on the priestess's shoulder. In a different tone she said, 'I bring greetings for you from Luth of Baude, who now serves Rian with dignity on her Island.'

Blaise grimaced at the recollection. 'Luth couldn't serve a flask of ale with dignity,' he said, anger and confusion overcoming him.

'You do not mean that, you are only unsettled. You might also be surprised at what any man may do when he, too, feels centred in his own being.' The reproach was mild enough, but Blaise felt, as he had before with this woman, that there were meanings beneath the surface of her words, that she was speaking to a part of him that no one should have been able to address.

The very old woman who had burned on the Garsenc lands all those years ago had been pitiful more than anything else. A village neighbour had accused her at the year end god-moot of witching a cow so its milk would dry. Galbert had decided to make an example of the case. Every year, sometimes more often, such a course was needful, he had said to his sons.

The cow's milk had been unchanged even after the witch had died with her white hair blazing. Blaise had made a point of going back to the village, after, and asking about that. Something had sickened in him then, and did so again whenever the memory came back. He recalled, a memory thick and oppressive, his father's heavy hand on his shoulder at the burning, as Galbert made sure his recalcitrant younger child would not shame him by turning away. There had been no darkness, no secret, dangerous power in the terrified woman screaming until she choked among black smoke and the tongues of flame and the smell of burning flesh. Somehow Blaise had known it even then.

But there *was* magic in the High Priestess of Rian. He had felt it on that island. She had known about Rosala. That, in itself, was an almost impossible thing to deal with, or forget. And as for the poison tonight: Bertran was here laughing, had been gleefully wagering with Ariane de Carenzu. Valery *could* not be dead. Even with syvaren on the arrow.

Something clenched and hurtful in Blaise, that had been present since he'd seen the white-and-black shaft fly, began to loosen its grip inside him. Rudel Correze, he thought abruptly, was going to be a profoundly disconcerted man one day not far from now. A part of him wanted to smile at that, but instead Blaise found himself sinking back down into his chair and reaching for his wine. He cradled the silver goblet in both hands without drinking. He was going to have to be careful now, he thought, looking at the two women and the man. Extremely careful.

'How much power do you have?' he asked, keeping his voice even, looking at the blind woman. She was still standing behind the divan.

And unexpectedly — she was always unsettling him, it seemed — the priestess laughed. 'What? Would you have a dissertation now on the Natural, Celestial and Ceremonial powers, with a subsidiary digression on the three Principal Harmonies? You think I am a lecturer at the university, perhaps? You haven't even offered me a fee, Northerner!'

Blaise flushed at the mockery. But even as the High Priestess ended, laughing still, Ariane de Carenzu's cool voice interceded, precise and sharp as a stiletto between the ribs. 'However captivating the issue raised might be, I am afraid the furthering of your education will have to be delayed a short while. You might recall that I have a question proposed first. You declined to answer until you knew who was behind the door. That was fair enough. Now you know. I would be grateful for a reply.'

What happened after you left the river? she had asked. The offered question and the heart of danger in this room tonight. Bertran de Talair stopped his restless pacing. He had picked up a crystal from one of the tables and held it now in one hand, turning it this way and that, accepting and diffusing candlelight, but his blue eyes were steady on Blaise's as he waited.

Blaise turned — as he seemed always to be turning — back to the High Priestess in her rough grey robe. Quietly, he said, 'If you know my mind, as you seemed to when last we met, you can answer all such questions for them, can't you.' He said it flatly; it was not a question.

Her expression, oddly, grew gentler, as if he'd sounded an unexpected chord. She shook her head. 'I also told you that night that our powers are less than our desires would have them be, and they grow weaker when we are farther from the hearthstones of Rian. On the goddess's Island I could read some things in your heart and in your history, largely to do with love and hate, you will remember. I said I could tell your future. That was a lie. Nor can I read your mind right now. If you have things to tell us you will have to tell them yourself.'

'Not all things,' Blaise said calmly. 'You could tell them who I am, for example.'

There was a short silence, then:

'We all *know* who you are, Blaise de Garsenc.' Bertran laid down the crystal as he spoke. His voice actually held a faint irritation. 'Did you honestly think you were travelling in such secrecy? That you entered my service without my knowing whom it was I was hiring?' The candlelight on the clever, cynical face exposed his old white scar.

Blaise swallowed. Events were moving very fast. Abruptly, he recalled something. 'But you asked me. You wanted to know who I was when first we met. If you knew, why ask?'

Bertran shrugged. 'I learn more sometimes from questions I know the answers to. Really, Blaise, whatever you — or I, for that matter — may think of your father, he is one of the powers of our world today, and his younger son has been, for a number of years, a coran of some reputation of his own. It was no secret — among certain circles, at any rate — that

Galbert de Garsenc's son left Gorhaut immediately after the Treaty of Iersen Bridge was signed. And when a distinctively tall, reddish-bearded Gorhaut coran of considerable skills was reported to be in Castle Baude some time after . . . it wasn't difficult to make an obvious guess. At which point I went to investigate matters for myself. Incidentally, I've never seen another man match arrows with my cousin at that distance before.'

Feeling bludgeoned by the increasing pace of revelations, Blaise shook his head. 'I didn't match him. And as it happens, the man who shot Valery tonight may well be better than either of us.' He wasn't sure he'd actually meant to say that.

'Ah, well now,' murmured Ariane de Carenzu, the words like a slow caress in the stillness of the room. 'This brings us somewhere, finally.' Blaise looked at her. Her lips were parted slightly, her eyes bright with anticipation.

'I had intended to tell the duke in the morning,' he said carefully. 'I undertook to wait until then.'

'Was such an undertaking yours to give?' The caressing note was gone as swiftly as it had come. She had spoken this way in the tavern, to Talair and Miraval. Blaise hadn't liked it then, and he didn't now. He let his eyes grow wide, holding and challenging hers. It was curious, and something he would have to think about afterwards, but with his identity out in the open he felt rather more equal to these people now. He had a suspicion that when he considered the matter he wouldn't be happy about it, since any such feeling would be derived, ultimately, from being his father's son, but it was there, it was undeniably there.

'You will remember,' he said quietly to the duchess of Carenzu, 'that I was under the impression that En Bertran would be mourning the death of his cousin this evening.'

'How solicitous of you.' It was Bertran. 'And was that the reason for your undertaking?'

'In part,' Blaise said, turning back to him. 'There were others.'

'Which were?'

Blaise hesitated. There was danger here. 'The desire to avoid an extremely delicate political problem for us all, and another reason which is private to me.'

'I am not certain we can value that privacy, tonight, and I rather think the people in this room can shape their own judgments and responses to any political problems, however delicate, that might emerge from what you say. I think you had best tell me who this person is.' The duke's posture and voice were as lazy as ever, but Blaise had been with him long enough now not to be fooled by that.

'*Don't be obtuse, Bertran. We know exactly who this person is.*' A fifth voice in the room, from one of the two chairs before the fire, assured, quite uncompromising. Blaise wheeled swiftly around but saw no one at all, until the speaker rose, with caution, and he finally understood. The others, he noted grimly, had not been surprised.

He had looked over at those chairs when he first entered the room, of course; they were wide, richly upholstered and straight-backed, facing the fireplace, but not so large as to conceal a man.

But this was Arbonne, and a woman was another matter. Particularly a small, fine-boned, white-haired woman whom he knew to be — for he had seen her before, bestowing honours at tournaments — Signe de Barbentain, countess of Arbonne.

She was looking at the duke. 'If you have been listening at all carefully, Bertran, then this should be one of those questions you already know the answer to. If so, you should not shame a coran who tells you he has given an undertaking not to speak. We do not behave that way here, whatever may happen elsewhere in this decaying world.'

She was clad in blue and a pale cream colour with pearl buttons, close set, running up the front of her gown. Her hair was held back with a golden diadem. She wore no other ornaments save for two rings on her fingers. She had been celebrated, Blaise knew, as the most beautiful woman in the world in her time. He could see it, even now. Her eyes were astonishing, so dark they were almost black.

He bowed, a straight leg forward, one hand brushing the carpet. His coran's training would have had him do so, even if his instincts had not.

She said, 'Mine cannot be the only sources of information that reported last year that the younger son of Galbert de

Garsenc spent a season in Mignano and Faenna at the palaces of the Delonghi. Nor can I be the only one to have heard certain rumours — which we need not now pursue — concerning the unfortunate death of Engarro di Faenna. But the name to be linked with all of this — a name that indeed would give rise to complexities in affairs of state, as well as eliciting a personal response from our friend here — is surely that of Rudel Correze. Who is, I am reliably informed, much sought-out as an assassin, in good part for his skill with a bow. You need not,' she added calmly, looking directly at Blaise for the first time, 'reproach yourself for an undertaking breached. You did not tell me this.'

Blaise cleared his throat. It sounded harsh in the silence. 'Evidently I did,' he said.

She smiled. 'You didn't even know I was here.'

Blaise found himself, unexpectedly, smiling back. 'Then I should reproach myself for that. It was unprofessional, and careless.' He drew a breath. 'My lady, I advised Rudel Correze to take ship tonight because I was going to inform the city authorities of his identity in the morning.'

'City authorities? You meant me, I dare assume.' Bertran had walked around the divan now to stand by Ariane. Beatritz, the High Priestess, had not moved or spoken for some time.

Blaise shook his head. 'He thinks he killed you. I did not disabuse him of the notion.'

After a moment Bertran threw back his head and laughed aloud. 'So he will sail away to claim whatever fee it was, from whoever paid him. Oh, splendid, Blaise! The embarrassment will be with him a long time.'

'I thought so too. And for using syvaren it is the least he should suffer. But I think you will agree it would have been impolitic to seize the favoured son of the Correze family. At this juncture of affairs.'

Ariane de Carenzu was nodding. 'Extremely impolitic. It could have been very awkward to have him in custody here.'

'I concluded as much,' Blaise said mildly. But he was delaying now, evading; there was an issue still buried here, waiting like a trap.

And so, naturally, it was the High Priestess who finally spoke, to ask, almost on cue with his own thought, 'Is there more we should know?' As she spoke, the white owl lifted suddenly, wings briefly spread, and alighted gently on the shoulder of the countess. Who was Beatritz's mother, Blaise suddenly remembered. Signe de Barbentain reached up and gently stroked the bird.

They would learn, he knew. They were going to find out soon enough, when the whole world did. He didn't want it to happen that way. He turned from the countess back to Bertran de Talair, who was, after all, the man who was to have been killed, and the man he was working for.

'There are two more things that matter. One is the fee.' He drew a breath. 'Rudel Correze was to be paid two hundred and fifty thousand in gold for killing you.'

It was a matter of some real satisfaction to see that En Bertran, the worldly, infinitely sophisticated duke of Talair, was no more able to conceal his shock at the size of the figure than Blaise had been in the Correze garden earlier that night. Ariane de Carenzu put a hand to her mouth. The countess was behind Blaise. The High Priestess did not move, nor did her face show any expression at all. He hadn't expected it to.

'Who, then?' Bertran asked finally, his voice showing strain for the first time. 'That is the second thing?'

Blaise nodded. The old anger was in him again, the difficult, continuous pain that seemed to be endlessly rising from this source as if from an underground spring that never dried. He was blunt, because he could not be anything else.

'My father,' he said. 'In the name of the king of Gorhaut.'

And was undone, he later realized, looking back, by the next words spoken in the room.

'But that must be *terrible* for you,' said the countess of Arbonne with passion.

They all turned to her. She was looking at Blaise, the magnificent dark eyes wide. 'He used your own friend for this? Amongst all the possible assassins? How he must hate you! What could you ever have done to make your father hate you so?'

There was, it seemed to Blaise, a lifetime's worth of compassion in those eyes. And some of it now was for him, remarkably. It was less than two years, he thought suddenly, as a stray piece of the story came back, since her husband had died. And theirs was said to have been that rarest thing, a true love match. He turned, on impulse, to look at the niece, Ariane, with her own dark eyes and a suddenly wistful expression, and then at the daughter, the priestess, whose eyes were gone and whose face showed only an intense concentration. There had been another daughter, he vaguely remembered. She was dead. There was a bitter tale there, too, one he probably should know but did not. Affairs in Arbonne had not occupied him greatly in his growing years or his time among the armies and the tournaments.

He turned back to the old woman whose beauty had been the talk of the world in her bright day, and he saw that now, at the late twilight of her time, she had another kind of splendour to her, shaped of sorrows and hard-learned things. For all the staggering import of what he had just told them, it was of his own most private pain that she had first spoken. Not even Rudel, who knew him so well and who had subtlety and cleverness to spare, had thought through to what Signe de Barbentain had immediately understood.

It was quiet in the room; distantly they could hear the late, lingering noises of Carnival. Blaise wondered if she really wanted an answer to the question. He said, roughly, 'Some men do not like being denied. In anything. I suppose a son's denial will cut deeper than most. I was to enter the clergy of the god, follow my father among the Elders of Corannos. It began with that. There have been other things. I am not blameless.'

'Are you excusing him?' She asked it gravely.

Blaise shook his head. 'Not that.' He hesitated. 'We are a hard family with each other. My mother should not have died.'

'At your birth?'

It was strange, to be talking to the countess of Arbonne about these things, and yet, in another way, it seemed unexpectedly apt. He nodded.

She tilted her head slightly to one side, a distinctive gesture. 'Would she have made a difference, do you really think? In Gorhaut?'

'I like to believe so,' Blaise said. 'It isn't the kind of thing we can know.'

'The dead,' said Bertran de Talair quietly, 'can drive you hard.'

Blaise and the women turned to him. The duke looked oddly unfocused, inward, as if he'd not really meant to say that, as if it opened him more than he wanted. Blaise had another memory in this night of inexorable, unbidden remembrance — that dark stairway in Castle Baude very late at night, a flask of seguignac passing back and forth, the weary sadness in the face of the man who'd just seduced a woman he hadn't even known a fortnight before.

'They can drive you away from the living, as well,' said Beatritz the priestess, and in her voice Blaise heard an asperity that told him this was not a new matter between her and the duke. These people had all known each other a long time, he reminded himself. Bertran's mouth narrowed.

'A loving, sisterly thought,' he said coldly. 'Shall we discuss families again?'

'Twenty years and more down the road, I would name it an adult thought,' the High Priestess replied, unperturbed. 'Tell me, my lord, what heir would be governing your lands tonight if that arrow had killed you? And if Ademar of Gorhaut chooses to bring an army south, would you say we are stronger or weaker for the hatred between Miraval and Talair? Pray share your thoughts. You will forgive me,' she added with sharp sarcasm, 'for asking questions about today's world, not requesting sweet verses from two decades ago.'

'*Enough*,' said Signe de Barbentain sharply. 'Please. Or you will both make me feel that I have lived too long.'

It was Ariane who took them past the moment. 'More than enough,' she murmured, reaching for her wine. She took a sip and set the goblet down, not hurrying. 'This is a tiresome, ancient wrangle, and there seem to be new matters that require our consideration. First of all, our bearded friend.' The dark eyes turned to Blaise, appraisingly. 'Are you?' she asked bluntly. 'Are you a friend?'

He had actually been ready for this. 'I am a hired coran in the service of the duke of Talair,' he replied. The correct answer, the professional one.

'Not good enough,' said Ariane calmly. 'Not any more. Your father paid a quarter of a million in gold to kill your employer. You will, I am afraid, have to elect to be more than you say, or less. Just as Rudel Correze is not merely another assassin among many, just as his name and lineage create dilemmas out of the ordinary, so, too, do yours. Under the circumstances, rather more so. There may be a war. You know the implications of Gorhaut having ceded lands in the Treaty of Iersen Bridge at least as well as we do. The son of Galbert de Garsenc cannot remain in Arbonne as an ordinary coran any more than Bertran can pretend to be just another troubadour drinking and dicing in The Liensenne.' Her voice was even and precise, carrying the tones, in fact, of a commander of men on a battlefield.

And what she said was true. He knew it, even as the old, sour anger came back. It was happening again: wherever he went in the world, alone or in company, in secret or carrying the bright flourish of his reputation into battle or tournament, it seemed that his father was there, with him or before him, barring and bolting doorways, a shadow across the light.

Blaise became aware that his hands were clenched at his sides. Deliberately he forced them to relax. He took a deep breath and turned to the duke.

'I honour my contracts,' he said. 'I believe you know that.'

Bertran gave his small shrug. 'Of course I do, but that hardly matters any more. Men, even kings and clerics of the god, do not spend two hundred and fifty thousand to dispose of a singer whose song they feel has embarrassed them. The game has changed, Blaise, it is larger than you and I and our private dealings. You are a player of significance now, whether you want to be or not.'

Stubbornly, Blaise shook his head. 'I am a coran for hire. Pay me enough and I will serve you in war or peace. Turn me off and I'll seek other employment.'

'Stop mouthing rote words, Blaise de Garsenc. It ill becomes you to pretend you do not understand what is being said.' Beatritz, tall and implacable, spoke in a voice of grim adjudication. 'You are the son of the most important man in Gorhaut. The king is a tool in Galbert's hands, and we all know it. Your family, whatever their inner turmoil, have holdings more powerful than any other in that country, the more so since all the northern lords have been dispossessed by the Treaty. Will you stand before us, before the countess of Arbonne, and claim that the only difference between you and Luth of Baude is that you are better with a sword? Have you been running from your father all these years because you will not oppose him?'

'Not *oppose* him?' Blaise echoed, shocked into genuine fury. 'I have spent my life opposing him, at home and then beyond our walls. I hate everything the Treaty represents. I left Gorhaut so as not to live in a country so stripped of its pride. Everyone there knows it. I have made my statement. What else would you have me do? Ride home in fell wrath and declare myself the true king of Gorhaut?'

And stopped, abashed and appalled by the quality of the silence that followed. By the intent, focused, deeply revealing expressions of the two women and the man by the divan. Blaise swallowed with difficulty; his mouth was dry. He closed his eyes for a moment, hearing his own last words as a weirdly distorted echo in the chamber of his skull. Opening his eyes again he turned, slowly, his heart pounding now as if he'd been running a long distance, and looked towards the fire, to where the countess of Arbonne was standing, small and delicate, white-haired, still beautiful, one hand on the back of a chair for support, her astonishing eyes gazing into his, and smiling, smiling now, he saw, with the radiant, indulgent approval of a mother for a child who has passed, all unexpectedly, a test thought to be beyond him.

No one spoke. In the rigid stillness of that room in Tavernel on Midsummer Night, at the hinge, the axis, the heart of the year, the white owl suddenly lifted itself, gliding silently on wide wings to settle on Blaise's shoulder like a benediction or a burden beyond all common measure.

CHAPTER·8

The crimson-clad guard of Carenzu took Lisseut through the late night streets and left her, with another flawless bow, at the doorway of The Liensenne. She stood there for a moment, undecided, listening to the uproar inside, a confused flurry of emotions working within her. As she hesitated, debating whether she wanted the conviviality of the tavern itself or the relative intimacy of a chamber upstairs, the noise subsided and a thin, reedy voice came drifting through the window, singing a plangent hymn to Rian.

Lisseut walked quickly around the corner, went down the laneway in back of the tavern, opened the rear door and started up the stairs. She was truly not of a mind just then to listen to Evrard of Lussan in his pious mode. On the stairway and then in the corridor she passed couples in ardent clinches — most of the chambers had been booked and overbooked long ago — before coming to the doorway of a room that was always reserved for this week and had been for years.

She knocked. It wouldn't be locked, she knew, but she had caused some embarrassment two years ago by walking in on three men and a woman, at what turned out to be an extremely inopportune time. Her difficult relations with Elisse dated from that moment.

By way of reply to her knocking, a reflective, mellifluous voice could be heard singing:

Alone am I and sorrowful for love has gone away,
Gone away on a white horse and left me here to mourn . . .

She smiled and opened the door. Aurelian, indeed alone,

was sitting on one of the two beds, leaning back against the wall as he fingered his lute. His shirt was open at the throat and he had taken off his boots. His long legs extended well out over the side of the bed. He gave her a grave smile of welcome and, still singing, indicated with a motion of his head the table where an open bottle of wine stood, a number of glasses beside it. There was a rumpled scattering of clothes on the other bed and Lisseut saw blood on a shirt. She poured herself some wine, took a quick, much-needed drink, and carried the bottle over to refill Aurelian's goblet as well. There was one small window in the room. She walked to it and looked down. It overlooked the alley; there was no one below, but she could hear sounds from the street and Evrard's music drifting up from the downstairs room.

Aurelian continued his own quiet singing, another song, the same theme:

My heart is lonely and brim-full of grief
When I remember the nights that are past,
When my sweet love would offer me
Delights beyond all earthly measure . . .

'I've never liked that verse,' he said, breaking off abruptly, 'but it isn't much good trying to talk to Jourdain about anything he's written, is it? I don't even know why I keep singing it.'

'The tune,' said Lisseut absently, still gazing out the window. 'I've told you that before. Jourdain's always better at the music than the words.'

Aurelian chuckled. 'Fine. You be the one to tell him that.' He paused; behind her she could almost feel his scrutiny. 'You're too pensive for a Carnival night, my dear. You do know that Valery is recovering?'

'*What?*' She spun around. 'I didn't . . . he's all right! *How?*'

'The High Priestess was in Tavernel tonight, don't ask this ignorant troubadour why. Affairs among the great. Valery should probably tithe the goddess from what he earns of Bertran for the rest of his life. She was able to deal with the poison, and the wound itself was minor. He'll be fine, they told us at the temple. So most of us came back here in a wonderful mood. Can't you hear? There are a great many people you know celebrating downstairs, why don't you go down?'

'Why don't you?' She and Aurelian knew each other very well.

He reached for his goblet. 'There's only so much carousing I can take these days, even at Midsummer. Am I getting old, Lisseut?'

Lisseut made a face at him. 'I don't know, most venerable sage. Are you?' Aurelian was, in fact, only two or three years older than she was, but he'd always been the quietest of them all, slightly removed from the wilder elements of the troubadour life.

'Where is Remy?' she asked, a natural extension of that last thought. She looked at the second, disordered bed, and back to Aurelian.

He arched one eyebrow elaborately. 'Silly question. Rather depends on the hour, I'd imagine. He had a few assignations arranged.'

'How is he?'

'Wounded pride. Nothing more, but a good deal of that. He'll probably drink himself into a fury tonight. We'd all best tread warily for a few days.'

Lisseut shook her head. 'Not I. He owes me for a hat and a shirt. Not to mention my own pride. I've no intention whatever of being nice to him. I plan to tell him that he looked like a sulky little boy when En Bertran was chastising him.'

Aurelian winced. 'The women of Vezét . . . what is it, do you think? The olive oil? Something about its sweetness that makes you all so fierce, to compensate?'

From the room below, the insistent voice of Evrard penetrated, still invoking Rian in the same tired ways. Feeling suddenly tired herself, Lisseut smiled wanly, laid her glass aside and sat beside Aurelian on the bed, leaning against his shoulder. Obligingly, he shifted a little and put a long arm around her.

'I don't feel very fierce,' she said. 'It's been a difficult night.' He squeezed her arm. 'I didn't like that Arimondan,' she said after a moment.

'Or the northerner, I saw. But don't think about them. It has nothing to do with us. Think about your song. Alain's downstairs, by the way, happy as a crow in a grainfield. They're all talking about it, you know, even with everything else that happened.'

'Are they? Oh, good. I'm so happy for Alain.'

'Be happy for his joglar, Lisseut. And don't sign any contracts tomorrow without talking to me first — you're worth a great deal more now than you were this afternoon. Believe it.'

'Then why don't you offer me a job?' An old tease, though his news was genuinely exciting. Too much had happened though, she couldn't reach through to any clear emotion, even for something like this.

Characteristically, he chose to take her seriously. 'If I write a woman's song like Alain did, trust me, it will be yours. But for the rest, I'm not proud, my dear . . . I sing my own work still. I started on the roads as a joglar, and I'll end as one, I expect.'

She squeezed his knee. 'I wasn't being serious, Aurelian.' One of the first rank of the troubadours, Aurelian was probably the very best of the joglars, with the possible exception of Bertran's own Ramir, who was getting old now and on the roads far less than he used to be.

Polite applause floated up from below. A new performer began tuning his instrument. Aurelian and Lisseut exchanged wry glances of relief, and then laughed quietly together. She lifted her head and kissed him on the cheek. 'How many years in a row now?' she asked, knowing the answer very well.

'Together at Carnival? I am aggrieved and affronted that the nights are etched on my heart while you can't even remember. Four, now, my dear. Does that make us a tradition?'

'Would you like to be one?' she asked. His hand had moved upwards, stroking the nape of her neck. He had a gentle touch; he was a gentle man.

'I would like to know you and be your friend for the rest of my life,' said Aurelian quietly. His dark head came down and they kissed.

Feeling a physical sense of release, and a genuine comfort on a night when she needed exactly that, Lisseut slid slowly back down on the bed and laced her fingers through his black, thick hair, pulling him down to her. They made love as they had before, three years running on this night . . . with tenderness and some laughter, and an awareness of shaping a still place together amid the wildness outside and the music below and the wheeling of the summer stars about the axis of the year.

Some time later, her head on his chest, his arm around her again, the two of them listened to a voice singing one of the oldest tunes, Anselme of Cauvas's most tender song. In The Liensenne someone always came back to it on Midsummer Eve:

> When all the world is dark as night
> There is, where she dwells, a shining light . . .

Softly, not entirely certain why she was asking, Lisseut said, 'Aurelian, what do you know about Lucianna Delonghi?'

'Enough to avoid her. It's Lucianna d'Andoria now, actually, since she's remarried, but no one but her husband's family will ever call her that. I would not place any sizable wager on Borsiard d'Andoria's long life or domestic happiness.'

'Then why did he marry her? He's a powerful man, isn't he? Why would he invite the Delonghi into Andoria?'

Aurelian laughed quietly. 'Why do men and women ever do anything less than rational? Why do the teachings of the metaphysicians of the university not guide us all in our actions? Shall we call it the influence of Rian on hearts and souls? The reason we love music more than rhetoric?'

This wasn't what she wanted to know.

'Is she beautiful, Aurelian?'

'I only saw her once, at a distance.'

'And?'

'Remy could describe her better.'

'Remy is out bedding someone or getting drunk. You tell me.'

There was a short pause. The music of Anselme's sweet song drifted up to them.

'She is as beautiful as obsidian in new snow,' said Aurelian slowly. 'She glitters like a diamond by candlelight. There is fire in her like a ruby or an emerald. What other jewellery shall I give her? She offers the promise of danger and dark oblivion, the same challenge that war or mountains do, and she is as cruel, I think, as all of these things.'

Lisseut swallowed with some difficulty. 'You sound like Remy when he's had too much wine,' she said finally, trying to manage a tone of irony. She had never heard Aurelian speak like that before. 'And all this from a distance?'

'From the far end of a table in Faenna,' he agreed calmly. 'I would never have dared go nearer, but that was near enough. She is not for having, that one. Were it not an impiety I would say that the dark side of the goddess is in her. She destroys what she is claimed by.'

'But still she is claimed.'

'There is darkness in all of us, and desires we might prefer to deny by day.' He hesitated. 'I dream of her sometimes.'

Lisseut was silent, unsettled again, sorry now that she had asked. Her confusion of before seemed to have come back in all its jangling discord. They lay together, listening to the music from below, and eventually it was the music that calmed her, as it almost always did. Before it ended they were both asleep. She dreamt, lying in Aurelian's arms, of arrows, though, and heard, in her dream, Rudel Correze's laughter in a garden.

In the morning she would waken with sunlight in the window to find Aurelian gone. Sprawled across the other bed, snoring and sodden, still in his boots and clothes, would be Remy of Orreze. Lisseut would hesitate only a moment, then, offering devout and genuinely grateful thanks to Rian and Corannos both, she would take the basin of water Aurelian had thoughtfully filled for her before he left, and empty it over the sleeping, fair-haired troubadour who'd been her first lover. Then she would flee through the door and down the stairs, leaving his shrieks of outrage behind to awaken all those who yet slumbered in The Liensenne on a bright Midsummer's Day.

She would feel much, much better after that.

†

Every second or third year, in the absence of war or plague, it had been the custom of Guibor IV, count of Arbonne, to spend Midsummer Night in Tavernel at the Carnival, in homage to the goddess and to affirm for his people in the south that he was ever mindful of his duties to them and of the importance of the sea to Arbonne. Once, when young, he had even essayed the Boats and Rings on the river, plucking three garlands before missing the fourth and dousing himself in the river, to emerge with the booming good-natured laughter that was a part of why his country loved him.

On those nights, Signe de Barbentain reflected, lying in a room in the temple of Rian with a small fire to take away the chill that afflicted her now, even in summer, she'd had no concerns about the ancient saying in Tavernel that it was unlucky to lie alone on Midsummer Eve. She had lain with her husband, and the wild sounds outside had seemed part of a fabric of enchantment in the dark.

Tonight, though, she was alone and feeling afraid. Not for herself; her own summons to Rian would come when it came, and was unlikely to lie far off. She had long since come to terms with that. Her fear was for the land, for the dangerous rush of events that seemed to be gathering speed all around them.

New parts to the pattern had been discovered tonight and, starkly awake, looking at the flickering shapes that fire and guttering candle cast on the walls of her room, the countess of Arbonne tried again to deal with these new things. Gorhaut was coming south. There could be no honest denial of that truth any longer. Roban, the chancellor, had flatly predicted it the very same day word of the Treaty of Iersen Bridge had come to Barbentain. And now there was this purposeful, extravagant payment made for the death of Bertran de Talair. He might indeed have died tonight, Signe thought, suppressing a shiver. Had the clouds not come when they did, or had Beatritz not been in Tavernel and the bearded coran, Blaise, not known the arrow and the assassin, and so guessed the presence of syvaren on the head, Bertran could so easily have died, leaving Talair without a proper heir and Arbonne without a man it needed desperately.

And that same Gorhaut coran, Blaise, was a matter unto himself. For the fiftieth time, or the hundredth, Signe tried to weigh risks and gains in this gamble that Beatritz and Bertran had jointly undertaken in trying to bind Galbert de Garsenc's younger son to their cause. Roban had wanted nothing to do with it, had stalked grimly about the perimeter of the council room when the matter was first raised. She couldn't really blame him; Beatritz and Bertran, so unlike each other in most ways, yet shared a confidence in their own judgment and a penchant for taking risks that could be quite unnerving at times.

Blaise de Garsenc wasn't the kind of man she'd been led to expect, either. Rumour had told of a hardened mercenary, with a reputation won in the tournaments and the wars of the six countries over many years. According to Roban, she herself had presented the man with a laurel at the Autumn Fair in Lussan six years past; she didn't remember. It was hard to remember all the young men now. They seemed to remain as young as ever while she grew older all the time.

This man wasn't the grim northern warrior she'd anticipated. He had anger in him, yes, and easy enough to see, but he was clever, and more bitter than anything else, she judged. He had clearly been hurt in Portezza before he came here; there were rumours about that as well. They were probably true. Well, he would not be the first young man whose heart had been left lying on the carpet outside Lucianna Delonghi's bedchamber door, and he was not going to be the last.

In the darkness, Signe rubbed her aching fingers together under the bedcovers; she always seemed to be cold these days. In her time, all the young men had fallen in love with her in that same way. She had known how to deal with it, though. How to deny them the grace they had to be denied while leaving them their pride and even binding them more closely to her — and so, more importantly, to Guibor and the causes of Arbonne in the world. There was an art to the rituals of courtly love, and a purpose. She knew: she was the one who had defined and shaped both the purpose and the art.

Thirty years ago there might have been arts she would have practised to bind this Gorhaut coran to her. Not now, though; those were the tools and contrivances of younger women and, she judged — and her judgment was extremely good in these matters — with a different man. Not so soon after Lucianna Delonghi was done with him would Blaise of Gorhaut tread the path a woman's allure offered or besought.

Which left anger and hatred as the emotions they could most easily invoke, neither of which came readily to her hand, either long ago in her youth or now, with Guibor gone and the world a sad and empty place. It fell not neatly to her to invoke a son's hatred of his father to achieve her own ends, however desperately needful those ends might be.

And yet. And yet the man had spoken the words himself, with none of them to goad or induce them: *What else would you have me do? Ride home in fell wrath and declare myself the true king of Gorhaut?*

He hadn't meant it, hadn't known he might even possibly mean it, but the pain of Iersen Bridge was so raw in him, and so was his knowledge of his father's designs. Most of the world that mattered knew that Galbert de Garsenc's younger son had left Gorhaut denouncing the treaty his father had devised.

It might be possible. It might indeed be barely possible to find a rift here to widen north of the mountains in Gorhaut. She felt old though, and tired. She wished she could sleep. She didn't want to deal with matters of war. She wanted music and what warmth the sun could offer as summer ripened the vines. She wanted the gentler warmth of memories.

There came a very quiet tapping at her door. Only one person she could think of would be knocking here this late at night.

'Come in,' she said. The fire and the single taper were still burning. By the flickering of their light she saw her last living child open and then close the door behind her, entering the room in a pale night-robe, with a sure tread that belied her blindness. The white owl lifted and flew to one of the bedposts.

Signe remembered the first time she'd seen Beatritz after her daughter's eyes had been sacrificed. It was not a memory she cared to relive. Even knowing the ancient, most holy reasons and the power gained, it was hard for a mother to see her child marred.

Beatritz came to stand beside the bed. 'Did I wake you?'

'No. I'm thinking too much to be able to sleep.'

'And I. Chasing too many thoughts on Rian's night.' Her daughter hesitated. 'Is there room for me, or will I disturb you? I'm troubled tonight, and fearful.'

Signe smiled. 'Child, there is always room for you beside me.' She pulled the coverings back and her daughter lay down with her. Signe lifted one arm to enfold her and began to stroke the greying hair, remembering how soft it had been,

how dark and shining and soft when Beatritz was a child.
There had been two brothers and a sister and a father then.
There are only the two of us left, Signe thought, humming a tune
she'd almost forgotten. *Only the two.*

†

Walking back from the chapel of the god to Bertran's city
palace, Blaise made a determined effort to empty his mind.
There would be time in the morning and the days to come to
think, to try to deal with the revelations of this night and the
improbable, treacherous pathways that seemed to have been
opened up before him. It was very late now, and he was bone-
weary.

The streets were quiet; only occasional couples or small
groups of apprentices went by, carrying wine and crumpled
masks. Both moons were over west and the clouds were gone,
chased by the breeze. It was still some time before dawn
though, even on this shortest night of the year; overhead the
stars were bright. They were said to be the god's lights in
Gorhaut, Rian's here; Blaise wondered, for the first time, how
much that difference mattered in the end. They would still be
there, still as remote and coldly bright, whichever power mortal man linked them with. There were said to be lands —
fabled and mysterious — far to the south beyond deserts and
seas where different gods and goddesses entirely were worshipped. Did the same stars shine there, and as brightly?

Blaise shook his head. These were late-night thoughts
and useless ones. He was ready to fall into his bed and sleep
for hours. In fact, he could probably drop off here in the street
like the figures he could see sprawled in doorways. Most of
those figures were not alone, and he could guess what had preceded their slumbers.

He had gone earlier to the largest of the domed temples
of Rian, his first time ever inside such a place. He'd wanted
to see Valery before the night was done. They'd let him in
without demur; he'd expected to have to offer blood or some
such ritual, but nothing of the sort took place. Valery had
been sleeping. They'd let him stand in the doorway of the
coran's room and look in by candlelight. Blaise could see that
the shoulder had been carefully bandaged; as for the other

healing thing that had happened here, that he had no way of judging, or even comprehending. In his experience syvaren had always killed.

On his way out he had seen an assembled company of people, both men and women, gathered in the largest part of the temple under the high dome. A priestess in a white robe was leading them through a service. Blaise hadn't lingered. He'd gone from there to the nearest house of Corannos, washed his hands ritually at the entrance, with both the supplication and the invocation spoken, and had knelt on the floor in the small, bare, stone-walled coran's chapel in front of the frieze. He'd been alone there, for the first time in a long time, and he'd tried to let the deep, enveloping silence lead him back into the presence and serenity of the god.

It hadn't happened though, not this night. Even in the chapel his mind had kept on circling back, like a hunting bird above a field where a hare has been seen, to that room in the Carenzu palace when he had said what he had said. He hadn't been serious, not even remotely so; the words had been meant to make clear to them all how helpless he truly was, whatever he might feel about what his father and King Ademar had done in Gorhaut. But they hadn't heard it that way, and in the silence that followed his outburst, when the white bird had lifted itself and settled on his shoulder, Blaise had felt the knock of his heart like a fist on the door of destiny.

He felt it again now, walking home through the quiet disarray of the streets, and he tried to force his mind away from such thoughts. He was too tired, this was too large.

Young Serlo was on guard under the lamps burning at the entrance to the duke's city palace. He nodded at Blaise from inside the iron gates, looked to left and right up the street and moved to open the gates. They hadn't been locked — one of the traditions of Midsummer here — but after an assassination attempt, a guard at the main entrance had seemed appropriate. Bertran's corans, led by Valery of Talair, were very good; there had been no training needed here, and even some things for Blaise to learn. The ongoing skirmishes with the corans of Miraval had had more than a little to do with that. A long-simmering feud among neighbouring castles shaped its own rules of conflict, very different from the clashes of armies.

'I looked in on Valery,' Blaise said as he entered. 'He's sleeping easily.'

Serlo nodded. 'I'll sleep more easily myself when we've found out who shot that arrow,' he said. 'I only hope the goddess and the god have decreed an eternal place of pain for men who use syvaren.'

'I've seen worse things in war,' Blaise said quietly. He had another thought, but he was too tired to shape it properly. 'Good night,' he said.

'Good night.'

He heard the gate swing shut behind him. He would have felt better himself if a key had turned in the lock; he had his own views about the traditions of Arbonne. On the other hand, knowing what he knew about Bertran de Talair, it was unlikely in the extreme that the duke was in the palace tonight. Blaise shook his head. He went across the courtyard, through the inner doors, up the stairs and then down the corridor to the small room his status as a mercenary captain had earned him. Not a minor benefit; most of the corans slept together in dormitories or the great hall of Talair, with seniority merely placing one nearer the fire in winter or the windows in the summer heat.

He opened his door, almost stumbling with fatigue. He was aware of the scent of perfume an instant before he saw the woman sitting on his bed.

'You may remember,' said Ariane de Carenzu, 'that we had a number of matters to consider, you and I. We seem to have only dealt with the most public ones.'

'How did you get past the guard?' Blaise said. His pulse had quickened again. He didn't feel tired any more. It was odd how swiftly that could happen.

'I didn't. There are other ways into this palace. And into mine, if it comes to that.'

'Does Bertran know you are here?'

'I rather hope not. I doubt it. He was going out himself, I think. It *is* Midsummer, Blaise, and we *are* in Tavernel.' He knew what that meant; the singer had told him just before this woman's soldiers had come to lead him away.

Her hair was down, of course, it always was, and her delicate scent imbued the small chamber with subtle, unsettling

nuances. But Blaise de Garsenc had his own rules and his own
code, and he had broken those rules and that code last summer in Portezza, enmeshed in a world of woman's perfume. He
said, 'I know where we are, actually. Where is the duke of
Carenzu?' He meant it to be wounding; he wasn't sure why.

She was unruffled, at least to his eye, by candlelight. 'My
husband? In Ravenc Castle with En Gaufroy, I suspect. They
have their own particular traditions at Midsummer and I'm
afraid women aren't a part of them.'

Blaise had heard about Gaufroy de Ravenc. His young
bride was said to be still a virgin after almost three years of
marriage. He hadn't heard the same sort of stories about
Thierry de Carenzu, but then he hadn't asked, or been much
interested.

'I see,' he said heavily.

'No you don't,' said Ariane de Carenzu sharply, irony and
amusement gone from her voice. 'I don't think you see at all.
You will have just now concluded that I am wandering in the
night because my husband's preference in bed partners is for
boys. You will be deciding that I am to be understood in the
light of that fact. Hear me then: I am here of my own choice,
and no taste or orientation of the man my father married me
to would affect that decision, short of physical restraint.'

'So pleasure is all? What of loyalty?'

She shook her head impatiently. 'When the day comes
that a man and woman of our society may wed because they
choose each other freely, then talk to me of loyalty. But so
long as women are coinage in a game of castles and nations,
even in Arbonne, then I will admit of no such duty and will
dedicate my life to changing the way of things. And this has
nothing, nothing at all to do with Thierry's habits or preferences.' She stood up, moving between him and the candle,
her vivid face suddenly in shadow. 'On the other hand, I know
nothing of your own habits or tastes. Would you prefer me to
leave? I can be gone quietly the same way I came in.'

'Why should it matter if you are quiet or not?' he said,
stubbornly holding to his anger. 'We're in Arbonne aren't we?
In Tavernel at Midsummer.'

He couldn't read her eyes, with the one flickering candle
behind her, but he saw again the impatient motion of her

head. 'Come, Blaise, you are cleverer than that. Discretion is at the heart of all of this. I am not here to bring shame to anyone, least of all myself. There is no public duty I owe my lord or my people in which I have been found wanting. I dare say that, and I know it to be true. Thierry has my respect and I am quite certain I have his. The duties I owe myself are different. What happens alone at night between two people who are adult about it need not impact upon the world in any way that matters.'

'Then why bother? Why bother to be together? Has your Court of Love ruled on that?' He meant to sound sardonic, but it didn't come out that way.

'Of course it has,' she said. 'We come together to glory in the gift of life the goddess gave us . . . or the god, if you prefer. Sometimes the best things in our lives come to us of a night and are gone in the morning. Have you never found that?'

He had found something very near to that, in fact, but the morning's ultimate legacy had been lasting pain. He almost said as much. There was a silence. In the shadows, her silhouetted form might almost have been Lucianna's. He could imagine the same feel to her black hair and remember the light touch that traced a path along . . .

But no. Remembering the past was where his anger lay. This woman had done him no wrong that he knew of, and was, by her own lights, honouring him with her presence here. He swallowed.

She said, 'It is all right. You are tired. I did not mean to offend you. I will leave.'

Blaise could not afterwards have said what sequence of movements brought them together. As he gathered her in his arms he was aware that he was trembling; he had not touched a woman since Rosala, and that night, too, carried its heavy burden of anger and self-reproach, both during and afterwards. Even as he lowered his mouth to Ariane's, breathing deeply of the scent that clung to her, Blaise was bracing himself to resist the alluring ways of yet another sophisticated woman of the south. Lucianna had surely taught him that much; if he had learned nothing from a spring and summer in Portezza he would be a man living an utterly wasted life. Blaise was prepared, defended.

He was not. For where Lucianna Delonghi had used love
and lovemaking as instruments, weapons in subtle, intricately
devised campaigns, a pursuit of pleasure and power through
binding men's spirits helplessly to her, Blaise was given a gift
that night in Tavernel of a strong soul's lovemaking, without
eluding, fierce as wind, with grace yet at the heart of it and
needs of her own, offered honestly and without holding back.

And in the turning, interwoven movements of that night
upon his bed in the city palace of Bertran de Talair, Blaise
found, for a short while in the darkness after the one candle
burned out, an easing of his own twin pains, the old one and
the new, and an access to sharing hitherto denied him. He
offered her what he had to give, and even, towards the end,
with irony pushed back far away, some of the things he'd
learned in Portezza, the skills and patterns of what men and
women could do lying with each other when trust and desire
came together. Accepting what he offered, laughing once,
breathlessly as if in genuine surprise, Ariane de Carenzu
bestowed upon him in turn something rich and rare, as a tree
that flowers at night without a leaf, and Blaise was, for all the
bitterness that lay within him, yet wise enough and deep
enough to accept it as such and let her sense his gratitude.

In the end he slept, holding her in his arms, breathing
the scent of her, slaked of hunger and need, returned to his
weariness as to a garden, through the thickets and brambles
of his history.

He woke some time later, disturbed by a sound outside in
the street. She was still with him, head on his chest, her dark
hair spread like a curtain to cover them both. He moved one
hand and stroked it, marvelling.

'Well,' said Ariane. 'Well, well, well . . .'

He laughed quietly. She had meant him to laugh. He
shook his head. 'This has been the longest night I can remember.' It was hard to believe how much had happened, in so
many different ways, since they had arrived in Tavernel in the
afternoon and walked through the thronged streets to The
Liensenne.

'Is it over?' Ariane de Carenzu asked in a whisper. Her
hand began moving slowly, fingernails barely brushing his skin.
'If the songs tell true we have until the lark sings at dawn.'

He felt desire returning, inexorable as the first beginning of a wave far out at sea. 'Wait,' he said awkwardly. 'I have a question.'

'Oh dear.'

'No, nothing terrible or very difficult. Just something about Arbonne, about people we know. Something I should have asked about a long time ago.'

Her hand was still, resting on his thigh. 'Yes?'

'What is it between Talair and Miraval? The hatred there?' It was true, what he'd said, what he'd come to realize earlier tonight: there was something unnatural about the refusal to learn that had carried him through his months here in Arbonne.

Ariane was silent for a moment, then she sighed. 'That *is* a terrible question, actually, and a difficult one. You'll have me chasing my own memories.'

'Forgive me, I —'

'No, it is all right. I have been thinking about them all in any case. The memories are never far away. They have shaped so much of what we are.' She hesitated. 'Have you at least heard of Aelis de Barbentain, who became Aelis de Miraval?'

He shook his head. 'I'm sorry. No.'

'The youngest child of Signe and Guibor. Heir to Arbonne because her sister Beatritz went to the goddess and the two brothers died of plague quite young. Wedded to En Urté de Miraval when she was seventeen years old. My cousin.' She hesitated, but only briefly. 'Bertran's lover, and I think the only real love of his life.'

There was a silence again. In it, Blaise heard once more, as if the speaker was actually in the room with them, Bertran's words on a dark stairway in the depths of another night: *The god knows, and sweet Rian knows I've tried, but in twenty-three years I've never yet found a woman to equal her.*

Blaise cleared his throat. 'I think, actually, that last will be true. He said something to me in Baude Castle that would fit . . . what you just said.'

Ariane lifted her head to look at him. 'He must have been in a strange mood to say anything about it at all.'

Blaise nodded his head. 'He was.'

'He must have trusted you, too, oddly enough.'

'Or known the words would mean nothing to me.'

'Perhaps.'

'Will you tell me the story? It's time I began to learn.'

Ariane sighed again, feeling ambushed almost by this entirely unexpected question. She had been thirteen that year, a bright, quick, laughing spirit, still a child. It had taken her a long time to recapture laughter afterwards, and the child in her had been lost forever the night Aelis died.

She was a grown woman now, with complex roles on the world stage and the burdens that came with those: queen of the Court of Love, daughter of one noble house, wedded into another. She was not a risk-taker by nature, not like Beatritz or Bertran; she thought things through more slowly before she moved. She would not have devised the scheme they had for this son of Galbert de Garsenc, nor had she approved when she was told of it. But by now she had made her own decisions about this man whose hard shell of bitterness so clearly served, like armour on a battlefield, to defend something wounded underneath.

So she told him the story, lying beside him after love on a bed in Bertran's palace, travelling back to the rhythm and cadence of her own words into the past as darkness outside slowly gave way to grey dawn. She told him all of it — quietly spinning the tale of sorrow from that long-ago year — save for one strand of the old weaving, the one thing she never told. It was not truly hers, that last secret, not hers to offer anyone, even in trust or by way of binding or in great need.

In the end, when she was done and fell silent, they did not make love again. It was difficult, Ariane had always found, to sustain any desires of her own in the present day when Aelis was remembered.

†

Elisse of Cauvas was vain, with, perhaps, some reason to be. She'd a ripe figure and a pleasing voice to go with the long-lashed, laughing eyes that made men feel wittier and more clever in her company than they normally did. Coming from the town that prided itself on being the birthplace of the first of the troubadours, Anselme himself, she often felt that she'd been destined to be a joglar and follow the life of the road, castle to castle, town to town. She considered herself miraculously released — and counted her blessings almost every morning when she awoke — from the tedium and premature ageing she associated with the life she might have expected as an artisan's daughter. Marry the apprentice, survive — if you were fortunate — too many childbrirths in too few years, struggle to feed a family and keep a leaking roof intact and the cold lash of the winter wind from coming in through chinks in the walls.

Not for her, that life. Not now. With perhaps a single irritating exception she was almost certainly the best-known of the women joglars following the musicians' circuit about Arbonne. As for that single exception, until very recently the only recognition Lisseut of Vezét ever received seemed to occur because her name was similar to Elisse's! Jourdain had told an amusing story about that a year ago, and they'd laughed together over it.

The latest touring season had changed things, though, or started to change them. In two or three towns and a highland castle in the hills near Götzland she and Jourdain had been asked their opinion of the wonderful music being made by Alain of Rousset and the girl who was his new joglar. And then, outrageously, Elisse had been asked by a fatuous village reeve, after a performance in a wealthy merchant's home in Seiranne, how the olive trees were faring back home in Vezét. When she realized what the man's mistake was, who he took her for, she'd been so furious she'd had to abandon the merchant's hall for a time, leaving Jourdain to amuse the guests alone while she regained her composure.

It wouldn't do, she thought, lying in an extremely comfortable bed on Midsummer Night, to dwell upon such things, or the unsettling success Lisseut had had with Alain's song earlier that evening — a frankly mediocre piece, Elisse had decided. Where had Jourdain's wits been, she thought, fighting a returning fury, when that glorious opportunity had arisen? Why hadn't he been quick enough to propose his own music for Ariane and the dukes, with Elisse to sing it? Only later, on the river, in the silly games men insisted upon playing, had her own troubadour, her current lover, pushed himself forward — to become an object of general amusement shortly afterwards, as he splashed into the water downstream.

Though 'current lover' might — it just possibly might — be an inappropriate phrase after tonight. Elisse stretched herself, cat-like, and let the bedsheet fall away, leaving her mostly uncovered in her nakedness. She turned her head towards the window, where the man she'd been lying with in the aftermath of love was now sitting on the ledge, picking at her lute. She didn't really like her lovers leaving her side without a word, as this one had, and she certainly didn't like other people handling the lute . . . but for this man she was prepared to make exceptions, as many exceptions and in whatever dimensions as proved necessary.

She'd brought the lute because she hadn't been entirely sure what was wanted from her. When Marotte, the owner of The Liensenne, had approached her with a whispered confidence earlier in the evening, telling her she'd be anxiously expected — those were his exact words — in the largest of the upstairs rooms after the third of the temple night chimes had sounded, Elisse had wondered if her singing days with Jourdain might possibly be winding to their close.

When she tapped at the room door though, wearing her best tunic, with a flower in her hair for Midsummer, the man who opened it gave her a slow, appraising smile that made her knees feel weak. It *was* Midsummer, and very late at night. She ought to have known it was not an audition she was being invited to. And, being honest, she didn't at all mind; there were many avenues to success in Arbonne for a woman of passion and spirit and some confidence in herself, and one of them was in this room.

One of them, in fact, was sitting on the window ledge, watching the eastern sky, his back to her, idly making music on her lute. He played very well, and when he lifted his voice — so softly she had to strain to hear, as if the words weren't meant for her at all — it was oddly sorrowful, though the song was not.

The song was his own, a very old one. A charming enough tune, Jourdain had dismissively called it once, tired of the endless springtime requests for it, even after all these years, and in preference to his own, far more musically intricate shapings.

Elisse, listening now to the quiet music and words, was prepared to disagree completely, if required — to regard this as the quintessence of all troubadour love songs. Lying in the wide bed alone, though with no complaint to offer about the hour just past, she had a feeling that her opinion would not be solicited, that it was, in fact, irrelevant. The man on the window ledge, she realized, had probably forgotten she was here.

That bothered her, but not unduly. In another man it might have been infuriating, cause enough to send her storming from the room, but this one was a different proposition from any other in her world, and Elisse of Cauvas was perfectly willing to take her cues from him, and only hope she was quick enough and, well, enjoyable enough, to make an impact of her own. She had never failed to do so before.

So she lay quietly and listened to Bertran de Talair play her lute and offer his own song to the coming of dawn above the empty street. She knew the words; everyone knew the words.

> *Even the birds above the lake*
> *Are singing of my love,*
> *And even the flowers along the shore*
> *Are growing for her sake.*
>
> *All the vines are ripening*
> *And the trees come into bud,*
> *For my love's footsteps passing by*
> *Are summoning the spring.*
>
> *Rian's stars in the night*
> *Shine more brightly over her,*
> *The god's moon and the goddess's*
> *Guard her with their light.*

It really was an almost childishly simple tune, with words to match, Elisse thought. Jourdain was right, of course; compared to the interwoven melodies he made her practise endlessly this was something a completely untrained person could sing, hardly worthy of the long apprenticeship demanded of the joglars of Arbonne.

Which made it even odder how near to tears she suddenly seemed to be, listening. Elisse couldn't remember the last time she'd cried, except in anger or frustration. It was because of Midsummer, she decided, and the extraordinary events of tonight, not least of which had been the long-imagined, though never really hoped for invitation to this room.

She reached for the pillow he had lain upon beside her in the dark and held it to herself for comfort, as the sweet refrain returned and brought the song to an end. The woman it celebrated was dead, she reminded herself, dead more than twenty years ago, before Elisse had even been born. She was dead, and would have been over forty years old by now had she lived, Elisse calculated. This wasn't real competition, she decided, she could allow these dawnsong memories without troubling herself. The dead were gone; she was the woman with him now, the one lying in his bed as Midsummer Night came to its end. The advantages, surely, were all hers. Elisse smiled, waiting for the moment when he would turn to see her waiting, her body offered to his sight, and for whatever else he wanted of her.

At the window, Bertran de Talair watched darkness surrender to grey in the streets below and then saw the first pale hues of morning streak the sky in the east. He wondered, idly, hopelessly, just how many dawns he had seen in this way, with the wrong woman waiting for him to come back to her in a bed he had abandoned. He wasn't going back to the bed. He pushed the very thought away, closing his eyes, letting his mind circle back, faithfully, to the ending of his song.

> Even the birds above the lake
> Are singing of my love,
> And even the flowers along the shore
> Are growing for her sake.

Dawn was breaking, the day was coming. There would be much to do, a world of complex things that demanded to be done. He opened his eyes, feeling her slipping away again as he did, slipping away in mist, in memory, with the child in her arms.

PART III

Autumn

CHAPTER·9

On the bright, mild morning in autumn when her life changes forever, Rosala de Garsenc is returning carefully from her favourite walk along the sloping, tree-lined path from the water mill back to the castle when she sees her father-in-law waiting for her astride his horse in the open space in front of the drawbridge.

Her breath quickening with the first stirrings of apprehension, she places her hands protectively in front of her rounded belly but resolutely does not alter her pace. Her husband is away at the court, and Galbert will know that.

'Good morrow, my lord,' she says as she comes slowly up to the courtyard. The drawbridge of the castle is down; inside the forecourt a handful of corans are noisily practising with quarterstaves, beyond them serfs are unloading sacks of harvested grain watched carefully by the reeve. It is a bustling tithe day at Garsenc Castle. No one is close enough though to overhear anything the two of them might say to each other.

Galbert de Garsenc, massive and imposing in his riding clothes, makes no immediate reply to her greeting, looking stonily down upon her from his horse. He ought to have dismounted, of course, simple courtesy to his son's wife demands that; his failure to do so is a first signal, an attempt to intimidate. Rosala knows by now that almost everything this man does is meant as a means of control.

'Will you come in?' she says, as if there is nothing untoward in his manner at all. 'You must know that Ranald is away, but I will gladly do what I may to make you comfortable.' She smiles, but only briefly; she will not abase herself before this man, she has sworn it to herself.

He jerks his reins to make the horse dance a little, quite close to her. She stands motionless; she certainly isn't afraid of horses, and she is quite sure, for the obvious reason, that her father-in-law will not risk doing her any physical harm just now.

Galbert clears his throat. 'Get in,' he says, the celebrated voice icy cold. 'Get into the castle immediately before you shame us further. I heard tell that you were walking abroad but refused to credit it. I came to see for myself, certain that the rumours must be idle and false. Instead I find you brazening about obscenely, parading in your condition before the serfs, exactly as I was told. Are you utterly corrupt that you do such things?'

She had actually thought it might be this. It is almost a relief to have been right, to know from what direction the latest attack is coming.

'You wrong me and cheapen yourself,' she says as calmly as she can manage. 'I am doing what the Savaric women have done for generations. You know it, my lord, do not feign otherwise. The women of my family have never kept to their rooms while carrying, they have always taken daily walks on the family estates.'

He jerks the reins again; the horse dances uneasily. 'You are a Garsenc now, not a Savaric.'

'False. I will always be a Savaric, my lord. Do not deceive yourself. What I was born to may not be taken from me.' She hesitates. 'It may only be added to.' That last is meant as conciliation; with Ranald away she really does not want a confrontation with his father. 'My husband and lord knows I am not lingering abed; I told him of my family tradition when we first learned I was carrying. He raised no objection.'

'Of course he didn't. Ranald is beneath contempt. A fool beyond words. He shames our ancestors.'

Rosala smiles sweetly. 'He did ask me to tell him if ever you spoke disparagingly of him to me. Would these words fit such a description?'

Be careful, she tells herself then. *This is a man who will not be crossed.* But it is hard to yield spinelessly to him; so very hard, remembering her own father and her home, to cringe before the High Elder, flush with his new ascendancy.

She sees Galbert check a too-swift reply. Ranald has a temper, and Blaise too, to a lesser degree. The father is as ice compared to both of them — his anger and his hate kept channelled, ruthlessly controlled.

'You are deliberately insolent,' he says. 'Shall I whip you for it?' His voice is incongruously mild speaking the words, as if he were merely offering to walk her about the grounds or summon a servant to her aid.

'Indeed,' Rosala says hardily. 'A worthy thought. You come here out of alleged concern for the child I carry, and then offer me a beating. A prudent course, my lord.'

His turn to smile. His smile frightens her more than anything else. She tries not to let that show.

'I can wait,' says Galbert de Garsenc softly. 'You are not a child. Discipline can be delayed and you will still know the cause. I am a patient man. Get into the castle now, though, or I will be forced to handle you in front of the corans and the servants. You carry the first of the new generation of the Garsenc line and you will not be permitted to jeopardize that with this folly.'

Rosala does not move. He is not going to hurt her. She knows that. A kind of reckless giddiness rises in her, a surge of hatred she cannot quite master. 'Forgive me my ignorance, and that of my family,' she says. 'You are clearly to be deferred to in these matters, my lord. You know so much about helping women survive childbirth.' A dangerous cut, one she might truly be made to pay for later. Galbert's first wife died, hours after giving birth to Blaise, and two subsequent wives did not survive their first confinements in this castle, with the children stillborn.

She has meant to wound, wisely or no, but nothing in his face shows that she has done so. 'As I said,' he murmurs, still smiling, 'a whipping may be given at any time.'

'Of course,' she replies. 'I live entirely at the mercy of your kindness, my lord. Though indeed, if you wound and scar me too greatly it might spoil the king's pleasure when he chooses to send for me, might it not?'

She hadn't planned to say anything like that; it has slipped out. She isn't sorry though, now that the words are spoken. The thought, and the fear behind it, are never far from her.

She sees the High Elder react for the first time. She wasn't even thought to have been aware of this aspect of things, she realizes. It is almost amusing: women are imagined to troop like so many sheep through the court, eyes down, dull minds shuttered, oblivious to whatever nuances might be passing about them. She could laugh, were her fears not so tangible.

Galbert de Garsenc's smile deepens now, the smooth-shaven, fleshy face creasing into something truly unpleasant. 'You are hungry for that moment, I see. You are already in lust. You would prefer to kill the child that you might come panting and hot to Ademar's bed the sooner, would you not? You have all the vile corruption of women in you, especially those of your lineage. I knew it when first I ever saw you.'

Rosala stiffens. She feels dizzy suddenly. The walk uphill, the bright sunlight overhead, and now this foul, streaming torrent of abuse. She actually wishes Ranald were home; his presence might have served to temper or at least deflect onto himself some of Galbert's viciousness. She has brought this upon herself, she thinks shakily. Better to have swallowed pride, to have meekly gone within. How can she, alone and at his mercy, possibly fight this man?

She looks up at him, a sickness within her. Her family is as good as this one, she tells herself fiercely, or so very nearly as to make no difference. She knows what has to be said now. Fighting for self-control, she speaks.

'Hear me. I will kill myself before I let him touch me. Do not ever doubt that this is so. And do not try to deny that you have encouraged the king's shameful thoughts, contemptuous of your son or any true sense of family honour, seeking only to bind a weak man more tightly to your use with whatever tools you may find. My lord, I am not a tool that will ever fit your hand. I will die before Ademar ever lies with me.'

She watches his face narrowly, and adds, 'Or you, my lord High Elder of Corannos. I will end my life before I suffer you to lay a hand or a lash upon this white flesh you dream about in the dark of the god's house at night.' A shaft loosed wildly that one, but she sees it hit, squarely. Galbert's ruddy face goes suddenly white, his eyes creasing to slits and flicking away from hers for the first time. Rosala feels no triumph, only a renewed wave of nausea.

She turns abruptly away and begins to walk across the drawbridge into the forecourt. The corans have stopped their duelling, their attention caught by something in the manner of the two of them here outside the walls. She holds her head high and walks with what composure she can achieve.

'My lady Rosala,' Galbert says from behind her, his voice raised slightly. She had known he would call her. He would need to have the final word. His nature will not permit otherwise. She thinks of not turning, of continuing on, but the corans have heard him call her. What she might do at some risk privately she dares not do in public: she might defy him to a certain point, but open shame he will not allow. A woman can be killed for that in Gorhaut.

She stops on the drawbridge and turns slowly back to look at him. After, she will remember that moment, the sun high, a breeze stirring the red and golden leaves of the chestnut trees along the avenue, birdsong in the branches, the stream beyond, glinting blue. A glorious autumn day.

'I wonder,' says Galbert de Garsenc, lowering his voice, moving the horse nearer, 'has your dear husband told you of our latest agreement? He has probably neglected to, in that forgetful way of his. We have decided that if you should bear a son it is mine. Ah! You seemed surprised, lady Rosala! It is just as I thought, the careless lad has not informed you. A boy is promised to Corannos, a daughter you may keep; a daughter is no use to me immediately, though I am sure I will devise a purpose for her later.'

Rosala is actually afraid she is going to faint. The sun swings in an erratic arc in the blue sky. She takes a stumbling, sidelong step to keep her balance. Her heart is a thudding hammer in her breast. She tastes blood; she has bitten through her lip.

'You . . . you would deprive your family of an heir?' she stammers, her brain stunned, refusing to believe what she has just heard.

'No, no, no, not necessarily.' He chuckles now, all benign good humour for the watching eyes of those inside the forecourt. 'Though we need another Elder in our family at least as much as we need an heir in this castle. Ranald's brother' — he never speaks Blaise's name — 'was to have followed me to the god. A great deal of our future depended upon that. His refusal has marred my planning, put me in a difficult position, but if you present me with a boy matters may yet be remedied. I will, of course, delay final consecration for a time, to judge how best to make use of the child — here at Garsenc or in the god's house. There will be many matters to be considered, but I daresay you will help me by having other children, dear daughter-in-law. And if you do not — seeing as it *did* take some time to conceive this one — why then I imagine Ranald could find a second wife who will. I am not greatly concerned on that score. And I must confess, I am looking forward to attending to a grandson's education and upbringing person- ally. I pray you, do not disappoint me, lady Rosala. Bear a strong boy child for me to take back to Corannos.'

She can say nothing at all. She seems to have lost the power of speech. She can scarcely stand. She feels suddenly ex- posed, naked in this place to the indifferent or mildly curious scrutiny of her household corans and the serfs of the estate.

'You really ought to go in now,' says Galbert kindly. 'You do not look at all well. You ought to be in your bed, my child. I would escort you there myself but I am afraid I have no time to linger for such domestic intimacies. The press of affairs demands my attention back at court. I do trust you have taken my meaning, though, and I will not have to come again?'

He turns, not waiting for any reply, lifting one hand to her that the corans might note his salute; it is the hand that holds his whip, though. That will not be an accident; noth- ing with this man is an accident. She sees that he is smiling as he rides away.

Inside the castle a short time later, alone in her suite of rooms, white-knuckled hands gripping each other, Rosala de Garsenc realizes, without knowing the actual moment of making her decision, that she is going to leave.

Galbert made a mistake, she thinks. He never meant to tell her about these plans, he must have known how she would feel about them; she had angered him though, revealed an awareness of his thoughts, and he replied rashly, to frighten and wound her, to have the final word.

She doesn't know how she is going to do it, she only knows she will not stay and surrender her child to that man.

I am at war now, she thinks, realizing that her only possible advantage is that she knows it and Galbert might not. Inside her, as if in response, the baby kicks hard against her ribs for the first time that morning.

'Hush,' she whispers. 'Hush, my love. It will not happen. Fear no harm, for none shall find you. Wherever in the world your father is, whether he ever comes to shelter you or no, I will guard you, little one. I swear it upon my life, and yours.'

†

Blaise was thinking of the child as the men of Talair rode north through the cool breezes of autumn in Arbonne: of Aelis de Miraval's son, and Bertran's. Since Ariane had told him the tale that Midsummer night three months ago, he had thought about it more often than he would have expected to, unable not to gaze curiously at such times at the man his own father had paid a quarter of a million in gold to have killed.

A tragedy had unfolded here some twenty-three years ago, and the effects of it were still rippling through Arbonne today. He remembered Ariane's quiet, measured voice telling him the tale as dawn broke over the littered streets and alleys of Tavernel.

'As I told you just now,' she had said, 'discretion is everything in love. My cousin Aelis had none, though she was very young, and that might be considered an excuse. There was something uncontrolled in her, something too fierce. Hatred and love drove her hard, and she was not a woman to accept her fate, or work within walls built to house her.'

'Neither are you,' Blaise remembered saying. 'What was the difference?'

She had smiled at that, a little sadly, and had not answered for a time.

'The difference, I suppose, is that I saw what she did, and what followed upon it. Aelis is the difference in my own life. She told her husband, you see. She hoarded the truth for a last, bitter swordstroke — with its own slow, killing poison, if you will. When the priestess who had come to her said she was not going to live they brought Urté to her confinement bed. He was sorrowful, I think. I have always thought he was genuinely in sorrow, though perhaps more for the loss of the

power she offered him than anything else. Aelis had no softness in her though, she was all pride and recklessness, even on
her deathbed. She pushed herself up in the bed and she told
Urté the child was Bertran de Talair's.'

'How do you know this?'

'I was there,' Ariane had said. 'As I say, that moment
altered my own life, shaped what I think I have become.
Those words she spoke to Urté changed our world, you know.
We would live in a differently ordered country had Aelis not
taken her vengeance.'

'Vengeance for what?' Blaise had asked, though he was
beginning, slowly, to understand.

'For not being loved,' Ariane had said simply. 'For being
valued at too much less than she was. For being exiled to the
dank, grim fastness of Miraval from the lights and laughter of
her father's court.'

He had thought it might be that. Once he would have
scorned such a thing as beneath contempt, another woman's
vanity marring the unfolding of the world. It had surprised
him a little that he didn't still see it that way; at least that
night in Tavernel, with Ariane de Carenzu in his arms he
didn't. It had occurred to him then, with a shock he had tried
to mask, that this new pattern of thought might be his own
deepest rebellion against his father.

'I can guess what you are thinking,' Ariane had said.

'No, I don't think you can,' he had replied without elab-
orating. 'What did Urté do?' he'd asked, pushing his own family affairs towards the back of his mind. There had been a
sadness in Blaise that night, hearing the old tale. The question was a formality. He was sure he knew what En Urté de
Miraval had done.

Ariane's answer had surprised him, though. 'No one
knows for certain. And that is the heart of Bertran's tragedy,
Blaise. There *was* a son born before Aelis died. I watched the
priestess bring him into the world. I heard him cry. Then Urté,
who had been waiting, took him away, and not Aelis nor the
priestess, and certainly not I at thirteen years of age, had the
power to stop him within his own walls. I remember how his
face changed when she told him who the father was; that I
will never forget. And I remember him bending down over

her, as she lay there, torn and dying, and whispering something into her ear that I could not hear. Then he left the room with Bertran's child crying in his arms.'

'And killed it.'

She shook her head. 'As I say, no one knows. It is likely, probable, knowing Urté, knowing how such a child would have been heir to so much . . . to Barbentain, and so to Arbonne itself, as Aelis's child. It is likely, but we do not know. Bertran doesn't know. Not with certainty. If the child lived, if it lives now, only Urté de Miraval knows where it is.'

Blaise had seen it clearly then, the harsh, ugly shape of Bertran's pain. 'And so Urté could not be killed all these years — cannot be killed now — because any possibility of finding the truth or the child will die with him.'

Ariane had looked up at him in the muted grey light of the room and nodded her head in silence. Blaise had tried to imagine what it would have been like to be thirteen years old and to have lived through such a night, to have it lying, like a weight of stones, in your own past.

'I would have killed him regardless,' he had said after a long time.

And she had answered only, 'You and Bertran de Talair are very different men.'

Riding north beside the river with Duke Bertran and the corans of Talair to the Autumn Fair in Lussan, Blaise thought again about that remark. It was very nearly the last thing she'd said to him that night before they'd dressed and she'd gone from his room alone, cloaked and hooded, with only a mild, chaste kiss of farewell in first grey light of day.

What made men so different from each other? Accidents of birth, of upbringing, of good fortune or tragedy? What sort of man would Blaise himself have become had he been the older son, the heir to Garsenc, and not the younger one for whom an unwanted destiny among the clergy of the god had been ordained by his father? What if his mother had lived, the question Signe de Barbentain had asked? Would she have made any difference? What if Galbert de Garsenc had somehow been a different, gentler, less power-obsessed man?

Though that last speculation was impossible, really; it was simply not possible to imagine his father as anything other than what he was. Galbert seemed absolute to Blaise, like a force of nature or some gigantic monument of the Ancients, one that spoke to nothing but power and had been in the world almost forever.

Bertran de Talair, too, was a younger son. Only the early death of his brother had brought him to the dukedom and set two great houses so harshly against each other. Before that he had followed the usual course: a sword for hire in battle and tournament, seeking fortune and a place in the world. The same path Blaise de Garsenc was to take, starting from Gorhaut, years after. The same path, that is, if one left out the music.

But the music could not be left out. It defined Bertran, just as it defined Arbonne, Blaise found himself thinking. He shook his head, almost amused at himself. Half a year now he had been here, and already his mind seemed to have this tendency to slide down channels it had never known before. Resolutely he pulled his wandering thoughts back to the present, to the high road of Arbonne built by the Ancients between the river and the grainfields to the east.

Looking ahead, squinting through the dust, Blaise was drawn from reverie. He was riding near the rear of the column, behind the long baggage-train of goods they were escorting to the fair — mostly barrels of Talair wine. He saw Bertran and Valery riding back towards him. Their pace was measured, but just quick enough to make him aware that something was happening at the front of the long column. Beyond the two of them he could make out banners in the distance. They seemed to be about to overtake someone. There was nothing in that, all the roads were crowded on the way to a fair, and the high road most of all. He raised his eyebrows as the two men came up and neatly turned their horses to fall into stride on either side of Blaise.

'Diversions, diversions,' said Bertran airily. He had a smile on his face that Blaise recognized by now; it made him uneasy. 'Unexpected pleasures of so many kinds await us. What,' the duke went on, 'can you tell me about someone named Rudel Correze?'

After a number of months with Bertran, Blaise was getting used to this sort of thing. It sometimes seemed to him that the Arbonnais preferred to be known as clever and witty more than anything else.

'He shoots fairly well,' he said drily, trying to match Bertran's tone. 'Ask Valery.'

The big coran, now fully recovered, grunted wryly.

'We have been,' said Bertran crisply, his tone changing without warning, 'collectively avoiding a decision all summer. I think it is time to make it.'

'Correze banners up ahead?' Blaise asked.

'Indeed there are. Among others. I think I recognized Andoria and Delonghi as well.'

It was odd how the ambushes of life came upon one so utterly unawares. Or perhaps it wasn't all that odd, Blaise corrected himself: they wouldn't be ambushes otherwise, would they? It stood to reason, didn't it? He felt suddenly cold, though. He wondered if the other two men could read a response in him, and then he wondered why it had never even occurred to him that Lucianna might be coming to the Lussan Fair.

There was more than enough of importance happening in the world, as autumn came, to make an appearance by the Delonghi an obvious thing to have expected at this annual gathering. They would come to trade, to watch and wager or fight in the tournament, to celebrate the harvests and share news of the six countries before winter's snow and rain made the roads impassable. And where the men of the Delonghi were likely to be present, the celebrated, notorious jewel of the family would almost certainly be found. Lucianna was not prone to be left behind, anywhere.

The immediate question had been about Rudel, though, and Bertran had raised another issue as well.

Blaise addressed the question, making his tone as precise as he could. 'You'll have to make a point of acknowledging Rudel himself, and his father if he's here. He might be. Once acknowledged, and under the truce of the fair Rudel will do nothing at all. In fact, it will probably amuse him to be seen in your company.'

'It will amuse me as well,' Bertran murmured, 'to no end. I think I will enjoy meeting this man.'

Most of the world knew now about the failed assassination and the money spent. A few people were aware of who it was who had fired that poisoned arrow and hit the wrong man. Rudel, so far as Blaise could judge, would have been seriously embarrassed — especially after heading straight to Götzland to claim the promised fee. Bertran's sources at the court of King Jörg — who were remarkably well informed — had sent word later about how Rudel had been forced to repay the sum. He had already spent part of it, it was reported, and so his father had been compelled to intervene and square the account. Blaise could quite easily imagine how his old friend had felt about that.

In his own way, he was looking forward to seeing Rudel again. In the complex sparring match of their relationship he had won a victory in that garden in Tavernel, and both of them would know it. He didn't win so cleanly very often; it would be something to savour.

Or it might have been, except that Lucianna was here, and Blaise knew from experience that Rudel would use whatever weapons he needed to to even a score if he felt himself on the losing side of the slate. Blaise shook his head. He would have to try to deal with that if and when it happened. There was something else still to be addressed here, and Bertran and Valery were both watching him in silence as they rode. There was a growing commotion up at the front of their column and they seemed to be slowing down. He could see the overtaken banners clearly now: Correze, Delonghi, Andoria, one or two others he didn't recognize.

He turned to Bertran. The duke was bareheaded as usual, in the nondescript riding clothes he favoured on the road. It had saved his life once, Valery had told Blaise, when another would-be assassin had been unable to tell which man in their party was de Talair himself.

'There's no decision to make, really. Not now.' Blaise kept his voice calm. Three men could now be seen riding back towards them, dust rising about their horses' hooves. 'If we're to ride with the Portezzans there are a number of them who know me. There's no point in my trying to remain unrecognized.'

'I thought as much,' Bertran said. 'Very well. From this time on may I assume it is Blaise de Garsenc who honours me by joining my corans for a time, despite his father's evident desire to have me killed?'

It was a watershed of sorts, a moment when many things could change. 'As you like,' said Blaise quietly.

The three riders had come nearer. He didn't recognize them. They were extravagantly garbed, even on the dusty road. Portezzans were like that.

'And on the other matter?' Bertran asked, the faintest hint of tension in his voice now. 'The one we have been delaying upon?'

Blaise knew what the duke meant, of course he knew: *What would you have me do, declare myself the true king of Gorhaut?* His own words.

He shook his head. Something in his chest grew tight and heavy whenever he thought about that. It was a step across a chasm so wide he had never thought to see such a thing, even in his mind's eye. 'No,' he said. 'Leave that. It is autumn now, and the truce of the fair. Gorhaut will do nothing here, if any of them even come, and then Ademar will have to wait until spring opens the mountains again. Let us wait and see what happens.'

Valery said in his measured voice, 'We might be doing things ourselves in winter, instead of waiting to see what others do.'

Blaise turned to him. 'I'm sorry,' he said sharply, 'if my reluctance to be used as a figurehead will spoil your winter.'

Bertran, on his other side, laughed aloud. 'Fair enough,' he said, 'though you are hardly a figurehead, if you are honest with yourself. If Ademar is seen as having betrayed his country with the Treaty of Iersen Bridge, is there a man in Gorhaut with a better claim to succeed him than you? Your brother, perhaps?'

'Perhaps,' Blaise said. 'He won't do anything, though. My father rules him.' He hesitated. 'Leave it, Bertran. Leave it for now.'

There was a silence. In it, the three riders came up, trailed by young Serlo. They were clad in a magnificent black and crimson livery Blaise knew. He realized abruptly whose these men must be. His heart began beating quickly again. It seemed that whatever he did, wherever he went, events drew him back into his past. The first of the riders pulled up his horse and bowed unctuously low in his saddle.

'Very well, we will leave it for now,' Bertran said quietly to Blaise. And then launched himself, almost before he'd finished speaking, in a hard, fluid, uncoiled movement from his horse.

He slammed into Blaise with his shoulder, knocking the wind from him, driving him from his own mount. The two of them landed hard in the dust of the road as the knife thrown by the second man in black and red whipped over the bowed head of the first and through the empty space where Blaise had been a moment before. Portezzans were legendary for their skill with knives.

But the corans of Bertran de Talair were the best trained in Arbonne. Valery killed the knife-thrower with a short, precise sword thrust, and Serlo, with an oath, dispatched the third man from behind without ceremony. Only the leader was left then, as Bertran and Blaise disentangled themselves and stood up. Bertran winced and flexed a knee.

Serlo and Valery had their blades levelled at the Portezzan from before and behind. It had all happened so quickly, so silently, that no one up ahead had even realized anything had taken place. There were two dead men on the ground, though. The Portezzan looked down at them and then at Bertran. He had a lean, tanned face and a carefully curled moustache. There were several rings on his fingers, over his riding gloves.

'I am perfectly content to surrender myself to your mercy,' he said calmly, in flawless, aristocratic Arbonnais. 'I will be ransomed by my cousin at a fair price, I can assure you of that.'

'Your cousin has just violated a truce formally guaranteed by the countess of Arbonne,' Bertran said icily. 'He will answer to her for that even more than you.'

'I am certain he will answer adequately,' the man said blandly.

Bertran's face grew pale; Blaise recognized the signs of real rage building. He was still too much in shock to frame his own response.

'I am rather less certain than you,' the duke said softly to the Portezzan. 'But in the interim, you will now make reply to me: why would you seek to kill one of my companions?'

For the first time the man's expression grew hesitant. He looked sidelong at Blaise as if to verify something. His face cleared, and as it did, even before he spoke, Blaise understood what had just happened. Something in him, in his heart actually, seemed to make a sound like a bowstring plucked or the string of a lute.

'My lord and cousin Borsiard d'Andoria has a mortal grievance against this man,' the Portezzan said. 'It has nothing to do with you, En Bertran. He has nothing but respect and affection for you, my lord, and for the countess of Arbonne.' The words were honeyed, mellifluous.

'An assault against a man in my company has a great deal to do with me, I'm afraid. And words of respect are meaningless when an assault takes place during the truce of a fair. Your lord and cousin has made a mistake.'

'And I have never met Borsiard d'Andoria in my life,' Blaise added. 'I would be interested to know what his mortal grievance is.' He knew, though, or thought he could guess.

'It is not a matter for proclaiming in public,' the Portezzan said haughtily. 'Nor do the Andoria explain themselves.'

'Another mistake,' said Bertran, in a blunt tone of finality. 'I see no reason to delay this. As a duke of Arbonne sworn to uphold the countess's peace, I have an obvious duty here.' He turned to Serlo. 'Take three corans and string this man from a tree. You will strip and brand him first. The whole world knows the punishment decreed for those who violate a truce.'

The Portezzan was a brave man, for all his posturing. 'I am a man of rank and cousin to Borsiard d'Andoria,' he said. 'I am entitled to the treatment appropriate to my status.'

Bertran de Talair shook his head. Blaise registered Valery's look of growing concern. He felt the same anxiety himself. The duke ignored them. He said, 'Your status is that of an attempted murderer, violator of a truce all six countries have sworn to keep. No one will speak for you today.' He turned back to Serlo. 'Hang him.'

Serlo had already summoned three other men. They pulled the Portezzan roughly from his horse. One man had a rope looped through his saddle. There was an oak tree at the edge of a field east of the road; they took him there.

'You cannot do this!' the Portezzan shouted, craning his neck to look back at Bertran, the first edge of fear entering his voice. He had truly never thought he might be in danger, Blaise realized. The immunity of his rank and kinship had led him to believe he could kill freely and be ransomed, that money and status could be an answer to anything.

'Are you sure of this?' Valery said quietly to his cousin. 'We may need the Andoria later.'

There was something nearly cruel in the blue eyes as Bertran de Talair watched his corans over by the tree. They were stripping the Portezzan; the man had begun to shout now. Bertran's voice was bleak as he answered Valery without turning, 'We need no one so much that we lose our honour in pursuing them. Wherever the fairs are, the ruler of that country is bound to uphold the truce that allows us all to trade. You know it. Everyone knows it. What just happened was an insult to the countess and to Arbonne so arrogant I will not countenance it. Let Borsiard d'Andoria do what he will, those three men have to die. When we reach Lussan and Barbentain, my advice to the countess will be to ban the Andoria from entry to the fair. I expect she will do so.'

He walked over and remounted his horse; Blaise, after a moment, did the same.

From up ahead, beyond the front of their column, a new commotion could now be heard. Beside the road, Bertran's corans had rigged a hanging rope around a branch of the tree. The condemned man had been stripped to his undergarments. Now Serlo resolutely pulled a knife from his belt, and while the others held the thrashing Portezzan, he set about carving onto his forehead the brand of an oathbreaker. Blaise had seen this before. He resisted an impulse to turn away. They heard the man scream suddenly, high and desperate. Five riders had now peeled away from the party in front of them and were galloping furiously back through the grass at the side of the road.

'Take as many men as you need,' said Bertran calmly to Valery. 'Surround the tree. If those people attempt to stop the hanging you are to kill them. Blaise, wait here with me.'

Without a word Valery moved to obey. The remaining corans of Talair had already begun moving swiftly into position, anticipating this. Swords out, arrows to bows, they

formed a wide ring around the hanging tree. At the rear of
the column beside Bertran, with two dead men on the ground
beside them, Blaise watched the third Portezzan bundled
onto the back of a horse, his hands tied before him, the knot-
ted rope around his neck. There was blood dripping down his
face from Serlo's branding. The five men racing back were
shouting now, gesticulating wildly. Serlo looked back to
Bertran, for confirmation. The duke nodded once. Serlo
stabbed the horse in the haunch with his blade. The animal
bolted forward. The Portezzan seemed to actually spring
backwards off the horse into the air. Then he dangled, swinging, an oddly disconnected figure. They had heard the cracking sound. He was already dead.

The five shouting Portezzans reined up hard at the very
edge of Valery's ring of men. They were hopelessly outnumbered, of course. The leader screamed something at Valery,
lashing his handsome horse in impotent rage. Bertran turned
to Blaise, as if bored by what was now happening.

'We have another small thing to sort out between us,' he
said, for all the world as if they were alone in the pleasant
autumn countryside. 'I have only just realized it myself. You
may not be ready to assert any sort of claim in Gorhaut, but
if we are riding to Lussan now with you clearly acknowledged
as who you are — and with what has just now happened that
decision has been made for us — then I cannot treat you as
simply another of my corans. You may not like this — for reasons I can appreciate — but it would ill behoove us both for
me to be seen giving you commands now. Will you accept a
discharge from my service? Will you accept the hospitality
and companionship of Talair as my friend and guest?'

It was, of course, the only action proper under the circumstances. And yes, Blaise *was* bothered by the change; it
marked a transition, yet another, in a year when his life
seemed to be careening with unsettling speed towards some
destination as yet hidden in the distance.

He managed a smile. 'I was wondering when my wages
would begin to grate upon you. I confess I had not thought
you were so careful with your money, my lord, it does go
against the image all the world has of you.'

Bertran, genuinely startled, laughed aloud. There was,

just then, a silence in the gesticulating knot of men by the tree. The sudden laughter carried. The five Portezzans turned to look at them. Their leader, a short, dark man on that splendid horse, stared across the distance for a long moment, ignoring the corans around him. Then he turned his horse without another word and rode back north. The other Portezzans followed.

'That,' said Bertran, 'was slightly unfortunate.'

'Who was that man?'

The duke turned to him with surprise. 'You were telling the truth, weren't you? You have really never met him. That was Borsiard d'Andoria, Blaise. You must at least have heard the name. He was recently married, in fact, to —'

'To Lucianna Delonghi. I know,' Blaise interrupted. And then added, 'That's why he wants to kill me.'

Even amid the churning of all the emotions of this morning there was, deep within Blaise, a curious flicker of pride. Even now, after everything, Lucianna would have been speaking of him; that had to be it, of course. Borsiard d'Andoria was seeking to kill his new wife's former lover from Gorhaut.

Bertran de Talair was very quick. 'Ah,' he said softly. 'Engarro di Faenna? It was true then, the rumour?'

'That I killed him for the Delonghi? Yes.' Blaise surprised himself with how easy it was to say this now to the duke. He hesitated over the next thing, but then went on: 'With Rudel Correze.'

He saw Bertran absorbing this. 'And so she wants you dead now?' He looked dubious.

Blaise shook his head. 'I doubt it. She wouldn't care enough to bother covering that trail. Borsiard does, though. He probably had a part in the assassination of Engarro, though I didn't know it then. He's uneasy about me. Afraid of what I might say or do. Rudel they'll trust; he's a Delonghi cousin. I'm an unknown quantity.' He stopped.

'And *that* would be his "mortal grievance" against you?'

Blaise looked at the duke. Bertran's blue eyes were searching, sceptical, and there was a glint in them now of something else.

'That would be a part of it,' Blaise said carefully.

Bertran nodded his head slowly. 'I thought so,' he said

after a moment. 'The jewel of the Delonghi, the exquisite Lucianna. He's a jealous man then, our friend Borsiard. That is worth knowing.' He nodded again. 'It begins to make sense. One day you must tell me more about her. Are all the stories true? I've spoken to her of course, but in a crowded room, nothing more, and that was years ago when she was very young. Should I be grateful for that limited exposure? Is she as deadly as word has it?'

Blaise shrugged. 'I have survived. So far.'

'Damaged?'

'Scars. I'm dealing with them.'

Bertran's mouth crooked. 'That is the most that can be said of any of us in such affairs.'

'You were in love,' said Blaise, surprising himself again. 'That goes deeper.'

'So does death.' After a moment Bertran shrugged, and then shook his head as if to break free of such thoughts. 'Are we friends? Are you visiting Talair and sparing me the cost of a trained coran?'

Blaise nodded. 'I suppose I am. This has become a strange path, though. Where do you think it will bring us out?'

Bertran looked amused. 'That, at least, is easy enough: Barbentain Castle and Lussan town below it. Hadn't you heard? There's a fair about to start.' He turned his horse and they began to ride.

Endlessly witty, Blaise thought, and at the price of almost everything else it sometimes seemed. He realized that he hadn't said anything to Bertran about saving his life.

On impulse he wheeled his horse and rode back a short way. Dismounting again, he found the dagger. The hilt was richly studded with gems in typically Portezzan fashion. He swung up into his saddle again and cantered to catch up with Bertran. The duke looked over, eyebrows raised, as he came up.

Blaise extended the blade, hilt foremost. 'A shame to leave it,' he said. 'Thank you. That was quick moving, for a man past his best.'

Bertran grinned. 'My knee certainly is, at any rate.' He took the dagger, examined it. 'Pretty work,' he said, 'if a trifle gaudy.' He put it in his belt.

Nothing more was said; nothing more would be said, Blaise knew. Men familiar with war had their codes in matters such as this. He had once thought that the Arbonnais corans would fall short in this, that they would be prone to commissioning rapturous troubadour verses to celebrate each minor deed of theirs in battle or tournament. It didn't happen that way, he had discovered. He seemed to have discovered a number of things in half a year, without really trying to do so.

The Portezzans ahead of them had begun to move, more quickly now. Borsiard d'Andoria would want to reach Barbentain ahead of Bertran. First complaint sometimes mattered in affairs such as this. They were two days' ride from the fair, though.

Valery, as if reading Blaise's mind, cantered up to them. Bertran looked at his cousin. 'I'm not going to try to pass them myself. We'll take our time. Pick five men and go ahead,' the duke said. 'Find the countess or Roban the chancellor, either one, both together if you can. It is my counsel that all the Portezzans may freely be allowed to enter Lussan or the castle save the Andoria. Tell them why.'

The big, greying coran turned to go.

'Valery,' said Bertran. His cousin reined his horse and looked back over his shoulder. 'Blaise de Garsenc is no longer in my service. He honours us at Talair with his company and his friendship. Perhaps he will even fight with our men in the tournament mêlée. Tell the countess.'

Valery nodded, looked briefly at Blaise and galloped away in a swirl of dust up the line of their column.

And so the decision was made. Given what had happened, it might have even seemed forced, obvious. With the speed of recent events, they had forgotten something though, all three of them. Under the circumstances that was, perhaps, not altogether surprising. Which did not make it less of an oversight.

On their right, as Bertran and Blaise went by, the dead man, almost naked, swayed from the oak tree, blood still dripping from his forehead where the oathbreaker's brand had been carved.

CHAPTER·10

Roban, the chancellor of Arbonne, had had an intensely trying few days, for all the usual reasons associated with the Autumn Fair. For more years than he could remember, his had been the responsibility of supervising the many-faceted preparations for the annual arrival of what sometimes seemed to be half the known world.

In the early days of the Lussan Fair, the burghers of the town had proudly taken charge of preparations themselves, but as the fair grew in importance and the tournament associated with it began to attract more and more of the celebrated figures of the six countries, including kings and queens on more than one occasion, the townsfolk were ultimately happy to swallow their pride and ask for help from the count in Barbentain. Faced with a matter as important, detail-oriented and essentially tedious as the logistics of preparing a month-long fair, the count had assigned the task to Roban. Naturally. As if he didn't have enough to do.

Of course the townsmen helped — as well they should, given how much wealth the Autumn Fair generated for Lussan — and the count had allocated monies adequate to let Roban appoint two Keepers of the Fair and two Keepers of the Seals to assist them. Having control of appointments was always vital, Roban had found; it let one choose men of competence instead of having to work with those who simply had favours owed to them. He was familiar with both scenarios after almost forty years in Barbentain.

In his first year of organizing the fair he had also picked a captain from among the Barbentain corans and empowered him to select and oversee one hundred serjans to police the

229

fairgrounds from sunrise to sunset. At night there was little point in policing anything. The count's guarantee — now the countess's — of safety in Lussan and on the roads approaching the fair was only good until sundown. No ruler in any of the six countries was really able to enforce security after dark, though Roban had had the idea years ago of spending the money to light the three main streets of Lussan for the duration of the fair.

Small touches like that were what had made Lussan's fair by far the most celebrated and best attended in the six countries. For all his frustrations and his chronic sense of being overburdened, Roban was proud of that; he'd always felt that it was worth doing a task properly if it was worth doing at all. That was part of his problem, of course; that was why he ended up with so much to do. It was also the source of his own particular pride: he knew — and he was certain the count, and more recently, the countess, knew — that there was simply no one else in Barbentain, in all of Arbonne, who could handle details such as these as well as he.

The tax officers of the fair were under his direct authority — the tariffs levied on all goods leaving Lussan went straight to the countess's coffers — but the burghers of the town were responsible for appointing and paying the inspectors, notaries, scribes, clerks and couriers. They sent out their own heralds, too, into hamlets throughout the countryside in the harvest season, to remind the farmers and villagers of Arbonne — as if anyone was likely to need reminding — that the Autumn Fair was coming, with its puppet shows and performing animals, its dancers and singers, men who swallowed burning coals and others who made pigeons disappear, and pedlars who sold trinkets and toys and pottery and cures for everything from infertility to indigestion. And there were also, of course, the women who gathered in Lussan for that month from all parts of the known world, and who could be bought in a tavern room for an hour or a night.

Roban was happy to leave the supervision of such things to the burghers; his own concern was for those coming with more tangible goods to trade, over the mountains or by water to Tavernel and then up the high road along the river. The merchants came from everywhere, in fact, travelling with silk and wool and wood, with medicines and perfumes and staggeringly costly spices from the east, with daggers from Arimonda, swords and armour from the forges of Aulensburg, longbows from Valensa, carved icons of Corannos from Gorhaut, gold and silver jewellery from Portezza, Valensan cloth and cheese, wine and olives and olive oil from the south of Arbonne itself. You could buy virtually anything at the Lussan Fair, see people from almost anywhere in the known world and, for the price of a beaker of ale bought in a tavern, hear tales told by sea captains of the fabled countries to the south, far beyond the boundaries of the known.

You could also find, in private houses that sheltered the princes and great merchants from too-close scrutiny, discussions going forward, in rooms shuttered against the sun or candlelit at night, that would shape the flow of events in the six countries for the year to come.

The Lussan Fair was always the last of each year before winter closed the roads and passes. It was the final opportunity for face-to-face discussions for months. Roban knew from long experience that it was what happened behind those forbidding, ornate doors that became the most important legacy of any fair.

That was especially true this year, perhaps more than any other in memory, for the Treaty of Iersen Bridge between Gorhaut and Valensa had completely altered the long balance of power among the six countries, and Arbonne in particular had reason to weigh and fear the consequences of that.

It was therefore not surprising that when the hard-pressed and chronically anxious chancellor of Arbonne learned that Duke Bertran's cousin Valery sought urgent audience with the countess and himself, he concluded, with the glum certainty of the innately pessimistic, that he was not about to receive tidings apt to soothe his jangling nerves.

This, of course, turned out to be the case. Aghast, Roban stood beside the countess's chair in her small private room behind the audience chamber and heard Valery of Talair calmly recount a murder attempt on the problematic Gorhaut coran, the killing of two Portezzans from Andoria in response and then the summary execution of the third — a cousin to Borsiard himself, and, it appeared, very possibly a favourite.

Valery was careful to spare them no details. The tensions that would ensue in the wake of all this, Roban calculated swiftly, were likely to ruin the fair before it began. They would also probably drive him to his bed for a day and a night with one of his blinding headaches.

It sometimes seemed to him that he'd spent his entire adult life here at Barbentain, with the count and now the countess, attempting to smooth over crises caused by the actions of the fractious, capricious noblemen of Arbonne. Roban was Arbonnais himself, of course, born to minor rank in Vaux Castle, but he'd been consecrated to Corannos early, in the way of younger sons of younger sons, then plucked from a chapel of the god by Guibor IV while still beardless, though with his abilities in numbers and letters already manifest.

He'd come to Barbentain and risen swiftly through the ranks of Guibor's court to the chancellorship. At the time of his appointment there had been much made of his youthful links with the clergy of the god — an act of careful political balancing by the count. That had been so long ago Roban doubted anyone even remembered any more. Few had objected to his precipitate ascent, even in an ambitious court. Even when he was young there had been something reassuringly earnest about Roban's manner. He was trusted. He *deserved* to be trusted, he often thought; if only he were *listened to* more often in this country of hot-blooded men and women with more passion for music than for orderly government.

Music was fine, Roban thought. He enjoyed the troubadours and joglars when he had the chance to hear them. He'd even written some verses himself long ago when formally courting the woman the count had suggested he marry. He couldn't remember the tunes or the lyrics very well — probably a good thing. There were limits to where music could take you, Roban had always thought, or, more properly, there were dimensions in affairs of state where it was necessary to leave aside the romantic troubadour strains and be ruthlessly practical. Roban was a pragmatic man, by his own estimation. He knew what implications flowed from what actions. He was aware that Bertran de Talair would know these things too, perhaps even better than he, but that much of the time the duke would simply not care. That was the way of things here in Arbonne, the chancellor thought gloomily. Witness what had happened two days ago on the high road beside the river.

There was no question that punishment had been called for, that something would have had to be done. What would have put the Andorians in a fury — and a contingent of them were reported to have also arrived today, coated in dust, horses lathered — was the summary action of the duke of Talair by the roadside. Noblemen were simply *not* executed in the manner of common thieves. Bertran had even had the man branded; Roban winced when Valery mentioned that, and turned away in a vain attempt to conceal his reaction. He tried to turn the motion into a coughing spasm, but suspected that the countess knew this was a subterfuge.

He was seldom able to conceal much from the countess. He had fallen in love the first time he'd ever seen her, forty years ago. He loved her yet, more than his life. He was almost certain that this, at least, she did not know — but it was one of the things that defined Roban of Vaux in his own eyes. He was a man who had loved one woman only and had done so for virtually all his days, notwithstanding his own marriage and children, notwithstanding their enormous difference in rank. He would die having loved the countess of Arbonne with the sustained, lifelong passion of his soul. He didn't even think about it any more, though there had been sleepless, sighing nights in a narrow bed long ago. By now, four decades later, it was simply a given, a fact upon which all else in his life had been founded.

In the room behind the audience chamber he smoothed his face, ran a hand down the front of his doublet in an habitual gesture and turned back to Bertran's cousin. Valery was pointing out, in a tone of calmly reasonable argument, that noblemen could not be allowed to violate a truce by attempting murder on the roads in the blithe expectation that a ransom of some sort would smooth things over for them. Bertran's extremely competent cousin — a man Roban approved of, actually — also noted that by acting summarily Bertran had decisively protected the countess's authority, while leaving her the option of chastising him and appeasing the Andoria, if she wished.

Roban, seeing a faint flicker of hope here, his mind quickly running through possibilities, tried to intercede at this point. He did not succeed. Bertran's own recommendation, Valery added smoothly without pausing for breath, was that no such appeasement should be contemplated. Roban closed his eyes. He was aware, just about then, that one of his headaches was indeed beginning to come on.

The countess's credibility as a woman ruling Arbonne, Valery of Talair said gravely, virtually demanded that she be seen to be as decisive as, say, Jörg of Götzland would have been in the same situation. Borsiard d'Andoria should be barred from the fair, that was Bertran's suggestion. Naturally it was, Roban thought bitterly: it was amazing to the chancellor that such things could be thought and said, could be casually proposed, by otherwise intelligent men.

'Götzland is not facing the real possibility of invasion next year,' he said bluntly to Valery, finally seizing the chance to speak. 'The countess has matters to consider that go beyond the protocols of trade fairs. It is a bad time — a *very* bad time — to be offending men as important as Borsiard d'Andoria.'

'You would have let him buy his man's life? Let him swan about with a new bride in Lussan at the fair and in this castle having attempted murder on our roads? What if the Gorhaut coran had died? What then?'

'His death might have simplified things,' Roban answered, too quickly. This was a sore spot for him. 'You know what I think of this insanity En Bertran has proposed.'

'It was my daughter who proposed it,' the countess said, speaking for the first time. It was a bad sign that her first words were to correct him. 'Bertran agreed with Beatritz's suggestion. I also agreed. You objected, made your arguments, and were presented with my decision. Do not be tiresome, Roban. I know your concerns here, but I do not see how we can do other than back what Bertran has already done. I am going to ban Borsiard d'Andoria from the fair.' The count, her husband, had been like that too, amazingly like that: hugely important decisions were made with a speed that stunned Roban.

'We will pay for it,' he said, feeling his face attaining the unfortunate pink hue that came with agitation. 'D'Andoria will be funding Gorhaut next year, I'll wager on it.'

Valery of Talair shrugged indifferently. 'They don't need funding, my lord chancellor. With the money they received from Valensa by the terms of Iersen Bridge they have more than enough. Look what they paid to assassinate Bertran. Did that appear to be the action of someone short of gold?'

'There is always a shortage of gold in wartime,' Roban said darkly. He'd actually had some privy information about the exact sums paid and still owing from Valensa to Gorhaut by the terms of the treaty. The numbers terrified him.

'That reminds me,' the countess said in a different tone, one Roban recognized apprehensively. 'Daufridi of Valensa must be desperately short of money these days if he paid so much to Gorhaut for the lands they ceded him.'

'I daresay he may have some problems,' Roban said cautiously. He had learned it was always wise to be cautious when he heard that tone — it usually meant some plan or other was about to be proposed. Usually those plans made him extremely nervous. His headache was growing worse.

He saw Valery grin just before the man brought a hand up quickly to cover his mouth. The men of Talair were so clever, it was almost unfair.

'We'll have to talk about that then,' the countess murmured. 'I do have an idea.'

Roban had no notion what she was referring to; it rankled him that Valery appeared to know. His was the endlessly vexing position of being the man left behind to attend to details and minutiae; he was surrounded by quicksilver people whose minds leapt effortlessly down channels he found perilously dark.

The countess was gazing pointedly at Valery; she had seen his smile as well. 'That is, if Bertran hasn't already had the same thought long before me.' Her tone was not nearly as stern as Roban felt it ought to have been. It was her weakness, he thought, not for the first time: she loved her gallant, irresponsible noblemen far too much to rein them in properly. And Bertran de Talair, among all of them, was a special case.

'I am sure,' Valery said gracefully, 'that any thoughts En Bertran might have on the subject of Valensa will be conveyed to you as soon as he arrives. I believe we can expect him by the end of the day.'

'I rather think,' Signe de Barbentain said drily, 'he will instead consent to inform me of measures he has already set in motion. Exactly as he did with those verses that nearly had him killed this summer. By the way,' she turned to Roban, 'this is important: I want Barbentain guards visible wherever the duke of Talair goes during the fair this month. No slight to Bertran's own corans, but anyone with designs upon him must be made aware that we are watching for them.' Roban nodded. This made sense; he liked it when she gave him commands that made sense.

'Rudel Correze is travelling with the Delonghi,' Valery said casually, almost as an afterthought. 'They were all in a party with the Andoria.'

'Wonderful,' the countess said tartly. It pleased Roban to see her angry with someone else, even though Bertran's cousin was hardly the appropriate target. 'Do I ban him, too? Do we spend this week antagonizing *every* important family in Portezza?' Signe de Barbentain seldom lost her temper, but Roban sensed it might be happening now. It gratified him that she understood and shared his concerns. He smoothed his doublet again.

Valery was shaking his head. 'Blaise de Garsenc says the man will do nothing here. That the Correze are too prudent to risk the economic hazards of violating a truce. He thinks Rudel has probably withdrawn from his contract in any case.'

'Why would he think that?' Roban asked testily. 'No one in that family turns their back on two hundred and fifty thousand in gold.'

Valery looked apologetic. 'I thought the same thing, my lord chancellor. Blaise tells me he knows Rudel Correze extremely well, though. He sees no danger from him now.'

'We are relying on that coran from Gorhaut rather a great deal, aren't we?'

'Enough, Roban!' He realized his mistake the moment she spoke — the anger building in her had abruptly turned on him. It always seemed to happen that way, as if he was the safe target, the one she knew she could snap at without risk. Which was true, he thought ruefully. It had been true for decades. Once, he'd wondered if his wife knew how he felt about the countess, and if she cared. He hadn't thought about such things for a long time.

'We will not go down that road again,' Signe was saying sternly. 'The man is not simply a coran from Gorhaut. He is the son of Galbert de Garsenc, and if we have any hope of dividing Gorhaut on this issue he is that hope. If he betrays us, I will admit you were right before we all die. Is that enough, Roban? Will that content you?'

The chancellor swallowed hard, feeling the way he always felt when she lashed out at him. When he was younger he had actually wept sometimes behind the closed doors of his own quarters after she'd spoken to him in this way. He didn't do that any more, but he sometimes felt like it. A terrible admission, the chancellor thought, for a man of his age and position. He wondered if she ever knew when his headaches were coming on, if she would have been more sympathetic, a little gentler perhaps, had he informed her.

Signe really didn't remember Roban ever being this obstinately tiresome when Guibor was alive. But then she hadn't had as much to do with him then; he was simply the efficient administrator in the background, and Guibor was not a man with whom advisers pushed their disagreements too hard. It looked as if she wasn't like that herself. Perhaps she depended on Roban too much, perhaps he felt she was weak and needed him to be stronger now. She didn't really know; it wasn't something she'd thought about very much. He was there, he had always been there, and she knew he could be trusted, that something assigned to him would be competently done if it was at all possible. He looked a little flushed today and there were circles under his eyes. It crossed her mind to wonder, as she watched him make his habitual little smoothing gesture down the front of his immaculate doublet, if Roban was over-burdened — the usual fate of competent men.

She didn't, in fact, feel especially strong herself at the moment, but that wasn't for anyone to see or guess, even Roban, even Valery. 'Send for Borsiard d'Andoria in Lussan,' she told the chancellor. 'I will give him an audience here. I will not ban him by fiat or decree. He will hear it from me in this castle.'

Which is what had happened later that same afternoon.

Borsiard had stormed into her audience chamber, raging in the most unpleasant manner, demanding Bertran de Talair's censure and death in redress for the slaughter of three noblemen of Andoria. He had actually had a belief that she might agree, Signe saw. He was seeing her as a woman, a woman who could be frightened by his rage, moved to do what he wanted her to do.

That realization was what had given her access to the cold anger she needed to quell the Portezzan. And he had been quelled. She had dealt with better men than he in the past. As soon as she'd begun to speak, slowly, letting her measured words fall like stones into the stillness of the room, Borsiard's bravado had seemed to leech away from him.

'Take your people and your goods and go,' she had said, speaking from the ancient throne of the counts of Arbonne. 'You will not be allowed trade or profit at a fair whose laws you have so vilely broken. The men who were killed were properly executed by the duke of Talair, who is our agent in this, as are all the nobility of Arbonne. Whatever your quarrel with Blaise de Garsenc of Gorhaut — a quarrel in which we have no interest whatever — the roads leading to the Lussan Fair were not the place to pursue it. In that, we have a great interest indeed. You will not be troubled as you leave Arbonne. Indeed, we will assign a company of our men to escort you safely to the Portezzan border . . . unless there is somewhere else you might wish to go?'

Guibor had taught her that; raise the issue yourself, take the initiative from the other person. And as if on cue, Borsiard d'Andoria's dark, handsome face had twisted with a spasm of malice. 'Indeed there is,' he had said. 'There are matters I should like to pursue in Gorhaut. I will travel north from here.'

'We have no doubt you will be welcome at the court of King Ademar,' Signe had said calmly. This was not a man to unsettle her, however much he might be worth, whatever Roban might fear. He was far too predictable. She wondered how long his marriage would last. She allowed herself to smile; she knew how to make her smile a weapon if need be. 'We only hope your lady wife does not find it cold in Cortil and dull there as winter comes to the north,' she murmured. 'If she prefers to go home we will be happy to offer her an escort. Indeed —' a thought born of the moment '— we will be most pleased to have her stay on at our court should you wish to go north without her. We imagine we could find ways to keep her amused. It would be unjust to deny a lady the pleasures of a fair because of her husband's transgressions. We do not behave that way in Arbonne.'

She wondered, lying in bed that same night, if she might have cause to regret the loss of temper that had led to that last invitation. It could prove awkward in many ways to have Lucianna Delonghi — it was almost impossible to think of her by any other name, despite her marriages — in Barbentain and Lussan this month. On the other hand, had the woman wanted to stay for the fair, she could simply have joined her father's contingent in any case. The invitation lent a sanction of control to what could hardly have been prevented. Signe hoped it might be seen that way, at any rate. She was also, privately, somewhat curious to meet the woman again. The last time Lucianna Delonghi had been in Barbentain was six or seven years ago, before the first of her marriages. Her father had presented her to the count and countess. She'd been clever, as all her family were, beautiful already, watchful, very young. A great deal had evidently happened to her in the intervening years.

It might be interesting to see exactly what. Later, though, Signe thought. She didn't want to see anyone at the moment. She had retired early, leaving to Roban and the Keepers of the Fair the task of carrying out her orders regarding the Andoria. She doubted there would be difficulties; Borsiard had few corans with him this far from home, and was unlikely to embarrass himself by forcing a public removal from Lussan. He was, however, quite likely to go north to Gorhaut — as Roban had gloomily predicted. The chancellor was usually right about such things. What Borsiard would do there was harder to guess. But the implications could not be lost on anyone: Andoria was one less source of funding for Arbonne, one less ally if war did come, and possibly one more contingent of arms in the field if Gorhaut asked for them.

Signe sighed in the darkness of her room. She knew Bertran had acted properly in what he'd done, that he'd made it easier for her by taking the burden upon himself. She only wished . . . she only wished he didn't seem to always find himself in situations where doing the proper thing meant so much trouble for all of them.

At the moment all she wanted to do was rest. There was sometimes a curious easing of care for her in the nighttime, in the embrace of sleep. It didn't always come to her easily, but when it did her dreams were almost always benign, comforting. She would be walking in the castle gardens, or with Guibor, young again, in that meadow she had loved beneath the Ancients' aqueduct near Carenzu, and sometimes the four children would be with them: clever Beatritz with her shining hair, the boys — Guibor eager and adventuresome, Piers watchful, a little apart — and then Aelis trailing behind them through the green, green grass. Aelis, in her mother's dreams, always seemed older than the others, though she was the youngest child. She would appear in the dreams as she had looked, coming into the flourish of her own late, fierce beauty, in the year before she died.

Signe reached towards sleep that night as a woman reaching for the last gentle lover of her days. The anxieties of day would still be waiting in the morning, with newer concerns appearing to join them, new dangers from the north . . . tonight she sought her dreams.

She was not allowed to have them.

The knocking at the outer door of her suite of rooms was so soft she would not have even heard it had she actually been asleep. One of the girls in the antechamber would have, though. Already Brisseau, the older of the two, hovered, anxious and wraithlike in her white night-robe, at the entrance to Signe's chamber.

'See who it is,' the countess said, though there was only one person it could be at this hour.

Roban waited in the outer room while she donned her own robe. She went out to him; she disliked receiving men or conducting affairs of state in her bedchamber. He was still in the doublet he'd worn earlier in the day. Signe understood, with something of a shock, that he had not yet even gone to bed. It was very late, and the chancellor did not look well. His face was haggard and in the light of the candles the girls were hastily lighting his eyes were deep-sunken. He looked older than his years, she thought suddenly: they had worn him down in their service, she and Guibor. She wondered if he felt the labours had been worth the price. She wondered, for the first time, what he actually thought of the two of them. Or of her, more properly. Guibor was dead; one thought nothing but good of the dead. She realized she didn't really know what her chancellor's opinion of her might be. Frivolous, she decided; he'd probably concluded she was frivolous and impetuous and needed a steady, guiding hand. That might answer her question of earlier in the day about why he had pushed his views so urgently of late.

He really didn't look well, though.

'Sit,' she said. 'Before you begin, sit down. Brisseau, a flask of cider for the chancellor.'

She thought Roban would refuse the chair but he did not; that only served to increase her own disquiet. Forcing herself to be patient she waited, sitting opposite him, until the cider had been brought and placed on the table. She waited again until he drank.

'Tell me,' she said, finally.

'My lady, a message came to me from Rian's temple in the town earlier tonight,' he said, his voice curiously faint. 'It purported to be from someone who could not possibly have been in Lussan, requesting audience and . . . and sanctuary with you.'

'Yes?'

'Yes, so I went down into town myself to see if it might possibly be a true message. I am afraid it is, my lady. I fear that we have the gravest crisis upon us now, one that makes the Andoria matter seem as nothing.'

'Who is it? Who is in the town?'

'Not in town any longer. I had no choice, my lady, I had to bring her up to the castle before anyone else knew she was here or what was happening.' The chancellor drew an unsteady breath. 'Countess, it seems that the Lady Rosala de Garsenc of Gorhaut has left the duke her husband without his knowledge. She seeks refuge with us. She is in Barbentain now, and, my lady . . . though I am far from expert in these matters, I believe that she may be about to give birth, even as we speak.'

†

Cadar de Savaric, defiantly named and surnamed for his mother's father and family, entered the world in Barbentain Castle shortly before dawn that night.

Brought early to his time by the rigours of his mother's journey through the mountains to Arbonne, he was nonetheless sturdy and pink when he emerged, letting out a loud cry his exhausted mother heard as triumphant when the priestesses of Rian, summoned hastily to the castle, drew him from her womb and clipped the birthing cord.

They washed him ceremoniously in milk warmed by the fire, as befitted a child of rank, and the older of the two priestesses swaddled him expertly in blue samite before handing him to the countess of Arbonne, who had remained in the room for the last long hours of Rosala's travail. Signe de Barbentain, white-haired, with the delicate blue veins showing in her pale, flawless skin, cradled the child and looked down upon it with an expression Rosala could not entirely comprehend but which she found deeply reassuring nonetheless. After a moment Signe walked over to the bed and laid the infant gently in his mother's arms.

Rosala had not expected the gentleness. She had not known what to expect. She had only realized, when Galbert de Garsenc had ridden away from her a week ago, that she was going to go south, however she possibly could. Beyond that she had not clearly thought.

The coming of the Lussan Fair had given her the chance. Garsenc lay near to the principal road that ran up into the mountain pass, and each day Rosala had seen small troupes of corans and tradesmen passing by their lands, often stopping to worship at the chapel, or do a bit of business in the castle or the village below.

Two days after her father-in-law's visit, Rosala wrote a note to her husband, saying that she was journeying north to her own family estate to await the birth of the child. She'd had a dream, she lied, a terrible nightmare of premonition. Too many infants and women had died in labour at Garsenc Castle, she wrote Ranald. It had frightened her for their child. She felt safer going home to Savaric. She hoped he would understand. She hoped he would come to her there when affairs at court allowed. She signed it with her name.

She left the castle, unseen, by the postern gate that same night. Her favourite horse was kept in the coran's stables out-side the walls so it could be readily exercised while she was unable to ride. There was no guard at the stables — no one would be rash enough to tempt the wrath of the Garsenc by approaching their horses. She had mounted awkwardly and ridden away, side-saddle, by the twin lights of the moons, the landscape both beautiful and frightening at night, the child large and heavy in her belly. She had only the faintest hope, dim as the stars beside bright Vidonne, of reaching her destination.

That one night was all she was capable of riding. Reluc-tantly, in real distress, she left the horse near a small hamlet be-fore dawn and made her way on foot back to the road. At sun-rise, walking slowly, hungry and extremely tired, she came upon the encampment of some travelling entertainers. Two women were bathing in a stream when she came up to them. They exclaimed at her condition. She used the first name that came into her head and told them she was travelling to Ar-bonne in search of aid in childbirth. Two infants had already died at birth, she lied, making the warding sign behind her hip. She was willing to do anything to save this one, she said.

That last was true. It was entirely true.

The women made their own warding signs at the hint that she was seeking magic but generously welcomed her into their company for the journey south. Rosala rode through the mountains in a jouncing, lurching wagon with two thievish grey monkeys, a talking bird from the northern swamplands, an adder in a basket and a garrulous animal-trainer, whose teeth were bizarrely blue. Poison, he explained, from the snake before it was defanged. He fed it mice and small lizards that he caught. Every time the wagon hit a rut in the road, and there were a great many as they went through the pass, Rosala looked anxiously to the basket, to make sure the clasp still held. The bear and the mountain cat, thankfully, rode in their own wagon just behind them.

She talked as little as she could, to avoid having to sus-tain an accent that would not give her away. It was relatively

easy with Othon in the wagon: he was one of those men who
would have pined away had he lost the use of his voice. He
was kind to her, though, bringing soups and bread back from
the communal fire at the dinner hour. She grew accustomed
to the drone of his voice and the endlessly reiterated stories
of past travels during the three slow days it took them to cross
from Gorhaut over the summit of the pass and come down
into Arbonne. It began to seem to her that she had always
been with these people, riding in this wagon, that Garsenc
Castle was the dream, something from another woman's life.

On the fourth morning, Rosala lifted the flap of the
wagon and stepped outside just as the sun was rising over the
hills east of them. She looked south over a landscape entirely
strange to her and saw a river, bright blue in the morning
light, flowing swiftly beside the road. In the distance, glittering, scarcely visible save for that shimmer in the sun, she
saw towers.

'That'll be Barbentain,' said Othon sagely from behind
her. She looked over her shoulder and managed a weak smile.
He scratched himself in several indelicate places, stretched
and grunted. 'Yon's the finest castle I've ever been to in all my
days. We'll be there tonight, I reckon. There was a count
there, not long ago — mayhap you heard of him — Guibor
Third, or Fourth he may have been. Huge man, tall as a tree,
fierce in war . . . and in love, as they all are down here.' He
chuckled lewdly, showing the blue teeth. 'Anyhap, he was the
finest figure of a man I ever saw in my days. His widow rules
now. Don't know much about her. They say she used to be
pretty but now she's old.' Othon yawned and then spat into
the grass. 'We all get old,' he pronounced and strolled away,
scratching, to attend to his morning functions in the bush.
One of the monkeys followed him.

Rosala placed a hand over her belly and looked along the
bright, sinuous line of the river away to the south. There were
cypresses on the ridges above them, and a species of pine she'd
not encountered before. On the terraced slopes west of the
road were the fabled olive trees of Arbonne.

She gazed at them for a moment, then turned back to
look again at the far, shimmering turrets of the castle, where
Guibor IV's widow ruled now. *Marry the bitch*, her husband

had advised Ademar of Gorhaut not so long ago. Rosala's father had said once that the countess of Arbonne was the fairest woman in the world in her day. One thing, at least, in which he appeared to agree with Othon the animal-trainer.

Rosala didn't need her to be beautiful. Only kind, and with a certain kind of courage that she knew her presence would put greatly to the test. She was too versed in the nature of things not to know what her arrival in Barbentain would mean, carrying a possible heir to Garsenc — or a successor to the High Elder of the god in Gorhaut. She honestly didn't see what choice she'd had, though, unless it was to surrender the child, and that was no choice at all.

Later in the day, with the sun high in a bright, clear autumn sky, she began feeling the first pains. She hid them as best she could, but eventually even Othon noticed and his endless flow of words slowly dried up. He sent for the women and they comforted her as best they could, but they had a long way to go yet to Lussan. It was, in fact, well past nightfall by the time they set her down at the temple of Rian.

It was a healthy, well-made baby boy, Signe thought, surprised at the pleasure she felt holding him. Under all the circumstances, she should have been feeling nothing but the deepest concern for her own people. This child and his mother represented danger in its purest form, they could easily be Gorhaut's excuse for war. In the room outside, Roban was pacing like a father desperate for an heir, but Signe knew the source of his disquiet was entirely otherwise. He was almost certainly hoping Rosala de Garsenc's child would be a girl. For a girl, the corans of Gorhaut were far less likely to be unleashed upon them.

No such luck, it seemed. Rian and Corannos both appeared to have a hand in the events unfolding here, and when the god and the goddess worked together, the old saying went, men and women could only kneel and bow their heads. Signe, bowing her head, smiled down upon the child, swaddled in aristocratic blue, and carried him to his mother. Rosala de Garsenc was almost bone-white in the candlelight, and her blue eyes were enormous in her drawn face, but the expression in those eyes was as resolute and unafraid now as it had been all night. Signe admired her greatly. She had heard the story in the dark of night, told in bursts through the birthing pains: the reason for this flight, the plea for sanctuary.

It was not a request she was capable of refusing; even Roban, to his credit, had brought the woman across to Barbentain. He would probably deny it in the morning, but Signe was almost certain her chancellor, too, had been moved by Rosala's story. It was more than pragmatism that had caused him to bring the woman to the castle. She was, she realized, proud of him.

She was also aware that this sympathy, this yielding to the human impulse, might well destroy them all. Rosala, quite evidently, knew this too. Through the long night of labour, talking almost incoherently through her pain, the woman had nonetheless revealed a formidable intelligence. Her courage, too, was obvious. One would need courage and something more to stand up to Galbert de Garsenc in the way this woman had.

'Your child is here, my lady,' Signe said softly by the bed, the formal words. 'Will it please his mother to give him his name?'

'Cadar,' said Rosala, lifting her voice to let the first speaking ring clearly in the world he had entered. 'His name is Cadar de Savaric.' She lifted her arms and Signe gave her the child.

There was more defiance here, the countess knew, to the point of provocation. She was glad Roban had not heard this; the chancellor had had enough stress for one day. She felt old and tired herself, weighted with the night and the years of her living. The time of music and laughter here in Barbentain seemed infinitely long ago, a dream, a troubadour's fantasy, not really part of her own history.

'He has a father,' she felt obliged to say. 'You are choosing to cut him off from that? What if his father wants to accept him, despite everything, to offer his protection? Will this name not be a bar to that?'

The woman was very tired, it was unfair to be taxing her in this way, but it was necessary, before the name went forth from this room. Rosala looked up with those clear blue northern eyes and said, 'If his father chooses to come for him and shelter him I will think on this again.' There was an intonation there, a stress on one word that stirred within Signe a new disquiet, like a note of music almost but not quite audible, sensed if not really heard.

Rosala said, 'He will need a man and a woman to stand for him before the god — and the goddess, too, if you have such a ritual in Arbonne.'

'We do. The Guardians of Rian and Corannos. We honour both here, I think you know that.'

'I do know that. Will you honour my child and myself by standing up for Cadar? Is this too much to ask?'

It was, in many ways. It redoubled all the dangers this child represented for Arbonne to have the countess herself so identified with him. Roban would have turned pink with the vigour of his reaction.

'I will,' said Signe de Barbentain, genuinely moved, looking down at the child. She had never seen her own grandson, born and lost on a winter's night so many years ago. Lost or dead, no one alive knew but Urté de Miraval, and he was not going to tell. He was not ever going to tell. Time and memory and loss seemed tangled and twisted tonight, with avenues to sorrow everywhere. She was looking down on this fair-haired woman and thinking of Aelis.

'The honour will be mine,' she said.

Rosala shifted the coverlet away and placed the infant against her breast. Blindly, with the most primal response of all, he began to suck. Signe was aware that she was dangerously close to tears. It was the sleepless night, she told herself sternly, but knew this was not so.

'And for the second Guardian?' she said. 'Is there anyone you know here you would want to ask?'

There is a next stage to the story of every man, every woman, every child, a point at which the new thing that happens shapes what follows irrevocably. Such a moment it was when Rosala looked up from her pillow, her pale hair matted and damp about her head, her son at her breast, and said to the countess of Arbonne: 'There is one, though it may be another presumption. My father said that whatever else was true of him, he was a brave and an honest man and, forgive me, I know he is an enemy of Galbert de Garsenc. That may not be the purest reason for naming a Guardian in the eyes of Corannos and Rian, but that *is* why my child needs guarding now. Is the duke of Talair in Lussan? Will he do this for us, do you think?'

Signe did weep then, and, moments later, frightening herself a little, she began to laugh, helplessly, through her tears. 'He is here. And if I ask him I think he will,' she said. There were already so many layers of interwoven memory here, so many echoes, and now one more, as Bertran, too, came into it.

She looked out the window; the first hint of grey was in the eastern sky. Something occurred to her then, far too late, one more thread in this dark, time-spun weaving: 'You do know that your husband's brother is with the duke of Talair?'

And saw then, having been carefully observant all her life, two things. First that the woman had not in fact known this; and secondly, that it mattered to her, very much. Signe's earlier disquiet, like a dissonance of almost-heard music, came back to her. She had a question suddenly, she had several questions, but it was not time for them, and it might never be time. She suddenly missed Beatritz very much, wished her daughter had elected to come north for the fair this year instead of remaining on Rian's Island.

Rosala de Garsenc said, speaking carefully, 'I would not want to see him yet. I would not want him to know I am here. Is this possible?'

'I do not think he would betray you, or try to send you back. We know a little of Blaise here now.'

Rosala shook her head. 'It isn't that. I am . . . too much entangled in that family. Would the duke tell him I was here?'

Signe shook her head, masking a growing unease. 'Bertran deals with women in his own ways, and he cannot be said to be the most predictable of men, but he will not betray a confidence.'

Rosala looked down at the child on her breast, trying to deal with what she had just learned. Cadar had an unexpectedly full head of hair, lying in whorls and ringlets upon his forehead. In the candlelight it was a distinctive shade of brown, nearly red. Very like his father's, she thought. This latest information should really not have surprised her so much; they had heard over the summer that Blaise had left Portezza again. She closed her eyes for a moment. It was difficult to have so many things to deal with just now. She was extremely tired.

She looked up at the countess. 'I am a very great burden for you. I know this is true. I could see no other choices, though, for the child. Thank you for allowing me here. Thank you for accepting Guardianship. Will you do one more thing? Will you ask the duke of Talair to stand up with you for my son this morning before Corannos and Rian and against all those who would do him harm in the world?'

In the end, Roban the chancellor went himself with two of the corans of his own household to find En Bertran de Talair. The duke was not in his own bed, but the chancellor persevered and found him soon enough, though not, unfortunately, alone. A mildly embarrassing incident ensued, but not one of sufficient importance to affect Roban's mission.

They rode back across the lowered bridge to the castle on its island just as the sun was rising beyond the river, sending light, finally, like a blessing into the room where Rosala lay. Bertran de Talair entered that room with the morning brightness, wearing his habitual amusement like a cloak, sardonic laughter barely hidden in his eyes. He looked at the countess first, and then to where the woman lay, and lastly he looked down, without speaking, upon the cradle at the foot of the bed and saw the sleeping child.

After a long time during which his expression could slowly be seen to change, he looked back at the mother lying in the bed. The priestesses of Rian had washed her and dressed her in a blue silk robe, and had helped her with her hair. It lay, long and golden in the mild sunlight, combed out upon the pillow and over the coverlet. Her eyes were as blue as his own.

'My congratulations,' he said formally. 'You have a handsome son. I wish him good fortune all his life.'

She was registering everything she could: the light, clear voice, the scar, the mutilated ear, the way his expressive face had altered when he allowed the irony to recede.

'Galbert de Garsenc, High Elder of Corannos in Gorhaut, would take this child from me,' she said, without preamble or pleasantry. Her voice was carefully measured; she had prepared these words while they waited for him to come. It was bald, graceless, but she was too weary to do this eloquently, she could barely manage to say what needed to be said.

'So I have been informed,' he replied gravely.

'I am afraid, under those circumstances, that accepting Guardianship for my child will be more than ceremonial.'

'Under the circumstances, I believe that to be so.'

'Will you take this upon yourself?' she asked.

'Yes,' he replied calmly. And then, after a pause, 'I will die myself before you lose this child to him.'

Her colour rose sharply, he saw, and her breathing quickened, as if released from a rigid effort of control. 'Thank you,' she whispered. There were tears now — for the first time all night, though he could not know that. She turned her head and looked at the countess. 'Thank you both. This makes him as safe as the world will let him be. I think I can rest now.'

They saw her close her eyes. She was asleep almost as soon as she finished speaking. Standing on either side of the bed Bertran and the countess exchanged a long glance. Neither spoke for several moments.

Finally the duke grinned; Signe had been more or less expecting that, it was almost a relief when it came, a breaking of the heavy spell of this night.

'You did this,' he said, 'not I. Never reproach me.'

'I did not think you would refuse a child,' she said quietly. 'There will be no reproach. We must be what we are, or we become our enemies.' It was morning, she hadn't slept all night. She didn't feel tired though, not any more. She walked to the eastern window and looked out over the island and the river and the red and golden autumn colours of her land.

In the doorway, Roban the chancellor heard those words exchanged and watched his countess move to stand at the window. She looked terribly small and fragile there, beautiful as ivory. He remained silent, smoothing down the front of his shirt again, unnecessarily. He was contemplating not only the nobility of the sentiments just expressed but the rapidly growing likelihood that they would all be conquered and dead by the summer of the year to come.

†

The taverns of Lussan were thronged at the time of the fair, and there were a great many of them. It was, therefore, only sheerest bad luck that led Othon the animal-trainer into The Arch late that night after he'd already visited three other inns and had commenced his enjoyment of the Lussan Fair in typically liquid fashion. Rendered even more garrulous than usual, Othon was holding forth at a table of sundry reunited performers, describing the unusual travelling companion he'd had in his wagon. For a man known to travel with a snake and monkeys to characterize any companion as unusual was sufficiently droll to earn him more attention than customary.

'Yellow-haired and blue-eyed, she was,' Othon declared, 'and very likely a beauty, though it was hard to see given her . . . condition, if you take my meaning.' He paused. Someone obligingly refilled his glass. 'Not many women look their best when about to drop a babe, in my experience.'

Someone made a lewd remark linking Othon's experience to his monkeys. Amid the laughter the animal-trainer drank again and then went on, with the placid tenacity of a story-teller used to holding the floor against difficult odds. He did not notice the three men at the next table who had stopped their own conversation to listen to what he was saying.

'She tried to pretend she was a farmer's wife or some such, a smith, a carter, but it was easy enough to see she was no such thing at all. I've been in enough castles in my time to recognize nobility, if you know what I mean.' The wit at his table attempted another jest, but Othon's voice rode over him this time. 'We left her at the goddess's temple here, and it is my personal wager that some lord of Gorhaut'll have a babe by now through the aid of the priestesses of Rian — and isn't that a jest?'

It might have been, but it was also somewhat near to the bone that autumn season. Everyone knew how tense affairs had become between Gorhaut and Arbonne, and no one wanted to be the first or the most obvious to laugh in a tavern filled with unfamiliar men from many countries. Disappointed, Othon subsided into silence for a few moments, before beginning, with impressive optimism, a new, discursive account of his last visit to Barbentain. He had lost his audience by then, though, and was largely talking to himself.

The three men at the next table had not only stopped listening, they had settled their account and left The Arch.

In the street outside, expensively lit by lanterns during the fair season, the three corans, who happened to be from Gorhaut, and more particularly from Garsenc Castle, had a hurried, highly agitated consultation among each other.

At first they considered drawing straws to see which of them would ride back to Garsenc with what they thought they'd learned. It could be done in two days if a man killed horses under him. A moment's further deliberation induced them to alter this plan. There might be some real risk in bearing these tidings, or there might be profit to be found — it was hard to tell with the lords of Gorhaut, and especially so with the de Garsenc.

In the end, they each elected to forego the ransoms they might earn in the tournament mêlée — the reason they'd come to Lussan in the first place — in favour of collectively riding north with the almost certain news that the missing wife of Duke Ranald was in Lussan at the moment. Carefully they avoided comment, even among themselves, on the possible implications of this. They returned to their own inn, paid their accounts, saddled horses and rode.

Part of the bad luck — all of it, in fact, from Othon the animal-trainer's point of view — was that one of the three pulled up suddenly just before the wide-open northern gates of walled Lussan and grimly pointed something out to the other two. Silent, visibly shaken by what he said, they exchanged frightened glances, each nodding agreement with this new conclusion.

They did draw straws then after all. The one who'd had the disturbing thought drew the short straw, perhaps appropriately. He bade farewell to the other two and watched them start off on the hard ride back through the mountain pass. He returned to their inn alone. Later that night he killed the animal-trainer with a knife between the ribs when the latter stumbled alone into an alley to relieve himself. It was an easy killing, in fact, though it brought him no particular satisfaction. No ruler could guarantee safety after sunset, even during a fair. He was breaching a truce by doing this, though, and, as it happened, he didn't much like doing that, but his own likes or dislikes weren't greatly important in a situation such as this one had become. He cleaned his blade at a splashing fountain and went back into The Arch for another flask of ale. Killing, he'd always found, gave him a thirst.

It would not do, he had said to the other two corans at the city gates, to have Ranald de Garsenc, or worse, the High Elder himself, asking why the loose-tongued old man had been permitted to continue prattling idly, spreading a vicious story that could only do harm to the family the three corans had sworn oaths to serve.

A crowded table had heard Othon tell his story, though, and rumour and gossip were the most vigorously traded items of any fair. It was all over Lussan by the end of the next day that a noblewoman from Gorhaut had come south to bear a child. A few people had even heard a second tale, that the countess herself, and the duke of Talair, had been seen together, first in Rian's temple and then the god's stone chapel in Barbentain just after dawn that morning. Some clever person mentioned the birth rites of Guardianship to someone else. That, too, was all over the fair by nightfall.

Othon's death passed virtually without comment. Knifings after dark among the travelling folk were too ordinary to be worth much discussion. The animals were sold to another trainer before the fair was over. One of the monkeys, surprisingly, refused to eat, and died.

CHAPTER·11

A *challenge!'* shouted the trovaritz from Aulensburg. The tavern was thronged, he wasn't loud enough, only those near him heard, and most of them laughed. The man, Lisseut saw from the next table over, was going to be persistent though. He climbed unsteadily onto his chair seat and then up on the table around which he and half a dozen other Götzland musicians were sitting. He was roaring drunk, she saw. Most of the people in The Senhal were by then. She'd had two or three glasses of wine herself, to celebrate the beginning of the fair. Jourdain and Remy, after successful summer tours, one in Arimonda, the other among the cities of Portezza, were taking turns buying for the table while trading competitive tales of increasingly improbable triumphs.

The Götzlanders began rhythmically banging their heavy flagons on the wooden table. The noise was so insistent it shaped a lull in the din of sound. Into that space in the noise the trovaritz on the table shouted again: 'A *challenge!'*

'Damn that man,' said Remy, in the middle of a story about a night in Portezzan Vialla when his music had been sung at the commune's summer feast while he had sat at the high table with the most powerful men of the city. Aurelian had been doing the singing, of course; Lisseut was still vexed at times that her lanky, dark-haired friend would continue to suspend his own steady rise among the ranks of the poets to revert to a joglar's role and spend a season lending the lustre of his voice to enhance Remy's name. *Friendship,* Aurelian had said mildly when she'd challenged him, and: *I like to sing. I like singing Remy's songs. Why should I deny myself those pleasures?* It was extremely hard to pick a fight with Aurelian.

'A challenge to the troubadours of Arbonne!' the Götz-lander roared. With the ebb in the tavern noise he was clearly heard this time. Even Remy turned around, his expressive face going still, to stare at the man balanced precariously on the next table top.

'Speak your challenge,' said Alain of Rousset from their own table. 'Before you fall and break your neck.' He was much more assertive these days, Lisseut noted, with some pleasure. She'd had something to do with that: the success of their partnership, the recognition now beginning to come for both of them.

'Won't fall,' said the trovaritz, very nearly doing exactly that. Two of his fellows had hands up, steadying him. A very crowded room had become remarkably quiet. The man reached downward urgently. Another of the Götzland musicians obligingly handed him up a flagon. The trovaritz took a long pull, wiped his moustache with the back of his hand and declaimed, 'Want you to show why we should keep following Arbonne. In our music. We do all your things in Aulensburg, there're singers in Arimonda 'n Portezza. Do *everything* you do now. Do it as well! S'time to come out from your shadow.' He drank again, swayed, added in the stillness, 'Specially 'cause you may not *be* here a year from now!'

Two of the others at his table had the grace to wince at that and haul the trovaritz down, but the thing had been said. Lisseut reached for anger but found only the sadness and the fear that seemed to have been with her since Midsummer. It didn't take brilliance to see enough of the future to be afraid.

There were four troubadours at their table, though she knew Aurelian would not volunteer his own music. He could sing for them, though. Remy and Jourdain exchanged a glance, and Alain cleared his throat nervously. Lisseut was about to speak her suggestion when someone took the matter away from all of them.

'I will make answer to that challenge, if I may.' She knew the voice, they all knew the voice, but they hadn't seen the man come in. No one had even reported that he was in Lussan. Looking quickly around, Lisseut saw Ramir of Talair, carrying his lute, coming slowly forward from a corner at the very back of the tavern, picking his way carefully between tables of people to the centre of the room.

Bertran's joglar had to be sixty years old now at least. He seldom toured for the duke any longer. Long past were the days when Ramir carried his lute and harp and Bertran de Talair's music to every castle and town of Arbonne, and into most of the major cities and fastnesses of the other five countries. He lingered in Talair mostly now, with a suite of rooms of his own and an honoured place by the fire in the hall. He hadn't even come to Tavernel for Midsummer the past two years. There had been some overly febrile speculation among the younger performers both seasons that it might soon be time for En Bertran to select a new joglar. There was no higher status imaginable for a singer; dreams or night-long sleeplessness could be shaped of such a fantasy.

Lisseut looked at the old performer with a mingling of affection and sadness. She had not seem him for a long time. He did look older now, frail. His round, kind face, scarred by a childhood pox, seemed to have been part of her world forever. A great deal would change when Ramir was gone, she realized, watching as he came shuffling forward. He didn't walk very well, she saw.

'Well, really — ' Remy began, under his breath.

'*Shut up.*' Aurelian spoke with uncharacteristic sharpness. The lanky troubadour's face had an odd expression as he looked at Ramir.

Alain rose from his seat and hurried to bring Ramir the performer's stool and footrest. With a gentle smile the old joglar thanked him. Troubadours didn't tend to assist joglars, but Ramir was different. Declining Alain's offered hand, the old man cautiously lowered himself onto the low stool. He stretched out his left leg with an audible sigh of relief. One of the Götzlanders laughed. Ramir had some trouble with the thong on his lute case and Lisseut saw an Arimondan at the table on the other side of them cover his mouth to politely hide a smile.

Ramir finally slipped his instrument out of the case and began tuning it. The lute looked to be as old as he was, but the sound, even in the tuning, was achingly pure. Lisseut would have given almost anything for such an instrument. She looked around The Senhal. The silence was a nervous one now, broken by whispers and murmuring. It was so crowded in the tavern it was hard to move. On the upper levels people had pushed to the railings to look down. Over on the eastern wall, on that higher level, Lisseut saw a gleam of long, dark hair by candlelight. She was a little surprised, but not greatly so. Ariane de Carenzu, her hair down, as ever, in defiance of tradition, sat beside a slender, handsome man, her husband. Lisseut knew Duke Thierry now. Before coming to Lussan she and Alain had spent a fortnight in Carenzu, at the particular request of the queen of the Court of Love. They each had a purse full of silver to show for it, and Lisseut had been given a crimson vest of fine wool trimmed with expensive squirrel fur against the coming cold. She had told Remy earlier in the evening that if he damaged her new vest in any way he would replace it or die. He had ordered a bottle of Cauvas gold wine by way of reply. They had been joking then, laughing about Midsummer, celebrating.

She looked back at Ramir. He was still tuning the lute, loosening his fingers as he did. Lisseut's uncle had taught her about that, one of the first lessons he had given her: whatever else you do, never rush the beginning. Start when you are ready to start, they will not leave as long as they see you preparing.

'We have a challenge here,' Ramir said, almost conversationally, one ear tilted down towards the lute, fingers busy on the strings. His voice was pitched so they all had to lean forward to hear. The silence abruptly became complete. Another old joglar's trick, Lisseut knew. She saw, out of the corner of her eye, that Remy was now smiling as well.

'A curious challenge, really.' For the first time Ramir looked briefly at the table of Götzlanders. 'How is one to fairly choose among the music of different countries, different heritages? Surely there is fine music made in Aulensburg and in Arimonda at the court of King Vericenna, as has just been urged upon us so . . . soberly . . . by our friend over there.' There was a titter of amusement. Gradually, almost imperceptibly, Ramir's voice had begun to chime and weave with the apparently random chords he was playing upon the lute. Aurelian's face as he listened, Lisseut saw, was entranced, rigorously attentive.

'We are asked, in the light of this truth, why Arbonne should be pre-eminent.' Ramir paused, looked around the room, not hurrying. 'We are also asked, in nearly as many words, what there will be to mourn if Arbonne is lost.'

He left a silence after that, save for the gentle, almost casual notes drawn from the instrument as if unconsciously. Lisseut swallowed abruptly, with difficulty. Ramir said, 'I am only a singer, and such questions are difficult to answer. Let me offer a song instead, with apologies if it should be found inadequate and fail to please.' The ancient phrasing, that, no one used it any more. 'I will sing a song of the first of the troubadours.'

'Ah,' said Remy under his breath. 'Ah, well.'

Ramir's fingers were busier now, the music beginning to take shape, the notes gathering as if from scattered places in the world at the joglar's bidding. 'Anselme of Cauvas was of modest birth,' Ramir said, and this too was of the old fashion, the *vidan*, the tale of the composer. No one in the newer generation did this any longer when beginning a song. 'Anselme was clever and gifted, though, and was brought into the chapel of the god at Cauvas, and then Duke Raimbaut de Vaux took him into his household, and finally he came to the attention of the count himself, Folquet, and the count honoured Anselme for his wisdom and discretion and employed him in many affairs of state in all of the six countries for many years. And Anselme had several great loves among the noble ladies of his day, but always he was chaste and honourable, and never did he speak the name of any of these women, but in his passion and desire he began composing songs for them, and this was the beginning of the troubadours of Arbonne.'

The music beneath the spoken words was beautiful, delicate as lace or the gems of a master jeweller, precise, many-faceted. Ramir said, 'I could sing a song of love of Anselme of Cauvas tonight, I could sing his love songs all night long until the dawn came to draw us out the doors, but we have been given a different kind of challenge here, and so I will sing a different kind of song. With the permission and by the grace of all those gathered here, I will sing a song Anselme wrote once when he was far from home.'

The music changed and was alone then, creating room for beauty by candle and lantern light in a thronged tavern, with the first cold breezes of autumn beginning to blow outside. Lisseut knew the tune immediately. Everyone at their table knew this tune. She waited, feeling close to tears, wanting to close her eyes but wanting also to watch Ramir, every movement he made, and a moment later she heard the joglar sing:

> *When the wind that comes from Arbonne*
> *Sweeps north across the mountains,*
> *Then my heart is full again, even in far Gorhaut,*
> *Because I know that spring has come to Tavernel and Lussan,*
> *To the olive groves above Vezét*
> *And the vineyards of Miraval,*
> *And nightingales are singing in the south.*

Ramir's rich voice paused again, as he let the simple, sweet notes of the music take them away with it. There was an old, plain roughness to the song, words and music both. It was worlds removed from Jourdain's intricate melodies or the subtle interplay of thought and image and changing form in Remy's best work or Alain's new songs. This, though, was the authentic voice of something at its very beginning. Lisseut knew her own origins were here, those of all the joglars and troubadours, and, yes, of that table of Götzland trovaritz, and all the Arimondan singers and Portezzan, and of those men in Gorhaut and Valensa who might actually venture to shape music of a different sort from the interminably thunderous battle hymns of those northern lands.

As if in answer to the flow of her thoughts, Ramir's voice was lifted again, not so vibrant perhaps as it once had been, but purified by years and the wisdom of those years into an instrument rare and fine as his lute:

> *Here in Gorhaut, so distant from my home,*
> *Among men who care nothing for music,*
> *And ladies who offer little of courtesy to poets*
> *And even less of love, the memory of songbirds*
> *In the branches of trees, of gardens watered*
> *By the sweetness of the Arbonne itself,*
> *Flowing from the mountains to the sea —*
> *Such a vision — a blessing of Rian! — guides*
> *Me to my rest at night with the promise of return.*

The singing ended. Ramir continued the music for only a little longer, after the old fashion again, and then his fingers on the lute, too, were still. It was silent in the tavern. Lisseut looked slowly around at her friends. They had all heard this song before, they had all sung it themselves, but not like this. Not ever like this. She saw that of all those sitting there it was Remy who had tears in his eyes. Her own heart was full, there was an ache in it.

His head lowered, Ramir was carefully slipping his lute back into its case. It took him a long moment to deal with the thong again. No one yet had made a sound. He finished putting away his instrument. With a grimace, he awkwardly shifted his bad leg and rose from the low stool. He bowed gravely towards the table of Götzlanders. Of course, Lisseut realized: they were the ones who had, after a fashion, called for his song. He turned to leave, but then, as if a new thought had just come to him, he looked back at the Götzlanders.

'I am sorry,' he said. 'Will you permit me to correct something I said before?' His voice was soft again, they had to lean forward to hear. And Lisseut heard him say then, would ever after remember hearing Ramir of Talair say, with his gentle, muted sadness, 'I told you I would not sing one of Anselme's songs of love. That is not true, on reflection. I did sing a love song after all.'

It was Ariane de Carenzu, a moment later, from her place on the upper level of the inn, who was first on her feet to begin the applause. Everyone at the troubadours' table stood as the noise in The Senhal began to grow and grow. And then Lisseut saw the Götzlanders rise, as one man, and begin pounding their fists and pewter mugs upon the dark oak wood of their table, shouting a fierce approval. She began to cry. Through the blurring rainfall of her sorrow and her pride she saw Ramir, clutching his lute in its case with both hands to his chest, walk slowly away. He didn't go back to his corner after all. He left the lights and the thunderous noise of the tavern and walked out into the autumn night under the stars.

†

There were some among the taverns and inns within and around Lussan that did their own highly successful business in the month of the fair by *not* remaining open during this lucrative season. The proprietor of The Silver Tree, a well-regarded country inn among fig and olive groves about three miles outside the city walls, had been surprised and more than pleased to join this small but select group. He accepted a considerable sum from Duke Bertran de Talair to house a number of the duke's corans and household during the fair. En Bertran himself would obviously spend most of his time in Lussan in his city palace there, or, indeed, in Barbentain itself with the countess, but he clearly found it useful to have a less conspicuous residence at his disposal, perhaps one where approaches to and from could be more closely monitored. The innkeeper speculated, but kept his thoughts to himself.

Sitting in the smaller, more comfortably furnished of the two ground-level rooms of that inn, with a fire blazing and the night wind blowing outside, Blaise fingered his wine glass and looked over again at Valery. He raised his eyebrows pointedly. Bertran's cousin merely shrugged. The duke himself was sitting at a table scribbling on a parchment, at times consulting other crumpled documents at hand. If Blaise hadn't known better he would have assumed that Bertran was dealing with affairs of importance. In fact, the duke was writing a song and had told them as much when he'd asked for silence some time ago.

They were waiting for someone. Corans were posted outside to warn them of an impending arrival. Bertran, needless to say, hadn't bothered to tell them who it was he was expecting. A surprise, he'd said blandly. Blaise didn't like surprises. He didn't like waiting. There were times when he wasn't sure if he liked Bertran de Talair.

The Talair wine, at least, was superb, and Blaise was comfortably warm in a deep-cushioned chair by the fire. There was food on a second, long table, and tapestries offered warmth and colour on the stone walls. He should, he told himself, be grateful for these blessings of continued life and give thanks to Corannos. He might so easily have died on the road four days ago. The talk since their arrival in Lussan was all about the banning of the Andoria from the fair. Blaise didn't normally spend much time listening to gossip and he didn't linger in places where he might hear it, but this was rather close to his own interests, and they had been given the details by Valery as soon as they'd entered the city.

They'd spent the first night in the Talair palace in town. Or rather, Blaise and Valery had. Bertran had had a nocturnal tryst he was characteristically unwilling to forego or postpone. There had been a curious incident when Roban, the chancellor of Arbonne — a hollow-cheeked, peremptory man Blaise had not met before — came looking for the duke in the hour before dawn. Valery, roused from sleep, had reluctantly named a house where Bertran might be found. The chancellor had grimaced in dismay. Valery had offered to go with the small party, but Roban, wrapped in fur against the cold, had declined. He'd looked over at Blaise with an expression of poorly concealed misgiving before riding off. Valery, seeing that look and catching Blaise's eye, had shrugged then, too. They'd yawned together and had gone back to their beds for what little remained of the night.

When they descended the stairs again Bertran had not yet returned. He came back later in the morning in a silent mood and had remained that way all day, venturing out alone twice for brief periods. He didn't enlighten them as to why. He went out again that night, smiling and scented, to a different house in the city. Blaise didn't bother asking Valery who lived there; he didn't want to know.

Towards the end of the next afternoon, the three of them had taken their horses and ridden out of Lussan and then along a winding country lane to The Silver Tree, where the larger part of the duke's men were staying. Bertran had again been silent during that ride. 'We're meeting someone,' was all he'd said when they set out. 'After dark.' Valery had only shrugged when Blaise looked at him. Blaise had decided that he was growing tired of Valery's shrugs, too.

He was gazing into the fire, trying with only marginal success to do some reflecting upon the larger, grimmer issues that awaited them, when Serlo appeared suddenly in the doorway leading to the larger room, making him start.

'Someone has come, my lord. He is alone, cloaked and hooded, with his face concealed. He will not reveal himself.'

Bertran shuffled his papers together before standing up. 'That's all right. Show him in as he is and then guard the door for us. We should not be disturbed, Serlo, unless I call for you.'

The young coran nodded and went out. Valery rose to his feet and Blaise did the same. There was a look of anticipation and of something else now — a kind of youthful, infectious delight — in the blue eyes of the duke. Blaise, against his will, began to feel a quickening excitement.

Serlo returned moments later escorting a man who was indeed wrapped in a long black mantle with a cloth wrapped about his face, concealing all but his eyes. The man wore a sword, but had, as Serlo noted, come alone. He waited until the young coran had withdrawn and closed the door behind himself. Then, with a neat sequence of movements, he let fall his cloak and hood and removed the scarf.

Blaise looked sharply over at Bertran, saw the genuine astonishment in the duke's expression and the swift beginning of anger, and then he began, helplessly, to laugh.

'Well, good evening to you all, at any rate,' said Rudel Correze brightly as no one spoke. 'I hope I'm not late, or early, or anything.'

Bertran's colour had risen; the scar showed white on his face. 'You had best tell me, very quickly, who you are and what you think you are doing,' he said icily. Valery had now moved forward, a hand to his sword hilt, his glance moving uncertainly towards Blaise and then to the man in the doorway again.

Still laughing at the sheer audacity of it all, Blaise said, 'Actually, you did say on the road to Lussan that you wanted to meet this man. Shall I perform the introductions?'

Bertran looked from Blaise back to the new arrival. 'Ah,' he said, his tone changing. He lifted one eyebrow. 'The Correze son? With the poisoned arrows?'

Rudel bowed deeply. His hair was bright in the blazing light of the fire and the candles. He grimaced wryly when he straightened. 'I do apologize for that. It was a long shot at night. I am glad to see you well, my lord.' He turned to Valery. 'And you. I trust you are recovered?'

'Entirely recovered, thank you,' said Valery politely, letting go of his sword. 'I am a walking tribute to the arts of the priestesses of Rian.' There was a flicker of amusement in his eyes, Blaise saw.

His old friend turned to him last of all. 'You must have greatly enjoyed that last conversation of ours,' Rudel Correze said quietly. 'Knowing what you knew, and chose to keep from me.'

'Not really,' Blaise said. 'Not at the time, at any rate. I thought Valery was dead, and you caught me unawares with almost everything you told me. I had a difficult time, actually. I wouldn't have told you about your mistake, though, even if I had been inclined to. If you had learned the duke was alive you might have felt obliged to try again, and I would have had to have you taken then, with problems for everyone in Arbonne.'

'Not to mention for myself,' Rudel said lightly. He was listening carefully though.

'You would have deserved it,' Blaise said. 'I'll concede that afterwards I did enjoy the thought of you showing up in Götzland to claim the money.'

Rudel made a sour face. 'I'm sure you did. You ensured I would arrive triumphantly in Aulensburg, report a successful mission, confirm the deposit of my ridiculous fee — and then deal with the discovery, a fortnight later, that the esteemed duke of Talair — ' he smiled briefly at Bertran ' — was engaged in ongoing diplomatic exchanges with King Jörg at Aulensburg and not, evidently, from beyond the grave.'

'So you gave the money back?' Blaise feigned ignorance. He was now enjoying this.

'I gave back what was left of it, under some impolite pressure from Gorhaut's ambassador to the court in Aulensburg. Not a pleasant man, I can tell you. I had to approach my father's branch bank for certain sums that were not . . . readily available to me privately.'

'After only a fortnight?' Blaise raised his eyebrows in feigned surprise. 'What did you buy? All the gems of the east? How much could you have spent in two weeks?'

'Enough,' said Rudel tersely, his handsome face colouring. 'Enough that you may consider our personal slate from that night in Tavernel to be balanced, at the very least. My father currently has a view of me that may well match the one yours has of you. Paying out money does that to him, I'm afraid.'

'Sad tidings,' said Bertran de Talair, his equanimity regained. Blaise recognized the tone and the glint in his eyes. 'But leaving, as I suppose we must, past trials for present affairs, I do think it reasonable to ask what you are doing here.'

'It is entirely reasonable.' Rudel paused, looked over at the long table by the far wall. 'I did hear you were known for serving a good wine,' he said politely.

Shaking his head, Valery walked over to the table and poured him a glass. He came back, handed it to the Portezzan, then stood near him, waiting. Bertran did not speak again, and neither, now, did Blaise. Rudel sipped, smiled his approval, and went on.

'I am sadly between contracts at the moment,' he said calmly, and Blaise saw Bertran and Valery both take the point. 'Given last summer's events, and the unexpected involvement of my old friend Blaise, I still had something of an interest in you, En Bertran. With nothing better to do before the tournament, I made a point of tracking your movements the past two days since we all arrived in Lussan and settled in for the fair — lamentably lacking the company of the choleric lord of Andoria.' He drank again, with obvious pleasure. 'When you took these quarters outside the walls in addition to your usual town residence, and then rode out here at day's end with only your cousin and my friend Blaise, it seemed appropriate to conclude that some meeting of a private nature was about to take place.'

However composed Rudel might be, the duke of Talair was a match for him. Coolly, not smiling now, Bertran said, 'Such a conclusion might indeed seem appropriate. The question is, why, having made that deduction, would you take it upon yourself to intrude upon that meeting?' There was something unreal, an almost hallucinatory quality to the dialogue taking place, Blaise thought. One of the men talking so pleasantly here had attempted to kill the other just three months ago for a quarter of a million in gold. He couldn't think of any other men he knew who could have had this conversation.

Rudel sipped his wine again. He favoured them all with his most brilliant smile. 'To be honest,' he murmured, 'I thought it might be amusing.'

Looking at his friend, at the clever, handsome face, Blaise knew with certainty that this was at least part of the truth, possibly even the largest part. He saw that Bertran realized it, too. The duke's own amusement was obvious. He shook his head and looked over at Valery. His cousin's expression was wry.

'Does this fellow remind you of anyone?' Bertran asked.

'Someone I grew up with, yes,' Valery said. 'A cousin I never expected to see reach the age you seem to have attained.' Blaise turned his head towards the door; he had heard voices, and now there were footsteps outside. 'What,' Valery went on calmly, 'do you want us to do with him?'

'I should mention,' Rudel said quickly, before Bertran could reply, 'that I had one more piece of information in solving this riddle. While I was watching by the walls this evening, at the gate from which you left, I did see a small party of men, one of them masked, the others hooded, ride out at darkfall. They were not in a hurry. It gave me the opportunity to have this most enjoyable encounter in private with you.'

There came a diffident knocking at the door.

'Yes, Serlo, what is it?'

The young coran's voice on the other side was angry and confused. 'I am sorry, my lord, but another party is here. A man in a mask who says he has a meeting with you here tonight. He has an escort with him.'

'Four men,' Rudel said helpfully.

'Four corans with weapons,' Serlo went on. 'I don't recognize the livery.'

'I don't think you are meant to,' Bertran said, opening the door. 'I think that is our proper guest. Escort him here, Serlo, and then entertain his escort. These may not, in the end, turn out to be friends, but they are guests tonight. Treat them accordingly.'

Serlo, looking unhappy, went away.

'I grow more and more curious,' said Rudel Correze cheerfully. 'I'm so glad you invited me in.'

Bertran swung the heavy door closed. His expression was quite sober. 'We have only a moment,' he said. 'I can have my corans render you unconscious, or bind and gag you in a back room somewhere. I may have to. One last time: is it only idle mischief that brings you here?'

Rudel's expression, not surprisingly, had also changed, but less than one might have expected — unless one knew the man. Eyes bright in the firelight, he said, 'I am not accustomed at this point in my career to having to solicit commissions, but I did tell you I was between engagements. You might spare my pride and regard that as a hint.'

There was another brief silence, and then Bertran de Talair began, helplessly, to laugh. Blaise, staring at his friend, followed suit a moment later. Rudel grinned back at them both, pleased. Whatever one might ever say about Rudel Correze, Blaise thought ruefully, things were seldom dull when he was around.

The same, for that matter, might be said of En Bertran de Talair. The duke said, 'You are seeking employment with me, is that correct?'

'I am.'

'Might I ask why?'

And now Rudel's expression finally became serious, and one was inescapably reminded that this was the scion of one of the wealthiest, most aristocratic banking houses in Portezza, with family connections to most of the nobility in that country. He laid down his glass on the small table beside him.

'Shall we say that I do not mind if my skills are bought? Indeed, my profession demands that this be the case. I do mind, however, rather a great deal, when my relationships are similarly exploited without my knowing it. I was not aware that Blaise was with you when I accepted his father's contract. I would not have done so had I known. I have reason to believe that Galbert de Garsenc chose me only because of my friendship with his son, and not for any flattering appraisal of my talents. This thought does not please me. I have formally relinquished his contract. It will satisfy my own sense of honour to work to ensure that no one else successfully fulfils it, if the sum is offered again.'

'I doubt it will be. They have made their point, and have a larger game to play now.'

'I think you are correct in that, my lord, but even so, I would be pleased and proud to enter your employment, En Bertran.'

Valery coughed. 'I rather doubt,' he said, 'that we could afford your current rates.'

Blaise grinned. Rudel did not. 'I will be happy to forget that. It was an unnatural offer in a number of ways. I will be honoured to accept whatever you are paying my friend Blaise at this moment, though I cannot, as I'm sure you'll appreciate, work for less.'

Blaise and Bertran exchanged a glance, looked over at Valery, and then all three of them began to laugh. Rudel attempted to look dignified which, Blaise reflected, is a difficult thing to do when three men are laughing at you.

This was, however, a friend, and one who had clearly been disturbed by the dangerous events of last summer. He was also proposing to join them — though Blaise still felt an inward disquiet when he tried to weigh his own complex allegiances here.

He let Rudel in on the jest. 'You have undervalued yourself, I fear. I am not now being paid anything at all. I've left the duke's employ. I'm with him as a friend and a companion in the tournament two days from now. I'm afraid you won't want to work for my current wages.'

Rudel reddened again. 'I see. I seem to be bound by what I just proposed, however. I can understand your amusement.'

Bertran shook his head, as another knock came at the door. 'Not so. I will be pleased to have you with me.' He grinned. 'And diverted as well, I rather suspect. I'll pay you what I was paying Blaise before he changed his status with us. We can discuss this further at our leisure — indeed, we will have to. For now, I'll greatly value discretion from all of you.' He turned to the door and opened it himself.

Serlo was there, standing a little behind an extremely tall, dark-bearded man with a lean, fighter's build. The man was indeed masked and hooded, clad in unrevealing black for the night ride. On the threshold he carefully took in the four of them, smiled thinly and removed his mask, revealing thick eyebrows and deep-set grey eyes.

'You have unexpected companions, de Talair,' he said in accented Arbonnais. 'In fact, if we count myself you seem to have assembled a room full of your enemies.' Notwithstanding this remark, he stepped across the threshold with easy confidence. Bertran closed the door behind him.

'My cousin Valery,' said the duke quietly. 'One friend at least. It appears you know both Blaise de Garsenc and Rudel Correze. And I am certain they both know you.'

Of course they did. If Rudel's appearance had been a shock to Blaise, this man's arrival was something stupefying. He had last seen those heavy-browed, calculating grey eyes almost two years ago on a frozen battlefield in the north. A wan sun had been setting, dead men piled in the crimson snow and three generations of war lying like a curse behind the savagely contested battle being waged.

Blaise bowed with briefest formality, masking his thoughts. Rudel and Valery bowed. And then Duke Bertran, turning back from making the introductions, did the same.

One bowed to the monarchs of this world.

'The younger Garsenc has prowess I have learned to fear,' said King Daufridi of Valensa, glancing at Blaise. 'As for the Correze scion, I would rather have thought his prowess was cause for your own fears, or were last summer's tales idle?'

'They were not, your highness,' Bertran said, straightening. 'But it seems, happily for my fragile peace of mind, that Rudel Correze now regrets accepting a contract to end the life of a man so inoffensive as myself and has joined my corans by way of redress. Is this not so?'

'It is,' said Rudel. 'I have seen the folly of my summer's ways, your highness. En Bertran has been good enough to allow me to display the truth of that in his employ.' His tone was neutral and composed, but Blaise knew that Rudel, too, would be struggling to absorb the shock of this encounter. It occurred to him, unexpectedly, to wonder if the countess of Arbonne knew anything about this meeting.

'I begin to fear,' said King Daufridi of Valensa, 'that your celebrated charms, de Talair, will prove too much for me as well. I shall have to firm my resolution by remembering your own, ah . . . inoffensive words about me, from last spring.' He crossed the room in three long strides, his boots resonating on the floorboards, and picked up Bertran's lute from the table. Striking three chords quite competently, he turned back to the four of them and chanted:

And what king lost to honour like craven Daufridi
Would retreat from that ice-field not to return?
Where went the manhood of Gorhaut and Valensa
When war was abandoned and pale peace bought

By weak kings and sons long lost to their lineage?

Bertran, at the side table pouring wine, paused in his movements, the decanter in one hand, a bemused expression on his face as he listened. Daufridi finished, struck a last chord and gently laid down the lute.

'Craven Daufridi,' he repeated musingly. 'I must admit, I was intrigued by what you thought you could achieve by inviting me here. I hadn't even planned on coming south to the fair this year. I'm getting too old for tournaments.'

Bertran lifted a glass and walked over with it to the king. 'I am pleased that I intrigued you sufficiently to have you join us. At the very least,' he murmured, 'I have now learned that your highness performs my music with skill. I have also been reminded that in my pursuit of balanced and well-shaped songs I ought to pay greater attention to possibilities the future might hold.'

Daufridi, with a chuckle, took the glass and sank down into a deep chair. He stretched out his long legs towards the fire and motioned graciously for the rest of them to sit. They did. The king looked at Bertran, irony manifest in his clever, bearded features. He was of an age with the duke, Blaise knew, but looked older. He too was scarred — the red weal of a sword wound ran down the left side of his throat to disappear beneath his clothing. Blaise happened to know how far that sword stroke ran. He had seen the blow. It had ended a battle, though the man who dealt it had died in the doing by Iersen Bridge.

'You will now proceed to tell me,' said Daufridi of Valensa, holding his wine up to admire its ruby colour in the firelight, 'that your lines about my shameful cowardice were simply inserted for poetic symmetry. That your real targets were King Ademar of Gorhaut and this man's father —' he gestured with the glass towards Blaise '— and any insult to me was deeply regrettable and most unfortunate and you sincerely apologize for it. Galbert de Garsenc, incidentally, invited me to contribute to last summer's assassination fee. I thought it greatly excessive and declined. Just so you know.' He drank from his glass. 'The wine,' he pronounced, 'is excellent.'

'Thank you. And so, I must say, is your reasoning and anticipation, your highness. You have completely pre-empted my own first words.' Bertran's expression and tone were grave.

Daufridi remained amused. 'I am disappointed now. Will political expediency cause a poet to so renounce his own creation?'

Blaise had heard tales about this king, about the keen-edged, fierce intelligence, a hitherto absent quality among the ale-sodden, brawling kings of watery Valensa. The very terms of the Treaty of Iersen Bridge, if nothing else, would speak to Daufridi's competence. Money given, if a great deal of it, in exchange for land sought and not won in fifty years of war. It didn't take a brilliant mind to judge who had gained the better of that treaty — if one left out what Gorhaut could now do with peace assured on its northern borders. Blaise wondered, for the first time, if those Portezzan negotiators Valensa had employed had really shaped the exchanges of letters and emissaries leading up to the treaty, or had merely acted as trained mouthpieces for the will of this shrewd, hard king.

He had wanted so much to kill this man two years ago.

He remembered hammering his way in grief-stricken rage towards Daufridi in the agonizing moments after his own King Duergar had toppled like a great tree from his saddle with that arrow in his eye, his death cry towering like a raven of the god in the frigid northern air. Blaise could hear it now, if he but closed his eyes. It had been Cadar de Savaric, Rosala's father, who had battled through to Daufridi first and inflicted that savage red wound, before dying under the maces and axes of the king's guard. Two giants of Gorhaut slain within moments of each other.

Two men who would have disembowelled themselves, Blaise thought bitterly, before signing the treaty of Iersen Bridge. The treaty his own father had so slyly devised, surrendering the ancient northlands of Gorhaut for Valensan gold, with his own designs dark-hidden in the shadows.

'I had always thought,' Daufridi was saying, smiling that thin, cool smile of his beneath the full, greying beard, 'that the troubadours valued nothing in this transitory world of ours so much as the sanctity of their art. Will you tell me now I was wrong all this time?'

Bertran, in the chair opposite the king, refused to be baited. Blaise sensed that the duke had prepared himself beforehand for something of this sort.

'All other things being equal,' Bertran said quietly, 'we value our work so highly because it might be the only thing we leave behind us for later generations, the only thing that will preserve our name after we die. One poet I know has gone so far as to say that everything men do today, everything that happens, whether of glory or beauty or pain, is merely to provide the matter of songs for those who come after us. Our lives are lived to become their music.'

Daufridi steepled his long fingers before his face. 'And you, de Talair? Do you believe this to be true?'

Slowly Bertran shook his head. 'It is too rare a thought for me, too pure. I am, somewhat to my own surprise, more caught in the toils of this world than that. I would not have thought it once. I lived when I was younger in an almost open courtship of death. You may, perhaps, remember a little of that time. I am older now. I did not expect to live this long, to be honest.' He smiled briefly. 'Rudel Correze is far from the first to seek to aid me in my passage to Rian. But I find myself still among the living, and I have discovered that I value this world for itself, not merely as matter for someone's song. I love it for its heady wines and its battles, for the beauty of its women and their generosity and pride, for the companionship of brave men and clever ones, the promise of spring in the depths of winter and the even surer promise that Rian and Corannos are waiting for us, whatever we may do. And I find now, your highness, long past the fires of my heart's youth and yours, that there is one thing I love more even more than the music that remains my release from pain.'

'Love, de Talair? This is a word I did not expect to hear from you. I was told you foreswore it more than twenty years ago. The whole world was speaking of that. This much I am certain I remember. My information, so far distant in our cold north, seems to have been wrong in yet another matter. What is the one thing, then, my lord duke? What is it you still love?'

'Arbonne,' said Bertran de Talair.

And with that, Blaise finally began to understand why they were here. He looked from Bertran, slight, controlled, but coiled, as always, like a Götzland crossbow, to the tall, hard figure of the king of Valensa, and he wondered, wrestling with difficult emotions of his own.

He didn't have long to wait. Daufridi of Valensa was not a sentimental man; Blaise could have told Bertran as much. Unlacing his fingers, the king of Valensa reached for his glass and took another sip of wine before saying, prosaically, 'We all love our countries, I daresay. It is not a novel emotion, de Talair.'

'I did not mean to suggest it was,' Bertran said quietly.

'I will confess to a similar passion for Valensa, and I doubt I would be wrong in attributing the same feeling for Gorhaut to young Garsenc here — whatever he might feel about certain . . . political decisions that have recently been implemented.' He smiled thinly at Blaise, the same cool look as before, and turned to Rudel. 'As for the Portezzans, they don't really have a country, do they? I imagine they offer the same love to their cities, or perhaps their families. Would that be fair, Correze?' He was being deliberately dry, almost pedantic, Blaise realized, smoothly resisting the emotional pull of Bertran's words.

'It would, your highness,' Rudel said. He coughed. 'I do hope my dear father becomes mindful again of that last.'

The king showed a flash of teeth. 'Ah. He is unhappy with you? You spent some of the money before you had to return it, didn't you? What a shame. But I'm certain your father will forgive you in time.' He turned back to Bertran, who had remained motionless through all of this, waiting.

The two men exchanged a long glance. Blaise had an eerie sense that he and Rudel, and Valery over by the fire, had been forgotten. It was as if they were not there.

Daufridi said, very softly, 'It is unwise to love anyone or anything too greatly, de Talair. People die, things are taken from us. It is the way of our lives in this world.'

'I have reason to know this. I have lived twenty-three years with that truth.'

'And have therefore moderated your passions?'

'And am therefore resolved that I will not live through the death of my country as I endured the death of the woman I loved.'

There was a silence then. Not daring to move, Blaise looked out of the corner of his eye at Rudel, and saw the rigid, focused expression on his friend's face.

'And so you asked me here,' Daufridi of Valensa said at length, 'to seek what aid I could give.'

'I did. Is this a surprise?'

'Hardly. Will it be a surprise in turn if I say I can give you nothing?'

'I should be grateful to know why.' Bertran was pale but quite composed.

Daufridi shrugged. 'I have a treaty signed, and I need five years, at least, to consolidate my hold on the lands they have ceded us. We need our own farmers there, we need to fill the villages with Valensans and give my own barons time to put down their roots in the castles that now are ours. Those men of Gorhaut who elect to stay — and some of them will — must be given time to feel that there are worse things than being subjects of the king of Valensa. In time, the treaty will offer us all the riches of that farmland north of the Iersen and more than recoup the money we have already paid and will pay out over the next three years. But I need peace to make all that happen.' He sipped from his wine again. 'It isn't very complex, de Talair. I would have expected you to know all this.'

'So you are happy Gorhaut is looking now to the south.'

Carefully Daufridi said, 'I am not entirely unhappy.'

Silence again. But into it there came now a light, cool voice. 'Forgive me,' said Rudel Correze, 'forgive my presumption, but I do have a question.' Daufridi and Bertran both turned to him. 'What do you imagine will happen to Valensa, your highness, if Gorhaut indeed comes south with fire and sword and conquers here?'

Blaise's own thought, his own question. Rudel had always been quicker to speak his mind. Portezzans tended to be. For the first time, he saw Daufridi shift in his seat a little uncomfortably.

'I have thought on that question,' he admitted.

'And what have you concluded after such thinking?' It

was Valery this time, from by the fire, his broad arms folded across his chest.

Bertran leaned forward a little in his chair and echoed his cousin softly. 'What can you possibly have concluded, your highness, should Gorhaut destroy Arbonne and have all the wealth of this land and its ports on the sea to draw upon? If there are five countries, not six, a year from now? Do you really think you would have your five years of peace then, to . . . as you say, solidify your hold on that farmland north of Iersen? How long do you think it would be before Ademar turned north again?'

Something curious began to happen to Blaise just about then. It seemed to him as though the words each man was speaking had become like preordained speeches in some temple ritual of the god, or the well-known opening moves of a tavern game, each following the other, each compelling the move that followed.

Daufridi said, a slight edge to his voice, 'As I say, I have considered this. I do not have any immediate conclusions.'

And so Blaise, seeing the next moves now as clearly as if they had already happened, said, 'Of course you do not. That is why you are here, isn't it, your highness? To see if the duke of Talair has a conclusion for you. And you find, to your disappointment, that what he wants is your help, which frightens you. You know — you *know* it is not in the interests of Valensa for Gorhaut to rule in Arbonne. Why will you then deny that aid, when asked for it?'

Daufridi of Valensa turned in his seat to look appraisingly at Blaise, his hard grey eyes almost lost beneath the heavy, drawn-together brows. 'I have a question of my own, first,' he said coolly. 'One I should have asked at the outset perhaps, before being as frank as I have been. Why are *you* here, Garsenc? Why are you not at Ademar's court in Cortil anticipating the glory of this conquest your father and king have set in motion? There might even be land for you. Younger sons always want land, don't they? We have spoken of love of country — where then is yours, de Garsenc?'

Blaise had been waiting for that: it was the next foreknown speech, the next move in the game being played. He wondered if Bertran had prepared this, if he had seen it coming or even steered them towards this moment.

It didn't really matter. The moment was upon them.

He said, 'Because I have set myself squarely against Ademar of Gorhaut. Because I think he is weak and unworthy of allegiance. Because it is my belief that he dispossessed and betrayed the people of my country with the Treaty of Iersen Bridge. Because the Gorhaut I love is the holy land where Corannos the god of the Ancients first came among the six countries we know, and the earliest corans swore their oaths to serve the god and their fellow men and walk a path of righteousness. Because the invasion of Arbonne would be a final straying from that path in pursuit of a dominion that could never, in the end, be preserved. Because my father knows that. He does not want to rule in Arbonne, he wants to put it to the fire. Because he has long ago lost whatever true communion with the god he ever had.'

He drew a needful breath to check this rush of words spilling out of him like a river in flood over a dam that has been breached. And he said the last thing then, made the next move in the game, chose:

'And because before the Lussan Fair is ended I will have named myself claimant to the crown of Gorhaut, to see if there are men of honour in my country — and elsewhere — who will rally to my name and this cause.'

He heard Rudel suck in his breath sharply. At least he'd surprised his friend, Blaise thought. If he did nothing else at all, he seemed to have succeeded in astonishing the unflappable scion of the House of Correze.

And the king of Valensa, too, he now saw. Daufridi's hands went to the arms of his chair and gripped there. He pushed for a moment, as if to lever himself to his feet, but then, with a visible effort, remained where he was.

It was silent in the room then. The only sound was the crackle of the fire and the strained breathing of four men. From outside, where the corans of the king were being entertained by Bertran's men, they heard a sudden loud burst of laughter.

'Ah, well,' said Daufridi of Valensa at length, very softly. 'Ah, well now. It seems we do have some things to talk about after all.'

Blaise felt light-headed, almost numb. He reached for his wine and drank. The motion itself seemed odd, unnaturally slow. He felt as if the owl should be in the room with them, Beatritz de Barbentain's white owl, settling on his shoulder again to mark him as a fool, or whatever else he was.

CHAPTER·12

I hope you realize I do not want her back,' Ranald de Garsenc says, glaring at the man on the far side of the room. He has expected this encounter, and has prepared himself, as much as he ever can be prepared for dealing with his father. The news of Rosala's flight to Arbonne, brought by two stammering, exhausted corans, was a shock but not, Ranald has come to realize during the course of the day, as much of one as might perhaps have been expected.

When he had learned — during this morning's earlier, furious discussion — about Galbert's visit to Garsenc and his claiming of the child, Ranald had laughed bitterly in his father's face.

'You did this, then,' he'd said. 'Not I, not anyone else. Your own folly, father. She angered you, didn't she? You *had* to say something, to put her in her place.' Galbert had scowled furiously, clenching and unclenching his big hands.

'That is exactly what happened, isn't it?' Ranald had gone on. '*You* are the fool and the weakling, father. You lashed out in the heat of the moment. You had to tell her, didn't you, to see if you could get a reaction. You should have known bet-ter than to threaten to take her child.'

'Threaten? *Her* child?' Galbert had made sure the instru-ment of his deep voice carried all possible nuances of con-tempt. 'Is that how you see it? Not your own child? Not ours? Are you truly so feeble? I am shamed by you in the eyes of the god and all men.'

There had been a servant in the room, and almost cer-tainly men listening on the outside of each of the three doors to the chamber where they'd been. King Ademar's palace in

Cortil was not the place for private discussions. Flushing, feeling suddenly defensive, Ranald had said, 'We will talk later, when you have calmed your choler. It is clear you are in no condition to be spoken with now. I will await you here at midday, father. Until then.'

He'd stalked quickly out of the room before Galbert could reply. A coran in the antechamber barely had time to be busy at the window. Ranald had ignored him. In fact he had been guardedly pleased with himself for that exit until, alone in his own rooms in the palace, he'd begun thinking more carefully through the implications of what his wife had done.

He'd sent a servant for ale and sat in a chair by the window looking out over a landscape where the sun was trying to break free of windblown autumn clouds. The king was hunting that morning. Someone had probably ridden out already to tell him the news; at Ademar's court ambitious men fell over each other to be the first to bring him tidings, particularly tidings damaging to the de Garsenc family. Galbert was seen as too powerful, Ranald knew. He probably *was* too powerful. Their family had blood as royal as Ademar's if one went back only two generations, and the High Elder was now first of all the king's advisers. Not much need to wonder why they were feared. There were those at court — and not a few of them — who would exult in Rosala's flight and their own discomfiture.

The servant had come back with a pitcher of beer and Ranald had gratefully drained his first flagon of the day. He'd stretched out his legs and closed his eyes. There was no comfort waiting for him though. His wife had lied to him in her last letter, had fled, carrying her child. His child. Had already given birth, it now appeared, in Arbonne. The corans who'd brought the tidings, riding north through the pass at horse-killing speed for two nights and a day, hadn't known if it was a boy or a girl. That mattered, of course, quite a lot. Ranald had found it hard to weigh political implications that morning though. He wasn't very good at it, for one thing. He would have preferred to be hunting with the king just then. In fact, what he really would have preferred was to be back at Garsenc, riding with his own men in his own forest. Slumped back, eyes closed, in that chair, he'd tried to picture Rosala with a babe. He had even tried, briefly, to imagine himself with one. He'd opened his eyes and filled his flagon from the pitcher on the table by his elbow.

He'd allowed himself no more. He would be meeting his father again at midday. It was necessary to be sober for such meetings, as he had learned, at a cost, over the years.

'I do not want her back,' he repeats. It is noon; the clouds are gone and the sun is high in a pale sky, shining through the western windows. Ranald tries to keep his voice calm. He even moves nearer to his father so they can speak more softly. The servants have been dismissed this time. Ranald doesn't want this discussion to be common knowledge through the palace — or all of Gorhaut, for that matter.

Galbert is quieter as well now, Ranald sees. In fact the High Elder appears to be dangerously composed. Before answering, he deliberately selects a chair and settles his bulk in it. He has changed his clothing: he is in the blue robes of Corannos now. Blaise, before he left, used to refuse to talk to their father when he wore the robes of the god. He'd called them a desecration once. That had been the last time they'd seen Blaise, actually, at the peak of yet another raging argument about the Treaty of Iersen Bridge. That one had ended with Ranald's younger brother storming out of the room and the castle swearing never to return to Gorhaut while that treaty stood. Thinking back to that night, Ranald suddenly has an image of his wife crying silently in her seat by the fire while the three of them screamed at each other.

'You are rejecting her. A most natural reaction,' his father says now, hands comfortably across his ample belly. He has gained weight, Ranald decides sourly. It goes with the increased power. 'Indeed, a better man would already have made arrangements to have her killed. Shall I do that for you?'

'The way you arranged for the duke of Talair? Thank you, but no. You aren't very efficient, father.' He can still trade barbs, to a point, but this subject makes Ranald uneasy. Truth is, he doesn't like the idea of Rosala dead. He doesn't want her back — that much is clear in his own mind — but that doesn't mean she has to be executed for reacting urgently to some threat by his father. He adds, 'We trivialize ourselves if we pursue her in that way.'

Galbert blinks, as if surprised. He probably is, his older son thinks. It isn't often that Ranald shows up for encounters in a state of such lucidity. He feels a tired self-contempt rising again. His father says, 'You would let her go, then? And have the world laugh at you.' Galbert uses the dismissive, flicking gesture Ranald has always hated. 'Well, so much is your own affair. I cannot play the man for you forever. You *will* concede,' he continues, in a tone of exaggerated civility, 'that there is an issue regarding the child?'

There is, of course. Though, in fact, Ranald has come to realize during the course of the morning that he is ambivalent about that, too. He is, he has long ago decided, an ambivalent man. Life was so much simpler in the days when, as King Duergar's appointed champion, all he had to do was unhorse and defeat whomever they sent against him. He'd been good at that ten years ago; he'd been extremely good.

He is less good at thinking through something like this. But if Rosala cares so much that she would risk death and accept exile to keep a child from Galbert's hands, well, Ranald, to be absolutely truthful, can understand such a feeling. The problem is, he can't give way to it. He is the duke of Garsenc, first among the nobility of Gorhaut; his father, who ought to have become duke himself when Ereibert his brother died childless, is High Elder of Corannos instead, with even more power accruing from that. Rosala's child — Ranald's child — is a pawn in an enormous game of power.

'If it is a boy,' Ranald says quietly, 'we take him back. I will offer her her life and her freedom to go where she will, but she gives back the babe — if it is a boy. If it is a girl child I truly do not care. Let them go. The king will free me to remarry. As soon as tomorrow, if I ask him. I'll beget other children. If only to make you happy, father.' He smiles bitterly again. 'Will you want all of them for your designs, or just a few?'

Galbert ignores that. 'You say we should take a boy child back. Why should you imagine that Rosala would consent to such a thing, if that is why she fled in the first instance?' His voice, too, is low. He won't want this conversation bruited about either.

Ranald shrugs. 'She too can have other children. For a life of freedom from us she might be willing to do this.'

'And if not?' his father pursues, dangerously calm. 'If she is not willing?'

Belatedly Ranald sees where this is going. It is going where almost everything Galbert de Garsenc has touched of late seems to go. He rises from his chair, suddenly agitated.

'Did you do this deliberately?' he snaps. 'Did you goad her into flight purposely? To create this situation?'

Galbert smiles complacently, his eyes crinkling, almost disappearing into the folds of his skin. 'What do you think? Of course I did,' he murmurs.

'You are lying, aren't you.' Ranald feels his hands forming into fists at his sides — his father's own gesture; he has tried and failed to break himself of it. 'The truth is she goaded you and you spat out something you didn't mean to say.'

His father shakes his head slowly back and forth, his jowls waggling with the motion. 'Don't be completely the fool, Ranald. Why do you think I went to see her at Garsenc in the first place? Why would I want a baby? What would I *do* with an infant? You seem sober this morning. Seize the opportunity: think. It will be in your own interests, incidentally — whatever you might privately imagine — to confirm my version of the story. I cannot conceive of events falling out better for our purposes.'

'*Our* purposes? Your own, you mean. You will now make war on Arbonne to bring back the child.' It is just barely possible that his father is telling the truth; that this entire escapade of Rosala's flight was cunningly engineered. It is the way he deals with people, the way he has proceeded all his life.

With a crash that shatters the stillness the largest door to the room bangs open and thuds against the stone wall. Father and son wheel swiftly. Massive in the doorway, beard and hair dripping with perspiration, blood and grass stains on his broad shoulders and chest, mud spattering breeches and boots, King Ademar of Gorhaut throws his riding whip down on the stone floor and snarls, 'I want her back! You hear me, Galbert? I want her back here immediately!' His face is a vivid red, his pale eyes are glassy with rage.

'Of course, my liege,' says the High Elder soothingly, recovering his poise with speed. 'Of course you do. You are conscious of the insult to our family and seek to help us respond. We are profoundly grateful. Indeed, my son and I were just discussing how next to proceed.'

'Proceed however you must! I want her back!' Ademar says again, running a gloved hand through his hair.

'And the child, too, of course,' Galbert murmurs. 'The child is so very important.'

His deep, calming tones seem finally to take effect. The king of Gorhaut takes a breath and shakes his head as if to clear it. He says, a little more lucidly, 'Of course. The child too. Very important. Heir to Garsenc, if it's a boy. Of course.' He looks at Ranald for the first time and his eyes flick away.

'If they keep a boy child from us,' Galbert de Garsenc says then, still in the quiet, assuaging voice, 'the world can scarcely dispute our right to go after him.'

Ademar bends suddenly and picks up his whip. He strikes it sharply against his own leg. 'Right. You do it. Götzland, Arimonda, the Portezzans . . . explain it, make it all sound right, whatever you need to do. *But I want her back.*'

He spins on his heel, not even looking at Ranald a second time, and strides heavily from the room. Behind him, expressionlessly, a servant reaches in and swings the heavy door closed, leaving the two Garsenc men alone again.

Registering his elder son's expression, Galbert begins, quietly, to laugh. 'Ah, well,' he says, not bothering to hide his amusement, his jowls shaking, 'you have just made a discovery. It seems that *someone* here at least desires the return of your lady wife. I do wonder why.'

Ranald turns away. He feels sick to his stomach and he needs a drink. The memory of the king, huge and wrathful in the doorway, seems imprinted on his brain. He can't shake free of the image. He wonders where his own rage is, where his capacity for such feelings seems to have gone over the years.

'It all works out so neatly for you, doesn't it?' he says quietly, looking out the window now on the inner courtyard of the palace. Ademar's corans are dismounting there in the bright sunlight, displaying the bloody trophies of their hunt.

'If they shelter the wife and heir of Garsenc,' his father says peacefully, in the deep, sonorous voice, 'they must not imagine they can do so with impunity. In the eyes of the world we will have the cause we need.'

'And if they do surrender them?' Ranald turns back from the window. He is wondering how long King Ademar has been coveting his wife. He wonders how he has never noticed it before. He wonders, finally, if his father has been quietly guiding that desire. Another tool, another instrument of policy. He ought to be challenging the king, he thinks. He almost has to. He knows he will do no such thing. Loathing himself, Ranald realizes that he is not going be able to continue this much longer without a drink.

His father is shaking his head. He asked Galbert a question, Ranald remembers. It has become difficult to concentrate. 'Surrender them? Arbonne? Woman-ruled Arbonne?' The High Elder is laughing. 'It will not happen. They will destroy themselves before they yield a woman and a new-born babe to us.'

Ranald feels a taste, as of bile, in his mouth. 'Or you will do the destroying for them.'

'I will indeed do so,' says Galbert de Garsenc, the glorious voice swelling now for the first time. 'In the name of Corannos and for his eternal glory I will indeed destroy that place of festering, blood-smeared, womanish corruption. It is the quest of my days, the reason for all I do.'

'And you are so close now, aren't you?' Ranald says, his own voice harsh. He is going to have to leave very soon, he knows. He is afraid he is about to be ill. He cannot get that image of the king out of his mind. 'Everything has come together for you. Duergar's death, the treaty, Rosala's flight now, Ademar in the palm of your hand.' He says that last too loudly, but he doesn't care any more. 'All you need now, to deal with the other countries, to make it all acceptable to them, is for the child to have been a boy.'

'You are correct,' his father agrees, smiling benignly. 'You astonish me, my son. I have prayed upon my knees to the god. I can only hope Corannos has heard my words and found me worthy to be answered, that I may strike soon with fire and sword in his most holy name. All I need, truly, as you say, is for the child to be a boy.'

†

Rosala came back down the corridor from the room where her

son lay sleeping. The wet-nurse they had found was with him, and the younger of the two priestesses who had been present at Cadar's birth was staying in Barbentain Castle for this first week. They were careful in Arbonne with babies, she was discovering, or, at least, careful with the babies of nobility. Some things were constant wherever in the world one went. Rosala doubted the same attention had been paid to the child of the wet-nurse in its village. She knew it had died; she didn't want to know how, or why. Children died in so many ways. The usual advice was not to grow too attached to them in the first year, lest the heart break if they were taken away. Rosala remembered hearing that years ago, and thinking it made sense; she didn't think that any more. She had no idea how women held back from loving the small, desperately needy infants in their arms. She was grateful beyond words for the care they were offering Cadar. Crossing the mountains south in that jostling wagon she seemed to have passed from an endless nightmare to a sheltering haven.

An illusory thought, she knew. She was too versed in the ways of the world to imagine that she would simply be allowed to live here peacefully with her child and the old countess, receiving troubadours and their joglars, listening to music and riding in the fields beside the river as the seasons followed each other and Cadar grew into a child and then a man. They had been known to kill women in Gorhaut for merely speaking impertinently to their husbands in a public place. What would they do to a woman who fled with a child? And not just any woman, or any child. The heir to the dukes of Garsenc was sleeping in the room she had just left, and Cadar was perilously near in succession to the throne itself while Ademar remained unwed. Third or fourth in line, actually, by one path of reckoning, depending on whether one counted the disinherited Blaise or not.

It didn't much matter. They would be coming for Cadar, and probably for her. It would begin with the formalities of statecraft, the richly clothed emissaries with their learned speeches and their gifts to the countess and the mellifluously written letters they would carry. The gifts would be elaborate; that was the way of things. The speeches would be eloquent and courteous. The demands in the letters would be unveiled and coldly precise, and backed by ultimatums that left nothing to the imagination.

Rosala wondered whether she should take ship for the east to release Arbonne from the burden of her presence. If somewhere in one of the fabled courts of magic in those far lands she might find a home for herself and Cadar. Another illusion, that. She knew the tales of what happened to fair-skinned women in the courts and bazaars of those lands of spice and silk. She knew what happened to their male children.

She could hear music, a murmur of voices and laughter spiralling up the stairwell from the great hall below. She couldn't remember the last time she'd heard laughter that didn't carry an edge of malice. They had told her that the music tonight, by a young man from Orrèze, would be of a very high order. She knew she would be welcome if she went downstairs. She still felt tired, though, and extremely tender, not ready for the demands of public spaces. Privacy was a rare thing in her world, something to be valued as much as any other gift they had offered her here in Barbentain.

She sat down carefully in a recessed window seat to listen. The stone bench was cushioned, for which she was grateful. She reached over and unlatched the window. It was of stained glass, etched wonderfully with the image of a green island in the sea. The breeze came in, and through the window she could see the unfiltered light of the blue moon. They called it Riannon here for the goddess, not Escoran for the god. Because of that difference, she reflected, Arbonne was to be destroyed.

After a moment she rejected the thought: too simple an argument and conclusion. Nothing was that simple in the world.

She could hear the river running below in the darkness, making a soft, continuous murmur beneath the singing of the joglar. It was cool tonight on the isle of Barbentain; Rosala wrapped the woollen robe they had given her more closely about herself. The fresh air revived her, though, and brought back with its clarity the reassuring awareness that she had, by coming here, done all she could do for Cadar. The next moves, in the larger game, were not hers to make. The scale of her own life had suddenly become much smaller, focused on a heartbeat. She felt an urge — and almost laughed at herself — to go back up the corridor to look in upon his sleep again. It was strange how swiftly, how completely, love could re-enter one's world.

The last person she had loved was her father, and he had died by Iersen Bridge almost two years ago. Her mother had gone before him, in the last plague year. Her brother Fulk elicited no real intensities of emotion, nor did she in him, Rosala knew. He would not lead the pursuit to bring her back, but neither would he speak up to stay it. He was a good steward of Savaric, though, and she respected him for that. The Savaric lands were terribly exposed now, wide open to raids from Valensa across the newly drawn border of the Iersen River. If the treaty ever ceased to hold they would be vulnerable to even more than that.

It wouldn't hold, Fulk had told her last year during one of the rare times when they were both at Cortil. Truces like this one never did, but lands lost for long enough were likely to be lost forever. He had said it quietly, for her ears alone. Not for cautious Fulk de Savaric the openly critical talk of a powerful lord, with a new king on the throne. Their father would have been loud in his denunciations, Rosala knew, whatever the consequences.

As Blaise de Garsenc had been before he left, both the first time and then again a year later, after his abortive return home.

Thoughts of Blaise were difficult. He was here in Lussan she now knew, with the duke of Talair. It would be easy to see him, to send a message as clear or cryptic as she wanted it to be. She wondered if he'd yet learned she was in the castle. The priestesses had told her the whole fair was gossiping about the high-born lady from Gorhaut who'd been brought to the temple so near to giving birth. *Othon,* she had thought ruefully: he would have been constitutionally incapable of not telling the tale, nor had she really any right to have expected him to withhold it.

Blaise had never been the sort to listen to gossip, though, and En Bertran de Talair had sworn an oath not to tell him until she was ready. It was even probable — a sharp, new thought — that Blaise hadn't even known she was with child.

There had been no communication at all since the night he'd gone away for the second time.

Rosala remembered that night. Sitting beside an open window in Arbonne with the murmuring river below and music wafting up the stairwell, she went back in her mind's eye to that wintry darkness, the stars lost and a storm wind howling, lashing snow and ice in rattling sheets against the windows of Garsenc Castle. She had listened to the father and the sons curse each other, heard the unforgivable names spoken, the vile things said, savagely wounding, more bitter than the night. She had wept silently, utterly ignored in her seat by the fire, ashamed of her own weakness, wanting so much to be gone from the room, from the tangled, savage hatreds of the Garsenc men, but unable to leave without Ranald's permission and unwilling to draw attention to herself by speaking. The father would turn on her she knew, viciously, the moment he remembered she was there.

Numb with cold beside the guttering fire none of them had bothered to tend, the servants having prudently absented themselves, Rosala had felt the cold tears on her cheeks and heard her brother-in-law, reaching some final apex of his fury, denounce his father and brother in a voice raw with anguish before he stormed from the room and the castle into the wild night: naming the one man as a traitor to Gorhaut, obscenely unworthy of the god, and the other as a drunkard and a coward. She had agreed with both assessments, even as she wept. He was a cold, hard, bitter man, Blaise de Garsenc, with no grace or kindness ever shown to her at all, but he was right, he was so right about the other two.

She remembered lying awake in her bed that night when they finally retired. Ranald in the connecting room had dropped into a snoring slumber she could hear through the closed door. He spoke to himself in the night sometimes, crying out in grief like a child in the darkness of his dreams. In the first months of their marriage she had tried to comfort him at such times; she didn't do that any more. Chilled and afraid, listening to the mad keening of the wind, she had waited, listening for the sound of Blaise coming back for his gear before leaving. When he did, when she heard his booted tread in the hallway, she had risen from her bed and gone to his room, her own feet bare on the bitter stones.

He had been packing a saddle-bag by candlelight when she walked in. She did not knock on the door. There was snow on his clothing, ice clumped in the tawny hair and beard. She had been clad in nothing but her sleeping-gown, her fair hair let down about her shoulders for the night. He would never have seen her hair down before. They had looked at each other for a frozen moment, silent within the midnight silence of the castle, then Rosala had said, softly, not to be heard at all outside this room, outside the small space of this single candle's glow, 'Will you not love me once? Only once before you go?'

And Blaise had crossed the room and lifted her in his arms and laid her down upon his bed, with her bright yellow hair spread out upon his pillow and her gown slipping with a rustle of sound above her waist as she raised her hips to let him move it so, and he had blown out the one candle and removed his wet clothing and taken her in darkness before he left his home again; taken her in silence, in rage and bitterness, and in the endless bone-deep anguish she knew he lived with because of his own lack of power. There had been no love that she could name in the room with the two of them, none at all.

And it had not mattered.

She had known what would be the things that might bring him to touch her that night, what would drive him, and she had not cared. *Whatever it takes*, she had thought in her own cold bed, summoning courage to her as from a far-off place while she waited for him to return. Whatever would bring him to take her for at least the one time.

And in his room later, in that darkness, with the unholy wind raging beyond the walls, the same thought again: she would accept and welcome — her hands grappling him hard to her, feeling him beginning to thrust with urgency, hearing the quickening pace of his breathing — whatever might bring him to give her the child Ranald could not.

He spoke her name once, after. She would remember that.

She did remember it, sitting in the window seat in Barbentain. Curiously, it had come to matter. Not so much for herself — she was not a woman who nurtured such illusions — but for

Cadar. Rational or not, it somehow seemed important to her now that at her child's conception that one spoken link between the two of them had been made manifest. It was an irony of sorts that it was the man who had done so; her own single-minded need had precluded such a reaching out. She wondered what the priestesses of the goddess would say about that, what their teaching would be. What happened, in their doctrine, when Corannos and Rian came together in love — if they did? She knew almost nothing about the rituals of worship here in Arbonne, only the twisted versions of them uttered with loathing in Gorhaut by the brethren of the god. She wondered if she would be here long enough to learn the truth.

There were footsteps in the corridor behind her. The wet-nurse, she thought, quickly concerned. She was about to lean out from the window seat but the steps halted just before where she sat, and Rosala heard a woman's voice she did not know, and then a man's. She remained motionless in the shadows of the alcove and realized, after a moment, that the voices were speaking of murder.

'It is to be done neatly and in silence,' the woman said nervously in accented Arbonnais. 'She told me to say as much.'

'I tend not to make a great deal of noise with a blade,' the man answered, amused. His voice was deep and assured.

'You do not understand. This must not be traced to her. The body will have to be disposed of, and no one the wiser. She said it would be best if he didn't even see you, lest he cry out.'

'Ah. She will be keeping him occupied? Oblivious to all else in the world? Does this sort of thing excite her? Will I have other duties, after?'

'You need not be vulgar,' the woman said primly.

The man laughed softly. 'Fear not. I will only follow your mistress's lead. If she wants to taste blood she will have to ask. He must see me, though, or there is no point to this. He must know who is killing him.'

'He might call for help. We cannot allow —'

'He will not. This is not a man inclined to call for help. And there will not be so very much time, I promise you. Come, which door? There is a ghost to be assuaged, and I have tarried.'

They went by her then, shadows behind them and then before as they passed under the wall torch in the empty corridor. Rosala shrank back against the window. The joglar in the great hall below was singing of endless love and unrequited desire. Neither the man nor the woman turned as they went by. She knew neither of them. At a doorway a little distance down their footsteps stopped. Holding her breath, Rosala leaned out slightly. She saw the man smile then and draw a knife from his belt. He opened the door and slipped inside, moving with silent, feline grace. The door closed behind him. There came no sound at all from within the room. The woman hesitated for a moment and Rosala saw her make a quick, warding sign before hurrying along the corridor and down another flight of stairs at the far end.

It was silent in the hallway, save for the distant voice of the singer drifting up from below, mournful and melodious. Rosala brought her hands up to her face. There was a horror about to happen. She could scream, she knew, to summon aid, and perhaps it would be in time, more likely not.

She was not a woman inclined to scream.

She took a steadying breath, struggling to decide what to do. Her first, her *only* duty, really, was to Cadar, to guard her own safety as his sole shelter in the world. There was no disputing that, or what choice it compelled.

Rosala de Savaric stood up, looked back along the corridor to where her new-born son was sleeping and resolutely began walking the other way. She was her father's daughter, and would not sit silent in a window seat or turn her back and let a man be murdered in a castle that had given her haven.

As it happened, she knew whose suite of rooms the man with the blade had just entered. The mingled scents of spices and perfume had been redolent in the corridor since that guest had arrived. The priestesses and the wet-nurse had been talking about her obsessively for two days. Rosala paused outside that doorway only long enough to look back one last time towards Cadar's room, then she squared her shoulders in a gesture that had also been her mother's, and she opened Lucianna Delonghi's door and stepped inside.

†

Daufridi and his escort left the inn first. Bertran gave them some time and then they rode back to Lussan themselves, passing under the trees and then along the west bank of the river beneath the blue moon. Just inside the gates of the city the duke insisted on parting from the three of them.

He looked at Blaise, hesitated, and then smiled wolfishly in the moonlight. 'I neglected to mention it to you — the baron of Castle Baude arrived this morning. I thought I would say hello to Mallin before retiring for the night. Shall I convey your good wishes?'

Even with what he had learned from Ariane de Carenzu last summer, there was still something disconcerting to Blaise about Bertran's indefatigable energy in this regard. With all that had just happened, with grim, huge discussions of his country's fate scarcely behind him, the duke of Talair was of a mind to go wandering in the night.

Blaise shrugged. 'Please do,' he murmured. 'And to Soresina, if you should happen to see her.'

Bertran's smile flashed briefly again. 'Don't wait up. Sunrise will see me homeward, when the morning breaks.' He always said that: the refrain of one of his own songs from years ago. He turned his horse and was gone into the shadows.

'Should he be alone?' Rudel asked. 'Under the circumstances?' There was something extraordinary about that, too, Blaise thought: the man raising the question had tried to kill Bertran three months ago.

'He won't be,' Valery replied quietly, looking down the lane where his cousin had ridden. 'Watch.' A moment later they saw three horsemen canter out from the darkness and set off after the duke. In their brief transit through the torchlight by the city walls, one of them waved briefly; Valery lifted a hand in return. Blaise recognized the livery and relaxed a little: the countess of Arbonne was evidently taking pains to guard her wayward duke.

'Do they ride into the bedrooms, too?' he asked.

Valery chuckled and twitched his horse's reins. 'In the bedrooms,' he said, 'we must assume he can take care of himself.'

Rudel laughed. 'Does he know he's being watched?'

'Probably,' said Valery. 'I think it amuses him.'

'Most things seem to,' Rudel assented.

Valery turned in the saddle to look at him. 'Most things, but not all. Don't be misled, not if you're joining us. What you heard him say to Daufridi this evening, how he dealt with him, was the real thing. Much of the rest, what he's doing now, is part of a long escape.'

There was a short silence. 'A successful one?' Rudel Correze was an extremely clever man. His tone was thoughtful.

Blaise was remembering that stairwell in Castle Baude again, a flask of seguignac passing back and forth. 'I don't think so,' he said quietly. 'That's why he works at it so hard. I think,' he said to Valery, 'that he should have killed Urté de Miraval a long time ago.'

Valery's face was hidden in the darkness as they rode under a covered archway spanning the street. 'So do I,' said Bertran's cousin finally. They came out into blue moonlight again, slanting down past the steep roofs of houses. 'But we aren't poets, are we, and there was a child.' An old, tired anger was in his voice; embers raked over but not dead.

'This,' said Rudel, 'is going to have to be explained to me.'

'Later,' said Blaise. 'Too tangled for tonight.'

They rode on. Some of the streets by the market were lit, but there were no great crowds. The Lussan Fair, as all the other fairs, was not like a carnival. For one thing, it lasted for a month, and not even Bertran de Talair, Blaise thought, would survive that much revelry. The fairs were for doing business, with some nocturnal activities for spice.

Rudel, perhaps predictably, seemed to be thinking about just that, as they came up to the two lanterns burning outside the honey-coloured walls of the Talair palace and walked their horses to the stables at the back. The ostler came sleepily forward from the shadows and took their mounts. The three of them went back around to the front doors. Under the lanterns again, Rudel had an expression on his face that Blaise knew well.

'There is an amusing tavern I know,' he said, 'just beyond the Portezzan quarter of the market. Are we really going to put the night to bed, or is there some life left in us? I would enjoy buying a drink for the pretender to the crown of Gorhaut.'

Valery looked around quickly, but Rudel's voice had been carefully low and the square before the house was empty. Even so, Blaise felt his pulse jump at the mention of what he'd said tonight. It had certainly had results.

It seems we do have some things to talk about after all, Daufridi of Valensa had said, looking with hard appraisal at Blaise, and then had listened intently, heavy brows drawn together, as Bertran de Talair outlined a number of propositions, some of them startling, one, at least, quite terrifying.

In the street outside the house Valery was shaking his head. 'I'm an old man tonight. Too many twists in the road for my poor head. I want a pillow more than I can say. You two go on. Be young a little longer yet.'

Blaise was torn, in fact, between equally strong desires: one for the quiet of his room, and another for some adequate external response to the excitement within himself. In the past when Rudel had suggested a night abroad, he had seldom demurred.

In those first months in Götzland and then Portezza, after he'd left Gorhaut the first time — the thought came suddenly, new-minted, to him — he himself seemed to have been performing his own driven search for an avenue of escape. It seemed, after all, that the winding route through so many taverns and towns, all the tournaments and courts and castles, the night and morning roads, dawn mist above battlefields and a murder in Faenna, had brought him back, on this cool autumn evening in Arbonne, to Gorhaut, to the country that was his home, and to the Treaty of Iersen Bridge, which he had twice sworn — the second time on his mother's blood on a night of storm at Garsenc — that he would never accept.

Oaths by younger sons, even those of the most powerful families, rarely meant a great deal in the world. It seemed, tonight, as if his own vow might just possibly be different. Either that, or the paths of folly were even wider and smoother and more welcoming than they were said to be, and he was squarely set upon one of them now.

He was not going to fall asleep, he realized. Valery, with a crooked smile at the two of them, walked up to the palace door and knocked softly. The viewing grille slid back, and then the door was opened by the coran on watch. 'Good night,' Bertran's cousin called, over his shoulder. 'Try to be quiet when you do come back. I promise you I'll be sleeping.'

Blaise watched him go in, then turned to Rudel. By the lamplight he saw his friend's head tilted to one side, eyebrows arched expectantly in that expression he well remembered. Valery had said earlier that the young Bertran had been much like this; it wasn't hard to see the similarity.

'Lead on,' he said. 'If events continue as they seem to have begun, and you do intend to stay the course with me, this may be the last chance we'll have to enter a tavern as corans for hire and nothing more.'

'Stay the course?' Rudel said, his voice swirling upwards as they began to walk. 'Do you think you could possibly get rid of me now?' He turned a corner, heading towards the distant glow of lights by the market. It was a lovely night, clear as a shepherd's dream. 'All the riches of my father wouldn't make me leave a game as diverting as this one has become.'

'Oh, good,' said Blaise dourly. 'I'm pleased to be amusing you again. What happens when I send you to your father to ask for all his riches to support us?'

Rudel Correze laughed. He was still laughing when six men ran out from the alley and blocked their path, before and behind, bows levelled at the two of them.

It was quiet in the dark street then, with the only lights a long way ahead or behind. Blaise, looking at the deadly purposeful shapes in front of them, had a brief image of Bertran somewhere in the city with Soresina de Baude, then another of Valery slowly climbing the winding stairs in the Talair city palace, heading peacefully to his rest.

'I find this,' he heard Rudel say, 'deeply offensive, I must say. I was greatly looking forward to that drink in The Senhal. You do know,' he said, raising his voice for the benefit of the silent men surrounding them, 'that I am the son of Vitalle Correze, and you are certainly dead men — dead in a most unpleasant fashion — if you molest us further.'

One thing about Rudel, Blaise thought, using the time his

friend was buying them to scan the shadowy street and alleys for possibilities of escape — he was never shy about invoking his father's name. Came with a good relationship, perhaps. Blaise would prefer to die before calling upon Galbert de Garsenc's even more prominent name as a means of succour.

A preference that might well be about to find its own grim realization. These weren't outlaws or renegades. With a sinking feeling, Blaise thought he recognized one of the bowmen. They wore no identifiable livery — naturally — but he was almost certain he'd seen the nearest man before: last summer, in Tavernel, standing with En Urté de Miraval in the entrance to The Liensenne on Midsummer Eve.

'I think I know them,' he murmured to Rudel. 'I'm afraid this is bad.'

'I didn't think it was particularly good,' Rudel replied tartly. 'You cut left, I go right?' They had swords, useless against archers. Blaise could think of no better plan. The streets were empty here. They were a long way from the market. They would have to hope uncertain light might make the bowmen miss.

'I'm sorry,' he said. 'You were better off being angry with me.'

'Not really. Bad for the heart and liver, anger. That's what my father's doctor says. Live a placid life, he advises. I think I might try that next.'

Poised, preparing to sprint as soon as Rudel moved, Blaise briefly wondered why none of the archers had spoken a word or even made a gesture of command.

Then, when four more men strode quickly out from the alley and came up behind them, he understood. Why give commands when all you want to do is freeze your victims long enough for their executioners to slaughter them? He recognized one of these men, too. It was his last clear thought.

'A placid life, that's the thing,' he heard Rudel repeat dreamily. Out of the corner of his eye he saw his slender, aristocratic friend crumple to his knees, just before the swinging blow from a wooden staff knocked him senseless too.

When he came to, it was with a headache so brutal the room lurched sickeningly as soon as he opened his eyes. He closed them quickly. What remained, as consciousness lingered tenuously, was an awareness that he was lying on something unexpectedly soft and there was a scent surrounding him. He knew that scent, it had associations for him, a great many. And an instant later, as full awareness returned, Blaise realized where he must be. His eyes snapped open with the shock and he twisted his head around to see. The movement made him immediately nauseated and he gasped with pain.

'I do regret that,' a woman's voice said, 'but I had to advise them you might not come willingly.'

'Why bother?' Blaise gasped. He couldn't see her. She was behind him. It was only when he tried, with another painful effort, to turn his body that he realized that his limbs were bound. He was on her bed, which explained the softness, and his hands and feet were tied to the four bedposts. The never-forgotten scent of her perfume was all around him. 'Why didn't you just have me killed in the street?'

'What?' said Lucianna Delonghi, moving at last into his field of vision. 'And deprive myself of this pleasure?'

He had not seen her for more than a year. She was clad in silk so diaphanous she might as well have been naked to his sight. The glitter of jewellery was all about her: a diadem in her hair, sapphires at each ear, diamonds and sea pearls around her throat. There were rings on her long fingers, gold and silver or ivory at each wrist and one spectacular, memorable pendant suspended between her breasts, red like the fire crackling on the hearth. She liked jewellery, he remembered, she liked fires in her rooms even when it wasn't cold, she liked cords and knots and toys in her bed.

His clothing and boots had been taken away; he was clad only in an undergarment that shielded his sex. He tried again, without success, to move his hands and realized, with a kind of despair, that what he was feeling, as much as fury and the several layers of pain, was the returning of desire, inexorable as the tides of the sea.

She was so beautiful it caused a kind of constriction around his heart. She was an incarnated vision from the legend of the paradise that waited for corans who died in battle. His mouth was dry. He looked at her, in her shining, long-limbed near-nakedness, and the memory of their lovemaking two summers ago, her body intertwined with his, legs wrapped high around him or straddling his waist as she rode above, her fingernails scoring his shoulders and arms, the eloquent, striving, backwards arch of her throat when she came to her culmination — it was with him again as if happening now, enveloping as the scent in the room. He became aware, helplessly, that his excitement would be visible. Lucianna, glancing downward, noted that. She had never been slow to observe such things. She looked away briefly, a small, satisfied smile curling about her lips.

'How sweet,' she murmured, in the nuanced, husky voice. She moved out of his sight for a moment and then came back. 'And all along I thought you left because you were angry, because you had lost your desire for me.' She looked down upon him from the side of the bed. 'I don't like it when men leave me, Blaise. Did I never tell you that?' There was a knife in her fingers now, taken from the bedside table. It too had gems in the hilt, rubies the colour of blood. She began to play with it, moving towards the foot of the bed, biting her lower lip as if thinking of something, chasing a memory, and then idly stroking the blade, as if unaware that she was doing so, along the sole of his foot. She twisted it suddenly and Blaise felt the point break the skin, drawing blood. He had been waiting for that.

'I left because you wanted me to, Lucianna. Do not pretend anything else.' It was difficult to be coherent amid both the aftermath of the blow and the increasingly intense reality of desire. Her scent was all around him, pushing clear thought even further away. She continued to move about the bed, the curves and planes of her body lit by the fire's glow. He said, 'Had you wanted to hold me you know you could have done so. I would not have been able to refuse, even after Engarro.'

'Ah,' she said, stopping now to look directly at him. Her skin was pale, flawless; it was still a shock sometimes to realize how young she was. 'But you would have *wanted* to refuse, wouldn't you, my dear? You would have stayed only against your better judgment, tangled in my dark toils . . . is that not how it would have been, Blaise?'

He swallowed with difficulty. She was her father's daughter; the subtlest woman he had ever known. She was also dancing the knife upwards now, along the inside of his thigh. 'I need a drink, Lucianna,' he said.

'I know what you need. Answer my question.'

Blaise turned his head away, and then back, to look her full in the eyes. 'As it happens, you are wrong. I was even more innocent than you knew. Rudel tried to warn me — I didn't want to listen. I thought, if you can believe it, that you were only the way you were because your father had forced you to be his tool, an instrument of policy. I thought you could still love truly if you made a free choice, and I thought you might actually give that love to me.' He felt the bitterness beginning to come back, step by step, mingled, as ever, with desire. 'I was even more a fool than I might have appeared.'

It occurred to him, incongruously, even as he was speaking, that Ariane de Carenzu had said something very like this to him in a different bed in summer, about choices and the paths of love. It also occurred to him, belatedly, that there was something more than a little absurd about this exchange; he had been brought here to die. He wondered where her husband was. Borsiard d'Andoria was probably waiting for her outside the city walls. It had been the corans of Miraval who had brought him here, though; a strange union this one had turned out to be. *When one's enemies take counsel together*, the proverb ran in Gorhaut, *one wants the wings of a bird to fly, or the strength of lions to fight.* He had neither at the moment. He was bound and helpless, head ringing like a temple bell, on Lucianna's bed.

'Do what you want,' he said tiredly as she remained motionless, saying nothing. Her dark eyes, shadings carefully applied above and below, were wide but unreadable. The pupils were larger than they should have been. She had taken her drugs, he realized. They heightened her pleasures. He wondered if she used them all the time now. He wondered how any mortal woman could possibly be so beautiful.

He tried once more to swallow. 'I would have thought the honour of your family, if nothing else, would preclude torturing a man who never did or meant you harm.' *I sound like a lawyer making a plea*, he thought sourly. 'If you must kill me, for your own reasons or your husband's, then have done with it, Lucianna.' He closed his eyes again.

'You really aren't in a position to make requests, are you, Blaise?' Her tone had sharpened. 'Or to comment unpleasantly on either my father's or my husband's courses of action.' He felt the knife point in his thigh. He refused to react. He kept his eyes closed; it seemed to be his only option of denial. That, and silence. Once, in Mignano, she had known he was displeased about something she had said at a banquet. Her woman had come to lead him to her chambers much later than usual that night. When they arrived, he had seen why. There had been easily a hundred candles of different shapes and sizes burning around the bed where Lucianna had lain, naked in the flicker and dance of all that light like an offering in some temple of dead and forgotten gods. She had been bound, wrist and ankle, as he was now.

She had waited for the woman to leave that night and had said, 'You are unhappy. You have no cause to be. Do with me as you will.' It had not been, he remembered noting even at the time, an apology. She was not a woman who apologized. Her body had glistened and shimmered with oil as she twisted slowly to left and right in the blaze of the candles, not smiling, her eyes enormous. Blaise had stood above the bed, looking down upon her for a long time. Slowly he had removed his own clothing as she lay bound beneath him in a dazzle of light, watching . . . and then he had untied all the knots that bound her before lowering himself to the bed.

Lucianna had laughed, he remembered. He had thought then it might be from a certain kind of relief. Now, living the moment again, he heard that laughter differently, as genuine amusement at his innocence: a war-trained Gorhaut coran in decadent Portezza, coupling with the least innocent woman in the world. Young as she was, Lucianna seemed never to have been young. The bitterness was in him again; there might always be that bitterness. Bertran de Talair, he thought suddenly, had never managed to move past what had happened to him in love when he was young.

She was silent still. Blaise kept his head averted, his eyes closed. He felt the knife blade withdraw and a moment later heard Lucianna say, 'I thought, back then . . . I remember thinking towards the end of that summer, before Engarro was killed . . . that I had met you too late.' An odd note in her voice. But that was not what finally caused Blaise to open his eyes. He had heard another sound, from the far end of the room, and felt the faintest thread of a draft across his skin.

When he looked up, Lucianna was turned away from him towards the door, and following her glance Blaise saw Quz-man of Arimonda standing there, white teeth bared in a luxurious smile, a blade in his hand, long as a small sword.

Lucianna glanced over and down at Blaise for an instant, her eyes wide and black with the drug; then she turned her back on him entirely and moved towards the fire, leaving only empty space between Blaise and the Arimondan who had come to end his life. It had indeed been corans of Miraval who had brought him here; the last piece of the puzzle fell into place.

'Staked out like a horse thief,' said Quzman with relish. 'Were this Arimonda I would have him in the desert beside a hive of blood ants, and would pour honey myself over his private parts and eyes and leave him there.' Lucianna said nothing. She was gazing into the depths of the fire.

'How fortunate for me that this is not Arimonda,' said Blaise stonily. He was not going to give this man any more satisfaction than the fact of his death would offer. 'Land of cowards and incestuous catamites.'

The Arimondan's smile never altered. 'You are foolish,' he said. 'You should not be goading me. Not with your sex easy to my blade. Your life ends here. My brother's ghost is hungry for your shade in the afterworld and it is in my hands whether your passage to the god is easy or very hard.'

'No it isn't,' said Lucianna quietly, her back to both of them. 'Do what you came to do, but quickly.'

'What I came to do? I came for an execution,' said the Arimondan, the smile deepening. 'And perhaps for some pleasure upon his body when he is dead.'

'You presume too greatly,' said Lucianna, still not turning from the fire. Her voice was toneless, very low. The Arimondan laughed and moved towards the bed.

'A severe penalty it does seem,' said Blaise to Lucianna, dragging his eyes away from the man with the blade towards the woman who had taught him all he knew about certain dimensions of joy and pain, 'for having met you too late. I do hope this pleases your new husband, and perhaps even the next one.'

She made a small sound; he thought it might be a kind of laugh. He didn't have time to decide, though, because just then, as he turned back to face his death the way a man does, with dignity and an acceptance of the infinite, eternal power of the god, the door opened again and, with utter stupefaction, Blaise saw his brother's wife step into the room behind the Arimondan.

'If you use that blade,' he heard Rosala announce in her crispest voice, 'I swear by holy Corannos I will have you brought into the presence of the countess of Arbonne before this night is over, and I will not rest until you are both dealt with for breaching a truce with murder.'

And then, with that spoken, as her own fierce inner momentum seemed to slow, all three of them staring at her, she registered for the first time — he actually saw it happen — who was lying on the bed, and she said, in a voice so completely different it could almost have made one laugh: '*Blaise?*'

It was Lucianna who laughed. 'How touching. A reunion,' she murmured, turning from the fire. She was still holding her own jewelled blade. 'The wandering children of Garsenc in the den of the dark lady. Someone will surely make a ballad of this.'

'I think not,' said Quzman of Arimonda. 'Since both of them must now be slain.'

His smile had gone. He took another step towards Blaise.

'*Now,*' said Lucianna Delonghi loudly, very clearly.

The inner doors on either side of the bed burst open. Through them, swords drawn, rushed half a dozen corans in the countess's colours, followed quickly by Roban, the chancellor of Arbonne, and then more slowly by a black-haired, sumptuously dressed, darkly handsome man. Last of all, moving with extreme caution, a compress held to one side of his head, came Rudel Correze.

The corans surrounded the Arimondan. One of them seized the dagger from him. Quzman's gaze, bleak and malevolent, did not move from Lucianna's face now. Returning a brief, glacially patrician glance, she said, 'You made an error and you are a crude, unpleasant man. The one might have been forgivable were the other not also the case. And both things, I might add, are equally true of the duke of Miraval, whom you serve in this matter.'

She said that last very clearly as well. Blaise saw the handsome man who was her father smile thinly as Roban the chancellor winced. It was becoming slowly clear to Blaise that he was not, for the moment at least, about to die. That Lucianna had set this whole thing up as a trap for . . . whom? Quzman? Urté? Both? He looked to his left and saw Rudel leaning against a bedpost for support, gazing down on him with an expression that might have managed to be amused if his face had not been quite so green.

'If you do not stop standing there uselessly and cut these cords,' Blaise snarled through clenched teeth, 'I will not be responsible for what I do to you later.'

'To *me?*' his friend replied with feeling. 'What can you possibly do beyond what has been done already? I have just been half killed by corans of Miraval in the interests of a ploy by my cursed cousin Lucianna that had nothing at all to do with me.' But he did begin, moving gingerly, to cut Blaise's bonds.

'You are, you understand, now taken into the custody of the countess of Arbonne,' the chancellor was saying to Quzman. He did not look happy. Blaise, finally able to sit up, slowly chafing his wrists, had some idea why. 'In the morning she will decide your fate,' Roban finished coldly.

The Arimondan was a brave man. 'My fate alone?' he said. 'You see how the woman had the northerner trussed up for me like a hog for slaughter? You know her husband tried to kill him on the road. Will you let her play this double game and laugh at all of us?' Blaise glanced over at Lucianna; she had moved towards the windows, and had put on a heavier robe. She didn't bother looking back at Quzman, or at any of them.

'I do not see anyone laughing,' said the chancellor. 'And if her game was doubled, it was only against yourself. She informed me of your proposal last night, immediately after it was first made.'

A good attempt at deflecting and controlling the damage, Blaise thought, but it was unlikely to succeed. Not with the other man who had entered the room standing there, listening attentively. He knew a fair bit about Massena Delonghi, actually. He had lived in his palaces two summers ago, sleeping with his daughter. He and Rudel Correze had killed a prince for him.

But it seemed, the way events were unfolding, that Lucianna had not intended to have Blaise murdered tonight after all, though the manner in which she had had him bound and what she had done and said still needed an answer. Or, he reflected, perhaps they did not. *I don't like it when men leave me, Blaise. Did I never tell you that?* Perhaps he had his answer. Perhaps she had said nothing more or less than truth. How . novel that would be, he thought wryly.

As he had expected, the chancellor's effort at diversion did not succeed. 'There is another person involved in this, though,' said Massena Delonghi, the sleek, suave man who was said to be seeking to dominate Portezza, and to be using his daughter's marriages in steady pursuit of that goal. 'This Arimondan, I am informed, is employed by the duke of Miraval. I understand from my dear daughter that it was the corans of Duke Urté who assaulted this young friend of ours, and our well-beloved cousin as well.'

'Thank you,' Rudel said brightly. 'I am so pleased someone remembered that.'

Roban did not look pleased at all. 'We will, of course, seek to hear what En Urté has to say about all of this in the morning. For the moment, there is only this man, caught by your daughter's . . . devices . . . in the act of attempting murder.'

'For which he will be branded and hanged, I trust?' Lucianna's brows were arched as she finally turned to look at them. Her voice and manner were a cool, glittering mirror of her father's. Blaise remembered this side of her too. She gazed at the chancellor: 'Precisely as that poor cousin of my dear husband was branded and hanged by the duke of Talair. *Precisely* in the same way, I dare suggest. Or indeed we will have sad cause to question the impartiality of the countess of Arbonne in her justice towards strangers and towards those who serve her own high lords.' The celebrated eyebrows remained pointedly high.

'And,' Massena Delonghi now added, in a tone more of sorrow than reproach, 'there must indeed be the morning's determination of Duke Urté's own responsibility for this most flagrant breach of the truce of the fair. A lamentable duty for the countess, I am sure, but if Portezzan noblemen are to be executed like common thieves, she surely cannot turn a blind eye to the transgressions of her own people, however lofty their rank.'

Lucianna's father was enjoying every moment of this, Blaise realized. It was exactly the sort of multi-faceted intrigue the Delonghi most loved. Massena would have little or nothing actually vested in Urté's downfall or the countess's embarrassment, but would take pleasure and — Blaise had no doubt — in the end find some gain in being the figure at the heart of both eventualities. If Arbonne had hoped to keep her internal feuds close to her breast, that hope was almost certainly ended now. Blaise wondered, cynically, if Massena Delonghi would be writing to Galbert de Garsenc soon in Gorhaut, or sending his factor in Cortil on an informal visit to King Ademar's court, to suggest some quiet transaction by way of compensation to the Delonghi for the discomfiture of Arbonne.

Rudel, proving belatedly useful, if not efficiently so, had finally finished with Blaise's ankle bonds. He'd also found, discarded in a corner of the room, the removed clothing and boots. Moving as well as his pounding head would allow, Blaise dressed himself. He saw that Rosala had taken a seat on a low bench by the door, sitting alone at some distance from everyone else. She was watching his every movement, though, with a curiously strained expression. It occurred to him, with something of a jolt, that he had also been unclothed the last time they'd seen each other. So, for that matter, had she.

The door to the room was still open beside her. Through it now, arresting that particular line of thought, came Lucianna's servant. Blaise remembered Imera well. Her knowing features had accompanied him on a great many silent night walks through one palace or another to her mistress's rooms. Imera stopped in the doorway, took in the scene and allowed herself the briefest smile imaginable as she observed the Arimondan ringed with swords.

It seemed to Blaise, looking at her, as if he were actually being made to journey backwards through the course of this night — first in that inn outside the walls with Rudel and King Daufridi, now here in Lucianna's room — through the layers of his own past. All that was needed now —

'The countess of Arbonne has come,' said Imera.

Of course, thought Blaise, tenderly probing the blood-encrusted lump on the back of his skull, preparing to kneel. He was not really surprised; he was even beginning to find the oddest element of humour in all of this. The small, elegant figure of Signe de Barbentain came briskly into the room, dressed in pale blue trimmed with pearls. She was followed — and this *was* a shock — by the bulky, grim-faced figure of Duke Urté de Miraval.

'My lady!' exclaimed Roban as they all sank down and then rose from their obeisances. 'I thought you to be asleep. I did not want to — '

'Asleep?' said the countess of Arbonne. 'With such beautiful music below and treachery above stairs in our palace? I have only the duke of Miraval to thank for bringing me here in time to deal with this. You and I, Roban, will have to have a talk in the morning.'

'But countess,' began the chancellor, a little too earnestly, 'it is the duke of Miraval himself who — '

'Who was informed by an Arimondan in his employ of a plot by the wife of the banned Borsiard d'Andoria, a second attempt against the life of our dear friend from Gorhaut.' Signe's voice and manner were chillingly austere.

'Quzman, I am sorry to say, has his own grievance against the northerner,' Urté added smoothly. 'So deep a hatred that he was willing to breach the truce of the fair to aid the lady of Andoria in her corrupt designs. I chose to allow the affair to proceed a certain distance, trusting it could be halted — and thereby exposing the Portezzan evil at its source. I am pleased to see that this has happened.' He was staring coldly at Lucianna.

Blaise looked over at Rudel and saw his friend smiling crookedly back at him, still holding a cloth to the side of his head. They turned, simultaneously, to the chancellor of Arbonne. Roban's surprise was just a little too extreme again.

This is a clever man, thought Blaise. *He may get away with it, after all.* Massena Delonghi, he noted, had paled a little beneath the dark tan, but he too was smiling slightly, showing a master's appreciation for the neatness of what was happening.

As if on cue to Blaise's thought, Roban said, 'But countess, there *was* no Portezzan plot. The gracious lady Lucianna Delonghi d'Andoria was acting only to expose this selfsame Arimondan. She personally informed me of his designs last night. She only pretended to accede to his scheme to prevent a more summary murder of the Gorhaut coran. It seems to be her understanding that, ah . . . the duke of Miraval was actively involved in his underling's designs.'

'Evidently a faulty understanding on my part,' Lucianna murmured silkily into the silence that followed this. 'One for which I must surely make amends to the duke when more private opportunity allows.' She smiled at Urté, her most dazzling smile.

'My dear daughter has such an impulsive nature,' Massena Delonghi added, playing out the game, 'and she was naturally so anxious to make redress for her . . . equally impulsive husband's earlier transgression.' He shrugged, and spread his hands. 'It seems we have *all* been acting in good faith here.'

'Except for one man,' said Signe de Barbentain icily. She was looking at the Arimondan.

Blaise had seen it before, and now he registered it again: Quzman of Arimonda was neither a coward nor a fool. The man was smiling, ringed about with steel and hostile glances.

'Ever the way of things, is it not?' he asked quietly, looking directly at his employer. Duke Urté, stone-faced, made no reply. 'I am the sacrifice after all, not the man who murdered my brother. I do wonder, though,' he said, turning with bold eyes and no deference at all to the countess of Arbonne, 'how I am presumed to have used ten of my lord of Miraval's corans tonight without his knowledge.'

The weak link, Blaise thought, racing through possibilities. *He's going to take Urté down with him.* But he'd underestimated the Arbonnais again.

'That is a matter of some grief to me,' En Urté de Miraval said, his deep voice conveying dimensions of regret. 'I chose to test the loyalty and prudence of my corans, electing not to caution them about Quzman's designs or undermine his plot. I am sorry to say that ten of them did, indeed, succumb to his undeniable persuasiveness. They have their own hatred of this Gorhautian coran, arising from the deaths of five of their fellows half a year ago in a most unfortunate incident. They agreed to assist in this terrible deed.'

'Then these men too must surely be punished,' said Massena Delonghi to the countess, shaking his head at this latest revelation of the world's depredations, the evils that seemed to flourish so brazenly in the midst of good and honest men.

Quzman of Arimonda was still smiling, Blaise saw — a terrible expression now, of complete understanding.

'They have been punished,' said Urté briefly. 'They are dead.'

And so the chancellor had indeed won, after all, Blaise realized. Given that his sole purpose here would have been to control the reverberations of this, to keep the countess from having to deal with the bitter feud between Miraval and Talair at this most sensitive juncture in Arbonne's affairs, he had almost certainly managed to do so. He turned to Rudel again and saw wry admiration in his friend's eyes as he looked towards the unassuming chancellor of Arbonne.

Impulsively, Blaise turned back towards the door, to the bench where Rosala was sitting, and read, without real surprise, an identically cynical understanding in her expression. She had always been that quick. It had been too easy to see her only as a woman at the beginning, the selected wife of his older brother — to fail to realize how clever she really was. But there had been moments, even in the few, brief intervals when he had been home, when Blaise had been forced to remind himself whose daughter Rosala was, and to remember that any child of Cadar de Savaric would know more than a thing or two about the world's affairs. Thinking so, he took a few steps towards her. Rosala was the last, in a real sense the largest, mystery of this night.

It was with a renewed surprise that he saw Signe de Barbentain turn as well, to smile at Rosala and then take a seat beside her on the bench. The countess of Arbonne took his sister-in-law's hands between her own. 'You thought you were saving a life, didn't you?' she asked. Her voice was low, but Blaise, moving nearer, was concentrating now on the two of them and he heard. Behind him the chancellor was ordering the binding of the Arimondan.

'I did think that,' he heard Rosala say. 'I didn't know who it was.'

'Which makes it a braver act, my dear. How is Cadar?'

Blaise blinked, and suddenly stopped where he was.

Rosala said, 'Sleeping down the hall, with his nurse.' She looked up at Blaise as she spoke those words, her clear blue eyes on his from across the room.

'Then why don't we leave these untidy affairs and go look in on your baby?' Blaise heard the countess say.

'I would like that,' his brother's wife murmured, rising. Blaise realized that his heart was pounding. 'You haven't seen him since the morning, have you?'

Signe stood up as well, smiling. 'But I have been thinking of him all day. Shall we go?'

Blaise wasn't quite certain how, but he seemed to have crossed the room towards the two of them. The countess looked at him, her elegant features composed. He was staring at Rosala though. He bent, carefully, and saluted her on both cheeks.

'My lady, this is a great surprise,' he said awkwardly, feeling himself flush. He had never been easy with her. 'Am I understanding correctly? Have you had a child? Have you had a child *here*?'

Her head was high, her handsome, intelligent features betrayed no distress at all, but up close now he could see marks of weariness and strain. She had burst into this room, even so, at the very real risk of her own life, following a man with a blade to save whoever it might have been who was in danger here.

She said gravely, 'I am sorry you are discovering it in this fashion. I was told you were here, but there seemed to be no easy way to inform you, given that I have left Garsenc without Ranald's knowledge and am not going back.' She paused for a moment, to let him begin dealing with that. 'I did give birth two days ago, by grace of Corannos, and Rian. My son

is asleep down the hall. His name is Cadar. Cadar de Savaric.'
She stopped a second time. Blaise was feeling as if he had been
struck again, a second blow to the head, in the same place the
staff had hit before. 'You may see him if you like,' his sister-
in-law concluded.

'How sweet this is, how truly touching,' came an amused
voice just behind him. 'The lost children of Gorhaut. Surely
I was right, there will *have* to be a ballad about this. Why don't
we *all* go dote upon the child?' He hadn't heard Lucianna
coming up; once, his whole being would have been focused
on knowing exactly where she was in any room. In the
strangest way, Blaise felt an obscure sadness in this change.

'I don't recall inviting you,' Rosala said calmly. 'You
might still feel like using the blade I saw.'

So she *had* seen that knife, and probably the blood on
him where the dancing blade had pricked. Blaise wondered
what she had thought. He wondered what there was to think.
Lucianna Delonghi, however, was not accustomed to being
discomfited by other women. 'I only stab babies when they
wake me at night,' she murmured in her laziest drawl. 'Grown
men tend to give greater cause, and different pleasures. Since
I am awake, your child is safe for the moment. From me, at
any rate. Are you not afraid, though, that dear, impetuous
Blaise will seize and spirit him home to his brother and
father?'

'Not really,' said Rosala. She looked at Blaise. 'Should I
be?'

Lucianna laughed. The countess of Arbonne stood quietly, looking at Massena Delonghi's daughter, her expression
thoughtful now, and under that level, appraising scrutiny Lucianna grew still. Blaise's mind was racing, despite the pulses of
pain, struggling to sort through the towering implications of all
of this. And there was something else as well, half-buried at the
base of that tower: a night of storm in Garsenc Castle eight
months ago, when he had left for the last time.

Quickly, he pushed that thought away. She had asked him
a question and was waiting for his reply. He said, 'Having left
them myself, I am unlikely to be the one to take anyone back
to that castle. As to that, at least, you need not be concerned.
You know they are unlikely to accept this, though.'

'We all know that,' asked Signe de Barbentain. 'There was some hope earlier that you might have a suggestion.'

'A suggestion about what?' asked Rudel, coming up to them. 'Cures for a cracked skull?'

'Family affairs,' Blaise said shortly, though it was more than that, a great deal more, given who and what his family were.

And it was precisely in that moment that the new thought appeared and immediately began, with unsettling speed, to take shape in him. He made the required introductions and then turned back to look at the others on the far side of the room. He was suddenly thinking hard, and there was a cold logic, a kind of inexorability to where those thoughts were leading him. They didn't make him happy though, not at all.

Urté de Miraval was talking quietly with Massena Delonghi beside the fire. Quzman the Arimondan was in the process of being bound by the corans of Barbentain; they weren't being especially gentle about it. The man's head was held arrogantly high, however; he didn't bother to struggle. Next to Blaise, Rudel Correze bowed to the countess and then bent low and kissed Rosala's hand. Lucianna murmured something to her cousin, under her breath; Blaise didn't hear what it was.

He took a deep breath. Life might be easier, he reflected just before he spoke, if he didn't keep making it harder for himself.

'One moment, if you will,' he said quietly, addressing the chancellor of Arbonne. It was interesting, actually: the other conversations stopped the moment he spoke, as if they had been waiting for him. He wasn't used to being the key to a gathering such as this. He wondered how it had happened. Lucianna was standing unnecessarily close to him. He tried to ignore that fact.

Roban the chancellor, who did not much like him, lifted an eyebrow.

Blaise said, 'I do have a suggestion to make. This affair ultimately concerns only that man and myself.' He nodded at the Arimondan. 'There is nothing that need involve the countess or the . . . wider issues of our time. I killed his brother when attacked some time ago. He sees that as cause for vengeance. I might say I would feel the same, had it been my own brother slain.' He heard Rosala make a small sound, an indrawn breath behind him. That was interesting too; of all of them, she seemed to be the first to sense where he was going. Or part of his path, at any rate. She could not know it all.

'What you say is not strictly true,' said Massena Delonghi, interjecting soberly. 'There remains the matter of the violated truce. Whatever might lie between the two of you, which is indeed your own affair, he was bound to hold back until the fair was over.'

'And it isn't even their own affair in any case,' said Rudel, irritatingly intruding himself. 'Correct me if I err, but I do seem to recall hearing last summer of a decree by the countess of Arbonne regarding killings between Talair and Miraval.'

Blaise understood what his friend was doing then, and reproached himself. He ought to have known better. Rudel wasn't intruding: he was handing Blaise the next thing to say, if he wanted to say it. And it seemed that he did want to say it, or he would not have begun this at all.

'As to that, I am in fact no longer a coran of Talair. Not since the attempt on my life on the road. With my identity revealed there it seemed inappropriate to Duke Bertran that he be giving Galbert de Garsenc's son commands as if to any other mercenary. I am with him now only as a friend. There is therefore no breach of the countess's decree in anything that passes between Quzman of Arimonda and myself.'

The Arimondan had begun, again, to smile, the white teeth showing against his dark skin. His magnificent body was ridged and corded with muscle. He was clever, and extremely dangerous.

'I propose,' said Blaise calmly, 'that this man and I fight each other at the tournament, and that all affairs of tonight be considered ended with whatever happens then.'

Quzman was looking at him. 'I might be forced to regard you as a man, after all,' he said. 'To the death?'

Blaise shrugged. It had come. 'Why bother, otherwise.

Behind him, Rudel Correze swore violently under his breath. Which meant that he had not, after all, seen exactly where this had been going. There was some small pleasure in that; he was rarely so far ahead of Rudel. Behind him, Rosala was silent now. It was the countess who spoke, very softly.

'I should not allow this. You have a reason, I dare hope?'

'I hope so as well,' Blaise said, not turning, his gaze holding the Arimondan's. The first moments of a challenge, he had been taught long ago, often determined what followed. It was important not to look away.

Urté de Miraval smiled broadly. 'One thousand in gold on the Arimondan,' he said. 'If anyone chooses to cover.'

'I will,' said Massena Delonghi. 'It will add spice to the watching.'

His daughter laughed.

'It appears,' said Signe de Barbentain, 'that I am expected to consent to this. I cannot imagine whence that expectation comes. Why should the Arimondan be allowed an even chance at his life?'

Blaise turned to the courageous, exquisitely beautiful woman who ruled this country. 'There is no reason but my asking it of you,' he said gravely. 'Arbonne has always been known for the greatness of its rulers and their generosity. There are those in Gorhaut who might prefer to deny that.' He paused; her blue gaze was intently searching his eyes. 'I am not one of them, your grace. Not any longer.'

He thought he saw a flicker of understanding, and then sorrow chasing it away, but he was certain of neither thing. Impulsively, he knelt before her. He felt her hand upon his head. The slender fingers curled in his hair and then down his cheek and beard. She lifted his chin to look at him.

'We are fond of you, Blaise of Gorhaut,' she said formally. 'We can only hope that this challenge does not bring us a new source of grief. We consent to it, because you have asked us to do so.' She looked out over Blaise's head. 'The Arimondan will remain in custody until this duel occurs, though he is not to be abused in any way. These two men will fight before us until one of them is dead, and this combat will take place on the first morning of the tournament by our decree. We will retire now. These matters are distasteful to us, and there is a child we have not seen all day.'

In the end, Blaise went down the hall with the countess and Rosala. When they walked in, the baby was awake and nursing with the wet-nurse they had found for him. Blaise looked at him for a long time and then turned to Rosala. He said nothing, nor did he find any answers to unspoken questions in her face. He had not, in fact, expected to.

On his way back down the corridor alone some time after, he saw Imera waiting for him at a dark place by the stairwell. He had been half expecting this. She gestured with one hand. Looking beyond her, he saw that Lucianna's door stood ajar. Torchlight flickered and shifted in the corridor.

Once again, desire for her was in Blaise like a wave, like the hard surge of the black, starlit sea against a stony shore. And Blaise understood, standing there in the shadows with Lucianna's servant, that he was unlikely ever to be wholly free of this. In the next heartbeat, he realized, with a feeling akin to that which sometimes came when the white moon broke free of clouds to shine serenely down upon the earth where men and women lived and died, that he could deal with that desire. He was not a slave to it. He could ride above the wave. He took a slow breath, shook his head gently and went past Imera down the dark, winding stairs.

There were people still awake and lights burning in the great hall of Barbentain. A lanky, dark-haired man was singing. Blaise paused in the doorway, listening for a moment. The voice was resonant and sad, quite beautiful actually. He thought he recognized the man, and one or two of the other musicians. Then he saw a woman he did know for certain: the joglar from Midsummer Eve, Lisseut. Her brown hair looked different tonight. He realized why after a moment: it was bright and clean, not soaked and tangled about her shoulders. Amused at the vivid memory, he waited until her gaze moved away from the singer to scan the room. When she saw him in the doorway, she smiled quickly and lifted a hand. Blaise, after a second, smiled back.

He was actually thinking about crossing the room to speak with her, but just then someone was at his elbow.

'I thought I'd wait a little while,' Rudel said. 'I wasn't entirely certain if you would be coming down before morning.'

Blaise looked over at his friend. 'Neither was I,' he said quietly, 'until just now. I feel free of something, actually.'

Rudel's expression was sober. 'Free to die?'

'We are always free for that. It is the god's gift and his burden.'

'Don't be so pious. Not all of us are fool enough to invite it, Blaise.'

Blaise smiled. 'Is this Rudel Correze I am hearing? The most reckless mercenary of us all? If it will make you feel happier I will let you tell me, on the way home, all the reasons why I am a fool.'

'It will make me feel a great deal happier,' Rudel said. And proceeded to take up the invitation, in meticulous, lucid detail, all the way back from the castle to Bertran de Talair's palace in Lussan.

Blaise listened, for the most part, but as they neared Bertran's house again his mind wandered away, touching and withdrawing and then reaching hesitantly back to touch again the last, most difficult thing of a difficult night.

He had never seen a new-born babe before. The child had had a surprisingly full head of reddish hair and the Garsenc nose already, indisputably. He looked like Ranald. He also looked like Blaise. Rosala, holding him when he had finished nursing with the woman, before he was swaddled again, had revealed nothing at all in words or with her eyes. Nothing, that is, save love, as Blaise watched her watch her son sleep in her arms.

They would be coming for him, of course.

There was no question at all but that his grandfather and the king of Gorhaut would be coming after that child. Rosala had told Blaise, tersely, about her last encounter with Galbert. He wondered if his father had provoked that clash deliberately. It wasn't a thought he could share with her.

'You haven't even uttered a word in your own defence,' Rudel complained sharply as they came up for the second time in a long night to stand beneath the lights burning outside Bertran's palace.

'I have none to offer. Every word you speak is true.'

'Well, then?'

Blaise was silent for a moment. 'Tell me, why did you spend so much of the assassination money on a jewel for Lucianna?'

Rudel grew still. It was quiet on the cobble-stoned street,

with the stars shining far above.

'How do you know that? Did she tell you I — '

'No. She would never do that. Rudel, I recognized it. You pointed out that red gem to me once, at that jeweller's in Aulensburg. It wasn't a difficult connection to make. Take my meaning though, Rudel: we are all foolish in our different ways.' It was quite dark where they stood, even with the two torches behind them. The sky was clear and a breeze was blowing. Both moons were down.

'I love her,' his friend said finally. 'I have no business calling any other man, living or dead, a fool.'

Blaise honestly hadn't known, not until he had seen that memorable crimson gem blazing between Lucianna's breasts tonight. There was a sadness in him, shaped of many things.

He smiled though, and touched his friend on the arm. 'You mentioned an amusing tavern quite some time ago. We appear to have been interrupted. If you are willing, I wouldn't mind trying again.'

He waited, and saw Rudel, slowly, return his smile.

Sunrise saw them homeward, when the morning broke.

CHAPTER·13

Tournaments in Arbonne and duels performed in the presence of women were under the aegis of the queen of the Court of Love. It was Ariane de Carenzu, therefore, who was responsible for supervising the formalities attendant upon the challenge issued at the Lussan Fair between Blaise de Garsenc of Gorhaut and Quzman di Peraño of Arimonda.

It was also Ariane who offered the most drily prosaic response of all to what Blaise had done the night before. They had gone to the Carenzu mansion in the morning: Blaise, Bertran, Valery and an extremely pale-looking Rudel Correze. A long night of drinking after a substantial blow to the head had not, it appeared, worked greatly to the advantage of the normally urbane scion of the Correze family.

For that matter, Blaise wasn't feeling entirely well himself, but he'd been more careful than Rudel in the tavern, and expected to become more functional as the day progressed; certainly by tomorrow at any rate, which was a good thing. Tomorrow he was going to be fighting a man to the death.

'I have no idea,' Ariane said, reclining prettily on an upholstered divan in the room where she received them, 'whether what you have done is sheerest folly or only moderately so.'

Her tone was astringent and sardonic, a controlling voice more than a little at odds with the morning freshness of her appearance. She was dressed in pale yellow, the fabric cut with sky blue at bodice and sleeve, with a soft hat of the same mild blue shade on her dark hair. She was looking at Blaise as she spoke and her expression was not particularly mild.

317

'I cannot decide, because I do not know how well you fight. I do know that Urté would not have hired the Arimondan — the two Arimondans — if they were not very good indeed.'

'Quzman? He *is* good,' Bertran de Talair murmured. He was pouring an early glass of wine from a flask on a tray. He seemed more amused now than anything else, though his first reaction, when they told him what had happened, had been one of grimly silent reflection. He hadn't shared those thoughts.

'So is Blaise,' said Rudel faintly from the depths of the chair into which he had carefully lowered himself. They could see only the top of his head. 'Consider the dead brother and five corans of Miraval.'

'Those were arrows,' Valery said quietly. Of all of them, he seemed the most unhappy this morning. 'This will be with swords.'

'It need not be,' Ariane said. 'I could easily — '

Blaise shook his head quickly. 'No point. He uses what he wants, so do I. I would be shamed by an attempt to control the weapons.'

'You may be killed by a failure to do so,' Ariane said tartly.

It was gradually becoming clear to Blaise, a knowledge accompanied by a growing bemusement, that the reactions of those around him to what was about to happen tomorrow were not entirely shaped by the pragmatic appraisal of risks and gains. They were concerned for him. The countess, Bertran and Valery, Rudel certainly, and now it was equally obvious — even to Blaise, who had never been good with understandings of this sort — that Ariane was speaking with more than an abstract interest in the rules of this challenge.

They had encountered her husband when they first entered the house, then Duke Thierry had gracefully excused himself when Bertran made it clear they were calling upon his wife in her formal capacity. The duke of Carenzu was a slender, well-built man, whose sexual tastes and appetites were in no way visible in his manner. He was also, Valery had said earlier, an exceptionally competent leader.

His wife, Blaise was thinking, was even more than that. He felt oddly unsettled now, meeting her lucid gaze, remembering, with unexpected clarity on this bright autumn morning, the summer night they had spent together, her words and manner as much as the act of love. It came to him that if they had been alone she might have been saying different things just now. For that matter, he might have been doing the same. This was a woman he trusted, Blaise suddenly realized, and he felt a momentary surprise.

They had told her about the meeting with King Daufridi. Bertran had discussed it with the countess and Roban as well; he had been in the palace early, before they came here this morning. Events were beginning to move with speed. With Rosala de Garsenc and a male child in Barbentain it was clear — it *had* to be clear to everyone, Blaise thought — that any number of dangerous things were likely to happen quickly. His head ached dully. He was beginning to regret the last part of the night almost as much as the first.

Looking at Ariane, drinking in her cool beauty like a reviving draught, he said, 'This whole exercise is about how we are seen in the eyes of the world. I lose too much if I am thought to be afraid of him, or to be arranging the affair to my obvious advantage. I am grateful for your concern, but there is no point to this challenge if we manipulate it.'

'And there *is* a point to this? We are entitled to assume that?' The same question the countess had asked. He ignored the sharp tone and gave her the same answer.

'I hope so. I hope there is.'

In truth, he wasn't certain. He was certain of nothing just now. He felt like one of those legendary dancers from Arimonda's distant past who were said to have leaped over the horns of bulls for the pleasure of their kings. He was in the middle of such a leap right now, grimly conscious of the gleaming, killing horns. It had seemed to Blaise, late last night — a thought shaped half of piety and half of simple fear — that Corannos had actually guided him here to Arbonne. That his journey south had not been fortuitous, not simply an escape from burdens and sorrows at home or in Portezza. It had been a movement towards destiny, the one chance the world might offer him to make good the vow he'd sworn when he left Garsenc Castle. He hadn't known he would say what he had said to Daufridi of Valensa. He hadn't prepared his challenge to Quzman in advance. He was a dancer with the bulls, moving with their movements, in flight now over the horns of his fate.

Drawing a breath to gather and hold his thoughts, he told Ariane then how he wanted certain things to be done on the morrow. Her features grew still and focused as she listened. Bertran came closer, resting a hand on the back of her divan. He added a suggestion when Blaise was done. Valery said nothing at all. He looked grimly unhappy. Blaise couldn't tell how Rudel looked; his friend was still slumped in his deep chair, only the fair, tousled hair visible from behind. He thought Rudel might even have fallen asleep, but discovered, when he was finished, that this was not so.

'My father was right,' said the heir to the Correze fortune in a musing tone. 'I will very probably go forth to repent this allegiance of mine more than all the other errors of my life. I ought surely to have known better than to leave the banking business and take up with madmen from Gorhaut.'

There were a number of replies that could be made to that, from the cutting, to the witty, to the soberly judicious. No one said anything, though.

†

'He will want to cut downwards on the angle and then back across low for your knees,' Valery said. Rudel was tightening the drawstrings on the leather armour to be worn by the two men fighting.

'I know,' said Blaise. 'It's the usual attack with a curved sword.' He wasn't really concentrating though, either on the words of advice or the increasing level of sound he could hear from the pavilions. When he and Quzman were ready to emerge from their tents the sounds would rise to a crescendo and then fall for the ceremony of introduction before beginning again, on a different note, when the killing began. It was the same all over the world. Blaise had seen a number of challenges to the death. He had fought in a foolish one, years before, when a Valensan coran had insulted the king of Gorhaut in the presence of one of that king's newest, youngest corans. Blaise had been lucky to survive and he knew it; the Valensan had taken his youthful opponent too casually and paid the price. Blaise had worn the dead man's armour for years.

'He'll have a knife in his belt and one behind his left calf,' Rudel murmured. 'And he won't hesitate to throw. He's known for that, and accurate with both hands. Keep your shield up.'

Blaise nodded again. They meant him a world of good, he knew; it was their anxieties that were producing this outpouring of instruction. He remembered being exactly the same way when serving as squire to friends in their challenges, including Rudel, three times if he remembered rightly.

He really wasn't paying close attention though. This had happened to him before: his mind wandered before battle, drifting along unexpected pathways. It kept him calm, until the moment the fighting began, when the sensation was akin to a muffling curtain pulled swiftly aside, and Blaise would feel all his senses converge like arrows upon the battleground.

Just now he was remembering Rudel's last comment in Ariane's chambers that morning. He thought about Vitalle Correze, who wanted his much-loved son to be a banker not a coran, and then about his relationship with his own father. He wasn't sure why his thoughts were turning that way. Perhaps as he grew older, saw more of the world and its interactions, he was coming to understand the degree to which the Garsenc men had poisoned each other. He suddenly wondered, for the first time, how Ranald would be feeling about Rosala's flight. He realized that he had no idea, absolutely none; he didn't know his brother very well.

Valery tapped him briskly on the shoulder and Blaise obediently sat down on the stool and straightened his legs in front of him. His friends knelt and began lacing and tying the supple Portezzan leather about his thighs and calves. Through a gap in the tent flap behind their bent heads Blaise could glimpse the dazzling colours of the pavilions in the morning sunlight, and the green grass where he would be fighting soon.

They hadn't raised the banner above his tent yet, following his instructions of yesterday. For most of the people in the pavilions or in the commoners' standing ground on the other side he was simply a Gorhautian coran enmeshed in some quarrel with an Arimondan. A quarrel that was about to offer them the most exciting entertainment there was. A handful of people knew more, and there would be rumours of course; there were usually rumours at a time like this.

He felt very calm. He was always calm before fighting now, though it hadn't been that way in the beginning, years ago. He had prayed last night, kneeling on the cold stone floor in the surprisingly handsome chapel of Corannos in Lussan. He had not asked for victory, a coran never did. Before the two tall candles above the frieze he had offered the ancient prayers for sunrise and sunset and for the strength of the god's life-giving golden light. The frieze itself had been masterfully done, a rendering of Corannos bestowing fire upon the first men, that the nights might hold less terror than before.

Perhaps he shouldn't have been so surprised by the serene grace of the god's houses here. They worshipped Corannos in Arbonne. He had always known that; there *were* corans here, after all, with the same rituals of initiation and invocation that he had passed through in Gorhaut, the same ones used in all six countries. It had been difficult, though, when he first arrived, in those early days at Castle Baude in the highlands, to overcome a lifetime of prejudice and vicious innuendo, much of it coming, of course, from his father. It was odd how often he was thinking about his father of late. Or perhaps not so odd after all, given what he was about to do. They said the mind reached backwards when one's life was in extreme peril.

Galbert de Garsenc had stipulated that his younger son follow him into the clergy of Corannos. It was not a matter for discussion; what the High Elder wanted, he was accustomed to receive. Blaise's repeated flights as a boy from the chapel school near Cortil, his silent endurance of the whippings he was given, both at home by Galbert's heavy hand and again when returned to the Elders, and then his obdurate, absolute refusal to speak the vows of consecration when he turned sixteen had represented a colossal thwarting of the High Elder's carefully laid plans.

They had tried to starve him into submitting to the vows — on his father's orders. Blaise had never forgotten those weeks. He woke sometimes in the night remembering them. Even today pangs of hunger made him panic irrationally, and he could not lash a man.

Would your mother have made a difference? Signe de Barbentain had asked the first night he met her. He didn't know.
He would never know. No man, with only the one life to live,
could answer such a question. He remembered learning, when
still a small boy, not to cry because there was no one in the
world who would come with comfort if he did. The brethren
in the chapel school were terrified of his father; none dared
offer succour to the unworthy, ingrate son. Not ever. Once, in
Garsenc, Ranald had slipped into Blaise's room at night with
a salve for his brother's lacerated back. In the morning, when
Galbert saw the healing ointment he had whipped Ranald
and then Blaise a second time. Ranald never tried to intervene in his punishments after that.

Blaise could have stopped running away. He could have
taken the vows they demanded of him. Neither possibility
ever occurred to him, not even as options to be considered.
When it became clear that Blaise would die of starvation
before he broke in this, Galbert calmly proposed to have him
publicly executed for his disobedience. It was King Duergar
himself, becoming aware of this savage family drama playing
itself out, who had forbidden that execution, who had insisted
on food and drink being brought for the starving boy, and it
was Duergar who accepted the sworn fealty of a gaunt, silent,
hollow-eyed sixteen-year-old one month later, and named
him a coran of Gorhaut.

Duke Ereibert de Garsenc, doughty and hoar, had died
childless when his two nephews were twenty-one and nineteen, his stern mastery in war allowing him to outface lifelong
rumours about his lack of heirs. Ranald inherited. He withdrew, of necessity, from his position as King's Champion and
became duke of Garsenc instead, lord of the richest, most
powerful estates in Gorhaut. Blaise *should* by then have been,
by his father's careful designs, firmly placed in the hierarchy
of the god's brotherhood, ready for a smooth ascent all the way
to the ultimate station Galbert held, as High Elder of Corannos, with kings and princes subject to his fiat. The Garsenc
family *should* have been poised for generations of power in
Gorhaut — the country held as if between the paws of the
rampant bear that was on their escutcheon — whomever
might nominally have been sitting on the throne.

Ranald would have sons to succeed him at Garsenc and to follow Blaise into the clergy; there would be daughters to bind other families with the hoops of marriage vows. And eventually, perhaps not so far in the future, there might be even more than all of this — there might be the throne itself. A Garsenc ruling in Cortil, and the borders of Gorhaut itself stretching all the time, though first — first if all things, of course — reaching across the mountain passes to the south, to Arbonne, where they were godless and heretical, ruled by women and womanish men steeped in their blood-soaked rites.

Blaise had known almost all of this from very early in his life. He had been the one Galbert talked to when the boys were young. There had been a brief time when he hadn't understood why that was so, and then a longer period when he'd felt sorry for Ranald. It had all been long ago.

'Boots,' said Rudel.

Blaise lifted first his left leg and then his right.

'All right,' said Valery. Blaise stood up, and Rudel reached around his waist and buckled on the long, Aulensburg-forged sword in its plain soldier's scabbard. From the table he hefted the light helmet. Blaise took it from him and set it on his head. Valery was waiting with the round, unornamented shield. Blaise took that too.

'Where do you want your knives?' Valery asked.

'One for the belt. I have the other.'

Valery asked no further questions, neither did Rudel. They, too, had both been through this before. Rudel, his face and manner sober, lifted a sleek black knife from the trunk beside the tent flap and handed it to Blaise.

Blaise smiled briefly at him. 'Do you remember? You gave me this one?'

Rudel made a quick, warding sign. 'I did no such thing. I *found* it for you. You paid me a copper piece for it. We don't give knives as gifts, you ignorant northerner.'

Blaise laughed. 'Forgive me. I forgot that you are a superstitious Portezzan farmer at heart. However did you get permission to leave your hoe in the vineyards to travel among men of rank?'

A frivolous gibe, not worthy of a response and receiving none, for the trumpets sounded then.

Valery and Rudel moved to stand on either side of the tent flaps. The tradition was for the squires to say nothing at this time; farewells of any sort were thought to be invitations to fate. Blaise knew this. He looked at each of them and smiled. He was still calm, but there was a slight tell-tale acceleration to his pulsebeat now, as silence settled like a bird to a branch outside.

He nodded, and Valery and Rudel each drew back a flap of the tent. He stepped past the two of them, ducking his head, and he came out into sunshine and the green grass of the battleground.

Quzman of Arimonda was the first person he saw, standing at the entrance to his own tent on the far side of the field. A banner was flying behind him: three black bulls on a crimson field. Blaise registered the curved sword worn across the Arimondan's back in the western fashion, and he saw the polished golden shield. He glanced east to check and remember the angle of the rising sun; that shield could blind him if the Arimondan used it to catch and throw back the light. Blaise was aware, but only as background, of excited, rapacious murmurs coming from all around them. A death challenge was the keenest sport there was.

The trumpets sounded again, briefly, and Blaise turned towards the central pavilion as the herald of Arbonne stepped forward. He was aware that his heart was beating even more rapidly now, but not from anticipation of the battle, not yet. There was something still to come, before the fighting.

The herald's rich voice rolled out, sonorously naming the most illustrious of those assembled there. Blaise saw King Daufridi of Valensa sitting next to the countess, his bearded features unreadable, betraying nothing more than idle, polite interest.

'To my left,' cried the herald at last, his trained voice carrying effortlessly over the grass and the densely packed pavilions, 'stands Quzman di Peraño of Arimonda, prepared to lay his life before Corannos and Rian in this matter of his family's honour.' He paused.

Blaise drew a breath. It had come.

'All right,' he said to the two men behind him. 'Do it.'

He didn't look back, but as the herald of Arbonne turned

towards him he heard the rustle and flap of two banners being run up to fly above his tent, and a moment later there came, truly like the roaring of sea surf in wind, a swelling of sound that nearly drowned the herald's urgently rising voice.

'To my other hand,' the herald proclaimed, 'equally prepared to defend the honour of his name, stands Blaise de Garsenc of Gorhaut, who here lays claim before this assembled gathering of the six nations and upon this holy field where the god and goddess are judges of honour and worth, to the crown of the Kingdom of Gorhaut, falsely now held by traitorous Ademar!'

People were on their feet; the herald was shouting now. 'En Blaise has also declared that this combat, freely entered into by him against a felon so proclaimed by the countess of Arbonne, shall serve as a warrant for the worth of his claim, and he willingly lays his life at hazard before you all in this moment of asserting his right to that same crown.'

The last was scarcely heard over the thunder of noise from the pavilions and the standing grounds on the other side. It didn't matter whether the herald was audible or not. The banners told the story. Blaise turned slowly — it was all theatre now, all symbol, until the killing began — and he nodded his head, as an equal to his equals, to Signe de Barbentain and then to Daufridi of Valensa. And the countess of Arbonne rose, in the presence of her people and those gathered from the other countries of the world, and gestured to Blaise with an extended hand in welcome, equal to equal. There was screaming now. Blaise ignored it. He waited. One long moment, then another, and finally, the hairs rising on the back of his neck, he saw Daufridi stand. Tall and proud, the king of Valensa turned to left and right, not hurrying, a master of moments such as this, and then very slowly, facing Blaise, he laid his right hand on his left shoulder in the coran's salute.

He had done it. There had been no way of knowing if he would. It was not quite the full gesture of welcome that Signe had offered — Daufridi had far too complex a game of his own to play for that to be possible — but he had given more than they'd had any right to expect: an acknowledgement that Blaise was worthy of a king's standing up to recognize him.

Blaise closed his eyes with relief, and then opened them quickly again. He must not be seen to have doubted, though of course he had. There had been no promises from Daufridi at all — and certainly none regarding an event so unexpectedly swift to develop as this one had been. Leaving that inn outside the walls two nights ago, he had offered only the unreassuring remark that he would think on what Bertran had said. He had done so, evidently. He was with them, at least this far. Blaise was under no illusions though: if the King of Valensa ever decided that they were a greater danger than Ademar and Galbert, he would be swift in his denunciation. But for the moment, in the midst of this tumultuous maelstrom of sound, he had risen to his feet to welcome Blaise to the stage of world affairs. It was something; it was, in fact, a great deal.

Keeping his expression as serene and unrevealing as he could, Blaise turned away from the pavilions to face his own tent, and so looked up for the first time at what flew above it now.

The rampant bear of Garsenc, crimson on its deep blue ground, carried its own full measure of significance for those who had not even known who he was until this moment. And above it, in pride and glory and most brazen declaration, flew the banner of the kings of Gorhaut.

Standing at the centre of a growing tidal wave of noise, Blaise looked up at that golden sun on its white ground, with the crown of kings above it and the sword of the god below, and it seemed to him, oddly, as if he had never really seen it before. In a way, he never had; not like this. Not lifted in the breeze and the light by his own command. It had begun. With this banner flying above his head and raised in his own name before the eyes of all the world, it had truly begun. He bowed low before the emblem of his country's kings as the noise from all around grew to a climax, louder than he would ever have thought possible.

He knew how to quell that sound. To bring the pavilions and the standing grounds back, like hunting dogs to heel, to what lay ahead of them now on this green grass beneath the morning sun. It had begun here, and it might end here, for there was still the affirmation of the god to be sought. Of

Corannos, and of the goddess of Arbonne. For the first time in his life Blaise of Gorhaut offered a prayer to Rian. Then he turned to the Arimondan and he drew his sword.

Jousts for pleasure and sport were done on horseback in full tournament regalia, horse and rider armoured magnificently, the display lying as much in the glitter of the coran's equipment as in anything else. No one ever enjoyed losing — it could be hideously expensive for one thing — but the armour prevented all but the rare serious injury, and in the long run, save for a handful of the most celebrated fighters, wins and losses tended to even themselves out. Tournaments were entertainments, a parading of wealth and success, a revelation of prowess, diversions for the pavilions and the commons both, and they were regarded as such.

Challenges to the death were contested on foot. Only limited protection was allowed. There was no glitter to them, no elaborately ornate breastplate or decorated helm. Death fights were primitive encounters, even holy ones, reaching back to far distant times before the Ancients had come, most purely testing a man's courage and will and the power of his goddesses or gods. They were an entertainment too, of course, as the excitement of the assembled watchers now attested, but of a darker sort, with a grim, foreknown destination: a man broken and dying on trampled grass, mortality made harshly manifest for those gathered to bear witness and be reminded of their own end.

It was because of this more than anything else that when Blaise drew his sword the screaming stopped. In the dining halls of the sanctuary retreats of Corannos, where men and women sometimes withdrew from the world as they felt their endings draw near, there were always tapestries or paintings hung upon the walls, and in every sanctuary at least one of these works would show the gaunt, laughing figure of Death, bearing the mace with which he ground the life from men, leading a winding procession over a wintry hill to the west where the sun was going down. And always, by long tradition, the first figure in that procession, even before the crowned kings and queens of earth, hand in hand with Death himself, would be a tall coran in the prime of his days, his sword useless in its scabbard as Death led him away.

Quzman di Peraño, with a smile, reached up and pulled his curved blade from the sheath on his back. He drew upon a clasp and let the scabbard fall behind him on the grass. One of his appointed squires from Miraval quickly knelt and picked it up. The Arimondan moved forward, light on his feet as a tumbler for all his size, and Blaise, watching closely, saw that his first steps carried him a little west. As expected. He had seen this manoeuvre before, the last time he'd fought a challenge with a man from Arimonda. He had almost died that day.

Moving to meet the man whose brother he had slain, Blaise regretted, not for the first time, that he knew so little about his foe and how he fought. For all Valery's words about the propensities of those using curved swords — tendencies Blaise knew well — they had little actual knowledge of Quzman beyond what was obvious. He was a big man, cat-quick, and brave, with a longing for revenge and nothing at all to lose today. *I could*, Blaise thought, *be dead before the sun rises much higher*.

It had always been possible. There was no honour to be sought or found in a meaningless challenge, no elevation in the eyes of the gathered world beneath the banner of Gorhaut's kings — which was, of course, the point of all of this.

Moving forward, Blaise found what he was looking for. His small round shield rested on his left forearm, leaving his fingers free. He transferred his sword to that hand and stooped quickly. In the same motion, as Quzman came straight towards him, he seized and hurled a clump of earth squarely at the Arimondan's gleaming shield. Quzman stopped, surprised, and Blaise had time to rattle another dulling handful of mud against the shield before straightening and reclaiming his sword in his fighting hand.

Quzman was no longer smiling. It was Blaise who grinned now, with deliberate mockery. 'Too pretty a toy,' he said. It was quiet now, he did not have to raise his voice. 'I'll have it cleaned when you are dead. How many men have you killed by blinding them first like a coward?'

'I wonder,' said Quzman after a short silence, his beautiful voice thickened by passion, 'if you have any idea how much pleasure your death will bring me?'

'I probably do. Blood ants on the plain. You told me already. By contrast, though,' Blaise replied, 'your life or death mean almost nothing to me at all. Welcome to the dance. Do you want to talk all morning or are you actually able to use that blade you carry?'

He was. He was more than able, and sorely provoked. The first stroke, exactly as Valery had predicted, was a downward angled slash on his backhand. Blaise parried smoothly, guiding it short of his body — but then was only barely quick enough, even with the anticipation, to block the vicious return sweep of the curved blade along the level of his knees. The impact, a grinding collision of weapons, was almost enough to numb his wrist. The man was strong, enormously so, and his reactions were even quicker than Blaise had guessed they would be.

Even as he thought this, Blaise was twisting desperately and dropping, guided only by reflexes of his own, an utterly instinctive movement shaped by years of combat in tournament and war, the primitive drive for survival letting him react to the curved sword abruptly planted, quivering, in the earth, to Quzman's gloved hand reaching for the back of his calf and the knife blade flung in a blurred motion for his throat. It went by, almost. Blaise felt a searing pain at the side of his head. He brought his sword hand quickly up to his ear and it came away soaked with blood. He heard a sound from the pavilions then, deep and low, like wind on a moor.

Quzman, his sword recaptured before it had even stopped vibrating in the ground, was smiling again, the white teeth gleaming. 'Now *that*,' he said, 'is pretty. Why don't you throw some mud on it like a peasant? You do seem to enjoy scrabbling in the earth.'

The pain was bad and would probably get worse, but Blaise didn't think his ear was gone. Not entirely, at any rate. He seemed to still be hearing sounds from that side. He thought of Bertran suddenly, with his own missing ear lobe. He thought of how much depended on his walking alive from this field. And with that his anger was upon him fully, the familiar, frightening daemon that came to him in battle.

'Spare your breath,' he said thickly, and surged up from the ground to engage the other man. There were no words then, no space for words and indeed no breath, only the quick chittering clatter of blades glancing and sliding from each other, or the harder, heavier clang as sword met blocking shield, the controlled grunting of two men as they circled each other, probing with cold metal and cold eyes for an avenue along which they could kill.

Quzman of Arimonda was indeed good, and driven by the fierce pride of his country and his family, and he had a sworn vengeance to claim. He fought with the fluid, deadly passion of a dancer and Blaise was wounded twice more, in the forearm and across the back of his calf, in the first three engagements.

But Quzman's thigh was gashed, and the leather armour over his ribs was not quite equal to the scything blow it took on a forehand slash from an Aulensburg sword wielded by a man with a passion and rage of his own.

Blaise didn't stop to gauge how badly he had wounded the man. He drove forward, attacking on both sides, parried each time with impacts that sent shocks up his elbow and shoulder. He registered the welling of blood at Quzman's left side, ignoring as best he could the stiffening protest from his own leg as he pushed off it. He could easily have been crippled by that low blow, he knew. He hadn't been. He was still on his feet, and before him was a man who stood in the path of . . . what?

Of a great many things, his own dream of Gorhaut not least of all. Of what his home *should* be, in the eyes of the world, in the sight of Corannos, in his own soul. He had said this two nights ago, words very like this, to King Daufridi of Valensa. He'd been asked if he loved his country.

He did. He loved it with a heart that ached like an old man's fingers in rain, hurting for the Gorhaut of his own vision, a land worthy of the god who had chosen it, and of the honour of men. Not a place of scheming wiles, of a degraded, sensuously corrupt king, of people dispossessed of their lands by a cowardly treaty, or of ugly designs under the false, perverted aegis of Corannos for nothing less than annihilation here south of the mountains.

It was one thing to have ambitions for one's homeland, dreams of scope and expansion. It was another to use the sky-blue cloak of the god to hide a smoke-shrouded inferno of men and women — a nation of them — thrown to burn on heretics' pyres. Blaise had seen such fires as a boy. He would never forget the first time. His father had clutched his shoulder and had not let him turn away.

He knew exactly what Galbert wanted, what Ademar of Gorhaut would be guided to do when he came south. He knew how strong, how wealthy the army of Gorhaut would be by the time the snows melted in spring. He had seen those pyres; he would not watch another burn. He had sworn it to himself those long years ago, watching an old woman die screaming, flames in her white hair. And to stop them, to stop his father and his king, he had first to defeat this Arimondan who stood now in his way with a curved sword already reddened by Blaise's own blood.

The most celebrated troubadours and the better known joglars did not watch the tournaments from the commons' standing ground. By courtesy of Ariane de Carenzu, as a sign of their high favour in Arbonne, they were given a pavilion, not far down the lists from her own. An invitation to sit among those in the pavilion was one of the prime measures of success each year among the musicians, and this autumn marked the first time Lisseut had found herself included in the elect. She owed it to Alain, she knew, to his own growing reputation, and to the little man's brash assertiveness that memorable night in Tavernel when she had sung his song to the queen of the Court of Love and the dukes of Talair and Miraval.

And to the red-bearded Gorhaut coran who was now battling for his life on the grass before them. It seemed he wasn't just a coran, though. Not since those two bright banners had been run up above his tent and the herald's voice had fought to be heard over a roar of sound. She had known since Midsummer who Blaise de Garsenc was and had kept faith by telling no one. Now he had revealed his identity to the world, and had done something rather more than that. The man she had upbraided so caustically in The Liensenne a season ago, and had then followed to the Correze gardens later that same night, was laying claim to the crown of Gorhaut.

It was with a sense of deep unreality that Lisseut remembered inviting him to come back with her that night in Tavernel. *Unlucky to spend tonight alone in this city*, she had told him. Unluckier still to have a degree of presumption as rash as her own. Her mother would likely be forced to take to her bed if she found out about any of this. Even now, months after, Lisseut could not stop herself from flushing at the memory.

Looking up at those two banners in the wind, she wondered what he must have thought of her, of the wet and straggle-haired, interfering, impertinent singer who had accosted him twice in a night and then taken his arm in the street and invited him to bed with her. He didn't even *like* singing, she remembered. Lisseut, among friends in a bright pavilion, had winced at that thought, too. No one had noticed. The others were busy wagering on the coming fight, laying odds on a man's death.

Then thoughts of herself and memories of summer had gone flying far away, for the two men on the grass had drawn their blades, the straight sword and the curved one, and had advanced upon each other. Blaise had bent to throw grass and mud at the other man's shield, something she hadn't understood until Aurelian, without being asked, had quickly stooped to speak an explanation in her ear. She had not turned to him. She had been unable to take her eyes from the two men on the grass, though a part of her was recoiling in horror even as she watched. They spoke to each other, but none of them could hear the words. She saw the Arimondan react as if scalded by something said, and then spring to attack. She saw him parried, once and then twice, as her breath caught in her throat. Death was here. This was not for show. The reality of that came home to her, and just then she saw the curved sword planted, unexpectedly, in the earth.

And it had been in the next moment, precisely then, she would afterwards remember — the Arimondan's flung dagger slicing through Blaise's ear as he twisted away, then the swift, bright flowering of blood — that Lisseut of Vezét realized, with a cold dawning of despair, that her heart was gone from her. It had left without her knowing, like a bird in winter, flying north to a hopelessly wrong destination where no haven or warmth or welcome could even be imagined.

'Oh, mother,' she whispered then, softly, to a woman far away among olive groves above a coastal town. No one paid any attention to her. Two men were trying to kill each other in front of them, and one of them had claimed a crown. This was matter for song, whatever happened; it was matter for tavern and castle talk for years to come. Lisseut, her hands gripping each other tightly in her lap, spoke a prayer then to sweet Rian, and watched, even as she felt the flight of her heart from her breast across the bright green grass.

Some things about fighting Blaise had had to teach himself, or learn from his brother at those rare intervals when he was at home and Ranald would consent to give him a secret lesson: Blaise was heading for the brethren, what use would skill with a blade be for him? Other elements he had learned from the men who guided him in swordsmanship, quite a few years later than most young men in Gorhaut, in the year after the king had already made him a coran, more as a rebuke to his High Elder than through any recognition of Blaise's merits.

But the greater part of his education had come in the field, in war and in the tournament mêlées, the nearest thing to warfare that peacetime offered. He was lucky he had survived in those first months and years. He knew that now. He'd been far too callow and untutored to have had any right to expect to walk away from battlefields at Thouvars or Graziani or Brissel, or those early tourneys at Aulensburg or Landeston in Valensa. By the time of Iersen Bridge, though, he had known the craft of killing and surviving extremely well. And it was there on that winter field that he had come nearest of all to dying: which was, of course, the darkest of many ironies at the heart of a soldier's life.

In any case, what Blaise proceeded now to do was as obvious to him as the direction of sunrise or the proper flight of birds in winter. The Arimondan was badly hurt on his left side. The task then was to make him use his shield again and again, to lift it high against forehand blows aimed towards shoulder or head. It didn't matter if the blows landed; against a good man they wouldn't be expected to. But with each one warded by a shield thrust upward in defence, Quzman's wound would be forced open more and his arm and side would grow weaker. It was straightforward, routine; any competent soldier would know this to be so.

Blaise became aware after a time that this was exactly what was happening. It began to be visible in the Arimondan's face, though his expression of arrogant concentration never really changed. There was more blood now, welling from the wound in his side. Meticulously, with the precision all field surgeons claimed and most lacked, Blaise set about exploiting the injury he had inflicted.

His focus was calmly precise, unhurried, patient, so much so that he nearly died.

He ought to have been killed, for he was badly fooled. What Quzman did was feint a throw with another knife. For the second time he stepped backwards and stabbed his sword into the flattened grass, reaching towards his leg with his freed hand. Blaise, alert for the throw, was already dodging, twisting downwards again, when Quzman, on one knee, hurled his heavy shield instead like an athlete's disc with his left hand, cracking Blaise so savagely across the shins it sent him sprawling, crying out with the pain. The Arimondan seized his sword again and was up with frightening speed, lunging forward with a downward slash intended to decapitate.

Blaise rolled desperately backwards and flopped to one side, gasping at the pain in both legs. The descending sword bit earth a blade's width from his head, but Quzman was reaching in earnest now for his second knife, at quarters too close for swords as he fell forward upon Blaise.

He never reached that blade.

Years ago, during one of the endless campaigns against Valensa, King Duergar of Gorhaut, who had continued to take an interest in Galbert de Garsenc's curiously rebellious younger son, had called for Blaise to ride out alone with him one morning in the king's circuit of his army's encampment. On that springtime ride, as a purely passing remark, he had offered a suggestion as to where a useful blade might be secreted upon one's person, before pointing out how cherry trees in blossom were a good place for archers to hide.

In real pain, his sword useless, Blaise rolled again desperately and released his grip on his shield. And as he did so he claimed his own hidden dagger from the iron sheath he'd had made for it, at his king's suggestion, on the inside face of the shield. Jamming his right arm against the ground at the end of his awkward roll he rang the shield hard off Quzman's shoulder and then, pulling his left hand free with the blade, he stabbed the Arimondan twice, once deep in the muscles of the sword arm, and then a raking gash across the ribs already wounded.

Then he twisted out from under his writhing foe and struggled to his feet. He quickly regained his sword. Quzman, twisting in pain, his sword arm now useless, his left side streaming with fresh blood, lay on the smeared grass beneath him. There was a sound of people shouting in the distance, oddly remote. Blaise was aware that he was swaying unsteadily on his feet. His ear felt as if it were shredded, on fire. His legs, from the first sword wound and then the last shield blow, could barely support him. But he was upright, and he had his sword again, and the other man was down.

He set the point, as steadily as he could, at Quzman's throat. The Arimondan's black eyes gazed up at him implacably, without fear, even as death arrived for him.

'Do it,' he said, 'that my spirit may rejoin my brother's.'

Blaise said, breathing in hard, short gasps, 'I am free of your blood before the god? It was fairly done? I have your dispensation?'

Quzman managed a bitter smile. 'It matters to you?' He dragged a breath. 'You have it. It was fairly done.' Another harsh breath. 'It was more than fair, after the woman's rooms. You are free of my death. Do it.'

The shouts and screaming had stopped. It was eerily silent now all around the ground where they stood. One man called out something from the commons' side. In the stillness his voice rose and fell away, leaving silence again. There was, Blaise realized, one more thing he could do this morning. And it seemed, remarkably, that he wanted to do it in any case.

He said, the words coming slowly as he struggled to control his breathing, 'Your wounds are not mortal. I will need good men with me to do what I must do. I killed your brother when attacked by six corans and only after they first shot at me. Will you let this combat settle the past for us? I am loath to kill a brave man. I do not want your death on my hands, even with dispensation.'

Quzman shook his head, his expression curiously tranquil now. 'I might have agreed,' he said, his breathing quick and shallow, 'were it not for one thing. My brother carried no bow, he never did, and he died of an arrow in the throat. You ought to have fought him, Northerner. For killing him at a distance you must die, or I must.'

Blaise shook his head. There was a great weariness in him now. 'Need it be written before the god that we be enemies?' He fought off a renewed wave of pain. He could feel blood dripping from his ear. 'It was not a tourney that day by the lake. I was fighting six men for my life. I am not going to kill you, Arimondan. If I ask, they will let you go from here. Do what you will with your life, but know that I will be pleased to have you in my company.'

'Do not do this,' said Quzman of Arimonda.

Blaise ignored him. He turned and began to walk — cautiously, because he could not move any other way just yet — towards the pavilion where the countess sat with Ariane and Bertran and the king of Valensa. It seemed a long way off. And it was very nearly the hardest thing he had ever done, not to try to move faster, not to look back and see.

He took five or six steps only. He had thought it might be thus. The man was an Arimondan, after all. There had been a slim chance, no more.

'I told you to kill me!' Quzman di Peraño cried. Blaise heard footsteps crossing the grass. He flung a prayer outwards, to whoever might hear him from this field in Arbonne, the god, or the goddess who was more than his maiden daughter here. And with his silent invocation, he heard the impact of arrows.

Behind him the Arimondan grunted queerly and spoke a name, and there came the sound of a body falling on the grass.

For a long moment Blaise stood motionless, dealing with an unexpected regret. When he did turn it was towards his tent, to see Valery of Talair and Rudel Correze approaching, the two best archers he knew, both grim-faced, both with bows to hand and the arrows gone. He went slowly back to stand above the body of the Arimondan. Quzman lay face down in the grass, still gripping his splendid sword, but Blaise, gazing upon him, saw something he could not understand.

There were four arrows, not two, in the dead man's body. He looked limp, almost comical, stuck full of arrows like a sorcerer's pin-doll. An ugly ending for a proud man.

Blaise looked up, his brow furrowing, and saw a third man with a bow step forward as if he had been waiting to be noticed. The man began hesitantly to come across the grass towards them from the far end of the pavilions. A moment later Blaise blinked in astonished recognition. It had been a long shot, that one, but he remembered Hirnan of Baude, the best coran there, as being exceptionally good with his bow.

Hirnan came up to him and bowed, his expression awkward and anxious. 'I must ask your forgiveness,' he said. 'I saw him rise up with the sword. I did not know the others had instructions from you.'

'They didn't,' Blaise said mildly. 'I didn't know I was going to do that.' He extended a hand and touched the big coran on the shoulder. 'Well met again, Hirnan, and hardly a time to be asking forgiveness — you might have saved my life just there.'

Hirnan took a relieved breath but did not smile. He seemed uneasy here on the grass with so many people watching them. 'I heard what the herald said,' he murmured. 'We never knew who you were, you understand.' He looked Blaise in the eye. 'But I made my own judgment last spring. I claim no very great skills or dignity, but if you can use a man you can trust in your company I would be honoured. My lord.'

Blaise felt a truly unexpected feeling of warmth beginning to steal through him, pushing away the pain. He liked this man and respected him. 'The honour will be as much my own,' he said gravely. 'I made my own judgments too, in the highlands. But you are a sworn coran of the lord of Baude Castle. I doubt Mallin will be eager to lose one such as you.'

For the first time, Hirnan allowed the trace of a smile to cross his face. 'Look again,' he said. 'It was En Mallin himself who told me to ready my bow, there at the end when the Arimondan fell and you stood talking to him. I truly do not think he will object if I join you now.'

Blaise did look over then, where Hirnan was indicating, to a bright yellow pavilion far down the lists, and he saw that Mallin de Baude was on his feet. Even at this distance he could

see that the young baron was smiling. Memories of the springtime came flooding back as Blaise lifted a hand in salute. And
then Mallin de Baude, as if born to such gestures, to performing them before the eyes of the gathered world, saluted Blaise
in return with a lifted hand, and then he bowed to him, the way
one bows to kings. Beside him, with exquisite grace, Soresina
de Baude, in a skirt green as the grass, sank low to the ground
and remained thus for a moment before she rose. There was a
murmur from the pavilions and the commons, both.

Blaise swallowed, struggling without great success to
adjust his own thinking to this sort of thing. It was difficult to
resist the urge to return the salute in kind, but a man claiming a crown did not bow to minor barons. The rules of the
game were changing; as of this morning they had changed for
the rest of his life, however long or short that might be. There
was something frightening in that thought.

Behind him there came a dry cough. He looked over his
shoulder at Rudel and Valery. 'That ear will need looking to.
And there is a fourth arrow here,' Valery said prosaically.

Rudel's expression was odd, as if astonishment were
vying with hilarity for mastery in him. 'And the man who fired
it is making his appearance even as we speak, like the
unmasked coran at the end of a puppet play. This *is* the end
of the play, Blaise. You'd best think quickly. Look to the other
tent.'

Blaise looked. From behind the Arimondan's tent, very
much indeed as from behind a stage curtain, resplendent in
green and gold, with a longbow in one hand, came Urté de
Miraval.

He was seen now by the pavilions and the commons
both, and so the noise, not surprisingly, began to grow again.
In the midst of it, Urté began walking towards them with a
measured, unhurried tread, as if he were doing no more than
stroll the grounds of Miraval.

He came up to Blaise and stopped, his carriage straight
as a spear for all his years. There was a stillness where they
stood, though the sounds continued to grow all around them.

'Do not,' Urté said, 'expect another salute. The last time
I looked into the matter, Ademar was king of Gorhaut. I'm
afraid I do not bow to the presumption of pretenders.'

'Why do you save their lives, then?' It was Rudel who asked as Blaise kept silent, thinking as swiftly as he could.

The duke didn't bother to look at Rudel. His eyes held Blaise's as he smiled thinly. 'The Arimondan was a disappointment. He cost me ten corans two nights ago, and a thousand in gold to Massena Delonghi this morning. And I didn't really want to be the sworn liege lord of a coran who killed his man from behind in a challenge. Bad for my own image, you understand.'

'I think I do, actually,' Blaise said. A cold anger was rising in him. 'You were at risk if he survived, weren't you? Since you betrayed him in Lucianna's rooms, he might have continued to talk about how you were really part of that attempt on my life two nights ago. Very bad for your image, I agree. You didn't save me, my lord, you killed an inconvenient man.'

The duke was undisturbed. 'A fair reason to kill a man, I would say. You might want to take care to avoid becoming inconvenient yourself, as well as presumptuous.'

Rudel gave a bark of shocked laughter. 'Are you mad? Are you threatening him?'

Again Urté did not even look at him. Blaise said then, very deliberately, 'Does it matter greatly what I do? I'd heard simple error was enough to cause you to kill, actually. Musicians who sang the wrong tune, loyal corans who made the mistake of obeying your instructions at the wrong time.' He paused, and fixed his gaze on Urté. He knew he shouldn't say this, but there was a rage working through him now, and he didn't care any more: 'And then there was a child who had the regrettably bad judgment to be sired by the wrong man, and a young wife who — '

'I believe that is enough,' said Urté de Miraval. His smile was gone.

'Do you? What if I do not believe so, my lord? What if I choose to suggest otherwise? To become truly inconvenient, as you put it? To denounce you myself for plotting to have me slain? And for other things, however long ago?' Blaise felt his hands beginning to tremble. 'If you wish, I will be pleased to fight you now. I have my attendants here, and there are two corans of Miraval already waiting by that tent. I will be happy to engage you. I don't like men who kill babies, my lord of Miraval.'

Urté de Miraval's expression had grown thoughtful. He was calm again, if very pale now. 'De Talair told you that?'

'He told me nothing. I have never asked him. This has nothing to do with Bertran.'

The duke smiled again. It was not a pleasant smile this time either. 'Ah, then,' he murmured, 'it was Ariane, last summer. Of course. I ought to have guessed. I love the woman dearly, but she loosens her tongue when bedded.'

Blaise's head snapped back. 'I have just offered once. Need I do so again? Will you fight me, my lord?'

After a moment, Urté de Miraval shook his head, seeming now to have fully recovered his composure, to be genuinely amused. 'I will not. You are hurt, for one thing, and are possibly of some importance to us right now, for another. You fought bravely this morning, Northerner. I can honour a man for that, and I do. Look, the women are waiting for you. Go play out the game and then have your ear dealt with, coran. I rather fear you are going to look like de Talair when that blood is cleaned away.'

It was a dismissal, in fact, a high lord speaking as if to some promising young swordsman, but Blaise, though recognizing that clearly, didn't quite know how to turn it into something else. Valery did it for him.

'There remains one unanswered question, my lord,' Bertran's cousin murmured to the duke. And Urté turned to him as he had not done for Rudel. 'Is it shame that keeps your back so straight just now? Shame because you have been off with an Arimondan on a dark trail of murder while the rest of us, including En Bertran, are trying to save Arbonne from a ruin we know to be coming. How far into the present *will* you carry the past, my lord, whether or not you killed the child?'

For an instant Urté was rendered speechless, and in that moment, feeling an easing of his own fury and a rush of satisfaction like a cool breeze, Blaise nodded politely to him and then turned his back, in the sight of all those watching. He heard his friends following as he began to walk towards the pavilion of the countess of Arbonne and the queen of the Court of Love, leaving the duke of Miraval standing alone on the grass with his bow, beside the body of his dead coran, the sunlight falling clearly upon the two of them.

Roban, the chancellor, standing discreetly but readily available towards the back of the countess's golden and white pavilion, saw the son of Galbert de Garsenc turn his back upon Urté de Miraval and begin to walk towards them. He winced. He hadn't heard a word of what had been spoken, of course, but the cool effrontery of the gesture carried its own message.

The messages were coming fast and furious this morning, all tending towards the same end. He still didn't like what was happening — it was too flamboyant, far too provocative for Roban — but he had to concede that the Gorhautian was carrying it off with real grace. Given what had just happened, he couldn't honestly claim to doubt the man any more. He might fail in this, they might all fail, but Blaise de Garsenc had abandoned any chance to betray them when he'd had the banner of the kings of Gorhaut raised above his tent this morning.

Roban made an unobtrusive gesture and one of his own people came hurrying over from the cleared space behind the pavilion. He sent the man running for the countess's physician and the priestess of healing as well.

In the middle of the field he saw En Urté make a belatedly imperious gesture, summoning the two Miraval corans to remove the body of the Arimondan. Roban had spent most of his life at court. He knew perfectly well why Urté had fired that long, splendid arrow shot from behind the tent. The duke, he was certain, had fully expected to find Blaise of Gorhaut already dead when he arrived at the Delonghi woman's rooms with the countess two nights ago. It wasn't any particular hatred of the young coran that would have driven him — de Miraval very possibly hadn't even known who Blaise really was — it would have been simply another blow, one more stupid, trivial, destructive blow in the endless war of Miraval and Talair. Bertran valued the Gorhautian and kept him close: therefore, and needing no other reason, Urté de Miraval would be pleased to see him slain. After which the Arimondan would have been abandoned to his fate, exactly as he had been in any event, and the unsettling, possibly dangerous lady from Portezza left to the countess. And to Roban, of course; the hard things were always left to Roban.

He watched as Blaise de Garsenc approached, walking with obvious difficulty. Some distance behind him the two green-garbed Miraval corans were running across the grass in response to their lord's summons. Roban was a thoughtful man, and it had long struck him as strange — and did so again now — that none of the blows between the warring dukes were ever directed at each other. It was as if — in some unspoken, unacknowledged fashion — they needed each other to keep alive the clear, bitter memories of that long-ago year, to give each other, however inexplicable it might appear, a reason to continue living.

It was ridiculous to Roban, hopelessly irrational, dark as pagan ritual, but at the same time something the countess had once said still rang true for him: it was virtually impossible ever to think of either man without immediately calling the other to mind. They were bound and grappled together, Roban thought, as in a net, by the death of Aelis de Miraval. Roban looked over and saw Bertran, relaxed and at ease in a chair under the countess's golden canopy. He was smiling broadly as he watched Urté stalk before his corans as they bore the Arimondan's body from the field.

It never stopped. It would not ever stop while the two of them lived. And who knew what people — and nations — they would draw down into the dark net with them, suspended forever in that time more than twenty years ago when a black-haired woman had died in Miraval?

The man who had just claimed the throne of Gorhaut was standing before the countess now. He looked, Roban thought, somewhat changed from before, even making allowance for the fact that he'd been bound and nearly naked on a woman's bed the last time the chancellor had seen him. The Gorhautian, for all the evident pain of his wounds — the gashed ear was dripping blood — carried himself with composure as he faced the two reigning ladies of Arbonne and the king of Valensa. He wasn't as young as Roban had first thought him to be, either. The look in his face just now included, unexpectedly, a hint of sadness. It was not the expression of a youthful man.

Behind him stood Bertran's cousin and Vitalle Correze's son, and a third coran in the livery of Castle Baude. They already looked like an entourage, the chancellor thought. Or was it only the manner of the Gorhautian himself that made that seem the case? Could the mere assertion of a claim effect so much of a change? It could, Roban decided, if the claim was as large as this one was. Men were often no more or less than what others saw in them, and no one in the world would ever look at this tall northern coran the same way ever again. That might, he thought suddenly, explain the sadness.

The countess rose, gesturing for those beside her to remain seated. Roban couldn't see her face, but he knew she would not be smiling. Not now, with so much cast into hazard this morning. She said, her light, clear voice carrying, 'You have acquitted yourself on this field with honour Blaise de Garsenc, and have received the favour of Rian and Corannos. We call upon all those here to bear witness that the matter of blood between yourself and Quzman di Peraño is ended and resolved forever.' She glanced deliberately over to where the banner of the Gorhaut kings was snapping in the breeze above his tent. 'As for other matters that have emerged this morning, we will have much to say to each other in the days to come, and we doubt not that the king of Valensa will wish to offer his wise counsel in these affairs. Such matters will be dealt with soon. For the moment, we offer you the care of our healers in Barbentain — ' she glanced briefly back towards Roban, who nodded '— and we shall say nothing more at this time but an offered prayer that holy Rian will bless you with her grace.'

Although that, Roban thought grimly, was a great deal to have said. The countess had made the point already when she rose to salute the Gorhautian at the first running up of his banners, but this was signalling it again, and quite unmistakably. The chancellor looked over his shoulder. The physician and the priestess had arrived; they were coming swiftly over, almost running. But there was one more thing to be done, Roban knew, before Blaise de Garsenc could be released from the public gaze into their care. This was theatre, and he was on the stage.

As the countess took her seat again it was Ariane who rose, beautiful in autumn hues of russet and pale gold. Sunrise and sunset, the chancellor thought, looking at the two women, or, since Ariane was not really young any more, perhaps noontide and twilight would better suit as images. The beauty of the lady of Carenzu was almost dazzling in the clear light. His own love, though, was for the older woman, for the grace of the ending day, and it would be until he died.

There was a rose to be given now. Mildly curious, in fact, as to what the Gorhautian would do, Roban heard Ariane's formal words spoken to invoke the symbolic rituals of the Court of Love. He was not a troubadour, not a coran, not a dancer or a wit or the sort of man who set styles of fashion at court among ladies. Even so, Roban the chancellor loved his country with his own enduring passion, with an inward, private flame, and he knew that these rituals, frivolous as they might seem, were what defined Arbonne and set it apart from the rest of the world. And he too, prosaic and dry and sober as he might be in the castle corridors of day, had had his own dreams of winning this rose and offering it — of course — to the countess before cheering multitudes. Not for some time had he had that dream, but it was not so very long ago, either.

'We have our traditions here in Arbonne,' Ariane was saying. 'Here, where Rian the goddess is so much more than merely Corinna, maiden daughter of the god. She has many incarnations, our goddess, and both death and life are contained in her. Which is why,' she said, her clear, strong voice now the only sound among the pavilions, 'which is why, at the end of a death challenge, there is a ceremony to honour Rian and the mortal women who are all her daughters. We ask the victor, the chosen of the goddess and the god, to give a rose.' She paused. 'Sometimes, as a higher recognition of his worth, we invite him to offer three.'

She opened the coffer they had given her, and Roban saw that she had indeed chosen to invoke the full ceremony this morning. It was seldom done, but it was obvious that Signe and Ariane were marking this moment and this man as indelibly as they could. He wondered if the Gorhaut coran could possibly be aware of how much he had taken upon himself today. He wondered how long the man would live — but that, of course, was bound up in how long any of them could expect to live with a war coming, certain as winter and the spring to follow.

'White is for fidelity,' Ariane said, holding the coffer up to be seen. There was a murmuring all along the pavilions, of anticipation and speculation. The morning was offering more than anyone could have imagined. 'Yellow is for love, and red is for desire.' She smiled. 'You may bestow them as you choose, my lord de Garsenc. We will all be honoured by your doing so.'

Blaise of Gorhaut, grass-stained and bloody, bowed to Ariane and took the coffer from her long fingers. It was purest ceremony, Roban knew, a spectacle intended entirely for those in the other pavilions and the commons' standing grounds, and for the words and music of the troubadours and joglars who would carry it to castles and villages far beyond this field when the fair was over. Knowing this, having seen it so many times before, he was nonetheless moved.

Gravely the man handed the open coffer to Vitalle Correze's son and took from it the white rose. He looked upon it in silence for a moment, before turning back to the queen.

'Fidelity I offer where it is most richly deserved, if I might be allowed to name a woman who is not with us at this field. May I ask you to guard this for her and have it laid at her feet in my name when the time allows?'

Gravely Ariane nodded. 'You may and I shall. Where should I carry it?'

'To my sister,' said Blaise, and Roban was almost certain the emotion in his voice was not feigned. 'To Rosala de Savaric de Garsenc, who kept faith with her child and her own vision of Gorhaut. And say to her, if you will, that I shall never break faith with her while I live.'

The woman was still in the castle, Roban knew. This open ground was no place for someone only days past childbirth. The herald was declaiming her name now that all might hear it. There had been rumours, but this would be the first formal confirmation of who the mysterious woman in Barbentain was. They were going be talking about this morning in all six countries for a long time, Roban thought, shaking his head.

Blaise had already turned to take the red rose. He seemed to be hesitating, brow furrowed, but then Roban saw him smile slightly for the first time since he'd approached. Carrying it before him, laid across both palms, he limped a short distance down the row of pavilions and stopped before the handsomely carved and decorated chair of Lucianna Delonghi, who had bound him in ropes two nights ago, and cut him with her dagger. Extending both hands he gave her, with another low bow, the red rose of desire.

Roban, watching with frank curiosity, saw the woman go pale, even as the father, beside her, smiled — and then slowly stopped smiling as implications came home to him. Lucianna Delonghi said nothing at all; her composure seemed shaken for the first time the chancellor could remember. With a court-bred instinct Roban turned just then to look at Ariane, and saw how thin her mouth was as she watched. *A new twist here*, he thought. *I wonder when that happened?*

'I begin to think,' murmured Bertran de Talair, speaking for the first time, 'that we may have all found more than we bargained for in this man. I may yet learn to fear him. He has just taken his full revenge upon Borsiard d'Andoria.'

It was true, Roban realized. This was a very public rose of desire offered to a married woman whose husband had been banned from the fair for trying to have Blaise killed. Everyone in the pavilions and most of the commons would now be certain they knew why. No wonder Massena Delonghi was no longer smiling. Turning back to the Portezzan pavilion, Roban was in time to see the Gorhautian speak one word to the woman, and the chancellor's line of vision was clear enough that he was very nearly certain that the word was *farewell*. The revenge, he considered, might not be only upon the husband.

The herald was busily crying Lucianna d'Andoria's name as Blaise came back for the yellow rose.

He took it in both hands, as he had held the other two, and turned to the countess and the queen. He looked from one to the other and then said, calmly in the stillness of the morning air, 'This one, if you will allow, I shall keep for a time. In my own country of Gorhaut we speak love privately before we declare it to the world.'

And then, before either woman could reply, without any dramatics at all, he fainted.

And that, thought the chancellor of Arbonne sagely as

he motioned urgently for the healers, is probably the first act of this entire morning that wasn't meant for an audience.

As it happened, he was wrong.

'*You might consider fainting if this goes on too long and you want to get out of here,*' Rudel had murmured, not moving his lips, as Blaise had taken the first rose. '*Gallant victor pushed to his very limits. They'll like that.*'

Towards the end, as he walked back from Lucianna's pavilion, Blaise had decided that it was, indeed, going on too long. He hadn't, actually, expected to see real pain in her eyes. Anger yes, and perhaps a scornful pride, but not that sudden pain.

Following upon everything else, it made him feel extremely strange. He didn't want to actually collapse, so he took Rudel's advice and allowed himself to seem to do so, slipping to the grass and letting his eyes fall closed. He heard voices of sharp concern above him, the countess calling for aid, Bertran's voice guiding the physician through the pavilion's seats to where he lay. Rudel and Valery quickly contrived a litter to carry him upon, and he heard Hirnan's brisk, highland accent clearing a path as they bore him away, out of the too-bright sun and the scrutiny of so many people.

Part of the way back towards the castle Blaise did, in fact, lose consciousness, but not before the thought came to him, quite unexpectedly, along the momentarily undefended pathways of his mind, that Rosala's child, Cadar, was almost certainly his own son.

Most of the troubadours were loudly, even wildly expressive in their enthusiasm for what had just happened. Even when En Blaise de Garsenc fell to the ground in a faint it did not check their exuberant spirit. Remy, it seemed, had elected to forget about his swordspoint encounter with the man at Midsummer. He would probably end up regarding it as an early bond of blood between the two of them. Jourdain and Alain were already speaking of a hurried collaboration this afternoon, to have at least one song ready for the evening's banquet in Barbentain.

'You don't look well. What is it?' Aurelian, of course, the one who always noticed, even in the midst of pandemonium.

Lisseut managed a shaky smile for him. 'I don't much like this kind of thing, I've just discovered.'

'Neither do I, and I learned that some time ago. It is over now. We can go.' He hesitated, looking down at her thoughtfully. 'He will be all right, you know. I saw the physician and a priestess coming over.'

'I did too. I'm sure he's all right.' She was aware that there was an expression of knowledge on his part in what he had just said, and an admission in her brief reply. She didn't care. He had given out the white rose to his brother's wife, and the red to Lucianna Delonghi, who was as beautiful as Aurelian had said she was. He had kept the yellow one.

Beside her, Aurelian was silent for a moment. She saw some children running about on the grass now, play-acting battles. People were beginning to leave their pavilion and all the others, joining the milling, feverish crowd. The inns were about to become extremely busy in Lussan.

'And you, my dear?' Aurelian asked finally. 'Will you be all right?'

'I don't know,' she answered, truthfully.

CHAPTER·14

The blue moon is full tonight, Ranald realizes belatedly, lending its strange luminosity to the trees and rocks of the mountain pass. The creatures of the otherworld are rumoured to be able to move between their own land and this one on nights when Escoran is full. The mountains, in the shepherds' tales, are the haunts of many of them: ethereal creatures the size of flowers; hairy, great-footed monsters who can seize and devour an unwary horse and rider and leave nothing but bones for the morning sun to find; or the spirits who steal babies from their cradles by the fire and take them away under barrow and hill forever.

Ranald tries, again, to decide exactly why he is so unhappy to be here. He likes hunting, and night certainly holds no terrors for him, especially not in the company of fifty of the king's best men. In a sense this is simply a larger, more wide-ranging hunt.

In another sense, a more honest one, it is no such thing at all.

He looks over to his left and stares for a long moment at the grim profile of the only man who seems even less pleased than he to be here. Fulk de Savaric had the misfortune to be paying one of his rare visits to Cortil when the message came of his sister's flight and the king decided that same evening to ride. Ademar had made it clear that the dukes of Garsenc and Savaric were not merely being given the opportunity to join his company. They were expected to do so. Loyalty, the message was explicit, was very much at issue on this ride.

For two days and a night, with a second night upon them now, they have been in the saddle, changing horses

three times, eating at speed and usually at a gallop. Ranald
has never seen King Ademar like this, so intense, so focused
in his rage.

This, he decides, is probably what is disturbing him most.
That the king is visibly so much more incensed than he himself by Rosala's flight with the child. It is almost as if she fled
from Ademar and not Ranald. In some ways that might even
be true. Not that he harbours illusions about the strength of
his relationship with his wife, but Ranald does wonder, almost
wistfully, if she would have risked so much, including the life
of the unborn child, just to leave Garsenc and his own company if his father and the king had not also been part of the
picture. Large parts, both of them, with Galbert threatening
to take the babe, and Ademar threatening . . . what? A seduction of the wife of the most powerful duke in the country? A
ravishing of her if she proved unwilling?

It seems, on the evidence, that she has indeed proven
unwilling, has chosen the astonishing, surely terrifying option
of flight alone to another country rather than trust her husband to guard and shelter her from his father and their king.
And what, he wonders, whether one considers it by the light
of day or the blue shining of this moon, do all of these things
say about the character and strength of Ranald, duke of
Garsenc, who is even now riding, however unwillingly, in the
wake of his king across the mountain pass towards a slaughter
in Arbonne?

In the end it is precisely as easy as any experienced soldier might have predicted it would be. The three Arbonnais
corans in the watch-tower on the southern slopes of the range
are accustomed to traffic from the north during the month of
the Lussan Fair, and utterly confident — as they have every
right to be — of the truce that always accompanies a fair.

Ademar halts his full company out of sight and sends five
corans down towards the tower. They are greeted with courtesy by the guards, offered shelter and food and straw for the
night. The three Arbonnais are killed even as these offers are
being made. On the instructions of the king, as the signal is
given and the rest of the company rides up, the three guardsmen are decapitated and castrated and the wooden buildings
beside the stone tower are set on fire.

They ride more swiftly then, to be ahead of any message in the flames. A short time later they sweep down upon the nearby hamlet of Aubry like a wild hunt out of the shepherds' night terrors: fifty howling men on horses, swords out, torches in their free hands, burning and slaying without warning, without reason offered, without respite. This raid in a time of truce is a message, and the message is to be made as unambiguous as it can be.

Ranald, aware that he is being watched by the king and by the Elder who is here as his father's representative, makes a point, slightly sickened, of seeking out those few villagers who have some sort of weapon in their hands as they stumble from the huts amid the screaming of animals and small children. He is a very good fighter, once a celebrated one, though his brother latterly might have had the reputation, travelling the world in search of tournaments and wars. But it was Ranald who first taught Blaise anything about swordsmanship, and it was Ranald de Garsenc who, the year he turned nineteen, was named King's Champion in Gorhaut by Ademar's father, Duergar.

That had been, he has often thought, easily the best time of his life. Honoured by the king and the court for his prowess, excited by the attention of women of high rank and low, continually gratified by his own smooth, effortless skills, immersed in the oblivious, expansive confidence of youth, and free — more than anything else, free of his father for a little while.

Then his uncle, Ereibert de Garsenc, had died and Ranald had become duke, with all the defining burdens and powers of rank, and the specific implications of being near to an often-disputed throne. A new champion had been named ceremoniously, even as Ranald returned to Garsenc Castle in the south, and his father, again, began to tell him what to do. More than ten years ago, that was. For all those years he has mostly been doing what Galbert tells him. He wonders what he could point to, if he tried, that has given him real pleasure in that time.

Certainly not this slaughter, or the meaning of it, in a time of truce. Ranald de Garsenc is hardly a sentimental man, and he has no trouble with warfare, or even the idea of conquest here in Arbonne. This isn't a war though, not yet. This is something ugly and vengeful. It is supposed to be his own revenge, he knows. He has not been consulted on the issue; he has only ridden, as required by his king, to deliver a message in blood and fire.

There is a small temple to the goddess Rian not far from the village, the northernmost temple in Arbonne, the nearest to Gorhaut. That is why they are here. The thirty or forty inhabitants of Aubry, awakened in the middle of the night, are killed, down to the last child. Like the guardsmen in the burning tower, the men — mostly shepherds and farmers — are decapitated and their genitals are hacked off. Ademar of Gorhaut knows exactly how to say what he thinks of the men in woman-ruled Arbonne.

Then they ride on to the temple.

Under the light of Escoran at its full and the just-risen crescent of Vidonne, the eight priestesses of Rian in that small sanctuary are taken from their beds and are burned alive. The soldiers are made free of them first, by order of the king. Ademar moves his big horse restlessly back and forth, watching first one cluster of corans with a woman and then another. There is a great deal of screaming and a growing roar from the swiftly gathered bonfire of dry autumn wood. At one point, his pale yellow hair reddened in the firelight, Ademar looks over at Ranald and laughs.

'Do you not want a woman, my lord of Garsenc? A gift from your king, solace for your great loss?' He shouts it so others can hear.

Ranald, his sword still in his hand, though unnecessarily now, says, 'Not before you, my liege. I will follow in this, as in all things.'

Ademar throws his head back and laughs again. For a moment, Ranald is afraid the king will indeed dismount and join his corans among the pinioned women, but Ademar only slashes his horse again and moves nearer to where the Elder that Galbert has sent is watching the pyre. Ranald watches the king go, a bleakness in his heart. He knows what he should do. He knows he will not do it. In the mingling of firelight and the moons his eyes briefly meet those of Fulk de Savaric. Both men look away without speaking.

He has seen burnings before, has ordered a number of them himself on the Garsenc lands, following his father's regime of having one such spectacle every year or so to keep the serfs and villagers properly subdued. He has watched impassively, time after time, setting an example. He has never seen eight women burned at once, though. The numbers shouldn't matter, but, when it finally begins, it appears that they do make a difference.

Through the screaming and the terrified noises of the farm animals all around, Ranald hears his father's designated Elder intone the ritual of denunciation and the formal curse of Corannos, and then, his voice rising in genuine triumph, invoking the god's gift of fire to eradicate heresy.

A scourging of the god, Galbert called this raid in the throne room of Cortil, when the king came out from a meeting with his High Elder and announced that he would be riding for Arbonne that same night.

The screaming continues among the flames until the smoke stops it, which is what always happens. The women slowly begin to turn black and the smell of burning flesh is strong. Ademar decides to leave. Having done what he came to do, his fury slaked for the moment, the king of Gorhaut leads his corans back towards the mountain pass. As they go past the still-smouldering outbuildings beside the lone watchtower one coran begins to sing, and soon almost all of them are doing so — a song of Gorhaut victorious in battle, the chosen warriors of Corannos in his most beloved land.

Three guardsmen in a tower, a hamlet of shepherds and farmers, eight priestesses raped and set on fire. A scourging of the god.

It is a beginning.

†

The west wind blew the smoke the other way, so he was able to see, quite clearly from the ridge at the fringe of the forest, exactly what was happening below. He watched the massacre in the village without expression, and felt a disturbing but unmistakable stirring in his loins when he saw men he knew dragging the women out from the temple, some naked, some in night-robes that were quickly ripped away. He was quite close, actually, though hidden among the trees. He heard not only the screams but the shouted jests of the corans. He recognized the king immediately, and a moment afterwards saw his own liege lord, the duke of Garsenc. These were, in fact, the men he had been riding north to find.

He was bothered by the burning, though in itself that would not have been enough to make him pause. He did pause however, silent and watchful on his horse above Aubry, as the corans of Gorhaut finished their games and their work and the screaming died away. Nor did he move, though it was clearly past time to ride down, when he saw the king make a sudden, sweeping gesture and fifty horsemen swiftly remount and ride away, east and north towards the pass.

He was trembling, in fact, confused and unsettled by his own hesitation, visited, as he had been all day, by thoughts he would never have entertained before this morning. Habit and fear, the compulsions of his discipline, had sent him riding north from Lussan at midday to carry news to Cortil of what he had seen on the tournament ground that morning. He had stopped at a roadside inn for ale, and had then lingered there absurdly long, telling himself over and over that it was time to get up in the saddle again, that his tidings were critical, dangerous, that he was even at risk of suspicion if he delayed too long.

It was very nearly day's end, though, when he left that inn, riding at a gallop but not straining his horse. It was a long way to Cortil, he told himself, he had to be careful not to exhaust his mount. In the darkness under Escoran's blue light he had approached Aubry, preparing to bypass it on the road towards the pass, when he heard the sounds of horses and shouting men and stopped at the forest's edge to see, astonishingly, the king he had been riding north to warn.

And he stayed up there watching, motionless, as they slaughtered the people of a village and a temple and rode away. He wasn't especially shocked by what the corans were doing to the priestesses, nor even, really, by the burning of the women after they were done, though no halfway normal man could really *enjoy* such a thing. That wasn't what kept him silent up on the ridge. He had seen worse, or as bad at any rate, in the brutal years of war against Valensa, especially among the farms and towns on either side of the border. The longer a war went on, his father had told him once, the more terrible the things one saw, and did. It seemed to him to have been a true thing to say; he felt that way about much of what his father had told him over the years.

It wasn't even, though this was a part of it, the thrill he had felt that morning, straight up his spine and tingling in his hair, when Blaise de Garsenc had raised the banner of the kings above his tent and gone forth to battle. He had always thought — and had once or twice even said, though only to trusted friends — that the youngest of the de Garsenc was much the best of the three of them.

That wouldn't have made the difference, not in and of itself. A coran in Gorhaut learned, early, to keep his thoughts where they belonged: away from any actions he might be ordered to perform. His own sworn liege lord was Ranald, duke of Garsenc, and if the duke took most of his own orders from the father in Cortil, well, the corans of Garsenc were not expected to have any thoughts at all about that.

He would have gone down with his tidings, he realized finally, still sitting silently on his horse long after the king's company had gone, watching the burning fires spread from two of the wooden houses to a third, if it hadn't been for the one additional thing, drawn slowly up from his own history during this long day like a bucket from a well.

There was no sound now save the crackle of the flames and the wailing, very faint, of a child or an animal that was somehow not yet dead. After a moment that crying also stopped and there was only the rising sound of wind and the fires, growing to a roar as the last of the wooden houses caught.

What had kept him here, rooted to this ridge, watching his king and liege lord and corans he had known for years, was the memory of his father's last year.

His own family home had been a small tract of farmland proudly entered in their own name on the baron's records since the last plague had made labour scarce and left too many farms untended. A small bit of land, but his father's own, after a grinding lifetime of brutally labouring for someone else. It had been in the good grainlands in the north of Gorhaut, that farm. Or, to speak properly now, in the north of what had *been*

Gorhaut. It was Valensa now, since the treaty that had surrendered land kept safe by King Duergar's own sword and the corans of the king and the courage of farmers and villagers fighting for what was theirs.

He had fought at Iersen Bridge himself. Fought and won in ice and blood among the army of Gorhaut, though grieving sorely for his king after swords were sheathed and spears laid aside. A season later, no more than that, back in the south at Garsenc Castle where he served the young duke as an anointed coran, to the vast pride of his family, he had learned that his parents, along with all the other farmers and the inhabitants of entire villages of the north, were being told to pack and travel south to wherever they would, wherever they could find shelter.

It was only for a time, they were advised by the messengers of the new king, Ademar. The new king, in his wisdom, had taken thought for them, the messengers said — there would be wider, richer lands for all of them very soon. In the meantime, his father's lifelong dream and prayer of his own farm was gone, handed over to the Valensans they had been fighting for fifty years. Just like that.

His parents had actually been among the fortunate, in a way of thinking, finding a place with his mother's sister's husband east of Cortil; working for someone else again, but with a roof over their heads at least. He had seen his father twice there, but though the old man said little at the best of times, after the northern fashion, his eyes didn't convey any sense of good fortune to his son.

Everyone knew where the promised new lands were supposed to be. It was common talk in the country as much as in the taverns and castles. His father had said only one thing about that, at the end of his second visit, his last, to the farmyard hut that was now his parents' home.

They had been walking out together, he and his father, at twilight, looking out over the grey moorland in a drizzle of rain. 'What,' his father had said, turning aside to spit into the mud, 'do I know about olive trees?'

His son had not replied. He had watched the thin rain falling on the moor. There was nothing to say. Nothing, that is, that would not be treason, or a lie.

This morning, though, on a challenge ground in Arbonne under a clear sky he had heard the younger son of Garsenc name Ademar a traitor and claim the throne of Gorhaut before lords and ladies of all six countries. And the simple truth was, he realized finally, sitting his horse on that ridge above a burning hamlet, he agreed with Blaise de Garsenc.

His father would have felt the same way, he knew with certainty, though he would never have put such a thought into words. They were people of Gorhaut, their lives and lands charged to the protection of the king — and their safety and history and trust had been given away by him with a signed piece of paper. It was said that Galbert the High Elder had been behind the whole thing. That he wanted to destroy Arbonne because of the goddess they had down here.

He didn't know much about that or very much care, but he had seen his father destroyed by living on another man's farm far from the northern lands he had known all his life. His father had died at the end of that same summer, taking to his bed one morning, the scribe's letter had said, and passing to the god four days after without any last word spoken. He had not appeared to be in great pain, the scribe wrote. His mother had made her mark at the end, after the part wishing him all best fortune. He still carried it, that letter.

He looked down a last time on the burning of Aubry. He drew a long breath, finally clear in his mind, though not any the less afraid for that. When he began to ride again it was south, the way he had come, carrying a different message, grim with fire and death and with more of each to come, certain as mortal man was born to die.

He had actually made his choice, he realized, on the evening of that last walk with his father in the rain. He had had no way to put that decision into action. Now he did.

He put spurs to his horse, leaving the fires of Aubry behind him. His eyes were on the empty road before him, seeing how bright and strange it had become in the mingling of the moons.

†

Blaise hadn't been happy about it, but the priestess and the physician, agreeing with each other, had insisted that he drink an herbal concoction that led him to sleep for most of the day.

When he awoke, in a room in Barbentain, the western sky outside his window was soft with the hues of sunset, dark rose and purple, with the blue-black of twilight soon to come. He couldn't see the river from his bed, but through the open window he could hear it rushing past; in the middle distance lights were beginning to come on in the houses of Lussan. He watched for a while, feeling curiously at peace though conscious of pain in his legs and aware of bandages about his left ear. He brought one hand up and felt them.

Tentatively he turned his head back the other way and so realized, for the first time, that he was not alone.

'It could have been worse,' Ariane said quietly. She was sitting in a chair halfway to the door. 'You lost part of the earlobe, but they say it will be no more than that. Much the same as Bertran, actually.'

'How long have you been here?'

'Not long. They said you would sleep until sundown. I asked if I could speak with you alone when you woke.'

She had changed to sober clothing from the bright regalia of the morning; her gown was a dark blue in colour, with her customary crimson only in the trim of the sleeves. She looked very beautiful to him. She smiled. 'Bertran has been going about the castle all day claiming that the two of you are now clearly revealed as long-separated brothers. The current version is that you were stolen by brigands from your cradle in Talair Castle and sold for three goats in a village in Gorhaut.'

'Three goats? I'm outraged,' Blaise said with a sigh. 'Five at least. Tell him I refuse to be undervalued, even in a story.'

Ariane's smile faded. 'You are unlikely to be undervalued, Blaise, here or anywhere else. Not after this morning. Your problems are almost certainly going to be of the opposite kind.'

He nodded slowly. It seemed that he could do that much without pain. With an effort, he pushed himself up until he was sitting. There was a flask on a table by the bed.

'What is this?' he asked.

'More of what you had before. They said you might want it.'

He shook his head. 'Is there anything else?'

There was wine, in a decanter by the far wall. There was food as well, cold meats and cheeses and fresh-baked bread from the castle kitchen. He was, he discovered, ravenous. Ariane watered the wine and brought him a tray. Blaise ate swiftly for a few moments, then looked up again. She was smiling, scrutinizing him carefully from her chair.

'They said the herbs might make you hungry when you woke.'

He grunted. 'What else did they say, since they seem to know me so well?'

'That I wasn't to agitate or excite you.' Her expression was demure.

Blaise felt oddly happy suddenly. A feeling of well-being suffused him, looking at the woman, feeling the calm and silence of the twilight. When he did leave this room the burdens of the world were waiting to be taken up. For the moment though, however brief the moment might be, all of that seemed agreeably remote. He was aware of her scent again, subtle as ever, but very much her own.

He said, 'You aren't very good at not doing that, you know.'

Surprisingly, she flushed. Blaise grinned. He shifted position and moved the lacquered tray to the chest beside his bed. She remained seated where she was.

'Has anything happened that I need to know about?' he asked. He really did feel remarkably well. More than well, actually. He wondered if the two physicians had predicted this, too. 'Anything that requires me, or you, for the next little while?'

Ariane, her dark eyes wide, shook her head.

'Is there a lock on that door?'

The hint of a smile returned to her face. 'Of course there is. And there are also four guards of the countess outside who would hear any key turning. Everyone knows I am here, Blaise.'

She was right, of course. Deflated, he leaned back against the pillows.

Ariane rose then, tall and slender, her black hair down as it always was. 'On the other hand,' she murmured, walking to

the door, 'the corans of Barbentain are legendary for their discretion.' She turned the key in the lock with a click. 'And since
the whole castle knows I'm here, we couldn't possibly be doing
anything but discussing what happens next, could we?'

She walked slowly back towards him and stood by the
edge of the bed. Blaise looked up at her, drinking in, as a
draught of cool, reviving wine, the dark-eyed, flawless beauty
of her.

'I had been wondering about that,' he said after a
moment. Her hand was playing idly with the coverlet, pulling
it back a little from his chest and then tugging it up again. He
was naked beneath. 'What happens next, I mean.'

Ariane laughed then, and drew the coverlet fully back
from him. 'We'll have to discuss it,' she said, and, sitting on
the bed, lowered her mouth to his. The kiss was brief, delicate, elusive. He remembered this about her. Then her lips
moved down, found the hollow of his throat, and then down
again, across his chest, and down again.

'Ariane,' he said.

'Hush,' she murmured. 'I did promise not to make you
agitate yourself. Don't make a liar out of me.'

His turn to laugh, helplessly, and then, not long after, to
stop laughing as other sensations took control of him. It had
grown dark in the room by then, night deepening outside.
They had lit no candles. In the shadows he saw her lift her
head from his body and then rise to stand by the bed, another
shadow, and slip free of her clothing. Then she moved again,
in a swirl of scent and a rustle of sound, to rise up over him
where he lay.

'Now remember, you aren't to get excited,' Ariane de
Carenzu said gravely as, with a smooth, liquescent motion,
she lowered herself upon his sex.

Lights were shining now in the town across the water,
someone's footsteps came down the hall, a voice answered a
quiet challenge from the guards and then the footsteps went
on. The river ran softly below, aiming for the distant sea.
Blaise felt Ariane's movements above him like the rhythm of
a tide. He lifted his hands to her breasts, and then began to
trace the outline of her face in the darkness like a blind man.
He slid his fingers over and over through the long glory of her

hair. Once again, aware of how unfair such a thing was, he could not help but contrast her to Lucianna. It was the difference, he suddenly thought, between lovemaking as a process of sharing and as an act of art. There were dangers in both, Blaise thought, for the unwary. It occurred to him that he might very easily have given the morning's red rose to this woman, had he not wanted to send a private and a public message beneath the canopy of the Portezzan pavilion.

He must have slept, afterwards, he didn't know for how long. Ariane had dressed herself, and there were candles burning throughout the room. She had not left him, though, she was watching from the chair again, as if this were his first awakening. There was something deeply reassuring about waking to find her watching him; he wondered if she knew that was so. He felt differently this time, drowsier. He looked from her calm face to the window again. The feel of the night had changed while he slept; a moment later he realized why: the blue moon, which would be full tonight, was riding above the castle and the world.

Blaise turned back to Ariane. And with the movement, remembrance of the morning came flooding back over him, the clear, sunlit image of that banner of the kings flying in his name. He lifted one hand, in an instinctive gesture. And still half-asleep said, in a whisper near to dream, 'But I don't *want* to be king of Gorhaut.'

'I know,' Ariane said, without moving. 'I know you don't.' With her night-black hair and her pale, almost translucent skin she looked like a ghost, a racoux, in the candlelight. She smiled ironically. 'I wouldn't worry about it, Blaise. We are unlikely to live so long.'

She left a little while after that. Bertran came in and visited briefly, sharing his new jest about their fraternity, deliberately avoiding anything of more weight or substance. Rudel and Valery came by. Blaise ate again while they were with him, a proper meal this time, brought by Hirnan; he was still hungry. The doctor and the priestess arrived afterwards and urged him to drink more of their herbal infusion. He declined. He felt all right, actually. Some pain in the ear, rather more at the moment across his shins and the back of his calf where the Arimondan's sword had caught him, but, on the whole, he was better off than he'd any right to be. He didn't want to be drugged again.

They left him alone for a time, going downstairs to the banquet and the singers. Blaise dozed a while, then got out of bed and sat by the window looking out. Faintly he could hear the music from below. He was thinking of Rosala, as it happened, when there came a knocking at his door again, and the countess herself came in, with Ariane and Bertran. Rudel was just behind them, and the chancellor, Roban. Their faces were grim. Ariane, Blaise saw immediately, had been crying. Before anyone could speak he made himself take a slow, deep breath as if pulling himself back to the world.

'There is a man who has come,' said Bertran as the countess, very pale, kept silent. Her face was a mask, a carving in marble. There was a look in her eyes though, a depth of anger he had never seen before. 'A man from Gorhaut. He has given us some extremely bad news and asked leave to be brought to you.'

Valery and Hirnan ushered the man in. Blaise knew him, if only slightly. A coran of Garsenc, one of the better ones, he remembered Ranald saying once. The man, without a word spoken, sank to his knees before Blaise. His hands were uplifted and pressed together in position for the oath. Slowly, aware that this too was a beginning of something irrevocable, Blaise rose from the window seat and cupped his own hands around those of the coran. He heard the ancient oath of Corannos spoken to him then in that high room in Barbentain Castle as if he had never heard the words before. Exactly as with the banner, he thought: it was different when it was meant for you. For a moment he looked over at Ariane. She was weeping again. He turned back to the coran, concentrating on the words.

'I swear to you in the name of the high god Corannos of fire and light, and on the blood of my father and his father, that I will keep faith with you. I offer my service to the gates of death. I acknowledge you in the eyes of men and the most holy god as my liege lord.'

The man paused. Blaise, just then, remembered his name: Thaune. He was from the northlands, the accent had given that away in any case. Thaune looked up and met his eyes for the first time. 'And I acknowledge you also,' he said, his voice surprisingly strong now as he spoke words that went beyond the ancient oath, 'as my true king. I will not lie easy at night nor unclasp my sword belt until you are upon the throne in Cortil in the stead of the traitor now sitting there. In the name of Corannos, all this I swear.'

Blaise cleared his throat. There was a feeling of dread in him; Ariane's tears, the silence of those around him. He said, 'I accept your homage. I take you as my man, Thaune of Gorhaut. I offer you shelter and succour and my own sworn oath of fidelity before the god as your liege. I bid you rise.' He shifted his hands and helped the coran stand. 'And now,' he said, 'you had better tell me what has happened.'

Thaune did so. In the midst of the telling, Blaise discovered, with some real urgency, that he wasn't as fully recovered as he had thought he was. It was Hirnan, watching closely, who moved the chair by the window quickly over for him. Blaise sank down into it.

It seemed that his father and King Ademar had not begun with messengers and elegantly phrased demands for Rosala's return with her child. They had begun with fire.

†

Cadar was having an odd night, waking often to feed and then falling asleep again almost as soon as the wet-nurse put him to the breast. The priestess was indulgent, unworried. It took a week or two, she said, for some of the little ones to learn that the dark hours were for sleeping more and eating less. Rosala, aware that under normal circumstances at home she would be far removed from her baby at this stage, with Cadar and his nurse living in another wing of the castle, or indeed, elsewhere entirely, had still not been able to stop herself from walking down the corridor to look in on him when he cried.

She was coming sleepily back up the hallway clad only in the night-robe the countess had given her when she saw someone waiting in the shadows outside her door. She stopped, instinctively afraid, a hand fumbling to more properly close her robe.

'Forgive me,' said the duke of Talair, moving forward into light. 'I did not mean to frighten you.'

Rosala took a shaky breath. 'I am easily frightened of late. I never used to be.'

'You are in a strange place,' En Bertran murmured gravely, 'and have a new responsibility. It is not unnatural, I think.'

'Will you enter?' she asked. 'I think I have wine left from earlier this evening. I can send a servant for more.'

'No need,' he said, 'but thank you, yes, I will come in. There are tidings you should hear.'

It was late at night. Something thumped within Rosala: her heart, pounding as if on a drum. 'What has happened?' she asked quickly.

He made no immediate reply, opening her door instead and ushering her in. He waited until she had taken one of the chairs by the fire and he sat down on the low bench opposite. In the firelight his eyes were remarkably blue, and the scar on his cheek showed white.

'Is it Blaise?' she asked. She had been told about this morning, several times already, by many people. The duchess of Carenzu had brought her a white flower and explained the meaning of it. The flower was in a vase by the window now. She had sat looking at it for a long time after Ariane had left, thinking of what Blaise had done, and had surprised herself by beginning to cry.

'He is fine,' said Bertran de Talair, reassuringly. He fingered his ear. 'I'm afraid he is going to rather resemble me, in one regard at least, when the bandages come off, but other than that he is not seriously harmed.' He hesitated. 'I don't know how much it means to you, at this point, but I can say that he honoured his name and his country's this morning.'

'So I have been told. It does mean something to me, obviously, given what he declared before the challenge began. They will not wait long before coming after him.'

The duke of Talair shifted a little in his seat then and left a small silence.

'I see,' Rosala said, clasping her hands tightly in her lap. 'They have come already.'

'They have, but not for him. They will not learn about him for some days yet. They destroyed a village named Aubry tonight, killing everyone, and then they burned the priestesses of the temple there.'

Rosala closed her eyes. Her hands began to tremble. 'That was for me, then,' she said. Her own voice unsettled her; it was dry and thin as a stream in a season of drought. It seemed to be coming from someone else, a long way off. 'It was because of me.'

'I'm afraid so.'

'How many people?'

'We aren't certain yet. Perhaps fifty.'

'Who was there? From Gorhaut, I mean.' Her eyes were still closed. She brought her arms up to wrap them around herself. She felt cold, suddenly.

His voice was gentle, but he was not shielding her from any of this. She understood that there was a large measure of respect for her in his not doing so. 'The king himself, we are told.' He hesitated. 'Your husband and your brother as well.'

Rosala opened her eyes. 'They would have had no choice. I don't think either of them would willingly have done this.'

Bertran de Talair shrugged. 'I would not know. They were there.' He looked closely at her a moment and then rose to tend to the fire. It had burned low, but there was fresh wood and kindling beside it, and he knelt, busying himself with them. She watched him, the neat, precise movements. He had not turned out to be what she'd expected from his verses, or from the tales told of his dealings with women in many countries.

'How do we know of this?' she asked at length.

He said, without turning, 'A coran from Garsenc who was here for the tournament. He watched Blaise this morning and was riding north to tell the king what had happened.'

'Why did he change his mind?'

Bertran looked briefly over his shoulder and shook his head. 'That I do not know. I'll have to ask Blaise later.' He turned back to the fire, shifting the wood. First one side caught, and then a moment later the other did. With a grunt of satisfaction he rose. 'He swore fealty to Blaise tonight, as his liege lord and true king. He named Ademar as a traitor.'

'Iersen Bridge, then,' said Rosala quietly. 'That is why he did it. He was probably a man from the north. There will be many who feel that way about the treaty.'

'How many?' asked the duke of Talair. She realized that he meant the question seriously, that he was treating her as someone whose views on this would matter.

'That is hard to judge,' she said. The fire had caught now, warming her. 'Not enough, I don't think. Most of the men of rank who might matter are afraid of the king, and the common folk are even more afraid of the brethren of Corannos — who are ruled by my father-in-law.'

He was silent. Looking into the fire Rosala saw a future there shaped of flame. Fifty people had died tonight for her. She closed her eyes again, but the imprint of the fire was still against her eyelids. The shock was beginning to pass.

'Oh, my son,' she said. 'Oh, Cadar.' And then, 'I will have to take him back. I cannot let them do this to people here. It is because he is a boy, you see. They will not let us be.'

It seemed that she was crying again, the tears spilling to slide down her face before the fire. She heard the sound of a chair scraping the floor, and then a rustling, and then competent, capable hands had taken her and laid her head against a strong shoulder. His arm went around her.

'Neither of you is going back,' said Bertran de Talair, his voice roughened. 'The countess herself stood up for your child before Corannos and Rian and so did I. I swore an oath to you the night Cadar was born. I did not do so carelessly. I will swear it again: neither of you is going back to them while I live.'

Something hard and tight in Rosala seemed to loosen, or she let go of her hold upon it, and she allowed herself to weep without shame in the arms of the duke of Talair. She wept for Cadar, for herself, for the dead and burned of that night, for all the dying and burning yet to come. His clasp was firm holding her, his voice low, murmuring words of comfort and heart's ease. No one had held her like this, Rosala thought, since her father had died. She wept for that, as well.

She could not know it, but Bertran de Talair's thoughts just then were almost a mirror of her own: he was thinking that he could not remember the last time he had held a woman in this way, offering shelter and strength and not simply the passion of a moment. And then, a moment later, he realized that this was untrue: that he *could* remember the last time, quite well actually, if he allowed the memory in through his barriers.

The last woman he had held this way, his own heart beating as if for hers, had later died in Miraval giving birth to his child, twenty-three years ago.

Blaise stopped outside the partially open door of Rosala's room. He had been coming to tell her of the news that had reached them that night, feeling the dread of all such message-bearers, but not wanting her to learn it badly, from a stranger. Ranald had been at Aubry, Thaune had said, and Fulk de Savaric, her brother. About to knock, he heard two voices, and realized a moment later that he had been anticipated in his errand. He felt an unexpected mixture of emotions. Relief, mostly, in the end.

Uncertain whether to enter or leave, he heard Rosala abruptly speak in a stricken voice of taking the child back to Gorhaut. Grieving for her, understanding exactly what she meant, and humbled again by what it seemed she was, he heard Bertran de Talair, unexpectedly gruff, repeating an oath he'd evidently sworn to her before. Blaise heard Rosala begin to weep then, and through the angle of the door, in the light of the fire's glow, he saw the duke move to the arm of her chair to hold her while she cried.

He felt an intruder, a cause of the distress the other man was trying to assuage. He ought to have been comforting her himself, he thought. He owed her that much. He owed her at least that much. Blaise looked back up the corridor and saw Hirnan waiting discreetly at the farther end. Feeling his wounds again and weary still, but with a suddenly urgent need to at least finish what he had begun with the white rose this morning, he knocked on the door and said, quietly, so as not to startle them too greatly, 'For what it is worth, I have an oath of my own from this morning to repeat.'

They both looked up; Bertran calmly, Rosala wiping quickly at her eyes. She shifted a little then and the duke rose, allowing her to stand and then walk forward. A little too late Blaise realized what she was about to do. Quickly, trying to forestall her, he moved into the room so that, in the end, they ended up on their knees, both of them, facing each other before the fire. He wouldn't have blamed Bertran for laughing, but the duke was silent and watchful.

The lost children of Gorhaut, Lucianna had said two nights ago. Truth to that, Blaise thought. Through her tears he saw Rosala offer the glimmer of a smile.

'Will you not accept my homage, my lord?'

He shook his head.

'You will have to become accustomed to this,' she murmured. 'Kings can't go about kneeling to women.'

'I am not a king yet,' he said, 'and to some women I think they can. I understand the duke of Talair has vowed that he will not let them take you while he lives.' He looked at Bertran, whose expression remained devoid of irony. 'Hear me, then. In the name of the most holy god, I swear I will keep faith with you, Rosala. My claim to the throne is as nothing if we surrender you and Cadar.' He heard the roughness in his own voice at the end.

It was the first time he had actually spoken the child's name. It sounded strange to him as an infant's name. Cadar was a name of power for Blaise, for an entire generation in Gorhaut, given their vivid images of Rosala's father. It was a name of pride, of hope . . . if the child lived long enough.

Rosala shook her head. 'We should not matter so much, he and I,' she murmured. 'There is too much at stake here.'

Behind her, Bertran said quietly, 'Sometimes people end up mattering more than one might expect. My lady, the two of you *are* what is at stake. They will use you to begin the war. They already have.'

'Then send us back,' she whispered. She was looking at Blaise, not at Bertran.

'It would make no difference,' the duke answered quietly. 'Not now. They would kill you and keep him and still find a reason to come down on us. They have all the dispossessed of their northlands hungry to be assuaged. This isn't like the old romances: Elienna carried off to Royaunce and an army going after her. This is pure politics now, the hard game of nations. My lady Rosala, Arbonne is the last clause, if you will, of the Treaty of Iersen Bridge.'

Blaise, closely watching her, saw the handsome, intelligent features accept the truth of Bertran's words. She knew as much about these things as Ariane or Lucianna, or indeed, he and Bertran. She always had. There were tears still on her cheeks, revealed by the firelight; awkwardly, regretting how difficult such gestures seemed to be for him, he brought up a hand and brushed them away. He wished he were more graceful, more at ease with himself. He said, 'You owe no homage to me, Rosala.'

She looked again as if she would protest, but in the end said only, 'I may thank you for the flower?'

Blaise found that he could smile. 'I would expect you to.'

Bertran laughed quietly. Rosala, a second later, returned the smile tremulously, but then she lowered her face into her hands.

'How can we speak thus?' she cried. 'They burned women tonight. Because of me. They never even knew who I was and they were taken from their beds and raped by Ademar's corans and — say nothing, I know they were! — and then they were burned alive. With all that the two of you know, will you tell me how I am to live with that? I can hear them screaming now.'

Blaise opened his mouth and closed it. He looked past her at Bertran, whose eyes were shadowed and dark with the fire behind him. The duke said nothing either. *With all that the two of you know.* He knew nothing, in the face of this. There were no words he could think of to say.

So he spoke her name. What was it about the speaking of a name? Slowly he brought up his arms again and gently took her head between his hands and, leaning forward, he kissed her on the brow. He wished there were more he could do, but there didn't seem to be. Women had been burned tonight, on a pyre of his father's long dreaming. Men had been slain and mutilated. He, too, could hear the screaming.

'In the morning . . .' he said roughly. 'We will all be stronger in the morning.' Lame words, an empty truth. It was this night that needed dealing with. He looked over at the duke again for a moment and then rose and left the room. Bertran would be better at this, he thought, than he himself would be. There was less history here for the duke, he knew women so much better. There was an ache inside Blaise, though, walking from her chamber.

Oh, Ranald, he thought; said it aloud, actually, softly in the empty corridor. *She might even have made a man of you, this one, if she had been allowed.* His brother had been at Aubry tonight. Blaise was nearly certain that Ranald wouldn't have wanted to be, but that didn't matter, did it? He had been there.

Heavy with burdens, of past and future both, Blaise suddenly stopped and stood very still. A child had cried out in a room behind him. He listened but there was no other sound. A cry in a dream that must have been. Cadar's.

Did new-born infants dream? Blaise didn't know. He only knew that he could not turn back, could not now, if ever, ask Rosala the question in his heart. *It doesn't matter,* he told himself. *It makes no difference at all to anything.*

A lie, of course, but the sort of lie that lets one carry on.

✝

By the time she reached the top of the stairway and saw the guards outside the door, Lisseut was already regretting she had come. She had no business here, no claim to this man's attention, especially so late at night after he had been seriously wounded in combat. She didn't even know exactly what she wanted to do, or say, if he should happen to be still awake, and should happen to receive her. Someday, she thought despairingly, she really was going to have to absorb her mother's so-often-repeated lesson and accept that one did not *always* have to follow the path lit by impulse and first reactions.

More than anything else, she knew, it had been the news from Aubry that had drawn her here. It hadn't taken long for the tidings to sweep downstairs through Barbentain and race along the great hall, where those joglars and troubadours honoured with places in the morning's pavilion were offering their performances after dinner.

The music had stopped, of course. One did not sing liensennes of courtly, unrequited love or ribaldries of enthusiastically answered passion in the forests of Arbonne when news came of a village destroyed and women burned alive by the king of Gorhaut. Love had no place in the scheme of things in the wake of such horror.

But if that were the case, what, in truth, was she doing here, hesitantly approaching a doorway on this upper level of

Barbentain? Alain had agreed to wait a little while for her downstairs. She didn't much want to walk back to the inn alone. An old man had been murdered in an alley a few nights ago. There were too many unknown people from too many countries wandering in the darkness of Lussan during the fair. She hadn't had the courage to ask Aurelian to wait — he knew too much, after this morning. It was the first time Lisseut could remember that she'd wanted to hold something back from him. Alain was easier; they had their understandings after two seasons together now. He wouldn't even speculate.

The horror of the tidings from Aubry had drawn her back, in a single dark leap of memory, to that garden in Tavernel last summer, when she had listened from a place of hiding on the wall and learned who the bearded northern coran was, and heard him speak with Rudel Correze of war coming with Gorhaut. Now everyone knew who he was, since this morning, and war was no longer coming, it was upon them. And the coran she had impulsively followed that Midsummer night had claimed Gorhaut's crown today.

On that thought she almost did turn back, but she had reached a place where the wall torches lit the corridor, and she realized that the guards outside his door were watching her. One of them she knew, a coran from Vezét, from a farm not far from her father's. She wasn't sure whether she was happy about that or not.

Having been seen, though, and almost certainly recognized, she was not about to turn and skulk away. Grateful that she looked presentable, at least, in her newest tunic bought for the fair and the vest Ariane had given her, and aware that if the guards knew her they would almost certainly also know she'd been among the selected performers tonight, Lisseut walked forward with her head high.

'Hello, Fabrise,' she said to the man she knew. 'I didn't realize you were in Barbentain. Is your father well?'

He grimaced briefly in response. 'He is, I thank you. Will you tell us what you are doing here?' Formal, extremely formal. No warmth at all. They had clearly been instructed that guard duty tonight outside this door was not ceremonial. After Blaise's declaration this morning it stood to reason, and after the attack on Aubry tonight every coran in Arbonne would be on edge. Again, Lisseut wondered why she had never listened to her mother more attentively.

She said hardily, 'I thought if Blaise de Garsenc was awake he might be willing to speak with me.' There was no reply at all to that. 'We are friends,' she added — it was almost true, in a manner of speaking — 'and I wanted to see how he was. Is he sleeping?'

For a long moment four grim corans regarded her in silence. Finally one of them, evidently concluding that whatever she was, it was something other than an immediate danger, made a wry face. 'What is it,' he said, addressing Fabrise, 'about your women from Vezét, will you tell me?'

Fabrise frowned. Lisseut felt herself flushing. This was pretty much what she'd feared would happen. *Oh, mother,* she thought. It had actually occurred to her several times during the day that it might be a good time for a visit home. She could sleep in her old bed, see people she'd grown up with, talk with her mother while they did the endless needlework in the doorway, or with her father, walking among the olive groves. It might be a good thing to do, she'd thought. It had been a long time since she'd been back, and home sometimes was a place where the heart could be eased.

'I know this woman. She is not like that,' said Fabrise of Vezét; her pulse quickened at his loyalty.

'Nor is this a night,' she said, emboldened, unwilling as ever to have someone else fight a battle for her, even a small one, 'when a man of Arbonne should speak any ill of the women of his country. I will accept an apology, coran, if you offer one.'

There was a great deal to be said for the training that regular appearances in public gave one. She was easily able to outface the coran who had made that jest. He lowered his head and mumbled words that did sound contrite. He looked young, Lisseut thought. He had probably meant no real offense, though he did have a great deal to learn.

On the other hand, what innocuous reason *could* she offer for being here? Truth was, the young coran was right, if not about the women of Vezét, then rather definitely about this particular one. *We are friends*, she had said. If a friendship could be built on a night's clandestine spying like an audrade on a garden wall followed by a rejected invitation to share her Midsummer bed. He had smiled at her two nights ago here in Barbentain. Did that count? She had even thought he was about to come over to her, before Rudel Correze had appeared at his elbow and the two men had walked away.

That had been before this morning's challenge, though: before everything had changed. These corans in the hallway were, she made herself repeat it again in her mind, the guards appointed for a man who had claimed a throne.

She bit her lip. Began her retreat. 'It *is* late, I know...' she murmured.

'He is awake,' Fabrise said, 'but not in his room. He went to see his sister. His brother's wife, I mean. The one who gave birth last week. I think he wanted to be the one to tell her the news.'

'Her husband was there,' the coran she'd reprimanded now confided, as if anxious to make amends. 'At Aubry, I mean. And also her —' He stopped with a grunt as one of the others sank an elbow in his ribs.

The four men looked quickly down the corridor, and so Lisseut turned with them — to see Blaise de Garsenc approaching from the shadows.

'And also her brother,' Blaise said, finishing the sentence. He was walking quite slowly, limping a little; he looked pale beneath the beard and there were smudged circles of fatigue under his eyes. He came up to them and stopped, looking at the four men, not at her. 'There is going to be gossip, of course, but we might appropriately leave it to others, don't you think?'

It was mildly said, but the young coran went crimson to the roots of his hair. Lisseut actually felt sorry for him. Then she forgot about the man entirely as she met Blaise's scrutiny.

'Hello, Lisseut,' he said. She hadn't been positive he would remember her name. He seemed unsurprised to find her in the hallway outside his room.

She took a breath and said, straining for a normal tone, 'I'm not sure, do I curtsey?'

'I'm not sure either,' he said calmly. 'Why don't we omit it for now? I thought I heard your voice earlier. The song from Midsummer, the woman singing in the garden?'

'I didn't think you had listened so carefully back then,' she said.

'I didn't either,' he murmured. 'Evidently some of it stayed with me. Will you come in?' He opened the door to his room and stepped aside for her to enter.

Feeling suddenly shy, Lisseut walked in. He followed, closing the door behind them. There were candles on chests beside and at the foot of the bed and on the two tables in the room. They were guttering low, though, and others had gone out. He busied himself for a moment lighting new ones.

'There is wine by the far wall,' he said over his shoulder. 'Pour us each a cup, if you will.' Glad of something to do, she moved to the sideboard and did so. A faint scent of perfume lingered in the air. She thought that if she tried she would recognize it; she didn't try. She carried the cups back and stood uncertainly in the middle of the room. The bed, she noticed, was rumpled, the covers in disarray. He seemed to notice this at about the same time, moving over to smooth them as best he could.

'Forgive me,' he said. 'This room is in no condition to receive a lady.'

He was being astonishingly kind, she thought. Kindness wasn't what she needed, though. She said, 'Even the sort of lady who spies on you at night?'

He grinned, though his fatigue was still evident. He came over and took his wine, motioning her to one of the chairs by the window. He sank into the other, with a half-suppressed sigh of relief.

'You *are* in pain,' Lisseut said quickly. 'I have no right to keep you awake.'

'You won't be able to for very long,' he said, somewhat ruefully. 'Much as I'd like to talk, they gave me some herbal thing earlier and I'm still sleepy with it. They wanted me to have more but I said no.'

'You probably should have taken it,' she said.

He grinned mockingly. She remembered that quickness from Midsummer. It had been one of the things she hadn't expected from a coran of Gorhaut. 'I wouldn't have taken you for so obedient a woman. Do you always do what you're told?' he asked.

She smiled then herself, for the first time. 'Always,' she said. 'I can't remember the last time I didn't obey instructions.'

He laughed, and sipped his wine. 'I saw you in the troubadours' pavilion this morning,' he said, surprising her again. 'Ariane told me only those of the first rank are invited there. Is this new for you? Should I be offering congratulations?'

Ariane. That was the perfume. *Of course*, she told herself: they would have had a council here when the tidings came. But what she was remembering was five corans in crimson escorting him away on Midsummer Eve.

He had asked a question; Lisseut shook her head, pushing such thoughts away. She said, 'Congratulations? Wouldn't that be absurd? After you didn't let me salute you?'

His eyes were bright in the light of the candle on the table and the beard showed quite red. 'Go ahead if you really want to. Curtsey *and* kneel. Kiss my foot three times. You'll help me get used to it.' There was a bitterness she hadn't expected in his voice. He paused a moment. 'I'm not a king yet, you know. I probably never will be. I'm only someone who's made a large and foolish claim because I hate what's happened to my country.'

'From what I understand of the men of Gorhaut, that's worthy of honour in itself,' she murmured.

His expression changed. 'I'm not sure that isn't as much an attack as a compliment.'

'Can you blame me, tonight?'

There was a silence. Without speaking, he shook his head. She took a quick sip of her wine and averted her eyes. This wasn't at all how she had wanted this conversation to go. She didn't really know what she had wanted, but it wasn't this. Thinking quickly, reaching for a new direction, she said, 'You did miss something . . . unique in the hall tonight. A canzone about your morning's triumph, written at dazzling speed, rhymed in triplets, with a refrain that was simply your name sung four times on a descending scale.'

'*What?*'

She kept her tone blandly innocuous. 'We should be fair about that last bit, though: 'Garsenc' *is* a difficult rhyme in Arbonnais.'

He looked pained. 'You're not being serious?'

'I'm a serious person, hadn't you noticed? It was composed by an old companion of yours, too. Evrard of Lussan.'

'An old *what?*' He blinked. '*Evrard?* He called himself
that?' He looked so astonished she had to laugh. 'How . . . how
does anyone know my connection with him?'

She was smiling now, enjoying this. 'From Rian's Island?
He began telling us all about it immediately after the challenge this morning. No one knew before, but as of today you
are a link worth exploiting. Apparently you yourself and no
lesser mortal were entrusted by En Mallin de Baude with the
delicate task of assuaging Evrard's wounded sensibilities last
spring. Is it true, Blaise?'

He was slowly shaking his head, though in wonder, not
denial. 'I thought he was a pompous, offensive fool, but Mallin
asked me to bring him back so I did. Unconscious, actually.
My companion.' He snorted. 'We slung him like a sack of
grain into a skiff. I wouldn't have been greatly distressed if
he'd fallen overboard.' He shook his head again, as if bemused
by the memory. 'I thought all the troubadours were like that.'

'And all the joglars? Do you still think so?'

'Hardly,' he said directly, not bothering to make a jest of
it or a compliment, or anything at all. He met her gaze for a
moment, and it was Lisseut who looked away, out the window.
There was silence then for a while. She sat gazing out at the
late-night stars, listening to the river. It was not a difficult
stillness, she decided.

'May I ask something of you?' he said at length, quietly.
She looked back at him. 'I am genuinely weary, Lisseut. I'm
afraid I'm too tired to entertain you properly. I'm almost too
tired to sleep, and there is a great deal to be done tomorrow.
I don't know if this is an imposition, something one doesn't
ask of a professional, but will you sing for me, to help me rest?'
A faint smile in the flickering light. 'To show me again that
all of you aren't like Evrard?'

'I didn't think you liked music.' She was sorry the moment
she'd said that. Why was she always challenging him?

He didn't take offense, or else he was being very patient
with her. 'If I said that I regret it. I grew up with music in
Gorhaut, however different it might have been. One day I will
want to try to explain to you that my country is not only . . .

what it has been made to be tonight.' He hesitated, choosing his words. 'I think there are . . . parts of the troubadour world here, courtly love, that I find unsettling. Perhaps I needed time to understand it better. I thought once it made your men weak, your women presumptuous.' He paused again. 'There is no weakness I have found in the men of Arbonne.'

'And the women?'

He had been waiting for that, she realized. 'The women are intolerably presumptuous.' She knew that tone though, by now, and he was grinning at her again, tired as he was. She found that she could smile back.

'I will be happy to sing for you,' she said quietly. 'It is no imposition. Not when asked of a friend.' There, she had said it.

He looked surprised again, but not uncomfortably so. He opened his mouth and closed it. She silently willed him to voice whatever thought he was struggling with, but all he said after a moment was, 'Thank you.' He rose, with a difficulty he didn't bother to hide, and limped over to stretch out on the bed. He pulled off his boots but didn't bother with the covers or his clothing.

Nothing of any great import had been done, nothing said, but Lisseut stood up as well, feeling a warmth inside and an unexpected calm. Moving quietly about the room she began blowing out the candles. She left two burning, one on the sideboard and one on the small table by the window, and then, in the near darkness, she began to sing. Not of love or war or the goddess or the god, or anything at all of the adult world. On the night he had named himself king of Gorhaut, the night Aubry had burned, Lisseut sang for Blaise of Gorhaut lullabies of childhood, the ones her mother had sung to her so many years ago.

Only when she was certain, from the steady rise and fall of his breathing, that he was asleep did she allow herself a last song for her own heart's easing. It was another very old melody this one, so ancient no one was certain who had written it, or even what dim, half-remembered legend or tale it recounted. It had always seemed to Lisseut to be almost unbearably sad. She had never thought she would feel it applying to her own life. But in Blaise de Garsenc's room that night, while he slept, she sang it softly for herself, and when she came to the verses

at the end, she realized that she was very nearly offering them
as a prayer:

Thy table set with rarest wine,
Choice meats, sweet ripened fruit
And candlelight when we dine
In Fionvarre.

On we two the high stars will shine
And the holy moon lend her light.
If not here you will be mine
In Fionvarre.

Her uncle had taught her that song in Vezét, long before
he had taken her from her father's house and offered her the
life of the singers on the road. And the roads had been good
to her, had given her friends and companions, a generous measure of success, fame almost, and they had led her here
tonight, following, as ever, the quick impulses of her spirit,
and now the unbidden need of her heart.

Strangely at peace now, Lisseut realized that she had
come looking for an answer in this room and she had found it
after all. This was not a man whose life she had a right to
share. He was a friend; she knew that now, knew that he would
make some place for her in the pattern of his days, however
long or short they were to be. But for more than that, more
than that small place, she had no right and he no proper space
in what his life had now become. The banner in the wind this
morning had made this so.

And it would be all right, Lisseut thought, as she ended
the song. She was no longer a child. Life did not always or
even normally grant one the wishes of the heart. Sometimes
it came near, sometimes not very near at all. She would
accept, with gratitude, what seemed to have been allowed her
tonight — with a hope, a prayer to Rian, that there might be
more such moments graciously allowed, before the goddess
called either or both of them back to her.

She left him sleeping, with the last two candles burning
down and the moons long set and the river murmuring its own
infinitely older, endless song far below the window.

PART IV

Winter

*Until the Sun Falls and
the Moons Die . . .*

CHAPTER·15

On the night appointed there was fog at Garsenc Castle. Rolling in from the east with the darkness at day's end it swallowed up the donjon and the outer watch-towers of the castle like some mist-dragon out of the old tales of the days before Corannos moved the sun.

Alone on the ramparts above the drawbridge Thaune of Garsenc shivered, despite the woollen overshirt and the fur vest he wore in winter. He was thinking about an oath he had sworn three months ago, a vow of fealty that had turned him from a coran of humble birth and modest future into a conspirator with a substantial prospect of dying before this night was over.

He watched his breath make puffs of smoke in the grey cold, adding to the fog; he couldn't see any further than that. The moons were invisible, of course, and the stars. They had chosen a time when both moons should have been bright and high, lending light for the crossing of the pass, but men could not control what the god sent in the way of weather, and more than one campaign of the past — including the not-so-distant past — had been undone by the elements. He remembered the savage cold at Iersen Bridge. He would always remember that. He placed both hands on the stone and peered out into the swirling grey darkness. Nothing. There could have been a hundred men below him outside the walls, and if they were quiet enough not he nor anyone else in Garsenc would have known they were there.

From the small guardhouse beside the portcullis he heard the murmur of voices. There were four men posted at night. They would be playing at dice by firelight. He couldn't even see the light down there through the fog. It didn't matter. He could hear the voices, muffled in the greyness, and three of them were with him. The fourth would be dealt with, as necessary.

Not killed though. His instructions had been clear. Blaise de Garsenc wanted a minimum of killing in these first days. He seemed to have known exactly what he wanted, even back in the autumn, in the days after his first declaration. He had sent Thaune north among the other corans of Gorhaut to carry word freely of what had been done and said before that challenge at the fair. All the Gorhautians attending the fair had been assembled in an enormous room in Barbentain, Thaune remembered, and after the countess of Arbonne had ordered them out of the country and confiscated their goods Blaise had spoken to them with a cool precision that had been genuinely impressive. Because of the Treaty of Iersen Bridge, he'd said — a treaty that was a betrayal in itself — King Ademar was about to embroil Gorhaut in another war here in Arbonne. It was a war they did not need, brought on by a treaty that should never have been signed. He invited those assembled to think about his words, and he promised they would be allowed passage north through the mountains unharmed.

They had even contrived a pretended assassination attempt, an arrow landing carefully short of Blaise as he walked out from the castle the next morning. The tournament mêlée had been cancelled, in the wake of the events at Aubry and in the watch-tower south of the pass: they had found the three maimed guards by then. The court of Signe de Barbentain had collectively attended mourning services in the Temple of Rian, and in their midst — walking beside the countess, in fact — had been Blaise de Garsenc.

Thaune was instructed to claim responsibility for that attempted killing of the pretender, both on the road north through the pass and again when he arrived home at the castle — a Garsenc coran would need such a story, Blaise had told him. Thaune, remembering the fears that had led him to kill the animal-trainer, had acceded gratefully. It was strange, actually, to be working for a leader who thought of so many details concerning his men. Thaune had even, after hesitating, told Blaise about that killing in the alley. He didn't want hidden things between him and this man.

Blaise had looked regretful, but not judgmental. 'You were afraid,' he'd said, 'and doing your duty out of fear. That is how things have always been at Garsenc. I hope you will do what you see as your duty now, but without the fear.'

Thaune remembered that. He had done what he could, which, as it turned out, was quite a bit. He'd more of a knack than he would have guessed for such intrigues. There had been only a dozen soldiers in his party on the ride north — Gorhaut corans seldom went south to tournaments in Arbonne, they hadn't done so for years.

There were no rules about such things, but corans of reputation usually waited another month and went east to Aulensburg for the tourney there. Götzland was seen as better than Arbonne; it was acceptable to fight there. Only the younger ones, and a handful of spies sometimes, went south to Lussan in the autumn with the merchants and entertainers. There were no spies in this small party, though, Thaune was certain of it. The young men listened, a little awed, to his snarling tale of wind pushing a long bowshot short.

They were probably wishing they had tried the same thing, he had mused that first night in the roadside inn among the falling leaves of autumn. Probably even dreaming of having done so, and having succeeded, and riding back to King Ademar in triumph unimaginable. Young men had such dreams.

Two of the corans on that ride, he'd decided, might be thinking, or dreaming, along somewhat different lines. He'd taken a chance and spoken to one of them before they parted ways. Turned out he had judged rightly; taking careful chances was what he'd been sent back to do. Before their roads divided, his to Garsenc, the other coran's towards the palace in Cortil, Thaune had won his first recruit to the cause of Blaise de Garsenc's rebellion. The accent had been what decided him. You could almost always trust a northland man to be unhappy with King Ademar.

On the ramparts of Garsenc he leaned forward, suddenly tense, peering blindly into the fog. It was thick as the mist was said to be above the river to the land of the dead. He could see nothing, but he thought he'd heard a sound from the grassy space beyond the outer wall and the dry moat.

†

The sky above another castle, beyond the mountains to the south, was brilliantly clear that same night, the stars like diamonds, the two moons bright enough to lend shadows to the trees bending in the path of the sirnal — the north wind that swept down the Arbonne Valley with the bitter force of winter behind it.

Fires were burning on all the hearths of Barbentain, and Signe had dressed herself in layers of fine-spun wool with fur trim at the collar and sleeves and a fur-lined hat covering her head, even indoors. She hated the winter, she always had, especially when the sirnal blew, making her eyes stream and her fingers ache. Usually she and Guibor had been south by this time, in Carenzo with Ariane and Thierry, or in the winter palace in Tavernel for their sojourn there. It was always milder in the south, the depredations of the sirnal less harrowing, tempered by the shape of the land and the influence of the sea.

This year was different. She needed to be in Barbentain because this winter would not be the customary time of sheltering behind castle and village walls while the wind whipped down the valleys and empty roads. Events were taking place this season that were going to define the future for all of them, one way or another. In fact, they were taking place tonight, beneath the brightness of these two moons beyond the mountains, in Gorhaut. She wondered what Vidonne and blue Riannon were seeing there as they looked down.

Almost unbearably anxious, unable to keep still, she paced back and forth from one fire to another in her sitting room. She was disturbing her waiting-women she knew, and almost certainly doing the same to Rosala, who sat calmly nonetheless, hands busy at needlework in her chair drawn close to one fire. She wondered how the woman could be so placid, knowing — as indeed she did know — what was at stake tonight in the north.

It had come down to Blaise de Garsenc, as Beatritz had said it might almost a year ago when they'd first become aware

that the new coran in Baude Castle was rather more than he
seemed. Rather more. A very great deal more, in fact. The
countess wished, again, that Beatritz was with her now,
instead of on the island so far to the south in the sea. Images
of the past year had been with her all evening, dancing in the
flicker of the fires. It sometimes seemed to her that she spent
half her life now walking with images of the past. But she
wasn't thinking of Guibor now. She was remembering Bertran
at the challenge ground as the northerner stood before the
Portezzan pavilion offering a red rose: *We may have all found
more than we bargained for in this man*, Bertran had said.

Another image rose up then, a memory from within this
castle, in autumn as well, when they had summoned all the
merchants and corans of Gorhaut the morning after Aubry
and told them they were confiscating their trade goods and
sending them home from the fair.

Urté de Miraval had wanted to execute them all, and
Signe, a hard rage running through her, had had to resist the
same desire. There were even precedents for such a thing.
Every citizen of a country was personally responsible for the
truce-breaking of their lords. It had been Blaise who had
requested, insisted actually, that the merchants be let go, and
had given cause why this should be so.

'I have nothing at all to offer in Gorhaut just yet,' he'd
said, speaking earnestly in this very room before they had all
gone down to deal with those assembled. 'They must go home
knowing I've saved their lives — lives put in hazard by Ademar's truce-breaking. They must go home and talk about that.
Will you give me that much?' He'd paused. 'Or are we no better than what we are trying to fight?'

She'd been genuinely angry with him then, a Gorhautian speaking so to her on the morning after so many of her
people had been slain. But she was a countess of a land in
peril, and she had always been able to master her emotions
when it was time to advise Guibor on his decisions, or to make
them herself. Blaise was speaking truth, she finally decided,
and she gave him what he asked.

In the room below when she came before the merchants
one of them had protested loudly at the announced seizure of
their goods, astonishingly oblivious to how close all of them

had been to being executed that same morning: no more
innocent than the villagers and priestesses of Aubry. The man
complained furiously a second time, and then a third, speaking with choler and no respect, interjecting while she was still
addressing them. In an odd, unsettling way, she had actually
been glad of it. She had nodded at Urté, who had been looking at her expectantly, only waiting for a signal. The duke of
Miraval had calmly declared the merchant's life to be forfeit.
The man had begun shouting then, and the palace corans had
moved in quickly to take him from the room.

Blaise had looked as if he wanted to object even to that,
but had held himself in check as the struggling merchant was
dragged away by the guards. There was another message that
had to be sent here, and Signe knew it; she had been governing a nation for some time, after all, with Guibor and now
alone. Images of power mattered: in Gorhaut they could
not be allowed to think they were so weak and soft here in
woman-ruled Arbonne. They already had that impression,
Signe knew. They could not be allowed to indulge in it. She
had looked at Blaise, her expression forbidding, and had
waited for him to nod his head.

'I cannot save a fool,' he'd said to the merchants and
corans of Gorhaut. The right thing to say; it would be remembered by the others. He was learning quickly. Later that morning they executed the man, though cleanly, without branding
or breaking him; he was a symbol, not a truce-breaker himself. Here in Arbonne they were *not* the same as those they
were now to fight. She would defend that assertion to the last
of her days.

That had all been back in the autumn, with the grape
harvest in and the leaves turning. Now, in the cold, clear glitter of a winter's night, she listened to the sirnal rattle the windows like a spirit of the dead and sipped at her mulled, spiced
wine, holding the goblet in both hands, its warmth comforting her as much as the scent and taste of the wine. The two
girls were sitting on their benches near the door, their hands
cupped around hollow silver balls with burning coals inside
them. Bertran had brought that idea back, years ago she
remembered, from a journey into the wild places east of Götzland. He had done a great deal of such dangerous travelling

in the years after Aelis died. 'He is blaming himself,' Guibor had said patiently. 'There is nothing we can do about it.'

Looking more closely at the two girls, Signe saw that Perrette, the younger one, was shivering. Impatiently, she shook her head. 'In Rian's name, come nearer the fire, both of you,' she said, sounding more irritated than she meant to. 'You'll be no use to me at all if you catch a chill and die.'

This was wrong, of course, she shouldn't be taking out anxieties on those around her. But what was there for her to do, otherwise? She was an old woman in a cold castle in winter. She could only sit or stand by a fireside now and wait to see if the goddess and the god would allow them to throw successfully at dice with so many lives and two nations' destinies.

Nervously, the girls hastened to obey her. Rosala glanced up from her work and smiled.

'How are you so calm?' Signe demanded abruptly. 'How can you sit there so easily?'

The smile faded. Mutely Rosala held up her work, and the countess saw, for the first time, the raddled, spoiled stitching and the visibly trembling hands that were lifting it for her to see.

†

The fog made things horrendously difficult. Thaune still couldn't see a thing down below, though he kept straining his eyes into the thick, grey gloom. There was to have been a single torch lit briefly at the edge of the woods and then doused. He couldn't have seen a torch from these ramparts tonight if it was directly below where he stood.

Even sounds were muffled, but not so much that — just there! — he could not make out, finally, the jingle of a horse's harness and then the same sound a second time, not far away. They had come. It was time. With an awareness of all that might turn on this in the next moments, and with the fear that came — that *had* to come — hand-in-glove with that, Thaune went quickly along the rampart walk to the stairwell and started down to the guardhouse, one hand on the wall for balance in the murk.

When he appeared in the doorway all four guards jumped up from the table. He nodded his head briefly.

'It is time,' he said.

'Time for what?' said Erthon, just before Girart brought the hilt of his knife smartly down on the back of his fellow guard's head. Erthon, whom Thaune hadn't been able to decide whether or not to trust, slumped forward, and Thaune had to be quick to catch him before he knocked over the table and sent the dice rattling.

'My luck,' said Girart. 'I was about to win for the first time all night.' Thaune was able to smile; the other two guards, younger, visibly nervous, were not.

'We're in a bigger game now,' Thaune said. 'Say your prayers and open the gate and the bridge.' He went out to stand behind the iron portcullis as it began rolling up. There was a noise, of course, as the chains turned, but for once the fog was useful and Thaune doubted anyone would hear the muffled sound from across the courtyard inside the castle.

When the bars were high enough he stepped forward, ducking to pass under the lowest spikes, and waited again, staring out into the cold mist of the night. No torches yet, nothing at all to be seen, only the sound of horses again, faintly, through the low, drifting fog. Then another noise behind him as the portcullis slotted with a clang into its niche at the top of the gate and the guards began quickly winding down the drawbridge over the dry moat.

When the bridge was down, Garsenc Castle lay open to those waiting in the fog, and the first part of what Thaune had come home to do was accomplished. The easy part.

He stepped out onto the wooden bridge and felt more than he heard the simultaneous tread of someone approaching from the other end. He still could not see. The mist redoubled his anxiety, inducing primitive, irrational feelings of dread. He couldn't even make out the planks of the bridge beneath his boots. He stopped walking. 'Light your torch,' he said, his tone as calm as he could make it. The sound of his voice went out feebly into the enveloping darkness and was swallowed up.

There was silence as the approaching footsteps also came to a halt. Thaune felt as if he were wrapped in a grey shroud, ready for burial. He shuddered at the thought.

'Light your torch,' he said again to the silent figures on the bridge with him.

Finally he heard the scraping sound of flint being struck, and a moment later the resinous scent of a torch catching came to him. In the fog the light spun out only a little way, a small circle, a tenuous island of illumination on the bridge.

Bright enough to reveal Galbert de Garsenc, the High Elder of Gorhaut, huge and unmistakable, standing directly in front of him with two corans on either hand.

'I am most happy to oblige you,' said the High Elder in his unforgettable voice. 'To illuminate the first of the traitors we will now be pleased to burn. I will light your own pyre with the torch you requested.'

Thaune felt as if the world had dropped away beneath his feet, as if the final darkness at the end of time had come. His breath was snatched away in horror. He couldn't move. He was actually afraid he was going to fall down.

'Do not even think about fleeing,' Galbert added, the deep tones conveying infinite contempt. 'There are four archers behind me with their bows trained on you, and this light is more than good enough for them.'

Another tread resounded on the far side of the bridge, approaching from behind the Elder, just beyond the spill of light. 'It would be good enough, I agree,' said a lighter, cooler voice. 'If they were still conscious and therefore still holding their bows. It is all right, Thaune,' said Blaise de Garsenc, 'we have this under control.'

There came another sound, twice in quick succession, and the corans beside Galbert grunted and slid to the planks, their swords rattling on the wood. The torch was dropped but then seized by an invisible hand before it could go out.

'Do tell me, father,' said Blaise, coming forward into the light, 'what is it that makes you so anxious to burn people alive?' His words were flippant but Thaune could hear the stiff tension running beneath them. He wondered when father and son had last seen each other. Galbert said nothing at all; the rage in his eyes was genuinely frightening in the torchlight.

'Blaise,' came a Portezzan accent from the murk beyond, 'it seems your brother is here too.'

'How splendid! A reunion!' said Blaise, again with that forced gaiety. 'Bring him, Rudel, let me see those dear, kind features again.'

Galbert still had not spoken. Thaune was unable to look at the High Elder's face. He heard footsteps again, and two men brought forward a third between them.

'We have dealt with all the others,' said a voice Thaune remembered from Arbonne. 'About fifteen of them, as you guessed.' They were lighting more torches now; by their light Thaune recognized Bertran de Talair.

'Nicely done, Thaune,' Blaise said, not taking his eyes from his father and the handsome figure of Ranald de Garsenc beside him. 'We had to make the assumption that there would be an informer though, that you would need to trust too many people for them all to be reliable. We were here two days earlier than I told you, and I had men watching the roads east to see who might be coming. I thought my father might want to do the honours himself. After all,' he added, with sudden, corrosive irony, 'it has been *months* since he had anyone burned, and that hardly counts because he wasn't able to be at Aubry himself. Tell me, dear brother, did *you* enjoy it there? Was it a fine hunt? Did the women scream amusingly?' Ranald de Garsenc shifted his feet but made no reply.

Men were walking up now, passing Thaune on either side, entering the castle. The big Arbonnais coran named Valery stopped beside him. 'Well done,' he said quietly. 'Now tell me the numbers inside. Do we have a fight on our hands?'

'How many of you are there?'

'Only fifty. Trained mercenaries, though, from Portezza and Götzland. This isn't an invasion of Gorhaut from Arbonne. This is a rising from within. We hope.'

Thaune cleared his throat. 'I think about half the castle will be with us.' He reached for his belt and unhooked a large key ring. 'This unlocks the weapons room — to the right across the courtyard, the double doors with the arch. Girart, who is just behind me, will show you. You may trust him with anything. There might be a hundred, perhaps more, who resist, but they will not be well armed.' He cleared his throat again. 'I think if En Blaise lets them know he is here there may be fewer who fight.'

Blaise heard that. 'Let them know?' he echoed in mock indignation. 'Of course I'll let them know. I'm the wayward son come home to his father's open arms. There ought to be music, a feast, wine and burning women for my delight. Perhaps *that* is why you came, father? To surprise me with the warmth of your welcome?' His tone was brittle, febrile. Beside Thaune, Valery of Talair made a small sound but said nothing.

Thaune became aware that the High Elder had now begun murmuring softly, but not to any of them. Somehow the quality of the man's voice, his inward, intense manner, shaped a silence on the bridge in the mist, and gradually, with a growing horror that bit deeper than the cold, Thaune became aware that the High Elder was intoning the denunciation of the god.

'. . . to the infinite cold that was before the world was or the moons were spoken, before the sun was moved and the stars allowed their light. O, most holy Corannos of ice and all the sacred tongues of fire, unworthy as I surely am in your sight, I beseech thee, in the name of your own ancient gifts to us, that there shall be for this man torments without number to the ending of time. Maggots beneath the skin and worms in his heart, the rotting sickness and the black blood that cannot be stanched. I pray that you send down upon this man who is my son no longer —'

'That is enough.' A second voice, cold with distaste. Bertran de Talair. Blaise himself was silent, immobile in the face of what his father was doing.

'— foul madness and a twisting agony in his bowels, blindness, boils, the stinking corruption of his flesh —'

'*I said that is enough!*'

'— all of these and more, O most holy Corannos. I pray that he be stricken also with the pestilence that —'

Bertran came around in front of Galbert and, in the midst of this pronunciation of the blackest curse known to the Elders of Corannos, struck him full in the face with an open palm, the way one might slap a servant. Galbert stopped, out of genuine shock as much as anything else. Blaise still hadn't moved. He opened his mouth to speak, and then closed it wordlessly. Ranald de Garsenc looked pale and unsteady beside his father.

'You *will* be silent,' Bertran said savagely. 'Ten more words and an archer will shoot. Your son may be unwilling to give such an order, for reasons that escape me, but be assured that I am not. Do not put this, I beg you, to the test.'

'Who are you?' Galbert snarled, through gritted teeth.

En Bertran laughed aloud then, as strange a sound in the fog as Thaune had heard all night. 'That is three words,' he said. 'Seven left. Hoard your store. I am sorely offended, though, I would have thought you would surely know the appearance of a man you paid so much to kill last summer.'

'Bertran de Talair,' said Ranald de Garsenc, his first words. 'I remember you from the tournaments.'

Galbert's eyes narrowed to slits, but he kept silent, his body rigid with anger. His gloved hands, Thaune saw, were ceaselessly working, opening and closing at his sides, as if longing for someone's throat.

Ranald turned from the duke of Talair to stare at his brother. 'What have you done? Turned traitor entirely? Invaded with Arbonne?'

'Hardly,' said Blaise, beginning to regain his composure but carefully not looking at his father. 'Bertran is here as a friend. My men are mercenaries recruited by Rudel Correze for me, you'll very likely know a number of them — mostly from Götzland. This is a seizing of Garsenc Castle from you, brother. I am sorry, but it seems a necessary first step, since you yourself are doing nothing at all. Worse than nothing, actually. I intend to take Gorhaut from Ademar with my own countrymen, and without burning women, either.'

'I had no choice about that,' Ranald said fiercely.

'Not so.' It was, surprisingly, Valery of Talair, behind Thaune by the portcullis. He was invisible in the fog, his disembodied voice flat and final as that of some judge at the iron gates of the afterworld. 'We can say no and die. It is a choice, my lord of Garsenc. In the face of some things asked of us it is the only choice.'

No one spoke in reply. There was silence on the bridge, heavy as the fog. Thaune heard only quick footsteps and saw cloaked and hurrying shapes as Blaise's mercenaries went by him into the forecourt. There had been no alarm raised within Garsenc; the world was wrapped in mist like a creation of dream.

And it was in that stillness, as if it were a part of such a dreaming, that Thaune then heard the rumble of hoofbeats to the east. A great many, as if the horsemen of the Night Ride were come down among them from the sky, from the train of the god, to ride over the fog-shrouded earth and destroy.

'What is that?' Valery took two steps forward and stopped.

'Get the men inside!' said Blaise sharply. 'We have to control the castle. They did send an army! Thaune, have the the portcullis lowered, quickly!'

Thaune was already moving, shouting a command to his two guardsmen. From beyond, in the fog, the drum roll of unseen hooves grew louder. There were torches visible now, and shadowy horses, and from the distance between the first and the last of those carried flames, Thaune realized that an army had indeed come.

It had always been likely they would fail. He had not made his choice last autumn because of any measured assessment of the chances of success. He did not want to die on a pyre, though. His only prayer in that moment was that so much mercy might be allowed. He wondered if, when he crossed to the god, he would be allowed to walk with his father again, in the wide meadows of Corannos, in the gentle light.

'I shall set the torch to your burning myself,' said Galbert de Garsenc, speaking to his son, as if giving voice to Thaune's own terror. He was smiling again now, a glittering triumph in his eyes, reflecting the torches' glow.

'That,' said Bertran de Talair, 'is two words too many.'

'Bertran!' said Blaise quickly.

'Valery,' said the duke of Talair in the same moment. And simultaneous with the two names spoken something sang past Thaune in the fog and he heard the High Elder of Corannos cry out as an arrow embedded itself in his shoulder through the links of the mail he wore.

'Ten more,' said Bertran de Talair calmly, 'and we will twin that in your other arm. Tell me — in less than ten words, mind you — do you think these horsemen will attack us at risk of your life, my lord High Elder? Why don't we wait for them here and consider the question at leisure?'

He was, thought Thaune, unbelievably calm.

The hoofbeats had been a rolling as of thunder but gradually stopped now beyond the end of the bridge in the wide, clear space before the woods. There were a great many torches; Thaune could see the outline of horses and riders, bulky figures heavily armed.

'We have the High Elder here, and the duke of Garsenc,' Blaise called out, his voice knifing into the fog. 'Have a care for their lives. Will you declare yourselves?'

His father, clutching at his left arm, laughed then. A harsh, ugly sound, at odds with the effortless beauty of his voice. 'Who do you *think* it is?' he snarled.

'Six words,' said Bertran quietly.

From amid the mist and the weaving torches a voice called back, cold and austere, 'There is no hostage you could name who will stay my hand or those of my men if we are minded to strike. Is it Blaise de Garsenc to whom I speak?'

'Careful!' said Rudel Correze sharply, under his breath.

'No point denying it,' Thaune heard Blaise reply softly. 'Our only hope is the hostages, whatever he says. He might be bluffing. He *must* be bluffing.'

There was a sound of horses approaching the far end of the bridge, and then the creak of an armoured rider dismounting. From behind, Thaune finally heard the rattle and the clang of the portcullis as the guards finished lowering it. Valery of Talair was beside him, another arrow to his bow. Thaune drew his sword.

'I am Blaise de Garsenc,' said the tall coran Thaune had sworn an oath to serve and to have for his king.

'I thought it might be so,' said the unseen man in a voice crisp with resolution. 'I had hoped my information was correct, that I would find you here tonight.'

And into the torchlight, heavily cloaked against the cold, strode Fulk de Savaric, to kneel on the planks of the bridge before Blaise.

He looked up, and the hovering torchlight fell upon the square, fair-haired, intelligent features he shared with all his family. Thaune, catching his breath, taking an involuntary step forward, saw that the duke of Savaric was not smiling. 'My lord, will you accept my sworn homage and the hand of a friend? Can you make use of a thousand men from Savaric and the lands of the north who share your feelings about the Treaty of Iersen Bridge and the men who rule us now?'

Long afterwards, Thaune remembered looking up then, almost expecting to see the moons appear like beacons in the fog, as if the heavens and the dark earth around them must somehow mirror the glow that seemed to be emanating from this bridge. It was still thick as river mud overhead, though, the sky lost to sight in the fog and only the nearest torches lending their light to the tableau before him as he looked back down to see En Blaise take Fulk de Savaric's offered hands formally between his own.

It was in his heart, not in the sky, Thaune realized, that the moons were beginning to shine again. The cold of the long night seemed lessened by the warmth of that inner light. He wondered, after, if the others on the bridge had had such an illusion, if they had all looked up to see if the sky had truly changed.

That might have been an explanation, though not, by any means, an excuse for what happened.

What happened was that Galbert de Garsenc, in the very moment his younger son was formally accepting the homage of the most powerful lord of the northern marches of Gorhaut, rammed one burly shoulder into the coran on his right, hammered a muscled forearm into the face of his other guard and leaped off the bridge, an arrow still quivering in his left arm, to disappear into the shrouded darkness of the dry moat.

After a frozen moment there was a babble of sound on the bridge. Valery of Talair and Rudel Correze hurtled into the moat after him. Thaune heard a snarled Portezzan obscenity as the latter landed badly on the uneven, rock-strewn surface below.

'He won't get far,' said Fulk de Savaric as Blaise helped him to his feet. Over his shoulder, de Savaric snapped commands in the darkness. A moment later Thaune heard horses galloping and saw torches moving again in the mist.

Of all of them it was Blaise who seemed least surprised. 'If he makes the woods,' he said, almost musingly, 'I doubt we'll find him.'

'He has to get out of the moat first,' said Bertran de Talair, 'and he's got a wounded arm.'

'Not badly wounded,' Blaise said, shaking his head, still with that detached air about him, as if he had almost anticipated this. 'He wears heavy mail, double-linked. I doubt the arrow went deep. Ring the moat, though,' he said to Fulk de Savaric. 'There's at least a chance your men might see him climbing out.'

There came the sound of laughter then, laced with mockery, with something else in it that Thaune could not quite identify. 'He won't be climbing out,' said Ranald, duke of Garsenc, to his brother. 'He's under the castle already, and will be out from it and gone before morning. There's a tunnel in from the moat that no one knows about, and another from the dungeon level that leads away. A long distance away. You won't find him, brother.' In silence the two men looked at each other.

'Blaise, quickly, *do* you know where it leads? We can get to the exit before him.' It was Bertran, speaking with urgency for the first time. Galbert de Garsenc, Thaune abruptly remembered, had offered two hundred and fifty thousand in gold last summer for the death of de Talair.

Blaise was shaking his head though, looking at his brother. 'This was done after I left.' His mouth twisted slightly. 'Ranald wouldn't have mentioned it otherwise.'

'We could make you tell us where the tunnels are,' said En Bertran to Ranald de Garsenc very quietly. There was something frightening in his voice now. Thaune wondered how he could ever have arrived at the notion that the Arbonnais men were soft.

The duke of Garsenc was still a handsome man, tall and well built, the image of what a lord should be. He looked down upon the slight, unprepossessing figure of the duke of Talair and said contemptuously, 'Really, my lord? What will you do? Set me on fire?'

Blaise said something then that Thaune could not hear. His brother did hear it though, and turned quickly back to him, his arrogance fading.

'Go ahead,' Blaise said, more loudly. 'I mean it. If you want to go with him you will not be stopped or followed.'

Ranald's expression had become confused, hesitant. He looked like a man who wanted a drink, thought Thaune. A cruel thought, he knew, but it was there. He had lived in this castle long enough. He knew the duke.

'If you want to, though, you can stay,' Blaise added. 'I will trust you among us if you give me your oath. I have never known you to lie, Ranald. I will not assume you would do so now. If you can see anything clearly tonight you must surely realize that this is the chance of your life. Probably the last chance, brother. Do you want to free yourself from him or not? He is gone, down that tunnel, away from both of us, back to Ademar. You don't have to follow him, Ranald, and I will not make you stay. You have the first free choice you've had in a long time.'

'If I kneel and swear fealty to a younger brother who ought to have been a cleric of Corannos? Is that my choice?'

'Is it so evil a course? Does it matter what he was supposed to become all those years ago?' It was Fulk de Savaric who spoke, as Blaise remained silent looking at his brother by the wan light of the torches in the mist.

Beyond the bridge, Thaune could hear men shouting and the galloping horses as corans raced to surround the moat. He shared Ranald's certainty: they were not going to find Galbert de Garsenc, not in the mists of this night, not in the morning, even if the sun returned. At the back of his mind, behind his awareness of the miracle of their triumph and Fulk de Savaric's sworn allegiance, he felt a flicker of fear, like a tongue of flame.

Blaise cleared his throat, oddly tentative with his brother, as he had been with the father. 'I do not request that you kneel before me, only that you follow my lead, Ranald.' He hesitated. 'I think you know, if the roles were reversed I would have been proud to swear homage to you.' He stopped again, visibly struggling for words, as if wrestling with something difficult. 'I also think you know there was a time I would have followed you to the end of the earth had you asked me to.'

'But why,' said Duke Ranald de Garsenc, after a silence, 'would I ever have wanted to go to such a place? Or to have you there with me?'

Blaise said nothing at all to that. He lowered his head.

'You are a greater fool than I even guessed,' said Bertran de Talair, but softly now, almost with regret. 'Bring my lord Ranald his horse,' he called out to the invisible corans beyond the end of the bridge. 'The most puissant duke of Garsenc is leaving our poor company for the pleasure of his father's and the high grace of Ademar's court.'

Blaise was still silent. Thaune, behind him, could not see his face. In a way he was glad of that. Even after years in this castle he found that what lay between the three men of Garsenc — like a thicket of spear shafts in the earth, iron heads angled to kill — was too much for him sometimes. Tonight, suddenly, had become one of those times, as if the destiny of nations was bound up in the darkness of this castle, a darkness that went far deeper than the mist and fog of a winter's night. They heard a horse being led up onto the bridge.

'Someone help the duke to mount,' Bertran said, with the same grim courtesy.

'No need,' said Ranald shortly, and he mounted in one smooth motion. He curvetted his horse and looked down upon his brother. 'Are you expecting me to thank you now?' he asked. Again there was that note in his voice, the one Thaune could not quite identify.

Blaise looked up. He shook his head. 'I thought you might ask about your son though.' A cruel question, though perhaps not cruelly meant. Thaune wasn't sure; he didn't understand the younger son either. He saw Ranald's jaw tighten. Blaise added, in a flat voice, 'I am proposing to name him my heir in Gorhaut, with Fulk as regent, should I die in this war. Does that interest you at all?'

He had to be quick, Thaune thought, he had to be very fast to have thought of this already. He turned to look at Fulk de Savaric, but there was nothing to be read there at all, nor in the features of Bertran de Talair beside Fulk. These were men used to the play of power, and to hiding their responses to it.

Ranald de Garsenc was less able to mask his feelings. 'How touching,' he shot back, as if firing a crossbow bolt. 'How wonderful to see that everyone in my family has plans for my son. It does free me of a father's anxiety, I must say.'

Blaise said, still gravely, 'Given that you haven't even cared to ask of his condition or even his name, it ill behooves you to take such a tone, brother.'

There was a silence. The very calmness of the words made the lash of them bite harder. Thaune felt that he and the others on the bridge had become extraneous, mere hangers-on at the edges of this long, bitter struggle within the de Garsenc family.

'Well?' said Ranald finally, as if that one word cost him a great effort. 'Tell me.'

From behind, Thaune saw Blaise lower his head again for a long moment, and then lift it once more. 'He is well. A handsome, healthy child. He looks like a Garsenc. His name is Cadar, for his grandfather of Savaric.'

Ranald laughed then, the same quick, bitter, corrosive sound as before, when his father had escaped. 'Of course it is,' he said. 'She *would* do that.'

'Can you blame her?'

Surprisingly, Ranald de Garsenc's laughter ended. He shook his head. He said, 'You will not believe me, but I told father and the king both that I was prepared to let her go if she sent back the child. Neither would agree, not that she would have done so in any case.' He paused. 'I faced summary execution if I did not ride with Ademar to Aubry last autumn. Ask the duke of Savaric, your brave new ally. He was at that burning too, for the same reason.'

It was Blaise's turn to be silent. 'I know he was,' he said at length. 'I know why you were there, Ranald. But Fulk de Savaric has made his response to that tonight. He is with us now. You are about to ride back to Cortil. To the ugliness there. I don't understand. I *can't* understand. Ranald, will you not tell me why?' There was pain in the question. Every man on the bridge heard it.

Slowly Ranald de Garsenc shook his head again. 'No,' he said finally. 'I do not owe you that much.' He paused, seeming more composed than his younger brother on the ground now. 'Nor will I thank you for not torturing me to find the location of the tunnel. I will say this much —' he turned to the duke of Talair, ' — I am not going back to Cortil. Forget not, in your urge to mock and diminish your foes, who and what it is you are dealing with. I never forget it, not ever, during any day or night of my life.'

He turned back to his brother. 'Farewell, little Blaise, who would be king of all of us. I can recall teaching you to use that sword you carry. I wonder if you remember?'

He turned then, and was gone into night and fog, only the drumming of his horse's hooves in the mist telling them he was riding east.

'Of course I remember,' said Blaise, to no one in particular.

He turned then and began walking up the bridge towards the castle, past the two dukes and all the corans, who quickly made way for him. He stood motionless before the portcullis bars until they had been rolled up again, allowing him to pass within, into his ancestral home.

Feeling buffeted by the speed of events, Thaune of Garsenc was more than a little eased to note heightened colour and hints of bemusement in the expressions of others when they gathered in the great hall.

There had been no resistance in the end. The announced arrival of Blaise de Garsenc, coupled with the even more tangible presence of nearly a thousand armed men with the duke of Savaric, induced any corans of Garsenc who might have been otherwise inclined to make their peace with the current situation.

That wasn't the problem. The problem emerged when the explanations began, while the castle servants scurried to provide wine and food and sleeping arrangements, not only for those in the hall but for the northern soldiers, and for the farmers who had also come with Fulk, carrying a variety of arms.

It was the presence of the farmers Fulk had been ordered to bring that raised the issue. It was winter, after all. Corans often followed their lord wherever he went, and it was not unusual for a duke to bring part of his household with him if he travelled to Cortil to spend the cold months drinking and brawling among the retinue of the king. It was a custom of long standing. That, they had assumed, was why Garsenc Castle was unlikely be heavily defended. But if the ordinary men of the land were being ordered by Ademar to take up arms in the dead of winter something else was afoot.

Fulk de Savaric knew that. He didn't know *what* was unfolding, though, because he hadn't yet reached Cortil when his instructions had been changed. His tale was simple. He had been instructed to bring as many men south as he could. Given the mood of the king since autumn, Fulk had not regarded these orders as being the sort he could comfortably ignore. They were mobilizing early for an attack in the spring, he had concluded; it had always been the most likely course of events.

Halfway to Cortil he had been met by a messenger from the High Elder, changing his orders, instructing him to turn west to Garsenc Castle and meet Galbert there. There was a threat from the south, the messenger reported, treachery abroad in the wintry heartland of Gorhaut. Fulk knew, as most of Gorhaut had known by then, that Blaise de Garsenc had claimed the throne last autumn.

Duke Fulk was his own man, if he lacked his father's flamboyance or the confidence of the monarch that Cadar de Savaric had had. He'd turned his thousand men as ordered, riding along a valley path laced with snow, but he had stopped them by a frozen river bed two days later, a half day's ride still from Garsenc Castle. And there, under grey skies, he had made a speech.

He was not a man for speeches, nor were the men of the north greatly inclined to listen to orations, especially in the cold. What he said was as terse and clear as he could make it, and the words marked a changing of his life. He would have denied that Aubry had led him to that moment, but he wouldn't have said it had nothing to do with it, either.

He had never liked the Treaty of Iersen Bridge, he told his assembled men, shouting the words into the rising wind. He had never liked the authority the High Elder of Corannos had over an increasingly self-indulgent king. He felt contempt and real anger for the way in which a quarter of the people of Gorhaut had been dispossessed of their land and ordered to find shelter somewhere, anywhere, while the king and his High Elder plotted a conquest in the south. Fulk de Savaric did not think they could hold any lands they took south of the passes; they wouldn't be allowed to, he said, by the other countries of their world. The balance would be too greatly shifted. They would only trade a border war with Valensa for an enormous combat against *all* the other nations, and the Arbonnais, he said, would die before they lay quiet under a Gorhaut yoke of occupation. They would be forced out of Arbonne, he told his men, leaving ruin and ashes and legions of the dead behind them.

That, said Fulk, probably didn't even matter to the High Elder, whose war this was. The real point of what was happening now had little to do with land for the dispossessed of the north. Galbert wanted only to destroy Arbonne and its goddess, and the Treaty of Iersen Bridge had been the first devious step towards that. Fulk de Savaric didn't much care either way about Arbonne's goddess; she had never bothered him, he said by that frozen river. What *did* bother him, what enraged him, he said, were the uprooted people of the northlands. Their king had sold them to Valensa for silver and gold, to raise an army for burning women in Arbonne.

There were others, he told his silent company, who felt the same way as he. Blaise de Garsenc, the younger son of the High Elder was probably known to many of them. He wasn't even a northlander, but he had left Gorhaut entirely rather than live with the terms of the Treaty of Iersen Bridge. He was very likely coming home now, perhaps even tonight, leading a rising against these very wrongs Fulk was speaking of. The duke proposed to join him, for the honour of the northland and in memory of his father and King Duergar who had truly loved and served Gorhaut. He invited those of his army who thought the same thing and who trusted his judgment to come with him. Those who felt otherwise were free to leave, with his honest gratitude for their service in the past.

That was all he said. Wind blew down the valley, sliding snow into mounds on the banks of the frozen river, shaking it down from the branches of bare trees.

Eighteen men left, from a company of almost a thousand.

The men of the northland had their own hard creed, always, and the lords of Savaric had seldom played them false, whatever the kings in Cortil might have done. Duke Cadar de Savaric had died defending their lands and his own at

Iersen Bridge. His son had shepherded the interests of the
north with a cautious diligence in the upheavals that followed
King Ademar's accession and the treaty he had signed. If the
time for caution now had ended, the time for loyalty had not,
and loyalty to the north was the first law of the north.

Not a man prone to the sweep of powerful emotions, Fulk
de Savaric had nonetheless been moved by what had followed
his words on that wintry afternoon. He was speaking treason,
after all.

There was no shouting when he ended, no cries of approval or swift cheers raised in his name. That was not their
way. There was only the grim, stern silence that had always
defined the north, as six horsemen and twelve men on foot detached themselves from the company, to proceed east from
that icy stream towards Cortil and King Ademar, who was still,
when all else was said and done, the anointed of the god.

The rest had followed him here to Garsenc Castle and
would follow him now, he said soberly to Blaise and Bertran
and the others gathered in the great hall, wherever he asked
them to go.

'That last,' said Blaise, 'is the real question, I fear.' He
seemed to have gradually recovered his composure after the
encounters with his father and brother. 'We had planned to
take this castle, use it as a winter base, a rallying point, for any
men who might join our cause, and then see what the spring
brought us, in numbers and possibilities. I didn't propose to
fight a war in winter.'

'We did once, in the time leading up to Iersen Bridge,'
said Fulk de Savaric.

'I know that. I was there. That was against an invader,
with no choice offered us. There's another thing: I don't want
to begin attacking across the countryside myself, ruining castles or towns. If I possibly can I want this to end up as one battle
against Ademar and only one. My army — if I have one —
against his on a field somewhere. If I am to come home as the
saviour of Gorhaut — the man who takes us back to the god
and our true destiny — I can't begin by killing my own people
and destroying their homes and fields. I won't do that, Fulk, for
the same reason I won't invade with an army from Arbonne.'

'Did they offer you one?' Fulk de Savaric asked.

Blaise turned to Bertran de Talair. The duke's expression was oddly inward, Thaune saw, as if he hadn't been closely following the last part of the conversation. And a moment later, Thaune realized that this, in fact, was so.

'Do you remember,' Bertran asked Blaise softly, not answering the question, 'what your brother said just before he left? His last words to me?' There was something strange in his voice, something that made the room feel cold again, despite the fires now burning on all the hearths. Thaune, by the doorway to the corridor, tried to remember what it was that Ranald de Garsenc had said.

'He said he wasn't going back to Cortil.' Blaise had been standing by the largest of the fires. Now he took two steps towards the duke of Talair and stopped.

'Would he have been telling you something?' asked Rudel Correze sharply. He rose from his seat. 'Because if he was . . .'

'If he was,' Duke Bertran finished flatly, 'then we know why Fulk was ordered to bring all the men he could. And why your brother wasn't going to Cortil. Ademar isn't *at* Cortil.'

'How did you come through the mountains?' Fulk de Savaric asked abruptly. He, too, had now risen from his chair.

'Lesser Gaillard Pass to the west,' said Blaise. 'There were only fifty of us, no wagons or goods. We didn't want to be seen. We might have been spotted had we gone through the High Road Pass.'

'Of course,' said Fulk. 'But if En Bertran is right about this . . .'

'Then Ademar and his army were moving south from Cortil towards the High Road Pass even while we were coming north.' Bertran de Talair had put down his wine glass. His face, Thaune saw, was very white, an old scar showing in sharp relief. 'That is what has happened, I am certain of it. It fits what we know. They decided not to wait for spring, after all. This *is* a winter war, my friends. In Arbonne. They might even be there already.'

'And what do we do here with a thousand men? Capture Cortil? Raise the country in revolt?' Rudel Correze's eyes were bright in the firelight. Blaise said nothing; his eyes were on the duke of Talair.

'There is no country to raise,' said Fulk de Savaric slowly. 'All of the men who can fight will be with the king. I think I see what he is thinking: he doesn't *care* what you do here. If he takes Arbonne quickly enough — and it will probably be wide open to him now in winter, however many men he loses to the mountains — he can come home with an army in triumph from the sack of that land and deal with us in spring, wherever Blaise is.'

'That isn't Ademar thinking, you do realize,' said Blaise finally. You could hear the bitterness. 'This is my father's cunning, and his dream. He has always wanted Arbonne destroyed. Always. He told me stories as a boy of how the temples of Rian had to be brought down to save the whole world from their corruption. And he knows me. He *knew* I would not bring an army here, that Ademar would be safe to leave Gorhaut almost undefended, and then come back, as Fulk says, to deal with whatever happens while he's gone.' He turned to Bertran. 'You know what he's going to do, don't you?'

The other man's expression was bleak as the winter night. Slowly he nodded his head. 'He won't bother with the castles or the cities. He won't try sieges in winter. He's going to force our corans out by making war on the villages and the temples. As he did at Aubry.'

'As he did at Aubry,' echoed Blaise.

'Shall we ride, then?' asked Fulk de Savaric. 'You wanted one battle, Blaise. It looks as if you might get it, but it will be in Arbonne.'

'Of course it will,' said the duke of Talair with savage irony. 'It is warmer there, isn't it? The sun shines, even in winter. If you go far enough south there's no snow at all. You can even catch the scent of the sea.'

'Through the smoke,' said Blaise shortly. 'Let's go.'

They left two hundred of Fulk's men to hold Garsenc Castle and to spread word as best they could that they were there. The rest of their company set out that same night in the fog and the cold on the long road back to the mountains. At one point during the night the mist finally began to lift and they caught a glimpse through tattered windblown clouds of white Vidonne low in the west before morning came.

CHAPTER·16

Roche the priest was in disgrace on Rian's Island in the sea. Someone foraging for winter firewood had smelled burning by a cove on the southern shoreline and had gone to investigate; the risk of the forests burning, though rather less in winter, was always real. A small fire-pit had been found, dug in the cold sand, covered with a flat slab of stone. Lifting the stone with a long branch revealed half a dozen lampfish grilling underneath.

Roche would have even tried to deny being the culprit, had he not been discovered moments later by the same interfering woodsman in a small shelter not far away, dozing in happy anticipation with a fishing line beside him and the smell of fish on his hands.

Awakened by an insolent prod of the woodsman's branch, he had stammered an offer to share his morning's secret catch under the mild winter sun while they looked out from the beach at the gentle swells of the sea. The woodsman was not moved, either by the idyllic setting nor even the succulent promise of lampfish. He was one of those depressingly pious fellows who left their homes after some night vision or other to come and serve the goddess on her island, labouring for the priests and priestesses, often becoming more sturdily attached to the doctrines and codes of conduct than the clergy were themselves.

It was fixed law, the woodsman pronounced with obdurate, finger-wagging satisfaction, that all fish and fowl around the shores of the island were interdicted to mortal men and women, sacred, he intoned virtuously, to holy Rian in her incarnation as protectress of the beasts.

Roche tried, without real hope, to explain that this applied only to fishermen or hunters from the mainland. As he'd expected, the woodsman knew better than that. Such an impiety, the man declared self-righteously, would have to be taken directly to the High Priestess herself. He shouldered his bundle of wood, took the reins of his equally burdened donkey and started briskly back north towards the temple compound. They always wanted to go straight to the High Priestess, Roche thought miserably, watching him go. As if she had nothing better to do than listen to reports of minor transgressions by her priests and priestesses.

This was, however, his third such minor transgression — for the same offence — in a year. Despairingly, he wondered if he would be sent away, demoted to service in some temple in the grainlands or the mountains. He didn't want to leave Rian's Island. He didn't want to leave the sea. He'd grown up by the ocean; it was what he knew and loved — as he loved the gracious harvests Rian in her generosity allowed them from the waves. Especially lampfish; most especially lampfish.

Morosely depressed, cursing his own weakness and the fact that he'd been stupid enough to fall asleep so near the fire-pit, he considered catching up to the woodsman, trying to forestall him, or concocting some tale that would serve his cause before they both got back to the compound. There was, he decided glumly, no point. Roche felt so miserable he almost lost his appetite.

The fish were ready, he could tell from the wafting aroma. With a heavy sigh, Roche went back to the fire-pit and looked sadly down on his six treasures sizzling invitingly beneath their carefully assembled and sprinkled herbs. As he did so he was somewhat surprised, given the extreme gravity of his plight, to discover that his hunger seemed to be returning after all.

He wandered back to the compound somewhat later, though in plenty of time for his tour of duty in the temple. He was a *good* priest, Roche told himself, he just liked fish.

As he'd anticipated, he was ordered to attend upon the High Priestess forthwith. He saw the woodsman with his donkey by the bakehouse door. The man looked smugly virtuous as Roche walked past. Wiping his mouth and rubbing at the stains on his robe, Roche ignored him as best he could.

On the far side of the temple dome, where the High Priestess and the Inner Circle had their chambers and meeting rooms, Roche was admitted by a stone-faced woman from Cauvas. He had never liked people from Cauvas — or anywhere inland, he suddenly thought. It took folk raised by the sea to understand the rhythms of life on the water. He wondered if he could say that to the High Priestess. She was from Barbentain, though; he didn't think it would be a prudent notion to present her with this particular proposition.

He waited in gloomy silence, alone in the antechamber, dabbing futilely at intervals at the tell-tale streaks on his robe. He sniffed his hands suddenly and grimaced. He ought to have had a wash, he realized. He was carrying the evidence of his sin right into Rian's temple. And this was the third time in a year. He was going to be sent north, Roche decided with real despair. He *deserved* to be sent to the mountains, far from his beloved ocean waters and their seductive bounty. He had no self-control at all, he reproached himself, no proper respect for the traditions of holy Rian which he had vowed to uphold for life, no true sense of his own solemn responsibility to set an example for —

The door opened. Another grim-faced servant nodded coldly to him. The lay-folk always loved it when a priest or priestess was in trouble. Roche wiped his hands on his robe one last time and walked in, with what dignity he could command while smelling of lampfish and charcoal, to be told his fate by the High Priestess of Rian in Arbonne.

He came out of the room shortly afterwards seriously unsettled. The High Priestess had barely even bothered to take note of his transgression. She had reprimanded him briefly, never even turning to him or taking her blind gaze from the fire on the hearth. She had pardoned him almost absently, with a ritually phrased injunction to pray in the temple for the strength to resist his weaknesses. That had been all. For the third offense in a year. He'd been dismissed. Not even her white owl had seemed to care enough to look over at him.

Roche couldn't understand it. His had been a fairly serious malfeasance, a terrible example for the lay workers. How could the High Priestess take an indifferent view of such a thing, he wondered? How could the customs of the goddess be properly preserved if the great ones of the temple paid so little attention to them? He felt almost indignant at his casual reprieve. Why, he deserved a temporary exile at the very least! Though he would have felt *miserable* at such a punishment, he had certainly deserved it. But what was this — an absent-minded lecture and a quick dismissal?

Something, Roche decided, was seriously wrong. He was only a lowly priest, but he couldn't help wondering if the upper hierarchies of Rian's clergy were serving her properly these days. He shook his head. What was the world coming to?

On the way out, though, he couldn't forebear grinning broadly at the dour-faced woman at the door, and as he walked back past the bakehouse through the crisp afternoon sunshine he offered the woodsman a positively cheerful wave. Not, perhaps, the most judicious thing to do, but some temptations, Roche had learned, he was ill-equipped to resist.

When he finished his tour of duty in the sanctuary that evening, he washed himself carefully, hands and face and body, in the growing chill of evening after the sun had gone down, and he donned clean raiment before going back to pray in the temple for two full watches of the evening. As he had been admonished to do, Roche humbly asked the goddess to vouchsafe him the strength to resist his inappropriate desires, and then, as an afterthought, he prayed for Rian to lend her holy wisdom and eternal presence to the High Priestess, who seemed troubled of late by burdens beyond his own poor understanding.

He felt better when he finally rose, though his knees and back creaked stiffly in the cold. He left the temple to return to the dormitory and his bed under the winter stars and both moons.

On the way out from the dome he saw a cluster of his fellow priests and priestesses standing together in the atrium around the one small fire there. It was very late; this was unusual. He went over to join them, and as they made room for him in their midst it was Maritte, very near now to delivering the child he and she had conceived last spring, who told Roche that word had just arrived that the army of Gorhaut had been seen two days ago in the High Road Pass through the mountains coming south into Arbonne with the engines of war.

†

It had always been likely, more than that, even.

From the moment the Treaty of Iersen Bridge had been signed, Beatritz had been certain Gorhaut would be coming to them. *Until the sun falls and the moons die, Gorhaut and Arbonne shall not lie easily beside each other.* That was the ancient saying — in both countries. The sun had not fallen and both moons were in the winter sky tonight she knew, aware of them as presences though she could not see their light.

Deep in her cushioned chair she was also aware of the fire on the hearth, as a warmth certainly, and a welcome one, but also as something else, not sound or heat, certainly not light — a source of danger and knowledge, both. It was such a complex world she had walked into on the night she had given up her eyes for this other sight of Rian. She saw so differently now, better in the darkness, best on the island, not at all without Brissel on her shoulder. She reached up and stroked the owl; she could feel his disquiet, or rather, she could feel him reacting to her own. She tried to send calming thoughts, to go with the gentling hand, but it was hard. It was hard tonight.

Aubry had been a blow to her heart, heavy as a descending hammer, and it had only been an opening move, no more than a small number of Gorhaut corans writing a first message in fire last autumn. There was an army now, and it seemed Galbert de Garsenc's long dream of burnings in Arbonne was about to be fulfilled.

And there was next to nothing she could do about it. She had already done what she could, keeping her lines of knowledge flung far, leaving the island more than she ought to have done, neglecting the localized but vital needs of her priests and priestesses to meet with her mother and Roban and the most important of the nobility — Bertran, Thierry and Ariane, Urté. It had been Beatritz, feeling the rare pulse of the goddess within her, who had counselled that a careful approach be made to Blaise de Garsenc, who was known to have left Gorhaut in anger. She remembered the first reactions to that: he was the son of the High Elder, their purest enemy. An ignorant, unpleasant mercenary soldier, Roban the chancellor had named him derisively.

He is more than that, Beatritz had told them, trusting her intuition and the silence of her owl. Bertran was the one who had agreed with her, though almost in a spirit of amusement, and also because — as they only afterwards understood — her proposal coincided neatly with a seduction he was then pursuing. It was that way with Bertran, sometimes. You took him for what he was, which was not inconsiderable, and tried to keep private the inward lament for how much more he might have been.

She had known she was right about Blaise de Garsenc when Rian, in holy intercession, had acted to bring the man to the island even before Bertran went to Castle Baude. Beatritz had done what she could here, too, trying to frighten him out of the grim complacency that was obvious and reach past his barriers to touch the shielded thing she sensed within. Brissel had let her know that he, too, felt something there, and long ago she had learned to listen when the owl told her such things.

She remembered Brissel flying from her shoulder on Midsummer Night in Tavernel when Blaise had first spoken of the crown of Gorhaut. She had not expected that, either the man's words or the white owl's sudden flight to him. She was truly blind when Brissel was not with her, but her mother had reached up to take her hand and had told her quietly where the bird had gone, and Beatritz had felt the presence of Rian in that moment.

If only it were a presence she could invoke more often. If only she had a tenth of the magic and the mental powers the superstitious attributed to her. But magic in Arbonne was a tenuous, very nearly non-existent thing — whatever it might be in those uncharted countries storm-blown mariners had told her lay beyond the deserts to the south. Magic here was wholly confined to small things, the coinage of hearth and heart. Control of conception, foreknowledge of a child's sex — and that last not always with certainty. Knowledge of sorrows, some access to easing them. A skill with the gifts of the earth: herbs, flowers, fruits, trees. A certain awareness Beatritz herself had — though only here on the island or the isle in Lake Dierne, and only since her blinding — of inward life, in matters of love and hate. Some powers of healing, though these as much a matter of herbal and other lore handed down as anything else.

That was the sum of their magic; that was their dangerous power. It had been useful to have others think there was more; a fear of the clergy of Rian and their night gatherings could be a kind of defence.

Until that fear became so deep and cold a terror that it became the very reason for their peril. Galbert de Garsenc seemed to have crossed over that line one day or night in his own past. His fear of the women of Arbonne, his hatred of Rian and all the goddess meant, was the reason there was an army in the mountains in the midst of winter, whipped into a killing frenzy by the High Elder of Corannos. They would be out of the mountains by now, Beatritz corrected herself, her heart aching, a slow, cold dread moving through her like a poison in the blood.

She didn't know what to do. That was the worst of it. She could pray, gather everyone on the island under the temple dome to offer hymns and incantations all day and night, seeking some access to the goddess, invoking her intercession. Rian could not be compelled, though. That was the oldest, deepest law; she was capricious and inviolate, and death was a part of her dominion — it was, in fact, one of her incarnations. She was mother, she was bride, but she was also gatherer of the dead.

It might even be that Rian herself had ordained this scourge as a punishment, a cleansing of the evils of their time. Beatritz didn't know what their great acts of evil might be, but she was only a servant of the goddess, not privy to divine awareness. She would have thought — she would have said — that there was no darkness or evil in Arbonne deserving of what had happened to the corans in that watch-tower below the High Pass last autumn, or to the priestesses of the temple of Aubry that same night.

She would have said as much to holy Rian herself. As if it would matter. The owl ruffled his feathers, bringing her mind back. She'd been considering options, responses. She remembered how her father used to do that, crisply running through possibilities aloud before decisively choosing his path. It was still difficult for her sometimes to accept that he was dead, that the burdens were her mother's now and her own, with such aid as could be invoked from the bitterly divided nobility of Arbonne.

There was no heir. That had always been a problem, and Guibor IV of Barbentain had been unable to name one in his last years for fear of tearing the country apart. He had even tried to make Beatritz leave the sanctuary of the goddess in the year after Aelis died with her child in Miraval. Guibor had anticipated this trouble in the time that followed the death of his youngest child. He had always anticipated a great deal; it was a fault of his, to try to make too many things fall right at the same time. It had been that way with Aelis's marriage to Urté de Miraval in the first place: a powerful duke, one of the mightiest in the country, a choice that could not be impeached, and a man anxious to father children, a son or even a daughter to rule Arbonne when Guibor died.

But Aelis had died first, and so too, almost certainly, had her son. No one could be absolutely sure, though everyone knew what she had told her husband on her deathbed about the fathering of the child: in doing so she had given dreadful, calamitous life to the feud that had shaped Arbonne ever since. Urté could not even be approached or spoken to on this issue. Beatritz had tried once, at the end of the year after Aelis died — and had received the most stinging rebuke of her life. They would have had to put the duke of Miraval to torture to even try to make him speak. And he wouldn't have, they all knew that: he wouldn't have said what had happened to the child even then.

Not even Guibor the count had been able to quell or control what Aelis had begun between Talair and Miraval on that night so long ago. So, searching for alternatives, he had tried to make Beatritz leave the clergy, come back to Barbentain, prepare herself to marry, to have a child of her own.

It was then that she'd had herself blinded, in that small temple in the Götzland mountains, taking the step no priestess had taken for years upon years, aligning herself irrevocably with Rian. She had become High Priestess two years later and had come to the island.

Her father had never truly forgiven her. That had always hurt, for she had loved him. Not as her mother did, with an undying passion of the soul, and not even as her sister Aelis had, with something complex and yearning at its core. Beatritz had known her father's weaknesses and his flaws too well, had seen him too clearly for either of those kinds of love: she understood his pride, how he wished to control and shape far too much in too many different ways, his own guiding hands on the reins of everyone and everything. Of course she understood such a thing: it was her own besetting vice. She was Guibor's child. Her call to Rian had been real, though, the truest thing in her life, and she had known it young.

Her mother had understood, surprisingly. Signe, beautiful and glittering like an ornamental jewel under torchlight in Barbentain, seemed nonetheless to have understood a great deal, always. Beatritz ached for her tonight, picturing her in the wintry castle with these brutal tidings newly come and the terrible, crushing knowledge that she might be the ruler of Arbonne in the time it died forever.

The owl grew restive again, a motion of admonition. Options. She had been considering her options. She could start north herself, leaving the island and the seat of any power or foreknowledge she might be given, to lend her purely mortal strength, what wisdom she had, to her mother and those who would be with the countess now.

They didn't need her, she realized with a gnawing helplessness. She had counsels to offer in times of peace or preparation, of smaller and larger intrigues, the tidings her own network of informants might gather, but what did she know about waging war?

It was, she told herself with bitterness, time for the men now. The irony was coruscating. Arbonne was to be destroyed because of its women, because of the goddess who shared in their love and devotion with Corannos in the sky, because it was ruled by a woman now, because of the symbols and the music of the Court of Love and the examples of grace set by figures like Signe and Ariane. And yet now that ruin had come to them with sword and axe and carried brand, now that images of rape and fire would dance behind the closed eyelids of every woman in Arbonne, it was the men who would have to save them after all.

And despite more than twenty years of her father's striving before he died, and then her mother's afterwards, despite patience and wiles and even Guibor's attempts at absolute commands, the two most powerful men in Arbonne still hated each other with a ferocity, with a savage, time-locked obsession that had never let them go, and would never do so, never let them act together, even to save themselves and their land.

Beatritz knew this. She knew it with a despair that almost overwhelmed her. *This* had always been the weakness at the heart of Arbonne in their time, the thing that left them wide open to destruction. Not the fact of a woman ruling them. Not the rumoured softness of their corans; that was false and manifestly so. Not the corrupting influence of the troubadours and their music; there was no corruption in the flourish of that art. Their danger, their crippling wound, was Talair and Miraval.

Her sister Aelis, Beatritz thought, with an old, unrelenting bitterness, had much to answer for.

It was an unfair thought, she supposed. Her mother had told her as much, over and again through the years. Unfair or not, it was there, she was thinking it, she would think it until she died, and she would die remembering Aelis, dark and slender, far too proud, with her will like forged iron and that unwillingness, ever, to forgive.

Like Bertran, that last quality, Beatritz thought. Like Urté. And then a newer thought, as she reached up again to gentle her restive owl: *Like me.*

'Oh, Aelis,' she murmured aloud. 'Oh, sister, did we all begin to die the night you died, with or without the child?'

It was possible, she thought. There were ripples to events, and they went a long way sometimes across the dark pools of time and the world.

Brissel shifted on her shoulder again and then suddenly flexed his sharp talons in a way she knew. It was always like this: without any warning at all the presence of the goddess might come to her. Catching her breath, feeling the familiar speeding up of her pulse, Beatritz waited, and was answered, assuaged, with images in her darkness, images swirling to take shape as out of some primal fog before the world was made.

She saw two castles and recognized them immediately.

Miraval and Talair — she had known those proud, twinned assertions all her life. Another image quickly: an arch, immeasurably old, massive, humbling, carvings of war and conquest stamped upon it like foreshadowings from long ago. And then, as she released her breath in a spasm of love and pain she could not quite hold in, the High Priestess of Rian saw a lake in her mind, a small, delicate isle in the midst of it, three plumes of smoke rising straight as swords into the windless winter sky. The last thing she saw was a tree. Then the images were gone and she was left with only darkness again, and Brissel on her shoulder.

It came like this, and it went, never coerced, never subject to entreaty. The goddess remembered her children sometimes and sometimes she forgot them in the caprice of her nature. She could shower gifts like blessed rain in spring, or she could turn her back and let ice and fire have their way. She had a face of laughter and one of desire, a countenance of true compassion and a terrible visage of judgment. In the teachings of Arbonne it was Corannos the god who was kinder, more soberly caring for men and women. Rian suffered them, and loved them, but she could be cruel as nature was cruel. It was the god who held their mortal children always in mind, who did not fail to see their sufferings upon the earth. So it had been taught in Arbonne for generations.

The teachings were different elsewhere. They were very different in Gorhaut.

She was going to have to stay here, Beatritz understood. Only on the island could she have access to any such precognitions as this one. A message would have to go to Barbentain tonight. She would ask the two young troubadours who were wintering with them here. They would not deny her; these were not men to hide in the sea when death and ruin were coming down from the north. She would send them to the countess, warning her, telling them all where the culmination was to be.

It would be in the place of this vision, she was being told: by that small isle in Lake Dierne, by the arch, the two castles, it would end there.

Of course, she thought, aware of an inner stillness in the aftermath of the presence of Rian. *Of course it will be there.*

She felt the nudge of an old sorrow. *I should have known. That is where it began.*

She was wise and no longer young, Beatritz de Barbentain, deeply conversant with the ways of power in the world, and long since accustomed to her darkness and the occasional gateways to knowledge it gave her. She was, in fact, more privy to the paths of Rian than she allowed herself to acknowledge, for she had always wanted more than she had. It was the nature of her family, the legacy of her blood. Still, the goddess had never yet abandoned her entirely, however long the intervals might be. She knew a great deal, having been granted, at moments such as this, clear, sharp visions through rifts in time hidden from all the other living children of Corannos and Rian.

On the other hand, there were things even the High Priestess on her island did not know and had never known, whether of future or present or the widening ripples of the shaping past. Nor would it have been proper if she had. Oaths sworn to the dying were sacrosanct in Arbonne.

†

When they come down at last from the snows of the pass into Arbonne, the crusading army of Gorhaut are halted by their spiritual leader, and on a high plateau they kneel in their armour, every man of them, to hear the High Elder's prayer of thanksgiving to the god.

They have come through the mountains with humbling, awe-inspiring ease, only some few hundred men and horses lost to the high cold and the icy, treacherous path and the one — amazingly, only the one — avalanche that missed the main army by less than a bowshot, taking only the rear guard down into a white death with no true burial.

It might have been — it *ought* to have been — so much worse, this folly of taking an army through the mountains in winter to seize the advantage of surprise. Even the High Elder himself narrowly escaped losing his life. Standing beside their tall king, he speaks to the army with an arrow held aloft in one hand and a crimson bandage on his left arm, brilliant against his blue robe and the white of the snow behind him. He had caught up to them, wounded as he was, in the midst of the pass, riding alone — which every man there knows to have been foolhardy beyond words. Foolhardy, that is, for one not perfectly trusting of Corannos, not favoured — as Galbert de Garsenc, High Elder of Gorhaut so manifestly is — by the blessing and the protection of the god. Which means that they, too, in his company, are so blessed, the chosen, the elect, the weapons of Corannos.

This, in fact, is his message to them when the prayer is over and they rise. He holds up for all to see the Arbonnais arrow — fired by a coward, and not in a time of war — that might have killed him in his own castle. The god is with us, he tells them all, we are his agents and his instrument.

It is hard not to agree, and the men of the army of Gorhaut, in the presence of their king, are not inclined to be cynical or doubting at a time like this. They have come miraculously through the mountains in winter, and before them now, bright and fair as a dream under blue skies lies the land that has been promised them.

Promised, that is, after the scourging is done. They are the hammers of the god, the High Elder proclaims. The temples and villages of Arbonne and the depraved, unclean women who inhabit them are the anvils upon which their most holy, cleansing blows must fall.

The temples are first, the castles will come after, he tells them. Everything will come to them if they but follow their great king. The men of Arbonne are cowards, they are woman-mastered, cuckolded as a matter of course by their own musicians and barnyard servants. What, Galbert de Garsenc asks, what will such soft men do when they come face to face with the assembled might of Gorhaut sweeping down upon them with the power of the god?

They will die, he tells them, answering his own question, as a sound shaped of hunger and excitement rises among the army. They will die like the craven unbelievers they are, and when all is done, when holy Corannos is worshipped properly again in this land, then shall the men of Gorhaut have shown themselves worthy of the great favour the god has always bestowed upon them. Then shall the whole world know their worth. Then shall this sunlight, these high green valleys, vineyards and castles and grainfields, the rich cities and harbours and the great sea beyond — all shall be truly given over to Gorhaut by the high, pure grace of Corannos.

Shall this not be the way of it, he cries to them, the magnificent instrument of his voice carrying the question down on the breeze to all those gathered below.

They give him his answer, fervent, exalted, with one voice of their own.

The king rides down from that high place, then, the High Elder beside him with the arrow still held aloft. They take their places together, handsome men, stern and majestic, at the forefront of an army. Near to them but a proper distance behind rides the lord Borsiard d'Andoria at the head of a company of his own men. The Portezzan's presence among them, the army has been told, is a mark of how not only the god but all the countries of the world are with them in this purging of dark unholiness.

King Ademar of Gorhaut lifts a hand and the trumpets of Gorhaut are heard in the clean, cool air under a sky where birds are wheeling and darting in the sunlight. Before them the slopes fall away southward, green with winter grass. In the middle distance the river most of them have never seen sparkles blue, then white where there are rapids, then blue again, rushing towards the distant sea. The ports on that sea will be theirs soon; they have been promised this. The god is with them.

They start south, the invading warriors of Gorhaut, in a vast glitter of spears and armour. Later that same day the vanguard rides past and above the ruined, empty village of Aubry and comes to the next hamlet beyond. And there, with sword and mace and brand, amid the screaming of the corrupt women and their heretic, unsouled children and the desperate cries of craven men — farmers, labourers, artisans, cowards all of them — the harrowing of Arbonne is begun.

The god is with his army. After the grey cold of the mountains and the miracle of their passage they can feel it in the shining grace of his holy sun above them. Everything they ride past is bright, is welcoming, gleams wondrously in the light.

They are the hammers of Corannos, the scourges of heresy, this war is blessed from the sky; every man of them knows it now, and so as they kill, they sing.

Let Arbonne learn the battle songs of Gorhaut. Let it hear them sung by brave men, true warriors of the north, amid the steady crackling of the fires.

†

'They are not in any great hurry,' said the countess grimly in her council chamber. 'They are waiting for us to come out.' It was four days after the first burning of the war. The army of Gorhaut was reported to be moving slowly, methodically south, destroying as it went.

'They are taking each village, burning every temple,' she went on. Rosala, sitting on one of the benches, hands clasped in her lap, marvelled at the control in her voice; she knew Signe well enough by now to know how hard-won such a dispassionate tone would be. There were some twenty men and women in the room, assembled in Barbentain by the countess's command. Signe said, 'They have no interest in besieging us in the castles or cities. Not in winter, with food a problem for them.'

'That is mostly true, but not entirely so, your grace. Food is not their problem I am afraid,' said Urté de Miraval heavily. He was leaning against the mantel of the larger fireplace, bulky and formidable, dressed in a dark green, fur-lined robe. 'I have recent information about that. They have used their monies from Valensa, the enormous price they received for the northern lands they ceded, to ensure a flow of supplies to follow them here from Götzland. With our villagers taking refuge in the cities and castles we will be at risk of hunger before them. We might want to consider an attack against their supply line.'

'That will not be necessary,' said Bertran de Talair, briefly, dismissively, from the opposite wall. Rosala turned to look at him.

He had arrived only the night before, with Blaise and his mercenaries and eight hundred armed men of Gorhaut. The assembled council was still dealing with that last fact, and the presence among them this morning of Duke Fulk de Savaric. Rosala was struggling to adjust to it as well, if for different reasons. Pride and fear and disbelief swept over her whenever she looked at her brother. They had not yet had a chance to speak privately.

'I would be very interested in learning why,' Urté said to Bertran, gazing inimically at the other man across the room. 'Have military strategies changed so greatly in recent years?'

'Hardly at all.' Bertran, dressed in nondescript brown riding clothes, turned away from de Miraval to the countess. 'You will remember, your grace, that I had dealings with King Daufridi of Valensa during the Lussan Fair.' He paused. There was a stir in the room at this; it was news to most of them. Bertran ignored the reaction. 'These dealings have borne useful fruit, though not, I'm afraid, dramatically so. Daufridi has persuaded Jörg of Götzland that their joint interests will not be served by a swift destruction of Arbonne. They will not go so far as to intercede for us, but the promised supplies from the east will be sadly late in arriving, I am informed. The food, when it reaches the army of Gorhaut, will be of dangerously poor quality, most of it inedible. King Jörg will be profusely apologetic to Ademar, of course. He will promise an enquiry, offer to return some of the money he has been paid. It helps,' he added with a straight face, 'to have up-to-date information in wartime.'

'It helps,' said the countess of Arbonne icily, 'if the commanders serving us share their information with each other and ourself.'

Bertran looked unabashed, despite the rare, admonitory use of royal language by the countess. 'I only returned last night,' he said mildly. 'I found confirmation from Valensa waiting for me. I might have expected to receive approval from my countess and those assembled here for what I have done, rather than condemnation.'

'You presumptuous peacock!' rasped Urté de Miraval. Comparing the garb of the two men, Rosala found the word almost amusing. But there was really no room for levity just then. 'An army more than twice as large as any we can raise is burning its way through Arbonne,' Urté snapped, glaring at Bertran, 'and you seek praise like a vain child, preening yourself on small triumphs of diplomacy.'

'Small perhaps, my lord — I began by saying as much myself, you will recall — but do favour us with an account of what you have achieved in the same interval.' Bertran's hard blue eyes met those of Urté and this time neither man looked away. Rosala felt hatred in the room like a wintry, congealing presence.

'It would be most pleasant,' Bertran went on, in a voice that was not pleasant at all, 'to be able to report richer results of my efforts with Valensa, but we can hardly blame Daufridi or the Götzlanders for being careful here, can we? We might perhaps make some comments instead about lords of Arbonne whose principal activity this past year seems to have been to sanction, if not instigate, the attempted murder of a friend and ally.'

Rosala, vividly remembering that night in Lucianna Delonghi's rooms, saw Blaise step forward then. 'That's enough, I think,' he said quietly to Bertran. 'We'll get nowhere useful retracing old paths.' His tone was interesting; he had changed in the short time since going north and coming back. His father and Ranald had both been at Garsenc, she had been told by Rudel Correze just before the meeting began. The one had escaped and the other had been set free; it was hard not to wonder about what had happened there.

'Enough? Is it really?' Bertran de Talair said, turning away from Urté again. 'I'm dreadfully sorry. Do please forgive my lamentable penchant for excess.' His voice was etched in acid but he didn't argue, Rosala noticed, or pursue the matter. Blaise looked at him a moment longer, but said nothing more.

'We forgive almost everything just now because we have little choice.' It was the countess again, reclaiming control of the room. They turned back to her. Her hands clasped about one of the small metal warming balls her women favoured, Signe waited a moment, deliberately, and then added: 'And also because we have desperate and perilous need of you, my lord of Talair, with all your . . . penchants. After taking most careful thought on this, we are resolved to appoint you herewith to lead our armies in this war. Into your hands we now entrust the sovereignty of Arbonne and the destiny of our children.'

Rosala closed her eyes for a moment. Cadar was with his nurse upstairs; it occurred to her to wonder if Fulk would ask to see him. She didn't think so. She looked up. Signe had paused again, looking with her famous eyes into the equally celebrated blue ones of the duke of Talair. When she spoke again her tone was very different.

'Bertran, it may be unfair to say "Fail me not," for I know what Ademar of Gorhaut has brought against us, but I am going to say it nonetheless, for if you do fail we are lost and from the burning that must follow there will be no rising from ashes.'

'*No. You cannot do this!*' In the stark silence that followed the countess's words, the voice of Urté de Miraval sounded harsh and raw. There was passion in it and a real pain.

Rosala saw him step awkwardly forward from the fireside and drop heavily to his knees before the countess. 'I am prostrate before you, my lady,' he said fiercely. 'I will not ask but beg. Do not do this thing. Do *not* put me in this position, I beg of you, your grace. I will not serve under him. I cannot. You *know* I cannot. For love of Arbonne, for the memory of your husband, for any honour at all in which you may yet hold my name, choose another leader! It need not be myself, it *cannot* be myself or you do the same thing to de Talair — but choose another leader, countess, lest you break me into pieces.' Under the short-cropped grey hair, his still-handsome, fleshy face was vivid with stricken intensity.

Signe de Barbentain's features, by contrast, were like a mask, beautiful and implacable, as she looked down at the duke on his knees before her. 'Have you ever thought,' she said with frigid clarity, 'how like children the both of you are?' She drew a breath then, and Rosala winced in premonitory anticipation of what was coming. Nor was she wrong.

'My daughter Aelis,' said the countess of Arbonne deliberately, 'was willful and proud and a child herself when she died. It was twenty-three *years* ago, in the name of our most holy goddess! Can neither of you realize that?' Rosala saw Urté flinch at the spoken name; Bertran turned his head away. Signe ignored both reactions, went on, her voice blunt as a hammer. 'She deceived Urté with Bertran. We all know this. She bore a son that was not her husband's and told him as much. We know this too. It was a desperately foolish thing to do. The child died or did not die. My daughter died. It is an old story. Do you hear me, both of you? *It is an old story!* Let it rest! Let Aelis lie in her grave, with her child or without him. I will not let Arbonne lie buried in that same grave, or be trapped in the maze you two have shaped for each other from that history. It is over! It *must* be over. Make no mistake, I am naming as leader this morning the man who understands Gorhaut better than any other here and who has Blaise de Garsenc and Fulk de Savaric beside him. This is my firm decision. It is not subject to the tired, worn-out passions of ancient history, my lord de Miraval.'

Silence then. A stillness as after a storm has passed. And into it, at length, came the quiet, careful voice of Bertran de Talair, unwontedly diffident. 'Your grace, I am deeply mindful of the honour you offer me. I will say that I have no difficulty at all in stepping aside for another if it will . . . ease matters among us. I will be proud to serve under Duke Thierry for example, or your brother of Malmont if you would prefer.'

'I would *not* prefer.' Signe's voice was brittle. 'Bertran, understand me, this is not a request, it is a command. If you refuse I will regard it as treason in wartime and act accordingly.'

'My lady!' began Ariane de Carenzu, her own colour high. 'Countess, this is something that — ' She stopped abruptly at a swift, imperious gesture from the countess. Signe hadn't even bothered to look at her. She was still gazing at Bertran de Talair, daring him to speak again. 'You lead our armies, my lord,' she said flatly. 'This is a command.' And then, very clearly, with an emphasis on each word: '*Fail me not.*'

Urté de Miraval rose slowly, heavily, to his feet. Rosala, watching him, felt an oppressive burden settling upon her like a weight of stones. It wasn't even her history, her country, but she thought she knew what was coming and what it would mean. The whole room, all those gathered here in Barbentain, seemed somehow to be caught and suspended in a dark, entangling web spun long ago.

'He leads those armies then without the men of Miraval,' Urté said with a grave, unnatural calm that was somehow a match for Signe's own manner. 'And so on your shoulders, countess, must lie the burden of that. You might perhaps have remembered, since you chose to speak so freely of the dead, that in this room I am the nearest thing to a son that you have.' And turning on his heel he strode to the door.

'My lord, wait!' called Thierry de Carenzu.

Urté did not turn. He opened the door and passed through and they heard it close with a reverberant finality behind him.

Echoes, Rosala thought, swallowing hard. Echoes of a past that threatened to destroy the present. She looked about the room, registering nuances of grave apprehension. Only the countess seemed immune, only Signe showed no fear or doubt.

'How many men does this mean?' It was Fulk, her brother's first words spoken and, characteristically, addressing the most prosaic aspect of all of this.

'Fifteen hundred, somewhat more. Almost all of them trained.' Thierry de Carenzu, who had been the only man to try to stay Urté's departure, gave the answer. It was a very large number and Rosala had been in Arbonne long enough to know why: two decades of clashes between Talair and Miraval had led both dukes to gather around them substantial armies of fighting men. And this morning those same bone-deep hostilities had just cost them half those men.

'I see,' said Fulk quietly. Her brother was not a man prone to elaboration of his thoughts. They were not needed here; every man and woman in the room knew the implications of Urté's leaving them. 'Are you going to have him arrested?' Fulk asked.

No one answered him. Bertran was staring out the window, visibly shaken. Rosala saw the chancellor, Roban, leaning against the wall, as if for desperately needed support; he was white as a bone. So were most of the others in the room, she saw. Only the countess, small, rigidly erect, seemed to have retained her composure.

Rosala cleared her throat. 'Will he really stay away?' she asked. It seemed incredible to her, and yet somehow, in some terrifying way, predestined at the same time. For some reason she found herself turning to Ariane de Carenzu as she spoke.

Ariane's face was also pale. In a thin voice far removed from her customary crisp authority, she said, 'I'm afraid he will. If he doesn't do even more than that.'

'That is unfair!' her husband said quickly, gesturing sharply. Thierry de Carenzu shook his head. 'He is not a traitor.'

'No?' It was Blaise again. Still with that slightly un-settling new control in his tone. 'What would you call a man who does what he just did, regardless of what course he takes afterwards?'

It was a fair question, if a harsh one. It was what Fulk had been asking. The answer was easy enough: you called such a man a traitor.

Rosala looked at her brother and saw that he was gazing steadily back at her for the first time that morning. In his eyes, identical to her own, she read the same answer. Were this Gorhaut, she thought suddenly, Urté de Miraval would never have been allowed to leave this room alive.

There was something genuinely frightening about that thought. She was beginning to glimpse a part of the price Arbonne paid for its freedoms and its subtle graces.

She wondered how much of that price was yet to be paid.

And it was at that precise moment, Rosala remembered afterwards, that the knocking came at the door and the guards opened it to admit two exhausted, travel-stained troubadours, one fair-haired, one dark, with a message from Rian's Island in the sea: a message that the High Priestess had had a vision from the goddess of a battle by Lake Dierne.

CHAPTER·17

The identical message by a different messenger came to the lake isle that same morning. Lisseut, who, wisely or otherwise, had not gone home for the winter to her mother after all, heard the tidings when she came across the green towards the dining hall for breakfast.

It was not a great surprise. They had known that the army of Gorhaut was likely to be coming to them. This isle was the holiest sanctuary of Rian in the north of Arbonne and by now everyone knew that the warriors of Gorhaut were on a crusade in the name of the god. It didn't matter that Corannos was worshipped here as well. Had such things mattered, Lisseut thought bitterly, then priestesses and children and those who had tried to defend them would not now be lying charred and dead.

She moved a little distance away from the knot of anxiously talking priests and priestesses. It was not easy to find privacy within the narrow confines of the isle and, perhaps surprisingly for someone who had come to adulthood within the intensely social world of the troubadours, she seemed to be drawn to solitude of late. More precisely, since the night she'd sung Blaise de Garsenc to sleep with lullabies of childhood and then left his room to walk back with Alain to their inn. There was no fierce turmoil in her any more, however, no sharp pain. That seemed to be behind her now that winter had come. A stone makes a splash when it strikes the water, Lisseut had thought, standing by this same shore on the day she'd arrived near the end of autumn, but no sound at all as it sinks down to the lake's deep bed. That was how she felt, she had decided — or how she *had* been feeling, until war came with the harrowing reports of deaths and burnings and thoughts of such private matters were trivialized and driven far away.

She looked out across the choppy waters of Lake Dierne, past the honey-coloured stones of Talair on the northern shore and up beyond the grass of the valley to the winter vine-yards and the forest rising in the distance. Somewhere out there an army was coming, axes and swords and brands, sev-ered heads dancing on pikes above them. The survivors, fleeing south before the fury of Gorhaut, had brought tales of such horrors with them.

Lisseut plunged her hands into the folds of the vest she'd been given by Ariane in Carenzu. It was a cold morning, dia-mond-bright, the stiff wind pushing the three plumes of smoke almost due south. The air was fresh and clean and she could see a long way. To the west, when she turned, the massive stones of the Arch of the Ancients showed clearly at the end of the row of marching elms. Lisseut hated that arch. She had from the moment she'd first seen it years ago: there was too much op-pressive power stamped upon it, the sculptor's undeniable art wholly given over to the brutally explicit message. The arch re-minded her now, every day, of what was coming.

She would have been safer at home, she knew. Vezét couldn't be reached by an invading army for a long time yet and, if it came to that, a well-known joglar could take ship from the coast and find a ready welcome in Portezza or Arimonda.

That last thought hadn't even lingered long enough to be seriously considered. Even when it had become clear that the flattering invitation she and Alain had accepted — to winter on Rian's Isle — had brought them squarely into the path of death, Lisseut knew she would not leave.

There was a reason she could have offered if anyone had asked, but no one did ask. It had been Ramir's song though, in Lussan at the Autumn Fair that, more than any other sin-gle thing, had shaped her feelings now. If there was a role, any role at all for her to play in this appalling time it would not lie in hiding away south by the sea or fleeing across the water. The imagined presence of that stone inside her, sinking silently down as through dark, still lake waters, might have had something to do with it, too. She would have admitted that; she was usually honest with herself, and the worst part of that pain seemed to be gone now. It had been months since the Lussan Fair; she didn't even know where Blaise was. She called him by his name in her mind now. Surely that much could be allowed?

Alain had stayed on the isle as well. She had thought he would. Her affection for the little troubadour had grown with each passing day. He had even begun practising with a sword, rowing across to join the corans of Talair every afternoon. He was not very good. Lisseut had gone to watch him one day, and foreboding had lain within her like a different kind of weight.

That grim sense of premonition was with her again now as she gazed out across the whitecaps at the stones of the arch beyond the western shore, trying to deal with the tidings that had come with the messenger from the High Priestess.

'Will they build their own arch, do you think, if they destroy us all?'

She hadn't heard Rinette approaching. Not entirely happy, for she still hadn't worked out her feelings about the coolly arrogant young priestess, she turned and regarded the other woman.

As always, it was the owl that gave her pause. Only the High Priestesses at each temple, or those named and being trained as their successors, carried the birds. Rinette, no older than Lisseut herself, was very young to be marked as heir to the High Priestess of Rian's Isle. Once she'd ascended to that rank she would be second only to Beatritz de Barbentain herself among the hierarchy of the goddess in Arbonne. Lisseut had even heard talk among the priests and priestesses of the isle that Rinette intended to follow Beatritz down the paths of blindness when that day came.

Lisseut of Vezét, child of this world, finding her pleasures and griefs among men and women, had found herself unsettled by the very thought. If Rinette had been older, a dour, pious zealot, it might have been easier to deal with, but the brown-haired priestess was beautiful and drily clever, and she seemed to know and enjoy the troubadours' repertoire of songs almost as well as Lisseut and Alain did themselves. Once she had even corrected Alain on a line-reading during his recitation of one of the old speak-pieces of Count Folquet. Lisseut, genuinely shocked by the interjection, had quickly searched her own recollection and realized that the priestess was right. Not that this made her any happier to have heard an audience member interrupt a troubadour.

What, she remembered thinking, was the world coming to?

A remarkably inconsequential issue that seemed since the winter invasion and now this morning's news. She was made aware, looking at the tall, slender woman beside her, that Rinette's fate if Gorhaut conquered was even more brutally clear than her own, and the priestess, by her sworn oath to the goddess, lacked even the options of flight south or overseas. Given that, given the darkness of the time, it suddenly seemed profoundly ungracious to be carrying a grievance against the woman for correcting the misreading of a verse. The world had greatly changed since Ademar of Gorhaut had led an army through the mountains into the green hills and valleys of Arbonne.

'A second arch?' she said quietly, addressing the question asked. 'I wonder. Do they build anything, these northerners?'

'Of course they do. They are not inhuman, they are not really so different from us,' Rinette replied calmly. 'You know that. They are badly taught, that is all.'

'There seems a great deal of difference to me,' Lisseut said sharply, 'if they burn women alive and cut the heads and sexual parts off dead men.'

'Badly taught,' Rinette repeated. 'Think of how much of the mystery and the power of life they have lost by denying Rian.'

'You'll forgive me, but I can't spare a great deal of time just now for pitying them that. I'm surprised you can.'

Rinette gave a small, graceful shrug, looking out at the western shore and the arch beyond. 'We are trained to think that way. The times are evil,' she said. 'Mortal men and women are what they have always been. Five hundred years from now we will all be dust and forgotten, and our fates, but Rian and Corannos will still steer the course of the world.'

It was rather too much for Lisseut, this holy posturing. 'I wonder,' she said harshly, good intentions forgotten, 'if you will take such a long view when we see the army of Gorhaut coming across the lake with torches in their hands.'

And regretted the words the moment they were spoken.

Rinette turned to her, and Lisseut saw then in the clear light of morning that the other woman's eyes were not nearly so tranquil as her voice and words might have suggested. She recognized, belatedly, that what she had been hearing was an attempt to master fear.

'I do not welcome the prospect of being burned alive, if that is what you mean,' Rinette of the Isle said. 'If that isn't what you mean, perhaps you'll tell me what you *are* trying to say.'

And after that of course there was nothing for Lisseut to do but apologize as best she could, and then carry on through the day, and the next two, wrapped in her vest against the wind and the coldness of her own deep fears. Alain rowed across the whitecaps of the lake to Talair each day, carrying a borrowed sword. He came back the second afternoon with a vivid red contusion on his forehead. He made a small joke about deceiving people with a show of clumsiness, but Lisseut had seen that his hands were trembling.

On the fourth day the armies came.

†

It was, in fact, a near thing. High on the ramparts of Talair at midday after the brutal, forced march from Barbentain and Lussan, Blaise looked down at their exhausted men in the open space below, and then north in the clear light for the first sign of those they were to fight. He was uneasily aware that besides the eerie precognition of the High Priestess, the only thing that had given them even a chance to reach Lake Dierne with an army in time had been the disciplined, prudent caution of Thierry de Carenzu.

The stupefying surprise of a winter invasion through the mountains would have caught Arbonne hopelessly unprepared — *no one* risked the passes in large numbers in winter — had the duke of Carenzu not issued orders at the end of the Lussan Fair in the countess's name for a gradual assembling of the armies of Arbonne under the barons and dukes. The idea was to have them armed and trained in the castles over the winter months, in preparation for the spring assault they all expected.

Blaise had never been comfortable with men who preferred their own sex in bed, and his nights with Ariane had rather complicated this particular issue, but he had to acknowledge a rapidly growing respect for the duke of Carenzu. Thierry was sober and pragmatic and conspicuously reliable. In a country where the two other most important noblemen were the dukes of Talair and Miraval these were not, Blaise concluded, inconsiderable virtues.

Because of these preparations, when word had come that Gorhaut was actually through the pass and coming down from the mountains, the men of Arbonne had been far more prepared than they otherwise would have been. They were able to move with order and some speed — though the southern roads were muddy with the winter rains — north towards Barbentain, and from there, when Beatritz's message came, here to Talair and the lake.

Bertran's own corans had been waiting for them and Blaise knew the soldiers of Miraval were not far away, but these were lost to their army now, if not worse.

For the hundredth time since that meeting in Barbentain four days ago Blaise found himself wrestling with the wisdom of the countess's decision to name Bertran to lead the armies. She *had* to have known that Urté would react as he had. Even Blaise, an oblivious stranger to that bitter tale only a year ago, could have guessed how Urté would bridle at submitting to Bertran's authority. Granting that de Talair was the obvious man to lead Arbonne, was that worth fifteen hundred men? Would Thierry de Carenzu have been so terrible a choice?

Or was it possible that Signe had expected Urté to rise above what lay between Talair and Miraval, with so much at stake now? With everything, really, in the balance. If so, she had been wrong, and Blaise was well-enough versed in the histories of war to know that Arbonne would not be the first country to fall to an invader because it could not set aside its own internal wars.

On Bertran's castle ramparts in the brilliant sunlight he shook his head but kept grimly silent, as he had in the council chamber and ever since. In some ways it might all be purely a matter for historians and dry philosophers to come: the men who picked over the bones of dead years like the scavengers who came out at night after a battle to despoil the slain and dying.

The stark reality today was that even with the corans of
Miraval they would have needed an enormous number of mercenaries to have had any real chance of defending themselves,
and the winter invasion had eliminated that possibility. They
were brutally outnumbered by the army Ademar of Gorhaut
had brought safely through the mountains. Ademar, and Galbert: Blaise knew, as surely as he knew anything in the world,
that this winter war was his father's strategem — cunning and
long planning mingled with a sublime, unwavering certainty
that the god would see him through the pass. And the frightening thing, of course, was that Corannos had. The army of
Gorhaut, which was the army of the god, was in Arbonne, and
Blaise, looking north from the ramparts with Bertran and Fulk
de Savaric and others, felt fear like a hard object lodge against
his heart.

Only fools and madmen do not know fear before a battle. His
first captain had told him that, and Blaise had offered the
same reassurance over the years to young men under his command. He was positive, though, that his father had no fear just
now, riding here in pursuit of his life's long dream. What that
meant, he really didn't know.

'We'll array ourselves at the south-east end of the valley,'
he heard Bertran explaining to the three men who had just
joined them. Barons from the south. One of them was Mallin
de Baude. He and Blaise had had time for no more than a
quick greeting and an exchange of glances. There might never
be time for more. 'The castle and the lake,' Bertran went on,
'will be behind us so they can't flank around. There is a slight
slope downward — if you look closely you can see it — in the
valley to the west that will help. It'll give the archers a little
more distance if nothing else.' Bertran, Blaise thought, knew
this land like a melody from his childhood. He surprised himself with the image. Perhaps, he thought, he should start being
less surprised: he was among the army of Arbonne, after all.

'What about Rian's Isle?' one of the new barons asked.
'Can they reach it from the western shore of the lake if we're
leaving them access to that side?'

'No boats. We've brought them all to our wharf or across
to the isle itself. I don't think they'll be thinking about that
in any case until they're done with us.' Bertran's voice was

calm. Blaise was impressed, though not especially surprised: he'd had some time now to take the measure of this man. He trusted him and he liked him, and only a year ago he wouldn't have expected either to ever be true.

Bertran was bareheaded as always, and without armour, clad in his usual outdoor garb of unassuming brown hues. When Blaise had first seen him riding up to Baude Castle last spring those rough-spun clothes had seemed a perverse affectation on the part of a lord of such immense power and wealth; now, in a curious fashion, Bertran's appearance seeeemed entirely apt to a war-leader on the eve of a battle. It was as if, in some inexplicable manner, de Talair had always been readying himself for this. Blaise wondered if that might actually be true: he remembered — another image crowding in — the biting, sardonic verses the duke had sung in Baude Castle about Ademar and Galbert and Daufridi of Valensa. The man who had written those words might well have anticipated a response to them. The first response had been an arrow dipped in syvaren, Blaise recalled, glancing at Rudel a little further along the wall walk. The second response seemed to be war.

He looked away west. The massive Arch of the Ancients shone in the sunlight at the end of its elms. A little nearer he saw the strand beside the roadway where six corans of Miraval had killed his horse and pack pony and then died by his arrows. He remembered the young priestess from the isle coming to bear him to Talair. *We have been waiting for you,* she had said, assured and arrogant as they all seemed to be. He had never properly understood what that had meant. It was part of the same unsettling web of mystery that had brought them here now in response to Beatritz's warning.

Who knows what the women do when they go out in the woods at night? His father's words once, before burning another presumed witch on Garsenc lands. He preferred not to remember such things. There would be fires here, though, an almost unimaginable inferno if Galbert conquered. With some effort Blaise forced himself to push that thought away, to think back, instead, to the music that had been playing as he'd entered this castle for the first time beside Valery that day in spring. It seemed a long time ago.

Fulk de Savaric moved closer, resting his elbows on the stone in front of them. Without taking his eyes from the northern end of the valley, he murmured wryly, 'Do you have anything extremely clever in mind?'

Blaise's mouth twitched. 'Of course I do,' he said, matching Fulk's tone. 'I intend to challenge Ademar to single combat. When he foolishly accepts I'll kill him, take command of his grateful army and we'll all ride home to Gorhaut in time for spring planting.'

Fulk gave a snort of amusement. 'Sounds good to me,' he said. 'Do I get to deal with your father?'

Blaise didn't smile this time. 'There are a few people who might want to do that,' he said.

'Including you?' Fulk turned to look at him.

'I suppose so.' He didn't meet the other man's gaze, and after a moment Fulk de Savaric turned away.

In the distance to the south-west, clearly visible from this height in the windswept winter air, Blaise could see the towers of Miraval. Even now, with all he had learned, and with the image of Duke Urté on his knees before Signe de Barbentain, then striding from the council chamber, there was a part of him that could not quite believe that fifteen hundred fighting men would stay within those walls if battle came.

Whether that was cause for a sliver of hope or a deeper, colder dread he did not know.

What he did know was that he had spent most of his own life pursuing a dream or a vision of Gorhaut, what it should be, what it once had been, and that vision had had Corannos at the very heart of it. And now, having rashly claimed a crown for himself, he was about to go to battle amongst the men of woman-ruled Arbonne in a goddess's name against his own country and king — and father if it came to that — and against an army marching beneath the banner of the god he had vowed to serve with honour all his days.

How, Blaise thought, did one trace back the line of a life to see where the fork appeared that had led to these ramparts? He couldn't answer that. Perhaps a poet could, or a priestess, but he was a soldier and, yes, a would-be king, and the time —

'There they are,' said Rudel quietly, his archer's eyes catching the first far glint of sunlight finding metal among the trees.

— and the time for such thoughts was gone now, like a leaf on the wind, a wave on the stony shore, like all the mornings of the vanished past. The army of Gorhaut had come to Lake Dierne.

Blaise saw them then, moving down the road that wound out of the woods, and their banners were the banners of his home, their voices — they could just hear them now — were lifted in a song he knew, and he could recognize, even from so far because of the clear light that was Arbonne's, the king he had named a traitor, and the father . . . the father whose long dream this army was. He saw Ranald ride around the curve of the road and, without real surprise, recognized the pennon of Andoria as Borsiard appeared at the head of his company of men. That is a man I will be happy to kill, he thought.

And then, as if mocking such a thought, there came into sight waving, jiggling pikes carried by foot-soldiers, and riding on the top of some of those pikes, spitted like meat for broiling were the severed heads of men.

Bertran de Talair made a sudden harsh gesture and a sound of denial that might have been a name, and a moment later Blaise registered a memorable mane of blond hair and realized that he, too, recognized the foremost of those severed heads. A sickness passed over him, forcing him to grip hard on the stones of the wall for support. A moment later it grew even worse. In the midst of the singing, gesticulating army of Gorhaut a rolling platform came into view, and on it they saw a man bound naked to a pole set in the centre of the platform. His genitals were gone; there was a blackened clotting of blood at his groin. Dead birds — owls, Blaise saw — were slung in mockery from ropes around his bowed, averted neck.

He thought this man, too, was dead, until the head was somehow lifted — in agonized response to what inner message, Blaise never knew — and even from the ramparts they could see the holes where his eyes had been gouged out.

Of course, Blaise thought with loathing, fighting sickness. It was part of the mockery: the blindness, and the birds of Rian. And then, with deepening horror, Blaise realized that he knew this maimed, dark-haired man as well. He looked over again to the head on the highest of the bobbing pikes and then turned, speechless, to Bertran de Talair. He saw that the duke had lowered his head so as not to have to see.

The landscape and the men on the ramparts grew oddly unfocused, and Blaise became aware that he was near to weeping, he who had killed so many men in war, or beside the shore of this same lake, or in the close darkness of a Portezzan night, and had seen others slain in terrible ways, and had regarded all of it as no more than the coinage of his profession. But he had never burned a helpless old woman naming her a witch, or dragged a priestess screaming from her bed, and he had never maimed or broken men in the way that these had been. This was warfare of a different kind.

He was remembering, almost against his will, Midsummer Night in Tavernel. Remy had been the fair-haired one, with more spirit and art than mature wisdom in him perhaps, and Aurelian was the darker, quieter man. They were musicians, not soldiers, both of them, and both were young. It was these two who had carried Beatritz's tidings to Barbentain from the island; they must have gone north together, Blaise realized, after delivering the High Priestess's message. He didn't know why; they might never know why.

'Look there,' he heard someone say. Rudel, his voice strained in the sound of the wind.

Blaise passed a hand across his eyes and looked down again. Following where Rudel was pointing, he saw, among the army of Arbonne spread out below the walls, a dozen archers, crimson-clad, moving neatly forward from the ranks. He did not know who had given this order; perhaps no one had. Perhaps this was simply the instinctive response of some of the best-trained men in the country, those sworn to guard, and to uphold the honour of the queen of the Court of Love — to whom all the troubadours of Arbonne had sworn their life's service and devotion.

Blaise saw the Carenzu archers set themselves in a line, draw back bowstrings together and then let their arrows fly, high into the face of the wind. Among the ranks of Gorhaut a sudden volley of shouts brought the singing to a ragged halt; men flung up shields and hastily lowered their helms.

They need not have done so. The arrows were not an attack. They had been sent out like arching prayers, in grief and passion and rage, in an anguished attempt to put the ruined man on the platform out of pain. Most fell short. Three did not, and one of those arrows pierced him through the heart. The dark-haired man's head was flung sharply back so the holes of his eyes stared blankly up at the bright, lost sun. They saw his mouth open then but no sound came forth. No sound at all as Aurelian died, no last note like a swan, though all his days he had been celebrated for the pure, transcendent beauty of his voice.

'Oh, Lady,' whispered Bertran de Talair. 'Oh, goddess, heal and shelter them now within the infinite mercy of your arms.' Blaise realized that his own hands were shaking. He gripped them together on the stone in front of him.

'You will excuse me,' Thierry de Carenzu said, visibly working to maintain his composure. 'I think I must go down and tell Ariane. She ought not to learn this from anyone else.'

Blaise said nothing. He could think of nothing to say. There was someone else, he thought suddenly, who ought properly to hear of these two deaths from someone who cared for her, but he didn't know where Lisseut was, and he didn't think it was his place, given who had done this thing. He watched his father remove his war helm in the valley below and then his tall, handsome, anointed king did the same. Blaise's eyes were dry and his hands grew steady then as he looked down at the two of them.

†

In this windy green valley by Lake Dierne, Ademar of Gorhaut is a happy man. The presence of the Arbonnais army here before them is a surprise of sorts, but not an unpleasant one. The High Elder has been telling him from the beginning that this lake will see the battle that ends Arbonne. They had expected things to follow a slightly different sequence, anticipating that it would be their sacking and burning of the Isle of Rian that would bring the goddess-afflicted soldiers of this land out from their walls to battle.

They did not anticipate an army waiting for them, but Ademar turns away from the now-dead singer on the platform

— one of the two fools they caught spying on their line of march — and sees his High Elder smiling as well.

'It is well,' Galbert says, the deep voice rich with satisfaction. 'They are ignorant as well as cowardly. Had they known about our shortage of food they would not be here. As it is, this will be over tomorrow, my liege, and the granaries of Arbonne will lie open to us with everything else. See their numbers? See our own? Look up at the god's sun over us.'

'It is well,' Ademar says briefly. At times he tires of Galbert's intoned pieties, and even his jaded appetites are nearly sated by now of the High Elder's passion for fire and maiming. Ademar has come to conquer a rich land and to scotch the whiff of rebellion shaped by the younger Garsenc son and Fulk de Savaric. Galbert is here for something else. The god will have his due and more, the king has promised as much. He only hopes it does not last too long, and leaves him some fields to sow and harvest and a country to rule when the last of the burning is done. The numbers are indeed very good though, Galbert speaks truth there, and there are surprises in reserve.

'If we are to fight tomorrow,' says Borsiard d'Andoria, moving his splendid horse nearer, 'then may I ask that the High Elder's disinherited son, the pretender, be left for me to deal with? I have reasons of my own, you understand.'

Ademar doesn't like this vain, choleric man, but he has been made to accept the importance that a Portezzan company in their ranks will have for the days after the war. At times it seems to him that he accepts rather too much from the High Elder, but the king of Gorhaut is willing to be tolerant yet. A great deal has been promised him and those promises are about to bear fruit.

Another horse approaches and he hears its rider laugh sardonically. 'My brother,' says Duke Ranald de Garsenc to the elegantly garbed Portezzan, as the three men turn to look at him, 'could slice you into pieces while attending to other business at the same time. Be not so hasty, my lord, to single him out unless you want your dear wife widowed again and free for another marriage.' The words are a little slurred. Ranald does not look well. It is a fair assumption that he has already been drinking during the morning's ride. His father scowls, but Ademar is genuinely amused, not at all unhappy to observe the de Garsenc at odds again, or the Portezzan's flushed discomfiture.

'Well, if we are speaking of dear wives — ' Borsiard d'Andoria begins waspishly.

'We are *not* speaking of them,' Ademar says quickly, asserting his control. He does not want this discussed, not now, and not ever in public. He wonders if Rosala de Garsenc is in Talair Castle now or still in Barbentain. Shrewdly he guesses she has come with the army, that the countess of Arbonne, too, is within those walls by the lake. If so, it will all truly be over tomorrow, Galbert will have been right. He remembers, amused again, that it was Ranald who suggested once that he marry Signe de Barbentain in order to gain control of Arbonne. That is not going to be necessary, it seems.

'There are formalities,' his High Elder is now saying, as he turns his back on his elder son. 'Shall I send the herald to speak your demands, my liege?' This, too, diverts the king, the so-careful observance of protocols and rituals despite what they have been doing to unarmed men and women and to children all the way south. That, Ademar thinks sagely, is what happens when one marries a religious crusade with a war of conquest.

'Send him,' he says lazily, 'but let us ride with him ourselves to see who they have sent against us. Who knows, my lord High Elder, we might even have a chance to speak with your ambitious younger son. I do still wonder how he came by that dangerous trait.'

'No son of mine!' Galbert says, a little too quickly, scenting danger. 'I disowned him formally in the sanctuary of Corannos in the mountains. You were with me, my liege.'

Ademar laughs aloud this time. He enjoys the ease with which he can set his counsellors on edge, even Galbert, who bears close watching. The king discovers just then, somewhat to his surprise, that he feels the need for a woman. Perhaps it is not so surprising after all. He has been watching his soldiers take their pleasure of the priestesses since they came down from the pass. He has held himself aloof, with some self-congratulation, to preserve the dignity of the crown on this holy crusade. He looks briefly over his shoulder at Ranald de

Garsenc and then back up at the ramparts of Talair. He is, in fact, quite certain that she is within those walls.

Tomorrow, he thinks, and smiles. He is not actually a man accustomed to waiting to slake his needs, but sometimes there is, in fact, a certain heightening of satisfaction if one delays a little time. Not too long, mind you, but a little. He regards this as a truth about the world he has discovered for himself. He looks back at the husband and then away again.

†

Lisseut saw what had been done to two of the men she had loved when she rode out with the countess of Arbonne and a number of their people to parley with the king of Gorhaut.

Had they not been warned by Thierry beforehand, the sickness that passed over her when the bodies came into sight might have undone all her resolutions. It was the hardest thing she had ever had to do in her life, to ride past what was left of Remy and Aurelian and not give way to the clawing grief that rose up within her. She kept her eyes fixed on the straight-backed figure of the countess in front of her and gripped her horse's reins in hands that would not stop shaking. She kept wanting to scream. She could not let herself scream.

She had been with Ariane and the countess and Rosala de Garsenc in the music gallery of Talair when the duke of Carenzu had come down from the tower to tell them that Gorhaut had come, and that something terrible had been done to men they all knew.

She would have expected to burst into desperate tears, to faint, to feel her mind slamming shut like a door. Perhaps it was the shock, or an inward refusal to believe, but she had done none of these things, nor had any of the other women there. Ariane, to whom her husband had formally told the news about Remy and Aurelian, had risen stiffly from where she sat and walked away, to stand with her back to the room, staring into the fire. After an interval of time, though, she had turned and come back. She had been very pale, but her flawless features were carefully composed. She had sat beside the countess and reached for one of Signe's hands, holding it between both of her own.

Of all the people in that room, Alain of Rousset had been the only one who wept openly, and Lisseut had gone over to him. The little troubadour had been wearing his sword. He was still awkward with it, but he was here to join the soldiers in Talair, had rowed across the water to fight with them.

It seemed that Remy and Aurelian had been thinking in the same way, spying on the army of Gorhaut as it moved south. Lisseut would have thought the two of them might even have been good at that, but she didn't know much about warfare.

Neither had they.

She had found herself meeting the clear blue gaze of the woman named Rosala. There was pain there, and something else as hurtful, if harder to understand, but Lisseut had taken resolution and a certain comfort from that exchange of glances, and tried, as best she could, to give back the same two things.

'There should be a song for them,' the countess had said, rising from her chair and turning to where Lisseut was standing beside Alain. The little troubadour had lifted his head, wiping his eyes. 'I will not ask for it now, though,' Signe de Barbentain went on. 'This is not a time for music.'

It was then that they had heard footsteps in the corridor again, and Bertran had come into the room with a number of other men. One of whom was Blaise. There was something bleak and forbidding about him, as if a part of the winter had passed into him on the ramparts. He had looked at Rosala first — his brother's wife — and nodded his head in greeting. But then he had turned to Lisseut and, after a moment, had made a small, helpless gesture with his hands. She did feel like crying then. She could remember him wounding Remy with his sword. She had come forward to challenge him for that. Midsummer, it had been. Midsummer Carnival in Tavernel. Hard to believe that there once had been a time of celebration in Arbonne.

'They have blown the horns and are coming to parley,' Bertran had said to the countess. 'Ademar is riding with his herald.'

'Then I should be with ours,' Signe had said calmly. 'If you think it right.'

'We are your servants, your grace. But yes, I think it right. I think you should come, and Ariane. This is a war being waged against our women, as much as anything, and I think the army, both armies, should see you here.'

'And I,' said Rosala de Garsenc then, rising. 'I am their excuse for war.' Bertran had looked quickly over at her, an odd expression in his face. He had looked as if he wanted to demur, but did not.

When Lisseut expressed the same intention to be present no one gainsaid her. She hadn't expected them to. She didn't even see herself as being presumptuous. Not with this. It seemed to her that there might even be a shared feeling now that one of the musicians should be there.

She had actually forgotten, for the moment, that Bertran de Talair was a troubadour too.

The king of Gorhaut, it soon appeared, had not. The two groups met within sight of the armies but at a careful distance removed. There were archers of skill in both ranks. The place chosen by the heralds was to the west, along the northern shore of Lake Dierne, beside a rocky strand of beach. They could see the great stone arch not far away, and in the distance, to the south-west, the towers of Miraval reared up like an illusion over the forest between.

Amid that company, beside the whitecapped lake, the voice of Signe de Barbentain rang out, colder than the waters or the wind. 'I thought Gorhaut had fallen somewhat since your father's death,' she said, looking straight at the broad-shouldered figure of Ademar. 'I had not realized until very lately how great that fall was. The man on that platform was honoured in all the countries of the world. Are you not ashamed before Corannos to have done this foul thing?'

'The god's name is profanity in your mouth,' said Galbert de Garsenc quickly, before Ademar could reply. The king gave him a sharp glance.

'Cannot your king at least speak *some* answers for himself?' Signe asked with deceptive mildness. Lisseut saw Ademar flush. She saw him look at Rosala de Garsenc before replying.

'He was captured as a spy.' The voice was unexpectedly light, but controlled. 'He would have been dealt with and executed as such, and the yellow-haired one as well, but he made a mistake.' Ademar turned to Bertran de Talair. 'He elected, unwisely, to sing some verses of a song you wrote, my lord. The wrong verses, the wrong song. And the other man chose to laugh. You might say you are responsible for what happened to them.'

For the first time he smiled. Lisseut shivered, seeing that. She saw Rosala de Garsenc turn away. But then, despite her own fear, or perhaps because of it, and because it was now clear what had happened, she dared speak, even in that company, for the sake of the two dead men she had loved. She said, to the king of Gorhaut:

'He sang for you? You didn't remotely deserve such an honour. Were these the lines by any chance? *What manner of man, with his father new-fallen, would destroy with a pen-stroke a long dream of glory?*' She felt an anger such as she had never known in her life. Almost snarling the words she added, 'Or did he ask the other, obvious question in the same song: *Where went the manhood of Gorhaut . . . ?* Where indeed. They are asking that question all through the world, about a nation that burns helpless women.' She spoke the words with all the passion of her heart.

And she was met, brutally, by laughter. 'I would have thought the question of lost manhood would apply to the one on the platform, actually.' King Ademar's amusement faded, the small pale eyes held hers. 'But since you have chosen to raise the issue, I will make a point of remembering your unremarkable face, and personally dealing with that question when we are finished doing what we have come to do tomorrow.'

'Your father,' said Bertan de Talair quietly, speaking for the first time, 'never blustered. I remember that about him.'

'Ah,' said Ademar, turning quickly to him. 'It comes back to fathers, does it?' He looked pointedly towards the distant towers of Miraval. 'I was told it had as much to do with a bastard son and a lusting woman, legs wide for any man but her own husband. What a shame the cuckolded duke of Miraval is not here to offer you his wise counsel. And what a great shame as well,' he added, turning from Bertran, whose face had gone white, 'that you have had to find such frail vessels from the north to fill out your sorry ranks.'

Lisseut had wondered when they would get to Blaise. In the moments that followed, she was made to realize that she had not moved past longing into acceptance after all. The image of that stone sinking silently down through dark water left her then, and never returned.

Blaise, despite Ademar's hard gaze, utterly ignored him, as if the king of Gorhaut were some minor functionary, unworthy of attention. His own eyes were locked on his father's face, and Lisseut saw the forbidding figure of Galbert de Garsenc in his blue cleric's robe looking at his younger son with an expression that actually terrified her. She had thought, naively, that her travels had led her to understand something of the world. She realized now, seeing that exchange of glances, that she knew nothing. She also understood in that moment that, in a real sense, all of this came down to the two of them.

'In the Books of Othair,' said Blaise softly, 'which are the holiest writings of Corannos, it is told that the land of Gorhaut carries the god's burden of bringing justice into the world. It teaches that Corannos has bestowed upon us the holy task of guarding the helpless and the persecuted in all lands we pass through, in return for his great favour and the promise of his eternal shelter when we die.' He was silent, and in the silence was an indictment.

'You *dare* speak to me of the teachings of the god?' Galbert said, his rich voice rising, genuinely incredulous. Behind him Lisseut saw a man who, from his appearance, had to be the other son. He was sitting astride a handsome horse among the small number of men who had come with the High Elder and the king. His expression was strained, oddly suspended between bitter amusement and pain. Impulsively, she glanced over at Rosala. She was gazing steadily at her husband, her face unreadable. There were, Lisseut thought, layers and layers of grief here.

Blaise seemed to ignore his father's interjection. He went on, as if no one had spoken. 'You are, in the light of these teachings, as much a betrayer of Corannos as this falsely anointed king is a traitor to his people. Because you are my father and the god teaches us to respect our parents in their dotage you will not be executed, but you will be stripped of your office when we return to Gorhaut.'

'You are mad,' said King Ademar flatly, dismissively.

Only then did Blaise turn to him. 'I am enraged,' he said, a ferocity in his voice for the first time, a first blaze of heat. 'I am revolted. I loathe how you have allowed yourself and your country to be used. What king permits a counsellor's vile obsession to lead him so far down paths of unholiness and betrayal?'

'A false king,' said Fulk de Savaric, his sudden voice clear as a bell. 'One unworthy of his crown.'

'Or his life,' said Bertran de Talair quietly.

'Or of any remembrance at all in the world after the death Rian is even now making ready for him,' added the countess of Arbonne, and of all those there it was her voice that was grimmest of all, as if she were truly speaking for some power beyond the world.

For the first time the king of Gorhaut, turning from one of them to the other, looked shaken. And so smoothly, predictably, his adviser moved to fill the silence that followed.

'These,' Galbert said in the deep, commanding voice, 'are the last strident posturings of the doomed. Shall we quail before this mumbling? Rather, you should all be on your knees even now, begging the mercy of a gentle death.'

'You would like that, wouldn't you?' said Ariane de Carenzu, moving her horse forward a little. She was smiling, but not with her eyes. 'You would like the women of Arbonne kneeling before you, I see. I do see it now, actually. No wonder your son's wife fled from you. What does Corannos say about such desires, Galbert de Garsenc?'

'They are abominations,' said Blaise quietly. 'For which atonement must be made.' He himself was pale now.

'This,' said the king of Gorhaut, regaining his composure, 'has grown tedious. I am here only because the protocols of war compel this meeting of heralds. Hear me then: we have come south because the countess of Arbonne has given shelter and succour to a woman of Gorhaut and has refused to return her to us. All else, as the High Elder says, is posturing. I have patience for no more of it. Prepare yourselves to die on the morrow.'

'What if I do return?' said Rosala suddenly. 'If I come back north, will you take your army home?'

Galbert de Garsenc laughed thickly. He opened his mouth to reply but was forestalled by the king's lifted hand. 'This comes,' said Ademar softly, 'very much too late. There is a lesson now to be taught to those who have denied our most proper demands. I am pleased to see you eager to return, but it makes no matter at this point. There is no power here, or anywhere in the world, Rosala, that can stop me now from bringing you back to Cortil.'

'With the child,' said Galbert quickly.

He was ignored.

'To *Cortil*, my lord?' Rosala asked, lifting her voice. 'Are you so open about this now? Do you not mean: back to Garsenc and my lord husband?'

In the stillness that followed this, Lisseut realized that the king of Gorhaut had just made, in some fashion she did not entirely understand, a mistake.

†

A long way south, on the Island of Rian in the sea, where the wind was not blowing on this day and the waters lay calm and blue under the pale winter sun, Beatritz de Barbentain, High Priestess of Rian, rose suddenly from before a fire into which she had been gazing sightlessly for most of the day.

'Something has just happened,' she said aloud, though there was no one in her room with her save the white owl on her shoulder. 'Something that might matter. Oh, sweet Rian remember us, have mercy upon your children.'

She was silent then, waiting, reaching out in her darkness for the elusive, uncoercible vision of the goddess that might let her know at least a part of what was now happening so far away in the place of the wind.

†

And in that precise moment, by the lake, among that gathering of enemies, a voice was heard for the first time.

'I am afraid,' said Ranald, duke of Garsenc, moving his horse into the open space between the two companies, 'that this *is* rather too openly said for my taste and for the honour of my family.' He was staring at the king of Gorhaut. He had not used a title.

No one responded. No one else moved. It seemed to Lisseut, afterwards, that the duke's words had virtually frozen them all with astonishment. Ranald de Garsenc, the only moving figure in a still world, turned to his wife. He looked remarkably at ease now, as if this action or decision, this movement, had somehow granted him release from something. He said, 'Forgive me, my lady, but I must ask this, and I will accept the truth of what you say: has the king of Gorhaut been your lover?'

Lisseut realized she was holding her breath. Out of the side of her vision she saw that Blaise had gone bone-white. Sitting her horse easily, Rosala de Garsenc seemed almost as composed as her husband though. She said, as clearly as before, 'He has not, my lord, though he has sought to be that for some time now. He was only delaying while I was with child. Your father, I am sorry to say, has been urging the thought upon him for purposes of his own. I will swear to you though, upon the life of my child, that I have not lain with Ademar, and that I will die before I willingly do so.'

'This is why you left?' A different note in Ranald's voice, almost too exposed; it made Lisseut wish, suddenly, that she was not here. *None of us has a right to be listening to this*, she thought.

But Rosala said, her handsome, strong head held high, 'It is indeed why I left, my lord. I feared you could not, or would not, guard us against your father and your king, for the one had claimed the child I was carrying, as you know, and the other wanted me.'

Ranald was nodding slowly, as if the words were striking echoes within himself.

'Ranald, in the god's name, do not shame me,' Galbert de Garsenc began, the beautiful voice becoming harsh, 'by allowing this depraved, contemptible woman to give voice to such —'

'You be silent,' said the duke of Garsenc bluntly. 'I will consider how to deal with you after.' The tone was so curt it was shocking.

'After what?' asked Ademar of Gorhaut. His own head was lifted, his carriage in the saddle magnificent. There was a glitter to his gaze. *He knows*, Lisseut thought. *He knows the answer to that.*

'After I have publicly dealt with you for the dishonour you have willed upon my house. No king of Gorhaut has ever been free to wreak what havoc he will among the high lords of our land. I am not about to let you be the first. The wife of the duke of Garsenc is not a trinket to be played for, however blind the duke might be.' He paused for a moment, then: 'This is a formal challenge, Ademar. Will you fight me yourself, or name a champion to shelter behind?'

'Are you *mad?*' Galbert de Garsenc cried out.

'That,' said Ranald gravely, 'is the second time that question has here been asked of one of your sons. In fact, I think it is true of neither of us.' He turned to Rosala. 'Other accusations may fairly be made against me. I will hope to have a chance to address them after.'

She met his glance but said nothing, stern and proud, Lisseut thought, as some yellow-haired goddess of the north. But that, she realized immediately after, was idle fantasy: they didn't allow goddesses in the north.

Ranald turned back to Ademar. They all turned back to Ademar. The king of Gorhaut, past the first surprise of this, was smiling; only with his lips though, his eyes were hard as stone.

'We are in a foreign country and at war,' he said. 'You are a commander of my army. You are now proposing that we fight each other because your wife, whose flight from your home is the cause of our being here, alleges that I expressed a desire for her. Is this what I understand from you, my lord of Garsenc?'

It sounded absurd, mad indeed, when put that way, but Ranald de Garsenc did not quail. He, too, was smiling now, a smaller man than the king but as easy in the saddle. 'You might not remember it,' he said, 'but I was in that room in Cortil with my father last autumn when you came in and demanded that Rosala be brought back. Back to you, you said.' They saw the king's expression change. His eyes flicked away from Ranald's, and then returned.

The duke went on. 'I should have made this challenge then, Ademar. You have been using Rosala's flight from me as your excuse for war — my father's idea, of course. You aren't nearly clever enough. She didn't fly from me, Ademar, I think

I dare say that. She left her husband and put our child at terrible risk because of you and my father. I think I am seeing things clearly for the first time in a great many years. If you have any honour or courage left in you, draw your sword.'

'I will have you arrested and then gelded before burning,' Galbert de Garsenc snarled, pointing a gauntleted finger at his older son.

Ranald actually laughed. 'More burning? Do what you will,' he said. 'The king might well be grateful for that protection. I will not, however,' he added, still with that unnatural calm, 'speak further to procurers.' He had not even bothered to look away from Ademar. To the king he said: 'There have been allegations of treason thrown about freely here. At my brother, by my brother at my father, at you. I find it all a game of words. I prefer to name you what you are, Ademar: a dupe, and a coward hiding behind his counsellor, unwilling to use his own sword in a matter of honour.'

'Ranald,' said Ademar, almost gently, 'Ranald, Ranald, you know I can kill you. You have done nothing but drink for ten years — *that* is why your wife fled south. I doubt you have given her a night's satisfaction in years. Do not deceive yourself before you go to the god.'

'This means, I take it, that you will fight.'

'He will do no such thing!' Galbert snapped.

'Yes, I will fight,' said Ademar in the same moment. 'The sons of my High Elder have finally grown too tiresome to endure. I would be done with them.'

And the king of Gorhaut drew his sword.

There came a sound from among the armies north of them, for the light was brilliantly clear and all men there could see that blade drawn. Then the sound changed, grew high-pitched with surprise, as Ranald de Garsenc drew his own blade in reply, and moved his horse apart from the others by the lake. Ademar followed him. As he lowered the visor of his helmet, they saw that the king was smiling. To the west, not far away, the stones of the Arch of the Ancients gleamed, honey-coloured in the light.

'Well?' Lisseut heard Bertran murmur under his breath.

'Ten years ago,' said Fulk de Savaric softly, 'it might have been a match. Not now, I am sorry to say.'

Blaise said nothing, though he had to have heard that. He was watching his brother with something hurtful in his eyes. Rosala was watching too, but there was nothing to be read in her expression at all. Ranald, Lisseut noted, had not bothered to lower his helm.

'It will make no difference, you know that,' said Galbert de Garsenc heavily, speaking to the Arbonne party. 'Even if Ademar dies we will destroy you tomorrow. And he will not die. Ranald has been drinking all day. He would never have done this otherwise. Look at his face. He is about to meet the judgment of the god, sodden and disgraced.'

'Redeemed, I should have said.' Blaise's voice was hollow. He did not take his eyes from the two men circling each other now on the roadway by the strand.

And what they saw then, as the long, bright swords touched for the first time, delicately, and then again with a sharp, wrist-grinding clash, was indeed redemption of a kind. There *is* a grace here, thought Lisseut suddenly, resisting the thought. She had never seen Ranald de Garsenc before and so she had never seen him fight. He had been King's Champion of Gorhaut once, for Ademar's father, someone had told her. That had been a long time ago.

For a moment it seemed not to have been, as he pivoted his war horse using knees and hips and rang a hard, quick downward blow against Ademar's side. The curved armour caught the blade and deflected it, but the king of Gorhaut swayed in his saddle, and there came a rumble again from the armies. Lisseut looked over at Blaise, she couldn't help herself, but then she turned away from what she saw in his face, back to the two men fighting in the road.

Blaise didn't even see Ranald's first blow land. He had actually closed his eyes when the combat began. He heard the clang of sword on armour, though, and looked up in time to see Ademar rock in his saddle before righting himself to deliver a slashing backhand of his own. Ranald blunted that with a twist of his sword-arm and sidled his horse away from Ademar's attempt at a cut back the other way.

It was that horseman's movement, the instinctive, almost unconscious product of a lifetime in the saddle with blade in hand, that took Blaise back, in a blur and rush of time, to his childhood and those first clandestine lessons his brother had given him, at a time when Galbert had forbidden Blaise to touch a sword. Both boys had been whipped when the deception was uncovered, though Blaise hadn't actually known about Ranald's punishment until long after, and then only because one of the corans had spoken of it. Ranald had never said a word. There had been no more lessons though. Galbert had had his way. He almost always did.

Blaise looked over at his father then, at the smooth-cheeked, commanding features. The furrow of concern on Galbert's brow had gone; he was actually smiling now, a smug, thin-mouthed expression Blaise knew well. And why should he not smile? Ranald was ten years past his fighting days, and Ademar was very possibly the strongest warrior in Gorhaut. The result of this had been assured from the moment the challenge was made, and Galbert, Blaise understood in that moment, cared nothing at all for the life of his son. Ranald's death would even simplify matters. He had become almost irrelevant to the High Elder, except, as here, when he became a nuisance and a distraction, or even a threat to Galbert's power over the king.

In fact, if Rosala's story was true — and of course it would be true — the honour or dignity of Garsenc had ceased to be important to Galbert in any way that signified. All that seemed to matter to the High Elder was his control of Ademar and this great burning in Arbonne that was allowing him. Ripened fruit of his long dream. That was what mattered, and one thing more: Cadar. His grandson was also a part of Galbert's cold stalking of power in Gorhaut and Arbonne's obliteration.

He must not have him, Blaise thought.

He wondered — the terrible thought intruding like a spear — if Rosala had given orders to have the baby killed if they lost the battle here. It was probable, he realized, in fact it was almost certain.

Grief, from all directions it seemed, closed in upon him as he turned from his father to look at his brother again, seeing Ranald strangely now, as if from a distance, as if he were fading already into the past, into mist, on a day in Arbonne brilliant with light.

Ranald de Garsenc is also thinking of the past as he lets his body respond intuitively to the demands of combat. For the moment, as the overwhelmingly familiar first steps of the dance begin, he is all right, he is even, in some unexpected fashion, nearly happy. He knows, absorbing a sequence of blows on shield and sword, slashing in response, that this cannot be sustained. He is not that much older than the king but he is far past his best years, while Ademar, strong as a tree, is as close to his peak as he will ever be.

As if to make explicit what both of them know, the sheer strength of the king drives his blade through a tardy attempt at warding and the sword hammers into the light armour Ranald wears. He has always preferred to be lighter in the saddle, relying on quickness. Now, wincing at a hard lance of pain in his ribs, pulling his horse back out of range, he realizes that most of that quickness is gone.

Ten years ago, Ranald thinks, though without bitterness, *I would have had him on the ground by now.* There is no false pride in the thought either: ten years ago he had been named by King Duergar as his court champion, and for two full years, fighting in the king's name, he did not lose a single combat in any tournament from Götzland to southern Portezza to the Arimondan court. Then, on a night in the dead of winter, Ereibert de Garsenc had died and Ranald became duke after the obligatory candlelit vigil in the chapel of Corannos. The tournaments and banquets and the celebrations of his prowess among women and men gave way to estate administration at Garsenc and an inexorable, trammelling immersion into his father's designs. Not as a confidant of course: Galbert trusted in Ranald no more than his son shared thoughts with him. Ranald, as duke of Garsenc, became a tool for Galbert's schemes, no more, and at times rather less. It was all a long time ago. Those were the days when ale and wine first became his comforts, avenues to oblivion.

But his thoughts do not linger among those memories. Even as he parries another barrage of blows, feeling the weight of the king's assault jarring his arm and shoulder almost numb, he finds his mind going even further back, much further actually.

Unlike Blaise, who never saw her, Ranald has a memory
of his mother.

Two or three images, in fact, though when he first spoke
of them as a child he was sternly told by his tutor that these
were false recollections, unworthy fantasies for a warrior-to-
be. Ranald was two years old when his mother died. Boys that
age could not remember things, the tutor decreed. When
Ranald tried, not long after, to ask his father about the recur-
ring image he had of a red-haired woman singing to him by
candlelight, Galbert flatly forbade him, on pain of a whipping,
to mention it again. Ranald was six years old. It was the last
time he'd attempted to confide something of importance to
his father. Or, he realizes abruptly now, to anyone else.

The memory of the red-haired woman has stayed with
him all these years, though he has never again spoken of it. It
occurs to him, for the first time, that he might have mentioned it to Rosala. It might have been something to share
with her. He guides his horse with a quick pressure of his left
knee and, ducking with a grunt under a wide side-sweeping
blow, delivers a backhand slash of his own, ringing it hard off
Ademar's armour. The king is prone to such flat, sidelong
blows he notes, a part of his mind still registering such things,
as if there is anything he is going to be able to do about it. *I
should have told her*, he is thinking. Rosala might have wanted
to hear of such a memory; in the beginning, at any rate. In the
later part of their time together he was less certain of her
interest but that, truly, was his own fault.

Just as it is his own fault that he is short of breath already.
He is feeling the effects of this morning's ale as a thick heav-
iness in his limbs, in the extra pulse of time between his
awareness of a threat or an opportunity and his body's slow
response. It is going to get worse, he knows. Ademar is not
even breathing hard but Ranald is grimly aware that his own
shield and armour are dented already by the king's blows. He
is afraid he may have broken ribs on his left side; it has become
difficult to do much more than parry.

Ademar seems to be aware of this. Through his lowered
black visor the king of Gorhaut speaks, contemptuously giving Ranald a respite. Softly, so that none of the others will
hear, he says, 'I could almost pity you, were you not such a

fool. She will be mine tomorrow, I want you to think of that. I hope you are thinking of it in the moment I kill you. Tomorrow night, when her hair is down and she wraps her mouth around my sex in the way that I shall teach her do you think she will mourn the poor, sad, drunken man she once had to lie beside?'

Ranald would reply, but he lacks the breath to spare for taunting, and there is nothing, actually, he can think of to say. His ribs are extraordinarily painful now; each breath drawn seems to slide a knife into his side. He suspects the king is wrong, though; he believes Rosala told no less than truth when she said she would die before lying with Ademar. This thought makes him abruptly aware of something: if the king kills him he is almost certainly killing Rosala as well. And — a second new thought like a lash of the cold wind — even more surely killing the child. The son he has never seen.

I am everything he says of me, Ranald de Garsenc thinks, and now there is bitterness. *I have wasted my life.*

He remembers — and with this memory as well there is sorrow now — his brother Blaise on the fogbound drawbridge of Garsenc only a little time ago: *You don't have to follow him, Ranald. You have the first free choice you've had in a long time.* He answered harshly, he remembers, almost choking in confused fury. Corannos knew, there had been so much anger in him that night. Wrongly directed though; he seems to have turned in wrong directions all his life.

There was a time when I would have followed you to the ends of the earth, Blaise also said that night. *I never knew that,* Ranald thinks, his eyes warily on the king of Gorhaut. Blaise is here too, watching him, has claimed a crown, defied their father — even named Corannos to witness his doing so. He is walking a path of honour, one that might make a man proud, even a brother.

Ademar lifts his sword and points it forward like an executioner. He is playing to the armies now, Ranald knows. He can hear them to the north, a constant murmur of sound broken by sharp sudden cries. It is about to begin again. And end, Ranald de Garsenc thinks. He looks up for a moment at the bright sun shining above the fields and the forests of this land of Arbonne.

He is genuinely not afraid, only sorrowful and full of regrets, but it really is too late, he thinks. There would never have been enough time to make amends for so many errors and weaknesses. He thinks of the red-haired woman singing him a lullaby. He wonders if she is waiting for him, if the god might allow a grace like that to such a man as he has been. He thinks of his brother again, and then, lastly, of his wife and the child he has let slip away. Cadar. A strong name, one of honour in the world. Far better than the memory of his own name will be, he thinks, and it is this, at the end, that hurts most of all. And spurs him to a last gesture, an attempt at redress.

Ignoring the pain in his side Ranald thrusts his own sword above his head, theatrical and arresting. Ademar hesitates.

Ranald sucks precious air and cries out then, as loudly as he can through the open visor of his helm, hoping the armies can hear: 'Before our most holy god I name you a false king, Ademar, and I set my sword against you in the name of Gorhaut.' He hears a new sound rising to the north and knows his words have carried. He stops, sucks air, speaks again, to a coran in their party now, one of his own, a rasped command: 'Bergen, ride back to the army. These are my orders, you are charged with them: the corans of Garsenc are not to fight for this man.' He pauses, then says it: 'Follow my brother now.'

It is done, spoken, and not actually so hard as he would have expected it to be. He takes his eyes from the king long enough to meet those of the leader of his corans. He sees Bergen hesitate, then nod, a movement jerky with surprise and fear. He sees him twitch his horse's reins to obey. He turns back then, because he must, to deal with the onrush of the suddenly enraged king.

Ranald de Garsenc offers his soul then, in genuine diffidence, to Corannos, and decides, on impulse, to do one last thing, more for the bittersweet irony of it than anything else. Something from childhood to leave them with. He wonders if anyone will actually realize or recognize what it is he is doing. *Blaise might*, he thinks wistfully, and then stops thinking for there is no time, Ademar's sword is swinging and the dance is nearly done.

For those watching, events happened very quickly then.

Blaise had turned from the fight when Ranald, sword flamboyantly raised, shouted to the armies and then spoke his astonishing instructions to Bergen, the long-time captain of the Garsenc corans. His heart jumped as he realized what his brother was doing, and he saw Bergen, dead loyal all his life, acknowledge and move to obey.

Bergen of Garsenc was felled by a swordstroke from behind before he had even fully turned his horse. Borsiard d'Andoria, elegant, unsmiling, slid his long blade carelessly free of the coran's body and they saw Bergen fall to the ground. The Portezzan looked deliberately over at Blaise, and then he did smile.

There came a shout of anger and unease from among the army of Gorhaut. They had heard Ranald's cry and had now seen the Portezzan slay one of their own. Some men from each army began moving closer, which was dangerous.

Blaise had no time to deal with that, or with Borsiard just then, for even as he was registering these things a stray, random memory was being jogged from far back in childhood, from the days when he used to watch his brother train with the corans in the courtyard. There had been something about that elaborately showy, sword-upraised gesture of Ranald's, a deliberate echo of something, a game, a frivolity.

And then memory sprang clear, and with a sound that he only realized afterwards had been his brother's name, Blaise wheeled back to watch what was going to be the ending, one way or the other.

He had only ever seen this done as a jest among friends, and that had been twenty years ago. The uplifted sword was the invitation, almost too transparent, luring one's opponent to venture a backhanded side-stroke at the exposed right side. What used to follow, when this was tried in the tiltyard at Garsenc, was a silly, undignified manoeuvre that had usually left both combatants rolling in the dust, swearing and laughing.

There was no laughter by the shore of Lake Dierne. Blaise watched the king of Gorhaut succumb completely to the ruse, driven by his fury at Ranald's orders to his men. Ademar launched a wild stroke of such force it would have half-severed Ranald's torso through the links of his armour had it landed.

It didn't land. Ranald de Garsenc flattened himself on his horse's neck and let fall his sword as Ademar's blade whistled over his head biting nothing but air. The king's motion carried him lurching sideways in his saddle and partly turned his horse. By the time he began, cursing, to straighten, Ranald, lightly armoured as always, had hurled himself from his horse towards the back of the king's saddle. Very much like a boy, Blaise was thinking, like the boy for whom all of this had been discovery and exhilaration, with pain and sorrow and ageing quite inconceivable concepts.

Ranald actually made it. Landed, almost neatly, behind Ademar, swinging a leg across the horse's rump. He was already grappling at his waist for the knife that would kill the king when the crossbow dart caught him above the collarbone and buried itself in his throat.

The half-drawn dagger fell from splayed fingers and a moment later Ranald de Garsenc slid slowly to the ground to lie beside it in the winter grass. Blood was pulsing from his neck, bright red in the sunlight.

Above him, controlling his horse with an effort, Ademar of Gorhaut looked down upon him, and then at the man who had fired that small, hidden crossbow.

'You interfered in a challenge,' said the king of Gorhaut. His voice was thin, disbelieving. He was visibly shaken.

'Would you prefer to be dead right now?' asked Galbert de Garsenc, High Elder of Gorhaut. He didn't even look at the body of his son. Ademar made no reply. There was a growing tumult now to the north of them.

'Watch him,' Blaise said to no one in particular, and slid from his horse. Ignoring Ademar completely, he knelt beside his brother. He heard footsteps behind him but did not turn. Ranald's eyes were closed; he was still alive, but only just. With all the care in the world Blaise shifted him a little, so he could lay his brother's head in his lap. Blood from the wound had already soaked the ground; now it began to seep into his clothing.

From above and behind he heard his father say to the king of Gorhaut, 'I have not come this close to be balked by a drunkard's folly or your own carelessness.'

Ranald opened his eyes then, and Blaise saw that his

brother was aware of him. A faint, genuine smile, crossed Ranald's face.

'It would have worked,' he whispered. 'I only tried it as a jest.'

'Spare your strength,' Blaise murmured.

Ranald shook his head slightly. 'No point,' he managed to say. 'I can feel poison. There is syvaren on the dart.'

Of course. Of course there was. This time it was Blaise who closed his eyes, feeling grief and a terrible, ancient rage threatening to overwhelm him. He fought desperately for control, and when he opened his eyes again saw that Ranald's gaze had moved away now, to someone beyond Blaise.

'I have no right to ask for anything,' he heard his brother whisper. Blaise looked over his shoulder then and saw Rosala standing there, tall and grave.

'I know you do not,' she agreed quietly, adhering, even at the last, to her own inner laws. 'But I have the right to grant what I wish.' She hesitated, and Blaise thought she would kneel but she did not. She said, very calmly, 'It was bravely done at the end, Ranald.'

There was a silence. Far off, Blaise heard noises that sounded like men fighting. He ought to turn, he knew, this mattered so much, but he could not.

Ranald said, 'Guard him if you can. Cadar, I mean.' And then, so softly it was difficult to hear, 'It is a fine name.' It was in that moment that Blaise thought he felt his heart beginning to break, hearing the unspoken thing, the lost lifetime of sorrow beneath those words.

And Rosala seemed to hear it too, for she did kneel then, neatly, in the blood-soaked grass beside her husband. She did not reach out to touch him, but Blaise heard her say, in that same grave, calm voice, 'Cadar Ranald de Garsenc now. You have earned as much. If it pleases you, my lord.'

Through a blurring of tears Blaise saw his older brother smile then for the last time and heard him say, no more than a breath now, 'It pleases me, my lady.'

He seemed to be gripping both of Ranald's hands — he couldn't actually remember taking them — and he was almost certain he felt a pressure then, the strong fingers squeezing his for a moment, before they went slack.

Blaise looked down at his dead brother, feeling the cold wind passing over the two of them. He slipped one hand free after a time and closed Ranald's eyes. He had seen a great many dead men. Sometimes their faces seemed to become calm and peaceful when life passed out of them and they began their second journey to the god. Ranald looked as he always had, though; perhaps when it was someone you knew well the comforting illusions of grace were harder to find.

He hadn't actually said farewell, he realized. He hadn't said anything. *Spare your strength*, had been his only words. Fatuous, really, to a man with a dart in his neck and syvaren running coldly through him. Perhaps the touching, their hands holding each other, perhaps that would have been enough. It would have to be; there was never going to be more.

He made himself look up. Ademar, still visibly shaken by what had happened, was on his horse above them. Blaise said nothing to him at all. He looked over his shoulder and saw that his father was still holding the tiny, lethal crossbow he had brought hidden to this place. The ancient rules of such things, the rituals and laws of parleys or challenges, would mean nothing to Galbert. Blaise had always known that. Ademar hadn't, it seemed.

The king of Gorhaut would be wondering how he was going to hold up his head among the nations now — even before his own people — after being so shamefully rescued in the midst of a formal challenge. It would probably make sense to taunt him, to unsettle him further, but Blaise had no heart for that at all. In fact, at another time, another place in the world, he might even have been able to feel sorry for Ademar, who would only now perhaps be discovering the degree to which even he was simply another instrument of Galbert de Garsenc's designs.

He seemed to be looking down at his brother again, as if trying to memorize Ranald's features, so like and yet unlike his own. 'You had best get up,' he heard Rosala say, as if from a distance. She herself had risen again. He looked up at her. She had never appeared to him to so much resemble one of the spear-maidens of Corannos, straight-backed and proud, a figure from a chapel frieze, her face seeming as if sculpted in stone. Her level gaze met his. 'He died as a man worth mourning,' said Rosala de Savaric de Garsenc, 'but it seems that this battle has begun.'

It seemed that it had.

He slipped his hands under Ranald's head and lifted it so he could slide himself free, then he laid his brother down again on the grass. Rising, he looked at Ademar and said formally, over the growing clamour to the north, 'As his brother I lay claim to this body. Do you challenge me for it?'

Ademar shook his head. 'Believe me, I do not want it.'

Blaise nodded. 'Very well.' He felt very calm now, almost eerily so. A kind of numbness was setting in. 'I will look for you at sunset if we are both alive.'

Ademar's eyes flicked over to where Ranald lay but then came back to meet Blaise's. He had never been a coward, whatever else might be said of him. 'I shall not be hard to find,' he said, and wheeled his horse north towards the battlefield.

Only then did Blaise turn to his father.

Galbert, watching the others leave, seemed to have been waiting for him. The large, smooth features were a little flushed perhaps, but otherwise unruffled. Blaise said, choosing his words with care, 'I will not be the man that kills you, for I would not want a father-slaying marked against my soul, but there is a journey to the god that awaits you, whether it comes today or soon or late and Corannos will know how to judge you for this deed.' He paused. 'And so will Rian, for a parley and a challenge breached, for a son's murder here.'

Galbert gave a bark of laughter and opened his mouth to reply.

'Be gone from this place,' said Bertran de Talair before the High Elder could speak. 'I have never slain a man in the presence of heralds in my life, but I could do so now.'

'What?' said Galbert mockingly. 'And face the same judgment as me?' And saying so he turned his horse and began riding away. The nearest companies of the armies were now engaging each other, banners whipped by the wind, in that valley north of Talair.

Blaise looked over at his dead brother on the ground, and then back to his father riding north, a huge, bulky man, yet easy and even graceful in the saddle. There was something deeply unreal about the two images for him, as if his mind were somehow refusing to accept this conjunction. But there were men battling now and he reached out towards that single hard truth, the urgency of it, as a pathway out of the numbness that seemed to be trying to claim him.

He heard a grating sound behind him and turned to see two boats being pulled up on the stony strand. The women began boarding them. In one of the boats he recognized, without surprise, the tall, slender young priestess he had met beside this lake when he first came here. There had been dead men on the ground then, too, he remembered. She looked at him, but only briefly and without expression, then she reached out a hand to the countess and helped her into the boat.

The other women were quickly on board and the boats were pushed back out into the choppy water. Sails were run up that the north wind might take them away. As he watched, hesitating beside that stony strand, Blaise saw Ariane turn back to look for him, her dark hair blown out behind her by the wind. Their glances held for a beat of time before she turned away. A moment later, in the other boat, Blaise saw that Lisseut of Vezét, who had also lost men she loved this day, had turned to look back as well. She began, awkwardly, to lift one hand, but then let it fall to her side. He could see that she was crying.

Rosala did not turn around at all, and so he did not see her face at the end. He only saw her from behind, sitting straight-backed beside the small, delicate figure of the countess of Arbonne as the two boats swept back across Lake Dierne towards the isle, leaving behind the grassy space by the stones of the northern shore where her husband's body lay.

Blaise drew a slow breath, and then another. He turned away from the women in the boats. Bertran de Talair came up to him.

'Are you all right?' the duke asked quietly. Blaise saw Fulk de Savaric behind Bertran, the same question in his eyes.

There was a third boat being pulled up even now on the strand, grating on the stones. They had come for Ranald, he realized. He would have to let them deal with him, and trust the clergy of Rian to do his brother honour. He had no choice in this, no time. Time was what had been taken away. His task was elsewhere now, among the living, and those he meant to kill.

'It doesn't matter how I am,' he said to the duke of Talair, a little frightened by the sound of his own voice. 'It really doesn't matter. Let's go.'

CHAPTER·18

The battle that ended Gorhaut and Arbonne as the world had known them started a day too soon. In the tumultuous wake of the aborted parley by the lake the nearest companies of the two armies engaged, and once that happened there was nothing, short of an actual manifestation of a goddess or a god in the sky above, that could have separated them. Whatever advantages of tactics and knowledge of the terrain that Bertran de Talair might have been able to call into play, given time to prepare, were swept away in the tumult of spontaneously begun fighting that turned, almost immediately, into headlong, screaming chaos.

In such a battle, Blaise knew, enmeshed in the fighting nearest the lake, sheer numbers would almost always tell. The smaller army could only have a chance if the larger one was cowardly, or poorly led, or composed of mercenaries who might be prone to cut their losses early.

None of these things were true in the valley by Lake Dierne. He had learned, in most of a year here south of the mountain passes, that the men of Arbonne were never to be lightly dismissed — and they were fighting now for their country and on their own land. Even so, the warriors of Gorhaut had been raised and trained in a single-minded purity that exalted Corannos of Battles as the highest incarnation of the god, squarely in the tradition of the Ancients who had come to conquer, and whose arch loomed west of this valley like a brooding presence.

It had always been that way in the nations of the north, in Gorhaut, Valensa, Götzland. The southern countries had no such fixed, warlike obsession in their make-up, and Arbonne worshipped a goddess above the god. All of these things involved nuances and subtleties to which he would have been oblivious a year ago, Blaise knew — but the primal inferno of a battlefield was no place for subtleties. They didn't matter here. Weapons mattered, and training, and the will of the men who wielded them. And, in the end, the numbers on either side.

It would take a miracle, he thought, immersing himself in battle that winter afternoon like a man with a bitter thirst to slake. Blaise had always given Corannos his faith and he was coming, amazingly, to have some sense of the very different power of Rian, but he still didn't believe in miracles. The men and women he knew — and he included himself in this — were simply not deserving of such holy intercession. He hewed and slashed with his sword, a mortal man dealing in death, knowing that he was killing men he'd fought beside at Iersen Bridge and many times before. It was only with an effort of will that he was able to keep the meaning of that from breaking through to undo him entirely.

Square on in that windswept valley the armies of two countries crashed into each other in the clear light of mid-winter in Arbonne and Blaise knew that the weight of numbers was going to push them back. Back to the lake, to the edge of the castle moat, to the ending of their lives. Courage and skill and the rightness of a cause were sometimes not enough. They were seldom enough, he thought, tasting that truth like poison in his mouth: Corannos and Rian had shaped a world in which this was so. He was aware of death hovering in the blue brightness of the sky, preparing to descend, to cloak the world in darkness.

He had a sudden, searing image in his mind of night fires on Rian's Isle when their army was destroyed. He saw Signe de Barbentain, small, elegant, proud, bound and burning on one of his father's pyres, her mouth open in a soundless scream, her white hair in flames. A rage rose up in him then, a fury of denial, and the numbness that had fallen upon him like a blanket of fog when Ranald died was finally pushed away.

Blaise looked around, as if seeing the field clearly for the first time and in doing so he pushed past his inward griefs and accepted the role that lay waiting for him, the burden that had been his from the moment he'd claimed a crown.

He was commanding the left flank; with him were Rudel and Fulk and the barons and corans of southern Arbonne, including Mallin de Baude. Bertran and Valery held the centre, mostly with the men of Talair, and Thierry de Carenzu, with the corans of the east, was on the right. As best he could tell — eyes narrowed in the sunlight — they were still holding ground on all fronts. He could see Ademar in the forefront of the Gorhaut army, not far from Bertran in fact, though there were hundreds of men between them. Galbert was beside the king, a black mace in his right hand. Even as Blaise watched, his father leaned over in his saddle, huge, powerful, to hammer the mace into the skull of an Arbonnais pikeman. The man didn't even have a chance to scream as his head was crushed. He crumpled to the earth like so much spilled grain.

Men died in battle. People one had known and loved died in battles. You could not let that make you falter. They were holding ground, but they were not going to do so for much longer. Blaise, in the grip of a sudden clarity, made his decision.

And that same swift clear-headedness made him understand that this, too, was one of the things that came with the role on the world's stage that he'd claimed for himself: one gave orders in a battle such as this that could shape the destinies of nations.

It was true, it was about to be made true even now, and Blaise realized that he would have to accept that weight because his only other alternative was to withdraw into the shadows and die, betraying all those who believed in him. He made his choice then, and prepared himself to answer for it before the god when his hour came.

Drawing back sharply from the crush at the front of the lines he wheeled his horse over towards Fulk de Savaric, gesturing urgently. Fulk saw him coming and drew back as well.

'We can't do this much longer!' Rosala's brother shouted over the roar of combat. A man beside them fell, dropping his sword, clutching with both hands at an arrow in his throat.

'I know! Listen to me! Pull your men back and try to flank around. We'll hold as best we can. Get in behind Ademar if you can! Drive towards Bertran.'

'You can't hold here without us!' Fulk screamed. There was blood on his face, dripping into his yellow beard. Blaise couldn't tell if it was Fulk's own blood or someone else's.

'Have to try!' he shouted. 'Nothing else is going to break this up, and we can't keep fighting twice our numbers face to face.'

He had another thought then and looked away from Fulk towards the front again. He saw that Rudel was looking back at him, waiting. They had fought beside each other often enough; it wasn't really a great surprise. He saw his friend arch his eyebrows in silent enquiry, and Blaise nodded his head.

'Do it!' he cried, and knew that Rudel understood. His friend turned to a mercenary beside him and spoke a one word command.

A moment later there came a fierce, ragged shout from Fulk's men of Savaric as over their heads, gripped by that coran beside Rudel, the banner of the kings of Gorhaut rose up to fly beside the standard of Arbonne. *Two of us under the same banner*, Blaise thought. *Will it matter?*

A moment later he realized, with a quickening of his heart, that it might.

'Look!' Fulk shouted, pointing.

Blaise had already seen.

'*To me!*' he roared, pulling at his horse's reins, driving towards the standard Rudel had raised. '*In the name of Gorhaut, to me, men of Garsenc!*'

And as he screamed it at the top of his voice, he saw that there were indeed corans of his family estate, from the company behind his father and Ademar, pulling back from the fight in the centre and making their way, swords uplifted in salute, towards him.

Ranald's last shouted words *had* been heard, Blaise realized. And these men would have watched one of their own, Bergen of Garsenc, felled by a Portezzan as he prepared to ride back to them. And sure, *surely*, there would be those among the corans he had grown up among who had not been filled with joy at the prospect of burning women and mutilating helpless men.

He saw his father turn, alerted by a change in the sounds behind him. Galbert visibly checked at what he saw, then his own magnificent, stentorian voice rang out over the battlefield like the voice of doom, of a god, 'Stop those men!' he trumpeted. 'There are traitors among us!'

Confusion reigned. Some corans turned obediently in the Gorhaut ranks and began slashing at others who, moments before, had been fighting beside them. In front of Blaise the warriors of Gorhaut turned towards the centre to see what was happening, and in the respite shaped by that brief hesitation the men of Arbonne pushed forward beside Rudel's hard-bitten mercenaries, fighting now beneath the incongruous banner of the kings of Gorhaut. Blaise saw Mallin de Baude drive forward, first man into the gap.

'Go quickly now!' he cried over his shoulder to Fulk. 'We have a chance!'

With no more words spoken, Fulk de Savaric barked orders to his captains and moments later — more swiftly than Blaise could have hoped — the men of Savaric had peeled back and begun swinging south towards the lake in a desperate attempt at flanking around.

It was going to *have* to be swift, Blaise realized grimly, as nearly half the men in their sector melted away. Rudel looked back at him, grasped what was happening and, improbably, grinned.

'It this some sort of vengeance upon me?' he cried, leaning over in his saddle towards Blaise. 'For youthful sins I have long forgotten?'

'What else could possibly be guiding me now?' Blaise shouted back, moving his horse up beside his friend. Rudel laughed aloud. Then he stopped laughing, for the warriors of Gorhaut, seeing empty space open up before them and the numbers of their foes suddenly diminished, returned, with a collective cry and a new urgency, to their own assault.

After that there was little chance to do so much as look up, let alone assert leadership on any grand scale. Battles were always like this at their peak, breaking down into islands of desperately close combat, the screams and the sweaty press of men and horses, the living and dying and dead, preventing any chance at grasping an overall picture. Blaise lost sight of Mallin. He knew Bertran must be holding in the centre, or they would by now have been under hopeless pressure from that side. He knew this had to be true, but he couldn't spare a moment to look up and see.

The world shrank to the smallest, bloodiest dimensions, to a sword lifting and falling, the scream of a dying horse, the jarring impact of his blade on armour or the different sucking feel as it bit into flesh, an awareness of Rudel on his left side and another man, a mercenary he didn't know beside him on the right. When that man fell, moments later, another coran pushed forward to take his place. It was Hirnan of Baude, and Blaise belatedly understood that they were guarding him. That he was no longer just one of the captains here. He was the man in whose name the banner above them was flying.

That was the moment, really, when Blaise was made aware of what being a king might entail. The knowledge came to him on that desperate battlefield as a weight and an exaltation, both. The rash folly he had begun in Tavernel last summer and then continued in the fall — claiming a crown at the Lussan Fair — became, in that valley north of Talair, something tangible and fully incarnate for him.

A man with an axe appeared in front of him on a dark grey horse; Rudel Correze, with an elegant, almost casual movement in the saddle, slid his sword into the man's throat between armour and helm and Blaise watched him fall. Hirnan immediately drove his horse forward to cut off the space in front of Blaise.

They were guarding him, he understood, at risk of their own lives.

In that instant, utterly calm in the midst of wild battle, with a dead man trampled into the ground at his feet, Blaise de Garsenc came into his true awareness of power. On a field of death, fighting his countrymen on the day his father had killed his brother, Blaise realized that he really did know what he wanted for Gorhaut, and that he thought he could achieve it if given but half a chance.

He did not expect, pushing forward between Rudel and Hirnan, feeling his horse's hooves unavoidably trample the body below, to live long enough to do anything about it.

Later he would remember how that last bleak thought had come to him even before he heard Rudel, his companion on so many battlefields, speak a malediction of bitter ferocity, and Blaise, looking over to the west, saw what his friend had seen and felt something colder than winter enter his heart with the awareness of treachery and of the final, inexorable revenge of the past.

On the forested ridge of land west of the valley a company of men could be seen at the edge of the trees. A very large company, arrayed in precise rows, well armed and armoured. Above their heads were flying not one but two banners. One was a green device Blaise had come to know well in Arbonne. The other was that of the kings of Gorhaut.

Urté de Miraval had come to war, and their worst nightmares were made real as those grim, meticulous ranks began to move down the slope. Fulk de Savaric, Blaise saw, had somehow managed to fight his way around by the shore of the lake. He and his men had turned north and were even now poised to turn and strike at Ademar's centre from behind.

It didn't matter any more. They were going to be annihilated, their backs completely exposed to the men of Miraval, who were gathering speed now as they swept into the valley. If Fulk turned to face Urté they would be equally helpless before Ademar's corans. Blaise had sent those men to the worst sort of death.

With their own soon to follow. Blaise looked a long way over then — there seemed to be a respite here on their flank as men in both armies turned to see what was happening — and he picked out the fiercely battling figure of Bertran de Talair. Once he had thought the man no more than a lord who debased his rank by consorting with singers and frivolously pursuing any woman who came under his blue gaze. These things were true, there was no gainsaying them, but there was nothing in the man he saw just then that could have been called less than lordly as Bertran fought for his land in the face of betrayal and what would have to be the knowledge, bitter as poison, that Urté de Miraval was the source of their undoing.

With a horrified fascination — the way one watches a coiled snake before it strikes — Blaise saw the corans of Miraval, fifteen hundred of them, sweep down from their ridge behind the majestic figure of the duke. He saw them come up beside the first of Fulk's wheeling, scrambling men, swords and spears and axes uplifted and levelled and poised.

And he saw them go straight past those desperate men, no horse or man of Urté's company so much as breaking stride, to crash, with a sound and an impact that seemed to shake the earth, full into the rear of the army of Gorhaut.

In the instant before that impact, just as he realized, with a wild surging in his heart, exactly what was happening, Blaise heard his father's voice rise up again — to tower like a presence over the valley, crying the name of the god in his need. There was no answer though, no reply from Corannos in the cold blue sky. Only the huge thunder of hooves on hard earth and the screams of terrified men as the racing corans of Miraval smashed into the rear of Ademar's men, with the warriors of Savaric turning swiftly to join them and Bertran's men coming forward from the other side, roaring in exultation, to pincer them mercilessly.

'*He fooled them!*' Rudel screamed in Blaise's ear. 'He fooled them completely!' It was true, Blaise saw: the disruption in the Gorhaut ranks caused by the first Garsenc defections earlier had turned into utter chaos. Corans of Garsenc Castle, men he had known all his life, were joining with Fulk de Savaric now, closing in upon Ademar's own guards even as he watched.

'Come on!' Blaise cried. In front of them the men on their flank were falling back in panic, fearing to be cut off. Blaise drove his horse recklessly forward into the gap between the armies. It seemed to him as if something oppressive had been lifted from his shoulders, a weight from the darkness of the past. He felt light, invulnerable, and he wanted Ademar. He didn't even look back to see if anyone was following him. He knew now that they would be; he was their leader, and a chance, a hope, a promise like a lantern's glow seen from afar in a night forest, had appeared for them where none could ever have been foreseen.

He was driving in to the centre, straight towards Ademar, and so was actually quite close when he saw Duke Urté de

Miraval meet the king of Gorhaut in the midst of the roiling
tumult.

†

Ademar feels as if he might actually choke in the heat of his
fury. It is hard to breathe. Even with the chill of the winter
afternoon he is sweltering in his armour and helm. He knows
it is rage that is doing this to him. He is almost dizzied by
wrath. First the Garsenc betrayals: it has *always* been the de
Garsenc who have balked him, he thinks, slashing savagely at
a Miraval foot-soldier, almost severing the man's head with
the blow. Swearing, he drags his sword free. He cannot
believe, he cannot *believe*, that with victory so easy, so assured,
those Garsenc corans have been mad enough to turn upon
their own ranks. Surely any sane man with a sense of self-
preservation would have known better than to rally to that
doomed pretender's pennon!

That was before he realized that Fulk de Savaric —
another traitor, *another* man who ought to have been by his
side! — had somehow managed to bring his company around
behind him. There had been some real danger there, and
Ademar was snapping urgent commands when one of his
captains pointed triumphantly upwards to the west, and the
king of Gorhaut, looking there, had felt his choler recede,
eased and cooled by something near to joy. He had never
been afraid, he was not a man inclined to fears, but with the
sight of the Miraval corans on that ridge beneath the banner
of Gorhaut, Ademar laughed aloud, tasting the sweetness
to come.

He had a few moments to think that way, to watch the
well-trained men of Duke Urté start smoothly down the slope,
gaining speed, bringing the end of this war with them and the
final exaltation of Gorhaut.

Then it all went wrong; wildly, desperately wrong.

There was one moment, when Urté de Miraval whipped
his warhorse straight past the corans of Savaric, when Ademar did know fear — just for an instant. Then he felt the
impact of those thundering Miraval horsemen as they
smashed into the rear of his ranks, driving men back before
them like so many helpless children.

Now, buffeted in the midst of a nightmare chaos, rage is foaming like a river in flood through the king of Gorhaut. Ademar hears his High Elder trumpet his call to the god and he curses in his heart the very name of Galbert de Garsenc who has brought him to this, who persuaded him that the duke of Miraval, whose overtures to them in the past few days were direct and explicit, was a necessary man to enlist in their cause, to act as first regent of Arbonne after their conquest.

It was a trap. It is clear now that everything Urté did was a trap, and they are in the jaws of it, between the corans of Talair and Miraval, with Fulk de Savaric and the renegades of Garsenc coming hard against them. Ademar lashes his horse westward, screaming in fury, and as men fall back before him he comes swiftly up to the man he needs to kill now, right now, *immediately*, before this battle turns hopelessly against them. He is aware, vaguely, that his own corans have also fallen back, that a ring of men has formed around the two of them, as if even in the midst of war there is a sense that this combat must take place. And so Ademar of Gorhaut begins his second single-challenge of this day.

Wordlessly, for he is beyond words now and none could be heard in any case, he swings his sword in a huge, sweeping arc towards the helmeted head of the duke of Miraval. He misses, as Urté, unexpectedly quick for a man of his size and past sixty years of age, ducks beneath the blade. A second later Ademar rocks wildly in the saddle as he absorbs a colossal blow on his own helm. He feels the world go momentarily black. His helmet has been knocked askew; he cannot see. There is a sticky, warm running of blood down the side of his face.

Roaring like a man beset by furies, Ademar hurls away his shield and rips his helm off with both hands, feeling a tearing and then a fierce pain at his left ear. He throws the helmet at de Miraval's face and then the king of Gorhaut follows that up with the hardest blow with a sword he has ever delivered in all his days.

The descending blade catches the armour of the duke just where it shields neck and shoulder and it drives straight down through the mesh, biting deeply into flesh. Ademar sees, through the blurring and darkening of his own vision, how the duke of Miraval lurches heavily over to one side in his saddle, and knowing the cursed, deceiving old man is falling, is as good as dead already, he rips free his blade, nonetheless, to blot him out of life.

The king of Gorhaut never does see the arrow that kills him.

The arrow that comes down out of the empty heavens above to take him in the eye — exactly as his own father was killed two years ago among the ice and the piled bodies by Iersen Bridge.

The king of Gorhaut, dead instantly, never does see that the shaft of that arrow is a deep crimson hue, like blood. Nor does he ever realize, as others do soon after, coming up to where the dead king lies on the ground beside the mortally wounded figure of Urté de Miraval, that the feathers with which that arrow has been fletched are — a thing without known precedent — the feathers of an owl, crimson-hued as well.

Men see these things and cannot understand them, nor can they comprehend whence that terrifying, death-dealing arrow might have been loosed, to have fallen, as it truly seems, straight down upon the king from the sky. Corans in both armies can be seen to be making the warding sign against darkness and the unknown.

The king of Gorhaut is dead of a crimson arrow fallen from the heavens, fletched with the feathers of an owl. Even the warriors of Gorhaut know what bird is sacred to Rian. The tale of an immortal goddess's vengeance for her servants defiled and slain begins to sweep immediately across the valley. It will not stop there. The story has a long way to travel. Such tales, of the deaths of kings, always do.

†

After that it became easy, in fact. Easier than it ought to have been, Blaise thought. At Iersen Bridge, King Duergar had died yet Gorhaut had still prevailed on a bitter field. The death of a king need not mean utter disarray among the ranks of his army.

That afternoon, though, it did. Blaise could have offered many reasons why, and any and all of those reasons might have been a part of it, but the truth — brilliantly clear in the afternoon light — was that the army of Gorhaut was undone from the time Urté de Miraval appeared against them and that red arrow came down to kill their king.

Blaise, battling in towards Bertran, began to recognize individual men in both armies nearer to the centre of the fighting. *Sunset*, he had said to Ademar. He had been denied that battle after all. Looking around, he remembered that there was someone else on this field he wanted for his own. Then he saw that man, some distance away, and realized that this, too, was going to be denied him.

Bertran de Talair came up to the Portezzan, Borsiard d'Andoria, on a tummock of grass in the midst of the side-slipping centre of the battle. It was clear that words were exchanged, but Blaise was too far away to hear them. Then he watched Bertran, who had set out on the road of a fighter more than twenty years ago after Aelis de Miraval had died in her husband's castle, dispatch the lord of Andoria with a precision that almost made a mockery of the notion of single combat. Two blows on the forehand, a feint, and then, slipping past the parry, a straight-ahead thrust that took Borsiard in the throat. It was more an execution than a duel, and when it was over Blaise's first thought was that Lucianna had just been widowed again.

His second thought, as he saw the Andorians begin, predictably, to throw down their weapons and hastily submit themselves as prisoners to the nearest of Bertran's men, was that he had something to do now that was going to be harder than any combat had been. He looked quickly around for Rudel and realized that his friend was no longer by his side. He had no time to wonder about that. Even as he watched, the battle of Lake Dierne was becoming a slaughter.

And he had to stop it. Stop it, even though the men of Arbonne could see the severed heads spitted on pikes at the back of the Gorhaut ranks, could still see what a hideous ruin had been made of the singer named Aurelian, and would all be carrying within them anguished images of women burning through the north of their land. They would not be inclined to clemency and moderation in this moment when certain defeat had turned into victory. Every man in the army of Arbonne would know what his fate and that of his family would have been had Gorhaut triumphed here.

Bertran was going to be no help to him now, Blaise saw. The duke had turned from his ruthless dispatching of Borsiard and, moving straight past the surrendering Portezzans, was cutting a deadly swath through the nearest men of Gorhaut. Valery, beside him, was doing exactly the same thing.

Urging his horse after them, Blaise lifted his voice over the screams of the dying and the fierce, wild shouts of the corans of Arbonne: 'Enough!' he cried. 'Bertran, it is enough!'

Valery slowed, and turned. The duke did not hear him or, if he did, paid no heed at all. Over to his left, behind the Gorhaut centre, Blaise saw Fulk de Savaric lift his head to his cry, raise a hand in response, and then turn to relay urgent orders to his men. The corans of Miraval were still attacking, driving in to meet Bertran, with panic-stricken soldiers of Gorhaut spinning and wheeling between them, implacable foes on all sides now, and men from their own ranks gone over to their enemies.

Blaise came up to the nearest of the Garsenc corans, the ones who had rallied to him when Rudel first raised the banner. 'No more killing!' he ordered the nearest of them. 'Make them throw down their weapons! They won't be killed if they do!' He was almost certain that was true, but not entirely so. There was a mood in the army of Arbonne that was near to being out of control.

He moved on, churning in the wake of the duke of Talair. He understood very well what had happened to Bertran, how battle-fury could overmaster the most clear-sighted of men — and he also knew that Bertran de Talair had more reason than a man should ever need to be killing men of Gorhaut just now.

In the end it was Thierry de Carenzu, over on the right flank, nearest the severed heads and the maimed, dead troubadour, who had the horns sounded to put a halt to the slaughter of men.

It was Thierry who did it, Blaise would always remember that; he himself was of Gorhaut, he could not have halted the army of Arbonne that day.

Even Bertran pulled up his horse when he heard the high clear sweet notes of those horns rising above the valley. It was music of a sort, among the dying and the dead. Blaise, forcing his way forward, was finally able to catch up with him.

'Bertran stop, you *must* stop. These are only soldiers now. Farmers and villagers. Ademar is dead, it is over!' The duke of Talair turned then to look at him and Blaise was sobered and chilled by what he saw in the other man's eyes.

'But I did not kill him,' Bertran said slowly, as if in a trance. There was something terrible in the words.

Drawing a deep breath, Blaise said carefully, 'Nor did I, with as much cause, perhaps. It must not be allowed to matter, Bertran, for either of us. We have won. And look, the men of Garsenc are forcing the others to surrender.'

It was true. The soldiers of Gorhaut, the crusading army of the god, could be seen throwing down their weapons even as they spoke. Blaise saw Thierry riding towards them. He shouted as he approached: 'We must not kill unarmed men, Bertran.'

'Will you tell me why? I seem to have forgotten.' Bertran's eyes were still wild, lost.

'No you haven't,' said Valery from behind his cousin. They turned to him; his own features were calm again, though Blaise could see that that control was costing Valery a great deal. 'You haven't forgotten at all. You just want to forget. So do I. Oh, Bertran, so do I, but if we do that we become what we have just defeated.'

Blaise had said the same thing once, in the serenity of a council chamber. This was a battlefield, and there was a kind of madness in the blue eyes of the man Valery was addressing. Bertran stared coldly for a long moment at his cousin. Then Blaise saw him shake his head several times, as if trying to slip free of something. He understood; he understood better than Bertran could have known, how hard it was to move past battle-rage to anything else at all.

But when Bertran turned back to him and to Thierry beside him, Blaise saw that the his expression was one he knew.

'Very well,' said the duke of Talair, 'we will accept their surrender. There is a last thing that is still be done, though it might grieve you, Blaise, I don't know.' He paused only briefly. 'Where is the High Elder of Gorhaut?'

Amazingly, Blaise had managed to push his father from his mind; or perhaps, given all that had now broken into fragments in the world, it wasn't so amazing after all. He turned towards the knot of men west of them, and standing in their midst — unhorsed but towering above even the tallest man there — he saw his father.

Galbert had removed his helm, or had had it taken from him. He stood bareheaded in the light of late afternoon. There was blood on his face and on his blue robe. A space had been cleared around him and, looking, Blaise realized belatedly where Rudel had gone. His friend was standing with Galbert inside that space, sword drawn, calmly levelling it at the man who, a little more than half a year ago, had offered him a quarter of a million in gold to kill Bertran de Talair.

This was, Blaise understood finally, one more score being settled, as the sun moved west in the winter sky. He wondered why his father had not killed himself rather than be given over in this fashion to his enemies. It was only a brief thought though, that one. Galbert was not a man to take such a way out, and it was, in any event, an action forbidden by the god.

It seemed to have grown quiet in the valley. Some clouds appeared in the northwest. He watched them move across the sun and then away. It was colder now, late in the day, and in the aftermath of so much exertion. It seemed to be over though; the clash of weapons had stopped. Men were moaning, crying out in pain from many parts of the field. That would go on a long time, Blaise knew. He shivered.

'I have a cloak for you.' It was Hirnan. Blaise turned to look at the Arbonnais coran who had been guarding him all afternoon. They had gone to Rian's Island in the sea once, in springtime, to fetch a poet back. It had begun there; for Blaise it seemed to have begun there with the High Priestess in the wood, the dark hollows of her eyes, the white owl on her shoulder.

After a moment he nodded his head and Hirnan draped a heavy cloak of a dark purple hue over Blaise's shoulders. Blaise wondered where he'd got it; purple was the colour of kings. He had a suspicion though, a guess as to whence that cloak had come. And that thought made him turn for a moment, away from his father in the ring of swords, to look briefly at Thierry, and then away from him and all the others, back towards the isle in the lake where the women were.

†

It was just possible, now that the fighting had stopped, to make out individual figures in the valley across the water. Standing with others on the northern shore of the isle, Ariane could see her husband; from the way he sat his horse it seemed he was all right. Not far from Thierry she watched Hirnan of Baude lay the purple cloak she had entrusted to him over Blaise de Garsenc's shoulders, and she began to cry.

There was a great deal of weeping taking place now; they did not yet know how many had died, or who. The countess was not with them here on the strand; she had joined the priestesses and the priests in the temple for a service of thanksgiving. Ariane knew she ought to be with them, but her thoughts just now, since the blowing of the horns, were entirely of this world.

The small boats were crossing continuously back and forth across the choppy water; they had been doing so all through the battle. The last messenger had told them that the king of Gorhaut was dead, of a crimson arrow in the eye. No one knew who had shot that arrow, the priest said, kneeling on the sands of the goddess. The feathers, he said, had been those of an owl. The arrow had dropped straight down from the sky.

He had also told them that Urté de Miraval, who had saved them in the end, despite everything, was dying, if he was not already dead. And these last tidings, for Ariane, meant more than they did to anyone else on the isle or, indeed, anyone else alive.

They meant that the term of an oath she had kept since the end of her childhood was over, a secret she had sworn to keep was hers to offer to the world. And it was because of this that she was weeping on that shore, looking north to the valley, at the figure of her husband in his red surcoat and the tall man cloaked in purple beside him, and at the third, smaller man with the two of them, the one who had, so many years ago, surprised a travelling party among the elm trees she could see even now beside the arch to the west.

She moved away from the others on the strand, with-drawing into memory. There was another boat coming with even newer tidings now; the other women moved anxiously towards it. Ariane walked a distance west instead and stood alone, gazing at the other shore, the one nearest Miraval.

It had been winter then, too, she remembered, that night twenty-three years ago, with a rain wind lashing the trees and lake when she came to that shore in the dark of night. Twenty-three years, and oh, it was as yesterday if she let her mind go back. It was as fierce and hard and terrible as if she were standing there now, thirteen years old, an oath newly sworn, sobbing wildly with grief and terror as she stood on that strand in the shelter of the signal hut.

She had been a child when that night had begun. A quick, curious, overly indulged young girl. She had not been young any longer when that long night was done and she watched the pale sun finally come up across the lake and listened to water dripping mournfully from the trees all around.

She had kept her promise. All these years she had kept the promise sworn to her cousin Aelis, whom she had loved. She could see herself so clearly even now: the thin, shivering girl riding in a wild storm, white face and black hair lost in the darkness except when the lightning flashed. And she had been crying, crying in the cruel lashing of the rain. She was crying again now, all these long years after, weeping for inno-cence lost, for the dead of that night and the awful burden she had been given then and had carried all these years.

After a long time Ariane wiped her eyes and squared her shoulders and turned away from that western shore and its weight of memory. She was the duchess of Carenzu, queen of the Court of Love in Arbonne, a woman of power in the world, and there was a great deal to be done.

Starting with the ending of a silence.

Aelis, she thought, whispered it to herself actually; only the name, nothing more than that, realizing as she did so that it was a kind of letting go. That almost brought her tears again, but she held them back this time.

She went along the curving path to the temple and waited there for the slow, beautifully chanted service to come to an

end. Then, after it was done, in the privacy of a small room beside the dome, with a necessary economy of words but as much
gentleness as she could command amid the fevered emotions
of that day, she told the first person who needed to know.

Afterwards, going back to the strand alone, she had herself rowed across the water into the wind, wrapping herself in
her crimson cloak against the chill at the end of day, and once
ashore she went looking for the second person who had to be
told before the whole world knew.

He had left the valley by then, they told her, and so, with
time only for a brief embrace of her husband and a whispered
word, she took horse to go after him. On the way, as she realized where it was he had gone, where she was following, she
began to cry again, unable to help herself, the tears cold on
her cheeks as the sun sank lower in the west, red as a fire.

†

Blaise had gone with Bertran and Thierry to where Urté de
Miraval lay dying on the ground, a folded cloak under his head
and another one, heavy and lined with fur, covering his body.
Urté was very pale, and Blaise saw at a glance that the cloths
they had used to try to stanch his bleeding were soaked
through. He had seen this before; it would not be long.

Urté was still conscious, though, and there was a hard
glint of triumph in his eyes. Thierry hesitated beside him and
then stepped carefully back and away so that Bertran de Talair
could stand alone next to Urté. The silence that followed was
taut as a drawn bowstring.

Another hesitation — nothing was being done easily
here, Blaise knew — and then Bertran knelt beside the
older man.

'We have won,' he said calmly. 'Your decision to join us
after all was what turned the battle.'

Urté de Miraval laughed then, a terrible sound, and the
movement started another flowing of blood. In obvious pain
he shook his head. '*After all?* You don't understand, do you?
There was no decision to make. We staged that scene in Barbentain when I walked out.'

Blaise felt his mouth fall open. He closed it with a snap.
He heard Thierry de Carenzu make a small sound.

'We?' said Bertran.

'The countess and I. I advised her the night before to name you leader of the army. We agreed that I would storm from the room and contact Ademar the next day.'

'Oh, sweet Rian, I don't believe it.' It was Thierry, the words like a prayer.

'Why not?' said the dying man, prosaically. 'We were going to be outnumbered, we had to devise some trap for them. It seems that it took two of the older generation to do it. The younger ones didn't have any ideas at all, did you?' He did not smile.

There was another silence.

'None at all,' said Bertran at length. 'I am astonished the countess didn't tell me.'

'I asked her not to,' Urté said. 'I told her you might alter your strategy, knowing what was coming. Make a move that might have alerted them that something was amiss. That was the reason I gave her.'

'It wasn't really the reason, was it?'

Urté de Miraval did smile then. 'Of course it wasn't,' he said.

Bertran slowly shook his head. 'As it happens, I had no strategies today. The battle started too soon.'

'I know. That is why we were late.'

Silence again. The westering sun sent a reddened light along the valley. Urté made a sudden, wry face that Blaise knew was that of a strong man wrestling with great pain.

'What shall I say to you?' asked Bertran de Talair.

A gasp that might have been laughter again. 'Spare me,' Urté whispered. But a moment later Blaise saw him turn his head a little so he was looking directly at Bertran. Urté opened his mouth and then closed it, as if wrestling with something inwardly, but then, very clearly, he said, 'I did not kill her. Or the child.'

Bertran became absolutely still, his face white as the dying man's.

'I took the child from her,' Urté said, his eyes holding Bertran's, 'after she told me . . . what she told me. I took it downstairs to the kitchen where there was a fire. It was very cold, there was a storm that night. You weren't here, you will not remember. I had the priestess thrown out of the castle. I left the child with the women in the kitchen. I didn't want Aelis to have him . . . after what she'd said, and I wasn't going to rear him as my own. I might have decided to kill him, I might have sent him away where he'd never be known or found. I was not thinking clearly and I knew it; I needed time. That child, if he had been mine, was heir to Miraval and Barbentain both, he would have ruled Arbonne.'

'But instead?' Bertran's voice was so low it could barely be heard. Blaise saw that he had laced his fingers tightly together.

'But instead Aelis was dead when I went back to her room. I was going up to tell her she would never see her child, that no one would ever know who he was, even if I chose to let him live. I wanted to . . . hurt her so much for what she had done. She cheated me, though. She was already dead when I returned. When I went back down again, after, I had them give me the child. I took him alone into the great hall and sat by the fire, holding him. I could see he was not strong. It wasn't very long before he died. They rarely live, born so soon. He was two months early.'

'I know. That's why I wasn't here.' Silence again. Blaise could hear the wind whistling down the valley and the cries of wounded and dying men. Overhead, very high, a flock of birds cut across the sun, heading south, late in the year. He could see that some of the priests and priestesses had crossed from the isle to tend to the injured. fires were being lit on the battlefield. He shivered again, in his heavy cloak.

'You might have told me this,' Bertran said, finally.

'Why?' Urté said. 'To ease your mind? Why would I have wanted to do that? I was happy to have you wondering if he was alive — that meant you could never kill me, didn't it?' That thin smile again. But after a moment his expression altered and he added, 'You wouldn't have believed me in any case. You know that.'

Slowly Bertran shook his head. 'No. I wouldn't have. I was almost certain you had killed them both.'

'I know. Almost certain, not quite. I enjoyed your thinking that. I hope it was in you like poison all these years.'

'It was. Like poison. All these years.'

'She was my wife,' said Urté de Miraval. 'What did you think I would do when I found out?'

Bertran was very still, his head lowered. When he spoke, it was in a voice scraped raw. 'I loved her. I have never stopped loving her. You never did, my lord. For you this has been about nothing but pride all these years.'

With a tremendous effort Urté managed to lift himself on one elbow. 'That would have been enough,' he said. 'More than enough. But you are wrong again. You have always been wrong about that, you and everyone else.' He paused to draw a difficult, gasping breath; blood was seeping from his wound. 'It was Aelis who didn't love me, not the other way around. I could never write songs, you see. I am glad we have won. Rian shelter this land of Arbonne forever in her arms.'

Slowly then, with a soldier's grace and considerable courage in the face of mortal pain, he lowered himself to the cold ground, and his eyes closed as he died.

Bertran remained on his knees beside the body for a long time. No one else moved or spoke. When Bertran finally rose, he turned to Thierry de Carenzu.

'May I leave what remains with you?' he asked, with toneless formality.

'Of course,' said the other man.

They watched as the duke of Talair walked back to where his horse was being held by a coran. Bertran mounted up without assistance and rode slowly from the valley, west, towards the avenue of trees that led to the arch.

Valery made an awkward movement as if minded to follow but then checked himself. Blaise, looking over at him, saw a huge, vivid grief stamped on the coran's normally calm features. He walked over to stand close by Valery, not touching him, but wanting to be near. Then, a moment later, he realized that Thierry was looking at him with unexpected compassion and he realized what was left to come. Blaise closed his eyes, and it was Valery who reached out and touched his shoulder briefly.

Blaise looked at Thierry de Carenzu. 'Have I the right to ask that it be done cleanly?' he said quietly.

'It will be,' said Ariane's husband. 'For you, and for ourselves, because of what we are, what we refuse to become.'

Blaise nodded his head. Thierry turned and Blaise followed him across the darkening field to where his father was still standing, ringed by men with swords.

'I am holding this man,' said Rudel Correze, speaking clearly and with unwonted gravity as they approached, 'for the judgment of Arbonne.'

'Final judgment,' said Thierry, 'belongs to Rian and Corannos, not to us, but punishment is, indeed, our duty now. Not for acts of war. Ransom and release could be granted if it were only those. For what has been done to the priestesses, though, this man must surely die.'

No one spoke. Only the cries of the wounded and the sound of the wind marred the stillness. There were fires all over the valley now, more for warmth than anything else; the light was still clear though the day was waning.

'Will you deny that the burning of women was by your command?' Thierry asked of the man in the ring.

'Hardly,' said Galbert de Garsenc.

No more than that. The High Elder stood, blood on his smooth, handsome face and on his blue robes, surrounded by mortal foes at the end of his life, and it seemed to his younger son as if he had, even now, nothing but contempt for any man here.

'Out of respect for your son, we will grant you a death by arrows,' Thierry said stolidly. Not far away, on his wheeled platform, Aurelian the singer had been unbound. Someone had covered his body with a cloak.

'I would like,' said Galbert de Garsenc, 'a few moments with my son before I die.' Blaise felt his mouth go dry. There was a silence. 'This is a last request,' added the High Elder of Gorhaut.

Thierry turned to Blaise, so did Rudel, concern in the eyes of both, a desire to shelter him from this. Blaise shook his head. He cleared his throat. 'I believe it is a fair request. One that we can honour.' He looked carefully at Thierry. 'If that is acceptable to you?'

Thierry nodded slowly. Rudel still looked as if he would protest, and Blaise heard Valery behind him murmur something fierce under his breath, but the duke of Carenzu, with a wave of his arm, motioned the circle of guards to draw back.

When they had done so Blaise walked forward. The ring
of men parted to let him through.

'It seems,' said his father calmly as he came up, 'that I
misjudged Urté de Miraval.' He might have been discussing
the wrong track a hunt had taken, or some mistaken crop rota-
tion on the Garsenc lands.

'He was hardly likely to join you after women were
burned.'

Galbert shrugged. 'Was that it, do you think? Did he
change his mind, or was it planned?'

'Planned,' said Blaise. 'By him and the countess. No one
else knew.'

'Clever, then,' said his father. He sighed. 'Ah, well, at
least I have lived long enough to know my son will rule in
Gorhaut.'

Blaise laughed bitterly. 'With so much aid and nurture
from you.'

'Well, of course,' said Galbert. 'I have been working
towards this for years.'

Blaise stopped laughing. 'That,' he said harshly, 'is a lie.'
Something hard and awkward seemed suddenly to have
lodged itself in his chest. He swallowed with difficulty.

'Is it?' said Galbert placidly. 'You are supposed to be the
clever one. Think, Blaise.'

He couldn't remember the last time his father had called
him by name.

'What is there to think about?' he snapped. 'You showed
your devotion to your family with Rosala and now here with
Ranald. You killed your son.'

'I gave him life and I took it away,' said Galbert, still
mildly, 'though I was sorry to have to do it. He was worthless
as a man until the end, but he was about to undo my one
chance to cleanse this land.'

'Of course. *That* is what you have been working towards
all these years.'

'Among other things. I would hardly have been worth
much myself if I had only one purpose in life. I wanted
Arbonne scourged if it could be done, I wanted a son of mine
on the throne of Gorhaut if it could be done. I never
expected to have both, but I did see reason to hope for one
or the other.'

'You are lying,' Blaise said again, hearing the note of desperation in his voice and fighting to control it. 'Why are you doing this? We know what you wanted: you intended me to follow you into the service of the god.'

'But naturally. You were the younger son, where else should I place you? Ranald was to become king.' Galbert shook his head, as if Blaise were being unexpectedly obtuse. 'Then you balked me, not for the first time or the last, and a little later it became clear that Ranald was . . . what he was.'

'You made him that.'

Again Galbert shrugged. 'If he could not deal with me he could not have dealt with kingship. You seemed to have found a way to do both. After I managed to drive you away with the Treaty of Iersen Bridge.'

Blaise felt himself losing colour. 'You are now going to tell me — '

'That I had a number of reasons for that treaty. Yes, I am. I did. *Think*, Blaise. Money for this war and a dagger at Ademar's back among the dispossessed of the north. *And* I finally made you leave Gorhaut, to go where you could become a focus for those who might oppose Ademar. And me,' he added as an afterthought.

'Incidentally,' Galbert went on, still in that same flat, calm manner, 'you are going to need a great deal of money to retake the northern marches, especially after our losses today. Fortunately Lucianna d'Andoria is a widow again. I was planning to have Borsiard killed here if no one in your army managed to do it. I saw her as a possible bride for Ranald if events fell out that way. You'll have to marry her now, which I know will make you almost as happy as it makes her father. With his daughter a queen he might even forego bringing her home to his own bed at intervals.' Galbert smiled; Blaise felt slightly faint. 'Watch him though, watch Massena Delonghi closely. Between the Correze and Delonghi banks, however, you should be able to deal with Valensa withholding the rest of the payments they owe by the terms of the treaty.'

Blaise felt his head beginning to ache, as if he were absorbing blows.

'You *are* lying, aren't you? Tell me why? What does it gain you now, at this point, to try to make me believe you planned all of this?'

'I didn't plan it all, Blaise, don't be a fool. I am a mortal servant of Corannos, not a god. After you left home for Göt-zland and Portezza I thought Fulk de Savaric and some of the other northern barons would send men after you with an offer of kingship. I didn't expect you to step forward yourself the way you did. I didn't know you had so much . . . rashness in you. I did consider that you might end up in Arbonne at some point, if only because you knew I would be coming here, but I didn't know how much . . . influence they would have on you. That, I will admit, has been a surprise.'

'Ademar,' said Blaise, still struggling. 'You did everything for him. You even tried to give him Rosala.'

His father's expression was contemptuous. 'I did nothing for Ademar but offer him rope for his hanging. He was never worth more than that. He was an instrument that would let me take Arbonne for the god. That is all.' He shrugged again. 'We seem to have failed in that. It is my grief as I die. I really thought we could not lose. In which case I expected the Cor-reze boy would take you away from here back to Portezza, and in time I might yet achieve both halves of my dream. Ademar would never have been able to hold Arbonne — not after what I intended to do here.' His beautiful voice, thought Blaise, was so seductively lucid. 'As for Rosala, really Blaise — that was to goad the barons further against him — and you, if you needed a further spur, and it was only to be *after* she'd borne her Garsenc child. Tell me, the boy, Cadar, he *is* yours isn't he?'

Blaise felt his hands beginning to shake. 'Will you soil everything you touch in your life, even at the end? Can noth-ing be clean?'

'My death, or so I have been promised,' said Galbert drily. His mouth quirked. 'Come, Blaise, if it isn't yours I will die wondering whose it is. I did some investigating after Ranald had been married some time without an heir. I dis-covered that in all the years he was King's Champion, with women clawing each other in their lust for his bed, he never fathered a single child that I could trace. You will remember that my brother failed to produce an heir either. There may be a flaw in our seed, though I seem to have escaped it. Did you?'

Blaise looked down at his shaking hands. He said, 'Nothing ever mattered except the goals, did it? Nothing had meaning in itself. We were all tools, every one of us, Ademar, Rosala, Ranald and I, even when we were boys.'

His father made a flicking gesture of dismissal. 'What did you want, Blaise? Lullabies? A pat on the back? A doting father's grip on the shoulder when you did well?'

'Yes,' said Blaise then, as evenly as he could. 'Yes, that is what I suppose I wanted.'

For the first time Galbert seemed to hesitate. 'You have managed all right without them.'

'Yes,' said Blaise again, taking a breath and letting it out slowly. 'I managed.' He looked at his father. 'Had we leisure to discuss it I might tell you something of my own sense of things, but I don't think I want to.' He paused. He felt very calm now. 'Is there more, father?'

A silence, then slowly Galbert shook his head. For another moment they looked at each other, then Blaise turned and went from the ring. The soldiers parted to make way for him. He saw that a company of archers in the crimson colours of Carenzu had come up to join the others now. Beyond them he saw his horse, with Hirnan holding the reins. He walked over and mounted up and began riding away. He didn't look back.

Behind him he heard Rudel's voice asking a question, and Thierry responding, very clearly, then he heard an order spoken and he heard the arrows sing.

CHAPTER·19

Blaise was unaware for the first part of his ride that he was following the same path Bertran had taken leaving the field. Heading west towards the reddening disc of the sun, he came to the avenue of elms that led to the arch. He stopped and looked back then at the fires dotting the battlefield. He felt very strange. It came to him, almost as an incidental fact, that he was alone in the world now.

It was then, glancing down, that he saw the fresh tracks of a single horse and realized that Bertran had come this way before him. The duke would be alone now, too, he thought, in a different way and yet the same. Ariane had said something about that a long time ago: Bertran had lost, with Urté's death, the passion of hatred that had ordered and shaped his life for more than twenty years. Hatred, Blaise thought, could be as powerful as love, though the singers might try to tell you otherwise.

He twitched the reins of his horse and started forward again. He passed under the dwarfing curve of the arch, briefly chilled, even with his cloak, as he entered its shade, then he came out on the other side again into the fading light of the sun. Overhead another flock of birds was flying south on the wind. His father was dead. His brother was dead. He was likely to be crowned king of Gorhaut very soon. Cadar Ranald de Savaric was probably his son. He had been struggling with that thought since autumn. It was not a thing to be told. He knew Rosala well enough to know she never would.

And that, predictably, carried his thoughts to Aelis de Miraval who had died so long ago, and for love of whom two strong men had twisted and ruined their lives. He rode on

through the silence, following the survivor of those two men
through the bare winter vineyards with the autumn grapes
long harvested and the first buds a long way off. The vines
gave way to grass eventually and a forest rose up before him
as he rode and in time Blaise came to a small charcoal-burner's
cabin at the edge of that wood and saw a horse he knew teth-
ered outside.

Sitting in the doorway, where a woman might sit at nee-
dle and thread at day's ending to catch the last of the good
light, was Bertran de Talair.

The duke looked up as Blaise dismounted. His expression registered surprise but was not unwelcoming. Blaise had
not been sure about that. He saw the flask of seguignac
clasped in Bertran's hands. Memory came with that, too,
clear as a temple bell. A stairway in Castle Baude. The
moons passing from the narrow window. That flask passing
back and forth between the two of them. Blaise brooding
upon Lucianna Delonghi in bitterness, Bertran speaking of a
woman dead more than twenty years and not of the one
whose bed he had just left.

The duke saw him looking at the flask and lifted it.
'There's a little left,' he said.

'My father is dead,' said Blaise. He hadn't expected to say
that. 'Thierry's archers.'

Bertran's expressive face grew still. 'There isn't enough
seguignac for that, Blaise. Not nearly enough for the needs of
this day, but sit down, sit with me.'

Blaise walked across the grass and sat down beside the
duke in the doorway. He took the offered flask and drank. The
clean fire ran through him. He drank again, feeling the
warmth, and handed back the flask.

'It is over?' Bertran asked.

Blaise nodded. 'They will all have surrendered by now.'

Bertran looked at him, his blue eyes ringed by dark circles. 'You were trying to stop me there at the end, weren't you.
I heard you calling my name.'

Blaise nodded again.

'I don't think I would have stopped. I don't think I could
have, if Thierry hadn't blown the horns.'

'I know. I understand.'

'I'm not very proud of that.' Bertran took another short pull at the flask.

'This isn't a time to be judging yourself. Women were burned. And the two troubadours . . .'

Bertran closed his eyes and Blaise fell silent. The duke looked up again after a moment and handed back the flask. Blaise cradled it, not drinking. The seguignac was already making him light-headed.

'I have a question for you,' said Bertran de Talair.

'Yes?'

'Do you have any great objection if I ask your brother's wife to marry me? If Rosala will have me, I would like to raise Cadar as my own, as heir to Talair.'

A remarkable sensation of warmth began to spread through Blaise, and he knew it wasn't coming from the seguignac this time. He looked over at Bertran and smiled for what was surely the first time in that long day. 'I have no say at all in what Rosala does, but nothing I can imagine would please me more.'

'Really? Do you think she will accept?' Bertran's tone was suddenly diffident.

Blaise laughed aloud. It was a strange sound in that space at the edge of the woods. 'You are asking *me* for guidance on a woman's thoughts?'

For a moment Bertran was still, and then he too laughed, more softly. After that there was silence again for a time.

'My father,' said Blaise finally, needing to say it, 'my father told me that Ademar was only his tool for destroying Rian in Arbonne. That his other goal all these years had been to place me on the throne of Gorhaut.'

Bertran was still again, in that manner he had of careful, focused gravity. 'That does not surprise me,' he said.

Blaise sighed and looked down at the flask in his hands. 'I would rather not accept it as true.'

'I can see that. Don't tell anyone else then. This need only be ours.'

'Which doesn't make it less true, that he was shaping even this.'

Bertran shrugged. 'Partly, not entirely. He couldn't have guessed what would happen to you in Arbonne.'

'He admitted that, actually.'

'You see? Blaise, we are shaped by so many different things it frightens me sometimes.' Bertran hesitated. 'This was the cabin where I used to meet Aelis. Where my son was conceived.'

It was Blaise's turn to grow still. He understood, and was deeply moved by the awareness, that Bertran was offering this to him as a truth of the heart in exchange for his own.

'I'm sorry,' Blaise said. 'I didn't set out to follow you, I just saw your tracks. Shall I go?'

Bertran shook his head. 'You might give me that, though, if you aren't drinking.' Blaise handed over the flask. Bertran lifted it, the metal glinting in the light, and finished the last of the seguignac. 'I don't think,' he said, 'that I can possibly deal with anything more today than I already have.'

A moment later they heard the sound of another horse approaching and looked up to see Ariane riding alone towards them through the winter grass.

She came up to where they were sitting together in the doorway of the cabin. She did not move to dismount. They could see that she had been weeping though she was not doing so now. She took a ragged breath and let it slowly out.

'I swore an oath to my cousin Aelis the night she died,' she said without greeting, without preamble. Blaise saw that she was controlling herself only with a great effort; he felt Bertran grow rigid at his side. 'An oath from which I have been released by Urté's death today.'

She was looking at the duke, Blaise saw, and so he made to rise and said again, 'I should leave. This is not something I have a right to — '

'No,' said Ariane, her voice bloodless, her exquisite features nearly white. 'This does concern you, as it happens.' Even as she was speaking, Bertran laid a hand on Blaise's knee to keep him from standing.

'Stay with me,' said the duke.

And so he stayed, he sat in a charcoal-burner's cabin doorway at the cold end of a day of death with wind blowing past them, pushing Ariane's black hair back from her face, stirring the tall grass behind her, and he heard her say, in that voice from which all resonance seemed to have bled away, leaving only the flat assertion of the words: 'There is something I can now tell you about the night Aelis died. There was a reason why she came early to her time, Bertran.' Another breath, the vivid evidence of a struggle for self-control. Ariane said, 'When Urté took your son from her arms and left the room with the priestess following him, trying to reclaim the boy, I was left alone in the birthing room with Aelis. And a few moments later we . . . realized she was carrying a second child.'

Beside Blaise, Bertan make a convulsive gesture with his hands. The flask fell on the grass. Bertran tried awkwardly to stand. His strength seemed to have left him though; he remained sitting in the doorway looking up at the woman on the horse.

Ariane said, 'I delivered your daughter into the world, Bertran. And then . . . then Aelis made me swear an oath to her, and we both knew she was dying.' She was weeping again now, tears bright as crystal on her cheeks.

'Tell me,' said Bertran. 'Ariane, tell me what happened.'

She had been weeping then, too, amid the terrors of that room. She had been thirteen years old, and had heard Aelis, dying, tell her husband that the boy child she was holding was Bertran de Talair's. Ariane had cowered in a corner of the room watching Urté's face grow blood-dark with a rage such as she had never ever seen in her life. She saw him seize the baby from its mother's arms where the priestess had gently laid it. Outside the walls of Miraval a winter storm had been howling, rain lashing the castle, thunder like an angry spirit overhead.

The duke and the priestess had rushed from the room; where, Ariane did not know. She was certain he was about to kill the child, though. Aelis had been sure of the same thing.

'Oh, my dear,' her cousin had said, lying amid blood on her bed, 'what is it I have done?' Ariane, distraught with fear and grief, had clutched her hand, unable to think of a single thing to say. Wanting only to be far away from that room, from that terrible castle.

And then, a moment later, Aelis had said something else, in a different tone. 'Oh, Rian,' she had said. And, 'Cousin, in the goddess's name, I think there is another child in me.'

There had been. A small babe, though larger than the first it seemed to Ariane. And this one was a girl, with her mother's dark hair and long limbs, and a strong voice when she raised her first cry amid the storms of the world she had entered.

It was Ariane who took her from Aelis's womb. Ariane who bit through the cord and wrapped the infant in the warm cloths that had been readied by the fire. Ariane who gave her, with trembling hands, to her mother. No one else had been in the room. No one else had heard that second cry.

And Aelis de Miraval de Barbentain had looked upon the dark-haired daughter in her arms, knowing that her own life was passing from her, and had said to her cousin, who was thirteen years old that year, 'I am binding you to something now as an oath to me on my deathbed. You must swear to do what I ask of you.'

Ariane had looked at the two of them, mother and child, and she had done so: had sworn to take the baby from that room by the back stairway, wrapped in those swaddling-clothes, hidden within her own cloak, and to bear it from Miraval into the wildness of that night storm.

And she swore an oath that night to tell no living soul, not even Bertran, of the existence of a second child for so long as Urté de Miraval was alive. 'After Urté dies,' her cousin had said, 'if you are alive and she is, I leave it to you. Judge what she has become, if you know where she is. I have no gift of foreknowledge, Ariane. Judge the needs of the time. It may even be that this child, my daughter, will be heir to Miraval or Talair, to Arbonne itself. I need you to become the sort of woman who will be able to make that judgment one day. And now kiss me cousin, and forgive me if you can, and go.'

And Ariane had bent and kissed the dying woman upon the mouth and had fled, alone down the twisting back stairway, wrapped in a dark cloak with a baby next to her heart. And she met no one at all on the stairs or in the corridor or passing out of the castle into the rain by the postern gate. At the stables the ostlers were nowhere to be seen in the storm, and so Ariane had taken her mare from its stall herself and had mounted up awkwardly from astride a bale of hay, and she had ridden bareback from the yard with only her cloak and hood to shield her and the child from the cold and the driving rain.

She never forgot that ride for the rest of her days or nights. It would come back to her in dreams, or with any sudden crack of thunder or flash of lightning in a storm. She would be back in the vineyards of Miraval then, riding east towards the lake, the twisted shapes of vines showing around her when lightning shredded earth and sky. The child had cried and cried at the beginning but had fallen silent after that, and Ariane had been terrified the baby was dead and had been afraid to open her cloak in the rain to see. And she had been weeping all through that ride.

She never knew how she managed to find the hut by the lake where they kept the wood and kindling dry for signalling the isle. She remembered dismounting there and tethering the horse and hurrying inside, to stand in the doorway, dripping wet, unable to stop crying. A vivid sheet of lightning had lit the whole of the sky then, and for a moment in its dazzling flash she had seen the Arch of the Ancients looming nearby, huge and black in the night, and she had screamed in fear. But then, as if in answer to her own cry, she had felt, oh, she had felt a stirring of the child next to her heart, and had heard her begin to wail again, a precarious, determined assertion of presence amid the terrors of the world.

Ariane had held her close, rocking back and forth, crooning wordlessly, watching as lightning flashed again and again and finally moved on, as the peals of thunder gradually grew fainter to the south, as, after what seemed a span of time without measure or end, the blue moon named for Rian showed briefly once and then appeared again through the swift racing of the clouds, and the rain stopped.

She had laid the baby down then, wrapping it as best she could on the blessedly dry floor of the cabin, and she took wood and kindling and flint for flame and lit a flare on the mound outside to summon the priestesses to come, and they came.

She saw a white sail running up on the near shore of the isle and watched as one small boat slipped across the now calm waters of the lake towards her, ineffably beautiful and strange in the blue moonlight, something graceful and delicate in a world from which those things had seemed to her forever gone.

Her robe was soaked and stained and torn. In the night they would not know it for a garment of wealth or privilege. She kept her hood up about her face. When the boat had almost reached the shore she unwrapped the baby, grieving, from the rich cloths of the castle and brought it out to them in a scrap of rag she found in the cabin.

Then she gave Aelis's child to the priestess who stood, tall and grave beside the prow of the boat on the strand. She made her voice quiver and stammer with accents of the farm-yard and told them it was her own child and her father would not let her keep her and, oh, would the good servants of sweet Rian shelter and guard her baby all her days? She had been crying then too, Ariane remembered.

It was not a rare thing, her request. It was one of the ways Rian's Isle and the goddess's Island in the sea received their necessary complement of servants and priests and priestesses through the turning of seasons and years. The two women asked no questions other than of her own health. She had reached out, Ariane remembered, and had taken the child in her thin, tired arms for a last time and had kissed her farewell full upon the mouth, as she had the mother. She told the two priestesses she would be all right.

She had told herself the same thing as she watched the boat going back across the stilled waters of the lake under the one moon and the thin, high, drifting clouds and the emerging glitter of the stars, carrying Aelis's daughter and Bertran's.

Aelis had said nothing to her about a name. Ariane, on that stony shore, had looked up at the blue crescent of the moon and had told the priestesses that the child was to be named, if they found her worthy, for that moon and so for the goddess.

'She lived,' Ariane de Carenzu said, twenty-three years after, astride another horse before the cabin where that child and her dead brother had been conceived. The tears had dried on her cheeks during the telling of the tale. 'I have kept watch over her all these years, whenever I could, as best I could. She remained on the isle, of course; they usually do. She is beau-tiful and clever and brave, Bertran. She looks very like her mother, I think. Her name is Rinette. She was to become High Priestess of Rian's Isle one day soon.'

'Was?' Bertran's voice was so low, the one word was almost inaudible. His hands were clasped together before him. They had been through the length of the tale. Blaise could see that they were trembling.

'I spoke to her before coming to you. I thought that was proper. I told her who she was and how she had come to Rian's Isle, and I explained some other things as well. I said . . . that because of who she was she might be more dearly needed now away from the isle, in the world of men and women, but that it was her own choice to make and . . . that I would ensure that that was so.'

'And?' Bertran looked older now, Blaise realized. He wanted to put an arm around the other man, but held back.

'She said that if what I had told her was true, it was obvious that she was indeed more important to Arbonne among the castles than among the sanctuaries. Those were her own words. She is very strong, Bertran. She is . . . really quite wonderful.' Her voice broke a little on the last words.

'I have seen her then,' the duke said, his tone holding wonder like a chalice. 'I must have seen her so many times and I never saw the resemblance.'

'Why should you have? There was nothing you were looking to find.'

Bertran shook his head. 'It must have been so hard for her, learning of this so suddenly. It must have been terrible.'

'It may become so. Not yet, I think,' said Ariane. 'I suspect, with everything, she is only half understanding what all of it will mean. She does know . . .' Ariane hesitated, and turned, inexplicably, to Blaise, 'she does know, because I told her, that she may possibly be expected to wed one day soon.'

And now he understood why she had wanted him to stay.

He looked up in the waning of that clear light and met Ariane's dark-eyed gaze. He was remembering many different things suddenly, but one conversation most of all, from a summer night in Tavernel.

It was, in the end, Bertran who looked from one to the other of them and rose first from that cabin doorway at the edge of the forest. 'I think,' said the duke, 'that I am going to ride back now.'

'Shall I come?' asked Blaise.

Bertran shook his head. He smiled crookedly, a ghost of his most habitual expression. 'I know the way,' he said. 'That much hasn't changed.'

Everything else seemed to have, though, as Blaise stood and watched the duke ride off. Ariane turned in the saddle to watch him as well. Only when Bertran had passed from sight, an unprepossessing figure in the torn and blood-stained garb of a fighting man, did she turn back to Blaise. She still made no movement to dismount.

He said bluntly, 'There was a woman who shared her bed with me on Midsummer Eve in Tavernel. She told me she would live her life to change the rules of the marriage game among men and women in our day.' He wasn't certain why, but he almost meant the words as a blow.

She took them that way, he saw, and realizing that, all anger and resentment passed from him as if swept by the wind. Ariane said, very quietly, 'I can control nothing here, nor do I want to try. I can see, even now, something that might happen. So can you, Blaise. You must know how difficult this is for me. Surely you must. Even with everything else that has happened.'

He did know, actually. He seemed to be a wiser man than he had been a year ago. He knew what truth of the heart she was holding out to him as an offering, and he felt, not for the first time, a humbling awareness of her honesty. This was the woman, he thought suddenly, who had freed him from Lucianna and the bitterness he had carried from Portezza.

'Ariane,' he said roughly, 'you are the reason Arbonne must never be allowed to die.'

'There are a world of reasons,' she said, but something flashed briefly in the darkness of her eyes.

'And you are the symbol and the heart of them. You are the queen of the Court of Love.'

'I thought you regarded that as folly.'

'I thought many things here to be folly that have turned out to be more true than anything I knew before.' He stopped, and then, because it absolutely needed to be said, added steadily, 'Ariane, your husband is the reason we were able to win this battle, whatever we might say about Urté and Bertran and Fulk de Savaric. And Thierry is also the reason we were able to prevent a slaughter of surrendering men.'

'I think I know this,' she said gravely.

'I cannot tell you how much respect I have for him.'

'And I,' she murmured. 'I told you as much in Tavernel. What are you saying, Blaise?'

He forced himself to meet her level gaze. Her eyes were so dark, deep enough for a man to lose his way in them. 'That I am still enough of a man of Gorhaut, and I think I always will be, to have a world of trouble speaking words of love to the wife of such a man.'

He saw her lower her head for a moment. 'I know this too,' she said, looking up at him again. 'I also know, to my sorrow, that we are what we are, and so are the times into which we have been born, and those words I spoke at Midsummer to you about freedom of choice are, truly, the only real folly either of us has ever offered to the other. You are about to be king of Gorhaut, Blaise, in the midst of a world turned upside-down. The heiress of Arbonne will be waiting at Talair, even now.'

'And you think I must take her? To begin the righting of the world?'

For the first time Ariane showed a flash of her old authority. 'I told you that I have no control over anything here. It is too soon, in any case. I do think — since you ask — that any man who shares his life with that one will be blessed beyond deserving all his days. Even you, Blaise.'

He had seen her, of course, twice. Rinette. Had exchanged hard, haughty words by the lake in spring after he'd killed six corans of Miraval. *We have been waiting for you,* she'd said to him, self-possessed beyond her years, and he had feared those words. Perhaps, he thought now, perhaps they had meant something other than what either of them had understood or guessed that spring day. Perhaps the goddess truly did work in ways men and women could not comprehend. He thought suddenly of the red arrow that had killed Ademar. He still had no idea — and was trying not to dwell upon the thought — how that arrow had come straight down from a clear sky.

He said, looking up at Ariane, 'I will see you? You will not leave my life?'

She smiled then. Said formally, 'The king of Gorhaut will always be welcome in Carenzu.'

She was guiding them back together to solid ground. Her gifts had always been generous, and this not the least of them. He tried to match her tone. 'And Carenzu's lord and lady, wherever I am.'

There was a short silence. She bit her lip. 'There were other words that were part of that Midsummer Night. A song sung in the tavern where we met. I wonder if you remember the ending of it?'

He shook his head. Lisseut of Vezét had sung that song, he remembered, but the words were lost to him. Ariane smiled then, with tenderness and sadness, and a returning hint of the wise, worldly awareness that had always seemed to be hers. 'Let me ride back alone, Blaise. If you don't mind. I don't think I'll be by myself very much in the next little while.'

He nodded his head. What else could he have done? Bring her down into his arms in the fading light? Not in this world, he thought. She touched a finger to her lips, still with that same smile, and turned away. She was as beautiful as any woman he had ever known. She would have offered so much comfort, he knew. Comfort and passion and wisdom. Offered, and taken whatever he had to give in return, had he but asked. His heart full, Blaise watched her ride slowly away from him at sunset through the tall grass. He was thinking of her at thirteen, with a new-born child in her arms.

That child had grown into the woman it seemed the world and his own growing understanding of it might have him wed. Nothing would or could be done swiftly, and indeed it might never be done at all; there were so many layers of complexity to this world he had entered now. She was waiting in Talair, Ariane had said. He let his mind move forward towards such a meeting. Only his thoughts, though: Blaise remained where he was for a long time, sitting quietly in the doorway as the sun slid down in the west and the colours of sunset gradually suffused the fields and the bare vineyards and the trees, and fell gently, like a late benediction, on that small cabin by the forest.

Blaise looked back once through the open doorway before he finally left, and he saw how that muted crimson light slanted through the western window to fall upon the small, neat bed against the wall. He stood there for a moment, motionless, and then he gently closed the door, that the wind and rain might not enter in after all these years.

†

It was dusk, the first faint stars shining in the east, when he rode back towards Talair. And because it was so nearly dark and he wasn't really thinking about his path — his thoughts ahead of him and far behind — he rode straight past the woman standing quietly beside her horse in shadow under the elms on the far side of the arch.

Lisseut had meant to call out to him, but in the moment he actually appeared and went by she found that her voice would not obey her. She could not say his name. She had seen the duke ride past earlier, and then Ariane de Carenzu, and she had remained out of sight beneath the trees, holding her thoughts close to her as the sun went down and the shadows grew deeper beneath the looming arch.

Her thoughts. No comfort there at all. The man she had followed, as she had followed him once before, was the king of Gorhaut, or would be before many days had passed. He was already wearing the cloak of royalty. She had seen it from the isle.

In the moment Blaise appeared she was thinking, actually, of her mother and father and of home, of sunrise seen through the window of her own small room, morning light filtering through the grey-green leaves of the olive trees, the air carrying the scent of the sea from below.

She had always been impetuous, always found herself pushing hardest when she thought, inwardly, that it might, in fact, be no time to push at all. Her mother had told her, endlessly, that it was a trait that could lead her greatly wrong one day.

Perhaps it was because of that memory of her mother's words, with the heart-breaking lucidity of that image of home, that Lisseut kept silent as the man went by, riding away from her, from the arch and the winter elms, back to the world that was waiting for him. She lost sight of Blaise in the darkness where the avenue of elms ended and the path curved east towards the shore of the lake.

She remained where she was; it had become curiously difficult to move just then. She clung to that image of home for a while yet, and then that too seemed to leave her. After a time in the deepening shadows, Lisseut found that her thoughts had turned elsewhere again, and then it seemed that her voice had come back to her and that, perhaps not surprisingly, there were words she needed to offer to the twilight and the empty path before her where she had watched him go:

Thy table set with rarest wine,
Choice meats, sweet ripened fruit
And candlelight when we dine
In Fionvarre.

On we two the high stars will shine
And the holy moon lend her light.
If not here you will be mine
In Fionvarre.

She sighed. There was truly no point in lingering here, she told herself. It was time to go back. She still felt this curious reluctance to move, though. It was cold in the night now but the elms blocked the worst of the wind and in the darkness the disturbing, sculpted shapes of prisoners and slaves on the arch could not be seen. It was, in fact, unexpectedly peaceful where she stood, holding the reins of a quiet horse.

She stayed quite a long time. It was much later, in fact, when she heard a single horseman go by along the edge of the woods behind her, heading south. She became a little frightened for the first time then, alone here in the darkness. She mounted up and began the ride back to where there would be lights and shelter and friends and such comfort as any and all of these might offer.

On the way, as she came up to the shore of the lake and rode alongside the water towards the distant castle, carrying loss and love, remembering home, trying to comprehend the shape of the future opening up before them all, Lisseut found herself thinking of a song. Not an old lullaby this time, its origins long lost, not a tune by Anselme of Cauvas, the first of all the troubadours, nor of Count Folquet or Alain or En Bertran, nor even of lost Remy or Aurelian.

This tune and its words belonged to none of them. This, for the first time ever, as she passed beside the shore of Lake Dierne in the starlit, wintry dark, riding towards the castle lights, was a song of her own.

†

It was cold here outside, but Rinette had felt awkwardly enveloped within the warm, firelit rooms of Talair Castle. She had asked them where the garden was and someone had escorted her there. Then, when she'd walked into the walled enclosure, she had asked if she could be left alone and they had done that for her as well. Everyone was being extraordinarily obliging, even beyond what could be expected by a ranking priestess of Rian.

But she was more than that, and less. She had left her owl behind, on the isle. That had been, actually, the first of the very hard things.

This is, Rinette thought, walking at twilight among bare trees and evergreens and bushes and shrubs and flowers that would be glorious come spring, *my own castle*. One of her castles. Barbentain itself was another, and even Miraval was part of her legacy, if one stretched a point only a little.

It was cold, but she did not mind the cold. Winter was something she could deal with. She was still wearing the robes of Rian under her grey cloak. It wasn't as if she'd had a great deal of time to change her garb. Or her sense of where she belonged in the world. When she had arisen this morning she had been a priestess of Rian on her holy Isle, the named successor to the High Priestess there, though wondering, with a fear every one of them had felt, if their lives would stretch beyond this winter. Or if their destiny was fire in the name of Gorhaut and the god it claimed to serve.

Then battle had come today, screaming horses and men, blood and chaos in the valley, and at the end, unlooked-for amid helpless terror, a victory so complete the mind and heart could scarcely absorb it. She had gone into the sanctuary, to help the High Priestess lead them through the ancient, holy ceremony of thanksgiving.

And had come out from under the dome to find the lady Ariane de Carenzu waiting for her with a story that changed her life forever.

It was hard, it was very hard, however she strove to deal with this as she had always tried to deal with everything — calmly and with as much clarity as she could command. The lady of Carenzu had ended by telling her what was obvious to any thinking person from the moment the story had begun to grow clear — that her place was almost certainly away from the isle now. That the blindness and inner sight of a High Priestess of Rian was not what Arbonne needed from her after this. Everything had changed.

Ariane had said something else, though, something unexpected: that she would defend with all her own power and honour any choice at all that Rinette made. She had been near to weeping as she said that, Rinette remembered. It was a deeply generous offer, but it actually didn't matter very much, not really. Rinette would not have been what she was had she been unable to see for herself the clear truth of what all of this meant.

She was heir to Arbonne. There was no one else.

With the offer of her hand in marriage, the future of her country, of the worship of holy Rian, could be safeguarded for a time. Perhaps a very long time. It was not an awareness from which one could turn away for the familiarity of the small isle that was all the home she'd ever known. The paths of holy blindness and the inward sight it might offer were not to be hers any more.

She was not going to follow the High Priestesses after all. Neither the one here, nor Beatritz herself on the island in the sea. The High Priestess on Rian's Island, the goddess's most holy servant, Rinette thought suddenly, putting her mind around this for the first time, was her mother's older sister.

She shook her head. It was going to be very hard. She could see them lighting torches in the garden now. They were being careful of her privacy, keeping at a distance from where she walked. The light in the west had become quite beautiful, crimson and purple and a softer range of dusky hues low down where the sun was nearly gone. The garden, she could see, was nowhere near its best in this depth of winter, but Talair was far enough south that there were still hints of colour all around, and the wind was gentler here, with the walls and the trees for shelter. She heard the sound of splashing water and walking a little further down a path of small stones she came to a fountain. The servants had been here before her; there were torches burning in brackets set into the soil. She stood close to one, holding her hands out for warmth.

She was heir to Arbonne. Heir to this castle of Talair as well, for En Bertran had never married and never named anyone to succeed him. *En Bertran*. The duke of Talair was her father.

She had seen him, of course; growing up on the isle so near this castle she had seen him so many times across the water. She could remember how she and the other acolytes had spent countless evenings when they were supposed to be asleep breathlessly repeating tales and rumours about him, carried by the troubadours and joglars who came to Rian's Isle. She knew all about Bertran de Talair and Duke Urté and the beautiful lady who had died, Aelis de Miraval. She even knew — everyone knew — the old song Bertran had written for his beloved beside the springtime shores of this same lake.

What she had never known was that the song was her father's for her mother, that she was a part of that tale. She seemed to be, in fact, the ending of the story.

There was the other man as well, the one who was soon to be made king of Gorhaut. He had fought for Arbonne today against his own people. She had seen him, too, twice. Once last spring and again this morning when they had come across the lake to take the countess from the parley. He was a tall man, that one, bearded as the northerners all were, grim-looking with that, but a message had come from Rian's Island last spring that he should be watched for, that he was coming their way and might be important to them. And only a little while ago this afternoon Ariane de Carenzu, who ought, Rinette supposed, to know about such things, had said that he was a good man, gentler than he looked, and wiser, carrying burdens with which he would need someone's help in the days and years to come.

She wondered if he would come to her here. If it would begin already. She wondered if her father would come. Abruptly she sat down on one of the stone benches by the fountain, ignoring the cold. Cold was easy to deal with. What had overtaken her today was not, despite the self-possession she had managed to preserve with Ariane. It had been an overwhelming day. She wished she could hide, sleep, not dream. She wanted . . . she didn't really know what she wanted.

She suddenly felt — and could not remember feeling this way since she'd been a small child — that she might even cry. It wasn't Ariane's fault, it wasn't *anyone's* fault. She was sitting in the walled garden of her father's castle, and all she knew of her father were the endlessly traded stories about a duke who wrote the finest music of his day and had fought in wars in many countries, and who had spent more than twenty years pursuing women all over the world with a flamboyance that everyone knew — *everyone* knew — was a lifelong attempt to deal with the death of the one lady he had ever loved. Her mother.

I am afraid, Rinette said to herself suddenly, and the admission, curiously, seemed to help her gather her self-control again. I am not going to burn alive, she admonished herself sternly. None of us are going to burn now. We have won, by grace of Rian, who has given us, again, more than we have ever deserved of her. These changes in her life, she told herself, were only that — changes in a life. Mortal men and women were not to know — they *could* not know — what the future held in store for them, except for the fleeting, wayward glimpses the goddess sometimes granted those who had blinded themselves in her name.

That was not to be her path. Her path began here in this garden, walking forth with whomever came to lead her into the brightness and the burdens shaped by what, it seemed, she was.

Surely it was all right to be a little afraid, though? Surely that could be allowed of someone sitting alone at dusk in a winter garden dealing with the loss of every expectation she had ever had of her life?

It was then that she heard a footfall on the walkway, from behind her, the way she had come. She looked up at the torches for a moment and then, a little blinded, beyond them until she could see the stars again. She drew a long breath and pushed her dark hair back from her face. Then Rinette rose, straight-backed, holding her head high, and turned to meet her future. There was a solitary figure standing at the end of the path that led to this fountain.

It was not the northerner who had come, nor, yet, her father, after all.

She knew who this was, of course. She sank to her knees on the cold ground.

'Oh, my dear,' said Signe de Barbentain, the countess of Arbonne, 'I am so desperately happy to see you, and so very sad just now. So many years we have lost, you and I. There is so much I have to tell you. About your father and your mother, and then about the grandfather you never knew, who would have loved you with all his heart.'

The countess came closer then, moving almost hesitantly into the light of the torches, and Rinette saw that she was crying, tears streaming down her face in the cold. Rinette rose quickly, instinctively, a queer feeling overtaking her, a constriction of the heart and throat. She heard herself make a sound that was very like a child's cry, and she moved forward, almost running, into the haven of her grandmother's arms.

†

It was full dark now in the valley where the battle had been. He had waited patiently, even happily, for this. The moons would rise soon, both very bright tonight, spilling their rich, mingled light. It was time to go. There were no fires near where he was, no soldiers of either army sleeping or on watch in the cold.

He made his way down from branch to branch, sure-footed in the dark. No one heard him; he made no sound for anyone to hear. Once on the ground he slipped away west, passing close by the forest, going the long way around to where he had left his horse two days before, north of the Arch of the Ancients.

The stallion was hungry, of course. He was sorry for that but there had been nothing to do about it. He had left food

in a sack nearby and he fed the horse now, patting and rubbing its long neck, speaking tenderly. He felt deeply at peace,
as one with the night and the murmuring trees all around him.
He knelt, on impulse, and prayed.

There was so much gratitude in his heart he felt it might
overflow. He had done exactly what he had come here to do.
What he had been preparing for — though in ignorance, following instructions only — since the early days of autumn.

It was time to go now, to be away south before the bright
moons rose. He saddled the horse and mounted and began
to ride.

I want you to learn a new way of shooting, the High Priestess had told him on the island in the sea. And she had sent
him to a place where no one ever went, to learn to do what
she wanted done. He had always been able to handle a bow,
but what she asked was odd, inexplicable. He didn't need
things explained, though; he was honoured beyond words to
have been chosen. He spent the whole of the autumn
practising, learning to hit targets with the high, arching tra-
jectories she had specified. Over and over, day by day as the
weeks passed, he went off alone to the eastern end of the
island and practised.

He learned. He told her one day that he thought he had
mastered that new, strange shooting as best he ever would.
She sent him back that very day to begin again, the same
arching bowshots aimed at the apex of the sky, but now he was
to do them while nestled in the branches of a tree. He did
that, too; day after day, week after week, as winter came to
Rian's Island and the first flocks of birds from the north filled
their skies.

Then, one day, the High Priestess summoned him again,
and alone in her chambers, with only the white owl to watch
his face as he reacted to what she said, she told him what his
task was to be, the thing he had been training to do.

The goddess, she told him, *will sometimes intercede for us,
but she always wants to see that we have tried to aid ourselves.* He
understood that, it made sense to him. In the natural world a
deer might come to you, but only if you were out in the forest, upwind and silent, not if you stayed at home on a bench
before the fire. She told him then — and her words made him

begin to tremble with awe — where he was to go, and she even described the tree he would climb before the armies came to the valley by Lake Dierne.

He was to wait in that tree, the High Priestess told him, her hands clasped together in her lap, for a moment that might come if Rian offered them her grace — a moment when he might kill the king of Gorhaut. No man or woman, she told him, not even any priest or priestess, knew what he was being sent to do. No one was ever to know. He had knelt before her then and sworn the holiest oath he knew. He had felt her strong fingers on his head as she granted him her blessing.

Then she had given him his arrows, crimson dyed, fletched with crimson owl feathers, and he'd concealed them in a covered quiver and had himself taken by boat to land. He bought a good horse with money she had given him and rode, travelling swiftly by day and night, until he came to the valley of which she had told him. Arriving at twilight, before either of the armies had come, he saw the tree she had so clearly described to him, and he climbed it in the darkness and settled in to wait.

The soldiers had come the next day. Battle began that afternoon. Late in the day, when En Urté de Miraval had brought his corans sweeping down the ridge from the west, the king of Gorhaut had battled Duke Urté and had swept off his dented helmet and hurled it away after taking a blow in that combat.

It was exactly as he had been told it might be. He offered his heart's most fervent prayer, speaking the words aloud, though softly, and he lifted his bow from where he sat among the branches of that tree above the valley, and he sent a crimson arrow almost straight up into the bright sky along the high pathway of Rian, the soaring arch he had mastered through those solitary weeks and months on the island.

He was not greatly surprised, only humbled and full of gratitude, beyond any words he could ever have encompassed, when he saw that arrow strike the king of Gorhaut in the eye and end his life.

After that it had been a matter of waiting silently, hidden in the branches of his tree, for darkfall, and then slipping away unseen.

In time, as he rode, he left the lake behind. Not long after, white Vidonne rose in the eastern sky lighting the road that stretched away before him to the south. There was no one else in sight. He was not weary at all. He felt exalted, blessed. *I could die now*, he thought.

The wind had lessened with the rising of the moon. It wasn't even cold any more, and he was heading south with a full heart to where it was never truly cold, where there were flowers throughout the year by the sweet grace of Rian.

When the blue moon also rose, following the white one up the sky, he could restrain himself no longer. Luth of Baude, who was Luth of Rian's Island since being taken in exchange for a poet last spring, and who thought he might even be found worthy now to be consecrated a priest of the goddess in her sanctuary, began to sing.

He was not a musician, not a very good singer at all; he knew that. But songs were not only for those who could perform them with artistry. He knew that, too. And so Luth lifted his voice without shame, feeling a deep richness, a glory in the night, as he galloped his horse down the winding, empty road to the south, past farm and castle, village and field and forest, under the risen moons and the stars above Arbonne.

From the vidan of the troubadour, Lisseut of Vezét . . .

Lisseut, who was one of the first and perhaps the greatest of the woman troubadours of Arbonne, was of reputable birth, the daughter of an olive merchant whose lands lay to the east of the coastal town of Vezét. She was of middling height for a woman, with brown-coloured hair and pleasing features. Her disposition was said to have been forthright in youth, and this trait appears to have remained with her all her life. Her mother's brother was himself a joglar of some small repute, and it was he who first noticed in the young Lisseut a purity of voice that led him to take her under his tutelage and train her in the craft and art of the joglars. It was not long, however, before Lisseut had greatly outstripped her uncle in renown . . .

It was in the time after the Battle of Lake Dierne, when Arbonne was saved from the peril of invasion from the north, that Lisseut's prowess moved into the realm of the troubadours and the shaping of her own songs. Her 'Lament for sweet music gone,' mourning two of her slain companions, was her first, and perhaps her most celebrated song. It became, in a short time, the anthem for all who had died in that war . . .

Lisseut was close in friendship all her days with the great King Blaise of Gorhaut, and also with both his first wife and his second, and many are of the view that her 'Elegy for the crown of all kings' written at the time of the death of King Blaise is her most accomplished and moving work . . . Lisseut of Vezét never married, though she had, as all know, one child, Aurelian, who will surely need no introduction for those reading or hearing these words. Many tales were spread during Lisseut's life and after her passage to Rian with respect to a person of the very highest renown who might have been the father of her son, but it is not our intent to repeat such idle speculations here, only those truths as may be ascertained with some certainty after all the years that have gone past since that time . . .